THE COUNT OF MONTE CRISTO

ALEXANDRE DUMAS

Includes student and book club study guides

Unabridged

Book 2 of 2

Contents

VOLUME THREE

CHAPTER 48

Ideology

If the Count of Monte Cristo had been for a long time familiar with the ways of Parisian society, he would have appreciated better the significance of the step which M. de Villefort had taken. Standing well at court, whether the king regnant was of the older or younger branch, whether the government was doctrinaire liberal, or conservative; looked upon by all as a man of talent, since those who have never experienced a political check are generally so regarded; hated by many, but warmly supported by others, without being really liked by anybody, M. de Villefort held a high position in the magistracy, and maintained his eminence like a Harlay or a Molé. His drawing-room, under the regenerating influence of a young wife and a daughter by his first marriage, scarcely eighteen, was still one of the well-regulated Paris salons where the worship of traditional customs and the observance of rigid etiquette were carefully maintained. A freezing politeness, a strict fidelity to government principles, a profound contempt for theories and theorists, a deep-seated hatred of ideality,—these were the elements of private and public life displayed by M. de Villefort.

M. de Villefort was not only a magistrate, he was almost a diplomatist. His relations with the former court, of which he always spoke with dignity and respect, made him respected by the new one, and he knew so many things, that not only was he always carefully considered, but sometimes consulted. Perhaps this would not have been so had it been possible to get rid of M. de Villefort; but, like the feudal barons who rebelled against their sovereign, he dwelt in an impregnable fortress. This fortress was his post as king's attorney, all the advantages of which he exploited with marvellous skill, and which he would not have resigned but to be made deputy, and thus to replace neutrality by opposition.

Ordinarily M. de Villefort made and returned very few visits. His wife visited for him, and this was the received thing in the world, where the weighty and multifarious occupations of the magistrate were accepted as an excuse for what was really only calculated pride, a manifestation of professed superiority—in fact, the application of the axiom, *Pretend to think well of yourself, and the world will think well of you*, an axiom a hundred times more useful in society nowadays than that of the Greeks, "Know thyself," a knowledge for which, in our days, we have substituted the less difficult and more advantageous science of *knowing others*.

To his friends M. de Villefort was a powerful protector; to his enemies, he was a silent, but bitter opponent; for those who were neither the one nor the other, he was a statue of the law-made man. He had a haughty bearing, a look either steady and impenetrable or insolently piercing and inquisitorial. Four successive revolutions had built and cemented the pedestal upon which his fortune was based.

M. de Villefort had the reputation of being the least curious and the least wearisome man in France. He gave a ball every year, at which he appeared for a quarter of an hour only,—that is to say, five-and-forty minutes less than the king is visible at his balls. He was never seen at the theatres, at concerts, or in any place of public resort. Occasionally, but seldom, he played at whist, and then care was taken to select partners worthy of him—sometimes they were ambassadors, sometimes archbishops, or sometimes a prince, or a president, or some dowager duchess.

Such was the man whose carriage had just now stopped before the Count of Monte Cristo's door. The valet de chambre announced M. de Villefort at the moment when the count, leaning over a large table, was tracing on a map the route from St. Petersburg to China.

The procureur entered with the same grave and measured step he would have employed in entering a court of justice. He was the same man, or rather the development of the same man, whom we have heretofore seen as assistant attorney at Marseilles. Nature, according to her way, had made no deviation in the path he had marked out for himself. From being slender he had now become meagre; once pale, he was now yellow; his deep-set eyes were hollow, and the gold spectacles shielding his eyes seemed to be an integral portion of his face. He dressed entirely in black, with the exception of his white tie, and his funeral appearance was only mitigated by the slight line of red ribbon which passed almost imperceptibly through his button-hole, and appeared like a streak of blood traced with a delicate brush.

Although master of himself, Monte Cristo, scrutinized with irrepressible curiosity the magistrate whose salute he returned, and who, distrustful by habit, and especially incredulous as to social prodigies, was much more despised to look upon "the noble stranger," as Monte Cristo was already called, as an adventurer in search of new fields, or an escaped criminal, rather than as a prince of the Holy See, or a sultan of the *Thousand and One Nights*.

"Sir," said Villefort, in the squeaky tone assumed by magistrates in their oratorical periods, and of which they cannot, or will not, divest themselves in society, "sir, the signal service which you yesterday rendered to my wife and son has made it a duty for me to offer you my thanks. I have come, therefore, to discharge this duty, and to express to you my overwhelming gratitude."

And as he said this, the "eye severe" of the magistrate had lost nothing of its habitual arrogance. He spoke in a voice of the procureur-general, with the rigid inflexibility of neck and shoulders which caused his flatterers to say (as we have before observed) that he was the living statue of the law.

"Monsieur," replied the count, with a chilling air, "I am very happy to have been the means of preserving a son to his mother, for they say that the sentiment of maternity is the most holy of all; and the good fortune which occurred to me, monsieur, might have enabled you to dispense with a duty which, in its discharge, confers an undoubtedly great honor; for I am aware that M. de Villefort is not usually lavish of the favor which he now bestows on me,—a favor which, however estimable, is unequal to the satisfaction which I have in my own consciousness."

Villefort, astonished at this reply, which he by no means expected, started like a soldier who feels the blow levelled at him over the armor he wears, and a curl of his disdainful lip indicated that from that moment he noted in the tablets of his brain that the Count of Monte Cristo was by no means a highly bred gentleman.

He glanced around, in order to seize on something on which the conversation might turn, and seemed to fall easily on a topic. He saw the map which Monte Cristo had been examining when he entered, and said:

"You seem geographically engaged, sir? It is a rich study for you, who, as I learn, have seen as many lands as are delineated on this map."

"Yes, sir," replied the count; "I have sought to make of the human race, taken in the mass, what you practice every day on individuals—a physiological study. I have believed it was much easier to descend from the whole to a part than to ascend from a part to the whole. It is an algebraic axiom, which makes us proceed from a known to an unknown quantity, and not from an unknown to a known; but sit down, sir, I beg of you."

Monte Cristo pointed to a chair, which the procureur was obliged to take the trouble to move forwards himself, while the count merely fell back into his own, on which he had been kneeling when M. Villefort entered. Thus the count was halfway turned towards his visitor, having his back towards the window, his elbow resting on the geographical chart which furnished the theme of conversation for the moment,—a conversation which assumed, as in the case of the interviews with Danglars and Morcerf, a turn analogous to the persons, if not to the situation.

"Ah, you philosophize," replied Villefort, after a moment's silence, during which, like a wrestler who encounters a powerful opponent, he took breath; "well, sir, really, if, like you, I had nothing else to do, I should seek a more amusing occupation."

"Why, in truth, sir," was Monte Cristo's reply, "man is but an ugly caterpillar for him who studies him through a solar microscope; but you said, I think, that I had nothing else to do. Now, really, let me ask, sir, have you?—do you believe you have anything to do? or to speak in plain terms, do you really think that what you do deserves being called anything?"

Villefort's astonishment redoubled at this second thrust so forcibly made by his strange adversary. It was a long time since the magistrate had heard a paradox so strong, or rather, to say the truth more exactly, it was the first time he had ever heard of it. The procureur exerted himself to reply.

"Sir," he responded, "you are a stranger, and I believe you say yourself that a portion of your life has been spent in Oriental countries, so you are not aware how human justice, so expeditious in barbarous countries, takes with us a prudent and well-studied course."

"Oh, yes—yes, I do, sir; it is the *pede claudo* of the ancients. I know all that, for it is with the justice of all countries especially that I have occupied myself—it is with the criminal procedure of all nations that I have compared natural justice, and I must say, sir, that it is the law of primitive nations, that is, the law of retaliation, that I have most frequently found to be according to the law of God."

"If this law were adopted, sir," said the procureur, "it would greatly simplify our legal codes, and in that case the magistrates would not (as you just observed) have much to do."

"It may, perhaps, come to this in time," observed Monte Cristo; "you know that human inventions march from the complex to the simple, and simplicity is always perfection."

"In the meanwhile," continued the magistrate, "our codes are in full force, with all their contradictory enactments derived from Gallic customs, Roman laws, and Frank usages; the knowledge of all which, you will agree, is not to be acquired without extended labor; it needs tedious study to acquire this knowledge, and, when acquired, a strong power of brain to retain it."

"I agree with you entirely, sir; but all that even you know with respect to the French code, I know, not only in reference to that code, but as regards the codes of all nations. The English, Turkish, Japanese, Hindu laws, are as familiar to me as the French laws, and thus I was right, when I said to you, that relatively (you know that everything is relative, sir)—that relatively to what I have done, you have very little to do; but that relatively to all I have learned, you have yet a great deal to learn."

"But with what motive have you learned all this?" inquired Villefort, in astonishment.

Monte Cristo smiled.

"Really, sir," he observed, "I see that in spite of the reputation which you have acquired as a superior man, you look at everything from the material and vulgar view of society, beginning with man, and ending with man—that is to say, in the most restricted, most narrow view which it is possible for human understanding to embrace."

"Pray, sir, explain yourself," said Villefort, more and more astonished, "I really do—not—understand you—perfectly."

"I say, sir, that with the eyes fixed on the social organization of nations, you see only the springs of the machine, and lose sight of the sublime workman who makes them act; I say that you do not recognize before you and around you any but those office-holders whose commissions have been signed by a minister or king; and that the men whom God has put above those office-holders, ministers, and kings, by giving them a mission to follow out, instead of a post to fill—I say that they escape your narrow, limited field of observation. It is thus that human weakness fails, from its debilitated and imperfect organs. Tobias took the angel who restored him to light for an ordinary young man. The nations took Attila, who was doomed to destroy them, for a conqueror similar to other conquerors, and it was necessary for both to reveal their missions, that they might be known and acknowledged; one was compelled to say, 'I am the angel of the Lord'; and the other, 'I am the hammer of God,' in order that the divine essence in both might be revealed."

"Then," said Villefort, more and more amazed, and really supposing he was speaking to a mystic or a madman, "you consider yourself as one of those extraordinary beings whom you have mentioned?"

"And why not?" said Monte Cristo coldly.

"Your pardon, sir," replied Villefort, quite astounded, "but you will excuse me if, when I presented myself to you, I was unaware that I should meet with a person whose knowledge and understanding so far surpass the usual knowledge and understanding of men. It is not usual with us corrupted wretches of civilization to find gentlemen like yourself, possessors, as you are, of immense fortune—at least, so it is said—and I beg you to observe that I do not inquire, I merely repeat;—it is not usual, I say, for such privileged and wealthy beings to waste their time in speculations on the state of society, in philosophical reveries, intended at best to console those whom fate has disinherited from the goods of this world."

"Really, sir," retorted the count, "have you attained the eminent situation in which you are, without having admitted, or even without having met with exceptions? and do you never use your eyes, which must have acquired so much *finesse* and certainty, to divine, at a glance, the kind of man by whom you are confronted? Should not a magistrate be not merely the best administrator of the law, but the most crafty expounder of the chicanery of his profession, a steel probe to search hearts, a touchstone to try the gold which in each soul is mingled with more or less of alloy?"

"Sir," said Villefort, "upon my word, you overcome me. I really never heard a person speak as you do."

"Because you remain eternally encircled in a round of general conditions, and have never dared to raise your wings into those upper spheres which God has peopled with invisible or exceptional beings."

"And you allow then, sir, that spheres exist, and that these marked and invisible beings mingle amongst us?"

"Why should they not? Can you see the air you breathe, and yet without which you could not for a moment exist?"

"Then we do not see those beings to whom you allude?"

"Yes, we do; you see them whenever God pleases to allow them to assume a material form. You touch them, come in contact with them, speak to them, and they reply to you."

"Ah," said Villefort, smiling, "I confess I should like to be warned when one of these beings is in contact with me."

"You have been served as you desire, monsieur, for you were warned just now, and I now again warn you."

"Then you yourself are one of these marked beings?"

"Yes, monsieur, I believe so; for until now, no man has found himself in a position similar to mine. The dominions of kings are limited either by mountains or rivers, or a change of manners, or an alteration of language. My kingdom is bounded only by the world, for I am not an Italian, or a Frenchman, or a Hindu, or an American, or a Spaniard—I am a cosmopolite. No country can say it saw my birth. God alone knows what country will see me die. I adopt all customs, speak all languages. You believe me to be a Frenchman, for I speak French with the same facility and purity as yourself. Well, Ali, my Nubian, believes me to be an Arab; Bertuccio, my steward, takes me for a Roman; Haydée, my slave, thinks me a Greek. You may, therefore, comprehend, that being of no country, asking no protection from any government, acknowledging no man as my brother, not one of the scruples that arrest the powerful, or the obstacles which paralyze the weak, paralyzes or arrests me. I have only two adversaries—I will not say two conquerors, for with perseverance I subdue even them,—they are time and distance. There is a third, and the most terrible—that is my condition as a mortal being. This alone can stop me in my onward career, before I have attained the goal at which I aim, for all the rest I have reduced to mathematical terms. What men call the chances of fate—namely, ruin, change, circumstances—I have fully anticipated, and if any of these should overtake me, yet it will not overwhelm me. Unless I die, I shall always be what I am, and therefore it is that I utter the things you have never heard, even from the mouths of kings—for kings have need, and other persons have fear of you. For who is there who does not say to himself, in a society as incongruously organized as ours, 'Perhaps some day I shall have to do with the king's attorney'?"

"But can you not say that, sir? The moment you become an inhabitant of France, you are naturally subjected to the French law."

"I know it sir," replied Monte Cristo; "but when I visit a country I begin to study, by all the means which are available, the men from whom I may have anything to hope or to fear, till I know them as well as, perhaps better than, they know themselves. It follows from this, that the king's attorney, be he who he may, with whom I should have to deal, would assuredly be more embarrassed than I should."

"That is to say," replied Villefort with hesitation, "that human nature being weak, every man, according to your creed, has committed faults."

"Faults or crimes," responded Monte Cristo with a negligent air.

"And that you alone, amongst the men whom you do not recognize as your brothers—for you have said so," observed Villefort in a tone that faltered somewhat—"you alone are perfect."

"No, not perfect," was the count's reply; "only impenetrable, that's all. But let us leave off this strain, sir, if the tone of it is displeasing to you; I am no more disturbed by your justice than are you by my second-sight."

"No, no,—by no means," said Villefort, who was afraid of seeming to abandon his ground. "No; by your brilliant and almost sublime conversation you have elevated me above the ordinary level; we no longer talk, we rise to dissertation. But you know how the theologians in their collegiate chairs, and philosophers in their controversies, occasionally say cruel truths; let us suppose for the moment that we are theologizing in a social way, or even philosophically, and I will say to you, rude as it may seem, 'My brother, you sacrifice greatly to pride; you may be above others, but above you there is God.'"

"Above us all, sir," was Monte Cristo's response, in a tone and with an emphasis so deep that Villefort involuntarily shuddered. "I have my pride for men—serpents always ready to threaten everyone who would pass without crushing them under foot. But I lay aside that pride before God, who has taken me from nothing to make me what I am."

"Then, count, I admire you," said Villefort, who, for the first time in this strange conversation, used the aristocratic form to the unknown personage, whom, until now, he had only called monsieur. "Yes, and I say to you, if you are really strong, really superior, really pious, or impenetrable, which you were right in saying amounts to the same thing—then be proud, sir, for that is the characteristic of predominance. Yet you have unquestionably some ambition."

"I have, sir."

"And what may it be?"

"I too, as happens to every man once in his life, have been taken by Satan into the highest mountain in the earth, and when there he showed me all the kingdoms of the world, and as he said before, so said he to me, 'Child of earth, what wouldst thou have to make thee adore me?' I reflected long, for a gnawing ambition had long preyed upon me, and then I replied, 'Listen,—I have always heard of Providence, and yet I have never seen him, or anything that resembles him, or which can make me believe that he exists. I wish to be Providence myself, for I feel that the most beautiful, noblest, most sublime thing in the world, is to recompense and punish.' Satan bowed his head, and groaned. 'You mistake,' he said, 'Providence does exist, only you have never seen him, because the child of God is as invisible as the parent. You have seen nothing that resembles him, because he works by secret springs, and moves by hidden ways. All I can do for you is to make you one of the agents of that Providence.' The bargain was concluded. I may sacrifice my soul, but what matters it?" added Monte Cristo. "If the thing were to do again, I would again do it."

Villefort looked at Monte Cristo with extreme amazement.

"Count," he inquired, "have you any relations?"

"No, sir, I am alone in the world."

"So much the worse."

"Why?" asked Monte Cristo.

"Because then you might witness a spectacle calculated to break down your pride. You say you fear nothing but death?"

"I did not say that I feared it; I only said that death alone could check the execution of my plans."

"And old age?"

"My end will be achieved before I grow old."

"And madness?"

"I have been nearly mad; and you know the axiom,—*non bis in idem.* It is an axiom of criminal law, and, consequently, you understand its full application."

"Sir," continued Villefort, "there is something to fear besides death, old age, and madness. For instance, there is apoplexy—that lightning-stroke which strikes but does not destroy you, and yet which brings everything to an end. You are still yourself as now, and yet you are yourself no longer; you who, like Ariel, verge on the angelic, are but an inert mass, which, like Caliban, verges on the brutal; and this is called in human tongues, as I tell you, neither more nor less than apoplexy. Come, if so you will, count, and continue this conversation at my house, any day you may be willing to see an adversary capable of understanding and anxious to refute you, and I will show you my father, M. Noirtier de Villefort, one of the most fiery Jacobins of the French Revolution; that is to say, he had the most remarkable audacity, seconded by a most powerful organization—a man who has not, perhaps, like yourself seen all the kingdoms of the earth, but who has helped to overturn one of the greatest; in fact, a man who believed himself, like you, one of the envoys, not of God, but of a supreme being; not of Providence, but of fate. Well, sir, the rupture of a blood-vessel on the lobe of the brain has destroyed all this, not in a day, not in an hour, but in a second. M. Noirtier, who, on the previous night, was the old Jacobin, the old senator, the old Carbonaro, laughing at the guillotine, the cannon, and the dagger—M. Noirtier, playing with revolutions—M. Noirtier, for whom France was a vast chess-board, from which pawns, rooks, knights, and queens were to disappear, so that the king was checkmated—M. Noirtier, the redoubtable, was the next morning *poor M. Noirtier,* the helpless old man, at the tender mercies of the weakest creature in the household, that is, his grandchild, Valentine; a dumb and frozen carcass, in fact, living painlessly on, that time may be given for his frame to decompose without his consciousness of its decay."

"Alas, sir," said Monte Cristo "this spectacle is neither strange to my eye nor my thought. I am something of a physician, and have, like my fellows, sought more than once for the soul in living and in dead matter; yet, like Providence, it has remained invisible to my eyes, although present to my heart. A hundred writers since Socrates, Seneca, St. Augustine, and Gall, have made, in verse and prose, the comparison you have made, and yet I can well understand that a father's sufferings may effect great changes in the mind of a son. I will call on you, sir, since you bid me contemplate, for the advantage of my pride, this terrible spectacle, which must have been so great a source of sorrow to your family."

"It would have been so unquestionably, had not God given me so large a compensation. In contrast with the old man, who is dragging his way to the tomb, are two children just entering into life—Valentine, the daughter by my first wife—Mademoiselle Renée de Saint-Méran—and Edward, the boy whose life you have this day saved."

"And what is your deduction from this compensation, sir?" inquired Monte Cristo.

"My deduction is," replied Villefort, "that my father, led away by his passions, has committed some fault unknown to human justice, but marked by the justice of God. That God, desirous in his mercy to punish but one person, has visited this justice on him alone."

Monte Cristo with a smile on his lips, uttered in the depths of his soul a groan which would have made Villefort fly had he but heard it.

"Adieu, sir," said the magistrate, who had risen from his seat; "I leave you, bearing a remembrance of you—a remembrance of esteem, which I hope will not be disagreeable to you when you know me better; for I am not a man to bore my friends, as you will learn. Besides, you have made an eternal friend of Madame de Villefort."

The count bowed, and contented himself with seeing Villefort to the door of his cabinet, the procureur being escorted to his carriage by two footmen, who, on a signal from their master, followed him with every mark of attention. When he had gone, Monte Cristo breathed a profound sigh, and said:

"Enough of this poison, let me now seek the antidote."

Then sounding his bell, he said to Ali, who entered:

"I am going to madame's chamber—have the carriage ready at one o'clock."

Study Guide Questions

For Students:

1. What are the elements of private and public life displayed by M. de Villefort?
2. Why does M. de Villefort pay a visit to the Count?
3. What is M. de Villefort's view of the justice system in Oriental Countries?

For Reading Club:

1. Do you think that modern-day magistrates are similar to M. de Villefort?
2. Do you think that Dantès' arguments are in fact his complaints to M. de Villefort?
3. Discuss the Count's ambition that he shares with M. de Villefort, what do you think of it?

CHAPTER 49

Haydée

It will be recollected that the new, or rather old, acquaintances of the Count of Monte Cristo, residing in the Rue Meslay, were no other than Maximilian, Julie, and Emmanuel.

The very anticipations of delight to be enjoyed in his forthcoming visits—the bright, pure gleam of heavenly happiness it diffused over the almost deadly warfare in which he had voluntarily engaged, illumined his whole countenance with a look of ineffable joy and calmness, as, immediately after Villefort's departure, his thoughts flew back to the cheering prospect before him, of tasting, at least, a brief respite from the fierce and stormy passions of his mind. Even Ali, who had hastened to obey the Count's summons, went forth from his master's presence in charmed amazement at the unusual animation and pleasure depicted on features ordinarily so stern and cold; while, as though dreading to put to flight the agreeable ideas hovering over his patron's meditations, whatever they were, the faithful Nubian walked on tiptoe towards the door, holding his breath, lest its faintest sound should dissipate his master's happy reverie.

It was noon, and Monte Cristo had set apart one hour to be passed in the apartments of Haydée, as though his oppressed spirit could not all at once admit the feeling of pure and unmixed joy, but required a gradual succession of calm and gentle emotions to prepare his mind to receive full and perfect happiness, in the same manner as ordinary natures demand to be inured by degrees to the reception of strong or violent sensations.

The young Greek, as we have already said, occupied apartments wholly unconnected with those of the count. The rooms had been fitted up in strict accordance with Oriental ideas; the floors were covered with the richest carpets Turkey could produce; the walls hung with brocaded silk of the most magnificent designs and texture; while around each chamber luxurious divans were placed, with piles of soft and yielding cushions, that needed only to be arranged at the pleasure or convenience of such as sought repose.

Haydée had three French maids, and one who was a Greek. The first three remained constantly in a small waiting-room, ready to obey the summons of a small golden bell, or to receive the orders of the Romaic slave, who knew just enough French to be able to transmit her mistress's wishes to the three other waiting-women; the latter had received most peremptory instructions from Monte Cristo to treat Haydée with all the deference they would observe to a queen.

The young girl herself generally passed her time in the chamber at the farther end of her apartments. This was a sort of boudoir, circular, and lighted only from the roof, which consisted of rose-colored glass. Haydée was reclining upon soft downy cushions, covered with blue satin spotted with silver; her head, supported by one of her exquisitely moulded arms, rested on the divan immediately behind her, while the other was employed in adjusting to her lips the coral tube of a rich narghile, through whose flexible pipe she drew the smoke fragrant by its passage through perfumed water. Her attitude, though perfectly natural for an Eastern woman would, in a European, have been deemed too full of coquettish straining after effect.

Her dress, which was that of the women of Epirus, consisted of a pair of white satin trousers, embroidered with pink roses, displaying feet so exquisitely formed and so delicately fair, that they might well have been taken for Parian marble, had not the eye been undeceived by their movements as they constantly shifted in and out of a pair of little slippers with upturned toes, beautifully ornamented with gold and pearls. She wore a blue and white-striped vest, with long open sleeves, trimmed with silver loops and buttons of pearls, and a sort of bodice, which, closing only from the centre to the waist, exhibited the whole of the ivory throat and upper part of the bosom; it was fastened with three magnificent diamond clasps. The junction of the bodice and drawers was entirely concealed by one of the many-colored scarves, whose brilliant hues and rich silken fringe have rendered them so precious in the eyes of Parisian belles.

Tilted on one side of her head she had a small cap of gold-colored silk, embroidered with pearls; while on the other a purple rose mingled its glowing colors with the luxuriant masses of her hair, of which the blackness was so intense that it was tinged with blue.

The extreme beauty of the countenance, that shone forth in loveliness that mocked the vain attempts of dress to augment it, was peculiarly and purely Grecian; there were the large, dark, melting eyes, the finely formed nose, the coral lips, and pearly teeth, that belonged to her race and country.

And, to complete the whole, Haydée was in the very springtide and fulness of youthful charms—she had not yet numbered more than nineteen or twenty summers.

Monte Cristo summoned the Greek attendant, and bade her inquire whether it would be agreeable to her mistress to receive his visit. Haydée's only reply was to direct her servant by a sign to withdraw the tapestried curtain that hung before the door of her boudoir, the framework of the opening thus made serving as a sort of border to the graceful tableau presented by the young girl's picturesque attitude and appearance.

As Monte Cristo approached, she leaned upon the elbow of the arm that held the narghile, and extending to him her other hand, said, with a smile of captivating sweetness, in the sonorous language spoken by the women of Athens and Sparta:

"Why demand permission ere you enter? Are you no longer my master, or have I ceased to be your slave?"

Monte Cristo returned her smile.

"Haydée," said he, "you well know."

"Why do you address me so coldly—so distantly?" asked the young Greek. "Have I by any means displeased you? Oh, if so, punish me as you will; but do not—do not speak to me in tones and manner so formal and constrained."

"Haydée," replied the count, "you know that you are now in France, and are free."

"Free to do what?" asked the young girl.

"Free to leave me."

"Leave you? Why should I leave you?"

"That is not for me to say; but we are now about to mix in society—to visit and be visited."

"I don't wish to see anybody but you."

"And should you see one whom you could prefer, I would not be so unjust—"

"I have never seen anyone I preferred to you, and I have never loved anyone but you and my father."

"My poor child," replied Monte Cristo, "that is merely because your father and myself are the only men who have ever talked to you."

"I don't want anybody else to talk to me. My father said I was his 'joy'—you style me your 'love,'—and both of you have called me 'my child.'"

"Do you remember your father, Haydée?"

The young Greek smiled.

"He is here, and here," said she, touching her eyes and her heart.

"And where am I?" inquired Monte Cristo laughingly.

"You?" cried she, with tones of thrilling tenderness, "you are everywhere!" Monte Cristo took the delicate hand of the young girl in his, and was about to raise it to his lips, when the simple child of nature hastily withdrew it, and presented her cheek.

"You now understand, Haydée," said the count, "that from this moment you are absolutely free; that here you exercise unlimited sway, and are at liberty to lay aside or continue the costume of your country, as it may suit your inclination. Within this mansion you are absolute mistress of your actions, and may go abroad or remain in your apartments as may seem most agreeable to you. A carriage waits your orders, and Ali and Myrtho will accompany you whithersoever you desire to go. There is but one favor I would entreat of you."

"Speak."

"Guard carefully the secret of your birth. Make no allusion to the past; nor upon any occasion be induced to pronounce the names of your illustrious father or ill-fated mother."

"I have already told you, my lord, that I shall see no one."

"It is possible, Haydée, that so perfect a seclusion, though conformable with the habits and customs of the East, may not be practicable in Paris. Endeavor, then, to accustom yourself to our manner of living in these northern climes as you did to those of Rome, Florence, Milan, and Madrid; it may be useful to you one of these days, whether you remain here or return to the East."

The young girl raised her tearful eyes towards Monte Cristo as she said with touching earnestness, "Whether *we* return to the East, you mean to say, my lord, do you not?"

"My child," returned Monte Cristo "you know full well that whenever we part, it will be no fault or wish of mine; the tree forsakes not the flower—the flower falls from the tree."

"My lord," replied Haydée, "I never will leave you, for I am sure I could not exist without you."

"My poor girl, in ten years I shall be old, and you will be still young."

"My father had a long white beard, but I loved him; he was sixty years old, but to me he was handsomer than all the fine youths I saw."

"Then tell me, Haydée, do you believe you shall be able to accustom yourself to our present mode of life?"

"Shall I see you?"

"Every day."

"Then what do you fear, my lord?"

"You might find it dull."

"No, my lord. In the morning, I shall rejoice in the prospect of your coming, and in the evening dwell with delight on the happiness I have enjoyed in your presence; then too, when alone, I can call forth mighty pictures of the past, see vast horizons bounded only by the towering mountains of Pindus and Olympus. Oh, believe me, that when three great passions, such as sorrow, love, and gratitude fill the heart, *ennui* can find no place."

"You are a worthy daughter of Epirus, Haydée, and your charming and poetical ideas prove well your descent from that race of goddesses who claim your country as their birthplace. Depend on my care to see that your youth is not blighted, or suffered to pass away in ungenial solitude; and of this be well assured, that if you love me as a father, I love you as a child."

"You are wrong, my lord. The love I have for you is very different from the love I had for my father. My father died, but I did not die. If you were to die, I should die too."

The count, with a smile of profound tenderness, extended his hand, and she carried it to her lips.

Monte Cristo, thus attuned to the interview he proposed to hold with Morrel and his family, departed, murmuring as he went these lines of Pindar, "Youth is a flower of which love is the fruit; happy is he who, after having watched its silent growth, is permitted to gather and call it his own." The carriage was prepared according to orders, and stepping lightly into it, the count drove off at his usual rapid pace.

Study Guide Questions

For Students:

1. Who is Haydée?
2. What favor does the Count ask of Haydée?
3. What kind of lifestyle does Haydée enjoy?

For Reading Club:

1. Discuss the relationship between the Count and Haydée, do you think their relationship glorifies patriarchy?
2. Do you think the Count has trapped Haydée in a golden cage? Why or why not?
3. Do you think Haydée's character and her dialogues are influenced by the male author?

CHAPTER 50

The Morrel Family

In a very few minutes the count reached No. 7 in the Rue Meslay. The house was of white stone, and in a small court before it were two small beds full of beautiful flowers. In the concierge that opened the gate the count recognized Cocles; but as he had but one eye, and that eye had become somewhat dim in the course of nine years, Cocles did not recognize the count.

The carriages that drove up to the door were compelled to turn, to avoid a fountain that played in a basin of rockwork,—an ornament that had excited the jealousy of the whole quarter, and had gained for the place the appellation of *The Little Versailles*. It is needless to add that there were gold and silver fish in the basin. The house, with kitchens and cellars below, had above the ground floor, two stories and attics. The whole of the property, consisting of an immense workshop, two pavilions at the bottom of the garden, and the garden itself, had been purchased by Emmanuel, who had seen at a glance that he could make of it a profitable speculation. He had reserved the house and half the garden, and building a wall between the garden and the workshops, had let them upon lease with the pavilions at the bottom of the garden. So that for a trifling sum he was as well lodged, and as perfectly shut out from observation, as the inhabitants of the finest mansion in the Faubourg St. Germain.

The breakfast-room was finished in oak; the salon in mahogany, and the furnishings were of blue velvet; the bedroom was in citronwood and green damask. There was a study for Emmanuel, who never studied, and a music-room for Julie, who never played. The whole of the second story was set apart for Maximilian; it was precisely similar to his sister's apartments, except that for the breakfast-parlor he had a billiard-room, where he received his friends. He was superintending the grooming of his horse, and smoking his cigar at the entrance of the garden, when the count's carriage stopped at the gate.

Cocles opened the gate, and Baptistin, springing from the box, inquired whether Monsieur and Madame Herbault and Monsieur Maximilian Morrel would see his excellency the Count of Monte Cristo.

"The Count of Monte Cristo?" cried Morrel, throwing away his cigar and hastening to the carriage; "I should think we would see him. Ah, a thousand thanks, count, for not having forgotten your promise."

And the young officer shook the count's hand so warmly, that Monte Cristo could not be mistaken as to the sincerity of his joy, and he saw that he had been expected with impatience, and was received with pleasure.

"Come, come," said Maximilian, "I will serve as your guide; such a man as you are ought not to be introduced by a servant. My sister is in the garden plucking the dead roses; my brother is reading his two papers, *la Presse* and *les Débats*, within six steps of her; for wherever you see Madame Herbault, you have only to look within a circle of four yards and you will find M. Emmanuel, and 'reciprocally,' as they say at the Polytechnic School."

At the sound of their steps a young woman of twenty to five-and-twenty, dressed in a silk morning gown, and busily engaged in plucking the dead leaves off a noisette rose-tree, raised her head. This was Julie, who had become, as the clerk of the house of Thomson & French had predicted, Madame Emmanuel Herbault. She uttered a cry of surprise at the sight of a stranger, and Maximilian began to laugh.

"Don't disturb yourself, Julie," said he. "The count has only been two or three days in Paris, but he already knows what a fashionable woman of the Marais is, and if he does not, you will show him."

"Ah, monsieur," returned Julie, "it is treason in my brother to bring you thus, but he never has any regard for his poor sister. Penelon, Penelon!"

An old man, who was digging busily at one of the beds, stuck his spade in the earth, and approached, cap in hand, striving to conceal a quid of tobacco he had just thrust into his cheek. A few locks of gray mingled with his hair, which was still thick and matted, while his bronzed features and determined glance well suited an old sailor who had braved the heat of the equator and the storms of the tropics.

"I think you hailed me, Mademoiselle Julie?" said he.

Penelon had still preserved the habit of calling his master's daughter "Mademoiselle Julie," and had never been able to change the name to Madame Herbault.

"Penelon," replied Julie, "go and inform M. Emmanuel of this gentleman's visit, and Maximilian will conduct him to the salon."

Then, turning to Monte Cristo,—"I hope you will permit me to leave you for a few minutes," continued she; and without awaiting any reply, disappeared behind a clump of trees, and escaped to the house by a lateral alley.

"I am sorry to see," observed Monte Cristo to Morrel, "that I cause no small disturbance in your house."

"Look there," said Maximilian, laughing; "there is her husband changing his jacket for a coat. I assure you, you are well known in the Rue Meslay."

"Your family appears to be a very happy one," said the count, as if speaking to himself.

"Oh, yes, I assure you, count, they want nothing that can render them happy; they are young and cheerful, they are tenderly attached to each other, and with twenty-five thousand francs a year they fancy themselves as rich as Rothschild."

"Five-and-twenty thousand francs is not a large sum, however," replied Monte Cristo, with a tone so sweet and gentle, that it went to Maximilian's heart like the voice of a father; "but they will not be content with that. Your brother-in-law is a barrister? a doctor?"

"He was a merchant, monsieur, and had succeeded to the business of my poor father. M. Morrel, at his death, left 500,000 francs, which were divided between my sister and myself, for we were his only children. Her husband, who, when he married her, had no other patrimony than his noble probity, his first-rate ability, and his spotless reputation, wished to possess as much as his wife. He labored and toiled until he had amassed 250,000 francs; six years sufficed to achieve this object. Oh, I assure you, sir, it was a touching spectacle to see these young creatures, destined by their talents for higher stations, toiling together, and through their unwillingness to change any of the customs of their paternal house, taking six years to accomplish what less scrupulous people would have effected in two or three. Marseilles resounded with their well-earned praises. At last, one day, Emmanuel came to his wife, who had just finished making up the accounts.

"'Julie,' said he to her, 'Cocles has just given me the last rouleau of a hundred francs; that completes the 250,000 francs we had fixed as the limits of our gains. Can you content yourself with the small fortune which we shall possess for the future? Listen to me. Our house transacts business to the amount of a million a year, from which we derive an income of 40,000 francs. We can dispose of the business, if we please, in an hour, for I have received a letter from M. Delaunay, in which he offers to purchase the good-will of the house, to unite with his own, for 300,000 francs. Advise me what I had better do.'

"'Emmanuel,' returned my sister, 'the house of Morrel can only be carried on by a Morrel. Is it not worth 300,000 francs to save our father's name from the chances of evil fortune and failure?'

"'I thought so,' replied Emmanuel; 'but I wished to have your advice.'

"'This is my counsel:—Our accounts are made up and our bills paid; all we have to do is to stop the issue of any more, and close our office.'

"This was done instantly. It was three o'clock; at a quarter past, a merchant presented himself to insure two ships; it was a clear profit of 15,000 francs.

"'Monsieur,' said Emmanuel, 'have the goodness to address yourself to M. Delaunay. We have quitted business.'

"'How long?' inquired the astonished merchant.

"'A quarter of an hour,' was the reply.

"And this is the reason, monsieur," continued Maximilian, "of my sister and brother-in-law having only 25,000 francs a year."

Maximilian had scarcely finished his story, during which the count's heart had swelled within him, when Emmanuel entered wearing a hat and coat. He saluted the count with the air of a man who is aware of the rank of his guest; then, after having led Monte Cristo around the little garden, he returned to the house.

A large vase of Japan porcelain, filled with flowers that loaded the air with their perfume, stood in the salon. Julie, suitably dressed, and her hair arranged (she had accomplished this feat in less than ten minutes), received the count on his entrance. The songs of the birds were heard in an aviary hard by, and the branches of laburnums and rose acacias formed an exquisite framework to the blue velvet curtains. Everything in this charming retreat, from the warble of the birds to the smile of the mistress, breathed tranquillity and repose.

The count had felt the influence of this happiness from the moment he entered the house, and he remained silent and pensive, forgetting that he was expected to renew the conversation, which had ceased after the first salutations had been exchanged. The silence became almost painful when, by a violent effort, tearing himself from his pleasing reverie:

"Madame," said he at length, "I pray you to excuse my emotion, which must astonish you who are only accustomed to the happiness I meet here; but contentment is so new a sight to me, that I could never be weary of looking at yourself and your husband."

"We are very happy, monsieur," replied Julie; "but we have also known unhappiness, and few have ever undergone more bitter sufferings than ourselves."

The count's features displayed an expression of the most intense curiosity.

"Oh, all this is a family history, as Château-Renaud told you the other day," observed Maximilian. "This humble picture would have but little interest for you, accustomed as you are to behold the pleasures and the misfortunes of the wealthy and industrious; but such as we are, we have experienced bitter sorrows."

"And God has poured balm into your wounds, as he does into those of all who are in affliction?" said Monte Cristo inquiringly.

"Yes, count," returned Julie, "we may indeed say he has, for he has done for us what he grants only to his chosen; he sent us one of his angels."

The count's cheeks became scarlet, and he coughed, in order to have an excuse for putting his handkerchief to his mouth.

"Those born to wealth, and who have the means of gratifying every wish," said Emmanuel, "know not what is the real happiness of life, just as those who have been tossed on the stormy waters of the ocean on a few frail planks can alone realize the blessings of fair weather."

Monte Cristo rose, and without making any answer (for the tremulousness of his voice would have betrayed his emotion) walked up and down the apartment with a slow step.

"Our magnificence makes you smile, count," said Maximilian, who had followed him with his eyes.

"No, no," returned Monte Cristo, pale as death, pressing one hand on his heart to still its throbbings, while with the other he pointed to a crystal cover, beneath which a silken purse lay on a black velvet cushion. "I was wondering what could be the significance of this purse, with the paper at one end and the large diamond at the other."

"Count," replied Maximilian, with an air of gravity, "those are our most precious family treasures."

"The stone seems very brilliant," answered the count.

"Oh, my brother does not allude to its value, although it has been estimated at 100,000 francs; he means, that the articles contained in this purse are the relics of the angel I spoke of just now."

"This I do not comprehend; and yet I may not ask for an explanation, madame," replied Monte Cristo bowing. "Pardon me, I had no intention of committing an indiscretion."

"Indiscretion,—oh, you make us happy by giving us an excuse for expatiating on this subject. If we wanted to conceal the noble action this purse commemorates, we should not expose it thus to view. Oh, would we could relate it everywhere, and to everyone, so that the emotion of our unknown benefactor might reveal his presence."

"Ah, really," said Monte Cristo in a half-stifled voice.

"Monsieur," returned Maximilian, raising the glass cover, and respectfully kissing the silken purse, "this has touched the hand of a man who saved my father from suicide, us from ruin, and our name from shame and disgrace,—a man by whose matchless benevolence we poor children, doomed to want and wretchedness, can at present hear everyone envying our happy lot. This letter" (as he spoke, Maximilian drew a letter from the purse and gave it to the count)—"this letter was written by him the day that my father had taken a desperate resolution, and this diamond was given by the generous unknown to my sister as her dowry."

Monte Cristo opened the letter, and read it with an indescribable feeling of delight. It was the letter written (as our readers know) to Julie, and signed "Sinbad the Sailor."

"Unknown you say, is the man who rendered you this service—unknown to you?"

"Yes; we have never had the happiness of pressing his hand," continued Maximilian. "We have supplicated Heaven in vain to grant us this favor, but the whole affair has had a mysterious meaning that we cannot comprehend—we have been guided by an invisible hand,—a hand as powerful as that of an enchanter."

"Oh," cried Julie, "I have not lost all hope of some day kissing that hand, as I now kiss the purse which he has touched. Four years ago, Penelon was at Trieste—Penelon, count, is the old sailor you saw in the garden, and who, from quartermaster, has become gardener—Penelon, when he was at Trieste, saw on the quay an Englishman, who was on the point of embarking on board a yacht, and he recognized him as the person who called on my father the fifth of June, 1829, and who wrote me this letter on the fifth of September. He felt convinced of his identity, but he did not venture to address him."

"An Englishman," said Monte Cristo, who grew uneasy at the attention with which Julie looked at him. "An Englishman you say?"

"Yes," replied Maximilian, "an Englishman, who represented himself as the confidential clerk of the house of Thomson & French, at Rome. It was this that made me start when you said the other day, at M. de Morcerf's, that Messrs. Thomson & French were your bankers. That happened, as I told you, in 1829. For God's sake, tell me, did you know this Englishman?"

"But you tell me, also, that the house of Thomson & French have constantly denied having rendered you this service?"

"Yes."

"Then is it not probable that this Englishman may be someone who, grateful for a kindness your father had shown him, and which he himself had forgotten, has taken this method of requiting the obligation?"

"Everything is possible in this affair, even a miracle."

"What was his name?" asked Monte Cristo.

"He gave no other name," answered Julie, looking earnestly at the count, "than that at the end of his letter—'Sinbad the Sailor.'"

"Which is evidently not his real name, but a fictitious one."

Then, noticing that Julie was struck with the sound of his voice:

"Tell me," continued he, "was he not about my height, perhaps a little taller, with his chin imprisoned, as it were, in a high cravat; his coat closely buttoned up, and constantly taking out his pencil?"

"Oh, do you then know him?" cried Julie, whose eyes sparkled with joy.

"No," returned Monte Cristo "I only guessed. I knew a Lord Wilmore, who was constantly doing actions of this kind."

"Without revealing himself?"

"He was an eccentric being, and did not believe in the existence of gratitude."

"Oh, Heaven," exclaimed Julie, clasping her hands, "in what did he believe, then?"

"He did not credit it at the period which I knew him," said Monte Cristo, touched to the heart by the accents of Julie's voice; "but, perhaps, since then he has had proofs that gratitude does exist."

"And do you know this gentleman, monsieur?" inquired Emmanuel.

"Oh, if you do know him," cried Julie, "can you tell us where he is—where we can find him? Maximilian—Emmanuel—if we do but discover him, he must believe in the gratitude of the heart!"

Monte Cristo felt tears start into his eyes, and he again walked hastily up and down the room.

"In the name of Heaven," said Maximilian, "if you know anything of him, tell us what it is."

"Alas," cried Monte Cristo, striving to repress his emotion, "if Lord Wilmore was your unknown benefactor, I fear you will never see him again. I parted from him two years ago at Palermo, and he was then on the point of setting out for the most remote regions; so that I fear he will never return."

"Oh, monsieur, this is cruel of you," said Julie, much affected; and the young lady's eyes swam with tears.

"Madame," replied Monte Cristo gravely, and gazing earnestly on the two liquid pearls that trickled down Julie's cheeks, "had Lord Wilmore seen what I now see, he would become attached to life, for the tears you shed would reconcile him to mankind;" and he held out his hand to Julie, who gave him hers, carried away by the look and accent of the count.

"But," continued she, "Lord Wilmore had a family or friends, he must have known someone, can we not—"

"Oh, it is useless to inquire," returned the count; "perhaps, after all, he was not the man you seek for. He was my friend: he had no secrets from me, and if this had been so he would have confided in me."

"And he told you nothing?"

"Not a word."

"Nothing that would lead you to suppose?"

"Nothing."

"And yet you spoke of him at once."

"Ah, in such a case one supposes—"

"Sister, sister," said Maximilian, coming to the count's aid, "monsieur is quite right. Recollect what our excellent father so often told us, 'It was no Englishman that thus saved us.'"

Monte Cristo started. "What did your father tell you, M. Morrel?" said he eagerly.

"My father thought that this action had been miraculously performed—he believed that a benefactor had arisen from the grave to save us. Oh, it was a touching superstition, monsieur, and although I did not myself believe it, I would not for the world have destroyed my father's faith. How often did he muse over it and pronounce the name of a dear friend—a friend lost to him forever; and on his death-bed, when the near approach of eternity seemed to have illumined his mind with supernatural light, this thought, which had until then been but a doubt, became a conviction, and his last words were, 'Maximilian, it was Edmond Dantès!'"

At these words the count's paleness, which had for some time been increasing, became alarming; he could not speak; he looked at his watch like a man who has forgotten the hour, said a few hurried words to Madame Herbault, and pressing the hands of Emmanuel and Maximilian,—"Madame," said he, "I trust you will allow me to visit you occasionally; I value your friendship, and feel grateful to you for your welcome, for this is the first time for many years that I have thus yielded to my feelings;" and he hastily quitted the apartment.

"This Count of Monte Cristo is a strange man," said Emmanuel.

"Yes," answered Maximilian, "but I feel sure he has an excellent heart, and that he likes us."

"His voice went to my heart," observed Julie; "and two or three times I fancied that I had heard it before."

Study Guide Questions

For Students:

1. Where does the Morrel Family live?
2. Who is part of the Morrel Family?
3. How much wealth does M. Morrel leave for his children?

For Reading Club:

1. Do you think that Emmanuel and Julie paint a very positive image of marital life?
2. The Morrel Family believes that true happiness is known to those who have been "tossed on the stormy waters of the ocean." Do you agree?
3. What does Maximilian tell the Count about his father's time near death?

CHAPTER 51

Pyramus and Thisbe

About two-thirds of the way along the Faubourg Saint-Honoré, and in the rear of one of the most imposing mansions in this rich neighborhood, where the various houses vie with each other for elegance of design and magnificence of construction, extended a large garden, where the wide-spreading chestnut-trees raised their heads high above the walls in a solid rampart, and with the coming of every spring scattered a shower of delicate pink and white blossoms into the large stone vases that stood upon the two square pilasters of a curiously wrought iron gate, that dated from the time of Louis XIII.

This noble entrance, however, in spite of its striking appearance and the graceful effect of the geraniums planted in the two vases, as they waved their variegated leaves in the wind and charmed the eye with their scarlet bloom, had fallen into utter disuse. The proprietors of the mansion had many years before thought it best to confine themselves to the possession of the house itself, with its thickly planted courtyard, opening into the Faubourg Saint-Honoré, and to the garden shut in by this gate, which formerly communicated with a fine kitchen-garden of about an acre. For the demon of speculation drew a line, or in other words projected a street, at the farther side of the kitchen-garden. The street was laid out, a name was chosen and posted up on an iron plate, but before construction was begun, it occurred to the possessor of the property that a handsome sum might be obtained for the ground then devoted to fruits and vegetables, by building along the line of the proposed street, and so making it a branch of communication with the Faubourg Saint-Honoré itself, one of the most important thoroughfares in the city of Paris.

In matters of speculation, however, though "man proposes," yet "money disposes." From some such difficulty the newly named street died almost in birth, and the purchaser of the kitchen-garden, having paid a high price for it, and being quite unable to find anyone willing to take his bargain off his hands without a considerable loss, yet still clinging to the belief that at some future day he should obtain a sum for it that would repay him, not only for his past outlay, but also the interest upon the capital locked up in his new acquisition, contented himself with letting the ground temporarily to some market-gardeners, at a yearly rental of 500 francs.

And so, as we have said, the iron gate leading into the kitchen-garden had been closed up and left to the rust, which bade fair before long to eat off its hinges, while to prevent the ignoble glances of the diggers and delvers of the ground from presuming to sully the aristocratic enclosure belonging to the mansion, the gate had been boarded up to a height of six feet. True, the planks were not so closely adjusted but that a hasty peep might be obtained through their interstices; but the strict decorum and rigid propriety of the inhabitants of the house left no grounds for apprehending that advantage would be taken of that circumstance.

Horticulture seemed, however, to have been abandoned in the deserted kitchen-garden; and where cabbages, carrots, radishes, peas, and melons had once flourished, a scanty crop of lucern alone bore evidence of its being deemed worthy of cultivation. A small, low door gave egress from the walled space we have been describing into the projected street, the ground having been abandoned as unproductive by its various renters, and had now fallen so completely in general estimation as to return not even the one-half per cent it had originally paid. Towards the house the chestnut-trees we have before mentioned rose high above the wall, without in any way affecting the growth of other luxuriant shrubs and flowers that eagerly dressed forward to fill up the vacant spaces, as though asserting their right to enjoy the boon of light and air. At one corner, where the foliage became so thick as almost to shut out day, a large stone bench and sundry rustic seats indicated that this sheltered spot was either in general favor or particular use by some inhabitant of the house, which was faintly discernible through the dense mass of verdure that partially concealed it, though situated but a hundred paces off.

Whoever had selected this retired portion of the grounds as the boundary of a walk, or as a place for meditation, was abundantly justified in the choice by the absence of all glare, the cool, refreshing shade, the screen it afforded from the scorching rays of the sun, that found no entrance there even during the burning days of hottest summer, the incessant and melodious warbling of birds, and the entire removal from either the noise of the street or the bustle of the mansion. On the evening of one of the warmest days spring had yet bestowed on the inhabitants of Paris, might be seen negligently thrown upon the stone bench, a book, a parasol, and a work-basket, from which hung a partly embroidered cambric handkerchief, while at a little distance from these articles was a young woman, standing close to the iron gate, endeavoring to discern something on the other side by means of the openings in the planks,—the earnestness of her attitude and the fixed gaze with which she seemed to seek the object of her wishes, proving how much her feelings were interested in the matter.

At that instant the little side-gate leading from the waste ground to the street was noiselessly opened, and a tall, powerful young man appeared. He was dressed in a common gray blouse and velvet cap, but his carefully arranged hair, beard and moustache, all of the richest and glossiest black, ill accorded with his plebeian attire. After casting a rapid glance around him, in order to assure himself that he was unobserved, he entered by the small gate, and, carefully closing and securing it after him, proceeded with a hurried step towards the barrier.

At the sight of him she expected, though probably not in such a costume, the young woman started in terror, and was about to make a hasty retreat. But the eye of love had already seen, even through the narrow chinks of the wooden palisades, the movement of the white robe, and observed the fluttering of the blue sash. Pressing his lips close to the planks, he exclaimed:

"Don't be alarmed, Valentine—it is I!"

Again the timid girl found courage to return to the gate, saying, as she did so:

"And why do you come so late today? It is almost dinner-time, and I had to use no little diplomacy to get rid of my watchful stepmother, my too-devoted maid, and my troublesome brother, who is always teasing me about coming to work at my embroidery, which I am in a fair way never to get done. So pray excuse yourself as well as you can for having made me wait, and, after that, tell me why I see you in a dress so singular that at first I did not recognize you."

"Dearest Valentine," said the young man, "the difference between our respective stations makes me fear to offend you by speaking of my love, but yet I cannot find myself in your presence without longing to pour forth my soul, and tell you how fondly I adore you. If it be but to carry away with me the recollection of such sweet moments, I could even thank you for chiding me, for it leaves me a gleam of hope, that if you did not expect me (and that indeed would be worse than vanity to suppose), at least I was in your thoughts. You asked me the cause of my being late, and why I come disguised. I will candidly explain the reason of both, and I trust to your goodness to pardon me. I have chosen a trade."

"A trade? Oh, Maximilian, how can you jest at a time when we have such deep cause for uneasiness?"

"Heaven keep me from jesting with that which is far dearer to me than life itself! But listen to me, Valentine, and I will tell you all about it. I became weary of ranging fields and scaling walls, and seriously alarmed at the idea suggested by you, that if caught hovering about here your father would very likely have me sent to prison as a thief. That would compromise the honor of the French army, to say nothing of the fact that the continual presence of a captain of Spahis in a place where no warlike projects could be supposed to account for it might well create surprise; so I have become a gardener, and, consequently, adopted the costume of my calling."

"What excessive nonsense you talk, Maximilian!"

"Nonsense? Pray do not call what I consider the wisest action of my life by such a name. Consider, by becoming a gardener I effectually screen our meetings from all suspicion or danger."

"I beseech of you, Maximilian, to cease trifling, and tell me what you really mean."

"Simply, that having ascertained that the piece of ground on which I stand was to let, I made application for it, was readily accepted by the proprietor, and am now master of this fine crop of lucern. Think of that, Valentine! There is nothing now to prevent my building myself a little hut on my plantation, and residing not twenty yards from you. Only imagine what happiness that would afford me. I can scarcely contain myself at the bare idea. Such felicity seems above all price—as a thing impossible and unattainable. But would you believe that I purchase all this delight, joy, and happiness, for which I would cheerfully have surrendered ten years of my life, at the small cost of 500 francs per annum, paid quarterly? Henceforth we have nothing to fear. I am on my own ground, and have an undoubted right to place a ladder against the wall, and to look over when I please, without having any apprehensions of being taken off by the police as a suspicious character. I may also enjoy the precious privilege of assuring you of my fond, faithful, and unalterable affection, whenever you visit your favorite bower, unless, indeed, it offends your pride to listen to professions of love from the lips of a poor workingman, clad in a blouse and cap."

A faint cry of mingled pleasure and surprise escaped from the lips of Valentine, who almost instantly said, in a saddened tone, as though some envious cloud darkened the joy which illumined her heart:

"Alas, no, Maximilian, this must not be, for many reasons. We should presume too much on our own strength, and, like others, perhaps, be led astray by our blind confidence in each other's prudence."

"How can you for an instant entertain so unworthy a thought, dear Valentine? Have I not, from the first blessed hour of our acquaintance, schooled all my words and actions to your sentiments and ideas? And you have, I am sure, the fullest confidence in my honor. When you spoke to me of experiencing a vague and indefinite sense of coming danger, I placed myself blindly and devotedly at your service, asking no other reward than the pleasure of being useful to you; and have I ever since, by word or look, given you cause of regret for having selected me from the numbers that would willingly have sacrificed their lives for you? You told me, my dear Valentine, that you were engaged to M. d'Épinay, and that your father was resolved upon completing the match, and that from his will there was no appeal, as M. de Villefort was never known to change a determination once formed. I kept in the background, as you wished, and waited, not for the decision of your heart or my own, but hoping that Providence would graciously interpose in our behalf, and order events in our favor. But what cared I for delays or difficulties, Valentine, as long as you confessed that you loved me, and took pity on me? If you will only repeat that avowal now and then, I can endure anything."

"Ah, Maximilian, that is the very thing that makes you so bold, and which renders me at once so happy and unhappy, that I frequently ask myself whether it is better for me to endure the harshness of my stepmother, and her blind preference for her own child, or to be, as I now am, insensible to any pleasure save such as I find in these meetings, so fraught with danger to both."

"I will not admit that word," returned the young man; "it is at once cruel and unjust. Is it possible to find a more submissive slave than myself? You have permitted me to converse with you from time to time, Valentine, but forbidden my ever following you in your walks or elsewhere—have I not obeyed? And since I found means to enter this enclosure to exchange a few words with you through this gate—to be close to you without really seeing you—have I ever asked so much as to touch the hem of your gown or tried to pass this barrier which is but a trifle to one of my youth and strength? Never has a complaint or a murmur escaped me. I have been bound by my promises as rigidly as any knight of olden times. Come, come, dearest Valentine, confess that what I say is true, lest I be tempted to call you unjust."

"It is true," said Valentine, as she passed the end of her slender fingers through a small opening in the planks, and permitted Maximilian to press his lips to them, "and you are a true and faithful friend; but still you acted from motives of self-interest, my dear Maximilian, for you well knew that from the moment in which you had manifested an opposite spirit all would have been ended between us. You promised to bestow on me the friendly affection of a brother. For I have no friend but yourself upon earth, who am neglected and forgotten by my father, harassed and persecuted by my stepmother, and left to the sole companionship of a paralyzed and speechless old man, whose withered hand can no longer press mine, and who can speak to me with the eye alone, although there still lingers in his heart the warmest tenderness for his poor grandchild. Oh, how bitter a fate is mine, to serve either as a victim or an enemy to all who are stronger than myself, while my only friend and supporter is a living corpse! Indeed, indeed, Maximilian, I am very miserable, and if you love me it must be out of pity."

"Valentine," replied the young man, deeply affected, "I will not say you are all I love in the world, for I dearly prize my sister and brother-in-law; but my affection for them is calm and tranquil, in no manner resembling what I feel for you. When I think of you my heart beats fast, the blood burns in my veins, and I can hardly breathe; but I solemnly promise you to restrain all this ardor, this fervor and intensity of feeling, until you yourself shall require me to render them available in serving or assisting you. M. Franz is not expected to return home for a year to come, I am told; in that time many favorable and unforeseen chances may befriend us. Let us, then, hope for the best; hope is so sweet a comforter. Meanwhile, Valentine, while reproaching me with selfishness, think a little what you have been to me—the beautiful but cold resemblance of a marble Venus. What promise of future reward have you made me for all the submission and obedience I have evinced?—none whatever. What granted me?—scarcely more. You tell me of M. Franz d'Épinay, your betrothed lover, and you shrink from the idea of being his wife; but tell me, Valentine, is there no other sorrow in your heart? You see me devoted to you, body and soul, my life and each warm drop that circles round my heart are consecrated to your service; you know full well that my existence is bound up in yours—that were I to lose you I would not outlive the hour of such crushing misery; yet you speak with calmness of the prospect of your being the wife of another! Oh, Valentine, were I in your place, and did I feel conscious, as you do, of being worshipped, adored, with such a love as mine, a hundred times at least should I have passed my hand between these iron bars, and said, 'Take this hand, dearest Maximilian, and believe that, living or dead, I am yours—yours only, and forever!'"

The poor girl made no reply, but her lover could plainly hear her sobs and tears. A rapid change took place in the young man's feelings.

"Dearest, dearest Valentine," exclaimed he, "forgive me if I have offended you, and forget the words I spoke if they have unwittingly caused you pain."

"No, Maximilian, I am not offended," answered she, "but do you not see what a poor, helpless being I am, almost a stranger and an outcast in my father's house, where even he is seldom seen; whose will has been thwarted, and spirits broken, from the age of ten years, beneath the iron rod so sternly held over me; oppressed, mortified, and persecuted, day by day, hour by hour, minute by minute, no person has cared for, even observed my sufferings, nor have I ever breathed one word on the subject save to yourself. Outwardly and in the eyes of the world, I am surrounded by kindness and affection; but the reverse is the case. The general remark is, 'Oh, it cannot be expected that one of so stern a character as M. Villefort could lavish the tenderness some fathers do on their daughters. What though she has lost her own mother at a tender age, she has had the happiness to find a second mother in Madame de Villefort.' The world, however, is mistaken; my father abandons me from utter indifference, while my stepmother detests me with a hatred so much the more terrible because it is veiled beneath a continual smile."

"Hate you, sweet Valentine," exclaimed the young man; "how is it possible for anyone to do that?"

"Alas," replied the weeping girl, "I am obliged to own that my stepmother's aversion to me arises from a very natural source—her overweening love for her own child, my brother Edward."

"But why should it?"

"I do not know; but, though unwilling to introduce money matters into our present conversation, I will just say this much—that her extreme dislike to me has its origin there; and I much fear she envies me the fortune I enjoy in right of my mother, and which will be more than doubled at the death of M. and Mme. de Saint-Méran, whose sole heiress I am. Madame de Villefort has nothing of her own, and hates me for being so richly endowed. Alas, how gladly would I exchange the half of this wealth for the happiness of at least sharing my father's love. God knows, I would prefer sacrificing the whole, so that it would obtain me a happy and affectionate home."

"Poor Valentine!"

"I seem to myself as though living a life of bondage, yet at the same time am so conscious of my own weakness that I fear to break the restraint in which I am held, lest I fall utterly helpless. Then, too, my father is not a person whose orders may be infringed with impunity; protected as he is by his high position and firmly established reputation for talent and unswerving integrity, no one could oppose him; he is all-powerful even with the king; he would crush you at a word. Dear Maximilian, believe me when I assure you that if I do not attempt to resist my father's commands it is more on your account than my own."

"But why, Valentine, do you persist in anticipating the worst,—why picture so gloomy a future?"

"Because I judge it from the past."

"Still, consider that although I may not be, strictly speaking, what is termed an illustrious match for you, I am, for many reasons, not altogether so much beneath your alliance. The days when such distinctions were so nicely weighed and considered no longer exist in France, and the first families of the monarchy have intermarried with those of the empire. The aristocracy of the lance has allied itself with the nobility of the cannon. Now I belong to this last-named class; and certainly my prospects of military preferment are most encouraging as well as certain. My fortune, though small, is free and unfettered, and the memory of my late father is respected in our country, Valentine, as that of the most upright and honorable merchant of the city; I say our country, because you were born not far from Marseilles."

"Don't speak of Marseilles, I beg of you, Maximilian; that one word brings back my mother to my recollection—my angel mother, who died too soon for myself and all who knew her; but who, after watching over her child during the brief period allotted to her in this world, now, I fondly hope, watches from her home in heaven. Oh, if my mother were still living, there would be nothing to fear, Maximilian, for I would tell her that I loved you, and she would protect us."

"I fear, Valentine," replied the lover, "that were she living I should never have had the happiness of knowing you; you would then have been too happy to have stooped from your grandeur to bestow a thought on me."

"Now it is you who are unjust, Maximilian," cried Valentine; "but there is one thing I wish to know."

"And what is that?" inquired the young man, perceiving that Valentine hesitated.

"Tell me truly, Maximilian, whether in former days, when our fathers dwelt at Marseilles, there was ever any misunderstanding between them?"

"Not that I am aware of," replied the young man, "unless, indeed, any ill-feeling might have arisen from their being of opposite parties—your father was, as you know, a zealous partisan of the Bourbons, while mine was wholly devoted to the emperor; there could not possibly be any other difference between them. But why do you ask?"

"I will tell you," replied the young girl, "for it is but right you should know. Well, on the day when your appointment as an officer of the Legion of Honor was announced in the papers, we were all sitting with my grandfather, M. Noirtier; M. Danglars was there also—you recollect M. Danglars, do you not, Maximilian, the banker, whose horses ran away with my stepmother and little brother, and very nearly killed them? While the rest of the company were discussing the approaching marriage of Mademoiselle Danglars, I was reading the paper to my grandfather; but when I came to the paragraph about you, although I had done nothing else but read it over to myself all the morning (you know you had told me all about it the previous evening), I felt so happy, and yet so nervous, at the idea of speaking your name aloud, and before so many people, that I really think I should have passed it over, but for the fear that my doing so might create suspicions as to the cause of my silence; so I summoned up all my courage, and read it as firmly and as steadily as I could."

"Dear Valentine!"

"Well, would you believe it? directly my father caught the sound of your name he turned round quite hastily, and, like a poor silly thing, I was so persuaded that everyone must be as much affected as myself by the utterance of your name, that I was not surprised to see my father start, and almost tremble; but I even thought (though that surely must have been a mistake) that M. Danglars trembled too."

"'Morrel, Morrel,' cried my father, 'stop a bit;' then knitting his brows into a deep frown, he added, 'surely this cannot be one of the Morrel family who lived at Marseilles, and gave us so much trouble from their violent Bonapartism—I mean about the year 1815.'

"'Yes,' replied M. Danglars, 'I believe he is the son of the old shipowner.'"

"Indeed," answered Maximilian; "and what did your father say then, Valentine?"

"Oh, such a dreadful thing, that I don't dare to tell you."

"Always tell me everything," said Maximilian with a smile.

"'Ah,' continued my father, still frowning, 'their idolized emperor treated these madmen as they deserved; he called them 'food for cannon,' which was precisely all they were good for; and I am delighted to see that the present government have adopted this salutary principle with all its pristine vigor; if Algiers were good for nothing but to furnish the means of carrying so admirable an idea into practice, it would be an acquisition well worthy of struggling to obtain. Though it certainly does cost France somewhat dear to assert her rights in that uncivilized country.'"

"Brutal politics, I must confess." said Maximilian; "but don't attach any serious importance, dear, to what your father said. My father was not a bit behind yours in that sort of talk. 'Why,' said he, 'does not the emperor, who has devised so many clever and efficient modes of improving the art of war, organize a regiment of lawyers, judges and legal practitioners, sending them in the hottest fire the enemy could maintain, and using them to save better men?' You see, my dear, that for picturesque expression and generosity of spirit there is not much to choose between the language of either party. But what did M. Danglars say to this outburst on the part of the procureur?"

"Oh, he laughed, and in that singular manner so peculiar to himself—half-malicious, half-ferocious; he almost immediately got up and took his leave; then, for the first time, I observed the agitation of my grandfather, and I must tell you, Maximilian, that I am the only person capable of discerning emotion in his paralyzed frame. And I suspected that the conversation that had been carried on in his presence (for they always say and do what they like before the dear old man, without the smallest regard for his feelings) had made a strong impression on his mind; for, naturally enough, it must have pained him to hear the emperor he so devotedly loved and served spoken of in that depreciating manner."

"The name of M. Noirtier," interposed Maximilian, "is celebrated throughout Europe; he was a statesman of high standing, and you may or may not know, Valentine, that he took a leading part in every Bonapartist conspiracy set on foot during the restoration of the Bourbons."

"Oh, I have often heard whispers of things that seem to me most strange—the father a Bonapartist, the son a Royalist; what can have been the reason of so singular a difference in parties and politics? But to resume my story; I turned towards my grandfather, as though to question him as to the cause of his emotion; he looked expressively at the newspaper I had been reading. 'What is the matter, dear grandfather?' said I, 'are you pleased?' He gave me a sign in the affirmative. 'With what my father said just now?' He returned a sign in the negative. 'Perhaps you liked what M. Danglars said?' Another sign in the negative. 'Oh, then, you were glad to hear that M. Morrel (I didn't dare to say Maximilian) had been made an officer of the Legion of Honor?' He signified assent; only think of the poor old man's being so pleased to think that you, who were a perfect stranger to him, had been made an officer of the Legion of Honor! Perhaps it was a mere whim on his part, for he is falling, they say, into second childhood, but I love him for showing so much interest in you."

"How singular," murmured Maximilian; "your father hates me, while your grandfather, on the contrary—What strange feelings are aroused by politics."

"Hush," cried Valentine, suddenly; "someone is coming!" Maximilian leaped at one bound into his crop of lucern, which he began to pull up in the most ruthless way, under the pretext of being occupied in weeding it.

"Mademoiselle, mademoiselle!" exclaimed a voice from behind the trees. "Madame is searching for you everywhere; there is a visitor in the drawing-room."

"A visitor?" inquired Valentine, much agitated; "who is it?"

"Some grand personage—a prince I believe they said—the Count of Monte Cristo."

"I will come directly," cried Valentine aloud.

The name of Monte Cristo sent an electric shock through the young man on the other side of the iron gate, to whom Valentine's *"I am coming"* was the customary signal of farewell.

"Now, then," said Maximilian, leaning on the handle of his spade, "I would give a good deal to know how it comes about that the Count of Monte Cristo is acquainted with M. de Villefort."

Study Guide Questions

For Students:

1. Who is Valentine and what is her relationship with Maximilian?
2. Who is Valentine's fiancé?
3. Why is Valentine's stepmother envious of her?

For Reading Club:

1. Maximilian is a good man with bright prospects but still not good enough for rich Valentine. Do you think such class discrimination is part of contemporary society?
2. Maximilian shares a piece of important news with Valentine. What does it tell you about his character?
3. Valentine seems confused about whether to choose Franz d' Epinay or Maximilian Morrel. Do you think such confusion is felt by modern women?

CHAPTER 52

Toxicology

It was really the Count of Monte Cristo who had just arrived at Madame de Villefort's for the purpose of returning the procureur's visit, and at his name, as may be easily imagined, the whole house was in confusion.

Madame de Villefort, who was alone in her drawing-room when the count was announced, desired that her son might be brought thither instantly to renew his thanks to the count; and Edward, who heard this great personage talked of for two whole days, made all possible haste to come to him, not from obedience to his mother, or out of any feeling of gratitude to the count, but from sheer curiosity, and that some chance remark might give him the opportunity for making one of the impertinent speeches which made his mother say:

"Oh, that naughty child! But I can't be severe with him, he is really *so* bright."

After the usual civilities, the count inquired after M. de Villefort.

"My husband dines with the chancellor," replied the young lady; "he has just gone, and I am sure he'll be exceedingly sorry not to have had the pleasure of seeing you before he went."

Two visitors who were there when the count arrived, having gazed at him with all their eyes, retired after that reasonable delay which politeness admits and curiosity requires.

"What is your sister Valentine doing?" inquired Madame de Villefort of Edward; "tell someone to bid her come here, that I may have the honor of introducing her to the count."

"You have a daughter, then, madame?" inquired the count; "very young, I presume?"

"The daughter of M. de Villefort by his first marriage," replied the young wife, "a fine well-grown girl."

"But melancholy," interrupted Master Edward, snatching the feathers out of the tail of a splendid paroquet that was screaming on its gilded perch, in order to make a plume for his hat.

Madame de Villefort merely cried, "Be still, Edward!" She then added, "This young madcap is, however, very nearly right, and merely re-echoes what he has heard me say with pain a hundred times; for Mademoiselle de Villefort is, in spite of all we can do to rouse her, of a melancholy disposition and taciturn habit, which frequently injure the effect of her beauty. But what detains her? Go, Edward, and see."

"Because they are looking for her where she is not to be found."

"And where are they looking for her?"

"With grandpapa Noirtier."

"And do you think she is not there?"

"No, no, no, no, no, she is not there," replied Edward, singing his words.

"And where is she, then? If you know, why don't you tell?"

"She is under the big chestnut-tree," replied the spoiled brat, as he gave, in spite of his mother's commands, live flies to the parrot, which seemed keenly to relish such fare.

Madame de Villefort stretched out her hand to ring, intending to direct her waiting-maid to the spot where she would find Valentine, when the young lady herself entered the apartment. She appeared much dejected; and any person who considered her attentively might have observed the traces of recent tears in her eyes.

Valentine, whom we have in the rapid march of our narrative presented to our readers without formally introducing her, was a tall and graceful girl of nineteen, with bright chestnut hair, deep blue eyes, and that reposeful air of quiet distinction which characterized her mother. Her white and slender fingers, her pearly neck, her cheeks tinted with varying hues reminded one of the lovely Englishwomen who have been so poetically compared in their manner to the gracefulness of a swan.

She entered the apartment, and seeing near her stepmother the stranger of whom she had already heard so much, saluted him without any girlish awkwardness, or even lowering her eyes, and with an elegance that redoubled the count's attention.

He rose to return the salutation.

"Mademoiselle de Villefort, my step-daughter," said Madame de Villefort to Monte Cristo, leaning back on her sofa and motioning towards Valentine with her hand.

"And M. de Monte Cristo, King of China, Emperor of Cochin-China," said the young imp, looking slyly towards his sister.

Madame de Villefort at this really did turn pale, and was very nearly angry with this household plague, who answered to the name of Edward; but the count, on the contrary, smiled, and appeared to look at the boy complacently, which caused the maternal heart to bound again with joy and enthusiasm.

"But, madame," replied the count, continuing the conversation, and looking by turns at Madame de Villefort and Valentine, "have I not already had the honor of meeting yourself and mademoiselle before? I could not help thinking so just now; the idea came over my mind, and as mademoiselle entered the sight of her was an additional ray of light thrown on a confused remembrance; excuse the remark."

"I do not think it likely, sir; Mademoiselle de Villefort is not very fond of society, and we very seldom go out," said the young lady.

"Then it was not in society that I met with mademoiselle or yourself, madame, or this charming little merry boy. Besides, the Parisian world is entirely unknown to me, for, as I believe I told you, I have been in Paris but very few days. No,—but, perhaps, you will permit me to call to mind—stay!"

The Count placed his hand on his brow as if to collect his thoughts.

"No—it was somewhere—away from here—it was—I do not know—but it appears that this recollection is connected with a lovely sky and some religious *fête*; mademoiselle was holding flowers in her hand, the interesting boy was chasing a beautiful peacock in a garden, and you, madame, were under the trellis of some arbor. Pray come to my aid, madame; do not these circumstances appeal to your memory?"

"No, indeed," replied Madame de Villefort; "and yet it appears to me, sir, that if I had met you anywhere, the recollection of you must have been imprinted on my memory."

"Perhaps the count saw us in Italy," said Valentine timidly.

"Yes, in Italy; it was in Italy most probably," replied Monte Cristo; "you have travelled then in Italy, mademoiselle?"

"Yes; madame and I were there two years ago. The doctors, anxious for my lungs, had prescribed the air of Naples. We went by Bologna, Perugia, and Rome."

"Ah, yes—true, mademoiselle," exclaimed Monte Cristo as if this simple explanation was sufficient to revive the recollection he sought. "It was at Perugia on Corpus Christi Day, in the garden of the Hôtel des Postes, when chance brought us together; you, Madame de Villefort, and her son; I now remember having had the honor of meeting you."

"I perfectly well remember Perugia, sir, and the Hôtel des Postes, and the festival of which you speak," said Madame de Villefort, "but in vain do I tax my memory, of whose treachery I am ashamed, for I really do not recall to mind that I ever had the pleasure of seeing you before."

"It is strange, but neither do I recollect meeting with you," observed Valentine, raising her beautiful eyes to the count.

"But I remember it perfectly," interposed the darling Edward.

"I will assist your memory, madame," continued the count; "the day had been burning hot; you were waiting for horses, which were delayed in consequence of the festival. Mademoiselle was walking in the shade of the garden, and your son disappeared in pursuit of the peacock."

"And I caught it, mamma, don't you remember?" interposed Edward, "and I pulled three such beautiful feathers out of his tail."

"You, madame, remained under the arbor; do you not remember, that while you were seated on a stone bench, and while, as I told you, Mademoiselle de Villefort and your young son were absent, you conversed for a considerable time with somebody?"

"Yes, in truth, yes," answered the young lady, turning very red, "I do remember conversing with a person wrapped in a long woollen mantle; he was a medical man, I think."

"Precisely so, madame; this man was myself; for a fortnight I had been at that hotel, during which period I had cured my valet de chambre of a fever, and my landlord of the jaundice, so that I really acquired a reputation as a skilful physician. We discoursed a long time, madame, on different subjects; of Perugino, of Raphael, of manners, customs, of the famous *aqua Tofana*, of which they had told you, I think you said, that certain individuals in Perugia had preserved the secret."

"Yes, true," replied Madame de Villefort, somewhat uneasily, "I remember now."

"I do not recollect now all the various subjects of which we discoursed, madame," continued the count with perfect calmness; "but I perfectly remember that, falling into the error which others had entertained respecting me, you consulted me as to the health of Mademoiselle de Villefort."

"Yes, really, sir, you were in fact a medical man," said Madame de Villefort, "since you had cured the sick."

"Molière or Beaumarchais would reply to you, madame, that it was precisely because I was not, that I had cured my patients; for myself, I am content to say to you that I have studied chemistry and the natural sciences somewhat deeply, but still only as an amateur, you understand."

At this moment the clock struck six.

"It is six o'clock," said Madame de Villefort, evidently agitated. "Valentine, will you not go and see if your grandpapa will have his dinner?"

Valentine rose, and saluting the count, left the apartment without speaking.

"Oh, madame," said the count, when Valentine had left the room, "was it on my account that you sent Mademoiselle de Villefort away?"

"By no means," replied the young lady quickly; "but this is the hour when we usually give M. Noirtier the unwelcome meal that sustains his pitiful existence. You are aware, sir, of the deplorable condition of my husband's father?"

"Yes, madame, M. de Villefort spoke of it to me—a paralysis, I think."

"Alas, yes; the poor old gentleman is entirely helpless; the mind alone is still active in this human machine, and that is faint and flickering, like the light of a lamp about to expire. But excuse me, sir, for talking of our domestic misfortunes; I interrupted you at the moment when you were telling me that you were a skilful chemist."

"No, madame, I did not say as much as that," replied the count with a smile; "quite the contrary. I have studied chemistry because, having determined to live in eastern climates I have been desirous of following the example of King Mithridates."

"*Mithridates, rex Ponticus*," said the young scamp, as he tore some beautiful portraits out of a splendid album, "the individual who took cream in his cup of poison every morning at breakfast."

"Edward, you naughty boy," exclaimed Madame de Villefort, snatching the mutilated book from the urchin's grasp, "you are positively past bearing; you really disturb the conversation; go, leave us, and join your sister Valentine in dear grandpapa Noirtier's room."

"The album," said Edward sulkily.

"What do you mean?—the album!"

"I want the album."

"How dare you tear out the drawings?"

"Oh, it amuses me."

"Go—go at once."

"I won't go unless you give me the album," said the boy, seating himself doggedly in an armchair, according to his habit of never giving way.

"Take it, then, and pray disturb us no longer," said Madame de Villefort, giving the album to Edward, who then went towards the door, led by his mother. The count followed her with his eyes.

"Let us see if she shuts the door after him," he muttered.

Madame de Villefort closed the door carefully after the child, the count appearing not to notice her; then casting a scrutinizing glance around the chamber, the young wife returned to her chair, in which she seated herself.

"Allow me to observe, madame," said the count, with that kind tone he could assume so well, "you are really very severe with that dear clever child."

"Oh, sometimes severity is quite necessary," replied Madame de Villefort, with all a mother's real firmness.

"It was his Cornelius Nepos that Master Edward was repeating when he referred to King Mithridates," continued the count, "and you interrupted him in a quotation which proves that his tutor has by no means neglected him, for your son is really advanced for his years."

"The fact is, count," answered the mother, agreeably flattered, "he has great aptitude, and learns all that is set before him. He has but one fault, he is somewhat wilful; but really, on referring for the moment to what he said, do you truly believe that Mithridates used these precautions, and that these precautions were efficacious?"

"I think so, madame, because I myself have made use of them, that I might not be poisoned at Naples, at Palermo, and at Smyrna—that is to say, on three several occasions when, but for these precautions, I must have lost my life."

"And your precautions were successful?"

"Completely so."

"Yes, I remember now your mentioning to me at Perugia something of this sort."

"Indeed?" said the count with an air of surprise, remarkably well counterfeited; "I really did not remember."

"I inquired of you if poisons acted equally, and with the same effect, on men of the North as on men of the South; and you answered me that the cold and sluggish habits of the North did not present the same aptitude as the rich and energetic temperaments of the natives of the South."

"And that is the case," observed Monte Cristo. "I have seen Russians devour, without being visibly inconvenienced, vegetable substances which would infallibly have killed a Neapolitan or an Arab."

"And you really believe the result would be still more sure with us than in the East, and in the midst of our fogs and rains a man would habituate himself more easily than in a warm latitude to this progressive absorption of poison?"

"Certainly; it being at the same time perfectly understood that he should have been duly fortified against the poison to which he had not been accustomed."

"Yes, I understand that; and how would you habituate yourself, for instance, or rather, how did you habituate yourself to it?"

"Oh, very easily. Suppose you knew beforehand the poison that would be made use of against you; suppose the poison was, for instance, brucine—"

"Brucine is extracted from the false angostura[1] is it not?" inquired Madame de Villefort.

"Precisely, madame," replied Monte Cristo; "but I perceive I have not much to teach you. Allow me to compliment you on your knowledge; such learning is very rare among ladies."

"Oh, I am aware of that," said Madame de Villefort; "but I have a passion for the occult sciences, which speak to the imagination like poetry, and are reducible to figures, like an algebraic equation; but go on, I beg of you; what you say interests me to the greatest degree."

"Well," replied Monte Cristo "suppose, then, that this poison was brucine, and you were to take a milligramme the first day, two milligrammes the second day, and so on. Well, at the end of ten days you would have taken a centigramme, at the end of twenty days, increasing another milligramme, you would have taken three hundred centigrammes; that is to say, a dose which you would support without inconvenience, and which would be very dangerous for any other person who had not taken the same precautions as yourself. Well, then, at the end of a month, when drinking water from the same carafe, you would kill the person who drank with you, without your perceiving, otherwise than from slight inconvenience, that there was any poisonous substance mingled with this water."

"Do you know any other counter-poisons?"

"I do not."

"I have often read, and read again, the history of Mithridates," said Madame de Villefort in a tone of reflection, "and had always considered it a fable."

"No, madame, contrary to most history, it is true; but what you tell me, madame, what you inquire of me, is not the result of a chance query, for two years ago you asked me the same questions, and said then, that for a very long time this history of Mithridates had occupied your mind."

"True, sir. The two favorite studies of my youth were botany and mineralogy, and subsequently, when I learned that the use of simples frequently explained the whole history of a people, and the entire life of individuals in the East, as flowers betoken and symbolize a love affair, I have regretted that I was not a man, that I might have been a Flamel, a Fontana, or a Cabanis."

[1] Brucea ferruginea.

"And the more, madame," said Monte Cristo, "as the Orientals do not confine themselves, as did Mithridates, to make a cuirass of his poisons, but they also made them a dagger. Science becomes, in their hands, not only a defensive weapon, but still more frequently an offensive one; the one serves against all their physical sufferings, the other against all their enemies. With opium, belladonna, brucea, snake-wood, and the cherry-laurel, they put to sleep all who stand in their way. There is not one of those women, Egyptian, Turkish, or Greek, whom here you call 'good women,' who do not know how, by means of chemistry, to stupefy a doctor, and in psychology to amaze a confessor."

"Really," said Madame de Villefort, whose eyes sparkled with strange fire at this conversation.

"Oh, yes, indeed, madame," continued Monte Cristo, "the secret dramas of the East begin with a love philtre and end with a death potion—begin with paradise and end with—hell. There are as many elixirs of every kind as there are caprices and peculiarities in the physical and moral nature of humanity; and I will say further—the art of these chemists is capable with the utmost precision to accommodate and proportion the remedy and the bane to yearnings for love or desires for vengeance."

"But, sir," remarked the young woman, "these Eastern societies, in the midst of which you have passed a portion of your existence, are as fantastic as the tales that come from their strange land. A man can easily be put out of the way there, then; it is, indeed, the Bagdad and Bassora of the *Thousand and One Nights*. The sultans and viziers who rule over society there, and who constitute what in France we call the government, are really Haroun-al-Raschids and Giaffars, who not only pardon a poisoner, but even make him a prime minister, if his crime has been an ingenious one, and who, under such circumstances, have the whole story written in letters of gold, to divert their hours of idleness and *ennui*."

"By no means, madame; the fanciful exists no longer in the East. There, disguised under other names, and concealed under other costumes, are police agents, magistrates, attorneys-general, and bailiffs. They hang, behead, and impale their criminals in the most agreeable possible manner; but some of these, like clever rogues, have contrived to escape human justice, and succeed in their fraudulent enterprises by cunning stratagems. Amongst us a simpleton, possessed by the demon of hate or cupidity, who has an enemy to destroy, or some near relation to dispose of, goes straight to the grocer's or druggist's, gives a false name, which leads more easily to his detection than his real one, and under the pretext that the rats prevent him from sleeping, purchases five or six grammes of arsenic—if he is really a cunning fellow, he goes to five or six different druggists or grocers, and thereby becomes only five or six times more easily traced;—

then, when he has acquired his specific, he administers duly to his enemy, or near kinsman, a dose of arsenic which would make a mammoth or mastodon burst, and which, without rhyme or reason, makes his victim utter groans which alarm the entire neighborhood. Then arrive a crowd of policemen and constables. They fetch a doctor, who opens the dead body, and collects from the entrails and stomach a quantity of arsenic in a spoon. Next day a hundred newspapers relate the fact, with the names of the victim and the murderer. The same evening the grocer or grocers, druggist or druggists, come and say, 'It was I who sold the arsenic to the gentleman;' and rather than not recognize the guilty purchaser, they will recognize twenty. Then the foolish criminal is taken, imprisoned, interrogated, confronted, confounded, condemned, and cut off by hemp or steel; or if she be a woman of any consideration, they lock her up for life. This is the way in which you Northerns understand chemistry, madame. Desrues was, however, I must confess, more skilful."

"What would you have, sir?" said the lady, laughing; "we do what we can. All the world has not the secret of the Medicis or the Borgias."

"Now," replied the count, shrugging his shoulders, "shall I tell you the cause of all these stupidities? It is because, at your theatres, by what at least I could judge by reading the pieces they play, they see persons swallow the contents of a phial, or suck the button of a ring, and fall dead instantly. Five minutes afterwards the curtain falls, and the spectators depart. They are ignorant of the consequences of the murder; they see neither the police commissary with his badge of office, nor the corporal with his four men; and so the poor fools believe that the whole thing is as easy as lying. But go a little way from France—go either to Aleppo or Cairo, or only to Naples or Rome, and you will see people passing by you in the streets—people erect, smiling, and fresh-colored, of whom Asmodeus, if you were holding on by the skirt of his mantle, would say, 'That man was poisoned three weeks ago; he will be a dead man in a month.'"

"Then," remarked Madame de Villefort, "they have again discovered the secret of the famous *aqua Tofana* that they said was lost at Perugia."

"Ah, but madame, does mankind ever lose anything? The arts change about and make a tour of the world; things take a different name, and the vulgar do not follow them—that is all; but there is always the same result. Poisons act particularly on some organ or another—one on the stomach, another on the brain, another on the intestines. Well, the poison brings on a cough, the cough an inflammation of the lungs, or some other complaint catalogued in the book of science, which, however, by no means precludes it from being decidedly mortal; and if it were not, would be sure to become so, thanks to the remedies applied by foolish doctors, who are generally bad chemists, and which will act in favor of or against the malady, as you please; and then there is a human being killed according to all the rules of art and skill, and of whom justice learns nothing, as was said by a terrible chemist of my acquaintance, the worthy Abbé Adelmonte of Taormina, in Sicily, who has studied these national phenomena very profoundly."

"It is quite frightful, but deeply interesting," said the young lady, motionless with attention. "I thought, I must confess, that these tales, were inventions of the Middle Ages."

"Yes, no doubt, but improved upon by ours. What is the use of time, rewards of merit, medals, crosses, Monthyon prizes, if they do not lead society towards more complete perfection? Yet man will never be perfect until he learns to create and destroy; he does know how to destroy, and that is half the battle."

"So," added Madame de Villefort, constantly returning to her object, "the poisons of the Borgias, the Medicis, the Renées, the Ruggieris, and later, probably, that of Baron de Trenck, whose story has been so misused by modern drama and romance—"

"Were objects of art, madame, and nothing more," replied the count. "Do you suppose that the real *savant* addresses himself stupidly to the mere individual? By no means. Science loves eccentricities, leaps and bounds, trials of strength, fancies, if I may be allowed so to term them. Thus, for instance, the excellent Abbé Adelmonte, of whom I spoke just now, made in this way some marvellous experiments."

"Really?"

"Yes; I will mention one to you. He had a remarkably fine garden, full of vegetables, flowers, and fruit. From amongst these vegetables he selected the most simple—a cabbage, for instance. For three days he watered this cabbage with a distillation of arsenic; on the third, the cabbage began to droop and turn yellow. At that moment he cut it. In the eyes of everybody it seemed fit for table, and preserved its wholesome appearance. It was only poisoned to the Abbé Adelmonte. He then took the cabbage to the room where he had rabbits—for the Abbé Adelmonte had a collection of rabbits, cats, and guinea-pigs, fully as fine as his collection of vegetables, flowers, and fruit. Well, the Abbé Adelmonte took a rabbit, and made it eat a leaf of the cabbage. The rabbit died. What magistrate would find, or even venture to insinuate, anything against this? What procureur has ever ventured to draw up an accusation against M. Magendie or M. Flourens, in consequence of the rabbits, cats, and guinea-pigs they have killed?—not one. So, then, the rabbit dies, and justice takes no notice. This rabbit dead, the Abbé Adelmonte has its entrails taken out by his cook and thrown on the dunghill; on this dunghill is a hen, who, pecking these intestines, is in her turn taken ill, and dies next day. At the moment when she is struggling in the convulsions of death, a vulture is flying by (there are a good many vultures in Adelmonte's country); this bird darts on the dead fowl, and carries it away to a rock, where it dines off its prey. Three days afterwards, this poor vulture, which has been very much indisposed since that dinner, suddenly feels very giddy while flying aloft in the clouds, and falls heavily into a fish-pond. The pike, eels, and carp eat greedily always, as everybody knows—well, they feast on the vulture. Now suppose that next day, one of these eels, or pike, or carp, poisoned at the fourth remove, is served up at your table. Well, then, your guest will be poisoned at the fifth remove, and die, at the end of eight or ten days, of pains in the intestines, sickness, or abscess of the pylorus. The doctors open the body and say with an air of profound learning, 'The subject has died of a tumor on the liver, or of typhoid fever!'"

"But," remarked Madame de Villefort, "all these circumstances which you link thus to one another may be broken by the least accident; the vulture may not see the fowl, or may fall a hundred yards from the fish-pond."

"Ah, that is where the art comes in. To be a great chemist in the East, one must direct chance; and this is to be achieved."

Madame de Villefort was in deep thought, yet listened attentively.

"But," she exclaimed, suddenly, "arsenic is indelible, indestructible; in whatsoever way it is absorbed, it will be found again in the body of the victim from the moment when it has been taken in sufficient quantity to cause death."

"Precisely so," cried Monte Cristo—"precisely so; and this is what I said to my worthy Adelmonte. He reflected, smiled, and replied to me by a Sicilian proverb, which I believe is also a French proverb, 'My son, the world was not made in a day—but in seven. Return on Sunday.' On the Sunday following I did return to him. Instead of having watered his cabbage with arsenic, he had watered it this time with a solution of salts, having their basis in strychnine, *strychnos colubrina*, as the learned term it. Now, the cabbage had not the slightest appearance of disease in the world, and the rabbit had not the smallest distrust; yet, five minutes afterwards, the rabbit was dead. The fowl pecked at the rabbit, and the next day was a dead hen. This time we were the vultures; so we opened the bird, and this time all special symptoms had disappeared, there were only general symptoms. There was no peculiar indication in any organ—an excitement of the nervous system—that was it; a case of cerebral congestion—nothing more. The fowl had not been poisoned—she had died of apoplexy. Apoplexy is a rare disease among fowls, I believe, but very common among men."

Madame de Villefort appeared more and more thoughtful.

"It is very fortunate," she observed, "that such substances could only be prepared by chemists; otherwise, all the world would be poisoning each other."

"By chemists and persons who have a taste for chemistry," said Monte Cristo carelessly.

"And then," said Madame de Villefort, endeavoring by a struggle, and with effort, to get away from her thoughts, "however skilfully it is prepared, crime is always crime, and if it avoid human scrutiny, it does not escape the eye of God. The Orientals are stronger than we are in cases of conscience, and, very prudently, have no hell—that is the point."

"Really, madame, this is a scruple which naturally must occur to a pure mind like yours, but which would easily yield before sound reasoning. The bad side of human thought will always be defined by the paradox of Jean Jacques Rousseau,—you remember,—the mandarin who is killed five hundred leagues off by raising the tip of the finger. Man's whole life passes in doing these things, and his intellect is exhausted by reflecting on them. You will find very few persons who will go and brutally thrust a knife in the heart of a fellow-creature, or will administer to him, in order to remove him from the surface of the globe on which we move with life and animation, that quantity of arsenic of which we just now talked. Such a thing is really out of rule—eccentric or stupid. To attain such a point, the blood must be heated to thirty-six degrees, the pulse be, at least, at ninety, and the feelings excited beyond the ordinary limit. But suppose one pass, as is permissible in philology, from the word itself to its softened synonym, then, instead of committing an ignoble assassination you make an 'elimination;' you merely and simply remove from your path the individual who is in your way, and that without shock or violence, without the display of the sufferings which, in the case of becoming a punishment, make a martyr of the victim, and a butcher, in every sense of the word, of him who inflicts them. Then there will be no blood, no groans, no convulsions, and above all, no consciousness of that horrid and compromising moment of accomplishing the act,—then one escapes the clutch of the human law, which says, 'Do not disturb society!' This is the mode in which they manage these things, and succeed in Eastern climes, where there are grave and phlegmatic persons who care very little for the questions of time in conjunctures of importance."

"Yet conscience remains," remarked Madame de Villefort in an agitated voice, and with a stifled sigh.

"Yes," answered Monte Cristo "happily, yes, conscience does remain; and if it did not, how wretched we should be! After every action requiring exertion, it is conscience that saves us, for it supplies us with a thousand good excuses, of which we alone are judges; and these reasons, howsoever excellent in producing sleep, would avail us but very little before a tribunal, when we were tried for our lives. Thus Richard III., for instance, was marvellously served by his conscience after the putting away of the two children of Edward IV.; in fact, he could say, 'These two children of a cruel and persecuting king, who have inherited the vices of their father, which I alone could perceive in their juvenile propensities—these two children are impediments in my way of promoting the happiness of the English people, whose unhappiness they (the children) would infallibly have caused.' Thus was Lady Macbeth served by her conscience, when she sought to give her son, and not her husband (whatever Shakespeare may say), a throne. Ah, maternal love is a great virtue, a powerful motive—so powerful that it excuses a multitude of things, even if, after Duncan's death, Lady Macbeth had been at all pricked by her conscience."

Madame de Villefort listened with avidity to these appalling maxims and horrible paradoxes, delivered by the count with that ironical simplicity which was peculiar to him.

After a moment's silence, the lady inquired:

"Do you know, my dear count," she said, "that you are a very terrible reasoner, and that you look at the world through a somewhat distempered medium? Have you really measured the world by scrutinies, or through alembics and crucibles? For you must indeed be a great chemist, and the elixir you administered to my son, which recalled him to life almost instantaneously—"

"Oh, do not place any reliance on that, madame; *one* drop of that elixir sufficed to recall life to a dying child, but three drops would have impelled the blood into his lungs in such a way as to have produced most violent palpitations; six would have suspended his respiration, and caused syncope more serious than that in which he was; ten would have destroyed him. You know, madame, how suddenly I snatched him from those phials which he so imprudently touched?"

"Is it then so terrible a poison?"

"Oh, no! In the first place, let us agree that the word poison does not exist, because in medicine use is made of the most violent poisons, which become, according as they are employed, most salutary remedies."

"What, then, is it?"

"A skilful preparation of my friend's the worthy Abbé Adelmonte, who taught me the use of it."

"Oh," observed Madame de Villefort, "it must be an admirable anti-spasmodic."

"Perfect, madame, as you have seen," replied the count; "and I frequently make use of it—with all possible prudence though, be it observed," he added with a smile of intelligence.

"Most assuredly," responded Madame de Villefort in the same tone. "As for me, so nervous, and so subject to fainting fits, I should require a Doctor Adelmonte to invent for me some means of breathing freely and tranquillizing my mind, in the fear I have of dying some fine day of suffocation. In the meanwhile, as the thing is difficult to find in France, and your abbé is not probably disposed to make a journey to Paris on my account, I must continue to use Monsieur Planche's anti-spasmodics; and mint and Hoffman's drops are among my favorite remedies. Here are some lozenges which I have made up on purpose; they are compounded doubly strong."

Monte Cristo opened the tortoise-shell box, which the lady presented to him, and inhaled the odor of the lozenges with the air of an amateur who thoroughly appreciated their composition.

"They are indeed exquisite," he said; "but as they are necessarily submitted to the process of deglutition—a function which it is frequently impossible for a fainting person to accomplish—I prefer my own specific."

"Undoubtedly, and so should I prefer it, after the effects I have seen produced; but of course it is a secret, and I am not so indiscreet as to ask it of you."

"But I," said Monte Cristo, rising as he spoke—"I am gallant enough to offer it you."

"How kind you are."

"Only remember one thing—a small dose is a remedy, a large one is poison. One drop will restore life, as you have seen; five or six will inevitably kill, and in a way the more terrible inasmuch as, poured into a glass of wine, it would not in the slightest degree affect its flavor. But I say no more, madame; it is really as if I were prescribing for you."

The clock struck half-past six, and a lady was announced, a friend of Madame de Villefort, who came to dine with her.

"If I had had the honor of seeing you for the third or fourth time, count, instead of only for the second," said Madame de Villefort; "if I had had the honor of being your friend, instead of only having the happiness of being under an obligation to you, I should insist on detaining you to dinner, and not allow myself to be daunted by a first refusal."

"A thousand thanks, madame," replied Monte Cristo "but I have an engagement which I cannot break. I have promised to escort to the Académie a Greek princess of my acquaintance who has never seen your grand opera, and who relies on me to conduct her thither."

"Adieu, then, sir, and do not forget the prescription."

"Ah, in truth, madame, to do that I must forget the hour's conversation I have had with you, which is indeed impossible."

Monte Cristo bowed, and left the house. Madame de Villefort remained immersed in thought.

"He is a very strange man," she said, "and in my opinion is himself the Adelmonte he talks about."

As to Monte Cristo the result had surpassed his utmost expectations.

"Good," said he, as he went away; "this is a fruitful soil, and I feel certain that the seed sown will not be cast on barren ground."

Next morning, faithful to his promise, he sent the prescription requested.

Study Guide Questions

For Students:

1. Why does the Count pay a visit to Villefort's house?
2. Why is the chapter named "Toxicology"?
3. Who is Abbé Adelmonte and what does Madame Villefort think of his existence?

For Reading Club:

1. Do you think Edward is smart or a spoiled child?
2. Discuss Madame Villefort's character. Do you think she is evil or justified?
3. What does the Count and Madame Villefort discuss about the absorption of poison? Do you think knowledge will be used by Madame Villefort?

CHAPTER 53

Robert le Diable

The pretext of an opera engagement was so much the more feasible, as there chanced to be on that very night a more than ordinary attraction at the Académie Royale. Levasseur, who had been suffering under severe illness, made his reappearance in the character of *Bertram*, and, as usual, the announcement of the most admired production of the favorite composer of the day had attracted a brilliant and fashionable audience. Morcerf, like most other young men of rank and fortune, had his orchestra stall, with the certainty of always finding a seat in at least a dozen of the principal boxes occupied by persons of his acquaintance; he had, moreover, his right of entry into the omnibus box. Château-Renaud rented a stall beside his own, while Beauchamp, as a journalist, had unlimited range all over the theatre. It happened that on this particular night the minister's box was placed at the disposal of Lucien Debray, who offered it to the Comte de Morcerf, who again, upon his rejection of it by Mercédès, sent it to Danglars, with an intimation that he should probably do himself the honor of joining the baroness and her daughter during the evening, in the event of their accepting the box in question. The ladies received the offer with too much pleasure to dream of a refusal. To no class of persons is the presentation of a gratuitous opera-box more acceptable than to the wealthy millionaire, who still hugs economy while boasting of carrying a king's ransom in his waistcoat pocket.

Danglars had, however, protested against showing himself in a ministerial box, declaring that his political principles, and his parliamentary position as member of the opposition party would not permit him so to commit himself; the baroness had, therefore, despatched a note to Lucien Debray, bidding him call for them, it being wholly impossible for her to go alone with Eugénie to the opera.

There is no gainsaying the fact that a very unfavorable construction would have been put upon the circumstance if the two women had gone without escort, while the addition of a third, in the person of her mother's admitted lover, enabled Mademoiselle Danglars to defy malice and ill-nature. One must take the world as one finds it.

The curtain rose, as usual, to an almost empty house, it being one of the absurdities of Parisian fashion never to appear at the opera until after the beginning of the performance, so that the first act is generally played without the slightest attention being paid to it, that part of the audience already assembled being too much occupied in observing the fresh arrivals, while nothing is heard but the noise of opening and shutting doors, and the buzz of conversation.

"Surely," said Albert, as the door of a box on the first circle opened, "that must be the Countess G—."

"And who is the Countess G—?" inquired Château-Renaud.

"What a question! Now, do you know, baron, I have a great mind to pick a quarrel with you for asking it; as if all the world did not know who the Countess G— was."

"Ah, to be sure," replied Château-Renaud; "the lovely Venetian, is it not?"

"Herself." At this moment the countess perceived Albert, and returned his salutation with a smile.

"You know her, it seems?" said Château-Renaud.

"Franz introduced me to her at Rome," replied Albert.

"Well, then, will you do as much for me in Paris as Franz did for you in Rome?"

"With pleasure."

There was a cry of "Shut up!" from the audience. This manifestation on the part of the spectators of their wish to be allowed to hear the music, produced not the slightest effect on the two young men, who continued their conversation.

"The countess was present at the races in the Champ-de-Mars," said Château-Renaud.

"Today?"

"Yes."

"Bless me, I quite forgot the races. Did you bet?"

"Oh, merely a paltry fifty louis."

"And who was the winner?"

"Nautilus. I staked on him."

"But there were three races, were there not?"

"Yes; there was the prize given by the Jockey Club—a gold cup, you know—and a very singular circumstance occurred about that race."

"What was it?"

"Oh, shut up!" again interposed some of the audience.

"Why, it was won by a horse and rider utterly unknown on the course."

"Is that possible?"

"True as day. The fact was, nobody had observed a horse entered by the name of Vampa, or that of a jockey styled Job, when, at the last moment, a splendid roan, mounted by a jockey about as big as your fist, presented themselves at the starting-post. They were obliged to stuff at least twenty pounds weight of shot in the small rider's pockets, to make him weight; but with all that he outstripped Ariel and Barbare, against whom he ran, by at least three whole lengths."

"And was it not found out at last to whom the horse and jockey belonged?"

"No."

"You say that the horse was entered under the name of Vampa?"

"Exactly; that was the title."

"Then," answered Albert, "I am better informed than you are, and know who the owner of that horse was."

"Shut up, there!" cried the pit in chorus. And this time the tone and manner in which the command was given, betokened such growing hostility that the two young men perceived, for the first time, that the mandate was addressed to them. Leisurely turning round, they calmly scrutinized the various countenances around them, as though demanding some one person who would take upon himself the responsibility of what they deemed excessive impertinence; but as no one responded to the challenge, the friends turned again to the front of the theatre, and affected to busy themselves with the stage. At this moment the door of the minister's box opened, and Madame Danglars, accompanied by her daughter, entered, escorted by Lucien Debray, who assiduously conducted them to their seats.

"Ha, ha," said Château-Renaud, "here come some friends of yours, viscount! What are you looking at there? don't you see they are trying to catch your eye?"

Albert turned round, just in time to receive a gracious wave of the fan from the baroness; as for Mademoiselle Eugénie, she scarcely vouchsafed to waste the glances of her large black eyes even upon the business of the stage.

"I tell you what, my dear fellow," said Château-Renaud, "I cannot imagine what objection you can possibly have to Mademoiselle Danglars—that is, setting aside her want of ancestry and somewhat inferior rank, which by the way I don't think you care very much about. Now, barring all that, I mean to say she is a deuced fine girl!"

"Handsome, certainly," replied Albert, "but not to my taste, which I confess, inclines to something softer, gentler, and more feminine."

"Ah, well," exclaimed Château-Renaud, who because he had seen his thirtieth summer fancied himself duly warranted in assuming a sort of paternal air with his more youthful friend, "you young people are never satisfied; why, what would you have more? your parents have chosen you a bride built on the model of Diana, the huntress, and yet you are not content."

"No, for that very resemblance affrights me; I should have liked something more in the manner of the Venus of Milo or Capua; but this chase-loving Diana, continually surrounded by her nymphs, gives me a sort of alarm lest she should some day bring on me the fate of Actæon."

And, indeed, it required but one glance at Mademoiselle Danglars to comprehend the justness of Morcerf's remark. She was beautiful, but her beauty was of too marked and decided a character to please a fastidious taste; her hair was raven black, but its natural waves seemed somewhat rebellious; her eyes, of the same color as her hair, were surmounted by well-arched brows, whose great defect, however, consisted in an almost habitual frown, while her whole physiognomy wore that expression of firmness and decision so little in accordance with the gentler attributes of her sex—her nose was precisely what a sculptor would have chosen for a chiselled Juno. Her mouth, which might have been found fault with as too large, displayed teeth of pearly whiteness, rendered still more conspicuous by the brilliant carmine of her lips, contrasting vividly with her naturally pale complexion. But that which completed the almost masculine look Morcerf found so little to his taste, was a dark mole, of much larger dimensions than these freaks of nature generally are, placed just at the corner of her mouth; and the effect tended to increase the expression of self-dependence that characterized her countenance.

The rest of Mademoiselle Eugénie's person was in perfect keeping with the head just described; she, indeed, reminded one of Diana, as Château-Renaud observed, but her bearing was more haughty and resolute.

As regarded her attainments, the only fault to be found with them was the same that a fastidious connoisseur might have found with her beauty, that they were somewhat too erudite and masculine for so young a person. She was a perfect linguist, a first-rate artist, wrote poetry, and composed music; to the study of the latter she professed to be entirely devoted, following it with an indefatigable perseverance, assisted by a schoolfellow,—a young woman without fortune whose talent promised to develop into remarkable powers as a singer. It was rumored that she was an object of almost paternal interest to one of the principal composers of the day, who excited her to spare no pains in the cultivation of her voice, which might hereafter prove a source of wealth and independence. But this counsel effectually decided Mademoiselle

Danglars never to commit herself by being seen in public with one destined for a theatrical life; and acting upon this principle, the banker's daughter, though perfectly willing to allow Mademoiselle Louise d'Armilly (that was the name of the young virtuosa) to practice with her through the day, took especial care not to be seen in her company. Still, though not actually received at the Hôtel Danglars in the light of an acknowledged friend, Louise was treated with far more kindness and consideration than is usually bestowed on a governess.

The curtain fell almost immediately after the entrance of Madame Danglars into her box, the band quitted the orchestra for the accustomed half-hour's interval allowed between the acts, and the audience were left at liberty to promenade the salon or lobbies, or to pay and receive visits in their respective boxes.

Morcerf and Château-Renaud were amongst the first to avail themselves of this permission. For an instant the idea struck Madame Danglars that this eagerness on the part of the young viscount arose from his impatience to join her party, and she whispered her expectations to her daughter, that Albert was hurrying to pay his respects to them. Mademoiselle Eugénie, however, merely returned a dissenting movement of the head, while, with a cold smile, she directed the attention of her mother to an opposite box on the first circle, in which sat the Countess G—, and where Morcerf had just made his appearance.

"So we meet again, my travelling friend, do we?" cried the countess, extending her hand to him with all the warmth and cordiality of an old acquaintance; "it was really very good of you to recognize me so quickly, and still more so to bestow your first visit on me."

"Be assured," replied Albert, "that if I had been aware of your arrival in Paris, and had known your address, I should have paid my respects to you before this. Allow me to introduce my friend, Baron de Château-Renaud, one of the few true gentlemen now to be found in France, and from whom I have just learned that you were a spectator of the races in the Champ-de-Mars, yesterday."

Château-Renaud bowed to the countess.

"So you were at the races, baron?" inquired the countess eagerly.

"Yes, madame."

"Well, then," pursued Madame G— with considerable animation, "you can probably tell me who won the Jockey Club stakes?"

"I am sorry to say I cannot," replied the baron; "and I was just asking the same question of Albert."

"Are you very anxious to know, countess?" asked Albert.

"To know what?"

"The name of the owner of the winning horse?"

"Excessively; only imagine—but do tell me, viscount, whether you really are acquainted with it or no?"

"I beg your pardon, madame, but you were about to relate some story, were you not? You said, 'only imagine,'—and then paused. Pray continue."

"Well, then, listen. You must know I felt so interested in the splendid roan horse, with his elegant little rider, so tastefully dressed in a pink satin jacket and cap, that I could not help praying for their success with as much earnestness as though the half of my fortune were at stake; and when I saw them outstrip all the others, and come to the winning-post in such gallant style, I actually clapped my hands with joy. Imagine my surprise, when, upon returning home, the first object I met on the staircase was the identical jockey in the pink jacket! I concluded that, by some singular chance, the owner of the winning horse must live in the same hotel as myself; but, as I entered my apartments, I beheld the very gold cup awarded as a prize to the unknown horse and rider. Inside the cup was a small piece of paper, on which were written these words—'From Lord Ruthven to Countess G—.'"

"Precisely; I was sure of it," said Morcerf.

"Sure of what?"

"That the owner of the horse was Lord Ruthven himself."

"What Lord Ruthven do you mean?"

"Why, our Lord Ruthven—the Vampire of the Salle Argentina!"

"Is it possible?" exclaimed the countess; "is he here in Paris?"

"To be sure,—why not?"

"And you visit him?—meet him at your own house and elsewhere?"

"I assure you he is my most intimate friend, and M. de Château-Renaud has also the honor of his acquaintance."

"But why are you so sure of his being the winner of the Jockey Club prize?"

"Was not the winning horse entered by the name of Vampa?"

"What of that?"

"Why, do you not recollect the name of the celebrated bandit by whom I was made prisoner?"

"Oh, yes."

"And from whose hands the count extricated me in so wonderful a manner?"

"To be sure, I remember it all now."

"He called himself Vampa. You see, it's evident where the count got the name."

"But what could have been his motive for sending the cup to me?"

"In the first place, because I had spoken much of you to him, as you may believe; and in the second, because he delighted to see a countrywoman take so lively an interest in his success."

"I trust and hope you never repeated to the count all the foolish remarks we used to make about him?"

"I should not like to affirm upon oath that I have not. Besides, his presenting you the cup under the name of Lord Ruthven—"

"Oh, but that is dreadful! Why, the man must owe me a fearful grudge."

"Does his action appear like that of an enemy?"

"No; certainly not."

"Well, then—"

"And so he is in Paris?"

"Yes."

"And what effect does he produce?"

"Why," said Albert, "he was talked about for a week; then the coronation of the queen of England took place, followed by the theft of Mademoiselle Mars's diamonds; and so people talked of something else."

"My good fellow," said Château-Renaud, "the count is your friend and you treat him accordingly. Do not believe what Albert is telling you, countess; so far from the sensation excited in the Parisian circles by the appearance of the Count of Monte Cristo having abated, I take upon myself to declare that it is as strong as ever. His first astounding act upon coming amongst us was to present a pair of horses, worth 32,000 francs, to Madame Danglars; his second, the almost miraculous preservation of Madame de Villefort's life; now it seems that he has carried off the prize awarded by the Jockey Club. I therefore maintain, in spite of Morcerf, that not only is the count the object of interest at this present moment, but also that he will continue to be so for a month longer if he pleases to exhibit an eccentricity of conduct which, after all, may be his ordinary mode of existence."

"Perhaps you are right," said Morcerf; "meanwhile, who is in the Russian ambassador's box?"

"Which box do you mean?" asked the countess.

"The one between the pillars on the first tier—it seems to have been fitted up entirely afresh."

"Did you observe anyone during the first act?" asked Château-Renaud.

"Where?"

"In that box."

"No," replied the countess, "it was certainly empty during the first act;" then, resuming the subject of their previous conversation, she said, "And so you really believe it was your mysterious Count of Monte Cristo that gained the prize?"

"I am sure of it."

"And who afterwards sent the cup to me?"

"Undoubtedly."

"But I don't know him," said the countess; "I have a great mind to return it."

"Do no such thing, I beg of you; he would only send you another, formed of a magnificent sapphire, or hollowed out of a gigantic ruby. It is his way, and you must take him as you find him."

At this moment the bell rang to announce the drawing up of the curtain for the second act. Albert rose to return to his place.

"Shall I see you again?" asked the countess.

"At the end of the next act, with your permission, I will come and inquire whether there is anything I can do for you in Paris?"

"Pray take notice," said the countess, "that my present residence is 22 Rue de Rivoli, and that I am at home to my friends every Saturday evening. So now, you are both forewarned."

The young men bowed, and quitted the box. Upon reaching their stalls, they found the whole of the audience in the parterre standing up and directing their gaze towards the box formerly possessed by the Russian ambassador. A man of from thirty-five to forty years of age, dressed in deep black, had just entered, accompanied by a young woman dressed after the Eastern style. The lady was surpassingly beautiful, while the rich magnificence of her attire drew all eyes upon her.

"Hullo," said Albert; "it is Monte Cristo and his Greek!"

The strangers were, indeed, no other than the count and Haydée. In a few moments the young girl had attracted the attention of the whole house, and even the occupants of the boxes leaned forward to scrutinize her magnificent diamonds.

The second act passed away during one continued buzz of voices—one deep whisper—intimating that some great and universally interesting event had occurred; all eyes, all thoughts, were occupied with the young and beautiful woman, whose gorgeous apparel and splendid jewels made a most extraordinary spectacle.

Upon this occasion an unmistakable sign from Madame Danglars intimated her desire to see Albert in her box directly the curtain fell on the second act, and neither the politeness nor good taste of Morcerf would permit his neglecting an invitation so unequivocally given. At the close of the act he therefore went to the baroness.

Having bowed to the two ladies, he extended his hand to Debray. By the baroness he was most graciously welcomed, while Eugénie received him with her accustomed coldness.

"My dear fellow," said Debray, "you have come in the nick of time. There is madame overwhelming me with questions respecting the count; she insists upon it that I can tell her his birth, education, and parentage, where he came from, and whither he is going. Being no disciple of Cagliostro, I was wholly unable to do this; so, by way of getting out of the scrape, I said, 'Ask Morcerf; he has got the whole history of his beloved Monte Cristo at his fingers' ends;' whereupon the baroness signified her desire to see you."

"Is it not almost incredible," said Madame Danglars, "that a person having at least half a million of secret-service money at his command, should possess so little information?"

"Let me assure you, madame," said Lucien, "that had I really the sum you mention at my disposal, I would employ it more profitably than in troubling myself to obtain particulars respecting the Count of Monte Cristo, whose only merit in my eyes consists in his being twice as rich as a nabob. However, I have turned the business over to Morcerf, so pray settle it with him as may be most agreeable to you; for my own part, I care nothing about the count or his mysterious doings."

"I am very sure no nabob would have sent me a pair of horses worth 32,000 francs, wearing on their heads four diamonds valued at 5,000 francs each."

"He seems to have a mania for diamonds," said Morcerf, smiling, "and I verily believe that, like Potemkin, he keeps his pockets filled, for the sake of strewing them along the road, as Tom Thumb did his flint stones."

"Perhaps he has discovered some mine," said Madame Danglars. "I suppose you know he has an order for unlimited credit on the baron's banking establishment?"

"I was not aware of it," replied Albert, "but I can readily believe it."

"And, further, that he stated to M. Danglars his intention of only staying a year in Paris, during which time he proposed to spend six millions.

"He must be the Shah of Persia, travelling *incog.*"

"Have you noticed the remarkable beauty of the young woman, M. Lucien?" inquired Eugénie.

"I really never met with one woman so ready to do justice to the charms of another as yourself," responded Lucien, raising his lorgnette to his eye. "A most lovely creature, upon my soul!" was his verdict.

"Who is this young person, M. de Morcerf?" inquired Eugénie; "does anybody know?"

"Mademoiselle," said Albert, replying to this direct appeal, "I can give you very exact information on that subject, as well as on most points relative to the mysterious person of whom we are now conversing—the young woman is a Greek."

"So I should suppose by her dress; if you know no more than that, everyone here is as well-informed as yourself."

"I am extremely sorry you find me so ignorant a *cicerone*," replied Morcerf, "but I am reluctantly obliged to confess, I have nothing further to communicate—yes, stay, I do know one thing more, namely, that she is a musician, for one day when I chanced to be breakfasting with the count, I heard the sound of a guzla—it is impossible that it could have been touched by any other finger than her own."

"Then your count entertains visitors, does he?" asked Madame Danglars.

"Indeed he does, and in a most lavish manner, I can assure you."

"I must try and persuade M. Danglars to invite him to a ball or dinner, or something of the sort, that he may be compelled to ask us in return."

"What," said Debray, laughing; "do you really mean you would go to his house?"

"Why not? my husband could accompany me."

"But do you know this mysterious count is a bachelor?"

"You have ample proof to the contrary, if you look opposite," said the baroness, as she laughingly pointed to the beautiful Greek.

"No, no!" exclaimed Debray; "that girl is not his wife: he told us himself she was his slave. Do you not recollect, Morcerf, his telling us so at your breakfast?"

"Well, then," said the baroness, "if slave she be, she has all the air and manner of a princess."

"Of the 'Arabian Nights'."

"If you like; but tell me, my dear Lucien, what it is that constitutes a princess. Why, diamonds—and she is covered with them."

"To me she seems overloaded," observed Eugénie; "she would look far better if she wore fewer, and we should then be able to see her finely formed throat and wrists."

"See how the artist peeps out!" exclaimed Madame Danglars. "My poor Eugénie, you must conceal your passion for the fine arts."

"I admire all that is beautiful," returned the young lady.

"What do you think of the count?" inquired Debray; "he is not much amiss, according to my ideas of good looks."

"The count," repeated Eugénie, as though it had not occurred to her to observe him sooner; "the count?—oh, he is so dreadfully pale."

"I quite agree with you," said Morcerf; "and the secret of that very pallor is what we want to find out. The Countess G— insists upon it that he is a vampire."

"Then the Countess G— has returned to Paris, has she?" inquired the baroness.

"Is that she, mamma?" asked Eugénie; "almost opposite to us, with that profusion of beautiful light hair?"

"Yes," said Madame Danglars, "that is she. Shall I tell you what you ought to do, Morcerf?"

"Command me, madame."

"Well, then, you should go and bring your Count of Monte Cristo to us."

"What for?" asked Eugénie.

"What for? Why, to converse with him, of course. Have you really no desire to meet him?"

"None whatever," replied Eugénie.

"Strange child," murmured the baroness.

"He will very probably come of his own accord," said Morcerf. "There; do you see, madame, he recognizes you, and bows."

The baroness returned the salute in the most smiling and graceful manner.

"Well," said Morcerf, "I may as well be magnanimous, and tear myself away to forward your wishes. Adieu; I will go and try if there are any means of speaking to him."

"Go straight to his box; that will be the simplest plan."

"But I have never been presented."

"Presented to whom?"

"To the beautiful Greek."

"You say she is only a slave?"

"While you assert that she is a queen, or at least a princess. No; I hope that when he sees me leave you, he will come out."

"That is possible—go."

"I am going," said Albert, as he made his parting bow.

Just as he was passing the count's box, the door opened, and Monte Cristo came forth. After giving some directions to Ali, who stood in the lobby, the count took Albert's arm. Carefully closing the box door, Ali placed himself before it, while a crowd of spectators assembled round the Nubian.

"Upon my word," said Monte Cristo, "Paris is a strange city, and the Parisians a very singular people. See that cluster of persons collected around poor Ali, who is as much astonished as themselves; really one might suppose he was the only Nubian they had ever beheld. Now I can promise you, that a Frenchman might show himself in public, either in Tunis, Constantinople, Bagdad, or Cairo, without being treated in that way."

"That shows that the Eastern nations have too much good sense to waste their time and attention on objects undeserving of either. However, as far as Ali is concerned, I can assure you, the interest he excites is merely from the circumstance of his being your attendant—you, who are at this moment the most celebrated and fashionable person in Paris."

"Really? and what has procured me so flattering a distinction?"

"What? why, yourself, to be sure! You give away horses worth a thousand louis; you save the lives of ladies of high rank and beauty; under the name of Major Black you run thoroughbreds ridden by tiny urchins not larger than marmots; then, when you have carried off the golden trophy of victory, instead of setting any value on it, you give it to the first handsome woman you think of!"

"And who has filled your head with all this nonsense?"

"Why, in the first place, I heard it from Madame Danglars, who, by the by, is dying to see you in her box, or to have you seen there by others; secondly, I learned it from Beauchamp's journal; and thirdly, from my own imagination. Why, if you sought concealment, did you call your horse Vampa?"

"That was an oversight, certainly," replied the count; "but tell me, does the Count of Morcerf never visit the Opera? I have been looking for him, but without success."

"He will be here tonight."

"In what part of the house?"

"In the baroness's box, I believe."

"That charming young woman with her is her daughter?"

"Yes."

"I congratulate you."

Morcerf smiled.

"We will discuss that subject at length some future time," said he. "But what do you think of the music?"

"What music?"

"Why, the music you have been listening to."

"Oh, it is well enough as the production of a human composer, sung by featherless bipeds, to quote the late Diogenes."

"From which it would seem, my dear count, that you can at pleasure enjoy the seraphic strains that proceed from the seven choirs of paradise?"

"You are right, in some degree; when I wish to listen to sounds more exquisitely attuned to melody than mortal ear ever yet listened to, I go to sleep."

"Then sleep here, my dear count. The conditions are favorable; what else was opera invented for?"

"No, thank you. Your orchestra is too noisy. To sleep after the manner I speak of, absolute calm and silence are necessary, and then a certain preparation—"

"I know—the famous hashish!"

"Precisely. So, my dear viscount, whenever you wish to be regaled with music come and sup with me."

"I have already enjoyed that treat when breakfasting with you," said Morcerf.

"Do you mean at Rome?"

"I do."

"Ah, then, I suppose you heard Haydée's guzla; the poor exile frequently beguiles a weary hour in playing over to me the airs of her native land."

Morcerf did not pursue the subject, and Monte Cristo himself fell into a silent reverie.

The bell rang at this moment for the rising of the curtain.

"You will excuse my leaving you," said the count, turning in the direction of his box.

"What? Are you going?"

"Pray, say everything that is kind to Countess G— on the part of her friend the vampire."

"And what message shall I convey to the baroness!"

"That, with her permission, I shall do myself the honor of paying my respects in the course of the evening."

The third act had begun; and during its progress the Count of Morcerf, according to his promise, made his appearance in the box of Madame Danglars. The Count of Morcerf was not a person to excite either interest or curiosity in a place of public amusement; his presence, therefore, was wholly unnoticed, save by the occupants of the box in which he had just seated himself.

The quick eye of Monte Cristo however, marked his coming; and a slight though meaning smile passed over his lips. Haydée, whose soul seemed centred in the business of the stage, like all unsophisticated natures, delighted in whatever addressed itself to the eye or ear.

The third act passed off as usual. Mesdemoiselles Noblet, Julia, and Leroux executed the customary pirouettes; Robert duly challenged the Prince of Granada; and the royal father of the princess Isabella, taking his daughter by the hand, swept round the stage with majestic strides, the better to display the rich folds of his velvet robe and mantle. After which the curtain again fell, and the spectators poured forth from the theatre into the lobbies and salon.

The count left his box, and a moment later was saluting the Baronne Danglars, who could not restrain a cry of mingled pleasure and surprise.

"You are welcome, count!" she exclaimed, as he entered. "I have been most anxious to see you, that I might repeat orally the thanks writing can so ill express."

"Surely so trifling a circumstance cannot deserve a place in your remembrance. Believe me, madame, I had entirely forgotten it."

"But it is not so easy to forget, monsieur, that the very next day after your princely gift you saved the life of my dear friend, Madame de Villefort, which was endangered by the very animals your generosity restored to me."

"This time, at least, I do not deserve your thanks. It was Ali, my Nubian slave, who rendered this service to Madame de Villefort."

"Was it Ali," asked the Count of Morcerf, "who rescued my son from the hands of bandits?"

"No, count," replied Monte Cristo taking the hand held out to him by the general; "in this instance I may fairly and freely accept your thanks; but you have already tendered them, and fully discharged your debt—if indeed there existed one—and I feel almost mortified to find you still reverting to the subject. May I beg of you, baroness, to honor me with an introduction to your daughter?"

"Oh, you are no stranger—at least not by name," replied Madame Danglars, "and the last two or three days we have really talked of nothing but you. Eugénie," continued the baroness, turning towards her daughter, "this is the Count of Monte Cristo."

The count bowed, while Mademoiselle Danglars bent her head slightly.

"You have a charming young person with you tonight, count," said Eugénie. "Is she your daughter?"

"No, mademoiselle," said Monte Cristo, astonished at the coolness and freedom of the question. "She is a poor unfortunate Greek left under my care."

"And what is her name?"

"Haydée," replied Monte Cristo.

"A Greek?" murmured the Count of Morcerf.

"Yes, indeed, count," said Madame Danglars; "and tell me, did you ever see at the court of Ali Tepelini, whom you so gloriously and valiantly served, a more exquisite beauty or richer costume?"

"Did I hear rightly, monsieur," said Monte Cristo "that you served at Yanina?"

"I was inspector-general of the pasha's troops," replied Morcerf; "and it is no secret that I owe my fortune, such as it is, to the liberality of the illustrious Albanese chief."

"But look!" exclaimed Madame Danglars.

"Where?" stammered Morcerf.

"There," said Monte Cristo placing his arms around the count, and leaning with him over the front of the box, just as Haydée, whose eyes were occupied in examining the theatre in search of her guardian, perceived his pale features close to Morcerf's face. It was as if the young girl beheld the head of Medusa. She bent forwards as though to assure herself of the reality of what she saw, then, uttering a faint cry, threw herself back in her seat. The sound was heard by the people about Ali, who instantly opened the box-door.

"Why, count," exclaimed Eugénie, "what has happened to your ward? she seems to have been taken suddenly ill.

"Very probably," answered the count. "But do not be alarmed on her account. Haydée's nervous system is delicately organized, and she is peculiarly susceptible to the odors even of flowers—nay, there are some which cause her to faint if brought into her presence. However," continued Monte Cristo, drawing a small phial from his pocket, "I have an infallible remedy."

So saying, he bowed to the baroness and her daughter, exchanged a parting shake of the hand with Debray and the count, and left Madame Danglars' box. Upon his return to Haydée he found her still very pale. As soon as she saw him she seized his hand; her own hands were moist and icy cold.

"Who was it you were talking with over there?" she asked.

"With the Count of Morcerf," answered Monte Cristo. "He tells me he served your illustrious father, and that he owes his fortune to him."

"Wretch!" exclaimed Haydée, her eyes flashing with rage; "he sold my father to the Turks, and the fortune he boasts of was the price of his treachery! Did not you know that, my dear lord?"

"Something of this I heard in Epirus," said Monte Cristo; "but the particulars are still unknown to me. You shall relate them to me, my child. They are, no doubt, both curious and interesting."

"Yes, yes; but let us go. I feel as though it would kill me to remain long near that dreadful man."

So saying, Haydée arose, and wrapping herself in her burnouse of white cashmere embroidered with pearls and coral, she hastily quitted the box at the moment when the curtain was rising upon the fourth act.

"Do you observe," said the Countess G— to Albert, who had returned to her side, "that man does nothing like other people; he listens most devoutly to the third act of *Robert le Diable*, and when the fourth begins, takes his departure."

Study Guide Questions

For Students:

1. What social event is taking place at the beginning of this chapter?
2. Who is Countess G? Why do Albert and Château-Renaud pay her a visit during orchestra break?
3. With whom does the Count attend orchestra?

For Reading Club:

1. Mademoiselle Eugénie is defined as a girl with masculine looks. What do you think of her physical description?
2. Discuss Mademoiselle Eugénie as a woman of the contemporary age.
3. Haydée attracts everyone's attention due to her 'gorgeous apparel and splendid jewels'. Do you think it shows that human society values appearances?

CHAPTER 54

A Flurry in Stocks

Some days after this meeting, Albert de Morcerf visited the Count of Monte Cristo at his house in the Champs-Élysées, which had already assumed that palace-like appearance which the count's princely fortune enabled him to give even to his most temporary residences. He came to renew the thanks of Madame Danglars which had been already conveyed to the count through the medium of a letter, signed "Baronne Danglars, *née* Hermine de Servieux."

Albert was accompanied by Lucien Debray, who, joining in his friend's conversation, added some passing compliments, the source of which the count's talent for finesse easily enabled him to guess. He was convinced that Lucien's visit was due to a double feeling of curiosity, the larger half of which sentiment emanated from the Rue de la Chaussée d'Antin. In short, Madame Danglars, not being able personally to examine in detail the domestic economy and household arrangements of a man who gave away horses worth 30,000 francs and who went to the opera with a Greek slave wearing diamonds to the amount of a million of money, had deputed those eyes, by which she was accustomed to see, to give her a faithful account of the mode of life of this incomprehensible person. But the count did not appear to suspect that there could be the slightest connection between Lucien's visit and the curiosity of the baroness.

"You are in constant communication with the Baron Danglars?" the count inquired of Albert de Morcerf.

"Yes, count, you know what I told you?"

"All remains the same, then, in that quarter?"

"It is more than ever a settled thing," said Lucien,—and, considering that this remark was all that he was at that time called upon to make, he adjusted the glass to his eye, and biting the top of his gold headed cane, began to make the tour of the apartment, examining the arms and the pictures.

"Ah," said Monte Cristo "I did not expect that the affair would be so promptly concluded."

"Oh, things take their course without our assistance. While we are forgetting them, they are falling into their appointed order; and when, again, our attention is directed to them, we are surprised at the progress they have made towards the proposed end. My father and M. Danglars served together in Spain, my father in the army and M. Danglars in the commissariat department. It was there that my father, ruined by the revolution, and M. Danglars, who never had possessed any patrimony, both laid the foundations of their different fortunes."

"Yes," said Monte Cristo "I think M. Danglars mentioned that in a visit which I paid him; and," continued he, casting a side-glance at Lucien, who was turning over the leaves of an album, "Mademoiselle Eugénie is pretty—I think I remember that to be her name."

"Very pretty, or rather, very beautiful," replied Albert, "but of that style of beauty which I do not appreciate; I am an ungrateful fellow."

"You speak as if you were already her husband."

"Ah," returned Albert, in his turn looking around to see what Lucien was doing.

"Really," said Monte Cristo, lowering his voice, "you do not appear to me to be very enthusiastic on the subject of this marriage."

"Mademoiselle Danglars is too rich for me," replied Morcerf, "and that frightens me."

"Bah," exclaimed Monte Cristo, "that's a fine reason to give. Are you not rich yourself?"

"My father's income is about 50,000 francs per annum; and he will give me, perhaps, ten or twelve thousand when I marry."

"That, perhaps, might not be considered a large sum, in Paris especially," said the count; "but everything does not depend on wealth, and it is a fine thing to have a good name, and to occupy a high station in society. Your name is celebrated, your position magnificent; and then the Comte de Morcerf is a soldier, and it is pleasing to see the integrity of a Bayard united to the poverty of a Duguesclin; disinterestedness is the brightest ray in which a noble sword can shine. As for me, I consider the union with Mademoiselle Danglars a most suitable one; she will enrich you, and you will ennoble her."

Albert shook his head, and looked thoughtful.

"There is still something else," said he.

"I confess," observed Monte Cristo, "that I have some difficulty in comprehending your objection to a young lady who is both rich and beautiful."

"Oh," said Morcerf, "this repugnance, if repugnance it may be called, is not all on my side."

"Whence can it arise, then? for you told me your father desired the marriage."

"It is my mother who dissents; she has a clear and penetrating judgment, and does not smile on the proposed union. I cannot account for it, but she seems to entertain some prejudice against the Danglars."

"Ah," said the count, in a somewhat forced tone, "that may be easily explained; the Comtesse de Morcerf, who is aristocracy and refinement itself, does not relish the idea of being allied by your marriage with one of ignoble birth; that is natural enough."

"I do not know if that is her reason," said Albert, "but one thing I do know, that if this marriage be consummated, it will render her quite miserable. There was to have been a meeting six weeks ago in order to talk over and settle the affair; but I had such a sudden attack of indisposition—"

"Real?" interrupted the count, smiling.

"Oh, real enough, from anxiety doubtless,—at any rate they postponed the matter for two months. There is no hurry, you know. I am not yet twenty-one, and Eugénie is only seventeen; but the two months expire next week. It must be done. My dear count, you cannot imagine how my mind is harassed. How happy you are in being exempt from all this!"

"Well, and why should not you be free, too? What prevents you from being so?"

"Oh, it will be too great a disappointment to my father if I do not marry Mademoiselle Danglars."

"Marry her then," said the count, with a significant shrug of the shoulders.

"Yes," replied Morcerf, "but that will plunge my mother into positive grief."

"Then do not marry her," said the count.

"Well, I shall see. I will try and think over what is the best thing to be done; you will give me your advice, will you not, and if possible extricate me from my unpleasant position? I think, rather than give pain to my dear mother, I would run the risk of offending the count."

Monte Cristo turned away; he seemed moved by this last remark.

"Ah," said he to Debray, who had thrown himself into an easy-chair at the farthest extremity of the salon, and who held a pencil in his right hand and an account book in his left, "what are you doing there? Are you making a sketch after Poussin?"

"Oh, no," was the tranquil response; "I am too fond of art to attempt anything of that sort. I am doing a little sum in arithmetic."

"In arithmetic?"

"Yes; I am calculating—by the way, Morcerf, that indirectly concerns you—I am calculating what the house of Danglars must have gained by the last rise in Haiti bonds; from 206 they have risen to 409 in three days, and the prudent banker had purchased at 206; therefore he must have made 300,000 livres."

"That is not his biggest scoop," said Morcerf; "did he not make a million in Spaniards this last year?"

"My dear fellow," said Lucien, "here is the Count of Monte Cristo, who will say to you, as the Italians do,—

"'Denaro e santità,
Metà della metà.'[2]

"When they tell me such things, I only shrug my shoulders and say nothing."

"But you were speaking of Haitians?" said Monte Cristo.

"Ah, Haitians,—that is quite another thing! Haitians are the *écarté* of French stock-jobbing. We may like bouillotte, delight in whist, be enraptured with boston, and yet grow tired of them all; but we always come back to *écarté*—it is not only a game, it is a *hors-d'œuvre*! M. Danglars sold yesterday at 405, and pockets 300,000 francs. Had he but waited till today, the price would have fallen to 205, and instead of gaining 300,000 francs, he would have lost 20 or 25,000."

"And what has caused the sudden fall from 409 to 206?" asked Monte Cristo. "I am profoundly ignorant of all these stock-jobbing intrigues."

"Because," said Albert, laughing, "one piece of news follows another, and there is often great dissimilarity between them."

"Ah," said the count, "I see that M. Danglars is accustomed to play at gaining or losing 300,000 francs in a day; he must be enormously rich."

"It is not he who plays!" exclaimed Lucien; "it is Madame Danglars; she is indeed daring."

"But you who are a reasonable being, Lucien, and who knows how little dependence is to be placed on the news, since you are at the fountain-head, surely you ought to prevent it," said Morcerf, with a smile.

"How can I, if her husband fails in controlling her?" asked Lucien; "you know the character of the baroness—no one has any influence with her, and she does precisely what she pleases."

"Ah, if I were in your place—" said Albert.

---

[2] 'Money and sanctity, Each in a moiety.'

"Well?"

"I would reform her; it would be rendering a service to her future son-in-law."

"How would you set about it?"

"Ah, that would be easy enough—I would give her a lesson."

"A lesson?"

"Yes. Your position as secretary to the minister renders your authority great on the subject of political news; you never open your mouth but the stockbrokers immediately stenograph your words. Cause her to lose a hundred thousand francs, and that would teach her prudence."

"I do not understand," stammered Lucien.

"It is very clear, notwithstanding," replied the young man, with an artlessness wholly free from affectation; "tell her some fine morning an unheard-of piece of intelligence—some telegraphic despatch, of which you alone are in possession; for instance, that Henri IV. was seen yesterday at Gabrielle's. That would boom the market; she will buy heavily, and she will certainly lose when Beauchamp announces the following day, in his gazette, 'The report circulated by some usually well-informed persons that the king was seen yesterday at Gabrielle's house, is totally without foundation. We can positively assert that his majesty did not quit the Pont-Neuf.'"

Lucien half smiled. Monte Cristo, although apparently indifferent, had not lost one word of this conversation, and his penetrating eye had even read a hidden secret in the embarrassed manner of the secretary. This embarrassment had completely escaped Albert, but it caused Lucien to shorten his visit; he was evidently ill at ease. The count, in taking leave of him, said something in a low voice, to which he answered, "Willingly, count; I accept." The count returned to young Morcerf.

"Do you not think, on reflection," said he to him, "that you have done wrong in thus speaking of your mother-in-law in the presence of M. Debray?"

"My dear count," said Morcerf, "I beg of you not to apply that title so prematurely."

"Now, speaking without any exaggeration, is your mother really so very much averse to this marriage?"

"So much so that the baroness very rarely comes to the house, and my mother, has not, I think, visited Madame Danglars twice in her whole life."

"Then," said the count, "I am emboldened to speak openly to you. M. Danglars is my banker; M. de Villefort has overwhelmed me with politeness in return for a service which a casual piece of good fortune enabled me to render him. I predict from all this an avalanche of dinners and routs. Now, in order not to presume on this, and also to be beforehand with them, I have, if agreeable to you, thought of inviting M.

and Madame Danglars, and M. and Madame de Villefort, to my country-house at Auteuil. If I were to invite you and the Count and Countess of Morcerf to this dinner, I should give it the appearance of being a matrimonial meeting, or at least Madame de Morcerf would look upon the affair in that light, especially if Baron Danglars did me the honor to bring his daughter. In that case your mother would hold me in aversion, and I do not at all wish that; on the contrary, I desire to stand high in her esteem."

"Indeed, count," said Morcerf, "I thank you sincerely for having used so much candor towards me, and I gratefully accept the exclusion which you propose. You say you desire my mother's good opinion; I assure you it is already yours to a very unusual extent."

"Do you think so?" said Monte Cristo, with interest.

"Oh, I am sure of it; we talked of you an hour after you left us the other day. But to return to what we were saying. If my mother could know of this attention on your part—and I will venture to tell her—I am sure that she will be most grateful to you; it is true that my father will be equally angry." The count laughed.

"Well," said he to Morcerf, "but I think your father will not be the only angry one; M. and Madame Danglars will think me a very ill-mannered person. They know that I am intimate with you—that you are, in fact; one of the oldest of my Parisian acquaintances—and they will not find you at my house; they will certainly ask me why I did not invite you. Be sure to provide yourself with some previous engagement which shall have a semblance of probability, and communicate the fact to me by a line in writing. You know that with bankers nothing but a written document will be valid."

"I will do better than that," said Albert; "my mother is wishing to go to the sea-side—what day is fixed for your dinner?"

"Saturday."

"This is Tuesday—well, tomorrow evening we leave, and the day after we shall be at Tréport. Really, count, you have a delightful way of setting people at their ease."

"Indeed, you give me more credit than I deserve; I only wish to do what will be agreeable to you, that is all."

"When shall you send your invitations?"

"This very day."

"Well, I will immediately call on M. Danglars, and tell him that my mother and myself must leave Paris tomorrow. I have not seen you, consequently I know nothing of your dinner."

"How foolish you are! Have you forgotten that M. Debray has just seen you at my house?"

"Ah, true."

"Fix it this way. I have seen you, and invited you without any ceremony, when you instantly answered that it would be impossible for you to accept, as you were going to Tréport."

"Well, then, that is settled; but you will come and call on my mother before tomorrow?"

"Before tomorrow?—that will be a difficult matter to arrange, besides, I shall just be in the way of all the preparations for departure."

"Well, you can do better. You were only a charming man before, but, if you accede to my proposal, you will be adorable."

"What must I do to attain such sublimity?"

"You are today free as air—come and dine with me; we shall be a small party—only yourself, my mother, and I. You have scarcely seen my mother; you shall have an opportunity of observing her more closely. She is a remarkable woman, and I only regret that there does not exist another like her, about twenty years younger; in that case, I assure you, there would very soon be a Countess and Viscountess of Morcerf. As to my father, you will not see him; he is officially engaged, and dines with the chief referendary. We will talk over our travels; and you, who have seen the whole world, will relate your adventures—you shall tell us the history of the beautiful Greek who was with you the other night at the Opera, and whom you call your slave, and yet treat like a princess. We will talk Italian and Spanish. Come, accept my invitation, and my mother will thank you."

"A thousand thanks," said the count, "your invitation is most gracious, and I regret exceedingly that it is not in my power to accept it. I am not so much at liberty as you suppose; on the contrary, I have a most important engagement."

"Ah, take care, you were teaching me just now how, in case of an invitation to dinner, one might creditably make an excuse. I require the proof of a pre-engagement. I am not a banker, like M. Danglars, but I am quite as incredulous as he is."

"I am going to give you a proof," replied the count, and he rang the bell.

"Humph," said Morcerf, "this is the second time you have refused to dine with my mother; it is evident that you wish to avoid her."

Monte Cristo started. "Oh, you do not mean that," said he; "besides, here comes the confirmation of my assertion."

Baptistin entered, and remained standing at the door.

"I had no previous knowledge of your visit, had I?"

"Indeed, you are such an extraordinary person, that I would not answer for it."

"At all events, I could not guess that you would invite me to dinner."

"Probably not."

"Well, listen, Baptistin, what did I tell you this morning when I called you into my laboratory?"

"To close the door against visitors as soon as the clock struck five," replied the valet.

"What then?"

"Ah, my dear count," said Albert.

"No, no, I wish to do away with that mysterious reputation that you have given me, my dear viscount; it is tiresome to be always acting Manfred. I wish my life to be free and open. Go on, Baptistin."

"Then to admit no one except Major Bartolomeo Cavalcanti and his son."

"You hear—Major Bartolomeo Cavalcanti—a man who ranks amongst the most ancient nobility of Italy, whose name Dante has celebrated in the tenth canto of *The Inferno*, you remember it, do you not? Then there is his son, Andrea, a charming young man, about your own age, viscount, bearing the same title as yourself, and who is making his entry into the Parisian world, aided by his father's millions. The major will bring his son with him this evening, the *contino*, as we say in Italy; he confides him to my care. If he proves himself worthy of it, I will do what I can to advance his interests. You will assist me in the work, will you not?"

"Most undoubtedly. This Major Cavalcanti is an old friend of yours, then?"

"By no means. He is a perfect nobleman, very polite, modest, and agreeable, such as may be found constantly in Italy, descendants of very ancient families. I have met him several times at Florence, Bologna and Lucca, and he has now communicated to me the fact of his arrival in Paris. The acquaintances one makes in travelling have a sort of claim on one; they everywhere expect to receive the same attention which you once paid them by chance, as though the civilities of a passing hour were likely to awaken any lasting interest in favor of the man in whose society you may happen to be thrown in the course of your journey. This good Major Cavalcanti is come to take a second view of Paris, which he only saw in passing through in the time of the Empire, when he was on his way to Moscow. I shall give him a good dinner, he will confide his son to my care, I will promise to watch over him, I shall let him follow in whatever path his folly may lead him, and then I shall have done my part."

"Certainly; I see you are a model Mentor," said Albert "Good-bye, we shall return on Sunday. By the way, I have received news of Franz."

"Have you? Is he still amusing himself in Italy?"

"I believe so; however, he regrets your absence extremely. He says you were the sun of Rome, and that without you all appears dark and cloudy; I do not know if he does not even go so far as to say that it rains."

"His opinion of me is altered for the better, then?"

"No, he still persists in looking upon you as the most incomprehensible and mysterious of beings."

"He is a charming young man," said Monte Cristo "and I felt a lively interest in him the very first evening of my introduction, when I met him in search of a supper, and prevailed upon him to accept a portion of mine. He is, I think, the son of General d'Épinay?"

"He is."

"The same who was so shamefully assassinated in 1815?"

"By the Bonapartists."

"Yes. Really I like him extremely; is there not also a matrimonial engagement contemplated for him?"

"Yes, he is to marry Mademoiselle de Villefort."

"Indeed?"

"And you know I am to marry Mademoiselle Danglars," said Albert, laughing.

"You smile."

"Yes."

"Why do you do so?"

"I smile because there appears to me to be about as much inclination for the consummation of the engagement in question as there is for my own. But really, my dear count, we are talking as much of women as they do of us; it is unpardonable."

Albert rose.

"Are you going?"

"Really, that is a good idea!—two hours have I been boring you to death with my company, and then you, with the greatest politeness, ask me if I am going. Indeed, count, you are the most polished man in the world. And your servants, too, how very well behaved they are; there is quite a style about them. Monsieur Baptistin especially; I could never get such a man as that. My servants seem to imitate those you sometimes see in a play, who, because they have only a word or two to say, aquit themselves in the most awkward manner possible. Therefore, if you part with M. Baptistin, give me the refusal of him."

"By all means."

"That is not all; give my compliments to your illustrious Luccanese, Cavalcante of the Cavalcanti; and if by any chance he should be wishing to establish his son, find him a wife very rich, very noble on her mother's side at least, and a baroness in right of her father, I will help you in the search."

"Ah, ha; you will do as much as that, will you?"

"Yes."

"Well, really, nothing is certain in this world."

"Oh, count, what a service you might render me! I should like you a hundred times better if, by your intervention, I could manage to remain a bachelor, even were it only for ten years."

"Nothing is impossible," gravely replied Monte Cristo; and taking leave of Albert, he returned into the house, and struck the gong three times. Bertuccio appeared.

"Monsieur Bertuccio, you understand that I intend entertaining company on Saturday at Auteuil." Bertuccio slightly started. "I shall require your services to see that all be properly arranged. It is a beautiful house, or at all events may be made so."

"There must be a good deal done before it can deserve that title, your excellency, for the tapestried hangings are very old."

"Let them all be taken away and changed, then, with the exception of the sleeping-chamber which is hung with red damask; you will leave that exactly as it is." Bertuccio bowed. "You will not touch the garden either; as to the yard, you may do what you please with it; I should prefer that being altered beyond all recognition."

"I will do everything in my power to carry out your wishes, your excellency. I should be glad, however, to receive your excellency's commands concerning the dinner."

"Really, my dear M. Bertuccio," said the count, "since you have been in Paris, you have become quite nervous, and apparently out of your element; you no longer seem to understand me."

"But surely your excellency will be so good as to inform me whom you are expecting to receive?"

"I do not yet know myself, neither is it necessary that you should do so. 'Lucullus dines with Lucullus,' that is quite sufficient."

Bertuccio bowed, and left the room.

Study Guide Questions

For Students:

1. Who visits the Count at the beginning of this chapter?
2. What does Albert's mother think of his union with Mademoiselle Danglars?
3. Why does the Count refuse to accept Albert's dinner invitation?

For Reading Club:

1. Do you think that Albert's concerns regarding marrying a girl richer than himself are felt by modern men as well?
2. The Count tells Albert that Mademoiselle Danglars 'will enrich you, and you will ennoble her.' Do you think it is a good reason to marry?
3. What does the Count propose to reduce the coldness between Comtesse de Morcerf and Madame Danglars?

CHAPTER 55

Major Cavalcanti

Both the count and Baptistin had told the truth when they announced to Morcerf the proposed visit of the major, which had served Monte Cristo as a pretext for declining Albert's invitation. Seven o'clock had just struck, and M. Bertuccio, according to the command which had been given him, had two hours before left for Auteuil, when a cab stopped at the door, and after depositing its occupant at the gate, immediately hurried away, as if ashamed of its employment. The visitor was about fifty-two years of age, dressed in one of the green surtouts, ornamented with black frogs, which have so long maintained their popularity all over Europe. He wore trousers of blue cloth, boots tolerably clean, but not of the brightest polish, and a little too thick in the soles, buckskin gloves, a hat somewhat resembling in shape those usually worn by the gendarmes, and a black cravat striped with white, which, if the proprietor had not worn it of his own free will, might have passed for a halter, so much did it resemble one. Such was the picturesque costume of the person who rang at the gate, and demanded if it was not at No. 30 in the Avenue des Champs-Élysées that the Count of Monte Cristo lived, and who, being answered by the porter in the affirmative, entered, closed the gate after him, and began to ascend the steps.

The small and angular head of this man, his white hair and thick gray moustaches, caused him to be easily recognized by Baptistin, who had received an exact description of the expected visitor, and who was awaiting him in the hall. Therefore, scarcely had the stranger time to pronounce his name before the count was apprised of his arrival. He was ushered into a simple and elegant drawing-room, and the count rose to meet him with a smiling air.

"Ah, my dear sir, you are most welcome; I was expecting you."

"Indeed," said the Italian, "was your excellency then aware of my visit?"

"Yes; I had been told that I should see you today at seven o'clock."

"Then you have received full information concerning my arrival?"

"Of course."

"Ah, so much the better, I feared this little precaution might have been forgotten."

"What precaution?"

"That of informing you beforehand of my coming."

"Oh, no, it has not."

"But you are sure you are not mistaken."

"Very sure."

"It really was I whom your excellency expected at seven o'clock this evening?"

"I will prove it to you beyond a doubt."

"Oh, no, never mind that," said the Italian; "it is not worth the trouble."

"Yes, yes," said Monte Cristo. His visitor appeared slightly uneasy. "Let me see," said the count; "are you not the Marquis Bartolomeo Cavalcanti?"

"Bartolomeo Cavalcanti," joyfully replied the Italian; "yes, I am really he."

"Ex-major in the Austrian service?"

"Was I a major?" timidly asked the old soldier.

"Yes," said Monte Cristo "you were a major; that is the title the French give to the post which you filled in Italy."

"Very good," said the major, "I do not demand more, you understand—"

"Your visit here today is not of your own suggestion, is it?" said Monte Cristo.

"No, certainly not."

"You were sent by some other person?"

"Yes."

"By the excellent Abbé Busoni?"

"Exactly so," said the delighted major.

"And you have a letter?"

"Yes, there it is."

"Give it to me, then." And Monte Cristo took the letter, which he opened and read. The major looked at the count with his large staring eyes, and then took a survey of the apartment, but his gaze almost immediately reverted to the proprietor of the room.

"Yes, yes, I see. 'Major Cavalcanti, a worthy patrician of Lucca, a descendant of the Cavalcanti of Florence,'" continued Monte Cristo, reading aloud, "'possessing an income of half a million.'"

Monte Cristo raised his eyes from the paper, and bowed.

"Half a million," said he, "magnificent!"

"Half a million, is it?" said the major.

"Yes, in so many words; and it must be so, for the abbé knows correctly the amount of all the largest fortunes in Europe."

"Be it half a million, then; but on my word of honor, I had no idea that it was so much."

"Because you are robbed by your steward. You must make some reformation in that quarter."

"You have opened my eyes," said the Italian gravely; "I will show the gentlemen the door."

Monte Cristo resumed the perusal of the letter:

"'And who only needs one thing more to make him happy.'"

"Yes, indeed but one!" said the major with a sigh.

"'Which is to recover a lost and adored son.'"

"A lost and adored son!"

"'Stolen away in his infancy, either by an enemy of his noble family or by the gypsies.'"

"At the age of five years!" said the major with a deep sigh, and raising his eye to heaven.

"Unhappy father," said Monte Cristo. The count continued:

"'I have given him renewed life and hope, in the assurance that you have the power of restoring the son whom he has vainly sought for fifteen years.'"

The major looked at the count with an indescribable expression of anxiety.

"I have the power of so doing," said Monte Cristo. The major recovered his self-possession.

"So, then," said he, "the letter was true to the end?"

"Did you doubt it, my dear Monsieur Bartolomeo?"

"No, indeed; certainly not; a good man, a man holding religious office, as does the Abbé Busoni, could not condescend to deceive or play off a joke; but your excellency has not read all."

"Ah, true," said Monte Cristo "there is a postscript."

"Yes, yes," repeated the major, "yes—there—is—a—postscript."

"'In order to save Major Cavalcanti the trouble of drawing on his banker, I send him a draft for 2,000 francs to defray his travelling expenses, and credit on you for the further sum of 48,000 francs, which you still owe me.'"

The major awaited the conclusion of the postscript, apparently with great anxiety.

"Very good," said the count.

"He said 'very good,'" muttered the major, "then—sir—" replied he.

"Then what?" asked Monte Cristo.

"Then the postscript—"

"Well; what of the postscript?"

"Then the postscript is as favorably received by you as the rest of the letter?"

"Certainly; the Abbé Busoni and myself have a small account open between us. I do not remember if it is exactly 48,000 francs, which I am still owing him, but I dare say we shall not dispute the difference. You attached great importance, then, to this postscript, my dear Monsieur Cavalcanti?"

"I must explain to you," said the major, "that, fully confiding in the signature of the Abbé Busoni, I had not provided myself with any other funds; so that if this resource had failed me, I should have found myself very unpleasantly situated in Paris."

"Is it possible that a man of your standing should be embarrassed anywhere?" said Monte Cristo.

"Why, really I know no one," said the major.

"But then you yourself are known to others?"

"Yes, I am known, so that—"

"Proceed, my dear Monsieur Cavalcanti."

"So that you will remit to me these 48,000 francs?"

"Certainly, at your first request." The major's eyes dilated with pleasing astonishment. "But sit down," said Monte Cristo; "really I do not know what I have been thinking of—I have positively kept you standing for the last quarter of an hour."

"Don't mention it." The major drew an armchair towards him, and proceeded to seat himself.

"Now," said the count, "what will you take—a glass of sherry, port, or Alicante?"

"Alicante, if you please; it is my favorite wine."

"I have some that is very good. You will take a biscuit with it, will you not?"

"Yes, I will take a biscuit, as you are so obliging."

Monte Cristo rang; Baptistin appeared. The count advanced to meet him.

"Well?" said he in a low voice.

"The young man is here," said the valet de chambre in the same tone.

"Into what room did you take him?"

"Into the blue drawing-room, according to your excellency's orders."

"That's right; now bring the Alicante and some biscuits."

Baptistin left the room.

"Really," said the major, "I am quite ashamed of the trouble I am giving you."

"Pray don't mention such a thing," said the count. Baptistin re-entered with glasses, wine, and biscuits. The count filled one glass, but in the other he only poured a few drops of the ruby-colored liquid. The bottle was covered with spiders' webs, and all the other signs which indicate the age of wine more truly than do wrinkles on a man's face. The major made a wise choice; he took the full glass and a biscuit. The count told Baptistin to leave the plate within reach of his guest, who began by sipping the Alicante with an expression of great satisfaction, and then delicately steeped his biscuit in the wine.

"So, sir, you lived at Lucca, did you? You were rich, noble, held in great esteem—had all that could render a man happy?"

"All," said the major, hastily swallowing his biscuit, "positively all."

"And yet there was one thing wanting in order to complete your happiness?"

"Only one thing," said the Italian.

"And that one thing, your lost child."

"Ah," said the major, taking a second biscuit, "that consummation of my happiness was indeed wanting." The worthy major raised his eyes to heaven and sighed.

"Let me hear, then," said the count, "who this deeply regretted son was; for I always understood you were a bachelor."

"That was the general opinion, sir," said the major, "and I—"

"Yes," replied the count, "and you confirmed the report. A youthful indiscretion, I suppose, which you were anxious to conceal from the world at large?"

The major recovered himself, and resumed his usual calm manner, at the same time casting his eyes down, either to give himself time to compose his countenance, or to assist his imagination, all the while giving an under-look at the count, the protracted smile on whose lips still announced the same polite curiosity.

"Yes," said the major, "I did wish this fault to be hidden from every eye."

"Not on your own account, surely," replied Monte Cristo; "for a man is above that sort of thing?"

"Oh, no, certainly not on my own account," said the major with a smile and a shake of the head.

"But for the sake of the mother?" said the count.

"Yes, for the mother's sake—his poor mother!" cried the major, taking a third biscuit.

"Take some more wine, my dear Cavalcanti," said the count, pouring out for him a second glass of Alicante; "your emotion has quite overcome you."

"His poor mother," murmured the major, trying to get the lachrymal gland in operation, so as to moisten the corner of his eye with a false tear.

"She belonged to one of the first families in Italy, I think, did she not?"

"She was of a noble family of Fiesole, count."

"And her name was—"

"Do you desire to know her name—?"

"Oh," said Monte Cristo "it would be quite superfluous for you to tell me, for I already know it."

"The count knows everything," said the Italian, bowing.

"Oliva Corsinari, was it not?"

"Oliva Corsinari!"

"A marchioness?"

"A marchioness!"

"And you married her at last, notwithstanding the opposition of her family?"

"Yes, that was the way it ended."

"And you have doubtless brought all your papers with you?" said Monte Cristo.

"What papers?"

"The certificate of your marriage with Oliva Corsinari, and the register of your child's birth."

"The register of my child's birth?"

"The register of the birth of Andrea Cavalcanti—of your son; is not his name Andrea?"

"I believe so," said the major.

"What? You believe so?"

"I dare not positively assert it, as he has been lost for so long a time."

"Well, then," said Monte Cristo "you have all the documents with you?"

"Your excellency, I regret to say that, not knowing it was necessary to come provided with these papers, I neglected to bring them."

"That is unfortunate," returned Monte Cristo.

"Were they, then, so necessary?"

"They were indispensable."

The major passed his hand across his brow. "Ah, *perbacco*, indispensable, were they?"

"Certainly they were; supposing there were to be doubts raised as to the validity of your marriage or the legitimacy of your child?"

"True," said the major, "there might be doubts raised."

"In that case your son would be very unpleasantly situated."

"It would be fatal to his interests."

"It might cause him to fail in some desirable matrimonial alliance."

"*O peccato!*"

"You must know that in France they are very particular on these points; it is not sufficient, as in Italy, to go to the priest and say, 'We love each other, and want you to marry us.' Marriage is a civil affair in France, and in order to marry in an orthodox manner you must have papers which undeniably establish your identity."

"That is the misfortune! You see I have not these necessary papers."

"Fortunately, I have them, though," said Monte Cristo.

"You?"

"Yes."

"You have them?"

"I have them."

"Ah, indeed?" said the major, who, seeing the object of his journey frustrated by the absence of the papers, feared also that his forgetfulness might give rise to some difficulty concerning the 48,000 francs—"ah, indeed, that is a fortunate circumstance; yes, that really is lucky, for it never occurred to me to bring them."

"I do not at all wonder at it—one cannot think of everything; but, happily, the Abbé Busoni thought for you."

"He is an excellent person."

"He is extremely prudent and thoughtful."

"He is an admirable man," said the major; "and he sent them to you?"

"Here they are."

The major clasped his hands in token of admiration.

"You married Oliva Corsinari in the church of San Paolo del Monte-Cattini; here is the priest's certificate."

"Yes indeed, there it is truly," said the Italian, looking on with astonishment.

"And here is Andrea Cavalcanti's baptismal register, given by the curé of Saravezza."

"All quite correct."

"Take these documents, then; they do not concern me. You will give them to your son, who will, of course, take great care of them."

"I should think so, indeed! If he were to lose them—"

"Well, and if he were to lose them?" said Monte Cristo.

"In that case," replied the major, "it would be necessary to write to the curé for duplicates, and it would be some time before they could be obtained."

"It would be a difficult matter to arrange," said Monte Cristo.

"Almost an impossibility," replied the major.

"I am very glad to see that you understand the value of these papers."

"I regard them as invaluable."

"Now," said Monte Cristo "as to the mother of the young man—"

"As to the mother of the young man—" repeated the Italian, with anxiety.

"As regards the Marchesa Corsinari—"

"Really," said the major, "difficulties seem to thicken upon us; will she be wanted in any way?"

"No, sir," replied Monte Cristo; "besides, has she not—"

"Yes, sir," said the major, "she has—"

"Paid the last debt of nature?"

"Alas, yes," returned the Italian.

"I knew that," said Monte Cristo; "she has been dead these ten years."

"And I am still mourning her loss," exclaimed the major, drawing from his pocket a checked handkerchief, and alternately wiping first the left and then the right eye.

"What would you have?" said Monte Cristo; "we are all mortal. Now, you understand, my dear Monsieur Cavalcanti, that it is useless for you to tell people in France that you have been separated from your son for fifteen years. Stories of gypsies, who steal children, are not at all in vogue in this part of the world, and would not be believed. You sent him for his education to a college in one of the provinces, and now you wish him to complete his education in the Parisian world. That is the reason which has induced you to leave Via Reggio, where you have lived since the death of your wife. That will be sufficient."

"You think so?"

"Certainly."

"Very well, then."

"If they should hear of the separation—"

"Ah, yes; what could I say?"

"That an unfaithful tutor, bought over by the enemies of your family—"

"By the Corsinari?"

"Precisely. Had stolen away this child, in order that your name might become extinct."

"That is reasonable, since he is an only son."

"Well, now that all is arranged, do not let these newly awakened remembrances be forgotten. You have, doubtless, already guessed that I was preparing a surprise for you?"

"An agreeable one?" asked the Italian.

"Ah, I see the eye of a father is no more to be deceived than his heart."

"Hum!" said the major.

"Someone has told you the secret; or, perhaps, you guessed that he was here."

"That who was here?"

"Your child—your son—your Andrea!"

"I did guess it," replied the major with the greatest possible coolness. "Then he is here?"

"He is," said Monte Cristo; "when the valet de chambre came in just now, he told me of his arrival."

"Ah, very well, very well," said the major, clutching the buttons of his coat at each exclamation.

"My dear sir," said Monte Cristo, "I understand your emotion; you must have time to recover yourself. I will, in the meantime, go and prepare the young man for this much-desired interview, for I presume that he is not less impatient for it than yourself."

"I should quite imagine that to be the case," said Cavalcanti.

"Well, in a quarter of an hour he shall be with you."

"You will bring him, then? You carry your goodness so far as even to present him to me yourself?"

"No; I do not wish to come between a father and son. Your interview will be private. But do not be uneasy; even if the powerful voice of nature should be silent, you cannot well mistake him; he will enter by this door. He is a fine young man, of fair complexion—a little too fair, perhaps—pleasing in manners; but you will see and judge for yourself."

"By the way," said the major, "you know I have only the 2,000 francs which the Abbé Busoni sent me; this sum I have expended upon travelling expenses, and—"

"And you want money; that is a matter of course, my dear M. Cavalcanti. Well, here are 8,000 francs on account."

The major's eyes sparkled brilliantly.

"It is 40,000 francs which I now owe you," said Monte Cristo.

"Does your excellency wish for a receipt?" said the major, at the same time slipping the money into the inner pocket of his coat.

"For what?" said the count.

"I thought you might want it to show the Abbé Busoni."

"Well, when you receive the remaining 40,000, you shall give me a receipt in full. Between honest men such excessive precaution is, I think, quite unnecessary."

"Yes, so it is, between perfectly upright people."

"One word more," said Monte Cristo.

"Say on."

"You will permit me to make one remark?"

"Certainly; pray do so."

"Then I should advise you to leave off wearing that style of dress."

"Indeed," said the major, regarding himself with an air of complete satisfaction.

"Yes. It may be worn at Via Reggio; but that costume, however elegant in itself, has long been out of fashion in Paris."

"That's unfortunate."

"Oh, if you really are attached to your old mode of dress; you can easily resume it when you leave Paris."

"But what shall I wear?"

"What you find in your trunks."

"In my trunks? I have but one portmanteau."

"I dare say you have nothing else with you. What is the use of boring one's self with so many things? Besides an old soldier always likes to march with as little baggage as possible."

"That is just the case—precisely so."

"But you are a man of foresight and prudence, therefore you sent your luggage on before you. It has arrived at the Hôtel des Princes, Rue de Richelieu. It is there you are to take up your quarters."

"Then, in these trunks—"

"I presume you have given orders to your valet de chambre to put in all you are likely to need,—your plain clothes and your uniform. On grand occasions you must wear your uniform; that will look very well. Do not forget your crosses. They still laugh at them in France, and yet always wear them, for all that."

"Very well, very well," said the major, who was in ecstasy at the attention paid him by the count.

"Now," said Monte Cristo, "that you have fortified yourself against all painful excitement, prepare yourself, my dear M. Cavalcanti, to meet your lost Andrea."

Saying which Monte Cristo bowed, and disappeared behind the tapestry, leaving the major fascinated beyond expression with the delightful reception which he had received at the hands of the count.

Study Guide Questions

For Students:

1. Who is Major Cavalcanti and why does he visit the Count?
2. What happened to Major Cavalcanti's son?
3. What is the name of Major Cavalcanti's son?

For Reading Club:

1. Discuss how the Count helps Major Cavalcanti.
2. What is the counter-story that the Count tells Major Cavalcanti to spread to everyone in Parisian society?
3. Why do you think the Count is capable of treating others like puppets?

CHAPTER 56

Andrea Cavalcanti

The Count of Monte Cristo entered the adjoining room, which Baptistin had designated as the drawing-room, and found there a young man, of graceful demeanor and elegant appearance, who had arrived in a cab about half an hour previously. Baptistin had not found any difficulty in recognizing the person who presented himself at the door for admittance. He was certainly the tall young man with light hair, red beard, black eyes, and brilliant complexion, whom his master had so particularly described to him. When the count entered the room the young man was carelessly stretched on a sofa, tapping his boot with the gold-headed cane which he held in his hand. On perceiving the count he rose quickly.

"The Count of Monte Cristo, I believe?" said he.

"Yes, sir, and I think I have the honor of addressing Count Andrea Cavalcanti?"

"Count Andrea Cavalcanti," repeated the young man, accompanying his words with a bow.

"You are charged with a letter of introduction addressed to me, are you not?" said the count.

"I did not mention that, because the signature seemed to me so strange."

"The letter signed 'Sinbad the Sailor,' is it not?"

"Exactly so. Now, as I have never known any Sinbad, with the exception of the one celebrated in the *Thousand and One Nights*—"

"Well, it is one of his descendants, and a great friend of mine; he is a very rich Englishman, eccentric almost to insanity, and his real name is Lord Wilmore."

"Ah, indeed? Then that explains everything that is extraordinary," said Andrea. "He is, then, the same Englishman whom I met—at—ah—yes, indeed. Well, monsieur, I am at your service."

"If what you say be true," replied the count, smiling, "perhaps you will be kind enough to give me some account of yourself and your family?"

"Certainly, I will do so," said the young man, with a quickness which gave proof of his ready invention. "I am (as you have said) the Count Andrea Cavalcanti, son of Major Bartolomeo Cavalcanti, a descendant of the Cavalcanti whose names are inscribed in the golden book at Florence. Our family, although still rich (for my father's income amounts to half a million), has experienced many misfortunes, and I myself was, at the age of five years, taken away by the treachery of my tutor, so that for fifteen years I have not seen the author of my existence. Since I have arrived at years of discretion and become my own master, I have been constantly seeking him, but all in vain. At length I received this letter from your friend, which states that my father is in Paris, and authorizes me to address myself to you for information respecting him."

"Really, all you have related to me is exceedingly interesting," said Monte Cristo, observing the young man with a gloomy satisfaction; "and you have done well to conform in everything to the wishes of my friend Sinbad; for your father is indeed here, and is seeking you."

The count from the moment of first entering the drawing-room, had not once lost sight of the expression of the young man's countenance; he had admired the assurance of his look and the firmness of his voice; but at these words, so natural in themselves, "Your father is indeed here, and is seeking you," young Andrea started, and exclaimed, "My father? Is my father here?"

"Most undoubtedly," replied Monte Cristo; "your father, Major Bartolomeo Cavalcanti." The expression of terror which, for the moment, had overspread the features of the young man, had now disappeared.

"Ah, yes, that is the name, certainly. Major Bartolomeo Cavalcanti. And you really mean to say; monsieur, that my dear father is here?"

"Yes, sir; and I can even add that I have only just left his company. The history which he related to me of his lost son touched me to the quick; indeed, his griefs, hopes, and fears on that subject might furnish material for a most touching and pathetic poem. At length, he one day received a letter, stating that the abductors of his son now offered to restore him, or at least to give notice where he might be found, on condition of receiving a large sum of money, by way of ransom. Your father did not hesitate an instant, and the sum was sent to the frontier of Piedmont, with a passport signed for Italy. You were in the south of France, I think?"

"Yes," replied Andrea, with an embarrassed air, "I was in the south of France."

"A carriage was to await you at Nice?"

"Precisely so; and it conveyed me from Nice to Genoa, from Genoa to Turin, from Turin to Chambéry, from Chambéry to Pont-de-Beauvoisin, and from Pont-de-Beauvoisin to Paris."

"Indeed? Then your father ought to have met with you on the road, for it is exactly the same route which he himself took, and that is how we have been able to trace your journey to this place."

"But," said Andrea, "if my father had met me, I doubt if he would have recognized me; I must be somewhat altered since he last saw me."

"Oh, the voice of nature," said Monte Cristo.

"True," interrupted the young man, "I had not looked upon it in that light."

"Now," replied Monte Cristo "there is only one source of uneasiness left in your father's mind, which is this—he is anxious to know how you have been employed during your long absence from him, how you have been treated by your persecutors, and if they have conducted themselves towards you with all the deference due to your rank. Finally, he is anxious to see if you have been fortunate enough to escape the bad moral influence to which you have been exposed, and which is infinitely more to be dreaded than any physical suffering; he wishes to discover if the fine abilities with which nature had endowed you have been weakened by want of culture; and, in short, whether you consider yourself capable of resuming and retaining in the world the high position to which your rank entitles you."

"Sir!" exclaimed the young man, quite astounded, "I hope no false report—"

"As for myself, I first heard you spoken of by my friend Wilmore, the philanthropist. I believe he found you in some unpleasant position, but do not know of what nature, for I did not ask, not being inquisitive. Your misfortunes engaged his sympathies, so you see you must have been interesting. He told me that he was anxious to restore you to the position which you had lost, and that he would seek your father until he found him. He did seek, and has found him, apparently, since he is here now; and, finally, my friend apprised me of your coming, and gave me a few other instructions relative to your future fortune. I am quite aware that my friend Wilmore is peculiar, but he is sincere, and as rich as a gold mine, consequently, he may indulge his eccentricities without any fear of their ruining him, and I have promised to adhere to his instructions. Now, sir, pray do not be offended at the question I am about to put to you, as it comes in the way of my duty as your patron. I would wish to know if the misfortunes which have happened to you—misfortunes entirely beyond your control, and which in no degree diminish my regard for you—I would wish to know if they have not, in some measure, contributed to render you a stranger to the world in which your fortune and your name entitle you to make a conspicuous figure?"

"Sir," returned the young man, with a reassurance of manner, "make your mind easy on this score. Those who took me from my father, and who always intended, sooner or later, to sell me again to my original proprietor, as they have now done, calculated that, in order to make the most of their bargain, it would be politic to leave me in possession of all my personal and hereditary worth, and even to increase the value, if possible. I have, therefore, received a very good education, and have been treated by these kidnappers very much as the slaves were treated in Asia Minor, whose masters made them grammarians, doctors, and philosophers, in order that they might fetch a higher price in the Roman market."

Monte Cristo smiled with satisfaction; it appeared as if he had not expected so much from M. Andrea Cavalcanti.

"Besides," continued the young man, "if there did appear some defect in education, or offence against the established forms of etiquette, I suppose it would be excused, in consideration of the misfortunes which accompanied my birth, and followed me through my youth."

"Well," said Monte Cristo in an indifferent tone, "you will do as you please, count, for you are the master of your own actions, and are the person most concerned in the matter, but if I were you, I would not divulge a word of these adventures. Your history is quite a romance, and the world, which delights in romances in yellow covers, strangely mistrusts those which are bound in living parchment, even though they be gilded like yourself. This is the kind of difficulty which I wished to represent to you, my dear count. You would hardly have recited your touching history before it would go forth to the world, and be deemed unlikely and unnatural. You would be no longer a lost child found, but you would be looked upon as an upstart, who had sprung up like a mushroom in the night. You might excite a little curiosity, but it is not everyone who likes to be made the centre of observation and the subject of unpleasant remark."

"I agree with you, monsieur," said the young man, turning pale, and, in spite of himself, trembling beneath the scrutinizing look of his companion, "such consequences would be extremely unpleasant."

"Nevertheless, you must not exaggerate the evil," said Monte Cristo, "for by endeavoring to avoid one fault you will fall into another. You must resolve upon one simple and single line of conduct, and for a man of your intelligence, this plan is as easy as it is necessary; you must form honorable friendships, and by that means counteract the prejudice which may attach to the obscurity of your former life."

Andrea visibly changed countenance.

"I would offer myself as your surety and friendly adviser," said Monte Cristo, "did I not possess a moral distrust of my best friends, and a sort of inclination to lead others to doubt them too; therefore, in departing from this rule, I should (as the actors say) be playing a part quite out of my line, and should, therefore, run the risk of being hissed, which would be an act of folly."

"However, your excellency," said Andrea, "in consideration of Lord Wilmore, by whom I was recommended to you—"

"Yes, certainly," interrupted Monte Cristo; "but Lord Wilmore did not omit to inform me, my dear M. Andrea, that the season of your youth was rather a stormy one. Ah," said the count, watching Andrea's countenance, "I do not demand any confession from you; it is precisely to avoid that necessity that your father was sent for from Lucca. You shall soon see him. He is a little stiff and pompous in his manner, and he is disfigured by his uniform; but when it becomes known that he has been for eighteen years in the Austrian service, all that will be pardoned. We are not generally very severe with the Austrians. In short, you will find your father a very presentable person, I assure you."

"Ah, sir, you have given me confidence; it is so long since we were separated, that I have not the least remembrance of him, and, besides, you know that in the eyes of the world a large fortune covers all defects."

"He is a millionaire—his income is 500,000 francs."

"Then," said the young man, with anxiety, "I shall be sure to be placed in an agreeable position."

"One of the most agreeable possible, my dear sir; he will allow you an income of 50,000 livres per annum during the whole time of your stay in Paris."

"Then in that case I shall always choose to remain there."

"You cannot control circumstances, my dear sir; 'man proposes, and God disposes.'" Andrea sighed.

"But," said he, "so long as I do remain in Paris, and nothing forces me to quit it, do you mean to tell me that I may rely on receiving the sum you just now mentioned to me?"

"You may."

"Shall I receive it from my father?" asked Andrea, with some uneasiness.

"Yes, you will receive it from your father personally, but Lord Wilmore will be the security for the money. He has, at the request of your father, opened an account of 5,000 francs a month at M. Danglars', which is one of the safest banks in Paris."

"And does my father mean to remain long in Paris?" asked Andrea.

"Only a few days," replied Monte Cristo. "His service does not allow him to absent himself more than two or three weeks together."

"Ah, my dear father!" exclaimed Andrea, evidently charmed with the idea of his speedy departure.

"Therefore," said Monte Cristo feigning to mistake his meaning—"therefore I will not, for another instant, retard the pleasure of your meeting. Are you prepared to embrace your worthy father?"

"I hope you do not doubt it."

"Go, then, into the drawing-room, my young friend, where you will find your father awaiting you."

Andrea made a low bow to the count, and entered the adjoining room. Monte Cristo watched him till he disappeared, and then touched a spring in a panel made to look like a picture, which, in sliding partly from the frame, discovered to view a small opening, so cleverly contrived that it revealed all that was passing in the drawing-room now occupied by Cavalcanti and Andrea. The young man closed the door behind him, and advanced towards the major, who had risen when he heard steps approaching him.

"Ah, my dear father!" said Andrea in a loud voice, in order that the count might hear him in the next room, "is it really you?"

"How do you do, my dear son?" said the major gravely.

"After so many years of painful separation," said Andrea, in the same tone of voice, and glancing towards the door, "what a happiness it is to meet again!"

"Indeed it is, after so long a separation."

"Will you not embrace me, sir?" said Andrea.

"If you wish it, my son," said the major; and the two men embraced each other after the fashion of actors on the stage; that is to say, each rested his head on the other's shoulder.

"Then we are once more reunited?" said Andrea.

"Once more," replied the major.

"Never more to be separated?"

"Why, as to that—I think, my dear son, you must be by this time so accustomed to France as to look upon it almost as a second country."

"The fact is," said the young man, "that I should be exceedingly grieved to leave it."

"As for me, you must know I cannot possibly live out of Lucca; therefore I shall return to Italy as soon as I can."

"But before you leave France, my dear father, I hope you will put me in possession of the documents which will be necessary to prove my descent."

"Certainly; I am come expressly on that account; it has cost me much trouble to find you, but I had resolved on giving them into your hands, and if I had to recommence my search, it would occupy all the few remaining years of my life."

"Where are these papers, then?"

"Here they are."

Andrea seized the certificate of his father's marriage and his own baptismal register, and after having opened them with all the eagerness which might be expected under the circumstances, he read them with a facility which proved that he was accustomed to similar documents, and with an expression which plainly denoted an unusual interest in the contents. When he had perused the documents, an indefinable expression of pleasure lighted up his countenance, and looking at the major with a most peculiar smile, he said, in very excellent Tuscan:

"Then there is no longer any such thing, in Italy as being condemned to the galleys?"

The major drew himself up to his full height.

"Why?—what do you mean by that question?"

"I mean that if there were, it would be impossible to draw up with impunity two such deeds as these. In France, my dear sir, half such a piece of effrontery as that would cause you to be quickly despatched to Toulon for five years, for change of air."

"Will you be good enough to explain your meaning?" said the major, endeavoring as much as possible to assume an air of the greatest majesty.

"My dear M. Cavalcanti," said Andrea, taking the major by the arm in a confidential manner, "how much are you paid for being my father?"

The major was about to speak, when Andrea continued, in a low voice:

"Nonsense, I am going to set you an example of confidence, they give me 50,000 francs a year to be your son; consequently, you can understand that it is not at all likely I shall ever deny my parent."

The major looked anxiously around him.

"Make yourself easy, we are quite alone," said Andrea; "besides, we are conversing in Italian."

"Well, then," replied the major, "they paid me 50,000 francs down."

"Monsieur Cavalcanti," said Andrea, "do you believe in fairy tales?"

"I used not to do so, but I really feel now almost obliged to have faith in them."

"You have, then, been induced to alter your opinion; you have had some proofs of their truth?" The major drew from his pocket a handful of gold.

"Most palpable proofs," said he, "as you may perceive."

"You think, then, that I may rely on the count's promises?"

"Certainly I do."

"You are sure he will keep his word with me?"

"To the letter, but at the same time, remember, we must continue to play our respective parts. I, as a tender father—"

"And I as a dutiful son, as they choose that I shall be descended from you."

"Whom do you mean by they?"

"*Ma foi,* I can hardly tell, but I was alluding to those who wrote the letter; you received one, did you not?"

"Yes."

"From whom?"

"From a certain Abbé Busoni."

"Have you any knowledge of him?"

"No, I have never seen him."

"What did he say in the letter?"

"You will promise not to betray me?"

"Rest assured of that; you well know that our interests are the same."

"Then read for yourself;" and the major gave a letter into the young man's hand. Andrea read in a low voice:

> "'You are poor; a miserable old age awaits you. Would you like to become rich, or at least independent? Set out immediately for Paris, and demand of the Count of Monte Cristo, Avenue des Champs-Élysées, No. 30, the son whom you had by the Marchesa Corsinari, and who was taken from you at five years of age. This son is named Andrea Cavalcanti. In order that you may not doubt the kind intention of the writer of this letter, you will find enclosed an order for 2,400 francs, payable in Florence, at Signor Gozzi's; also a letter of introduction to the Count of Monte Cristo, on whom I give you a draft of 48,000 francs. Remember to go to the count on the 26th May at seven o'clock in the evening.
>
> "(Signed) 'Abbé Busoni.'"

"It is the same."

"What do you mean?" said the major.

"I was going to say that I received a letter almost to the same effect."

"You?"

"Yes."

"From the Abbé Busoni?"

"No."

"From whom, then?"

"From an Englishman, called Lord Wilmore, who takes the name of Sinbad the Sailor."

"And of whom you have no more knowledge than I of the Abbé Busoni?"

"You are mistaken; there I am ahead of you."

"You have seen him, then?"

"Yes, once."

"Where?"

"Ah, that is just what I cannot tell you; if I did, I should make you as wise as myself, which it is not my intention to do."

"And what did the letter contain?"

"Read it."

"'You are poor, and your future prospects are dark and gloomy. Do you wish for a name? should you like to be rich, and your own master?'"

"*Parbleu!*" said the young man; "was it possible there could be two answers to such a question?"

"'Take the post-chaise which you will find waiting at the Porte de Gênes, as you enter Nice; pass through Turin, Chambéry, and Pont-de-Beauvoisin. Go to the Count of Monte Cristo, Avenue des Champs-Élysées, on the 26th of May, at seven o'clock in the evening, and demand of him your father. You are the son of the Marchese Cavalcanti and the Marchesa Oliva Corsinari. The marquis will give you some papers which will certify this fact, and authorize you to appear under that name in the Parisian world. As to your rank, an annual income of 50,000 livres will enable you to support it admirably. I enclose a draft for 5,000 livres, payable on M. Ferrea, banker at Nice, and also a letter of introduction to the Count of Monte Cristo, whom I have directed to supply all your wants.

"'Sinbad the Sailor.'"

"Humph," said the major; "very good. You have seen the count, you say?"

"I have only just left him."

"And has he conformed to all that the letter specified?"

"He has."

"Do you understand it?"

"Not in the least."

"There is a dupe somewhere."

"At all events, it is neither you nor I."

"Certainly not."

"Well, then—"

"Why, it does not much concern us, do you think it does?"

"No; I agree with you there. We must play the game to the end, and consent to be blindfolded."

"Ah, you shall see; I promise you I will sustain my part to admiration."

"I never once doubted your doing so." Monte Cristo chose this moment for re-entering the drawing-room. On hearing the sound of his footsteps, the two men threw themselves in each other's arms, and while they were in the midst of this embrace, the count entered.

"Well, marquis," said Monte Cristo, "you appear to be in no way disappointed in the son whom your good fortune has restored to you."

"Ah, your excellency, I am overwhelmed with delight."

"And what are your feelings?" said Monte Cristo, turning to the young man.

"As for me, my heart is overflowing with happiness."

"Happy father, happy son!" said the count.

"There is only one thing which grieves me," observed the major, "and that is the necessity for my leaving Paris so soon."

"Ah, my dear M. Cavalcanti, I trust you will not leave before I have had the honor of presenting you to some of my friends."

"I am at your service, sir," replied the major.

"Now, sir," said Monte Cristo, addressing Andrea, "make your confession."

"To whom?"

"Tell M. Cavalcanti something of the state of your finances."

"*Ma foi!* monsieur, you have touched upon a tender chord."

"Do you hear what he says, major?"

"Certainly I do."

"But do you understand?"

"I do."

"Your son says he requires money."

"Well, what would you have me do?" said the major.

"You should furnish him with some of course," replied Monte Cristo.

"I?"

"Yes, you," said the count, at the same time advancing towards Andrea, and slipping a packet of bank-notes into the young man's hand.

"What is this?"

"It is from your father."

"From my father?"

"Yes; did you not tell him just now that you wanted money? Well, then, he deputes me to give you this."

"Am I to consider this as part of my income on account?"

"No, it is for the first expenses of your settling in Paris."

"Ah, how good my dear father is!"

"Silence," said Monte Cristo; "he does not wish you to know that it comes from him."

"I fully appreciate his delicacy," said Andrea, cramming the notes hastily into his pocket.

"And now, gentlemen, I wish you good-morning," said Monte Cristo.

"And when shall we have the honor of seeing you again, your excellency?" asked Cavalcanti.

"Ah," said Andrea, "when may we hope for that pleasure?"

"On Saturday, if you will—Yes.—Let me see—Saturday—I am to dine at my country house, at Auteuil, on that day, Rue de la Fontaine, No. 28. Several persons are invited, and among others, M. Danglars, your banker. I will introduce you to him, for it will be necessary he should know you, as he is to pay your money."

"Full dress?" said the major, half aloud.

"Oh, yes, certainly," said the count; "uniform, cross, knee-breeches."

"And how shall I be dressed?" demanded Andrea.

"Oh, very simply; black trousers, patent leather boots, white waistcoat, either a black or blue coat, and a long cravat. Go to Blin or Véronique for your clothes. Baptistin will tell you where, if you do not know their address. The less pretension there is in your attire, the better will be the effect, as you are a rich man. If you mean to buy any horses, get them of Devedeux, and if you purchase a phaeton, go to Baptiste for it."

"At what hour shall we come?" asked the young man.

"About half-past six."

"We will be with you at that time," said the major. The two Cavalcanti bowed to the count, and left the house. Monte Cristo went to the window, and saw them crossing the street, arm in arm.

"There go two miscreants;" said he, "it is a pity they are not really related!" Then, after an instant of gloomy reflection, "Come, I will go to see the Morrels," said he; "I think that disgust is even more sickening than hatred."

Study Guide Questions

For Students:

1. Who is Lord Wilmore?
2. What does Andrea reveal when he meets Major Cavalcanti?
3. How does the Count convince two random men to behave like a father and son?

For Reading Club:

1. What does Andrea tell the Count about his past?
2. Andrea says that "in the eyes of the world a large fortune covers all defects". What do you think of the statement?
3. Why do you think Andrea seems to be more interested in his father's fortune than in anything else?

CHAPTER 57

In the Lucern Patch

Our readers must now allow us to transport them again to the enclosure surrounding M. de Villefort's house, and, behind the gate, half screened from view by the large chestnut-trees, which on all sides spread their luxuriant branches, we shall find some people of our acquaintance. This time Maximilian was the first to arrive. He was intently watching for a shadow to appear among the trees, and awaiting with anxiety the sound of a light step on the gravel walk.

At length, the long-desired sound was heard, and instead of one figure, as he had expected, he perceived that two were approaching him. The delay had been occasioned by a visit from Madame Danglars and Eugénie, which had been prolonged beyond the time at which Valentine was expected. That she might not appear to fail in her promise to Maximilian, she proposed to Mademoiselle Danglars that they should take a walk in the garden, being anxious to show that the delay, which was doubtless a cause of vexation to him, was not occasioned by any neglect on her part. The young man, with the intuitive perception of a lover, quickly understood the circumstances in which she was involuntarily placed, and he was comforted. Besides, although she avoided coming within speaking distance, Valentine arranged so that Maximilian could see her pass and repass, and each time she went by, she managed, unperceived by her companion, to cast an expressive look at the young man, which seemed to say, "Have patience! You see it is not my fault."

And Maximilian was patient, and employed himself in mentally contrasting the two girls,—one fair, with soft languishing eyes, a figure gracefully bending like a weeping willow; the other a brunette, with a fierce and haughty expression, and as straight as a poplar. It is unnecessary to state that, in the eyes of the young man, Valentine did not suffer by the contrast. In about half an hour the girls went away, and

Maximilian understood that Mademoiselle Danglars' visit had at last come to an end. In a few minutes Valentine re-entered the garden alone. For fear that anyone should be observing her return, she walked slowly; and instead of immediately directing her steps towards the gate, she seated herself on a bench, and, carefully casting her eyes around, to convince herself that she was not watched, she presently arose, and proceeded quickly to join Maximilian.

"Good-evening, Valentine," said a well-known voice.

"Good-evening, Maximilian; I know I have kept you waiting, but you saw the cause of my delay."

"Yes, I recognized Mademoiselle Danglars. I was not aware that you were so intimate with her."

"Who told you we were intimate, Maximilian?"

"No one, but you appeared to be so. From the manner in which you walked and talked together, one would have thought you were two school-girls telling your secrets to each other."

"We were having a confidential conversation," returned Valentine; "she was owning to me her repugnance to the marriage with M. de Morcerf; and I, on the other hand, was confessing to her how wretched it made me to think of marrying M. d'Épinay."

"Dear Valentine!"

"That will account to you for the unreserved manner which you observed between me and Eugénie, as in speaking of the man whom I could not love, my thoughts involuntarily reverted to him on whom my affections were fixed."

"Ah, how good you are to say so, Valentine! You possess a quality which can never belong to Mademoiselle Danglars. It is that indefinable charm which is to a woman what perfume is to the flower and flavor to the fruit, for the beauty of either is not the only quality we seek."

"It is your love which makes you look upon everything in that light."

"No, Valentine, I assure you such is not the case. I was observing you both when you were walking in the garden, and, on my honor, without at all wishing to depreciate the beauty of Mademoiselle Danglars, I cannot understand how any man can really love her."

"The fact is, Maximilian, that I was there, and my presence had the effect of rendering you unjust in your comparison."

"No; but tell me—it is a question of simple curiosity, and which was suggested by certain ideas passing in my mind relative to Mademoiselle Danglars—"

"I dare say it is something disparaging which you are going to say. It only proves how little indulgence we may expect from your sex," interrupted Valentine.

"You cannot, at least, deny that you are very harsh judges of each other."

"If we are so, it is because we generally judge under the influence of excitement. But return to your question."

"Does Mademoiselle Danglars object to this marriage with M. de Morcerf on account of loving another?"

"I told you I was not on terms of strict intimacy with Eugénie."

"Yes, but girls tell each other secrets without being particularly intimate; own, now, that you did question her on the subject. Ah, I see you are smiling."

"If you are already aware of the conversation that passed, the wooden partition which interposed between us and you has proved but a slight security."

"Come, what did she say?"

"She told me that she loved no one," said Valentine; "that she disliked the idea of being married; that she would infinitely prefer leading an independent and unfettered life; and that she almost wished her father might lose his fortune, that she might become an artist, like her friend, Mademoiselle Louise d'Armilly."

"Ah, you see—"

"Well, what does that prove?" asked Valentine.

"Nothing," replied Maximilian.

"Then why did you smile?"

"Why, you know very well that you are reflecting on yourself, Valentine."

"Do you want me to go away?"

"Ah, no, no. But do not let us lose time; you are the subject on which I wish to speak."

"True, we must be quick, for we have scarcely ten minutes more to pass together."

"*Ma foi!*" said Maximilian, in consternation.

"Yes, you are right; I am but a poor friend to you. What a life I cause you to lead, poor Maximilian, you who are formed for happiness! I bitterly reproach myself, I assure you."

"Well, what does it signify, Valentine, so long as I am satisfied, and feel that even this long and painful suspense is amply repaid by five minutes of your society, or two words from your lips? And I have also a deep conviction that heaven would not have created two hearts, harmonizing as ours do, and almost miraculously brought us together, to separate us at last."

"Those are kind and cheering words. You must hope for us both, Maximilian; that will make me at least partly happy."

"But why must you leave me so soon?"

"I do not know particulars. I can only tell you that Madame de Villefort sent to request my presence, as she had a communication to make on which a part of my fortune depended. Let them take my fortune, I am already too rich; and, perhaps, when they have taken it, they will leave me in peace and quietness. You would love me as much if I were poor, would you not, Maximilian?"

"Oh, I shall always love you. What should I care for either riches or poverty, if my Valentine was near me, and I felt certain that no one could deprive me of her? But do you not fear that this communication may relate to your marriage?"

"I do not think that is the case."

"However it may be, Valentine, you must not be alarmed. I assure you that, as long as I live, I shall never love anyone else!"

"Do you think to reassure me when you say that, Maximilian?"

"Pardon me, you are right. I am a brute. But I was going to tell you that I met M. de Morcerf the other day."

"Well?"

"Monsieur Franz is his friend, you know."

"What then?"

"Monsieur de Morcerf has received a letter from Franz, announcing his immediate return." Valentine turned pale, and leaned her hand against the gate.

"Ah heavens, if it were that! But no, the communication would not come through Madame de Villefort."

"Why not?"

"Because—I scarcely know why—but it has appeared as if Madame de Villefort secretly objected to the marriage, although she did not choose openly to oppose it."

"Is it so? Then I feel as if I could adore Madame de Villefort."

"Do not be in such a hurry to do that," said Valentine, with a sad smile.

"If she objects to your marrying M. d'Épinay, she would be all the more likely to listen to any other proposition."

"No, Maximilian, it is not suitors to which Madame de Villefort objects, it is marriage itself."

"Marriage? If she dislikes that so much, why did she ever marry herself?"

"You do not understand me, Maximilian. About a year ago, I talked of retiring to a convent. Madame de Villefort, in spite of all the remarks which she considered it her duty to make, secretly approved of the proposition, my father consented to it at her instigation, and it was only on account of my poor grandfather that I finally abandoned the project. You can form no idea of the expression of that old man's eye when he looks at me, the only person in the world whom he loves, and, I had almost said, by whom he is beloved in return. When he learned my resolution, I shall never forget the reproachful look which he cast on me, and the tears of utter despair which chased each other down his lifeless cheeks. Ah, Maximilian, I experienced, at that moment, such remorse for my intention, that, throwing myself at his feet, I exclaimed,—'Forgive me, pray forgive me, my dear grandfather; they may do what they will with me, I will never leave you.' When I had ceased speaking, he thankfully raised his eyes to heaven, but without uttering a word. Ah, Maximilian, I may have much to suffer, but I feel as if my grandfather's look at that moment would more than compensate for all."

"Dear Valentine, you are a perfect angel, and I am sure I do not know what I—sabring right and left among the Bedouins—can have done to merit your being revealed to me, unless, indeed, Heaven took into consideration the fact that the victims of my sword were infidels. But tell me what interest Madame de Villefort can have in your remaining unmarried?"

"Did I not tell you just now that I was rich, Maximilian—too rich? I possess nearly 50,000 livres in right of my mother; my grandfather and my grandmother, the Marquis and Marquise de Saint-Méran, will leave me as much, and M. Noirtier evidently intends making me his heir. My brother Edward, who inherits nothing from his mother, will, therefore, be poor in comparison with me. Now, if I had taken the veil, all this fortune would have descended to my father, and, in reversion, to his son."

"Ah, how strange it seems that such a young and beautiful woman should be so avaricious."

"It is not for herself that she is so, but for her son, and what you regard as a vice becomes almost a virtue when looked at in the light of maternal love."

"But could you not compromise matters, and give up a portion of your fortune to her son?"

"How could I make such a proposition, especially to a woman who always professes to be so entirely disinterested?"

"Valentine, I have always regarded our love in the light of something sacred; consequently, I have covered it with the veil of respect, and hid it in the innermost recesses of my soul. No human being, not even my sister, is aware of its existence. Valentine, will you permit me to make a confidant of a friend and reveal to him the love I bear you?"

Valentine started. "A friend, Maximilian; and who is this friend? I tremble to give my permission."

"Listen, Valentine. Have you never experienced for anyone that sudden and irresistible sympathy which made you feel as if the object of it had been your old and familiar friend, though, in reality, it was the first time you had ever met? Nay, further, have you never endeavored to recall the time, place, and circumstances of your former intercourse, and failing in this attempt, have almost believed that your spirits must have held converse with each other in some state of being anterior to the present, and that you are only now occupied in a reminiscence of the past?"

"Yes."

"Well, that is precisely the feeling which I experienced when I first saw that extraordinary man."

"Extraordinary, did you say?"

"Yes."

"You have known him for some time, then?"

"Scarcely longer than eight or ten days."

"And do you call a man your friend whom you have only known for eight or ten days? Ah, Maximilian, I had hoped you set a higher value on the title of friend."

"Your logic is most powerful, Valentine, but say what you will, I can never renounce the sentiment which has instinctively taken possession of my mind. I feel as if it were ordained that this man should be associated with all the good which the future may have in store for me, and sometimes it really seems as if his eye was able to see what was to come, and his hand endowed with the power of directing events according to his own will."

"He must be a prophet, then," said Valentine, smiling.

"Indeed," said Maximilian, "I have often been almost tempted to attribute to him the gift of prophecy; at all events, he has a wonderful power of foretelling any future good."

"Ah," said Valentine in a mournful tone, "do let me see this man, Maximilian; he may tell me whether I shall ever be loved sufficiently to make amends for all I have suffered."

"My poor girl, you know him already."

"I know him?"

"Yes; it was he who saved the life of your step-mother and her son."

"The Count of Monte Cristo?"

"The same."

"Ah," cried Valentine, "he is too much the friend of Madame de Villefort ever to be mine."

"The friend of Madame de Villefort! It cannot be; surely, Valentine, you are mistaken?"

"No, indeed, I am not; for I assure you, his power over our household is almost unlimited. Courted by my step-mother, who regards him as the epitome of human wisdom; admired by my father, who says he has never before heard such sublime ideas so eloquently expressed; idolized by Edward, who, notwithstanding his fear of the count's large black eyes, runs to meet him the moment he arrives, and opens his hand, in which he is sure to find some delightful present,—M. de Monte Cristo appears to exert a mysterious and almost uncontrollable influence over all the members of our family."

"If such be the case, my dear Valentine, you must yourself have felt, or at all events will soon feel, the effects of his presence. He meets Albert de Morcerf in Italy—it is to rescue him from the hands of the banditti; he introduces himself to Madame Danglars—it is that he may give her a royal present; your step-mother and her son pass before his door—it is that his Nubian may save them from destruction. This man evidently possesses the power of influencing events, both as regards men and things. I never saw more simple tastes united to greater magnificence. His smile is so sweet when he addresses me, that I forget it ever can be bitter to others. Ah, Valentine, tell me, if he ever looked on you with one of those sweet smiles? if so, depend on it, you will be happy."

"Me?" said the young girl, "he never even glances at me; on the contrary, if I accidentally cross his path, he appears rather to avoid me. Ah, he is not generous, neither does he possess that supernatural penetration which you attribute to him, for if he did, he would have perceived that I was unhappy; and if he had been generous, seeing me sad and solitary, he would have used his influence to my advantage, and since, as you say, he resembles the sun, he would have warmed my heart with one of his life-giving rays. You say he loves you, Maximilian; how do you know that he does? All would pay deference to an officer like you, with a fierce moustache and a long sabre, but they think they may crush a poor weeping girl with impunity."

"Ah, Valentine, I assure you you are mistaken."

"If it were otherwise—if he treated me diplomatically—that is to say, like a man who wishes, by some means or other, to obtain a footing in the house, so that he may ultimately gain the power of dictating to its occupants—he would, if it had been but once, have honored me with the smile which you extol so loudly; but no, he saw that I was unhappy, he understood that I could be of no use to him, and therefore paid no attention to me whatever. Who knows but that, in order to please Madame de Villefort and my father, he may not persecute me by every means in his power? It is not just that he should despise me so, without any reason. Ah, forgive me," said Valentine, perceiving the effect which her words were producing on Maximilian: "I have done wrong, for I have given utterance to thoughts concerning that man which I did not even know existed in my heart. I do not deny the influence of which you speak, or that I have not myself experienced it, but with me it has been productive of evil rather than good."

"Well, Valentine," said Morrel with a sigh, "we will not discuss the matter further. I will not make a confidant of him."

"Alas!" said Valentine, "I see that I have given you pain. I can only say how sincerely I ask pardon for having grieved you. But, indeed, I am not prejudiced beyond the power of conviction. Tell me what this Count of Monte Cristo has done for you."

"I own that your question embarrasses me, Valentine, for I cannot say that the count has rendered me any ostensible service. Still, as I have already told you, I have an instinctive affection for him, the source of which I cannot explain to you. Has the sun done anything for me? No; he warms me with his rays, and it is by his light that I see you—nothing more. Has such and such a perfume done anything for me? No; its odor charms one of my senses—that is all I can say when I am asked why I praise it. My friendship for him is as strange and unaccountable as his for me. A secret voice seems to whisper to me that there must be something more than chance in this unexpected reciprocity of friendship. In his most simple actions, as well as in his most secret thoughts, I find a relation to my own. You will perhaps smile at me when I tell you that, ever since I have known this man, I have involuntarily entertained the idea that all the good fortune which has befallen me originated from him. However, I have managed to live thirty years without this protection, you will say; but I will endeavor a little to illustrate my meaning. He invited me to dine with him on Saturday, which was a very natural thing for him to do. Well, what have I learned since? That your mother and M. de Villefort are both coming to this dinner. I shall meet them there, and who knows what future advantages may result from the interview? This may appear to you to be no unusual combination of circumstances; nevertheless, I perceive some hidden plot in the arrangement—something, in fact, more than is apparent on a casual view of the subject. I believe that this singular man, who appears to fathom the motives of everyone, has purposely arranged for me to meet M. and Madame de Villefort, and sometimes, I confess, I have gone so far as to try to read in his eyes whether he was in possession of the secret of our love."

"My good friend," said Valentine, "I should take you for a visionary, and should tremble for your reason, if I were always to hear you talk in a strain similar to this. Is it possible that you can see anything more than the merest chance in this meeting? Pray reflect a little. My father, who never goes out, has several times been on the point of refusing this invitation; Madame de Villefort, on the contrary, is burning with the desire of seeing this extraordinary nabob in his own house, therefore, she has with great difficulty prevailed on my father to accompany her. No, no; it is as I have said, Maximilian,—there is no one in the world of whom I can ask help but yourself and my grandfather, who is little better than a corpse—no support to cling to but my mother in heaven!"

"I see that you are right, logically speaking," said Maximilian; "but the gentle voice which usually has such power over me fails to convince me today."

"I feel the same as regards yourself." said Valentine; "and I own that, if you have no stronger proof to give me—"

"I have another," replied Maximilian; "but I fear you will deem it even more absurd than the first."

"So much the worse," said Valentine, smiling.

"It is, nevertheless, conclusive to my mind. My ten years of service have also confirmed my ideas on the subject of sudden inspirations, for I have several times owed my life to a mysterious impulse which directed me to move at once either to the right or to the left, in order to escape the ball which killed the comrade fighting by my side, while it left me unharmed."

"Dear Maximilian, why not attribute your escape to my constant prayers for your safety? When you are away, I no longer pray for myself, but for you."

"Yes, since you have known me," said Morrel, smiling; "but that cannot apply to the time previous to our acquaintance, Valentine."

"You are very provoking, and will not give me credit for anything; but let me hear this second proof, which you yourself own to be absurd."

"Well, look through this opening, and you will see the beautiful new horse which I rode here."

"Ah! what a beautiful creature!" cried Valentine; "why did you not bring him close to the gate, so that I could talk to him and pat him?"

"He is, as you see, a very valuable animal," said Maximilian. "You know that my means are limited, and that I am what would be designated a man of moderate pretensions. Well, I went to a horse dealer's, where I saw this magnificent horse, which I have named Médéah. I asked the price; they told me it was 4,500 francs. I was, therefore, obliged to give it up, as you may imagine, but I own I went away with rather a heavy heart, for the horse had looked at me affectionately, had rubbed his head against me and, when I mounted him, had pranced in the most delightful way imaginable, so that I was altogether fascinated with him. The same evening some friends of mine visited me,—M. de Château-Renaud, M. Debray, and five or six other choice spirits, whom you do not know, even by name. They proposed a game of *bouillotte*. I never play, for I am not rich enough to afford to lose, or sufficiently poor to desire to gain. But I was at my own house, you understand, so there was nothing to be done but to send for the cards, which I did.

"Just as they were sitting down to table, M. de Monte Cristo arrived. He took his seat amongst them; they played, and I won. I am almost ashamed to say that my gains amounted to 5,000 francs. We separated at midnight. I could not defer my pleasure, so I took a cabriolet and drove to the horse dealer's. Feverish and excited, I rang at the door. The person who opened it must have taken me for a madman, for I rushed at once to the stable. Médéah was standing at the rack, eating his hay. I immediately put on the saddle and bridle, to which operation he lent himself with the best grace possible; then, putting the 4,500 francs into the hands of the astonished dealer, I proceeded to fulfil my intention of passing the night in riding in the Champs-Élysées. As I rode by the count's house I perceived a light in one of the windows, and fancied I saw the shadow of his figure moving behind the curtain. Now, Valentine, I firmly believe that he knew of my wish to possess this horse, and that he lost expressly to give me the means of procuring him."

"My dear Maximilian, you are really too fanciful; you will not love even me long. A man who accustoms himself to live in such a world of poetry and imagination must find far too little excitement in a common, every-day sort of attachment such as ours. But they are calling me. Do you hear?"

"Ah, Valentine," said Maximilian, "give me but one finger through this opening in the grating, one finger, the littlest finger of all, that I may have the happiness of kissing it."

"Maximilian, we said we would be to each other as two voices, two shadows."

"As you will, Valentine."

"Shall you be happy if I do what you wish?"

"Oh, yes!"

Valentine mounted on a bench, and passed not only her finger but her whole hand through the opening. Maximilian uttered a cry of delight, and, springing forwards, seized the hand extended towards him, and imprinted on it a fervent and impassioned kiss. The little hand was then immediately withdrawn, and the young man saw Valentine hurrying towards the house, as though she were almost terrified at her own sensations.

Study Guide Questions

For Students:

1. What do Valentine and Eugénie discuss?
2. Why is Eugénie not interested in marriage?
3. Why does Madame Villefort want Valentine to stay unmarried?

For Reading Club:

1. Valentine and Eugénie are expected to marry men they do not love. What are your views on it?
2. Maximilian says that "girls tell each other secrets without being intimate". Do you think this statement is true?
3. Valentine is a very innocent girl but she seems to understand the Count's intentions very well. What does it tell you about her character?

CHAPTER 58

M. Noirtier de Villefort

We will now relate what was passing in the house of the king's attorney after the departure of Madame Danglars and her daughter, and during the time of the conversation between Maximilian and Valentine, which we have just detailed.

M. de Villefort entered his father's room, followed by Madame de Villefort. Both of the visitors, after saluting the old man and speaking to Barrois, a faithful servant, who had been twenty-five years in his service, took their places on either side of the paralytic.

M. Noirtier was sitting in an armchair, which moved upon casters, in which he was wheeled into the room in the morning, and in the same way drawn out again at night. He was placed before a large glass, which reflected the whole apartment, and so, without any attempt to move, which would have been impossible, he could see all who entered the room and everything which was going on around him. M. Noirtier, although almost as immovable as a corpse, looked at the new-comers with a quick and intelligent expression, perceiving at once, by their ceremonious courtesy, that they were come on business of an unexpected and official character.

Sight and hearing were the only senses remaining, and they, like two solitary sparks, remained to animate the miserable body which seemed fit for nothing but the grave; it was only, however, by means of one of these senses that he could reveal the thoughts and feelings that still occupied his mind, and the look by which he gave expression to his inner life was like the distant gleam of a candle which a traveller sees by night across some desert place, and knows that a living being dwells beyond the silence and obscurity.

Noirtier's hair was long and white, and flowed over his shoulders; while in his eyes, shaded by thick black lashes, was concentrated, as it often happens with an organ which is used to the exclusion of the others, all the activity, address, force, and intelligence which were formerly diffused over his whole body; and so although the movement of the arm, the sound of the voice, and the agility of the body, were wanting, the speaking eye sufficed for all. He commanded with it; it was the medium through which his thanks were conveyed. In short, his whole appearance produced on the mind the impression of a corpse with living eyes, and nothing could be more startling than to observe the expression of anger or joy suddenly lighting up these organs, while the rest of the rigid and marble-like features were utterly deprived of the power of participation. Three persons only could understand this language of the poor paralytic; these were Villefort, Valentine, and the old servant of whom we have already spoken. But as Villefort saw his father but seldom, and then only when absolutely obliged, and as he never took any pains to please or gratify him when he was there, all the old man's happiness was centred in his granddaughter. Valentine, by means of her love, her patience, and her devotion, had learned to read in Noirtier's look all the varied feelings which were passing in his mind. To this dumb language, which was so unintelligible to others, she answered by throwing her whole soul into the expression of her countenance, and in this manner were the conversations sustained between the blooming girl and the helpless invalid, whose body could scarcely be called a living one, but who, nevertheless, possessed a fund of knowledge and penetration, united with a will as powerful as ever although clogged by a body rendered utterly incapable of obeying its impulses.

Valentine had solved the problem, and was able easily to understand his thoughts, and to convey her own in return, and, through her untiring and devoted assiduity, it was seldom that, in the ordinary transactions of every-day life, she failed to anticipate the wishes of the living, thinking mind, or the wants of the almost inanimate body.

As to the servant, he had, as we have said, been with his master for five-and-twenty years, therefore he knew all his habits, and it was seldom that Noirtier found it necessary to ask for anything, so prompt was he in administering to all the necessities of the invalid.

Villefort did not need the help of either Valentine or the domestic in order to carry on with his father the strange conversation which he was about to begin. As we have said, he perfectly understood the old man's vocabulary, and if he did not use it more often, it was only indifference and *ennui* which prevented him from so doing. He therefore allowed Valentine to go into the garden, sent away Barrois, and after having seated himself at his father's right hand, while Madame de Villefort placed herself on the left, he addressed him thus:

"I trust you will not be displeased, sir, that Valentine has not come with us, or that I dismissed Barrois, for our conference will be one which could not with propriety be carried on in the presence of either. Madame de Villefort and I have a communication to make to you."

Noirtier's face remained perfectly passive during this long preamble, while, on the contrary, Villefort's eye was endeavoring to penetrate into the inmost recesses of the old man's heart.

"This communication," continued the procureur, in that cold and decisive tone which seemed at once to preclude all discussion, "will, we are sure, meet with your approbation."

The eye of the invalid still retained that vacancy of expression which prevented his son from obtaining any knowledge of the feelings which were passing in his mind; he listened, nothing more.

"Sir," resumed Villefort, "we are thinking of marrying Valentine." Had the old man's face been moulded in wax it could not have shown less emotion at this news than was now to be traced there. "The marriage will take place in less than three months," said Villefort.

Noirtier's eye still retained its inanimate expression.

Madame de Villefort now took her part in the conversation and added:

"We thought this news would possess an interest for you, sir, who have always entertained a great affection for Valentine; it therefore only now remains for us to tell you the name of the young man for whom she is destined. It is one of the most desirable connections which could possibly be formed; he possesses fortune, a high rank in society, and every personal qualification likely to render Valentine supremely happy,—his name, moreover, cannot be wholly unknown to you. It is M. Franz de Quesnel, Baron d'Épinay."

While his wife was speaking, Villefort had narrowly watched the old man's countenance. When Madame de Villefort pronounced the name of Franz, the pupil of M. Noirtier's eye began to dilate, and his eyelids trembled with the same movement that may be perceived on the lips of an individual about to speak, and he darted a lightning glance at Madame de Villefort and his son. The procureur, who knew the political hatred which had formerly existed between M. Noirtier and the elder d'Épinay, well understood the agitation and anger which the announcement had produced; but, feigning not to perceive either, he immediately resumed the narrative begun by his wife.

"Sir," said he, "you are aware that Valentine is about to enter her nineteenth year, which renders it important that she should lose no time in forming a suitable alliance.

Nevertheless, you have not been forgotten in our plans, and we have fully ascertained beforehand that Valentine's future husband will consent, not to live in this house, for that might not be pleasant for the young people, but that you should live with them; so that you and Valentine, who are so attached to each other, would not be separated, and you would be able to pursue exactly the same course of life which you have hitherto done, and thus, instead of losing, you will be a gainer by the change, as it will secure to you two children instead of one, to watch over and comfort you."

Noirtier's look was furious; it was very evident that something desperate was passing in the old man's mind, for a cry of anger and grief rose in his throat, and not being able to find vent in utterance, appeared almost to choke him, for his face and lips turned quite purple with the struggle. Villefort quietly opened a window, saying, "It is very warm, and the heat affects M. Noirtier." He then returned to his place, but did not sit down.

"This marriage," added Madame de Villefort, "is quite agreeable to the wishes of M. d'Épinay and his family; besides, he had no relations nearer than an uncle and aunt, his mother having died at his birth, and his father having been assassinated in 1815, that is to say, when he was but two years old; it naturally followed that the child was permitted to choose his own pursuits, and he has, therefore, seldom acknowledged any other authority but that of his own will."

"That assassination was a mysterious affair," said Villefort, "and the perpetrators have hitherto escaped detection, although suspicion has fallen on the head of more than one person."

Noirtier made such an effort that his lips expanded into a smile.

"Now," continued Villefort, "those to whom the guilt really belongs, by whom the crime was committed, on whose heads the justice of man may probably descend here, and the certain judgment of God hereafter, would rejoice in the opportunity thus afforded of bestowing such a peace-offering as Valentine on the son of him whose life they so ruthlessly destroyed." Noirtier had succeeded in mastering his emotion more than could have been deemed possible with such an enfeebled and shattered frame.

"Yes, I understand," was the reply contained in his look; and this look expressed a feeling of strong indignation, mixed with profound contempt. Villefort fully understood his father's meaning, and answered by a slight shrug of his shoulders. He then motioned to his wife to take leave.

"Now sir," said Madame de Villefort, "I must bid you farewell. Would you like me to send Edward to you for a short time?"

It had been agreed that the old man should express his approbation by closing his eyes, his refusal by winking them several times, and if he had some desire or feeling to express, he raised them to heaven. If he wanted Valentine, he closed his right eye only, and if Barrois, the left. At Madame de Villefort's proposition he instantly winked his eyes.

Provoked by a complete refusal, she bit her lip and said, "Then shall I send Valentine to you?" The old man closed his eyes eagerly, thereby intimating that such was his wish.

M. and Madame de Villefort bowed and left the room, giving orders that Valentine should be summoned to her grandfather's presence, and feeling sure that she would have much to do to restore calmness to the perturbed spirit of the invalid. Valentine, with a color still heightened by emotion, entered the room just after her parents had quitted it. One look was sufficient to tell her that her grandfather was suffering, and that there was much on his mind which he was wishing to communicate to her.

"Dear grandpapa," cried she, "what has happened? They have vexed you, and you are angry?"

The paralytic closed his eyes in token of assent.

"Who has displeased you? Is it my father?"

"No."

"Madame de Villefort?"

"No."

"Me?" The former sign was repeated.

"Are you displeased with me?" cried Valentine in astonishment. M. Noirtier again closed his eyes.

"And what have I done, dear grandpapa, that you should be angry with me?" cried Valentine.

There was no answer, and she continued:

"I have not seen you all day. Has anyone been speaking to you against me?"

"Yes," said the old man's look, with eagerness.

"Let me think a moment. I do assure you, grandpapa—Ah—M. and Madame de Villefort have just left this room, have they not?"

"Yes."

"And it was they who told you something which made you angry? What was it then? May I go and ask them, that I may have the opportunity of making my peace with you?"

"No, no," said Noirtier's look.

"Ah, you frighten me. What can they have said?" and she again tried to think what it could be.

"Ah, I know," said she, lowering her voice and going close to the old man. "They have been speaking of my marriage,—have they not?"

"Yes," replied the angry look.

"I understand; you are displeased at the silence I have preserved on the subject. The reason of it was, that they had insisted on my keeping the matter a secret, and begged me not to tell you anything of it. They did not even acquaint me with their intentions, and I only discovered them by chance, that is why I have been so reserved with you, dear grandpapa. Pray forgive me."

But there was no look calculated to reassure her; all it seemed to say was, "It is not only your reserve which afflicts me."

"What is it, then?" asked the young girl. "Perhaps you think I shall abandon you, dear grandpapa, and that I shall forget you when I am married?"

"No."

"They told you, then, that M. d'Épinay consented to our all living together?"

"Yes."

"Then why are you still vexed and grieved?" The old man's eyes beamed with an expression of gentle affection.

"Yes, I understand," said Valentine; "it is because you love me." The old man assented.

"And you are afraid I shall be unhappy?"

"Yes."

"You do not like M. Franz?" The eyes repeated several times, "No, no, no."

"Then you are vexed with the engagement?"

"Yes."

"Well, listen," said Valentine, throwing herself on her knees, and putting her arm round her grandfather's neck, "I am vexed, too, for I do not love M. Franz d'Épinay."

An expression of intense joy illumined the old man's eyes.

"When I wished to retire into a convent, you remember how angry you were with me?" A tear trembled in the eye of the invalid. "Well," continued Valentine, "the reason of my proposing it was that I might escape this hateful marriage, which drives me to despair." Noirtier's breathing came thick and short.

"Then the idea of this marriage really grieves you too? Ah, if you could but help me—if we could both together defeat their plan! But you are unable to oppose them,—you, whose mind is so quick, and whose will is so firm are nevertheless, as weak and unequal to the contest as I am myself. Alas, you, who would have been such a powerful protector to me in the days of your health and strength, can now only sympathize in my joys and sorrows, without being able to take any active part in them. However, this is much, and calls for gratitude and Heaven has not taken away all my blessings when it leaves me your sympathy and kindness."

At these words there appeared in Noirtier's eye an expression of such deep meaning that the young girl thought she could read these words there: "You are mistaken; I can still do much for you."

"Do you think you can help me, dear grandpapa?" said Valentine.

"Yes." Noirtier raised his eyes, it was the sign agreed on between him and Valentine when he wanted anything.

"What is it you want, dear grandpapa?" said Valentine, and she endeavored to recall to mind all the things which he would be likely to need; and as the ideas presented themselves to her mind, she repeated them aloud, then,—finding that all her efforts elicited nothing but a constant *"No,"*—she said, "Come, since this plan does not answer, I will have recourse to another."

She then recited all the letters of the alphabet from A down to N. When she arrived at that letter the paralytic made her understand that she had spoken the initial letter of the thing he wanted.

"Ah," said Valentine, "the thing you desire begins with the letter N; it is with N that we have to do, then. Well, let me see, what can you want that begins with N? Na—Ne—Ni—No—"

"Yes, yes, yes," said the old man's eye.

"Ah, it is No, then?"

"Yes."

Valentine fetched a dictionary, which she placed on a desk before Noirtier; she opened it, and, seeing that the old man's eye was thoroughly fixed on its pages, she ran her finger quickly up and down the columns. During the six years which had passed since Noirtier first fell into this sad state, Valentine's powers of invention had been too often put to the test not to render her expert in devising expedients for gaining a knowledge of his wishes, and the constant practice had so perfected her in the art that she guessed the old man's meaning as quickly as if he himself had been able to seek for what he wanted. At the word *Notary*, Noirtier made a sign to her to stop.

"Notary," said she, "do you want a notary, dear grandpapa?" The old man again signified that it was a notary he desired.

"You would wish a notary to be sent for then?" said Valentine.

"Yes."

"Shall my father be informed of your wish?"

"Yes."

"Do you wish the notary to be sent for immediately?"

"Yes."

"Then they shall go for him directly, dear grandpapa. Is that all you want?"

"Yes." Valentine rang the bell, and ordered the servant to tell Monsieur or Madame de Villefort that they were requested to come to M. Noirtier's room.

"Are you satisfied now?" inquired Valentine.

"Yes."

"I am sure you are; it is not very difficult to discover that." And the young girl smiled on her grandfather, as if he had been a child. M. de Villefort entered, followed by Barrois.

"What do you want me for, sir?" demanded he of the paralytic.

"Sir," said Valentine, "my grandfather wishes for a notary." At this strange and unexpected demand M. de Villefort and his father exchanged looks.

"Yes," motioned the latter, with a firmness which seemed to declare that with the help of Valentine and his old servant, who both knew what his wishes were, he was quite prepared to maintain the contest.

"Do you wish for a notary?" asked Villefort.

"Yes."

"What to do?"

Noirtier made no answer.

"What do you want with a notary?" again repeated Villefort. The invalid's eye remained fixed, by which expression he intended to intimate that his resolution was unalterable.

"Is it to do us some ill turn? Do you think it is worth while?" said Villefort.

"Still," said Barrois, with the freedom and fidelity of an old servant, "if M. Noirtier asks for a notary, I suppose he really wishes for a notary; therefore I shall go at once and fetch one." Barrois acknowledged no master but Noirtier, and never allowed his desires in any way to be contradicted.

"Yes, I do want a notary," motioned the old man, shutting his eyes with a look of defiance, which seemed to say, "and I should like to see the person who dares to refuse my request."

"You shall have a notary, as you absolutely wish for one, sir," said Villefort; "but I shall explain to him your state of health, and make excuses for you, for the scene cannot fail of being a most ridiculous one."

"Never mind that," said Barrois; "I shall go and fetch a notary, nevertheless." And the old servant departed triumphantly on his mission.

Study Guide Questions

For Students:

1. What is the condition of M. Noirtier de Villefort?
2. What is the news that M. de Villefort shares with M. Noirtier in Valentine's absence?
3. Why does M. Noirtier feel angry after knowing about Valentine's groom-to-be?

For Reading Club:

1. Why do you think M. Noirtier feels angry at M. de Villefort's proposition?
2. Discuss the conversation between M. Noirtier and Valentine that occurs at the end of the chapter.
3. Do you think modern-day girls should be as patient or submissive as Valentine? Why or why not?

CHAPTER 59

The Will

As soon as Barrois had left the room, Noirtier looked at Valentine with a malicious expression that said many things. The young girl perfectly understood the look, and so did Villefort, for his countenance became clouded, and he knitted his eyebrows angrily. He took a seat, and quietly awaited the arrival of the notary. Noirtier saw him seat himself with an appearance of perfect indifference, at the same time giving a side look at Valentine, which made her understand that she also was to remain in the room. Three-quarters of an hour after, Barrois returned, bringing the notary with him.

"Sir," said Villefort, after the first salutations were over, "you were sent for by M. Noirtier, whom you see here. All his limbs have become completely paralysed, he has lost his voice also, and we ourselves find much trouble in endeavoring to catch some fragments of his meaning."

Noirtier cast an appealing look on Valentine, which look was at once so earnest and imperative, that she answered immediately.

"Sir," said she, "I perfectly understand my grandfather's meaning at all times."

"That is quite true," said Barrois; "and that is what I told the gentleman as we walked along."

"Permit me," said the notary, turning first to Villefort and then to Valentine—"permit me to state that the case in question is just one of those in which a public officer like myself cannot proceed to act without thereby incurring a dangerous responsibility. The first thing necessary to render an act valid is, that the notary should be thoroughly convinced that he has faithfully interpreted the will and wishes of the person dictating the act. Now I cannot be sure of the approbation or disapprobation of a client who cannot speak, and as the object of his desire or his repugnance cannot be clearly proved to me, on account of his want of speech, my services here would be quite useless, and cannot be legally exercised."

The notary then prepared to retire. An imperceptible smile of triumph was expressed on the lips of the procureur. Noirtier looked at Valentine with an expression so full of grief, that she arrested the departure of the notary.

"Sir," said she, "the language which I speak with my grandfather may be easily learnt, and I can teach you in a few minutes, to understand it almost as well as I can myself. Will you tell me what you require, in order to set your conscience quite at ease on the subject?"

"In order to render an act valid, I must be certain of the approbation or disapprobation of my client. Illness of body would not affect the validity of the deed, but sanity of mind is absolutely requisite."

"Well, sir, by the help of two signs, with which I will acquaint you presently, you may ascertain with perfect certainty that my grandfather is still in the full possession of all his mental faculties. M. Noirtier, being deprived of voice and motion, is accustomed to convey his meaning by closing his eyes when he wishes to signify 'yes,' and to wink when he means 'no.' You now know quite enough to enable you to converse with M. Noirtier;—try."

Noirtier gave Valentine such a look of tenderness and gratitude that it was comprehended even by the notary himself.

"You have heard and understood what your granddaughter has been saying, sir, have you?" asked the notary. Noirtier closed his eyes.

"And you approve of what she said—that is to say, you declare that the signs which she mentioned are really those by means of which you are accustomed to convey your thoughts?"

"Yes."

"It was you who sent for me?"

"Yes."

"To make your will?"

"Yes."

"And you do not wish me to go away without fulfilling your original intentions?" The old man winked violently.

"Well, sir," said the young girl, "do you understand now, and is your conscience perfectly at rest on the subject?"

But before the notary could answer, Villefort had drawn him aside.

"Sir," said he, "do you suppose for a moment that a man can sustain a physical shock, such as M. Noirtier has received, without any detriment to his mental faculties?"

"It is not exactly that, sir," said the notary, "which makes me uneasy, but the difficulty will be in wording his thoughts and intentions, so as to be able to get his answers."

"You must see that to be an utter impossibility," said Villefort. Valentine and the old man heard this conversation, and Noirtier fixed his eye so earnestly on Valentine that she felt bound to answer to the look.

"Sir," said she, "that need not make you uneasy, however difficult it may at first sight appear to be. I can discover and explain to you my grandfather's thoughts, so as to put an end to all your doubts and fears on the subject. I have now been six years with M. Noirtier, and let him tell you if ever once, during that time, he has entertained a thought which he was unable to make me understand."

"No," signed the old man.

"Let us try what we can do, then," said the notary. "You accept this young lady as your interpreter, M. Noirtier?"

"Yes."

"Well, sir, what do you require of me, and what document is it that you wish to be drawn up?"

Valentine named all the letters of the alphabet until she came to W. At this letter the eloquent eye of Noirtier gave her notice that she was to stop.

"It is very evident that it is the letter W which M. Noirtier wants," said the notary.

"Wait," said Valentine; and, turning to her grandfather, she repeated, "Wa—We—Wi—" The old man stopped her at the last syllable. Valentine then took the dictionary, and the notary watched her while she turned over the pages.

She passed her finger slowly down the columns, and when she came to the word "Will," M. Noirtier's eye bade her stop.

"Will," said the notary; "it is very evident that M. Noirtier is desirous of making his will."

"Yes, yes, yes," motioned the invalid.

"Really, sir, you must allow that this is most extraordinary," said the astonished notary, turning to M. de Villefort.

"Yes," said the procureur, "and I think the will promises to be yet more extraordinary, for I cannot see how it is to be drawn up without the intervention of Valentine, and she may, perhaps, be considered as too much interested in its contents to allow of her being a suitable interpreter of the obscure and ill-defined wishes of her grandfather."

"No, no, no," replied the eye of the paralytic.

"What?" said Villefort, "do you mean to say that Valentine is not interested in your will?"

"No."

"Sir," said the notary, whose interest had been greatly excited, and who had resolved on publishing far and wide the account of this extraordinary and picturesque scene, "what appeared so impossible to me an hour ago, has now become quite easy and practicable, and this may be a perfectly valid will, provided it be read in the presence of seven witnesses, approved by the testator, and sealed by the notary in the presence of the witnesses. As to the time, it will not require very much more than the generality of wills. There are certain forms necessary to be gone through, and which are always the same. As to the details, the greater part will be furnished afterwards by the state in which we find the affairs of the testator, and by yourself, who, having had the management of them, can doubtless give full information on the subject. But besides all this, in order that the instrument may not be contested, I am anxious to give it the greatest possible authenticity, therefore, one of my colleagues will help me, and, contrary to custom, will assist in the dictation of the testament. Are you satisfied, sir?" continued the notary, addressing the old man.

"Yes," looked the invalid, his eye beaming with delight at the ready interpretation of his meaning.

"What is he going to do?" thought Villefort, whose position demanded much reserve, but who was longing to know what his father's intentions were. He left the room to give orders for another notary to be sent, but Barrois, who had heard all that passed, had guessed his master's wishes, and had already gone to fetch one. The procureur then told his wife to come up. In the course of a quarter of an hour everyone had assembled in the chamber of the paralytic; the second notary had also arrived.

A few words sufficed for a mutual understanding between the two officers of the law. They read to Noirtier the formal copy of a will, in order to give him an idea of the terms in which such documents are generally couched; then, in order to test the capacity of the testator, the first notary said, turning towards him:

"When an individual makes his will, it is generally in favor or in prejudice of some person."

"Yes."

"Have you an exact idea of the amount of your fortune?"

"Yes."

"I will name to you several sums which will increase by gradation; you will stop me when I reach the one representing the amount of your own possessions?"

"Yes."

There was a kind of solemnity in this interrogation. Never had the struggle between mind and matter been more apparent than now, and if it was not a sublime, it was, at least, a curious spectacle. They had formed a circle round the invalid; the second notary was sitting at a table, prepared for writing, and his colleague was standing before the testator in the act of interrogating him on the subject to which we have alluded.

"Your fortune exceeds 300,000 francs, does it not?" asked he. Noirtier made a sign that it did.

"Do you possess 400,000 francs?" inquired the notary. Noirtier's eye remained immovable.

"500,000?" The same expression continued.

"600,000—700,000—800,000—900,000?"

Noirtier stopped him at the last-named sum.

"You are then in possession of 900,000 francs?" asked the notary.

"Yes."

"In landed property?"

"No."

"In stock?"

"Yes."

"The stock is in your own hands?"

The look which M. Noirtier cast on Barrois showed that there was something wanting which he knew where to find. The old servant left the room, and presently returned, bringing with him a small casket.

"Do you permit us to open this casket?" asked the notary. Noirtier gave his assent.

They opened it, and found 900,000 francs in bank scrip. The first notary handed over each note, as he examined it, to his colleague.

The total amount was found to be as M. Noirtier had stated.

"It is all as he has said; it is very evident that the mind still retains its full force and vigor." Then, turning towards the paralytic, he said, "You possess, then, 900,000 francs of capital, which, according to the manner in which you have invested it, ought to bring in an income of about 40,000 livres?"

"Yes."

"To whom do you desire to leave this fortune?"

"Oh!" said Madame de Villefort, "there is not much doubt on that subject. M. Noirtier tenderly loves his granddaughter, Mademoiselle de Villefort; it is she who has nursed and tended him for six years, and has, by her devoted attention, fully secured the affection, I had almost said the gratitude, of her grandfather, and it is but just that she should reap the fruit of her devotion."

The eye of Noirtier clearly showed by its expression that he was not deceived by the false assent given by Madame de Villefort's words and manner to the motives which she supposed him to entertain.

"Is it, then, to Mademoiselle Valentine de Villefort that you leave these 900,000 francs?" demanded the notary, thinking he had only to insert this clause, but waiting first for the assent of Noirtier, which it was necessary should be given before all the witnesses of this singular scene.

Valentine, when her name was made the subject of discussion, had stepped back, to escape unpleasant observation; her eyes were cast down, and she was crying. The old man looked at her for an instant with an expression of the deepest tenderness, then, turning towards the notary, he significantly winked his eye in token of dissent.

"What," said the notary, "do you not intend making Mademoiselle Valentine de Villefort your residuary legatee?"

"No."

"You are not making any mistake, are you?" said the notary; "you really mean to declare that such is not your intention?"

"No," repeated Noirtier; "No."

Valentine raised her head, struck dumb with astonishment. It was not so much the conviction that she was disinherited that caused her grief, but her total inability to account for the feelings which had provoked her grandfather to such an act. But Noirtier looked at her with so much affectionate tenderness that she exclaimed:

"Oh, grandpapa, I see now that it is only your fortune of which you deprive me; you still leave me the love which I have always enjoyed."

"Ah, yes, most assuredly," said the eyes of the paralytic, for he closed them with an expression which Valentine could not mistake.

"Thank you, thank you," murmured she. The old man's declaration that Valentine was not the destined inheritor of his fortune had excited the hopes of Madame de Villefort; she gradually approached the invalid, and said:

"Then, doubtless, dear M. Noirtier, you intend leaving your fortune to your grandson, Edward de Villefort?"

The winking of the eyes which answered this speech was most decided and terrible, and expressed a feeling almost amounting to hatred.

"No?" said the notary; "then, perhaps, it is to your son, M. de Villefort?"

"No." The two notaries looked at each other in mute astonishment and inquiry as to what were the real intentions of the testator. Villefort and his wife both grew red, one from shame, the other from anger.

"What have we all done, then, dear grandpapa?" said Valentine; "you no longer seem to love any of us?"

The old man's eyes passed rapidly from Villefort and his wife, and rested on Valentine with a look of unutterable fondness.

"Well," said she; "if you love me, grandpapa, try and bring that love to bear upon your actions at this present moment. You know me well enough to be quite sure that I have never thought of your fortune; besides, they say I am already rich in right of my mother—too rich, even. Explain yourself, then."

Noirtier fixed his intelligent eyes on Valentine's hand.

"My hand?" said she.

"Yes."

"Her hand!" exclaimed everyone.

"Oh, gentlemen, you see it is all useless, and that my father's mind is really impaired," said Villefort.

"Ah," cried Valentine suddenly, "I understand. It is my marriage you mean, is it not, dear grandpapa?"

"Yes, yes, yes," signed the paralytic, casting on Valentine a look of joyful gratitude for having guessed his meaning.

"You are angry with us all on account of this marriage, are you not?"

"Yes?"

"Really, this is too absurd," said Villefort.

"Excuse me, sir," replied the notary; "on the contrary, the meaning of M. Noirtier is quite evident to me, and I can quite easily connect the train of ideas passing in his mind."

"You do not wish me to marry M. Franz d'Épinay?" observed Valentine.

"I do not wish it," said the eye of her grandfather.

"And you disinherit your granddaughter," continued the notary, "because she has contracted an engagement contrary to your wishes?"

"Yes."

"So that, but for this marriage, she would have been your heir?"

"Yes."

There was a profound silence. The two notaries were holding a consultation as to the best means of proceeding with the affair. Valentine was looking at her grandfather with a smile of intense gratitude, and Villefort was biting his lips with vexation, while

Madame de Villefort could not succeed in repressing an inward feeling of joy, which, in spite of herself, appeared in her whole countenance.

"But," said Villefort, who was the first to break the silence, "I consider that I am the best judge of the propriety of the marriage in question. I am the only person possessing the right to dispose of my daughter's hand. It is my wish that she should marry M. Franz d'Épinay—and she shall marry him."

Valentine sank weeping into a chair.

"Sir," said the notary, "how do you intend disposing of your fortune in case Mademoiselle de Villefort still determines on marrying M. Franz?" The old man gave no answer.

"You will, of course, dispose of it in some way or other?"

"Yes."

"In favor of some member of your family?"

"No."

"Do you intend devoting it to charitable purposes, then?" pursued the notary.

"Yes."

"But," said the notary, "you are aware that the law does not allow a son to be entirely deprived of his patrimony?"

"Yes."

"You only intend, then, to dispose of that part of your fortune which the law allows you to subtract from the inheritance of your son?" Noirtier made no answer.

"Do you still wish to dispose of all?"

"Yes."

"But they will contest the will after your death?"

"No."

"My father knows me," replied Villefort; "he is quite sure that his wishes will be held sacred by me; besides, he understands that in my position I cannot plead against the poor." The eye of Noirtier beamed with triumph.

"What do you decide on, sir?" asked the notary of Villefort.

"Nothing, sir; it is a resolution which my father has taken and I know he never alters his mind. I am quite resigned. These 900,000 francs will go out of the family in order to enrich some hospital; but it is ridiculous thus to yield to the caprices of an old man, and I shall, therefore, act according to my conscience."

Having said this, Villefort quitted the room with his wife, leaving his father at liberty to do as he pleased. The same day the will was made, the witnesses were brought, it was approved by the old man, sealed in the presence of all and given in charge to M. Deschamps, the family notary.

Study Guide Questions

For Students:

1. Who is M. Noirtier's interpreter?
2. How much is M. Noirtier's fortune?
3. What is M. de Villefort's reaction to the will?

For Reading Club:

1. Do you feel M. de Villefort does not want his father to draw a will?
2. Discuss M. Noirtier's will, how do you think it will help Valentine?
3. How does Valentine's marriage affair highlight patriarchy?

CHAPTER 60

The Telegraph

M. and Madame de Villefort found on their return that the Count of Monte Cristo, who had come to visit them in their absence, had been ushered into the drawing-room, and was still awaiting them there. Madame de Villefort, who had not yet sufficiently recovered from her late emotion to allow of her entertaining visitors so immediately, retired to her bedroom, while the procureur, who could better depend upon himself, proceeded at once to the salon.

Although M. de Villefort flattered himself that, to all outward view, he had completely masked the feelings which were passing in his mind, he did not know that the cloud was still lowering on his brow, so much so that the count, whose smile was radiant, immediately noticed his sombre and thoughtful air.

"*Ma foi!*" said Monte Cristo, after the first compliments were over, "what is the matter with you, M. de Villefort? Have I arrived at the moment when you were drawing up an indictment for a capital crime?"

Villefort tried to smile.

"No, count," he replied, "I am the only victim in this case. It is I who lose my cause, and it is ill-luck, obstinacy, and folly which have caused it to be decided against me."

"To what do you refer?" said Monte Cristo with well-feigned interest. "Have you really met with some great misfortune?"

"Oh, no, monsieur," said Villefort with a bitter smile; "it is only a loss of money which I have sustained—nothing worth mentioning, I assure you."

"True," said Monte Cristo, "the loss of a sum of money becomes almost immaterial with a fortune such as you possess, and to one of your philosophic spirit."

"It is not so much the loss of the money that vexes me," said Villefort, "though, after all, 900,000 francs are worth regretting; but I am the more annoyed with this fate, chance, or whatever you please to call the power which has destroyed my hopes and my fortune, and may blast the prospects of my child also, as it is all occasioned by an old man relapsed into second childhood."

"What do you say?" said the count; "900,000 francs? It is indeed a sum which might be regretted even by a philosopher. And who is the cause of all this annoyance?"

"My father, as I told you."

"M. Noirtier? But I thought you told me he had become entirely paralyzed, and that all his faculties were completely destroyed?"

"Yes, his bodily faculties, for he can neither move nor speak, nevertheless he thinks, acts, and wills in the manner I have described. I left him about five minutes ago, and he is now occupied in dictating his will to two notaries."

"But to do this he must have spoken?"

"He has done better than that—he has made himself understood."

"How was such a thing possible?"

"By the help of his eyes, which are still full of life, and, as you perceive, possess the power of inflicting mortal injury."

"My dear," said Madame de Villefort, who had just entered the room, "perhaps you exaggerate the evil."

"Good-morning, madame," said the count, bowing.

Madame de Villefort acknowledged the salutation with one of her most gracious smiles.

"What is this that M. de Villefort has been telling me?" demanded Monte Cristo "and what incomprehensible misfortune—"

"Incomprehensible is the word!" interrupted the procureur, shrugging his shoulders. "It is an old man's caprice!"

"And is there no means of making him revoke his decision?"

"Yes," said Madame de Villefort; "and it is still entirely in the power of my husband to cause the will, which is now in prejudice of Valentine, to be altered in her favor."

The count, who perceived that M. and Madame de Villefort were beginning to speak in parables, appeared to pay no attention to the conversation, and feigned to be busily engaged in watching Edward, who was mischievously pouring some ink into the bird's water-glass.

"My dear," said Villefort, in answer to his wife, "you know I have never been accustomed to play the patriarch in my family, nor have I ever considered that the fate of a universe was to be decided by my nod. Nevertheless, it is necessary that my will should be respected in my family, and that the folly of an old man and the caprice of a child should not be allowed to overturn a project which I have entertained for so many years. The Baron d'Épinay was my friend, as you know, and an alliance with his son is the most suitable thing that could possibly be arranged."

"Do you think," said Madame de Villefort, "that Valentine is in league with him? She has always been opposed to this marriage, and I should not be at all surprised if what we have just seen and heard is nothing but the execution of a plan concerted between them."

"Madame," said Villefort, "believe me, a fortune of 900,000 francs is not so easily renounced."

"She could, nevertheless, make up her mind to renounce the world, sir, since it is only about a year ago that she herself proposed entering a convent."

"Never mind," replied Villefort; "I say that this marriage *shall* be consummated."

"Notwithstanding your father's wishes to the contrary?" said Madame de Villefort, selecting a new point of attack. "That is a serious thing."

Monte Cristo, who pretended not to be listening, heard however, every word that was said.

"Madame," replied Villefort "I can truly say that I have always entertained a high respect for my father, because, to the natural feeling of relationship was added the consciousness of his moral superiority. The name of father is sacred in two senses; he should be reverenced as the author of our being and as a master whom we ought to obey. But, under the present circumstances, I am justified in doubting the wisdom of an old man who, because he hated the father, vents his anger on the son. It would be ridiculous in me to regulate my conduct by such caprices. I shall still continue to preserve the same respect toward M. Noirtier; I will suffer, without complaint, the pecuniary deprivation to which he has subjected me; but I shall remain firm in my determination, and the world shall see which party has reason on his side. Consequently I shall marry my daughter to the Baron Franz d'Épinay, because I consider it would be a proper and eligible match for her to make, and, in short, because I choose to bestow my daughter's hand on whomever I please."

"What?" said the count, the approbation of whose eye Villefort had frequently solicited during this speech. "What? Do you say that M. Noirtier disinherits Mademoiselle de Villefort because she is going to marry M. le Baron Franz d'Épinay?"

"Yes, sir, that is the reason," said Villefort, shrugging his shoulders.

"The apparent reason, at least," said Madame de Villefort.

"The *real* reason, madame, I can assure you; I know my father."

"But I want to know in what way M. d'Épinay can have displeased your father more than any other person?"

"I believe I know M. Franz d'Épinay," said the count; "is he not the son of General de Quesnel, who was created Baron d'Épinay by Charles X.?"

"The same," said Villefort.

"Well, but he is a charming young man, according to my ideas."

"He is, which makes me believe that it is only an excuse of M. Noirtier to prevent his granddaughter marrying; old men are always so selfish in their affection," said Madame de Villefort.

"But," said Monte Cristo "do you not know any cause for this hatred?"

"Ah, *ma foi!* who is to know?"

"Perhaps it is some political difference?"

"My father and the Baron d'Épinay lived in the stormy times of which I only saw the ending," said Villefort.

"Was not your father a Bonapartist?" asked Monte Cristo; "I think I remember that you told me something of that kind."

"My father has been a Jacobin more than anything else," said Villefort, carried by his emotion beyond the bounds of prudence; "and the senator's robe, which Napoleon cast on his shoulders, only served to disguise the old man without in any degree changing him. When my father conspired, it was not for the emperor, it was against the Bourbons; for M. Noirtier possessed this peculiarity, he never projected any Utopian schemes which could never be realized, but strove for possibilities, and he applied to the realization of these possibilities the terrible theories of The Mountain,—theories that never shrank from any means that were deemed necessary to bring about the desired result."

"Well," said Monte Cristo, "it is just as I thought; it was politics which brought Noirtier and M. d'Épinay into personal contact. Although General d'Épinay served under Napoleon, did he not still retain royalist sentiments? And was he not the person who was assassinated one evening on leaving a Bonapartist meeting to which he had been invited on the supposition that he favored the cause of the emperor?"

Villefort looked at the count almost with terror.

"Am I mistaken, then?" said Monte Cristo.

"No, sir, the facts were precisely what you have stated," said Madame de Villefort; "and it was to prevent the renewal of old feuds that M. de Villefort formed the idea of uniting in the bonds of affection the two children of these inveterate enemies."

"It was a sublime and charitable thought," said Monte Cristo, "and the whole world should applaud it. It would be noble to see Mademoiselle Noirtier de Villefort assuming the title of Madame Franz d'Épinay."

Villefort shuddered and looked at Monte Cristo as if he wished to read in his countenance the real feelings which had dictated the words he had just uttered. But the count completely baffled the procureur, and prevented him from discovering anything beneath the never-varying smile he was so constantly in the habit of assuming.

"Although," said Villefort, "it will be a serious thing for Valentine to lose her grandfather's fortune, I do not think that M. d'Épinay will be frightened at this pecuniary loss. He will, perhaps, hold me in greater esteem than the money itself, seeing that I sacrifice everything in order to keep my word with him. Besides, he knows that Valentine is rich in right of her mother, and that she will, in all probability, inherit the fortune of M. and Madame de Saint-Méran, her mother's parents, who both love her tenderly."

"And who are fully as well worth loving and tending as M. Noirtier," said Madame de Villefort; "besides, they are to come to Paris in about a month, and Valentine, after the affront she has received, need not consider it necessary to continue to bury herself alive by being shut up with M. Noirtier."

The count listened with satisfaction to this tale of wounded self-love and defeated ambition.

"But it seems to me," said Monte Cristo, "and I must begin by asking your pardon for what I am about to say, that if M. Noirtier disinherits Mademoiselle de Villefort because she is going to marry a man whose father he detested, he cannot have the same cause of complaint against this dear Edward."

"True," said Madame de Villefort, with an intonation of voice which it is impossible to describe; "is it not unjust—shamefully unjust? Poor Edward is as much M. Noirtier's grandchild as Valentine, and yet, if she had not been going to marry M. Franz, M. Noirtier would have left her all his money; and supposing Valentine to be disinherited by her grandfather, she will still be three times richer than he."

The count listened and said no more.

"Count," said Villefort, "we will not entertain you any longer with our family misfortunes. It is true that my patrimony will go to endow charitable institutions, and my father will have deprived me of my lawful inheritance without any reason for doing so, but I shall have the satisfaction of knowing that I have acted like a man of sense and feeling. M. d'Épinay, to whom I had promised the interest of this sum, shall receive it, even if I endure the most cruel privations."

"However," said Madame de Villefort, returning to the one idea which incessantly occupied her mind, "perhaps it would be better to explain this unlucky affair to M. d'Épinay, in order to give him the opportunity of himself renouncing his claim to the hand of Mademoiselle de Villefort."

"Ah, that would be a great pity," said Villefort.

"A great pity," said Monte Cristo.

"Undoubtedly," said Villefort, moderating the tones of his voice, "a marriage once concerted and then broken off, throws a sort of discredit on a young lady; then again, the old reports, which I was so anxious to put an end to, will instantly gain ground. No, it will all go well; M. d'Épinay, if he is an honorable man, will consider himself more than ever pledged to Mademoiselle de Villefort, unless he were actuated by a decided feeling of avarice, but that is impossible."

"I agree with M. de Villefort," said Monte Cristo, fixing his eyes on Madame de Villefort; "and if I were sufficiently intimate with him to allow of giving my advice, I would persuade him, since I have been told M. d'Épinay is coming back, to settle this affair at once beyond all possibility of revocation. I will answer for the success of a project which will reflect so much honor on M. de Villefort."

The procureur arose, delighted with the proposition, but his wife slightly changed color.

"Well, that is all that I wanted, and I will be guided by a counsellor such as you are," said he, extending his hand to Monte Cristo. "Therefore let everyone here look upon what has passed today as if it had not happened, and as though we had never thought of such a thing as a change in our original plans."

"Sir," said the count, "the world, unjust as it is, will be pleased with your resolution; your friends will be proud of you, and M. d'Épinay, even if he took Mademoiselle de Villefort without any dowry, which he will not do, would be delighted with the idea of entering a family which could make such sacrifices in order to keep a promise and fulfil a duty."

At the conclusion of these words, the count rose to depart.

"Are you going to leave us, count?" said Madame de Villefort.

"I am sorry to say I must do so, madame, I only came to remind you of your promise for Saturday."

"Did you fear that we should forget it?"

"You are very good, madame, but M. de Villefort has so many important and urgent occupations."

"My husband has given me his word, sir," said Madame de Villefort; "you have just seen him resolve to keep it when he has everything to lose, and surely there is more reason for his doing so where he has everything to gain."

"And," said Villefort, "is it at your house in the Champs-Élysées that you receive your visitors?"

"No," said Monte Cristo, "which is precisely the reason which renders your kindness more meritorious,—it is in the country."

"In the country?"

"Yes."

"Where is it, then? Near Paris, is it not?"

"Very near, only half a league from the Barriers,—it is at Auteuil."

"At Auteuil?" said Villefort; "true, Madame de Villefort told me you lived at Auteuil, since it was to your house that she was taken. And in what part of Auteuil do you reside?"

"Rue de la Fontaine."

"Rue de la Fontaine!" exclaimed Villefort in an agitated tone; "at what number?"

"No. 28."

"Then," cried Villefort, "was it you who bought M. de Saint-Méran's house!"

"Did it belong to M. de Saint-Méran?" demanded Monte Cristo.

"Yes," replied Madame de Villefort; "and, would you believe it, count—"

"Believe what?"

"You think this house pretty, do you not?"

"I think it charming."

"Well, my husband would never live in it."

"Indeed?" returned Monte Cristo, "that is a prejudice on your part, M. de Villefort, for which I am quite at a loss to account."

"I do not like Auteuil, sir," said the procureur, making an evident effort to appear calm.

"But I hope you will not carry your antipathy so far as to deprive me of the pleasure of your company, sir," said Monte Cristo.

"No, count,—I hope—I assure you I shall do my best," stammered Villefort.

"Oh," said Monte Cristo, "I allow of no excuse. On Saturday, at six o'clock. I shall be expecting you, and if you fail to come, I shall think—for how do I know to the contrary?—that this house, which has remained uninhabited for twenty years, must have some gloomy tradition or dreadful legend connected with it."

"I will come, count,—I will be sure to come," said Villefort eagerly.

"Thank you," said Monte Cristo; "now you must permit me to take my leave of you."

"You said before that you were obliged to leave us, monsieur," said Madame de Villefort, "and you were about to tell us why when your attention was called to some other subject."

"Indeed madame," said Monte Cristo: "I scarcely know if I dare tell you where I am going."

"Nonsense; say on."

"Well, then, it is to see a thing on which I have sometimes mused for hours together."

"What is it?"

"A telegraph. So now I have told my secret."

"A telegraph?" repeated Madame de Villefort.

"Yes, a telegraph. I had often seen one placed at the end of a road on a hillock, and in the light of the sun its black arms, bending in every direction, always reminded me of the claws of an immense beetle, and I assure you it was never without emotion that I gazed on it, for I could not help thinking how wonderful it was that these various signs should be made to cleave the air with such precision as to convey to the distance of three hundred leagues the ideas and wishes of a man sitting at a table at one end of the line to another man similarly placed at the opposite extremity, and all this effected by a simple act of volition on the part of the sender of the message. I began to think of genii, sylphs, gnomes, in short, of all the ministers of the occult sciences, until I laughed aloud at the freaks of my own imagination. Now, it never occurred to me to wish for a nearer inspection of these large insects, with their long black claws, for I always feared to find under their stone wings some little human genius fagged to death with cabals, factions, and government intrigues. But one fine day I learned that the mover of this telegraph was only a poor wretch, hired for twelve hundred francs a year, and employed all day, not in studying the heavens like an astronomer, or in gazing on the water like an angler, or even in enjoying the privilege of observing the country around him, but all his monotonous life was passed in watching his white-bellied, black-clawed fellow insect, four or five leagues distant from him. At length I felt a desire to study this living chrysalis more closely, and to endeavor to understand the secret part played by these insect-actors when they occupy themselves simply with pulling different pieces of string."

"And are you going there?"

"I am."

"What telegraph do you intend visiting? that of the home department, or of the observatory?"

"Oh, no; I should find there people who would force me to understand things of which I would prefer to remain ignorant, and who would try to explain to me, in spite of myself, a mystery which even they do not understand. *Ma foi!* I should wish to keep my illusions concerning insects unimpaired; it is quite enough to have those dissipated which I had formed of my fellow-creatures. I shall, therefore, not visit either of these telegraphs, but one in the open country where I shall find a good-natured simpleton, who knows no more than the machine he is employed to work."

"You are a singular man," said Villefort.

"What line would you advise me to study?"

"The one that is most in use just at this time."

"The Spanish one, you mean, I suppose?"

"Yes; should you like a letter to the minister that they might explain to you—"

"No," said Monte Cristo; "since, as I told you before, I do not wish to comprehend it. The moment I understand it there will no longer exist a telegraph for me; it will be nothing more than a sign from M. Duchâtel, or from M. Montalivet, transmitted to the prefect of Bayonne, mystified by two Greek words, *têle*, *graphein*. It is the insect with black claws, and the awful word which I wish to retain in my imagination in all its purity and all its importance."

"Go then; for in the course of two hours it will be dark, and you will not be able to see anything."

"*Ma foi!* you frighten me. Which is the nearest way? Bayonne?"

"Yes; the road to Bayonne."

"And afterwards the road to Châtillon?"

"Yes."

"By the tower of Montlhéry, you mean?"

"Yes."

"Thank you. Good-bye. On Saturday I will tell you my impressions concerning the telegraph."

At the door the count was met by the two notaries, who had just completed the act which was to disinherit Valentine, and who were leaving under the conviction of having done a thing which could not fail of redounding considerably to their credit.

Study Guide Questions

For Students:

1. Who visits M. de Villefort?
2. What does M. de Villefort tell the Count?
3. What does Madame Villefort wish to do after knowing M. Noirtier's will?

For Reading Club:

1. M. de Villefort says "A marriage, once concerted and then broken off, throws a sort of discredit on a young lady." Is this still true and applicable?
2. Discuss how the chapter highlights the theme of duty and honor.
3. Do you think that M. Noirtier and M. de Villefort want to impose their decisions on Valentine's and none of them care for Valentine's happiness?

CHAPTER 61

How a Gardener May Get Rid of the Dormice that Eat His Peaches

Not on the same night as he had stated, but the next morning, the Count of Monte Cristo went out by the Barrière d'Enfer, taking the road to Orléans. Leaving the village of Linas, without stopping at the telegraph, which flourished its great bony arms as he passed, the count reached the tower of Montlhéry, situated, as everyone knows, upon the highest point of the plain of that name. At the foot of the hill the count dismounted and began to ascend by a little winding path, about eighteen inches wide; when he reached the summit he found himself stopped by a hedge, upon which green fruit had succeeded to red and white flowers.

Monte Cristo looked for the entrance to the enclosure, and was not long in finding a little wooden gate, working on willow hinges, and fastened with a nail and string. The count soon mastered the mechanism, the gate opened, and he then found himself in a little garden, about twenty feet long by twelve wide, bounded on one side by part of the hedge, which contained the ingenious contrivance we have called a gate, and on the other by the old tower, covered with ivy and studded with wall-flowers.

No one would have thought in looking at this old, weather-beaten, floral-decked tower (which might be likened to an elderly dame dressed up to receive her grandchildren at a birthday feast) that it would have been capable of telling strange things, if,—in addition to the menacing ears which the proverb says all walls are provided with,—it had also a voice.

The garden was crossed by a path of red gravel, edged by a border of thick box, of many years' growth, and of a tone and color that would have delighted the heart of Delacroix, our modern Rubens. This path was formed in the shape of the figure of 8, thus, in its windings, making a walk of sixty feet in a garden of only twenty.

Never had Flora, the fresh and smiling goddess of gardeners, been honored with a purer or more scrupulous worship than that which was paid to her in this little enclosure. In fact, of the twenty rose-trees which formed the *parterre*, not one bore the mark of the slug, nor were there evidences anywhere of the clustering aphis which is so destructive to plants growing in a damp soil. And yet it was not because the damp had been excluded from the garden; the earth, black as soot, the thick foliage of the trees betrayed its presence; besides, had natural humidity been wanting, it could have been immediately supplied by artificial means, thanks to a tank of water, sunk in one of the corners of the garden, and upon which were stationed a frog and a toad, who, from antipathy, no doubt, always remained on the two opposite sides of the basin. There was not a blade of grass to be seen in the paths, or a weed in the flower-beds; no fine lady ever trained and watered her geraniums, her cacti, and her rhododendrons, in her porcelain *jardinière* with more pains than this hitherto unseen gardener bestowed upon his little enclosure.

Monte Cristo stopped after having closed the gate and fastened the string to the nail, and cast a look around.

"The man at the telegraph," said he, "must either engage a gardener or devote himself passionately to agriculture."

Suddenly he struck against something crouching behind a wheelbarrow filled with leaves; the something rose, uttering an exclamation of astonishment, and Monte Cristo found himself facing a man about fifty years old, who was plucking strawberries, which he was placing upon grape leaves. He had twelve leaves and about as many strawberries, which, on rising suddenly, he let fall from his hand.

"You are gathering your crop, sir?" said Monte Cristo, smiling.

"Excuse me, sir," replied the man, raising his hand to his cap; "I am not up there, I know, but I have only just come down."

"Do not let me interfere with you in anything, my friend," said the count; "gather your strawberries, if, indeed, there are any left."

"I have ten left," said the man, "for here are eleven, and I had twenty-one, five more than last year. But I am not surprised; the spring has been warm this year, and strawberries require heat, sir. This is the reason that, instead of the sixteen I had last year, I have this year, you see, eleven, already plucked—twelve, thirteen, fourteen, fifteen, sixteen, seventeen, eighteen. Ah, I miss three, they were here last night, sir—I am sure they were here—I counted them. It must be the son of Mère Simon who has stolen them; I saw him strolling about here this morning. Ah, the young rascal—stealing in a garden—he does not know where that may lead him to."

"Certainly, it is wrong," said Monte Cristo, "but you should take into consideration the youth and greediness of the delinquent."

"Of course," said the gardener, "but that does not make it the less unpleasant. But, sir, once more I beg pardon; perhaps you are an officer that I am detaining here." And he glanced timidly at the count's blue coat.

"Calm yourself, my friend," said the count, with the smile which he made at will either terrible or benevolent, and which now expressed only the kindliest feeling; "I am not an inspector, but a traveller, brought here by a curiosity he half repents of, since he causes you to lose your time."

"Ah, my time is not valuable," replied the man with a melancholy smile. "Still it belongs to government, and I ought not to waste it; but, having received the signal that I might rest for an hour" (here he glanced at the sun-dial, for there was everything in the enclosure of Montlhéry, even a sun-dial), "and having ten minutes before me, and my strawberries being ripe, when a day longer—by-the-by, sir, do you think dormice eat them?"

"Indeed, I should think not," replied Monte Cristo; "dormice are bad neighbors for us who do not eat them preserved, as the Romans did."

"What? Did the Romans eat them?" said the gardener—"ate dormice?"

"I have read so in Petronius," said the count.

"Really? They can't be nice, though they do say 'as fat as a dormouse.' It is not a wonder they are fat, sleeping all day, and only waking to eat all night. Listen. Last year I had four apricots—they stole one, I had one nectarine, only one—well, sir, they ate half of it on the wall; a splendid nectarine—I never ate a better."

"You ate it?"

"That is to say, the half that was left—you understand; it was exquisite, sir. Ah, those gentlemen never choose the worst morsels; like Mère Simon's son, who has not chosen the worst strawberries. But this year," continued the horticulturist, "I'll take care it shall not happen, even if I should be forced to sit by the whole night to watch when the strawberries are ripe."

Monte Cristo had seen enough. Every man has a devouring passion in his heart, as every fruit has its worm; that of the telegraph man was horticulture. He began gathering the grape-leaves which screened the sun from the grapes, and won the heart of the gardener.

"Did you come here, sir, to see the telegraph?" he said.

"Yes, if it isn't contrary to the rules."

"Oh, no," said the gardener; "not in the least, since there is no danger that anyone can possibly understand what we are saying."

"I have been told," said the count, "that you do not always yourselves understand the signals you repeat."

"That is true, sir, and that is what I like best," said the man, smiling.

"Why do you like that best?"

"Because then I have no responsibility. I am a machine then, and nothing else, and so long as I work, nothing more is required of me."

"Is it possible," said Monte Cristo to himself, "that I can have met with a man that has no ambition? That would spoil my plans."

"Sir," said the gardener, glancing at the sun-dial, "the ten minutes are almost up; I must return to my post. Will you go up with me?"

"I follow you."

Monte Cristo entered the tower, which was divided into three stories. The tower contained implements, such as spades, rakes, watering-pots, hung against the wall; this was all the furniture. The second was the man's conventional abode, or rather sleeping-place; it contained a few poor articles of household furniture—a bed, a table, two chairs, a stone pitcher—and some dry herbs, hung up to the ceiling, which the count recognized as sweet peas, and of which the good man was preserving the seeds; he had labelled them with as much care as if he had been master botanist in the Jardin des Plantes.

"Does it require much study to learn the art of telegraphing?" asked Monte Cristo.

"The study does not take long; it was acting as a supernumerary that was so tedious."

"And what is the pay?"

"A thousand francs, sir."

"It is nothing."

"No; but then we are lodged, as you perceive."

Monte Cristo looked at the room. They passed to the third story; it was the telegraph room. Monte Cristo looked in turn at the two iron handles by which the machine was worked. "It is very interesting," he said, "but it must be very tedious for a lifetime."

"Yes. At first my neck was cramped with looking at it, but at the end of a year I became used to it; and then we have our hours of recreation, and our holidays."

"Holidays?"

"Yes."

"When?"

"When we have a fog."

"Ah, to be sure."

"Those are indeed holidays to me; I go into the garden, I plant, I prune, I trim, I kill the insects all day long."

"How long have you been here?"

"Ten years, and five as a supernumerary make fifteen."

"You are—"

"Fifty-five years old."

"How long must you have served to claim the pension?"

"Oh, sir, twenty-five years."

"And how much is the pension?"

"A hundred crowns."

"Poor humanity!" murmured Monte Cristo.

"What did you say, sir?" asked the man.

"I was saying it was very interesting."

"What was?"

"All you were showing me. And you really understand none of these signals?"

"None at all."

"And have you never tried to understand them?"

"Never. Why should I?"

"But still there are some signals only addressed to you."

"Certainly."

"And do you understand them?"

"They are always the same."

"And they mean—"

"'*Nothing new; You have an hour;*' or '*Tomorrow.*'"

"This is simple enough," said the count; "but look, is not your correspondent putting itself in motion?"

"Ah, yes; thank you, sir."

"And what is it saying—anything you understand?"

"Yes; it asks if I am ready."

"And you reply?"

"By the same sign, which, at the same time, tells my right-hand correspondent that I am ready, while it gives notice to my left-hand correspondent to prepare in his turn."

"It is very ingenious," said the count.

"You will see," said the man proudly; "in five minutes he will speak."

"I have, then, five minutes," said Monte Cristo to himself; "it is more time than I require. My dear sir, will you allow me to ask you a question?"

"What is it, sir?"

"You are fond of gardening?"

"Passionately."

"And you would be pleased to have, instead of this terrace of twenty feet, an enclosure of two acres?"

"Sir, I should make a terrestrial paradise of it."

"You live badly on your thousand francs?"

"Badly enough; but yet I do live."

"Yes; but you have a wretchedly small garden."

"True, the garden is not large."

"And, then, such as it is, it is filled with dormice, who eat everything."

"Ah, they are my scourges."

"Tell me, should you have the misfortune to turn your head while your right-hand correspondent was telegraphing—"

"I should not see him."

"Then what would happen?"

"I could not repeat the signals."

"And then?"

"Not having repeated them, through negligence, I should be fined."

"How much?"

"A hundred francs."

"The tenth of your income—that would be fine work."

"Ah!" said the man.

"Has it ever happened to you?" said Monte Cristo.

"Once, sir, when I was grafting a rose-tree."

"Well, suppose you were to alter a signal, and substitute another?"

"Ah, that is another case; I should be turned off, and lose my pension."

"Three hundred francs?"

"A hundred crowns, yes, sir; so you see that I am not likely to do any of these things."

"Not even for fifteen years' wages? Come, it is worth thinking about?"

"For fifteen thousand francs?"

"Yes."

"Sir, you alarm me."

"Nonsense."

"Sir, you are tempting me?"

"Just so; fifteen thousand francs, do you understand?"

"Sir, let me see my right-hand correspondent."

"On the contrary, do not look at him, but at this."

"What is it?"

"What? Do you not know these bits of paper?"

"Bank-notes!"

"Exactly; there are fifteen of them."

"And whose are they?"

"Yours, if you like."

"Mine?" exclaimed the man, half-suffocated.

"Yes; yours—your own property."

"Sir, my right-hand correspondent is signalling."

"Let him signal."

"Sir, you have distracted me; I shall be fined."

"That will cost you a hundred francs; you see it is your interest to take my bank-notes."

"Sir, my right-hand correspondent redoubles his signals; he is impatient."

"Never mind—take these;" and the count placed the packet in the man's hands. "Now this is not all," he said; "you cannot live upon your fifteen thousand francs."

"I shall still have my place."

"No, you will lose it, for you are going to alter your correspondent's message."

"Oh, sir, what are you proposing?"

"A jest."

"Sir, unless you force me—"

"I think I can effectually force you;" and Monte Cristo drew another packet from his pocket. "Here are ten thousand more francs," he said, "with the fifteen thousand already in your pocket, they will make twenty-five thousand. With five thousand you can buy a pretty little house with two acres of land; the remaining twenty thousand will bring you in a thousand francs a year."

"A garden with two acres of land!"

"And a thousand francs a year."

"Oh, heavens!"

"Come, take them," and Monte Cristo forced the bank-notes into his hand.

"What am I to do?"

"Nothing very difficult."

"But what is it?"

"To repeat these signs." Monte Cristo took a paper from his pocket, upon which were drawn three signs, with numbers to indicate the order in which they were to be worked.

"There, you see it will not take long."

"Yes; but—"

"Do this, and you will have nectarines and all the rest."

The shot told; red with fever, while the large drops fell from his brow, the man executed, one after the other, the three signs given by the count, in spite of the frightful contortions of the right-hand correspondent, who, not understanding the change, began to think the gardener had gone mad. As to the left-hand one, he conscientiously repeated the same signals, which were finally transmitted to the Minister of the Interior.

"Now you are rich," said Monte Cristo.

"Yes," replied the man, "but at what a price!"

"Listen, friend," said Monte Cristo. "I do not wish to cause you any remorse; believe me, then, when I swear to you that you have wronged no man, but on the contrary have benefited mankind."

The man looked at the bank-notes, felt them, counted them, turned pale, then red, then rushed into his room to drink a glass of water, but he had no time to reach the water-jug, and fainted in the midst of his dried herbs. Five minutes after the new telegram reached the minister, Debray had the horses put to his carriage, and drove to Danglars' house.

"Has your husband any Spanish bonds?" he asked of the baroness.

"I think so, indeed! He has six millions' worth."

"He must sell them at whatever price."

"Why?"

"Because Don Carlos has fled from Bourges, and has returned to Spain."

"How do you know?" Debray shrugged his shoulders.

"The idea of asking how I hear the news," he said.

The baroness did not wait for a repetition; she ran to her husband, who immediately hastened to his agent, and ordered him to sell at any price. When it was seen that Danglars sold, the Spanish funds fell directly. Danglars lost five hundred thousand francs; but he rid himself of all his Spanish shares. The same evening the following was read in *Le Messager*:

"[By telegraph.] The king, Don Carlos, has escaped the vigilance of his guardians at Bourges, and has returned to Spain by the Catalonian frontier. Barcelona has risen in his favor."

All that evening nothing was spoken of but the foresight of Danglars, who had sold his shares, and of the luck of the stock-jobber, who only lost five hundred thousand francs by such a blow. Those who had kept their shares, or bought those of Danglars, looked upon themselves as ruined, and passed a very bad night. Next morning *Le Moniteur* contained the following:

"It was without any foundation that *Le Messager* yesterday announced the flight of Don Carlos and the revolt of Barcelona. The king (Don Carlos) has not left Bourges, and the peninsula is in the enjoyment of profound peace. A telegraphic signal, improperly interpreted, owing to the fog, was the cause of this error."

The funds rose one per cent higher than before they had fallen. This, reckoning his loss, and what he had missed gaining, made the difference of a million to Danglars.

"Good," said Monte Cristo to Morrel, who was at his house when the news arrived of the strange reverse of fortune of which Danglars had been the victim, "I have just made a discovery for twenty-five thousand francs, for which I would have paid a hundred thousand."

"What have you discovered?" asked Morrel.

"I have just discovered how a gardener may get rid of the dormice that eat his peaches."

Study Guide Questions

For Students:

1. Where does the Count go?
2. Whom does the Count meet?
3. Why does the Count bribe the telegraph man?

For Reading Club:

1. The telegraph man is a simple man with a simple hobby, why do you think he accepts the Count's bribe?
2. Do you think the chapter shows that social evils (corruption, bribery, etc.) have always been part of human society?
3. Discuss how does the Count's wrong telegraphic signal impact Danglars?

CHAPTER 62

Ghosts

At first sight, the exterior of the house at Auteuil gave no indications of splendor, nothing one would expect from the destined residence of the magnificent Count of Monte Cristo; but this simplicity was according to the will of its master, who positively ordered nothing to be altered outside. The splendor was within. Indeed, almost before the door opened, the scene changed.

M. Bertuccio had outdone himself in the taste displayed in furnishing, and in the rapidity with which it was executed. It is told that the Duc d'Antin removed in a single night a whole avenue of trees that annoyed Louis XIV.; in three days M. Bertuccio planted an entirely bare court with poplars, large spreading sycamores to shade the different parts of the house, and in the foreground, instead of the usual paving-stones, half hidden by the grass, there extended a lawn but that morning laid down, and upon which the water was yet glistening. For the rest, the orders had been issued by the count; he himself had given a plan to Bertuccio, marking the spot where each tree was to be planted, and the shape and extent of the lawn which was to take the place of the paving-stones.

Thus the house had become unrecognizable, and Bertuccio himself declared that he scarcely knew it, encircled as it was by a framework of trees. The overseer would not have objected, while he was about it, to have made some improvements in the garden, but the count had positively forbidden it to be touched. Bertuccio made amends, however, by loading the antechambers, staircases, and mantle-pieces with flowers.

What, above all, manifested the shrewdness of the steward, and the profound science of the master, the one in carrying out the ideas of the other, was that this house which appeared only the night before so sad and gloomy, impregnated with that sickly smell one can almost fancy to be the smell of time, had in a single day acquired the aspect of life, was scented with its master's favorite perfumes, and had the very light regulated according to his wish. When the count arrived, he had under his touch his books and arms, his eyes rested upon his favorite pictures; his dogs, whose caresses he loved, welcomed him in the antechamber; the birds, whose songs delighted him, cheered him with their music; and the house, awakened from its long sleep, like the sleeping beauty in the wood, lived, sang, and bloomed like the houses we have long cherished, and in which, when we are forced to leave them, we leave a part of our souls.

The servants passed gayly along the fine courtyard; some, belonging to the kitchens, gliding down the stairs, restored but the previous day, as if they had always inhabited the house; others filling the coach-houses, where the equipages, encased and numbered, appeared to have been installed for the last fifty years; and in the stables the horses replied with neighs to the grooms, who spoke to them with much more respect than many servants pay their masters.

The library was divided into two parts on either side of the wall, and contained upwards of two thousand volumes; one division was entirely devoted to novels, and even the volume which had been published but the day before was to be seen in its place in all the dignity of its red and gold binding.

On the other side of the house, to match with the library, was the conservatory, ornamented with rare flowers, that bloomed in china jars; and in the midst of the greenhouse, marvellous alike to sight and smell, was a billiard-table which looked as if it had been abandoned during the past hour by players who had left the balls on the cloth.

One chamber alone had been respected by the magnificent Bertuccio. Before this room, to which you could ascend by the grand, and go out by the back staircase, the servants passed with curiosity, and Bertuccio with terror.

At five o'clock precisely, the count arrived before the house at Auteuil, followed by Ali. Bertuccio was awaiting this arrival with impatience, mingled with uneasiness; he hoped for some compliments, while, at the same time, he feared to have frowns. Monte Cristo descended into the courtyard, walked all over the house, without giving any sign of approbation or pleasure, until he entered his bedroom, situated on the opposite side to the closed room; then he approached a little piece of furniture, made of rosewood, which he had noticed at a previous visit.

"That can only be to hold gloves," he said.

"Will your excellency deign to open it?" said the delighted Bertuccio, "and you will find gloves in it."

Elsewhere the count found everything he required—smelling-bottles, cigars, knick-knacks.

"Good," he said; and M. Bertuccio left enraptured, so great, so powerful, and real was the influence exercised by this man over all who surrounded him.

At precisely six o'clock the clatter of horses' hoofs was heard at the entrance door; it was our captain of Spahis, who had arrived on Médéah. "I am sure I am the first," cried Morrel; "I did it on purpose to have you a minute to myself, before everyone came. Julie and Emmanuel have a thousand things to tell you. Ah, really this is magnificent! But tell me, count, will your people take care of my horse?"

"Do not alarm yourself, my dear Maximilian—they understand."

"I mean, because he wants petting. If you had seen at what a pace he came—like the wind!"

"I should think so,—a horse that cost 5,000 francs!" said Monte Cristo, in the tone which a father would use towards a son.

"Do you regret them?" asked Morrel, with his open laugh.

"I? Certainly not," replied the count. "No; I should only regret if the horse had not proved good."

"It is so good, that I have distanced M. de Château-Renaud, one of the best riders in France, and M. Debray, who both mount the minister's Arabians; and close on their heels are the horses of Madame Danglars, who always go at six leagues an hour."

"Then they follow you?" asked Monte Cristo.

"See, they are here." And at the same minute a carriage with smoking horses, accompanied by two mounted gentlemen, arrived at the gate, which opened before them. The carriage drove round, and stopped at the steps, followed by the horsemen.

The instant Debray had touched the ground, he was at the carriage-door. He offered his hand to the baroness, who, descending, took it with a peculiarity of manner imperceptible to everyone but Monte Cristo. But nothing escaped the count's notice, and he observed a little note, passed with the facility that indicates frequent practice, from the hand of Madame Danglars to that of the minister's secretary.

After his wife the banker descended, as pale as though he had issued from his tomb instead of his carriage.

Madame Danglars threw a rapid and inquiring glance which could only be interpreted by Monte Cristo, around the courtyard, over the peristyle, and across the front of the house, then, repressing a slight emotion, which must have been seen on her countenance if she had not kept her color, she ascended the steps, saying to Morrel:

"Sir, if you were a friend of mine, I should ask you if you would sell your horse."

Morrel smiled with an expression very like a grimace, and then turned round to Monte Cristo, as if to ask him to extricate him from his embarrassment. The count understood him.

"Ah, madame," he said, "why did you not make that request of me?"

"With you, sir," replied the baroness, "one can wish for nothing, one is so sure to obtain it. If it were so with M. Morrel—"

"Unfortunately," replied the count, "I am witness that M. Morrel cannot give up his horse, his honor being engaged in keeping it."

"How so?"

"He laid a wager he would tame Médéah in the space of six months. You understand now that if he were to get rid of the animal before the time named, he would not only lose his bet, but people would say he was afraid; and a brave captain of Spahis cannot risk this, even to gratify a pretty woman, which is, in my opinion, one of the most sacred obligations in the world."

"You see my position, madame," said Morrel, bestowing a grateful smile on Monte Cristo.

"It seems to me," said Danglars, in his coarse tone, ill-concealed by a forced smile, "that you have already got horses enough."

Madame Danglars seldom allowed remarks of this kind to pass unnoticed, but, to the surprise of the young people, she pretended not to hear it, and said nothing. Monte Cristo smiled at her unusual humility, and showed her two immense porcelain jars, over which wound marine plants, of a size and delicacy that nature alone could produce. The baroness was astonished.

"Why," said she, "you could plant one of the chestnut-trees in the Tuileries inside! How can such enormous jars have been manufactured?"

"Ah! madame," replied Monte Cristo, "you must not ask of us, the manufacturers of fine porcelain, such a question. It is the work of another age, constructed by the genii of earth and water."

"How so?—at what period can that have been?"

"I do not know; I have only heard that an emperor of China had an oven built expressly, and that in this oven twelve jars like this were successively baked. Two broke, from the heat of the fire; the other ten were sunk three hundred fathoms deep into the sea. The sea, knowing what was required of her, threw over them her weeds, encircled them with coral, and encrusted them with shells; the whole was cemented by two hundred years beneath these almost impervious depths, for a revolution carried away the emperor who wished to make the trial, and only left the documents proving the manufacture of the jars and their descent into the sea. At the end of two hundred years the documents were found, and they thought of bringing up the jars. Divers descended in machines, made expressly on the discovery, into the bay where they were thrown; but of ten three only remained, the rest having been broken by the waves. I am fond of these jars, upon which, perhaps, misshapen, frightful monsters have fixed their cold, dull eyes, and in which myriads of small fish have slept, seeking a refuge from the pursuit of their enemies."

Meanwhile, Danglars, who had cared little for curiosities, was mechanically tearing off the blossoms of a splendid orange-tree, one after another. When he had finished with the orange-tree, he began at the cactus; but this, not being so easily plucked as the orange-tree, pricked him dreadfully. He shuddered, and rubbed his eyes as though awaking from a dream.

"Sir," said Monte Cristo to him, "I do not recommend my pictures to you, who possess such splendid paintings; but, nevertheless, here are two by Hobbema, a Paul Potter, a Mieris, two by Gerard Douw, a Raphael, a Van Dyck, a Zurbaran, and two or three by Murillo, worth looking at."

"Stay," said Debray; "I recognize this Hobbema."

"Ah, indeed!"

"Yes; it was proposed for the Museum."

"Which, I believe, does not contain one?" said Monte Cristo.

"No; and yet they refused to buy it."

"Why?" said Château-Renaud.

"You pretend not to know,—because government was not rich enough."

"Ah, pardon me," said Château-Renaud; "I have heard of these things every day during the last eight years, and I cannot understand them yet."

"You will, by and by," said Debray.

"I think not," replied Château-Renaud.

"Major Bartolomeo Cavalcanti and Count Andrea Cavalcanti," announced Baptistin.

A black satin stock, fresh from the maker's hands, gray moustaches, a bold eye, a major's uniform, ornamented with three medals and five crosses—in fact, the thorough bearing of an old soldier—such was the appearance of Major Bartolomeo Cavalcanti, that tender father with whom we are already acquainted. Close to him, dressed in entirely new clothes, advanced smilingly Count Andrea Cavalcanti, the dutiful son, whom we also know. The three young people were talking together. On the entrance of the new-comers, their eyes glanced from father to son, and then, naturally enough, rested on the latter, whom they began criticising.

"Cavalcanti!" said Debray.

"A fine name," said Morrel.

"Yes," said Château-Renaud, "these Italians are well named and badly dressed."

"You are fastidious, Château-Renaud," replied Debray; "those clothes are well cut and quite new."

"That is just what I find fault with. That gentleman appears to be well dressed for the first time in his life."

"Who are those gentlemen?" asked Danglars of Monte Cristo.

"You heard—Cavalcanti."

"That tells me their name, and nothing else."

"Ah! true. You do not know the Italian nobility; the Cavalcanti are all descended from princes."

"Have they any fortune?"

"An enormous one."

"What do they do?"

"Try to spend it all. They have some business with you, I think, from what they told me the day before yesterday. I, indeed, invited them here today on your account. I will introduce you to them."

"But they appear to speak French with a very pure accent," said Danglars.

"The son has been educated in a college in the south; I believe near Marseilles. You will find him quite enthusiastic."

"Upon what subject?" asked Madame Danglars.

"The French ladies, madame. He has made up his mind to take a wife from Paris."

"A fine idea that of his," said Danglars, shrugging his shoulders. Madame Danglars looked at her husband with an expression which, at any other time, would have indicated a storm, but for the second time she controlled herself.

"The baron appears thoughtful today," said Monte Cristo to her; "are they going to put him in the ministry?"

"Not yet, I think. More likely he has been speculating on the Bourse, and has lost money."

"M. and Madame de Villefort," cried Baptistin.

They entered. M. de Villefort, notwithstanding his self-control, was visibly affected, and when Monte Cristo touched his hand, he felt it tremble.

"Certainly, women alone know how to dissimulate," said Monte Cristo to himself, glancing at Madame Danglars, who was smiling on the procureur, and embracing his wife.

After a short time, the count saw Bertuccio, who, until then, had been occupied on the other side of the house, glide into an adjoining room. He went to him.

"What do you want, M. Bertuccio?" said he.

"Your excellency has not stated the number of guests."

"Ah, true."

"How many covers?"

"Count for yourself."

"Is everyone here, your excellency?"

"Yes."

Bertuccio glanced through the door, which was ajar. The count watched him. "Good heavens!" he exclaimed.

"What is the matter?" said the count.

"That woman—that woman!"

"Which?"

"The one with a white dress and so many diamonds—the fair one."

"Madame Danglars?"

"I do not know her name; but it is she, sir, it is she!"

"Whom do you mean?"

"The woman of the garden!—she that was *enceinte*—she who was walking while she waited for—"

Bertuccio stood at the open door, with his eyes starting and his hair on end.

"Waiting for whom?" Bertuccio, without answering, pointed to Villefort with something of the gesture Macbeth uses to point out Banquo.

"Oh, oh!" he at length muttered, "do you see?"

"What? Who?"

"Him!"

"Him!—M. de Villefort, the king's attorney? Certainly I see him."

"Then I did not kill him?"

"Really, I think you are going mad, good Bertuccio," said the count.

"Then he is not dead?"

"No; you see plainly he is not dead. Instead of striking between the sixth and seventh left ribs, as your countrymen do, you must have struck higher or lower, and life is very tenacious in these lawyers, or rather there is no truth in anything you have told me—it was a fright of the imagination, a dream of your fancy. You went to sleep full of thoughts of vengeance; they weighed heavily upon your stomach; you had the nightmare—that's all. Come, calm yourself, and reckon them up—M. and Madame de Villefort, two; M. and Madame Danglars, four; M. de Château-Renaud, M. Debray, M. Morrel, seven; Major Bartolomeo Cavalcanti, eight."

"Eight!" repeated Bertuccio.

"Stop! You are in a shocking hurry to be off—you forget one of my guests. Lean a little to the left. Stay! look at M. Andrea Cavalcanti, the young man in a black coat, looking at Murillo's 'Madonna'; now he is turning."

This time Bertuccio would have uttered an exclamation, had not a look from Monte Cristo silenced him.

"Benedetto?" he muttered; "fatality!"

"Half-past six o'clock has just struck, M. Bertuccio," said the count severely; "I ordered dinner at that hour, and I do not like to wait;" and he returned to his guests, while Bertuccio, leaning against the wall, succeeded in reaching the dining-room. Five minutes afterwards the doors of the drawing-room were thrown open, and Bertuccio appearing said, with a violent effort, "The dinner waits."

The Count of Monte Cristo offered his arm to Madame de Villefort. "M. de Villefort," he said, "will you conduct the Baroness Danglars?"

Villefort complied, and they passed on to the dining-room.

Study Guide Questions

For Students:

1. Who is the first guest to arrive at the Count's party?
2. Why is Bertuccio shocked to see Madame Danglars?
3. How does Bertuccio know Andrea Cavalcanti?

For Reading Club:

1. Discuss the changes in the Count's house.
2. Why do you think the Count is lying about Cavalcanti?
3. Discuss the relationship between M. de Villefort, Madame Danglars, and Andrea Cavalcanti.

CHAPTER 63

The Dinner

It was evident that one sentiment affected all the guests on entering the dining-room. Each one asked what strange influence had brought them to this house, and yet astonished, even uneasy though they were, they still felt that they would not like to be absent. The recent events, the solitary and eccentric position of the count, his enormous, nay, almost incredible fortune, should have made men cautious, and have altogether prevented ladies visiting a house where there was no one of their own sex to receive them; and yet curiosity had been enough to lead them to overleap the bounds of prudence and decorum.

And all present, even including Cavalcanti and his son, notwithstanding the stiffness of the one and the carelessness of the other, were thoughtful, on finding themselves assembled at the house of this incomprehensible man. Madame Danglars had started when Villefort, on the count's invitation, offered his arm; and Villefort felt that his glance was uneasy beneath his gold spectacles, when he felt the arm of the baroness press upon his own. None of this had escaped the count, and even by this mere contact of individuals the scene had already acquired considerable interest for an observer.

M. de Villefort had on the right hand Madame Danglars, on his left Morrel. The count was seated between Madame de Villefort and Danglars; the other seats were filled by Debray, who was placed between the two Cavalcanti, and by Château-Renaud, seated between Madame de Villefort and Morrel.

The repast was magnificent; Monte Cristo had endeavored completely to overturn the Parisian ideas, and to feed the curiosity as much as the appetite of his guests. It was an Oriental feast that he offered to them, but of such a kind as the Arabian fairies might be supposed to prepare. Every delicious fruit that the four quarters of the globe could provide was heaped in vases from China and jars from Japan. Rare birds, retaining their most brilliant plumage, enormous fish, spread upon massive silver dishes, together with every wine produced in the Archipelago, Asia Minor, or the Cape, sparkling in bottles, whose grotesque shape seemed to give an additional flavor to the draught,—all these, like one of the displays with which Apicius of old gratified his guests, passed in review before the eyes of the astonished Parisians, who understood that it was possible to expend a thousand louis upon a dinner for ten persons, but only on the condition of eating pearls, like Cleopatra, or drinking refined gold, like Lorenzo de' Medici.

Monte Cristo noticed the general astonishment, and began laughing and joking about it.

"Gentlemen," he said, "you will admit that, when arrived at a certain degree of fortune, the superfluities of life are all that can be desired; and the ladies will allow that, after having risen to a certain eminence of position, the ideal alone can be more exalted. Now, to follow out this reasoning, what is the marvellous?—that which we do not understand. What is it that we really desire?—that which we cannot obtain. Now, to see things which I cannot understand, to procure impossibilities, these are the study of my life. I gratify my wishes by two means—my will and my money. I take as much interest in the pursuit of some whim as you do, M. Danglars, in promoting a new railway line; you, M. de Villefort, in condemning a culprit to death; you, M. Debray, in pacifying a kingdom; you, M. de Château-Renaud, in pleasing a woman; and you, Morrel, in breaking a horse that no one can ride. For example, you see these two fish; one brought from fifty leagues beyond St. Petersburg, the other five leagues from Naples. Is it not amusing to see them both on the same table?"

"What are the two fish?" asked Danglars.

"M. Château-Renaud, who has lived in Russia, will tell you the name of one, and Major Cavalcanti, who is an Italian, will tell you the name of the other."

"This one is, I think, a sterlet," said Château-Renaud.

"And that one, if I mistake not, a lamprey."

"Just so. Now, M. Danglars, ask these gentlemen where they are caught."

"Sterlets," said Château-Renaud, "are only found in the Volga."

"And," said Cavalcanti, "I know that Lake Fusaro alone supplies lampreys of that size."

"Exactly; one comes from the Volga, and the other from Lake Fusaro."

"Impossible!" cried all the guests simultaneously.

"Well, this is just what amuses me," said Monte Cristo. "I am like Nero—*cupitor impossibilium*; and that is what is amusing you at this moment. This fish, which seems so exquisite to you, is very likely no better than perch or salmon; but it seemed impossible to procure it, and here it is."

"But how could you have these fish brought to France?"

"Oh, nothing more easy. Each fish was brought over in a cask—one filled with river herbs and weeds, the other with rushes and lake plants; they were placed in a wagon built on purpose, and thus the sterlet lived twelve days, the lamprey eight, and both were alive when my cook seized them, killing one with milk and the other with wine. You do not believe me, M. Danglars!"

"I cannot help doubting," answered Danglars with his stupid smile.

"Baptistin," said the count, "have the other fish brought in—the sterlet and the lamprey which came in the other casks, and which are yet alive."

Danglars opened his bewildered eyes; the company clapped their hands. Four servants carried in two casks covered with aquatic plants, and in each of which was breathing a fish similar to those on the table.

"But why have two of each sort?" asked Danglars.

"Merely because one might have died," carelessly answered Monte Cristo.

"You are certainly an extraordinary man," said Danglars; "and philosophers may well say it is a fine thing to be rich."

"And to have ideas," added Madame Danglars.

"Oh, do not give me credit for this, madame; it was done by the Romans, who much esteemed them, and Pliny relates that they sent slaves from Ostia to Rome, who carried on their heads fish which he calls the *mulus*, and which, from the description, must probably be the goldfish. It was also considered a luxury to have them alive, it being an amusing sight to see them die, for, when dying, they change color three or four times, and like the rainbow when it disappears, pass through all the prismatic shades, after which they were sent to the kitchen. Their agony formed part of their merit—if they were not seen alive, they were despised when dead."

"Yes," said Debray, "but then Ostia is only a few leagues from Rome."

"True," said Monte Cristo; "but what would be the use of living eighteen hundred years after Lucullus, if we can do no better than he could?"

The two Cavalcanti opened their enormous eyes, but had the good sense not to say anything.

"All this is very extraordinary," said Château-Renaud; "still, what I admire the most, I confess, is the marvellous promptitude with which your orders are executed. Is it not true that you only bought this house five or six days ago?"

"Certainly not longer."

"Well, I am sure it is quite transformed since last week. If I remember rightly, it had another entrance, and the courtyard was paved and empty; while today we have a splendid lawn, bordered by trees which appear to be a hundred years old."

"Why not? I am fond of grass and shade," said Monte Cristo.

"Yes," said Madame de Villefort, "the door was towards the road before, and on the day of my miraculous escape you brought me into the house from the road, I remember."

"Yes, madame," said Monte Cristo; "but I preferred having an entrance which would allow me to see the Bois de Boulogne over my gate."

"In four days," said Morrel; "it is extraordinary!"

"Indeed," said Château-Renaud, "it seems quite miraculous to make a new house out of an old one; for it was very old, and dull too. I recollect coming for my mother to look at it when M. de Saint-Méran advertised it for sale two or three years ago."

"M. de Saint-Méran?" said Madame de Villefort; "then this house belonged to M. de Saint-Méran before you bought it?"

"It appears so," replied Monte Cristo.

"Is it possible that you do not know of whom you purchased it?"

"Quite so; my steward transacts all this business for me."

"It is certainly ten years since the house had been occupied," said Château-Renaud, "and it was quite melancholy to look at it, with the blinds closed, the doors locked, and the weeds in the court. Really, if the house had not belonged to the father-in-law of the procureur, one might have thought it some accursed place where a horrible crime had been committed."

Villefort, who had hitherto not tasted the three or four glasses of rare wine which were placed before him, here took one, and drank it off. Monte Cristo allowed a short time to elapse, and then said:

"It is singular, baron, but the same idea came across me the first time I came here; it looked so gloomy I should never have bought it if my steward had not taken the matter into his own hands. Perhaps the fellow had been bribed by the notary."

"It is probable," stammered out Villefort, trying to smile; "but I can assure you that I had nothing to do with any such proceeding. This house is part of Valentine's marriage-portion, and M. de Saint-Méran wished to sell it; for if it had remained another year or two uninhabited it would have fallen to ruin."

It was Morrel's turn to become pale.

"There was, above all, one room," continued Monte Cristo, "very plain in appearance, hung with red damask, which, I know not why, appeared to me quite dramatic."

"Why so?" said Danglars; "why dramatic?"

"Can we account for instinct?" said Monte Cristo. "Are there not some places where we seem to breathe sadness?—why, we cannot tell. It is a chain of recollections—an idea which carries you back to other times, to other places—which, very likely, have no connection with the present time and place. And there is something in this room which reminds me forcibly of the chamber of the Marquise de Ganges[3] or Desdemona. Stay, since we have finished dinner, I will show it to you, and then we will take coffee in the garden. After dinner, the play."

Monte Cristo looked inquiringly at his guests. Madame de Villefort rose, Monte Cristo did the same, and the rest followed their example. Villefort and Madame Danglars remained for a moment, as if rooted to their seats; they questioned each other with vague and stupid glances.

"Did you hear?" said Madame Danglars.

"We must go," replied Villefort, offering his arm.

The others, attracted by curiosity, were already scattered in different parts of the house; for they thought the visit would not be limited to the one room, and that, at the same time, they would obtain a view of the rest of the building, of which Monte Cristo had created a palace. Each one went out by the open doors. Monte Cristo waited for the two who remained; then, when they had passed, he brought up the rear, and on his face was a smile, which, if they could have understood it, would have alarmed them much more than a visit to the room they were about to enter. They began by walking through the apartments, many of which were fitted up in the Eastern style, with cushions and divans instead of beds, and pipes instead of furniture. The drawing-rooms were decorated with the rarest pictures by the old masters, the boudoirs hung with draperies from China, of fanciful colors, fantastic design, and wonderful texture. At length they arrived at the famous room. There was nothing particular about it, excepting that, although daylight had disappeared, it was not lighted, and everything in it was old-fashioned, while the rest of the rooms had been redecorated. These two causes were enough to give it a gloomy aspect.

"Oh." cried Madame de Villefort, "it is really frightful."

Madame Danglars tried to utter a few words, but was not heard. Many observations were made, the import of which was a unanimous opinion that there was something sinister about the room.

---

[3] Elisabeth de Rossan, Marquise de Ganges, was one of the famous women of the court of Louis XIV. where she was known as "La Belle Provençale." She was the widow of the Marquis de Castellane when she married de Ganges, and having the misfortune to excite the enmity of her new brothers-in-law, was forced by them to take poison; and they finished her off with pistol and dagger.—Ed.

"Is it not so?" asked Monte Cristo. "Look at that large clumsy bed, hung with such gloomy, blood-colored drapery! And those two crayon portraits, that have faded from the dampness; do they not seem to say, with their pale lips and staring eyes, 'We have seen'?"

Villefort became livid; Madame Danglars fell into a long seat placed near the chimney.

"Oh," said Madame de Villefort, smiling, "are you courageous enough to sit down upon the very seat perhaps upon which the crime was committed?"

Madame Danglars rose suddenly.

"And then," said Monte Cristo, "this is not all."

"What is there more?" said Debray, who had not failed to notice the agitation of Madame Danglars.

"Ah, what else is there?" said Danglars; "for, at present, I cannot say that I have seen anything extraordinary. What do you say, M. Cavalcanti?"

"Ah," said he, "we have at Pisa, Ugolino's tower; at Ferrara, Tasso's prison; at Rimini, the room of Francesca and Paolo."

"Yes, but you have not this little staircase," said Monte Cristo, opening a door concealed by the drapery. "Look at it, and tell me what you think of it."

"What a wicked-looking, crooked staircase," said Château-Renaud with a smile.

"I do not know whether the wine of Chios produces melancholy, but certainly everything appears to me black in this house," said Debray.

Ever since Valentine's dowry had been mentioned, Morrel had been silent and sad.

"Can you imagine," said Monte Cristo, "some Othello or Abbé de Ganges, one stormy, dark night, descending these stairs step by step, carrying a load, which he wishes to hide from the sight of man, if not from God?"

Madame Danglars half fainted on the arm of Villefort, who was obliged to support himself against the wall.

"Ah, madame," cried Debray, "what is the matter with you? how pale you look!"

"It is very evident what is the matter with her," said Madame de Villefort; "M. de Monte Cristo is relating horrible stories to us, doubtless intending to frighten us to death."

"Yes," said Villefort, "really, count, you frighten the ladies."

"What is the matter?" asked Debray, in a whisper, of Madame Danglars.

"Nothing," she replied with a violent effort. "I want air, that is all."

"Will you come into the garden?" said Debray, advancing towards the back staircase.

"No, no," she answered, "I would rather remain here."

"Are you really frightened, madame?" said Monte Cristo.

"Oh, no, sir," said Madame Danglars; "but you suppose scenes in a manner which gives them the appearance of reality."

"Ah, yes," said Monte Cristo smiling; "it is all a matter of imagination. Why should we not imagine this the apartment of an honest mother? And this bed with red hangings, a bed visited by the goddess Lucina? And that mysterious staircase, the passage through which, not to disturb their sleep, the doctor and nurse pass, or even the father carrying the sleeping child?"

Here Madame Danglars, instead of being calmed by the soft picture, uttered a groan and fainted.

"Madame Danglars is ill," said Villefort; "it would be better to take her to her carriage."

"Oh, *mon Dieu!*" said Monte Cristo, "and I have forgotten my smelling-bottle!"

"I have mine," said Madame de Villefort; and she passed over to Monte Cristo a bottle full of the same kind of red liquid whose good properties the count had tested on Edward.

"Ah," said Monte Cristo, taking it from her hand.

"Yes," she said, "at your advice I have made the trial."

"And have you succeeded?"

"I think so."

Madame Danglars was carried into the adjoining room; Monte Cristo dropped a very small portion of the red liquid upon her lips; she returned to consciousness.

"Ah," she cried, "what a frightful dream!"

Villefort pressed her hand to let her know it was not a dream. They looked for M. Danglars, but, as he was not especially interested in poetical ideas, he had gone into the garden, and was talking with Major Cavalcanti on the projected railway from Leghorn to Florence. Monte Cristo seemed in despair. He took the arm of Madame Danglars, and conducted her into the garden, where they found Danglars taking coffee between the Cavalcanti.

"Really, madame," he said, "did I alarm you much?"

"Oh, no, sir," she answered; "but you know, things impress us differently, according to the mood of our minds." Villefort forced a laugh.

"And then, you know," he said, "an idea, a supposition, is sufficient."

"Well," said Monte Cristo, "you may believe me if you like, but it is my opinion that a crime has been committed in this house."

"Take care," said Madame de Villefort, "the king's attorney is here."

"Ah," replied Monte Cristo, "since that is the case, I will take advantage of his presence to make my declaration."

"Your declaration?" said Villefort.

"Yes, before witnesses."

"Oh, this is very interesting," said Debray; "if there really has been a crime, we will investigate it."

"There has been a crime," said Monte Cristo. "Come this way, gentlemen; come, M. Villefort, for a declaration to be available, should be made before the competent authorities."

He then took Villefort's arm, and, at the same time, holding that of Madame Danglars under his own, he dragged the procureur to the plantain-tree, where the shade was thickest. All the other guests followed.

"Stay," said Monte Cristo, "here, in this very spot" (and he stamped upon the ground), "I had the earth dug up and fresh mould put in, to refresh these old trees; well, my man, digging, found a box, or rather, the iron-work of a box, in the midst of which was the skeleton of a newly born infant."

Monte Cristo felt the arm of Madame Danglars stiffen, while that of Villefort trembled.

"A newly born infant," repeated Debray; "this affair becomes serious!"

"Well," said Château-Renaud, "I was not wrong just now then, when I said that houses had souls and faces like men, and that their exteriors carried the impress of their characters. This house was gloomy because it was remorseful: it was remorseful because it concealed a crime."

"Who said it was a crime?" asked Villefort, with a last effort.

"How? is it not a crime to bury a living child in a garden?" cried Monte Cristo. "And pray what do you call such an action?"

"But who said it was buried alive?"

"Why bury it there if it were dead? This garden has never been a cemetery."

"What is done to infanticides in this country?" asked Major Cavalcanti innocently.

"Oh, their heads are soon cut off," said Danglars.

"Ah, indeed?" said Cavalcanti.

"I think so; am I not right, M. de Villefort?" asked Monte Cristo.

"Yes, count," replied Villefort, in a voice now scarcely human.

Monte Cristo, seeing that the two persons for whom he had prepared this scene could scarcely endure it, and not wishing to carry it too far, said:

"Come, gentlemen,—some coffee, we seem to have forgotten it," and he conducted the guests back to the table on the lawn.

"Indeed, count," said Madame Danglars, "I am ashamed to own it, but all your frightful stories have so upset me, that I must beg you to let me sit down;" and she fell into a chair.

Monte Cristo bowed, and went to Madame de Villefort.

"I think Madame Danglars again requires your bottle," he said. But before Madame de Villefort could reach her friend, the procureur had found time to whisper to Madame Danglars, "I must speak to you."

"When?"

"Tomorrow."

"Where?"

"In my office, or in the court, if you like,—that is the surest place."

"I will be there."

At this moment Madame de Villefort approached.

"Thanks, my dear friend," said Madame Danglars, trying to smile; "it is over now, and I am much better."

Study Guide Questions

For Students:

1. What kind of feast is served to the guests at the dinner?
2. Who faints during the tour of the house at Auteuil and why?
3. What is the declaration made by the Count in presence of M. de Villefort?

For Reading Club:

1. Discuss the feelings of the guests on entering the dining room.
2. The Count mentions multiple times that he desires things that are impossible. What are your views on it?
3. Discuss the reaction of different guests to the sinister red room. Why do you think Madame Danglars is agitated the most?

CHAPTER 64

The Beggar

The evening passed on; Madame de Villefort expressed a desire to return to Paris, which Madame Danglars had not dared to do, notwithstanding the uneasiness she experienced. On his wife's request, M. de Villefort was the first to give the signal of departure. He offered a seat in his landau to Madame Danglars, that she might be under the care of his wife. As for M. Danglars, absorbed in an interesting conversation with M. Cavalcanti, he paid no attention to anything that was passing. While Monte Cristo had begged the smelling-bottle of Madame de Villefort, he had noticed the approach of Villefort to Madame Danglars, and he soon guessed all that had passed between them, though the words had been uttered in so low a voice as hardly to be heard by Madame Danglars. Without opposing their arrangements, he allowed Morrel, Château-Renaud, and Debray to leave on horseback, and the ladies in M. de Villefort's carriage. Danglars, more and more delighted with Major Cavalcanti, had offered him a seat in his carriage. Andrea Cavalcanti found his tilbury waiting at the door; the groom, in every respect a caricature of the English fashion, was standing on tiptoe to hold a large iron-gray horse.

Andrea had spoken very little during dinner; he was an intelligent lad, and he feared to utter some absurdity before so many grand people, amongst whom, with dilating eyes, he saw the king's attorney. Then he had been seized upon by Danglars, who, with a rapid glance at the stiff-necked old major and his modest son, and taking into consideration the hospitality of the count, made up his mind that he was in the society of some nabob come to Paris to finish the worldly education of his heir. He contemplated with unspeakable delight the large diamond which shone on the major's little finger; for the major, like a prudent man, in case of any accident happening to his bank-notes, had immediately converted them into an available asset. Then, after dinner, on the pretext of business, he questioned the father and son upon their mode of living; and the father and son, previously informed that it was through Danglars the one was to receive his 48,000 francs and the other 50,000 livres annually, were so full of affability that they would have shaken hands even with the banker's servants, so much did their gratitude need an object to expend itself upon.

One thing above all the rest heightened the respect, nay almost the veneration, of Danglars for Cavalcanti. The latter, faithful to the principle of Horace, *nil admirari*, had contented himself with showing his knowledge by declaring in what lake the best lampreys were caught. Then he had eaten some without saying a word more; Danglars, therefore, concluded that such luxuries were common at the table of the illustrious descendant of the Cavalcanti, who most likely in Lucca fed upon trout brought from Switzerland, and lobsters sent from England, by the same means used by the count to bring the lampreys from Lake Fusaro, and the sterlet from the Volga. Thus it was with much politeness of manner that he heard Cavalcanti pronounce these words:

"Tomorrow, sir, I shall have the honor of waiting upon you on business."

"And I, sir," said Danglars, "shall be most happy to receive you."

Upon which he offered to take Cavalcanti in his carriage to the Hôtel des Princes, if it would not be depriving him of the company of his son. To this Cavalcanti replied by saying that for some time past his son had lived independently of him, that he had his own horses and carriages, and that not having come together, it would not be difficult for them to leave separately. The major seated himself, therefore, by the side of Danglars, who was more and more charmed with the ideas of order and economy which ruled this man, and yet who, being able to allow his son 60,000 francs a year, might be supposed to possess a fortune of 500,000 or 600,000 livres.

As for Andrea, he began, by way of showing off, to scold his groom, who, instead of bringing the tilbury to the steps of the house, had taken it to the outer door, thus giving him the trouble of walking thirty steps to reach it. The groom heard him with humility, took the bit of the impatient animal with his left hand, and with the right held out the reins to Andrea, who, taking them from him, rested his polished boot lightly on the step.

At that moment a hand touched his shoulder. The young man turned round, thinking that Danglars or Monte Cristo had forgotten something they wished to tell him, and had returned just as they were starting. But instead of either of these, he saw nothing but a strange face, sunburnt, and encircled by a beard, with eyes brilliant as carbuncles, and a smile upon the mouth which displayed a perfect set of white teeth, pointed and sharp as the wolf's or jackal's. A red handkerchief encircled his gray head; torn and filthy garments covered his large bony limbs, which seemed as though, like those of a skeleton, they would rattle as he walked; and the hand with which he leaned upon the young man's shoulder, and which was the first thing Andrea saw, seemed of gigantic size.

Did the young man recognize that face by the light of the lantern in his tilbury, or was he merely struck with the horrible appearance of his interrogator? We cannot say; but only relate the fact that he shuddered and stepped back suddenly.

"What do you want of me?" he asked.

"Pardon me, my friend, if I disturb you," said the man with the red handkerchief, "but I want to speak to you."

"You have no right to beg at night," said the groom, endeavoring to rid his master of the troublesome intruder.

"I am not begging, my fine fellow," said the unknown to the servant, with so ironical an expression of the eye, and so frightful a smile, that he withdrew; "I only wish to say two or three words to your master, who gave me a commission to execute about a fortnight ago."

"Come," said Andrea, with sufficient nerve for his servant not to perceive his agitation, "what do you want? Speak quickly, friend."

The man said, in a low voice: "I wish—I wish you to spare me the walk back to Paris. I am very tired, and as I have not eaten so good a dinner as you, I can scarcely stand."

The young man shuddered at this strange familiarity.

"Tell me," he said—"tell me what you want?"

"Well, then, I want you to take me up in your fine carriage, and carry me back." Andrea turned pale, but said nothing.

"Yes," said the man, thrusting his hands into his pockets, and looking impudently at the youth; "I have taken the whim into my head; do you understand, Master Benedetto?"

At this name, no doubt, the young man reflected a little, for he went towards his groom, saying:

"This man is right; I did indeed charge him with a commission, the result of which he must tell me; walk to the barrier, there take a cab, that you may not be too late."

The surprised groom retired.

"Let me at least reach a shady spot," said Andrea.

"Oh, as for that, I'll take you to a splendid place," said the man with the handkerchief; and taking the horse's bit he led the tilbury where it was certainly impossible for anyone to witness the honor that Andrea conferred upon him.

"Don't think I want the glory of riding in your fine carriage," said he; "oh, no, it's only because I am tired, and also because I have a little business to talk over with you."

"Come, step in," said the young man. It was a pity this scene had not occurred in daylight, for it was curious to see this rascal throwing himself heavily down on the cushion beside the young and elegant driver of the tilbury. Andrea drove past the last house in the village without saying a word to his companion, who smiled complacently, as though well-pleased to find himself travelling in so comfortable a vehicle. Once out of Auteuil, Andrea looked around, in order to assure himself that he could neither be seen nor heard, and then, stopping the horse and crossing his arms before the man, he asked:

"Now, tell me why you come to disturb my tranquillity?"

"Let me ask you why you deceived me?"

"How have I deceived you?"

"'How,' do you ask? When we parted at the Pont du Var, you told me you were going to travel through Piedmont and Tuscany; but instead of that, you come to Paris."

"How does that annoy you?"

"It does not; on the contrary, I think it will answer my purpose."

"So," said Andrea, "you are speculating upon me?"

"What fine words he uses!"

"I warn you, Master Caderousse, that you are mistaken."

"Well, well, don't be angry, my boy; you know well enough what it is to be unfortunate; and misfortunes make us jealous. I thought you were earning a living in Tuscany or Piedmont by acting as *facchino* or *cicerone*, and I pitied you sincerely, as I would a child of my own. You know I always did call you my child."

"Come, come, what then?"

"Patience—patience!"

"I am patient, but go on."

"All at once I see you pass through the barrier with a groom, a tilbury, and fine new clothes. You must have discovered a mine, or else become a stockbroker."

"So that, as you confess, you are jealous?"

"No, I am pleased—so pleased that I wished to congratulate you; but as I am not quite properly dressed, I chose my opportunity, that I might not compromise you."

"Yes, and a fine opportunity you have chosen!" exclaimed Andrea; "you speak to me before my servant."

"How can I help that, my boy? I speak to you when I can catch you. You have a quick horse, a light tilbury, you are naturally as slippery as an eel; if I had missed you tonight, I might not have had another chance."

"You see, I do not conceal myself."

"You are lucky; I wish I could say as much, for I do conceal myself; and then I was afraid you would not recognize me, but you did," added Caderousse with his unpleasant smile. "It was very polite of you."

"Come," said Andrea, "what do you want?"

"You do not speak affectionately to me, Benedetto, my old friend, that is not right—take care, or I may become troublesome."

This menace smothered the young man's passion. He urged the horse again into a trot.

"You should not speak so to an old friend like me, Caderousse, as you said just now; you are a native of Marseilles, I am—"

"Do you know then now what you are?"

"No, but I was brought up in Corsica; you are old and obstinate, I am young and wilful. Between people like us threats are out of place, everything should be amicably arranged. Is it my fault if fortune, which has frowned on you, has been kind to me?"

"Fortune has been kind to you, then? Your tilbury, your groom, your clothes, are not then hired? Good, so much the better," said Caderousse, his eyes sparkling with avarice.

"Oh, you knew that well enough before speaking to me," said Andrea, becoming more and more excited. "If I had been wearing a handkerchief like yours on my head, rags on my back, and worn-out shoes on my feet, you would not have known me."

"You wrong me, my boy; now I have found you, nothing prevents my being as well-dressed as anyone, knowing, as I do, the goodness of your heart. If you have two coats you will give me one of them. I used to divide my soup and beans with you when you were hungry."

"True," said Andrea.

"What an appetite you used to have! Is it as good now?"

"Oh, yes," replied Andrea, laughing.

"How did you come to be dining with that prince whose house you have just left?"

"He is not a prince; simply a count."

"A count, and a rich one too, eh?"

"Yes; but you had better not have anything to say to him, for he is not a very good-tempered gentleman."

"Oh, be easy! I have no design upon your count, and you shall have him all to yourself. But," said Caderousse, again smiling with the disagreeable expression he had before assumed, "you must pay for it—you understand?"

"Well, what do you want?"

"I think that with a hundred francs a month—"

"Well?"

"I could live—"

"Upon a hundred francs!"

"Come—you understand me; but that with—"

"With?"

"With a hundred and fifty francs I should be quite happy."

"Here are two hundred," said Andrea; and he placed ten gold louis in the hand of Caderousse.

"Good!" said Caderousse.

"Apply to the steward on the first day of every month, and you will receive the same sum."

"There now, again you degrade me."

"How so?"

"By making me apply to the servants, when I want to transact business with you alone."

"Well, be it so, then. Take it from me then, and so long at least as I receive my income, you shall be paid yours."

"Come, come; I always said you were a fine fellow, and it is a blessing when good fortune happens to such as you. But tell me all about it?"

"Why do you wish to know?" asked Cavalcanti.

"What? do you again defy me?"

"No; the fact is, I have found my father."

"What? a real father?"

"Yes, so long as he pays me—"

"You'll honor and believe him—that's right. What is his name?"

"Major Cavalcanti."

"Is he pleased with you?"

"So far I have appeared to answer his purpose."

"And who found this father for you?"

"The Count of Monte Cristo."

"The man whose house you have just left?"

"Yes."

"I wish you would try and find me a situation with him as grandfather, since he holds the money-chest!"

"Well, I will mention you to him. Meanwhile, what are you going to do?"

"I?"

"Yes, you."

"It is very kind of you to trouble yourself about me."

"Since you interest yourself in my affairs, I think it is now my turn to ask you some questions."

"Ah, true. Well; I shall rent a room in some respectable house, wear a decent coat, shave every day, and go and read the papers in a café. Then, in the evening, I shall go to the theatre; I shall look like some retired baker. That is what I want."

"Come, if you will only put this scheme into execution, and be steady, nothing could be better."

"Do you think so, M. Bossuet? And you—what will you become? A peer of France?"

"Ah," said Andrea, "who knows?"

"Major Cavalcanti is already one, perhaps; but then, hereditary rank is abolished."

"No politics, Caderousse. And now that you have all you want, and that we understand each other, jump down from the tilbury and disappear."

"Not at all, my good friend."

"How? Not at all?"

"Why, just think for a moment; with this red handkerchief on my head, with scarcely any shoes, no papers, and ten gold napoleons in my pocket, without reckoning what was there before—making in all about two hundred francs,—why, I should certainly be arrested at the barriers. Then, to justify myself, I should say that you gave me the money; this would cause inquiries, it would be found that I left Toulon without giving due notice, and I should then be escorted back to the shores of the Mediterranean. Then I should become simply No. 106, and good-bye to my dream of resembling the retired baker! No, no, my boy; I prefer remaining honorably in the capital."

Andrea scowled. Certainly, as he had himself owned, the reputed son of Major Cavalcanti was a wilful fellow. He drew up for a minute, threw a rapid glance around him, and then his hand fell instantly into his pocket, where it began playing with a pistol. But, meanwhile, Caderousse, who had never taken his eyes off his companion, passed his hand behind his back, and opened a long Spanish knife, which he always carried with him, to be ready in case of need. The two friends, as we see, were worthy of and understood one another. Andrea's hand left his pocket inoffensively, and was carried up to the red moustache, which it played with for some time.

"Good Caderousse," he said, "how happy you will be."

"I will do my best," said the innkeeper of the Pont du Gard, shutting up his knife.

"Well, then, we will go into Paris. But how will you pass through the barrier without exciting suspicion? It seems to me that you are in more danger riding than on foot."

"Wait," said Caderousse, "we shall see." He then took the greatcoat with the large collar, which the groom had left behind in the tilbury, and put it on his back; then he took off Cavalcanti's hat, which he placed upon his own head, and finally he assumed the careless attitude of a servant whose master drives himself.

"But, tell me," said Andrea, "am I to remain bareheaded?"

"Pooh," said Caderousse; "it is so windy that your hat can easily appear to have blown off."

"Come, come; enough of this," said Cavalcanti.

"What are you waiting for?" said Caderousse. "I hope I am not the cause."

"Hush," said Andrea. They passed the barrier without accident. At the first cross street Andrea stopped his horse, and Caderousse leaped out.

"Well!" said Andrea,—"my servant's coat and my hat?"

"Ah," said Caderousse, "you would not like me to risk taking cold?"

"But what am I to do?"

"You? Oh, you are young while I am beginning to get old. *Au revoir*, Benedetto;" and running into a court, he disappeared.

"Alas," said Andrea, sighing, "one cannot be completely happy in this world!"

Study Guide Questions

For Students:

1. Who stops Andrea when he is leaving the Count's house?
2. What does the beggar ask of Andrea?
3. Who is the beggar?

For Reading Club:

1. Discuss Danglars as a materialistic man.
2. Discuss the conversation that takes place between Andrea and the beggar.
3. What is decided between Caderousse and Benedetto?

CHAPTER 65

A Conjugal Scene

At the Place Louis XV. the three young people separated—that is to say, Morrel went to the Boulevards, Château-Renaud to the Pont de la Révolution, and Debray to the Quai. Most probably Morrel and Château-Renaud returned to their "domestic hearths," as they say in the gallery of the Chamber in well-turned speeches, and in the theatre of the Rue Richelieu in well-written pieces; but it was not the case with Debray. When he reached the wicket of the Louvre, he turned to the left, galloped across the Carrousel, passed through the Rue Saint-Roch, and, issuing from the Rue de la Michodière, he arrived at M. Danglars' door just at the same time that Villefort's landau, after having deposited him and his wife at the Faubourg Saint-Honoré, stopped to leave the baroness at her own house.

Debray, with the air of a man familiar with the house, entered first into the court, threw his bridle into the hands of a footman, and returned to the door to receive Madame Danglars, to whom he offered his arm, to conduct her to her apartments. The gate once closed, and Debray and the baroness alone in the court, he asked:

"What was the matter with you, Hermine? and why were you so affected at that story, or rather fable, which the count related?"

"Because I have been in such shocking spirits all the evening, my friend," said the baroness.

"No, Hermine," replied Debray; "you cannot make me believe that; on the contrary, you were in excellent spirits when you arrived at the count's. M. Danglars was disagreeable, certainly, but I know how much you care for his ill-humor. Someone has vexed you; I will allow no one to annoy you."

"You are deceived, Lucien, I assure you," replied Madame Danglars; "and what I have told you is really the case, added to the ill-humor you remarked, but which I did not think it worth while to allude to."

It was evident that Madame Danglars was suffering from that nervous irritability which women frequently cannot account for even to themselves; or that, as Debray had guessed, she had experienced some secret agitation that she would not acknowledge to anyone. Being a man who knew that the former of these symptoms was one of the inherent penalties of womanhood, he did not then press his inquiries, but waited for a more appropriate opportunity when he should again interrogate her, or receive an avowal *proprio motu.*

At the door of her apartment the baroness met Mademoiselle Cornélie, her confidential maid.

"What is my daughter doing?" asked Madame Danglars.

"She practiced all the evening, and then went to bed," replied Mademoiselle Cornélie.

"Yet I think I hear her piano."

"It is Mademoiselle Louise d'Armilly, who is playing while Mademoiselle Danglars is in bed."

"Well," said Madame Danglars, "come and undress me."

They entered the bedroom. Debray stretched himself upon a large couch, and Madame Danglars passed into her dressing-room with Mademoiselle Cornélie.

"My dear M. Lucien," said Madame Danglars through the door, "you are always complaining that Eugénie will not address a word to you."

"Madame," said Lucien, playing with a little dog, who, recognizing him as a friend of the house, expected to be caressed, "I am not the only one who makes similar complaints, I think I heard Morcerf say that he could not extract a word from his betrothed."

"True," said Madame Danglars; "yet I think this will all pass off, and that you will one day see her enter your study."

"My study?"

"At least that of the minister."

"Why so!"

"To ask for an engagement at the Opera. Really, I never saw such an infatuation for music; it is quite ridiculous for a young lady of fashion."

Debray smiled. "Well," said he, "let her come, with your consent and that of the baron, and we will try and give her an engagement, though we are very poor to pay such talent as hers."

"Go, Cornélie," said Madame Danglars, "I do not require you any longer."

Cornélie obeyed, and the next minute Madame Danglars left her room in a charming loose dress, and came and sat down close to Debray. Then she began thoughtfully to caress the little spaniel. Lucien looked at her for a moment in silence.

"Come, Hermine," he said, after a short time, "answer candidly,—something vexes you—is it not so?"

"Nothing," answered the baroness.

And yet, as she could scarcely breathe, she rose and went towards a looking-glass. "I am frightful tonight," she said. Debray rose, smiling, and was about to contradict the baroness upon this latter point, when the door opened suddenly. M. Danglars appeared; Debray reseated himself. At the noise of the door Madame Danglars turned round, and looked upon her husband with an astonishment she took no trouble to conceal.

"Good-evening, madame," said the banker; "good-evening, M. Debray."

Probably the baroness thought this unexpected visit signified a desire to make up for the sharp words he had uttered during the day. Assuming a dignified air, she turned round to Debray, without answering her husband.

"Read me something, M. Debray," she said. Debray, who was slightly disturbed at this visit, recovered himself when he saw the calmness of the baroness, and took up a book marked by a mother-of-pearl knife inlaid with gold.

"Excuse me," said the banker, "but you will tire yourself, baroness, by such late hours, and M. Debray lives some distance from here."

Debray was petrified, not only to hear Danglars speak so calmly and politely, but because it was apparent that beneath outward politeness there really lurked a determined spirit of opposition to anything his wife might wish to do. The baroness was also surprised, and showed her astonishment by a look which would doubtless have had some effect upon her husband if he had not been intently occupied with the paper, where he was looking to see the closing stock quotations. The result was, that the proud look entirely failed of its purpose.

"M. Lucien," said the baroness, "I assure you I have no desire to sleep, and that I have a thousand things to tell you this evening, which you must listen to, even though you slept while hearing me."

"I am at your service, madame," replied Lucien coldly.

"My dear M. Debray," said the banker, "do not kill yourself tonight listening to the follies of Madame Danglars, for you can hear them as well tomorrow; but I claim tonight and will devote it, if you will allow me, to talk over some serious matters with my wife."

This time the blow was so well aimed, and hit so directly, that Lucien and the baroness were staggered, and they interrogated each other with their eyes, as if to seek help against this aggression, but the irresistible will of the master of the house prevailed, and the husband was victorious.

"Do not think I wish to turn you out, my dear Debray," continued Danglars; "oh, no, not at all. An unexpected occurrence forces me to ask my wife to have a little conversation with me; it is so rarely I make such a request, I am sure you cannot grudge it to me."

Debray muttered something, bowed and went out, knocking himself against the edge of the door, like Nathan in *Athalie.*

"It is extraordinary," he said, when the door was closed behind him, "how easily these husbands, whom we ridicule, gain an advantage over us."

Lucien having left, Danglars took his place on the sofa, closed the open book, and placing himself in a dreadfully dictatorial attitude, he began playing with the dog; but the animal, not liking him as well as Debray, and attempting to bite him, Danglars seized him by the skin of his neck and threw him upon a couch on the other side of the room. The animal uttered a cry during the transit, but, arrived at its destination, it crouched behind the cushions, and stupefied at such unusual treatment remained silent and motionless.

"Do you know, sir," asked the baroness, "that you are improving? Generally you are only rude, but tonight you are brutal."

"It is because I am in a worse humor than usual," replied Danglars. Hermine looked at the banker with supreme disdain. These glances frequently exasperated the pride of Danglars, but this evening he took no notice of them.

"And what have I to do with your ill-humor?" said the baroness, irritated at the impassibility of her husband; "do these things concern me? Keep your ill-humor at home in your money boxes, or, since you have clerks whom you pay, vent it upon them."

"Not so," replied Danglars; "your advice is wrong, so I shall not follow it. My money boxes are my Pactolus, as, I think, M. Demoustier says, and I will not retard its course, or disturb its calm. My clerks are honest men, who earn my fortune, whom I pay much below their deserts, if I may value them according to what they bring in; therefore I shall not get into a passion with them; those with whom I will be in a passion are those who eat my dinners, mount my horses, and exhaust my fortune."

"And pray who are the persons who exhaust your fortune? Explain yourself more clearly, I beg, sir."

"Oh, make yourself easy!—I am not speaking riddles, and you will soon know what I mean. The people who exhaust my fortune are those who draw out 700,000 francs in the course of an hour."

"I do not understand you, sir," said the baroness, trying to disguise the agitation of her voice and the flush of her face.

"You understand me perfectly, on the contrary," said Danglars: "but, if you will persist, I will tell you that I have just lost 700,000 francs upon the Spanish loan."

"And pray," asked the baroness, "am I responsible for this loss?"

"Why not?"

"Is it my fault you have lost 700,000 francs?"

"Certainly it is not mine."

"Once for all, sir," replied the baroness sharply, "I tell you I will not hear cash named; it is a style of language I never heard in the house of my parents or in that of my first husband."

"Oh, I can well believe that, for neither of them was worth a penny."

"The better reason for my not being conversant with the slang of the bank, which is here dinning in my ears from morning to night; that noise of jingling crowns, which are constantly being counted and re-counted, is odious to me. I only know one thing I dislike more, which is the sound of your voice."

"Really?" said Danglars. "Well, this surprises me, for I thought you took the liveliest interest in all my affairs!"

"I? What could put such an idea into your head?"

"Yourself."

"Ah?—what next?"

"Most assuredly."

"I should like to know upon what occasion?"

"Oh, *mon Dieu!* that is very easily done. Last February you were the first who told me of the Haitian funds. You had dreamed that a ship had entered the harbor at Le Havre, that this ship brought news that a payment we had looked upon as lost was going to be made. I know how clear-sighted your dreams are; I therefore purchased immediately as many shares as I could of the Haitian debt, and I gained 400,000 francs by it, of which 100,000 have been honestly paid to you. You spent it as you pleased; that was your business. In March there was a question about a grant to a railway. Three companies presented themselves, each offering equal securities. You told me that your instinct,—and although you pretend to know nothing about speculations, I think on the contrary, that your comprehension is very clear upon certain affairs,—well, you told me that your instinct led you to believe the grant would be given to the company called the Southern. I bought two thirds of the shares of that company; as you had foreseen, the shares trebled in value, and I picked up a million, from which 250,000 francs were paid to you for pin-money. How have you spent this 250,000 francs?—it is no business of mine."

"When are you coming to the point?" cried the baroness, shivering with anger and impatience.

"Patience, madame, I am coming to it."

"That's fortunate."

"In April you went to dine at the minister's. You heard a private conversation respecting Spanish affairs—on the expulsion of Don Carlos. I bought some Spanish shares. The expulsion took place and I pocketed 600,000 francs the day Charles V. repassed the Bidassoa. Of these 600,000 francs you took 50,000 crowns. They were yours, you disposed of them according to your fancy, and I asked no questions; but it is not the less true that you have this year received 500,000 livres."

"Well, sir, and what then?"

"Ah, yes, it was just after this that you spoiled everything."

"Really, your manner of speaking—"

"It expresses my meaning, and that is all I want. Well, three days after that you talked politics with M. Debray, and you fancied from his words that Don Carlos had returned to Spain. Well, I sold my shares, the news got out, and I no longer sold—I gave them away, next day I find the news was false, and by this false report I have lost 700,000 francs."

"Well?"

"Well, since I gave you a fourth of my gains, I think you owe me a fourth of my losses; the fourth of 700,000 francs is 175,000 francs."

"What you say is absurd, and I cannot see why M. Debray's name is mixed up in this affair."

"Because if you do not possess the 175,000 francs I reclaim, you must have lent them to your friends, and M. Debray is one of your friends."

"For shame!" exclaimed the baroness.

"Oh, let us have no gestures, no screams, no modern drama, or you will oblige me to tell you that I see Debray leave here, pocketing the whole of the 500,000 livres you have handed over to him this year, while he smiles to himself, saying that he has found what the most skilful players have never discovered—that is, a roulette where he wins without playing, and is no loser when he loses."

The baroness became enraged.

"Wretch!" she cried, "will you dare to tell me you did not know what you now reproach me with?"

"I do not say that I did know it, and I do not say that I did not know it. I merely tell you to look into my conduct during the last four years that we have ceased to be husband and wife, and see whether it has not always been consistent. Some time after our rupture, you wished to study music, under the celebrated baritone who made such a successful appearance at the Théâtre Italien; at the same time I felt inclined to learn dancing of the *danseuse* who acquired such a reputation in London. This cost me, on your account and mine, 100,000 francs. I said nothing, for we must have peace in the house; and 100,000 francs for a lady and gentleman to be properly instructed in music and dancing are not too much. Well, you soon become tired of singing, and you take a fancy to study diplomacy with the minister's secretary. You understand, it signifies nothing to me so long as you pay for your lessons out of your own cash box. But today I find you are drawing on mine, and that your apprenticeship may cost me 700,000 francs per month. Stop there, madame, for this cannot last. Either the diplomatist must give his lessons gratis, and I will tolerate him, or he must never set his foot again in my house;—do you understand, madame?"

"Oh, this is too much," cried Hermine, choking, "you are worse than despicable."

"But," continued Danglars, "I find you did not even pause there—"

"Insults!"

"You are right; let us leave these facts alone, and reason coolly. I have never interfered in your affairs excepting for your good; treat me in the same way. You say you have nothing to do with my cash box. Be it so. Do as you like with your own, but do not fill or empty mine. Besides, how do I know that this was not a political trick, that the minister enraged at seeing me in the opposition, and jealous of the popular sympathy I excite, has not concerted with M. Debray to ruin me?"

"A probable thing!"

"Why not? Who ever heard of such an occurrence as this?—a false telegraphic despatch—it is almost impossible for wrong signals to be made as they were in the last two telegrams. It was done on purpose for me—I am sure of it."

"Sir," said the baroness humbly, "are you not aware that the man employed there was dismissed, that they talked of going to law with him, that orders were issued to arrest him and that this order would have been put into execution if he had not escaped by flight, which proves that he was either mad or guilty? It was a mistake."

"Yes, which made fools laugh, which caused the minister to have a sleepless night, which has caused the minister's secretaries to blacken several sheets of paper, but which has cost me 700,000 francs."

"But, sir," said Hermine suddenly, "if all this is, as you say, caused by M. Debray, why, instead of going direct to him, do you come and tell me of it? Why, to accuse the man, do you address the woman?"

"Do I know M. Debray?—do I wish to know him?—do I wish to know that he gives advice?—do I wish to follow it?—do I speculate? No; you do all this, not I."

"Still it seems to me, that as you profit by it—"

Danglars shrugged his shoulders. "Foolish creature," he exclaimed. "Women fancy they have talent because they have managed two or three intrigues without being the talk of Paris! But know that if you had even hidden your irregularities from your husband, who has but the commencement of the art—for generally husbands *will* not see—you would then have been but a faint imitation of most of your friends among the women of the world. But it has not been so with me,—I see, and always have seen, during the last sixteen years. You may, perhaps, have hidden a thought; but not a step, not an action, not a fault, has escaped me, while you flattered yourself upon your address, and firmly believed you had deceived me. What has been the result?—that, thanks to my pretended ignorance, there is none of your friends, from M. de Villefort to M. Debray, who has not trembled before me. There is not one who has not treated me as the master of the house,—the only title I desire with respect to you; there is not one, in fact, who would have dared to speak of me as I have spoken of them this day. I will allow you to make me hateful, but I will prevent your rendering me ridiculous, and, above all, I forbid you to ruin me."

The baroness had been tolerably composed until the name of Villefort had been pronounced; but then she became pale, and, rising, as if touched by a spring, she stretched out her hands as though conjuring an apparition; she then took two or three steps towards her husband, as though to tear the secret from him, of which he was ignorant, or which he withheld from some odious calculation,—odious, as all his calculations were.

"M. de Villefort!—What do you mean?"

"I mean that M. de Nargonne, your first husband, being neither a philosopher nor a banker, or perhaps being both, and seeing there was nothing to be got out of a king's attorney, died of grief or anger at finding, after an absence of nine months, that you had been *enceinte* six. I am brutal,—I not only allow it, but boast of it; it is one of the reasons of my success in commercial business. Why did he kill himself instead of you? Because he had no cash to save. My life belongs to my cash. M. Debray has made me lose 700,000 francs; let him bear his share of the loss, and we will go on as before; if not, let him become bankrupt for the 250,000 livres, and do as all bankrupts do—

disappear. He is a charming fellow, I allow, when his news is correct; but when it is not, there are fifty others in the world who would do better than he."

Madame Danglars was rooted to the spot; she made a violent effort to reply to this last attack, but she fell upon a chair thinking of Villefort, of the dinner scene, of the strange series of misfortunes which had taken place in her house during the last few days, and changed the usual calm of her establishment to a scene of scandalous debate.

Danglars did not even look at her, though she did her best to faint. He shut the bedroom door after him, without adding another word, and returned to his apartments; and when Madame Danglars recovered from her half-fainting condition, she could almost believe that she had had a disagreeable dream.

Study Guide Questions

For Students:

1. What does Madame Danglars tell Debray about her sudden illness?
2. Why is M. Danglars angry at his wife?
3. Why does M. Danglars ask his wife for 175,000 francs?

For Reading Club:

1. How does the chapter comment on the husband/wife relationship?
2. Do you think that the all-knowing bold nature of Madame Danglars is one of the major causes of the dispute?
3. Discuss the accusation made by M. Danglars at the end of the chapter concerning Madame Danglars, her first husband, and M. de Villefort.

CHAPTER 66

Matrimonial Projects

The day following this scene, at the hour Debray usually chose to pay a visit to Madame Danglars on his way to his office, his *coupé* did not appear. At this time, that is, about half-past twelve, Madame Danglars ordered her carriage, and went out. Danglars, hidden behind a curtain, watched the departure he had been waiting for. He gave orders that he should be informed as soon as Madame Danglars appeared; but at two o'clock she had not returned. He then called for his horses, drove to the Chamber, and inscribed his name to speak against the budget. From twelve to two o'clock Danglars had remained in his study, unsealing his dispatches, and becoming more and more sad every minute, heaping figure upon figure, and receiving, among other visits, one from Major Cavalcanti, who, as stiff and exact as ever, presented himself precisely at the hour named the night before, to terminate his business with the banker.

On leaving the Chamber, Danglars, who had shown violent marks of agitation during the sitting, and been more bitter than ever against the ministry, re-entered his carriage, and told the coachman to drive to the Avenue des Champs-Élysées, No. 30.

Monte Cristo was at home; only he was engaged with someone and begged Danglars to wait for a moment in the drawing-room. While the banker was waiting in the anteroom, the door opened, and a man dressed as an abbé and doubtless more familiar with the house than he was, came in and instead of waiting, merely bowed, passed on to the farther apartments, and disappeared.

A minute after the door by which the priest had entered reopened, and Monte Cristo appeared.

"Pardon me," said he, "my dear baron, but one of my friends, the Abbé Busoni, whom you perhaps saw pass by, has just arrived in Paris; not having seen him for a long time, I could not make up my mind to leave him sooner, so I hope this will be sufficient reason for my having made you wait."

"Nay," said Danglars, "it is my fault; I have chosen my visit at a wrong time, and will retire."

"Not at all; on the contrary, be seated; but what is the matter with you? You look careworn; really, you alarm me. Melancholy in a capitalist, like the appearance of a comet, presages some misfortune to the world."

"I have been in ill-luck for several days," said Danglars, "and I have heard nothing but bad news."

"Ah, indeed?" said Monte Cristo. "Have you had another fall at the Bourse?"

"No; I am safe for a few days at least. I am only annoyed about a bankrupt of Trieste."

"Really? Does it happen to be Jacopo Manfredi?"

"Exactly so. Imagine a man who has transacted business with me for I don't know how long, to the amount of 800,000 or 900,000 francs during the year. Never a mistake or delay—a fellow who paid like a prince. Well, I was a million in advance with him, and now my fine Jacopo Manfredi suspends payment!"

"Really?"

"It is an unheard-of fatality. I draw upon him for 600,000 francs, my bills are returned unpaid, and, more than that, I hold bills of exchange signed by him to the value of 400,000 francs, payable at his correspondent's in Paris at the end of this month. Today is the 30th. I present them; but my correspondent has disappeared. This, with my Spanish affairs, made a pretty end to the month."

"Then you really lost by that affair in Spain?"

"Yes; only 700,000 francs out of my cash box—nothing more!"

"Why, how could you make such a mistake—such an old stager?"

"Oh, it is all my wife's fault. She dreamed Don Carlos had returned to Spain; she believes in dreams. It is magnetism, she says, and when she dreams a thing it is sure to happen, she assures me. On this conviction I allow her to speculate, she having her bank and her stockbroker; she speculated and lost. It is true she speculates with her own money, not mine; nevertheless, you can understand that when 700,000 francs leave the wife's pocket, the husband always finds it out. But do you mean to say you have not heard of this? Why, the thing has made a tremendous noise."

"Yes, I heard it spoken of, but I did not know the details, and then no one can be more ignorant than I am of the affairs in the Bourse."

"Then you do not speculate?"

"I?—How could I speculate when I already have so much trouble in regulating my income? I should be obliged, besides my steward, to keep a clerk and a boy. But touching these Spanish affairs, I think that the baroness did not dream the whole of the Don Carlos matter. The papers said something about it, did they not?"

"Then you believe the papers?"

"I?—not the least in the world; only I fancied that the honest *Messager* was an exception to the rule, and that it only announced telegraphic despatches."

"Well, that's what puzzles me," replied Danglars; "the news of the return of Don Carlos was brought by telegraph."

"So that," said Monte Cristo, "you have lost nearly 1,700,000 francs this month."

"Not nearly, indeed; that is exactly my loss."

"*Diable!*" said Monte Cristo compassionately, "it is a hard blow for a third-rate fortune."

"Third-rate," said Danglars, rather humble, "what do you mean by that?"

"Certainly," continued Monte Cristo, "I make three assortments in fortune—first-rate, second-rate, and third-rate fortunes. I call those first-rate which are composed of treasures one possesses under one's hand, such as mines, lands, and funded property, in such states as France, Austria, and England, provided these treasures and property form a total of about a hundred millions; I call those second-rate fortunes, that are gained by manufacturing enterprises, joint-stock companies, viceroyalties, and principalities, not drawing more than 1,500,000 francs, the whole forming a capital of about fifty millions; finally, I call those third-rate fortunes, which are composed of a fluctuating capital, dependent upon the will of others, or upon chances which a bankruptcy involves or a false telegram shakes, such as banks, speculations of the day—in fact, all operations under the influence of greater or less mischances, the whole bringing in a real or fictitious capital of about fifteen millions. I think this is about your position, is it not?"

"Confound it, yes!" replied Danglars.

"The result, then, of six more such months as this would be to reduce the third-rate house to despair."

"Oh," said Danglars, becoming very pale, how you are running on!"

"Let us imagine seven such months," continued Monte Cristo, in the same tone. "Tell me, have you ever thought that seven times 1,700,000 francs make nearly twelve millions? No, you have not;—well, you are right, for if you indulged in such reflections, you would never risk your principal, which is to the speculator what the skin is to civilized man. We have our clothes, some more splendid than others,—this is our credit; but when a man dies he has only his skin; in the same way, on retiring from business, you have nothing but your real principal of about five or six millions, at the most; for third-rate fortunes are never more than a fourth of what they appear to be, like the locomotive on a railway, the size of which is magnified by the smoke and steam surrounding it. Well, out of the five or six millions which form your real capital, you have just lost nearly two millions, which must, of course, in the same degree diminish your credit and fictitious fortune; to follow out my simile, your skin has been opened by bleeding, and this if repeated three or four times will cause death—so pay attention to it, my dear Monsieur Danglars. Do you want money? Do you wish me to lend you some?"

"What a bad calculator you are!" exclaimed Danglars, calling to his assistance all his philosophy and dissimulation. "I have made money at the same time by speculations which have succeeded. I have made up the loss of blood by nutrition. I lost a battle in Spain, I have been defeated in Trieste, but my naval army in India will have taken some galleons, and my Mexican pioneers will have discovered some mine."

"Very good, very good! But the wound remains and will reopen at the first loss."

"No, for I am only embarked in certainties," replied Danglars, with the air of a mountebank sounding his own praises; "to involve me, three governments must crumble to dust."

"Well, such things have been."

"That there should be a famine!"

"Recollect the seven fat and the seven lean kine."

"Or, that the sea should become dry, as in the days of Pharaoh, and even then my vessels would become caravans."

"So much the better. I congratulate you, my dear M. Danglars," said Monte Cristo; "I see I was deceived, and that you belong to the class of second-rate fortunes."

"I think I may aspire to that honor," said Danglars with a smile, which reminded Monte Cristo of the sickly moons which bad artists are so fond of daubing into their pictures of ruins. "But, while we are speaking of business," Danglars added, pleased to find an opportunity of changing the subject, "tell me what I am to do for M. Cavalcanti."

"Give him money, if he is recommended to you, and the recommendation seems good."

"Excellent; he presented himself this morning with a bond of 40,000 francs, payable at sight, on you, signed by Busoni, and returned by you to me, with your endorsement—of course, I immediately counted him over the forty bank-notes."

Monte Cristo nodded his head in token of assent.

"But that is not all," continued Danglars; "he has opened an account with my house for his son."

"May I ask how much he allows the young man?"

"Five thousand francs per month."

"Sixty thousand francs per year. I thought I was right in believing that Cavalcanti to be a stingy fellow. How can a young man live upon 5,000 francs a month?"

"But you understand that if the young man should want a few thousands more—"

"Do not advance it; the father will never repay it. You do not know these ultramontane millionaires; they are regular misers. And by whom were they recommended to you?"

"Oh, by the house of Fenzi, one of the best in Florence."

"I do not mean to say you will lose, but, nevertheless, mind you hold to the terms of the agreement."

"Would you not trust the Cavalcanti?"

"I? oh, I would advance ten millions on his signature. I was only speaking in reference to the second-rate fortunes we were mentioning just now."

"And with all this, how unassuming he is! I should never have taken him for anything more than a mere major."

"And you would have flattered him, for certainly, as you say, he has no manner. The first time I saw him he appeared to me like an old lieutenant who had grown mouldy under his epaulets. But all the Italians are the same; they are like old Jews when they are not glittering in Oriental splendor."

"The young man is better," said Danglars.

"Yes; a little nervous, perhaps, but, upon the whole, he appeared tolerable. I was uneasy about him."

"Why?"

"Because you met him at my house, just after his introduction into the world, as they told me. He has been travelling with a very severe tutor, and had never been to Paris before."

"Ah, I believe noblemen marry amongst themselves, do they not?" asked Danglars carelessly; "they like to unite their fortunes."

"It is usual, certainly; but Cavalcanti is an original who does nothing like other people. I cannot help thinking that he has brought his son to France to choose a wife."

"Do you think so?"

"I am sure of it."

"And you have heard his fortune mentioned?"

"Nothing else was talked of; only some said he was worth millions, and others that he did not possess a farthing."

"And what is your opinion?"

"I ought not to influence you, because it is only my own personal impression."

"Well, and it is that—"

"My opinion is, that all these old *podestàs*, these ancient *condottieri*,—for the Cavalcanti have commanded armies and governed provinces,—my opinion, I say, is, that they have buried their millions in corners, the secret of which they have transmitted only to their eldest sons, who have done the same from generation to generation; and the proof of this is seen in their yellow and dry appearance, like the florins of the republic, which, from being constantly gazed upon, have become reflected in them."

"Certainly," said Danglars, "and this is further supported by the fact of their not possessing an inch of land."

"Very little, at least; I know of none which Cavalcanti possesses, excepting his palace in Lucca."

"Ah, he has a palace?" said Danglars, laughing; "come, that is something."

"Yes; and more than that, he lets it to the Minister of Finance while he lives in a simple house. Oh, as I told you before, I think the old fellow is very close."

"Come, you do not flatter him."

"I scarcely know him; I think I have seen him three times in my life; all I know relating to him is through Busoni and himself. He was telling me this morning that, tired of letting his property lie dormant in Italy, which is a dead nation, he wished to find a method, either in France or England, of multiplying his millions, but remember, that though I place great confidence in Busoni, I am not responsible for this."

"Never mind; accept my thanks for the client you have sent me. It is a fine name to inscribe on my ledgers, and my cashier was quite proud of it when I explained to him who the Cavalcanti were. By the way, this is merely a simple question, when this sort of people marry their sons, do they give them any fortune?"

"Oh, that depends upon circumstances. I know an Italian prince, rich as a gold mine, one of the noblest families in Tuscany, who, when his sons married according to his wish, gave them millions; and when they married against his consent, merely allowed them thirty crowns a month. Should Andrea marry according to his father's views, he will, perhaps, give him one, two, or three millions. For example, supposing it were the daughter of a banker, he might take an interest in the house of the father-in-law of his son; then again, if he disliked his choice, the major takes the key, double-locks his coffer, and Master Andrea would be obliged to live like the sons of a Parisian family, by shuffling cards or rattling the dice."

"Ah, that boy will find out some Bavarian or Peruvian princess; he will want a crown, an El Dorado, and Potosí."

"No; these grand lords on the other side of the Alps frequently marry into plain families; like Jupiter, they like to cross the race. But do you wish to marry Andrea, my dear M. Danglars, that you are asking so many questions?"

"*Ma foi,*" said Danglars, "it would not be a bad speculation, I fancy, and you know I am a speculator."

"You are not thinking of Mademoiselle Danglars, I hope; you would not like poor Andrea to have his throat cut by Albert?"

"Albert," repeated Danglars, shrugging his shoulders; "ah, well; he would care very little about it, I think."

"But he is betrothed to your daughter, I believe?"

"Well, M. de Morcerf and I have talked about this marriage, but Madame de Morcerf and Albert—"

"You do not mean to say that it would not be a good match?"

"Indeed, I imagine that Mademoiselle Danglars is as good as M. de Morcerf."

"Mademoiselle Danglars' fortune will be great, no doubt, especially if the telegraph should not make any more mistakes."

"Oh, I do not mean her fortune only; but tell me—"

"What?"

"Why did you not invite M. and Madame de Morcerf to your dinner?"

"I did so, but he excused himself on account of Madame de Morcerf being obliged to go to Dieppe for the benefit of sea air."

"Yes, yes," said Danglars, laughing, "it would do her a great deal of good."

"Why so?"

"Because it is the air she always breathed in her youth."

Monte Cristo took no notice of this ill-natured remark.

"But still, if Albert be not so rich as Mademoiselle Danglars," said the count, "you must allow that he has a fine name?"

"So he has; but I like mine as well."

"Certainly; your name is popular, and does honor to the title they have adorned it with; but you are too intelligent not to know that according to a prejudice, too firmly rooted to be exterminated, a nobility which dates back five centuries is worth more than one that can only reckon twenty years."

"And for this very reason," said Danglars with a smile, which he tried to make sardonic, "I prefer M. Andrea Cavalcanti to M. Albert de Morcerf."

"Still, I should not think the Morcerfs would yield to the Cavalcanti?"

"The Morcerfs!—Stay, my dear count," said Danglars; "you are a man of the world, are you not?"

"I think so."

"And you understand heraldry?"

"A little."

"Well, look at my coat-of-arms, it is worth more than Morcerf's."

"Why so?"

"Because, though I am not a baron by birth, my real name is, at least, Danglars."

"Well, what then?"

"While his name is not Morcerf."

"How?—not Morcerf?"

"Not the least in the world."

"Go on."

"I have been made a baron, so that I actually am one; he made himself a count, so that he is not one at all."

"Impossible!"

"Listen my dear count; M. de Morcerf has been my friend, or rather my acquaintance, during the last thirty years. You know I have made the most of my arms, though I never forgot my origin."

"A proof of great humility or great pride," said Monte Cristo.

"Well, when I was a clerk, Morcerf was a mere fisherman."

"And then he was called—"

"Fernand."

"Only Fernand?"

"Fernand Mondego."

"You are sure?"

"*Pardieu!* I have bought enough fish of him to know his name."

"Then, why did you think of giving your daughter to him?"

"Because Fernand and Danglars, being both parvenus, both having become noble, both rich, are about equal in worth, excepting that there have been certain things mentioned of him that were never said of me."

"What?"

"Oh, nothing!"

"Ah, yes; what you tell me recalls to mind something about the name of Fernand Mondego. I have heard that name in Greece."

"In conjunction with the affairs of Ali Pasha?"

"Exactly so."

"This is the mystery," said Danglars. "I acknowledge I would have given anything to find it out."

"It would be very easy if you much wished it?"

"How so?"

"Probably you have some correspondent in Greece?"

"I should think so."

"At Yanina?"

"Everywhere."

"Well, write to your correspondent in Yanina, and ask him what part was played by a Frenchman named Fernand Mondego in the catastrophe of Ali Tepelini."

"You are right," exclaimed Danglars, rising quickly, "I will write today."

"Do so."

"I will."

"And if you should hear of anything very scandalous—"

"I will communicate it to you."

"You will oblige me."

Danglars rushed out of the room, and made but one leap into his *coupé.*

Study Guide Questions

For Students:

1. How much has M. Danglars lost in one month?
2. What according to the Count is the third-rate fortune?
3. What does M. Danglars say about the origin of M. de Morcerf?

For Reading Club:

1. Discuss why M. Danglars has paid a visit to the Count.
2. Discuss M. Danglars' matrimonial plans for his daughter.
3. Do you think M. Danglars is using his daughter like a commodity?

CHAPTER 67

The Office of the King's Attorney

Let us leave the banker driving his horses at their fullest speed, and follow Madame Danglars in her morning excursion. We have said that at half-past twelve o'clock Madame Danglars had ordered her horses, and had left home in the carriage. She directed her course towards the Faubourg Saint Germain, went down the Rue Mazarine, and stopped at the Passage du Pont-Neuf. She descended, and went through the passage. She was very plainly dressed, as would be the case with a woman of taste walking in the morning. At the Rue Guénégaud she called a cab, and directed the driver to go to the Rue de Harlay. As soon as she was seated in the vehicle, she drew from her pocket a very thick black veil, which she tied on to her straw bonnet. She then replaced the bonnet, and saw with pleasure, in a little pocket-mirror, that her white complexion and brilliant eyes were alone visible. The cab crossed the Pont-Neuf and entered the Rue de Harlay by the Place Dauphine; the driver was paid as the door opened, and stepping lightly up the stairs Madame Danglars soon reached the Salle des Pas-Perdus.

There was a great deal going on that morning, and many business-like persons at the Palais; business-like persons pay very little attention to women, and Madame Danglars crossed the hall without exciting any more attention than any other woman calling upon her lawyer.

There was a great press of people in M. de Villefort's antechamber, but Madame Danglars had no occasion even to pronounce her name. The instant she appeared the door-keeper rose, came to her, and asked her whether she was not the person with whom the procureur had made an appointment; and on her affirmative answer being given, he conducted her by a private passage to M. de Villefort's office.

The magistrate was seated in an armchair, writing, with his back towards the door; he did not move as he heard it open, and the door-keeper pronounce the words, "Walk in, madame," and then reclose it; but no sooner had the man's footsteps ceased, than he started up, drew the bolts, closed the curtains, and examined every corner of the room. Then, when he had assured himself that he could neither be seen nor heard, and was consequently relieved of doubts, he said:

"Thanks, madame,—thanks for your punctuality;" and he offered a chair to Madame Danglars, which she accepted, for her heart beat so violently that she felt nearly suffocated.

"It is a long time, madame," said the procureur, describing a half-circle with his chair, so as to place himself exactly opposite to Madame Danglars,—"it is a long time since I had the pleasure of speaking alone with you, and I regret that we have only now met to enter upon a painful conversation."

"Nevertheless, sir, you see I have answered your first appeal, although certainly the conversation must be much more painful for me than for you." Villefort smiled bitterly.

"It is true, then," he said, rather uttering his thoughts aloud than addressing his companion,—"it is true, then, that all our actions leave their traces—some sad, others bright—on our paths; it is true that every step in our lives is like the course of an insect on the sands;—it leaves its track! Alas, to many the path is traced by tears."

"Sir," said Madame Danglars, "you can feel for my emotion, can you not? Spare me, then, I beseech you. When I look at this room,—whence so many guilty creatures have departed, trembling and ashamed, when I look at that chair before which I now sit trembling and ashamed,—oh, it requires all my reason to convince me that I am not a very guilty woman and you a menacing judge."

Villefort dropped his head and sighed.

"And I," he said, "I feel that my place is not in the judge's seat, but on the prisoner's bench."

"You?" said Madame Danglars.

"Yes, I."

"I think, sir, you exaggerate your situation," said Madame Danglars, whose beautiful eyes sparkled for a moment. "The paths of which you were just speaking have been traced by all young men of ardent imaginations. Besides the pleasure, there is always remorse from the indulgence of our passions, and, after all, what have you men to fear from all this? the world excuses, and notoriety ennobles you."

"Madame," replied Villefort, "you know that I am no hypocrite, or, at least, that I never deceive without a reason. If my brow be severe, it is because many misfortunes have clouded it; if my heart be petrified, it is that it might sustain the blows it has received. I was not so in my youth, I was not so on the night of the betrothal, when we were all seated around a table in the Rue du Cours at Marseilles. But since then everything has changed in and about me; I am accustomed to brave difficulties, and, in the conflict to crush those who, by their own free will, or by chance, voluntarily or involuntarily, interfere with me in my career. It is generally the case that what we most ardently desire is as ardently withheld from us by those who wish to obtain it, or from whom we attempt to snatch it. Thus, the greater number of a man's errors come before him disguised under the specious form of necessity; then, after error has been committed in a moment of excitement, of delirium, or of fear, we see that we might have avoided and escaped it. The means we might have used, which we in our blindness could not see, then seem simple and easy, and we say, 'Why did I not do this, instead of that?' Women, on the contrary, are rarely tormented with remorse; for the decision does not come from you,—your misfortunes are generally imposed upon you, and your faults the results of others' crimes."

"In any case, sir, you will allow," replied Madame Danglars, "that, even if the fault were alone mine, I last night received a severe punishment for it."

"Poor thing," said Villefort, pressing her hand, "it was too severe for your strength, for you were twice overwhelmed, and yet—"

"Well?"

"Well, I must tell you. Collect all your courage, for you have not yet heard all."

"Ah," exclaimed Madame Danglars, alarmed, "what is there more to hear?"

"You only look back to the past, and it is, indeed, bad enough. Well, picture to yourself a future more gloomy still—certainly frightful, perhaps sanguinary!"

The baroness knew how calm Villefort naturally was, and his present excitement frightened her so much that she opened her mouth to scream, but the sound died in her throat.

"How has this terrible past been recalled?" cried Villefort; "how is it that it has escaped from the depths of the tomb and the recesses of our hearts, where it was buried, to visit us now, like a phantom, whitening our cheeks and flushing our brows with shame?"

"Alas," said Hermine, "doubtless it is chance."

"Chance?" replied Villefort; "No, no, madame, there is no such thing as chance."

"Oh, yes; has not a fatal chance revealed all this? Was it not by chance the Count of Monte Cristo bought that house? Was it not by chance he caused the earth to be dug up? Is it not by chance that the unfortunate child was disinterred under the trees?—that poor innocent offspring of mine, which I never even kissed, but for whom I wept many, many tears. Ah, my heart clung to the count when he mentioned the dear spoil found beneath the flowers."

"Well, no, madame,—this is the terrible news I have to tell you," said Villefort in a hollow voice—"no, nothing was found beneath the flowers; there was no child disinterred—no. You must not weep, no, you must not groan, you must tremble!"

"What can you mean?" asked Madame Danglars, shuddering.

"I mean that M. de Monte Cristo, digging underneath these trees, found neither skeleton nor chest, because neither of them was there!"

"Neither of them there?" repeated Madame Danglars, her staring, wide-open eyes expressing her alarm. "Neither of them there!" she again said, as though striving to impress herself with the meaning of the words which escaped her.

"No," said Villefort, burying his face in his hands, "no, a hundred times no!"

"Then you did not bury the poor child there, sir? Why did you deceive me? Where did you place it? tell me—where?"

"There! But listen to me—listen—and you will pity me who has for twenty years alone borne the heavy burden of grief I am about to reveal, without casting the least portion upon you."

"Oh, you frighten me! But speak; I will listen."

"You recollect that sad night, when you were half-expiring on that bed in the red damask room, while I, scarcely less agitated than you, awaited your delivery. The child was born, was given to me—motionless, breathless, voiceless; we thought it dead."

Madame Danglars moved rapidly, as though she would spring from her chair, but Villefort stopped, and clasped his hands as if to implore her attention.

"We thought it dead," he repeated; "I placed it in the chest, which was to take the place of a coffin; I descended to the garden, I dug a hole, and then flung it down in haste. Scarcely had I covered it with earth, when the arm of the Corsican was stretched towards me; I saw a shadow rise, and, at the same time, a flash of light. I felt pain; I wished to cry out, but an icy shiver ran through my veins and stifled my voice; I fell lifeless, and fancied myself killed. Never shall I forget your sublime courage, when, having returned to consciousness, I dragged myself to the foot of the stairs, and you, almost dying yourself, came to meet me. We were obliged to keep silent upon the dreadful catastrophe. You had the fortitude to regain the house, assisted by your nurse. A duel was the pretext for my wound. Though we scarcely expected it, our secret remained in our own keeping alone. I was taken to Versailles; for three months I struggled with death; at last, as I seemed to cling to life, I was ordered to the South. Four men carried me from Paris to Châlons, walking six leagues a day; Madame de Villefort followed the litter in her carriage. At Châlons I was put upon the Saône, thence I passed on to the Rhône, whence I descended, merely with the current, to Arles; at Arles I was again placed on my litter, and continued my journey to Marseilles. My recovery lasted six months. I never heard you mentioned, and I did not dare inquire for you. When I returned to Paris, I learned that you, the widow of M. de Nargonne, had married M. Danglars.

"What was the subject of my thoughts from the time consciousness returned to me? Always the same—always the child's corpse, coming every night in my dreams, rising from the earth, and hovering over the grave with menacing look and gesture. I inquired immediately on my return to Paris; the house had not been inhabited since we left it, but it had just been let for nine years. I found the tenant. I pretended that I disliked the idea that a house belonging to my wife's father and mother should pass into the hands of strangers. I offered to pay them for cancelling the lease; they demanded 6,000 francs. I would have given 10,000—I would have given 20,000. I had the money with me; I made the tenant sign the deed of resilition, and when I had obtained what I so much wanted, I galloped to Auteuil. No one had entered the house since I had left it.

"It was five o'clock in the afternoon; I ascended into the red room, and waited for night. There all the thoughts which had disturbed me during my year of constant agony came back with double force. The Corsican, who had declared the vendetta against me, who had followed me from Nîmes to Paris, who had hid himself in the garden, who had struck me, had seen me dig the grave, had seen me inter the child,—he might become acquainted with your person,—nay, he might even then have known it. Would he not one day make you pay for keeping this terrible secret? Would it not be a sweet revenge for him when he found that I had not died from the blow of his dagger? It was therefore necessary, before everything else, and at all risks, that I should cause all traces of the past to disappear—that I should destroy every material vestige; too much reality would always remain in my recollection. It was for this I had annulled the lease—it was for this I had come—it was for this I was waiting.

"Night arrived; I allowed it to become quite dark. I was without a light in that room; when the wind shook all the doors, behind which I continually expected to see some spy concealed, I trembled. I seemed everywhere to hear your moans behind me in the bed, and I dared not turn around. My heart beat so violently that I feared my wound would open. At length, one by one, all the noises in the neighborhood ceased. I understood that I had nothing to fear, that I should neither be seen nor heard, so I decided upon descending to the garden.

"Listen, Hermine; I consider myself as brave as most men, but when I drew from my breast the little key of the staircase, which I had found in my coat—that little key we both used to cherish so much, which you wished to have fastened to a golden ring—when I opened the door, and saw the pale moon shedding a long stream of white light on the spiral staircase like a spectre, I leaned against the wall, and nearly shrieked. I seemed to be going mad. At last I mastered my agitation. I descended the staircase step by step; the only thing I could not conquer was a strange trembling in my knees. I grasped the railings; if I had relaxed my hold for a moment, I should have fallen. I reached the lower door. Outside this door a spade was placed against the wall; I took it, and advanced towards the thicket. I had provided myself with a dark lantern. In the middle of the lawn I stopped to light it, then I continued my path.

"It was the end of November, all the verdure of the garden had disappeared, the trees were nothing more than skeletons with their long bony arms, and the dead leaves sounded on the gravel under my feet. My terror overcame me to such a degree as I approached the thicket, that I took a pistol from my pocket and armed myself. I fancied continually that I saw the figure of the Corsican between the branches. I examined the thicket with my dark lantern; it was empty. I looked carefully around; I was indeed alone,—no noise disturbed the silence but the owl, whose piercing cry seemed to be calling up the phantoms of the night. I tied my lantern to a forked branch I had noticed a year before at the precise spot where I stopped to dig the hole.

"The grass had grown very thickly there during the summer, and when autumn arrived no one had been there to mow it. Still one place where the grass was thin attracted my attention; it evidently was there I had turned up the ground. I went to work. The hour, then, for which I had been waiting during the last year had at length arrived. How I worked, how I hoped, how I struck every piece of turf, thinking to find some resistance to my spade! But no, I found nothing, though I had made a hole twice as large as the first. I thought I had been deceived—had mistaken the spot. I turned around, I looked at the trees, I tried to recall the details which had struck me at the time. A cold, sharp wind whistled through the leafless branches, and yet the drops fell from my forehead. I recollected that I was stabbed just as I was trampling the ground to fill up the hole; while doing so I had leaned against a laburnum; behind me was an artificial rockery, intended to serve as a resting-place for persons walking in the garden; in falling, my hand, relaxing its hold of the laburnum, felt the coldness of the stone. On my right I saw the tree, behind me the rock. I stood in the same attitude, and threw myself down. I rose, and again began digging and enlarging the hole; still I found nothing, nothing—the chest was no longer there!"

"The chest no longer there?" murmured Madame Danglars, choking with fear.

"Think not I contented myself with this one effort," continued Villefort. "No; I searched the whole thicket. I thought the assassin, having discovered the chest, and supposing it to be a treasure, had intended carrying it off, but, perceiving his error, had dug another hole, and deposited it there; but I could find nothing. Then the idea struck me that he had not taken these precautions, and had simply thrown it in a corner. In the last case I must wait for daylight to renew my search. I remained in the room and waited."

"Oh, Heaven!"

When daylight dawned I went down again. My first visit was to the thicket. I hoped to find some traces which had escaped me in the darkness. I had turned up the earth over a surface of more than twenty feet square, and a depth of two feet. A laborer would not have done in a day what occupied me an hour. But I could find nothing—absolutely nothing. Then I renewed the search. Supposing it had been thrown aside, it would probably be on the path which led to the little gate; but this examination was as useless as the first, and with a bursting heart I returned to the thicket, which now contained no hope for me."

"Oh," cried Madame Danglars, "it was enough to drive you mad!"

"I hoped for a moment that it might," said Villefort; "but that happiness was denied me. However, recovering my strength and my ideas, 'Why,' said I, 'should that man have carried away the corpse?'"

"But you said," replied Madame Danglars, "he would require it as a proof."

"Ah, no, madame, that could not be. Dead bodies are not kept a year; they are shown to a magistrate, and the evidence is taken. Now, nothing of the kind has happened."

"What then?" asked Hermine, trembling violently.

"Something more terrible, more fatal, more alarming for us—the child was, perhaps, alive, and the assassin may have saved it!"

Madame Danglars uttered a piercing cry, and, seizing Villefort's hands, exclaimed, "My child was alive?" said she; "you buried my child alive? You were not certain my child was dead, and you buried it? Ah—"

Madame Danglars had risen, and stood before the procureur, whose hands she wrung in her feeble grasp.

"I know not; I merely suppose so, as I might suppose anything else," replied Villefort with a look so fixed, it indicated that his powerful mind was on the verge of despair and madness.

"Ah, my child, my poor child!" cried the baroness, falling on her chair, and stifling her sobs in her handkerchief. Villefort, becoming somewhat reassured, perceived that to avert the maternal storm gathering over his head, he must inspire Madame Danglars with the terror he felt.

"You understand, then, that if it were so," said he, rising in his turn, and approaching the baroness, to speak to her in a lower tone, "we are lost. This child lives, and someone knows it lives—someone is in possession of our secret; and since Monte Cristo speaks before us of a child disinterred, when that child could not be found, it is he who is in possession of our secret."

"Just God, avenging God!" murmured Madame Danglars.

Villefort's only answer was a stifled groan.

"But the child—the child, sir?" repeated the agitated mother.

"How I have searched for him," replied Villefort, wringing his hands; "how I have called him in my long sleepless nights; how I have longed for royal wealth to purchase a million of secrets from a million of men, and to find mine among them! At last, one day, when for the hundredth time I took up my spade, I asked myself again and again what the Corsican could have done with the child. A child encumbers a fugitive; perhaps, on perceiving it was still alive, he had thrown it into the river."

"Impossible!" cried Madame Danglars: "a man may murder another out of revenge, but he would not deliberately drown a child."

"Perhaps," continued Villefort, "he had put it in the foundling hospital."

"Oh, yes, yes," cried the baroness; "my child is there!"

"I ran to the hospital, and learned that the same night—the night of the 20th of September—a child had been brought there, wrapped in part of a fine linen napkin, purposely torn in half. This portion of the napkin was marked with half a baron's crown, and the letter H."

"Truly, truly," said Madame Danglars, "all my linen is marked thus; Monsieur de Nargonne was a baron, and my name is Hermine. Thank God, my child was not then dead!"

"No, it was not dead."

"And you can tell me so without fearing to make me die of joy? Where is the child?"

Villefort shrugged his shoulders.

"Do I know?" said he; "and do you believe that if I knew I would relate to you all its trials and all its adventures as would a dramatist or a novel writer? Alas, no, I know not. A woman, about six months after, came to claim it with the other half of the napkin. This woman gave all the requisite particulars, and it was intrusted to her."

"But you should have inquired for the woman; you should have traced her."

"And what do you think I did? I feigned a criminal process, and employed all the most acute bloodhounds and skilful agents in search of her. They traced her to Châlons, and there they lost her."

"They lost her?"

"Yes, forever."

Madame Danglars had listened to this recital with a sigh, a tear, or a shriek for every detail. "And this is all?" said she; "and you stopped there?"

"Oh, no," said Villefort; "I never ceased to search and to inquire. However, the last two or three years I had allowed myself some respite. But now I will begin with more perseverance and fury than ever, since fear urges me, not my conscience."

"But," replied Madame Danglars, "the Count of Monte Cristo can know nothing, or he would not seek our society as he does."

"Oh, the wickedness of man is very great," said Villefort, "since it surpasses the goodness of God. Did you observe that man's eyes while he was speaking to us?"

"No."

"But have you ever watched him carefully?"

"Doubtless he is capricious, but that is all; one thing alone struck me,—of all the exquisite things he placed before us, he touched nothing. I might have suspected he was poisoning us."

"And you see you would have been deceived."

"Yes, doubtless."

"But believe me, that man has other projects. For that reason I wished to see you, to speak to you, to warn you against everyone, but especially against him. Tell me," cried Villefort, fixing his eyes more steadfastly on her than he had ever done before, "did you ever reveal to anyone our connection?"

"Never, to anyone."

"You understand me," replied Villefort, affectionately; "when I say anyone,—pardon my urgency,—to anyone living I mean?"

"Yes, yes, I understand very well," ejaculated the baroness; "never, I swear to you."

"Were you ever in the habit of writing in the evening what had transpired in the morning? Do you keep a journal?"

"No, my life has been passed in frivolity; I wish to forget it myself."

"Do you talk in your sleep?"

"I sleep soundly, like a child; do you not remember?"

The color mounted to the baroness's face, and Villefort turned awfully pale.

"It is true," said he, in so low a tone that he could hardly be heard.

"Well?" said the baroness.

"Well, I understand what I now have to do," replied Villefort. "In less than one week from this time I will ascertain who this M. de Monte Cristo is, whence he comes, where he goes, and why he speaks in our presence of children that have been disinterred in a garden."

Villefort pronounced these words with an accent which would have made the count shudder had he heard him. Then he pressed the hand the baroness reluctantly gave him, and led her respectfully back to the door. Madame Danglars returned in another cab to the passage, on the other side of which she found her carriage, and her coachman sleeping peacefully on his box while waiting for her.

Study Guide Questions

For Students:

1. Who visits the office of the King's Attorney?
2. What happened in the red room of the house in Auteuil?
3. What does M. de Villefort tell Madame Danglars about the casket?

For Reading Club:

1. Villefort believes that he has been a victim of circumstances. Do you agree?
2. Discuss Villefort's past relationship with Hermine.
3. What does M. de Villefort decide to do at the end of the chapter?

CHAPTER 68

A Summer Ball

The same day during the interview between Madame Danglars and the procureur, a travelling-carriage entered the Rue du Helder, passed through the gateway of No. 27, and stopped in the yard. In a moment the door was opened, and Madame de Morcerf alighted, leaning on her son's arm. Albert soon left her, ordered his horses, and having arranged his toilet, drove to the Champs-Élysées, to the house of Monte Cristo.

The count received him with his habitual smile. It was a strange thing that no one ever appeared to advance a step in that man's favor. Those who would, as it were, force a passage to his heart, found an impassable barrier. Morcerf, who ran towards him with open arms, was chilled as he drew near, in spite of the friendly smile, and simply held out his hand. Monte Cristo shook it coldly, according to his invariable practice.

"Here I am, dear count."

"Welcome home again."

"I arrived an hour since."

"From Dieppe?"

"No, from Tréport."

"Indeed?"

"And I have come at once to see you."

"That is extremely kind of you," said Monte Cristo with a tone of perfect indifference.

"And what is the news?"

"You should not ask a stranger, a foreigner, for news."

"I know it, but in asking for news, I mean, have you done anything for me?"

"Had you commissioned me?" said Monte Cristo, feigning uneasiness.

"Come, come," said Albert, "do not assume so much indifference. It is said, sympathy travels rapidly, and when at Tréport, I felt the electric shock; you have either been working for me or thinking of me."

"Possibly," said Monte Cristo, "I have indeed thought of you, but the magnetic wire I was guiding acted, indeed, without my knowledge."

"Indeed! Pray tell me how it happened."

"Willingly. M. Danglars dined with me."

"I know it; to avoid meeting him, my mother and I left town."

"But he met here M. Andrea Cavalcanti."

"Your Italian prince?"

"Not so fast; M. Andrea only calls himself count."

"Calls himself, do you say?"

"Yes, calls himself."

"Is he not a count?"

"What can I know of him? He calls himself so. I, of course, give him the same title, and everyone else does likewise."

"What a strange man you are! What next? You say M. Danglars dined here?"

"Yes, with Count Cavalcanti, the marquis his father, Madame Danglars, M. and Madame de Villefort,—charming people,—M. Debray, Maximilian Morrel, and M. de Château-Renaud."

"Did they speak of me?"

"Not a word."

"So much the worse."

"Why so? I thought you wished them to forget you?"

"If they did not speak of me, I am sure they thought about me, and I am in despair."

"How will that affect you, since Mademoiselle Danglars was not among the number here who thought of you? Truly, she might have thought of you at home."

"I have no fear of that; or, if she did, it was only in the same way in which I think of her."

"Touching sympathy! So you hate each other?" said the count.

"Listen," said Morcerf—"if Mademoiselle Danglars were disposed to take pity on my supposed martyrdom on her account, and would dispense with all matrimonial formalities between our two families, I am ready to agree to the arrangement. In a word, Mademoiselle Danglars would make a charming mistress—but a wife—*diable!*"

"And this," said Monte Cristo, "is your opinion of your intended spouse?"

"Yes; it is rather unkind, I acknowledge, but it is true. But as this dream cannot be realized, since Mademoiselle Danglars must become my lawful wife, live perpetually with me, sing to me, compose verses and music within ten paces of me, and that for my whole life, it frightens me. One may forsake a mistress, but a wife,—good heavens! There she must always be; and to marry Mademoiselle Danglars would be awful."

"You are difficult to please, viscount."

"Yes, for I often wish for what is impossible."

"What is that?"

"To find such a wife as my father found."

Monte Cristo turned pale, and looked at Albert, while playing with some magnificent pistols.

"Your father was fortunate, then?" said he.

"You know my opinion of my mother, count; look at her,—still beautiful, witty, more charming than ever. For any other son to have stayed with his mother for four days at Tréport, it would have been a condescension or a martyrdom, while I return, more contented, more peaceful—shall I say more poetic!—than if I had taken Queen Mab or Titania as my companion."

"That is an overwhelming demonstration, and you would make everyone vow to live a single life."

"Such are my reasons for not liking to marry Mademoiselle Danglars. Have you ever noticed how much a thing is heightened in value when we obtain possession of it? The diamond which glittered in the window at Marlé's or Fossin's shines with more splendor when it is our own; but if we are compelled to acknowledge the superiority of another, and still must retain the one that is inferior, do you not know what we have to endure?"

"Worldling," murmured the count.

"Thus I shall rejoice when Mademoiselle Eugénie perceives I am but a pitiful atom, with scarcely as many hundred thousand francs as she has millions." Monte Cristo smiled. "One plan occurred to me," continued Albert; "Franz likes all that is eccentric; I tried to make him fall in love with Mademoiselle Danglars; but in spite of four letters, written in the most alluring style, he invariably answered: 'My eccentricity may be great, but it will not make me break my promise.'"

"That is what I call devoted friendship, to recommend to another one whom you would not marry yourself." Albert smiled.

"Apropos," continued he, "Franz is coming soon, but it will not interest you; you dislike him, I think?"

"I?" said Monte Cristo; "my dear viscount, how have you discovered that I did not like M. Franz! I like everyone."

"And you include me in the expression everyone—many thanks!"

"Let us not mistake," said Monte Cristo; "I love everyone as God commands us to love our neighbor, as Christians; but I thoroughly hate but a few. Let us return to M. Franz d'Épinay. Did you say he was coming?"

"Yes; summoned by M. de Villefort, who is apparently as anxious to get Mademoiselle Valentine married as M. Danglars is to see Mademoiselle Eugénie settled. It must be a very irksome office to be the father of a grown-up daughter; it seems to make one feverish, and to raise one's pulse to ninety beats a minute until the deed is done."

"But M. d'Épinay, unlike you, bears his misfortune patiently."

"Still more, he talks seriously about the matter, puts on a white tie, and speaks of his family. He entertains a very high opinion of M. and Madame de Villefort."

"Which they deserve, do they not?"

"I believe they do. M. de Villefort has always passed for a severe but a just man."

"There is, then, one," said Monte Cristo, "whom you do not condemn like poor Danglars?"

"Because I am not compelled to marry his daughter perhaps," replied Albert, laughing.

"Indeed, my dear sir," said Monte Cristo, "you are revoltingly foppish."

"I foppish? how do you mean?"

"Yes; pray take a cigar, and cease to defend yourself, and to struggle to escape marrying Mademoiselle Danglars. Let things take their course; perhaps you may not have to retract."

"Bah!" said Albert, staring.

"Doubtless, my dear viscount, you will not be taken by force; and seriously, do you wish to break off your engagement?"

"I would give a hundred thousand francs to be able to do so."

"Then make yourself quite easy. M. Danglars would give double that sum to attain the same end."

"Am I, indeed, so happy?" said Albert, who still could not prevent an almost imperceptible cloud passing across his brow. "But, my dear count, has M. Danglars any reason?"

"Ah! there is your proud and selfish nature. You would expose the self-love of another with a hatchet, but you shrink if your own is attacked with a needle."

"But yet, M. Danglars appeared—"

"Delighted with you, was he not? Well, he is a man of bad taste, and is still more enchanted with another. I know not whom; look and judge for yourself."

"Thank you, I understand. But my mother—no, not my mother; I mistake—my father intends giving a ball."

"A ball at this season?"

"Summer balls are fashionable."

"If they were not, the countess has only to wish it, and they would become so."

"You are right; You know they are select affairs; those who remain in Paris in July must be true Parisians. Will you take charge of our invitation to Messieurs Cavalcanti?"

"When will it take place?"

"On Saturday."

"M. Cavalcanti's father will be gone."

"But the son will be here; will you invite young M. Cavalcanti?"

"I do not know him, viscount."

"You do not know him?"

"No, I never saw him until a few days since, and am not responsible for him."

"But you receive him at your house?"

"That is another thing: he was recommended to me by a good abbé, who may be deceived. Give him a direct invitation, but do not ask me to present him. If he were afterwards to marry Mademoiselle Danglars, you would accuse me of intrigue, and would be challenging me,—besides, I may not be there myself."

"Where?"

"At your ball."

"Why should you not be there?"

"Because you have not yet invited me."

"But I come expressly for that purpose."

"You are very kind, but I may be prevented."

"If I tell you one thing, you will be so amiable as to set aside all impediments."

"Tell me what it is."

"My mother begs you to come."

"The Comtesse de Morcerf?" said Monte Cristo, starting.

"Ah, count," said Albert, "I assure you Madame de Morcerf speaks freely to me, and if you have not felt those sympathetic fibres of which I spoke just now thrill within you, you must be entirely devoid of them, for during the last four days we have spoken of no one else."

"You have talked of me?"

"Yes, that is the penalty of being a living puzzle!"

"Then I am also a puzzle to your mother? I should have thought her too reasonable to be led by imagination."

"A problem, my dear count, for everyone—for my mother as well as others; much studied, but not solved, you still remain an enigma, do not fear. My mother is only astonished that you remain so long unsolved. I believe, while the Countess G— takes you for Lord Ruthven, my mother imagines you to be Cagliostro or the Count Saint-Germain. The first opportunity you have, confirm her in her opinion; it will be easy for you, as you have the philosophy of the one and the wit of the other."

"I thank you for the warning," said the count; "I shall endeavor to be prepared for all suppositions."

"You will, then, come on Saturday?"

"Yes, since Madame de Morcerf invites me."

"You are very kind."

"Will M. Danglars be there?"

"He has already been invited by my father. We shall try to persuade the great d'Aguesseau,[4] M. de Villefort, to come, but have not much hope of seeing him."

"'Never despair of anything,' says the proverb."

"Do you dance, count?"

"I dance?"

"Yes, you; it would not be astonishing."

"That is very well before one is over forty. No, I do not dance, but I like to see others do so. Does Madame de Morcerf dance?"

"Never; you can talk to her, she so delights in your conversation."

"Indeed?"

"Yes, truly; and I assure you. You are the only man of whom I have heard her speak with interest." Albert rose and took his hat; the count conducted him to the door.

"I have one thing to reproach myself with," said he, stopping Albert on the steps. "What is it?"

"I have spoken to you indiscreetly about Danglars."

"On the contrary, speak to me always in the same strain about him."

"I am glad to be reassured on that point. Apropos, when do you aspect M. d'Épinay?"

"Five or six days hence at the latest."

"And when is he to be married?"

---

[4] Magistrate and orator of great eloquence—chancellor of France under Louis XV.

"Immediately on the arrival of M. and Madame de Saint-Méran."

"Bring him to see me. Although you say I do not like him, I assure you I shall be happy to see him."

"I will obey your orders, my lord."

"Good-bye."

"Until Saturday, when I may expect you, may I not?"

"Yes, I promised you." The Count watched Albert, waving his hand to him. When he had mounted his phaeton, Monte Cristo turned, and seeing Bertuccio, "What news?" said he.

"She went to the Palais," replied the steward.

"Did she stay long there?"

"An hour and a half."

"Did she return home?"

"Directly."

"Well, my dear Bertuccio," said the count, "I now advise you to go in quest of the little estate I spoke to you of in Normandy."

Bertuccio bowed, and as his wishes were in perfect harmony with the order he had received, he started the same evening.

Study Guide Questions

For Students:

1. Who comes to visit the Count?
2. Who is hosting the summer ball?
3. Who according to Albert wants the Count to attend the ball?

For Reading Club:

1. Discuss Albert's opinion of his mother. What does it tell you about the mother-son relationship?
2. Why do you think the fathers (Villefort and Danglars) are keen on marrying their daughters without their consent?
3. Why do you think Madame de Morcerf likes the Count?

CHAPTER 69
The Inquiry

M. de Villefort kept the promise he had made to Madame Danglars, to endeavor to find out how the Count of Monte Cristo had discovered the history of the house at Auteuil. He wrote the same day for the required information to M. de Boville, who, from having been an inspector of prisons, was promoted to a high office in the police; and the latter begged for two days time to ascertain exactly who would be most likely to give him full particulars. At the end of the second day M. de Villefort received the following note:

"The person called the Count of Monte Cristo is an intimate acquaintance of Lord Wilmore, a rich foreigner, who is sometimes seen in Paris and who is there at this moment; he is also known to the Abbé Busoni, a Sicilian priest, of high repute in the East, where he has done much good."

M. de Villefort replied by ordering the strictest inquiries to be made respecting these two persons; his orders were executed, and the following evening he received these details:

"The abbé, who was in Paris only for a month, inhabited a small two-storied house behind Saint-Sulpice; there were two rooms on each floor and he was the only tenant. The two lower rooms consisted of a dining-room, with a table, chairs, and side-board of walnut, and a wainscoted parlor, without ornaments, carpet, or timepiece. It was evident that the abbé limited himself to objects of strict necessity. He preferred to use the sitting-room upstairs, which was more library than parlor, and was furnished with theological books and parchments, in which he delighted to bury himself for months at a time, according to his valet de chambre. His valet looked at the visitors through a sort of wicket; and if their faces were unknown to him or displeased him, he replied that the abbé was not in Paris, an answer which satisfied most persons, because the abbé was known to be a great traveller. Besides, whether at home or not, whether in Paris or Cairo, the abbé always left something to give away, which the valet distributed through this wicket in his master's name. The other room near the library was a bedroom. A bed without curtains, four armchairs, and a couch, covered with yellow Utrecht velvet, composed, with a *prie-Dieu,* all its furniture.

"Lord Wilmore resided in Rue Fontaine-Saint-Georges. He was one of those English tourists who consume a large fortune in travelling. He hired the apartment in which he lived furnished, passed only a few hours in the day there, and rarely slept there. One of his peculiarities was never to speak a word of French, which he however wrote with great facility."

The day after this important information had been given to the king's attorney, a man alighted from a carriage at the corner of the Rue Férou, and rapping at an olive-green door, asked if the Abbé Busoni were within.

"No, he went out early this morning," replied the valet.

"I might not always be content with that answer," replied the visitor, "for I come from one to whom everyone must be at home. But have the kindness to give the Abbé Busoni—"

"I told you he was not at home," repeated the valet.

"Then on his return give him that card and this sealed paper. Will he be at home at eight o'clock this evening?"

"Doubtless, unless he is at work, which is the same as if he were out."

"I will come again at that time," replied the visitor, who then retired.

At the appointed hour the same man returned in the same carriage, which, instead of stopping this time at the end of the Rue Férou, drove up to the green door. He knocked, and it opened immediately to admit him. From the signs of respect the valet paid him, he saw that his note had produced a good effect.

"Is the abbé at home?" asked he.

"Yes; he is at work in his library, but he expects you, sir," replied the valet. The stranger ascended a rough staircase, and before a table, illumined by a lamp whose light was concentrated by a large shade while the rest of the apartment was in partial darkness, he perceived the abbé in a monk's dress, with a cowl on his head such as was used by learned men of the Middle Ages.

"Have I the honor of addressing the Abbé Busoni?" asked the visitor.

"Yes, sir," replied the abbé; "and you are the person whom M. de Boville, formerly an inspector of prisons, sends to me from the prefect of police?"

"Exactly, sir."

"One of the agents appointed to secure the safety of Paris?"

"Yes, sir" replied the stranger with a slight hesitation, and blushing.

The abbé replaced the large spectacles, which covered not only his eyes but his temples, and sitting down motioned to his visitor to do the same. "I am at your service, sir," said the abbé, with a marked Italian accent.

"The mission with which I am charged, sir," replied the visitor, speaking with hesitation, "is a confidential one on the part of him who fulfils it, and him by whom he is employed." The abbé bowed. "Your probity," replied the stranger, "is so well known to the prefect that he wishes as a magistrate to ascertain from you some particulars connected with the public safety, to ascertain which I am deputed to see you. It is hoped that no ties of friendship or humane consideration will induce you to conceal the truth."

"Provided, sir, the particulars you wish for do not interfere with my scruples or my conscience. I am a priest, sir, and the secrets of confession, for instance, must remain between me and God, and not between me and human justice."

"Do not alarm yourself, monsieur, we will duly respect your conscience."

At this moment the abbé pressed down his side of the shade and so raised it on the other, throwing a bright light on the stranger's face, while his own remained obscured.

"Excuse me, abbé," said the envoy of the prefect of the police, "but the light tries my eyes very much." The abbé lowered the shade.

"Now, sir, I am listening—go on."

"I will come at once to the point. Do you know the Count of Monte Cristo?"

"You mean Monsieur Zaccone, I presume?"

"Zaccone?—is not his name Monte Cristo?"

"Monte Cristo is the name of an estate, or, rather, of a rock, and not a family name."

"Well, be it so—let us not dispute about words; and since M. de Monte Cristo and M. Zaccone are the same—"

"Absolutely the same."

"Let us speak of M. Zaccone."

"Agreed."

"I asked you if you knew him?"

"Extremely well."

"Who is he?"

"The son of a rich shipbuilder in Malta."

"I know that is the report; but, as you are aware, the police does not content itself with vague reports."

"However," replied the abbé, with an affable smile, "when that report is in accordance with the truth, everybody must believe it, the police as well as all the rest."

"Are you sure of what you assert?"

"What do you mean by that question?"

"Understand, sir, I do not in the least suspect your veracity; I ask if you are certain of it?"

"I knew his father, M. Zaccone."

"Ah, indeed?"

"And when a child I often played with the son in the timber-yards."

"But whence does he derive the title of count?"

"You are aware that may be bought."

"In Italy?"

"Everywhere."

"And his immense riches, whence does he procure them?"

"They may not be so very great."

"How much do you suppose he possesses?"

"From one hundred and fifty to two hundred thousand livres per annum."

"That is reasonable," said the visitor; "I have heard he had three or four millions."

"Two hundred thousand per annum would make four millions of capital."

"But I was told he had four millions per annum."

"That is not probable."

"Do you know this Island of Monte Cristo?"

"Certainly, everyone who has come from Palermo, Naples, or Rome to France by sea must know it, since he has passed close to it and must have seen it."

"I am told it is a delightful place?"

"It is a rock."

"And why has the count bought a rock?"

"For the sake of being a count. In Italy one must have territorial possessions to be a count."

"You have, doubtless, heard the adventures of M. Zaccone's youth?"

"The father's?"

"No, the son's."

"I know nothing certain; at that period of his life, I lost sight of my young comrade."

"Was he in the wars?"

"I think he entered the service."

"In what branch?"

"In the navy."

"Are you not his confessor?"

"No, sir; I believe he is a Lutheran."

"A Lutheran?"

"I say, I believe such is the case, I do not affirm it; besides, liberty of conscience is established in France."

"Doubtless, and we are not now inquiring into his creed, but his actions; in the name of the prefect of police, I ask you what you know of him.

"He passes for a very charitable man. Our holy father, the pope, has made him a knight of Jesus Christ for the services he rendered to the Christians in the East; he has five or six rings as testimonials from Eastern monarchs of his services."

"Does he wear them?"

"No, but he is proud of them; he is better pleased with rewards given to the benefactors of man than to his destroyers."

"He is a Quaker then?"

"Exactly, he is a Quaker, with the exception of the peculiar dress."

"Has he any friends?"

"Yes, everyone who knows him is his friend."

"But has he any enemies?"

"One only."

"What is his name?"

"Lord Wilmore."

"Where is he?"

"He is in Paris just now."

"Can he give me any particulars?"

"Important ones; he was in India with Zaccone."

"Do you know his abode?"

"It's somewhere in the Chaussée d'Antin; but I know neither the street nor the number."

"Are you at variance with the Englishman?"

"I love Zaccone, and he hates him; we are consequently not friends."

"Do you think the Count of Monte Cristo had ever been in France before he made this visit to Paris?"

"To that question I can answer positively; no, sir, he had not, because he applied to me six months ago for the particulars he required, and as I did not know when I might again come to Paris, I recommended M. Cavalcanti to him."

"Andrea?"

"No, Bartolomeo, his father."

"Now, sir, I have but one question more to ask, and I charge you, in the name of honor, of humanity, and of religion, to answer me candidly."

"What is it, sir?"

"Do you know with what design M. de Monte Cristo purchased a house at Auteuil?"

"Certainly, for he told me."

"What is it, sir?"

"To make a lunatic asylum of it, similar to that founded by the Count of Pisani at Palermo. Do you know about that institution?"

"I have heard of it."

"It is a magnificent charity." Having said this, the abbé bowed to imply he wished to pursue his studies.

The visitor either understood the abbé's meaning, or had no more questions to ask; he arose, and the abbé accompanied him to the door.

"You are a great almsgiver," said the visitor, "and although you are said to be rich, I will venture to offer you something for your poor people; will you accept my offering?"

"I thank you, sir; I am only jealous in one thing, and that is that the relief I give should be entirely from my own resources."

"However—"

"My resolution, sir, is unchangeable, but you have only to search for yourself and you will find, alas, but too many objects upon whom to exercise your benevolence."

The abbé once more bowed as he opened the door, the stranger bowed and took his leave, and the carriage conveyed him straight to the house of M. de Villefort. An hour afterwards the carriage was again ordered, and this time it went to the Rue Fontaine-Saint-Georges, and stopped at No. 5, where Lord Wilmore lived. The stranger had written to Lord Wilmore, requesting an interview, which the latter had fixed for ten o'clock. As the envoy of the prefect of police arrived ten minutes before ten, he was told that Lord Wilmore, who was precision and punctuality personified, was not yet come in, but that he would be sure to return as the clock struck.

The visitor was introduced into the drawing-room, which was like all other furnished drawing-rooms. A mantle-piece, with two modern Sèvres vases, a timepiece representing Cupid with his bent bow, a mirror with an engraving on each side—one representing Homer carrying his guide, the other, Belisarius begging—a grayish paper; red and black tapestry—such was the appearance of Lord Wilmore's drawing-room.

It was illuminated by lamps with ground-glass shades which gave only a feeble light, as if out of consideration for the envoy's weak sight. After ten minutes' expectation the clock struck ten; at the fifth stroke the door opened and Lord Wilmore appeared. He was rather above the middle height, with thin reddish whiskers, light complexion and light hair, turning rather gray. He was dressed with all the English peculiarity, namely, in a blue coat, with gilt buttons and high collar, in the fashion of 1811, a white kerseymere waistcoat, and nankeen pantaloons, three inches too short, but which were prevented by straps from slipping up to the knee. His first remark on entering was:

"You know, sir, I do not speak French?"

"I know you do not like to converse in our language," replied the envoy.

"But you may use it," replied Lord Wilmore; "I understand it."

"And I," replied the visitor, changing his idiom, "know enough of English to keep up the conversation. Do not put yourself to the slightest inconvenience."

"Aw?" said Lord Wilmore, with that tone which is only known to natives of Great Britain.

The envoy presented his letter of introduction, which the latter read with English coolness, and having finished:

"I understand," said he, "perfectly."

Then began the questions, which were similar to those which had been addressed to the Abbé Busoni. But as Lord Wilmore, in the character of the count's enemy, was less restrained in his answers, they were more numerous; he described the youth of Monte Cristo, who he said, at ten years of age, entered the service of one of the petty sovereigns of India who make war on the English. It was there Wilmore had first met him and fought against him; and in that war Zaccone had been taken prisoner, sent to England, and consigned to the hulks, whence he had escaped by swimming. Then began his travels, his duels, his caprices; then the insurrection in Greece broke out, and he had served in the Grecian ranks. While in that service he had discovered a silver mine in the mountains of Thessaly, but he had been careful to conceal it from everyone. After the battle of Navarino, when the Greek government was consolidated, he asked of King Otho a mining grant for that district, which was given him. Hence that immense fortune, which, in Lord Wilmore's opinion, possibly amounted to one or two millions per annum,—a precarious fortune, which might be momentarily lost by the failure of the mine.

"But," asked the visitor, "do you know why he came to France?"

"He is speculating in railways," said Lord Wilmore, "and as he is an expert chemist and physicist, he has invented a new system of telegraphy, which he is seeking to bring to perfection."

"How much does he spend yearly?" asked the prefect.

"Not more than five or six hundred thousand francs," said Lord Wilmore; "he is a miser." Hatred evidently inspired the Englishman, who, knowing no other reproach to bring on the count, accused him of avarice.

"Do you know his house at Auteuil?"

"Certainly."

"What do you know respecting it?"

"Do you wish to know why he bought it?"

"Yes."

"The count is a speculator, who will certainly ruin himself in experiments. He supposes there is in the neighborhood of the house he has bought a mineral spring equal to those at Bagnères, Luchon, and Cauterets. He is going to turn his house into a *Badhaus*, as the Germans term it. He has already dug up all the garden two or three times to find the famous spring, and, being unsuccessful, he will soon purchase all the contiguous houses. Now, as I dislike him, and hope his railway, his electric telegraph, or his search for baths, will ruin him, I am watching for his discomfiture, which must soon take place."

"What was the cause of your quarrel?"

"When he was in England he seduced the wife of one of my friends."

"Why do you not seek revenge?"

"I have already fought three duels with him," said the Englishman, "the first with the pistol, the second with the sword, and the third with the sabre."

"And what was the result of those duels?"

"The first time, he broke my arm; the second, he wounded me in the breast; and the third time, made this large wound." The Englishman turned down his shirt-collar, and showed a scar, whose redness proved it to be a recent one. "So that, you see, there is a deadly feud between us."

"But," said the envoy, "you do not go about it in the right way to kill him, if I understand you correctly."

"Aw?" said the Englishman, "I practice shooting every day, and every other day Grisier comes to my house."

This was all the visitor wished to ascertain, or, rather, all the Englishman appeared to know. The agent arose, and having bowed to Lord Wilmore, who returned his salutation with the stiff politeness of the English, he retired. Lord Wilmore, having heard the door close after him, returned to his bedroom, where with one hand he pulled off his light hair, his red whiskers, his false jaw, and his wound, to resume the black hair, dark complexion, and pearly teeth of the Count of Monte Cristo.

It was M. de Villefort, and not the prefect, who returned to the house of M. de Villefort. The procureur felt more at ease, although he had learned nothing really satisfactory, and, for the first time since the dinner-party at Auteuil, he slept soundly.

Study Guide Questions

For Students:

1. What information does Villefort receive about the Count at the beginning of this chapter?
2. Who according to Abbé Busoni is the Count's only enemy?
3. What is the information revealed at the end of the chapter about Abbé Busoni and Lord Wilmore?

For Reading Club:

1. What does Abbé Busoni say about the Count?
2. What does Lord Wilmore say about the Count?
3. Discuss the inquiry made by M. de Villefort in this chapter.

CHAPTER 70

The Ball

It was in the warmest days of July, when in due course of time the Saturday arrived upon which the ball was to take place at M. de Morcerf's. It was ten o'clock at night; the branches of the great trees in the garden of the count's house stood out boldly against the azure canopy of heaven, which was studded with golden stars, but where the last fleeting clouds of a vanishing storm yet lingered.

From the apartments on the ground floor might be heard the sound of music, with the whirl of the waltz and galop, while brilliant streams of light shone through the openings of the Venetian blinds. At this moment the garden was only occupied by about ten servants, who had just received orders from their mistress to prepare the supper, the serenity of the weather continuing to increase. Until now, it had been undecided whether the supper should take place in the dining-room, or under a long tent erected on the lawn, but the beautiful blue sky, studded with stars, had settled the question in favor of the lawn.

The gardens were illuminated with colored lanterns, according to the Italian custom, and, as is usual in countries where the luxuries of the table—the rarest of all luxuries in their complete form—are well understood, the supper-table was loaded with wax-lights and flowers.

At the time the Countess of Morcerf returned to the rooms, after giving her orders, many guests were arriving, more attracted by the charming hospitality of the countess than by the distinguished position of the count; for, owing to the good taste of Mercédès, one was sure of finding some devices at her entertainment worthy of describing, or even copying in case of need.

Madame Danglars, in whom the events we have related had caused deep anxiety, had hesitated about going to Madame de Morcerf's, when during the morning her carriage happened to meet that of Villefort. The latter made a sign, and when the carriages had drawn close together, said:

"You are going to Madame de Morcerf's, are you not?"

"No," replied Madame Danglars, "I am too ill."

"You are wrong," replied Villefort, significantly; "it is important that you should be seen there."

"Do you think so?" asked the baroness.

"I do."

"In that case I will go."

And the two carriages passed on towards their different destinations. Madame Danglars therefore came, not only beautiful in person, but radiant with splendor; she entered by one door at the time when Mercédès appeared at the door. The countess took Albert to meet Madame Danglars. He approached, paid her some well merited compliments on her toilet, and offered his arm to conduct her to a seat. Albert looked around him.

"You are looking for my daughter?" said the baroness, smiling.

"I confess it," replied Albert. "Could you have been so cruel as not to bring her?"

"Calm yourself. She has met Mademoiselle de Villefort, and has taken her arm; see, they are following us, both in white dresses, one with a bouquet of camellias, the other with one of myosotis. But tell me—"

"Well, what do you wish to know?"

"Will not the Count of Monte Cristo be here tonight?"

"Seventeen!" replied Albert.

"What do you mean?"

"I only mean that the count seems the rage," replied the viscount, smiling, "and that you are the seventeenth person that has asked me the same question. The count is in fashion; I congratulate him upon it."

"And have you replied to everyone as you have to me?"

"Ah, to be sure, I have not answered you; be satisfied, we shall have this 'lion'; we are among the privileged ones."

"Were you at the Opera yesterday?"

"No."

"He was there."

"Ah, indeed? And did the eccentric person commit any new originality?"

"Can he be seen without doing so? Elssler was dancing in *Le Diable boiteux*; the Greek princess was in ecstasies. After the cachucha he placed a magnificent ring on the stem of a bouquet, and threw it to the charming danseuse, who, in the third act, to do honor to the gift, reappeared with it on her finger. And the Greek princess,—will she be here?"

"No, you will be deprived of that pleasure; her position in the count's establishment is not sufficiently understood."

"Wait; leave me here, and go and speak to Madame de Villefort, who is trying to attract your attention."

Albert bowed to Madame Danglars, and advanced towards Madame de Villefort, whose lips opened as he approached.

"I wager anything," said Albert, interrupting her, "that I know what you were about to say."

"Well, what is it?"

"If I guess rightly, will you confess it?"

"Yes."

"On your honor?"

"On my honor."

"You were going to ask me if the Count of Monte Cristo had arrived, or was expected."

"Not at all. It is not of him that I am now thinking. I was going to ask you if you had received any news of Monsieur Franz."

"Yes,—yesterday."

"What did he tell you?"

"That he was leaving at the same time as his letter."

"Well, now then, the count?"

"The count will come, of that you may be satisfied."

"You know that he has another name besides Monte Cristo?"

"No, I did not know it."

"Monte Cristo is the name of an island, and he has a family name."

"I never heard it."

"Well, then, I am better informed than you; his name is Zaccone."

"It is possible."

"He is a Maltese."

"That is also possible.

"The son of a shipowner."

"Really, you should relate all this aloud, you would have the greatest success."

"He served in India, discovered a mine in Thessaly, and comes to Paris to establish a mineral water-cure at Auteuil."

"Well, I'm sure," said Morcerf, "this is indeed news! Am I allowed to repeat it?"

"Yes, but cautiously, tell one thing at a time, and do not say I told you."

"Why so?"

"Because it is a secret just discovered."

"By whom?"

"The police."

"Then the news originated—"

"At the prefect's last night. Paris, you can understand, is astonished at the sight of such unusual splendor, and the police have made inquiries."

"Well, well! Nothing more is wanting than to arrest the count as a vagabond, on the pretext of his being too rich."

"Indeed, that doubtless would have happened if his credentials had not been so favorable."

"Poor count! And is he aware of the danger he has been in?"

"I think not."

"Then it will be but charitable to inform him. When he arrives, I will not fail to do so."

Just then, a handsome young man, with bright eyes, black hair, and glossy moustache, respectfully bowed to Madame de Villefort. Albert extended his hand.

"Madame," said Albert, "allow me to present to you M. Maximilian Morrel, captain of Spahis, one of our best, and, above all, of our bravest officers."

"I have already had the pleasure of meeting this gentleman at Auteuil, at the house of the Count of Monte Cristo," replied Madame de Villefort, turning away with marked coldness of manner.

This answer, and especially the tone in which it was uttered, chilled the heart of poor Morrel. But a recompense was in store for him; turning around, he saw near the door a beautiful fair face, whose large blue eyes were, without any marked expression, fixed upon him, while the bouquet of myosotis was gently raised to her lips.

The salutation was so well understood that Morrel, with the same expression in his eyes, placed his handkerchief to his mouth; and these two living statues, whose hearts beat so violently under their marble aspect, separated from each other by the whole length of the room, forgot themselves for a moment, or rather forgot the world in their mutual contemplation. They might have remained much longer lost in one another, without anyone noticing their abstraction. The Count of Monte Cristo had just entered.

We have already said that there was something in the count which attracted universal attention wherever he appeared. It was not the coat, unexceptional in its cut, though simple and unornamented; it was not the plain white waistcoat; it was not the trousers, that displayed the foot so perfectly formed—it was none of these things that attracted the attention,—it was his pale complexion, his waving black hair, his calm and serene expression, his dark and melancholy eye, his mouth, chiselled with such marvellous delicacy, which so easily expressed such high disdain,—these were what fixed the attention of all upon him.

Many men might have been handsomer, but certainly there could be none whose appearance was more *significant,* if the expression may be used. Everything about the count seemed to have its meaning, for the constant habit of thought which he had acquired had given an ease and vigor to the expression of his face, and even to the most trifling gesture, scarcely to be understood. Yet the Parisian world is so strange, that even all this might not have won attention had there not been connected with it a mysterious story gilded by an immense fortune.

Meanwhile he advanced through the assemblage of guests under a battery of curious glances towards Madame de Morcerf, who, standing before a mantle-piece ornamented with flowers, had seen his entrance in a looking-glass placed opposite the door, and was prepared to receive him. She turned towards him with a serene smile just at the moment he was bowing to her. No doubt she fancied the count would speak to her, while on his side the count thought she was about to address him; but both remained silent, and after a mere bow, Monte Cristo directed his steps to Albert, who received him cordially.

"Have you seen my mother?" asked Albert.

"I have just had the pleasure," replied the count; "but I have not seen your father."

"See, he is down there, talking politics with that little group of great geniuses."

"Indeed?" said Monte Cristo; "and so those gentlemen down there are men of great talent. I should not have guessed it. And for what kind of talent are they celebrated? You know there are different sorts."

"That tall, harsh-looking man is very learned, he discovered, in the neighborhood of Rome, a kind of lizard with a vertebra more than lizards usually have, and he immediately laid his discovery before the Institute. The thing was discussed for a long time, but finally decided in his favor. I can assure you the vertebra made a great noise in the learned world, and the gentleman, who was only a knight of the Legion of Honor, was made an officer."

"Come," said Monte Cristo, "this cross seems to me to be wisely awarded. I suppose, had he found another additional vertebra, they would have made him a commander."

"Very likely," said Albert.

"And who can that person be who has taken it into his head to wrap himself up in a blue coat embroidered with green?"

"Oh, that coat is not his own idea; it is the Republic's, which deputed David[5] to devise a uniform for the Academicians."

"Indeed?" said Monte Cristo; "so this gentleman is an Academician?"

"Within the last week he has been made one of the learned assembly."

"And what is his especial talent?"

"His talent? I believe he thrusts pins through the heads of rabbits, he makes fowls eat madder, and punches the spinal marrow out of dogs with whalebone."

"And he is made a member of the Academy of Sciences for this?"

"No; of the French Academy."

"But what has the French Academy to do with all this?"

"I was going to tell you. It seems—"

"That his experiments have very considerably advanced the cause of science, doubtless?"

"No; that his style of writing is very good."

"This must be very flattering to the feelings of the rabbits into whose heads he has thrust pins, to the fowls whose bones he has dyed red, and to the dogs whose spinal marrow he has punched out?"

Albert laughed.

"And the other one?" demanded the count.

"That one?"

"Yes, the third."

"The one in the dark blue coat?"

"Yes."

"He is a colleague of the count, and one of the most active opponents to the idea of providing the Chamber of Peers with a uniform. He was very successful upon that question. He stood badly with the Liberal papers, but his noble opposition to the wishes of the court is now getting him into favor with the journalists. They talk of making him an ambassador."

"And what are his claims to the peerage?"

"He has composed two or three comic operas, written four or five articles in the *Siècle*, and voted five or six years on the ministerial side."

"Bravo, viscount," said Monte Cristo, smiling; "you are a delightful *cicerone*. And now you will do me a favor, will you not?"

---

[5] Jacques-Louis David, a famous French painter (1748-1825).

"What is it?"

"Do not introduce me to any of these gentlemen; and should they wish it, you will warn me." Just then the count felt his arm pressed. He turned round; it was Danglars.

"Ah! is it you, baron?" said he.

"Why do you call me baron?" said Danglars; "you know that I care nothing for my title. I am not like you, viscount; you like your title, do you not?"

"Certainly," replied Albert, "seeing that without my title I should be nothing; while you, sacrificing the baron, would still remain the millionaire."

"Which seems to me the finest title under the royalty of July," replied Danglars.

"Unfortunately," said Monte Cristo, "one's title to a millionaire does not last for life, like that of baron, peer of France, or academician; for example, the millionaires Franck & Poulmann, of Frankfurt, who have just become bankrupts."

"Indeed?" said Danglars, becoming pale.

"Yes; I received the news this evening by a courier. I had about a million in their hands, but, warned in time, I withdrew it a month ago."

"Ah, *mon Dieu!*" exclaimed Danglars, "they have drawn on me for 200,000 francs!"

"Well, you can throw out the draft; their signature is worth five per cent."

"Yes, but it is too late," said Danglars, "I have honored their bills."

"Then," said Monte Cristo, "here are 200,000 francs gone after—"

"Hush, do not mention these things," said Danglars; then, approaching Monte Cristo, he added, "especially before young M. Cavalcanti;" after which he smiled, and turned towards the young man in question.

Albert had left the count to speak to his mother, Danglars to converse with young Cavalcanti; Monte Cristo was for an instant alone. Meanwhile the heat became excessive. The footmen were hastening through the rooms with waiters loaded with ices. Monte Cristo wiped the perspiration from his forehead, but drew back when the waiter was presented to him; he took no refreshment. Madame de Morcerf did not lose sight of Monte Cristo; she saw that he took nothing, and even noticed his gesture of refusal.

"Albert," she asked, "did you notice that?"

"What, mother?"

"That the count has never been willing to partake of food under the roof of M. de Morcerf."

"Yes; but then he breakfasted with me—indeed, he made his first appearance in the world on that occasion."

"But your house is not M. de Morcerf's," murmured Mercédès; "and since he has been here I have watched him."

"Well?"

"Well, he has taken nothing yet."

"The count is very temperate."

Mercédès smiled sadly.

"Approach him," said she, "and when the next waiter passes, insist upon his taking something."

"But why, mother?"

"Just to please me, Albert," said Mercédès. Albert kissed his mother's hand, and drew near the count. Another salver passed, loaded like the preceding ones; she saw Albert attempt to persuade the count, but he obstinately refused. Albert rejoined his mother; she was very pale.

"Well," said she, "you see he refuses?"

"Yes; but why need this annoy you?"

"You know, Albert, women are singular creatures. I should like to have seen the count take something in my house, if only an ice. Perhaps he cannot reconcile himself to the French style of living, and might prefer something else."

"Oh, no; I have seen him eat of everything in Italy; no doubt he does not feel inclined this evening."

"And besides," said the countess, "accustomed as he is to burning climates, possibly he does not feel the heat as we do."

"I do not think that, for he has complained of feeling almost suffocated, and asked why the Venetian blinds were not opened as well as the windows."

"In a word," said Mercédès, "it was a way of assuring me that his abstinence was intended."

And she left the room.

A minute afterwards the blinds were thrown open, and through the jessamine and clematis that overhung the window one could see the garden ornamented with lanterns, and the supper laid under the tent. Dancers, players, talkers, all uttered an exclamation of joy—everyone inhaled with delight the breeze that floated in. At the same time Mercédès reappeared, paler than before, but with that imperturbable expression of countenance which she sometimes wore. She went straight to the group of which her husband formed the centre.

"Do not detain those gentlemen here, count," she said; "they would prefer, I should think, to breathe in the garden rather than suffocate here, since they are not playing."

"Ah," said a gallant old general, who, in 1809, had sung *Partant pour la Syrie,*— "we will not go alone to the garden."

"Then," said Mercédès, "I will lead the way."

Turning towards Monte Cristo, she added, "count, will you oblige me with your arm?"

The count almost staggered at these simple words; then he fixed his eyes on Mercédès. It was only a momentary glance, but it seemed to the countess to have lasted for a century, so much was expressed in that one look. He offered his arm to the countess; she took it, or rather just touched it with her little hand, and they together descended the steps, lined with rhododendrons and camellias. Behind them, by another outlet, a group of about twenty persons rushed into the garden with loud exclamations of delight.

Study Guide Questions

For Students:

1. What does Madame Villefort tell Albert about the Count?
2. How does Madame Villefort react to Maximilian Morrel?
3. What does Mercédès observe about the Count?

For Reading Club:

1. Why do you think everyone at the ball is interested in the Count?
2. Discuss the interaction between Dantès and Mercédès.
3. Do you think the chapter reveals the problems of the upper class?

CHAPTER 71

Bread and Salt

Madame de Morcerf entered an archway of trees with her companion. It led through a grove of lindens to a conservatory.

"It was too warm in the room, was it not, count?" she asked.

"Yes, madame; and it was an excellent idea of yours to open the doors and the blinds." As he ceased speaking, the count felt the hand of Mercédès tremble. "But you," he said, "with that light dress, and without anything to cover you but that gauze scarf, perhaps you feel cold?"

"Do you know where I am leading you?" said the countess, without replying to the question.

"No, madame," replied Monte Cristo; "but you see I make no resistance."

"We are going to the greenhouse that you see at the other end of the grove."

The count looked at Mercédès as if to interrogate her, but she continued to walk on in silence, and he refrained from speaking. They reached the building, ornamented with magnificent fruits, which ripen at the beginning of July in the artificial temperature which takes the place of the sun, so frequently absent in our climate. The countess left the arm of Monte Cristo, and gathered a bunch of Muscatel grapes.

"See, count," she said, with a smile so sad in its expression that one could almost detect the tears on her eyelids—"see, our French grapes are not to be compared, I know, with yours of Sicily and Cyprus, but you will make allowance for our northern sun." The count bowed, but stepped back.

"Do you refuse?" said Mercédès, in a tremulous voice.

"Pray excuse me, madame," replied Monte Cristo, "but I never eat Muscatel grapes."

Mercédès let them fall, and sighed. A magnificent peach was hanging against an adjoining wall, ripened by the same artificial heat. Mercédès drew near, and plucked the fruit.

"Take this peach, then," she said. The count again refused. "What, again?" she exclaimed, in so plaintive an accent that it seemed to stifle a sob; "really, you pain me."

A long silence followed; the peach, like the grapes, fell to the ground.

"Count," added Mercédès with a supplicating glance, "there is a beautiful Arabian custom, which makes eternal friends of those who have together eaten bread and salt under the same roof."

"I know it, madame," replied the count; "but we are in France, and not in Arabia, and in France eternal friendships are as rare as the custom of dividing bread and salt with one another."

"But," said the countess, breathlessly, with her eyes fixed on Monte Cristo, whose arm she convulsively pressed with both hands, "we are friends, are we not?"

The count became pale as death, the blood rushed to his heart, and then again rising, dyed his cheeks with crimson; his eyes swam like those of a man suddenly dazzled.

"Certainly, we are friends," he replied; "why should we not be?"

The answer was so little like the one Mercédès desired, that she turned away to give vent to a sigh, which sounded more like a groan. "Thank you," she said. And they walked on again. They went the whole length of the garden without uttering a word.

"Sir," suddenly exclaimed the countess, after their walk had continued ten minutes in silence, "is it true that you have seen so much, travelled so far, and suffered so deeply?"

"I have suffered deeply, madame," answered Monte Cristo.

"But now you are happy?"

"Doubtless," replied the count, "since no one hears me complain."

"And your present happiness, has it softened your heart?"

"My present happiness equals my past misery," said the count.

"Are you not married?" asked the countess.

"I, married?" exclaimed Monte Cristo, shuddering; "who could have told you so?"

"No one told me you were, but you have frequently been seen at the Opera with a young and lovely woman."

"She is a slave whom I bought at Constantinople, madame, the daughter of a prince. I have adopted her as my daughter, having no one else to love in the world."

"You live alone, then?"

"I do."

"You have no sister—no son—no father?"

"I have no one."

"How can you exist thus without anyone to attach you to life?"

"It is not my fault, madame. At Malta, I loved a young girl, was on the point of marrying her, when war came and carried me away. I thought she loved me well enough to wait for me, and even to remain faithful to my memory. When I returned she was married. This is the history of most men who have passed twenty years of age. Perhaps my heart was weaker than the hearts of most men, and I suffered more than they would have done in my place; that is all."

The countess stopped for a moment, as if gasping for breath. "Yes," she said, "and you have still preserved this love in your heart—one can only love once—and did you ever see her again?"

"Never."

"Never?"

"I never returned to the country where she lived."

"To Malta?"

"Yes; Malta."

"She is, then, now at Malta?"

"I think so."

"And have you forgiven her for all she has made you suffer?"

"Her,—yes."

"But only her; do you then still hate those who separated you?"

"I hate them? Not at all; why should I?" The countess placed herself before Monte Cristo, still holding in her hand a portion of the perfumed grapes.

"Take some," she said.

"Madame, I never eat Muscatel grapes," replied Monte Cristo, as if the subject had not been mentioned before. The countess dashed the grapes into the nearest thicket, with a gesture of despair.

"Inflexible man!" she murmured. Monte Cristo remained as unmoved as if the reproach had not been addressed to him.

Albert at this moment ran in. "Oh, mother," he exclaimed, "such a misfortune has happened!"

"What? What has happened?" asked the countess, as though awakening from a sleep to the realities of life; "did you say a misfortune? Indeed, I should expect misfortunes."

"M. de Villefort is here."

"Well?"

"He comes to fetch his wife and daughter."

"Why so?"

"Because Madame de Saint-Méran is just arrived in Paris, bringing the news of M. de Saint-Méran's death, which took place on the first stage after he left Marseilles. Madame de Villefort, who was in very good spirits, would neither believe nor think of the misfortune, but Mademoiselle Valentine, at the first words, guessed the whole truth, notwithstanding all the precautions of her father; the blow struck her like a thunderbolt, and she fell senseless."

"And how was M. de Saint-Méran related to Mademoiselle de Villefort?" said the count.

"He was her grandfather on the mother's side. He was coming here to hasten her marriage with Franz."

"Ah, indeed!"

"So Franz must wait. Why was not M. de Saint-Méran also grandfather to Mademoiselle Danglars?"

"Albert, Albert," said Madame de Morcerf, in a tone of mild reproof, "what are you saying? Ah, count, he esteems you so highly, tell him that he has spoken amiss."

And she took two or three steps forward. Monte Cristo watched her with an air so thoughtful, and so full of affectionate admiration, that she turned back and grasped his hand; at the same time she seized that of her son, and joined them together.

"We are friends; are we not?" she asked.

"Oh, madame, I do not presume to call myself your friend, but at all times I am your most respectful servant." The countess left with an indescribable pang in her heart, and before she had taken ten steps the count saw her raise her handkerchief to her eyes.

"Do not my mother and you agree?" asked Albert, astonished.

"On the contrary," replied the count, "did you not hear her declare that we were friends?"

They re-entered the drawing-room, which Valentine and Madame de Villefort had just quitted. It is perhaps needless to add that Morrel departed almost at the same time.

Study Guide Questions

For Students:

1. Where does Mercédès take the Count?
2. What does the Count tell Mercédès about Haydèe?
3. What does the Count tell Mercédès about his past love?

For Reading Club:

1. What does Mercédès say about sharing 'bread and salt', what do you think of the custom?
2. What do Dantès and Mercédès talk about?
3. Do you think the chapter revolves around the theme of loyalty and faithfulness?

CHAPTER 72

Madame de Saint-Méran

A gloomy scene had indeed just passed at the house of M. de Villefort. After the ladies had departed for the ball, whither all the entreaties of Madame de Villefort had failed in persuading him to accompany them, the procureur had shut himself up in his study, according to his custom, with a heap of papers calculated to alarm anyone else, but which generally scarcely satisfied his inordinate desires.

But this time the papers were a mere matter of form. Villefort had secluded himself, not to study, but to reflect; and with the door locked and orders given that he should not be disturbed excepting for important business, he sat down in his armchair and began to ponder over the events, the remembrance of which had during the last eight days filled his mind with so many gloomy thoughts and bitter recollections.

Then, instead of plunging into the mass of documents piled before him, he opened the drawer of his desk, touched a spring, and drew out a parcel of cherished memoranda, amongst which he had carefully arranged, in characters only known to himself, the names of all those who, either in his political career, in money matters, at the bar, or in his mysterious love affairs, had become his enemies.

Their number was formidable, now that he had begun to fear, and yet these names, powerful though they were, had often caused him to smile with the same kind of satisfaction experienced by a traveller who from the summit of a mountain beholds at his feet the craggy eminences, the almost impassable paths, and the fearful chasms, through which he has so perilously climbed. When he had run over all these names in his memory, again read and studied them, commenting meanwhile upon his lists, he shook his head.

"No," he murmured, "none of my enemies would have waited so patiently and laboriously for so long a space of time, that they might now come and crush me with this secret. Sometimes, as Hamlet says:

'Foul deeds will rise,
Though all the earth o'erwhelm them, to men's eyes;'

but, like a phosphoric light, they rise but to mislead. The story has been told by the Corsican to some priest, who in his turn has repeated it. M. de Monte Cristo may have heard it, and to enlighten himself—

"But why should he wish to enlighten himself upon the subject?" asked Villefort, after a moment's reflection, "what interest can this M. de Monte Cristo or M. Zaccone,—son of a shipowner of Malta, discoverer of a mine in Thessaly, now visiting Paris for the first time,—what interest, I say, can he take in discovering a gloomy, mysterious, and useless fact like this? However, among all the incoherent details given to me by the Abbé Busoni and by Lord Wilmore, by that friend and that enemy, one thing appears certain and clear in my opinion—that in no period, in no case, in no circumstance, could there have been any contact between him and me."

But Villefort uttered words which even he himself did not believe. He dreaded not so much the revelation, for he could reply to or deny its truth;—he cared little for that *mene, mene, tekel upharsin*, which appeared suddenly in letters of blood upon the wall;—but what he was really anxious for was to discover whose hand had traced them. While he was endeavoring to calm his fears,—and instead of dwelling upon the political future that had so often been the subject of his ambitious dreams, was imagining a future limited to the enjoyments of home, in fear of awakening the enemy that had so long slept,—the noise of a carriage sounded in the yard, then he heard the steps of an aged person ascending the stairs, followed by tears and lamentations, such as servants always give vent to when they wish to appear interested in their master's grief.

He drew back the bolt of his door, and almost directly an old lady entered, unannounced, carrying her shawl on her arm, and her bonnet in her hand. The white hair was thrown back from her yellow forehead, and her eyes, already sunken by the furrows of age, now almost disappeared beneath the eyelids swollen with grief.

"Oh, sir," she said; "oh, sir, what a misfortune! I shall die of it; oh, yes, I shall certainly die of it!"

And then, falling upon the chair nearest the door, she burst into a paroxysm of sobs. The servants, standing in the doorway, not daring to approach nearer, were looking at Noirtier's old servant, who had heard the noise from his master's room, and run there also, remaining behind the others. Villefort rose, and ran towards his mother-in-law, for it was she.

"Why, what can have happened?" he exclaimed, "what has thus disturbed you? Is M. de Saint-Méran with you?"

"M. de Saint-Méran is dead," answered the old marchioness, without preface and without expression; she appeared to be stupefied. Villefort drew back, and clasping his hands together, exclaimed:

"Dead!—so suddenly?"

"A week ago," continued Madame de Saint-Méran, "we went out together in the carriage after dinner. M. de Saint-Méran had been unwell for some days; still, the idea of seeing our dear Valentine again inspired him with courage, and notwithstanding his illness he would leave. At six leagues from Marseilles, after having eaten some of the lozenges he is accustomed to take, he fell into such a deep sleep, that it appeared to me unnatural; still I hesitated to wake him, although I fancied that his face was flushed, and that the veins of his temples throbbed more violently than usual. However, as it became dark, and I could no longer see, I fell asleep; I was soon aroused by a piercing shriek, as from a person suffering in his dreams, and he suddenly threw his head back violently. I called the valet, I stopped the postilion, I spoke to M. de Saint-Méran, I applied my smelling-salts; but all was over, and I arrived at Aix by the side of a corpse."

Villefort stood with his mouth half open, quite stupefied.

"Of course you sent for a doctor?"

"Immediately; but, as I have told you, it was too late."

"Yes; but then he could tell of what complaint the poor marquis had died."

"Oh, yes, sir, he told me; it appears to have been an apoplectic stroke."

"And what did you do then?"

"M. de Saint-Méran had always expressed a desire, in case his death happened during his absence from Paris, that his body might be brought to the family vault. I had him put into a leaden coffin, and I am preceding him by a few days."

"Oh! my poor mother!" said Villefort, "to have such duties to perform at your age after such a blow!"

"God has supported me through all; and then, my dear marquis, he would certainly have done everything for me that I performed for him. It is true that since I left him, I seem to have lost my senses. I cannot cry; at my age they say that we have no more tears,—still I think that when one is in trouble one should have the power of weeping. Where is Valentine, sir? It is on her account I am here; I wish to see Valentine."

Villefort thought it would be terrible to reply that Valentine was at a ball; so he only said that she had gone out with her step-mother, and that she should be fetched. "This instant, sir—this instant, I beseech you!" said the old lady. Villefort placed the arm of Madame de Saint-Méran within his own, and conducted her to his apartment.

"Rest yourself, mother," he said.

The marchioness raised her head at this word, and beholding the man who so forcibly reminded her of her deeply-regretted child, who still lived for her in Valentine, she felt touched at the name of mother, and bursting into tears, she fell on her knees before an armchair, where she buried her venerable head. Villefort left her to the care of the women, while old Barrois ran, half-scared, to his master; for nothing frightens old people so much as when death relaxes its vigilance over them for a moment in order to strike some other old person. Then, while Madame de Saint-Méran remained on her knees, praying fervently, Villefort sent for a cab, and went himself to fetch his wife and daughter from Madame de Morcerf's. He was so pale when he appeared at the door of the ball-room, that Valentine ran to him, saying:

"Oh, father, some misfortune has happened!"

"Your grandmamma has just arrived, Valentine," said M. de Villefort.

"And grandpapa?" inquired the young girl, trembling with apprehension. M. de Villefort only replied by offering his arm to his daughter. It was just in time, for Valentine's head swam, and she staggered; Madame de Villefort instantly hastened to her assistance, and aided her husband in dragging her to the carriage, saying:

"What a singular event! Who could have thought it? Ah, yes, it is indeed strange!"

And the wretched family departed, leaving a cloud of sadness hanging over the rest of the evening. At the foot of the stairs, Valentine found Barrois awaiting her.

"M. Noirtier wishes to see you tonight, he said, in an undertone.

"Tell him I will come when I leave my dear grandmamma," she replied, feeling, with true delicacy, that the person to whom she could be of the most service just then was Madame de Saint-Méran.

Valentine found her grandmother in bed; silent caresses, heartwrung sobs, broken sighs, burning tears, were all that passed in this sad interview, while Madame de Villefort, leaning on her husband's arm, maintained all outward forms of respect, at least towards the poor widow. She soon whispered to her husband:

"I think it would be better for me to retire, with your permission, for the sight of me appears still to afflict your mother-in-law." Madame de Saint-Méran heard her.

"Yes, yes," she said softly to Valentine, "let her leave; but do you stay."

Madame de Villefort left, and Valentine remained alone beside the bed, for the procureur, overcome with astonishment at the unexpected death, had followed his wife.

Meanwhile, Barrois had returned for the first time to old Noirtier, who having heard the noise in the house, had, as we have said, sent his old servant to inquire the cause; on his return, his quick intelligent eye interrogated the messenger.

"Alas, sir," exclaimed Barrois, "a great misfortune has happened. Madame de Saint-Méran has arrived, and her husband is dead!"

M. de Saint-Méran and Noirtier had never been on strict terms of friendship; still, the death of one old man always considerably affects another. Noirtier let his head fall upon his chest, apparently overwhelmed and thoughtful; then he closed one eye, in token of inquiry.

Barrois asked, "Mademoiselle Valentine?"

Noirtier nodded his head.

"She is at the ball, as you know, since she came to say good-bye to you in full dress." Noirtier again closed his left eye.

"Do you wish to see her?" Noirtier again made an affirmative sign.

"Well, they have gone to fetch her, no doubt, from Madame de Morcerf's; I will await her return, and beg her to come up here. Is that what you wish for?"

"Yes," replied the invalid.

Barrois, therefore, as we have seen, watched for Valentine, and informed her of her grandfather's wish. Consequently, Valentine came up to Noirtier, on leaving Madame de Saint-Méran, who in the midst of her grief had at last yielded to fatigue and fallen into a feverish sleep. Within reach of her hand they placed a small table upon which stood a bottle of orangeade, her usual beverage, and a glass. Then, as we have said, the young girl left the bedside to see M. Noirtier.

Valentine kissed the old man, who looked at her with such tenderness that her eyes again filled with tears, whose sources he thought must be exhausted. The old gentleman continued to dwell upon her with the same expression.

"Yes, yes," said Valentine, "you mean that I have yet a kind grandfather left, do you not." The old man intimated that such was his meaning. "Ah, yes, happily I have," replied Valentine. "Without that, what would become of me?"

It was one o'clock in the morning. Barrois, who wished to go to bed himself, observed that after such sad events everyone stood in need of rest. Noirtier would not say that the only rest he needed was to see his child, but wished her good-night, for grief and fatigue had made her appear quite ill.

The next morning she found her grandmother in bed; the fever had not abated, on the contrary her eyes glistened and she appeared to be suffering from violent nervous irritability.

"Oh, dear grandmamma, are you worse?" exclaimed Valentine, perceiving all these signs of agitation.

"No, my child, no," said Madame de Saint-Méran; "but I was impatiently waiting for your arrival, that I might send for your father."

"My father?" inquired Valentine, uneasily.

"Yes, I wish to speak to him."

Valentine durst not oppose her grandmother's wish, the cause of which she did not know, and an instant afterwards Villefort entered.

"Sir," said Madame de Saint-Méran, without using any circumlocution, and as if fearing she had no time to lose, "you wrote to me concerning the marriage of this child?"

"Yes, madame," replied Villefort, "it is not only projected but arranged."

"Your intended son-in-law is named M. Franz d'Épinay?"

"Yes, madame."

"Is he not the son of General d'Épinay who was on our side, and who was assassinated some days before the usurper returned from the Island of Elba?"

"The same."

"Does he not dislike the idea of marrying the granddaughter of a Jacobin?"

"Our civil dissensions are now happily extinguished, mother," said Villefort; "M. d'Épinay was quite a child when his father died, he knows very little of M. Noirtier, and will meet him, if not with pleasure, at least with indifference."

"Is it a suitable match?"

"In every respect."

"And the young man?"

"Is regarded with universal esteem."

"You approve of him?"

"He is one of the most well-bred young men I know."

During the whole of this conversation Valentine had remained silent.

"Well, sir," said Madame de Saint-Méran, after a few minutes' reflection, "I must hasten the marriage, for I have but a short time to live."

"You, madame?" "You, dear mamma?" exclaimed M. de Villefort and Valentine at the same time.

"I know what I am saying," continued the marchioness; "I must hurry you, so that, as she has no mother, she may at least have a grandmother to bless her marriage. I am all that is left to her belonging to my poor Renée, whom you have so soon forgotten, sir."

"Ah, madame," said Villefort, "you forget that I was obliged to give a mother to my child."

"A stepmother is never a mother, sir. But this is not to the purpose,—our business concerns Valentine, let us leave the dead in peace."

All this was said with such exceeding rapidity, that there was something in the conversation that seemed like the beginning of delirium.

"It shall be as you wish, madame," said Villefort; "more especially since your wishes coincide with mine, and as soon as M. d'Épinay arrives in Paris—"

"My dear grandmother," interrupted Valentine, "consider decorum—the recent death. You would not have me marry under such sad auspices?"

"My child," exclaimed the old lady sharply, "let us hear none of the conventional objections that deter weak minds from preparing for the future. I also was married at the death-bed of my mother, and certainly I have not been less happy on that account."

"Still that idea of death, madame," said Villefort.

"Still?—Always! I tell you I am going to die—do you understand? Well, before dying, I wish to see my son-in-law. I wish to tell him to make my child happy; I wish to read in his eyes whether he intends to obey me;—in fact, I will know him—I will!" continued the old lady, with a fearful expression, "that I may rise from the depths of my grave to find him, if he should not fulfil his duty!"

"Madame," said Villefort, "you must lay aside these exalted ideas, which almost assume the appearance of madness. The dead, once buried in their graves, rise no more."

"And I tell you, sir, that you are mistaken. This night I have had a fearful sleep. It seemed as though my soul were already hovering over my body, my eyes, which I tried to open, closed against my will, and what will appear impossible above all to you, sir, I saw, with my eyes shut, in the spot where you are now standing, issuing from that corner where there is a door leading into Madame Villefort's dressing-room—I saw, I tell you, silently enter, a white figure."

Valentine screamed.

"It was the fever that disturbed you, madame," said Villefort.

"Doubt, if you please, but I am sure of what I say. I saw a white figure, and as if to prevent my discrediting the testimony of only one of my senses, I heard my glass removed—the same which is there now on the table."

"Oh, dear mother, it was a dream."

"So little was it a dream, that I stretched my hand towards the bell; but when I did so, the shade disappeared; my maid then entered with a light."

"But she saw no one?"

"Phantoms are visible to those only who ought to see them. It was the soul of my husband!—Well, if my husband's soul can come to me, why should not my soul reappear to guard my granddaughter? the tie is even more direct, it seems to me."

"Oh, madame," said Villefort, deeply affected, in spite of himself, "do not yield to those gloomy thoughts; you will long live with us, happy, loved, and honored, and we will make you forget—"

"Never, never, never," said the marchioness. "When does M. d'Épinay return?"

"We expect him every moment."

"It is well. As soon as he arrives inform me. We must be expeditious. And then I also wish to see a notary, that I may be assured that all our property returns to Valentine."

"Ah, grandmamma," murmured Valentine, pressing her lips on the burning brow, "do you wish to kill me? Oh, how feverish you are; we must not send for a notary, but for a doctor!"

"A doctor?" said she, shrugging her shoulders, "I am not ill; I am thirsty—that is all."

"What are you drinking, dear grandmamma?"

"The same as usual, my dear, my glass is there on the table—give it to me, Valentine." Valentine poured the orangeade into a glass and gave it to her grandmother with a certain degree of dread, for it was the same glass she fancied that had been touched by the spectre.

The marchioness drained the glass at a single draught, and then turned on her pillow, repeating,

"The notary, the notary!"

M. de Villefort left the room, and Valentine seated herself at the bedside of her grandmother. The poor child appeared herself to require the doctor she had recommended to her aged relative. A bright spot burned in either cheek, her respiration was short and difficult, and her pulse beat with feverish excitement. She was thinking of the despair of Maximilian, when he should be informed that Madame de Saint-Méran, instead of being an ally, was unconsciously acting as his enemy.

More than once she thought of revealing all to her grandmother, and she would not have hesitated a moment, if Maximilian Morrel had been named Albert de Morcerf or Raoul de Château-Renaud; but Morrel was of plebeian extraction, and Valentine knew how the haughty Marquise de Saint-Méran despised all who were not noble. Her secret had each time been repressed when she was about to reveal it, by the sad conviction that it would be useless to do so; for, were it once discovered by her father and mother, all would be lost.

Two hours passed thus; Madame de Saint-Méran was in a feverish sleep, and the notary had arrived. Though his coming was announced in a very low tone, Madame de Saint-Méran arose from her pillow.

"The notary!" she exclaimed, "let him come in."

The notary, who was at the door, immediately entered. "Go, Valentine," said Madame de Saint-Méran, "and leave me with this gentleman."

"But, grandmamma—"

"Leave me—go!"

The young girl kissed her grandmother, and left with her handkerchief to her eyes; at the door she found the valet de chambre, who told her that the doctor was waiting in the dining-room. Valentine instantly ran down. The doctor was a friend of the family, and at the same time one of the cleverest men of the day, and very fond of Valentine, whose birth he had witnessed. He had himself a daughter about her age, but whose life was one continued source of anxiety and fear to him from her mother having been consumptive.

"Oh," said Valentine, "we have been waiting for you with such impatience, dear M. d'Avrigny. But, first of all, how are Madeleine and Antoinette?"

Madeleine was the daughter of M. d'Avrigny, and Antoinette his niece. M. d'Avrigny smiled sadly.

"Antoinette is very well," he said, "and Madeleine tolerably so. But you sent for me, my dear child. It is not your father or Madame de Villefort who is ill. As for you, although we doctors cannot divest our patients of nerves, I fancy you have no further need of me than to recommend you not to allow your imagination to take too wide a field."

Valentine colored. M. d'Avrigny carried the science of divination almost to a miraculous extent, for he was one of the physicians who always work upon the body through the mind.

"No," she replied, "it is for my poor grandmother. You know the calamity that has happened to us, do you not?"

"I know nothing." said M. d'Avrigny.

"Alas," said Valentine, restraining her tears, "my grandfather is dead."

"M. de Saint-Méran?"

"Yes."

"Suddenly?"

"From an apoplectic stroke."

"An apoplectic stroke?" repeated the doctor.

"Yes, and my poor grandmother fancies that her husband, whom she never left, has called her, and that she must go and join him. Oh, M. d'Avrigny, I beseech you, do something for her!"

"Where is she?"

"In her room with the notary."

"And M. Noirtier?"

"Just as he was, his mind perfectly clear, but the same incapability of moving or speaking."

"And the same love for you—eh, my dear child?"

"Yes," said Valentine, "he was very fond of me."

"Who does not love you?" Valentine smiled sadly. "What are your grandmother's symptoms?"

"An extreme nervous excitement and a strangely agitated sleep; she fancied this morning in her sleep that her soul was hovering above her body, which she at the same time watched. It must have been delirium; she fancies, too, that she saw a phantom enter her chamber and even heard the noise it made on touching her glass."

"It is singular," said the doctor; "I was not aware that Madame de Saint-Méran was subject to such hallucinations."

"It is the first time I ever saw her in this condition," said Valentine; "and this morning she frightened me so that I thought her mad; and my father, who you know is a strong-minded man, himself appeared deeply impressed."

"We will go and see," said the doctor; "what you tell me seems very strange." The notary here descended, and Valentine was informed that her grandmother was alone.

"Go upstairs," she said to the doctor.

"And you?"

"Oh, I dare not—she forbade my sending for you; and, as you say, I am myself agitated, feverish and out of sorts. I will go and take a turn in the garden to recover myself."

The doctor pressed Valentine's hand, and while he visited her grandmother, she descended the steps. We need not say which portion of the garden was her favorite walk. After remaining for a short time in the parterre surrounding the house, and gathering a rose to place in her waist or hair, she turned into the dark avenue which led to the bench; then from the bench she went to the gate. As usual, Valentine strolled for a short time among her flowers, but without gathering them. The mourning in her heart forbade her assuming this simple ornament, though she had not yet had time to put on the outward semblance of woe.

She then turned towards the avenue. As she advanced she fancied she heard a voice speaking her name. She stopped astonished, then the voice reached her ear more distinctly, and she recognized it to be that of Maximilian.

Study Guide Questions

For Students:

1. What is the news brought by Madame de Saint-Méran?
2. Why does Madame de Saint-Méran wish to hasten the marriage?
3. Why does Madame de Saint-Méran call a notary?

For Reading Club:

1. Do you think Valentine should have expressed her love for Maximilian before her family? Why or why not?
2. Madame de Saint-Méran is extremely disturbed by the death of her husband. Do you think a modern-day wife would be disturbed in the exact same way?
3. What do you think Valentine should do? Evaluate her options.

CHAPTER 73

The Promise

It was indeed Maximilian Morrel, who had passed a wretched existence since the previous day. With the instinct peculiar to lovers he had anticipated after the return of Madame de Saint-Méran and the death of the marquis, that something would occur at M. de Villefort's in connection with his attachment for Valentine. His presentiments were realized, as we shall see, and his uneasy forebodings had goaded him pale and trembling to the gate under the chestnut-trees.

Valentine was ignorant of the cause of this sorrow and anxiety, and as it was not his accustomed hour for visiting her, she had gone to the spot simply by accident or perhaps through sympathy. Morrel called her, and she ran to the gate.

"You here at this hour?" said she.

"Yes, my poor girl," replied Morrel; "I come to bring and to hear bad tidings."

"This is, indeed, a house of mourning," said Valentine; "speak, Maximilian, although the cup of sorrow seems already full."

"Dear Valentine," said Morrel, endeavoring to conceal his own emotion, "listen, I entreat you; what I am about to say is very serious. When are you to be married?"

"I will tell you all," said Valentine; "from you I have nothing to conceal. This morning the subject was introduced, and my dear grandmother, on whom I depended as my only support, not only declared herself favorable to it, but is so anxious for it, that they only await the arrival of M. d'Épinay, and the following day the contract will be signed."

A deep sigh escaped the young man, who gazed long and mournfully at her he loved.

"Alas," replied he, "it is dreadful thus to hear my condemnation from your own lips. The sentence is passed, and, in a few hours, will be executed; it must be so, and I will not endeavor to prevent it. But, since you say nothing remains but for M. d'Épinay to arrive that the contract may be signed, and the following day you will be his, tomorrow you will be engaged to M. d'Épinay, for he came this morning to Paris." Valentine uttered a cry.

"I was at the house of Monte Cristo an hour since," said Morrel; "we were speaking, he of the sorrow your family had experienced, and I of your grief, when a carriage rolled into the courtyard. Never, till then, had I placed any confidence in presentiments, but now I cannot help believing them, Valentine. At the sound of that carriage I shuddered; soon I heard steps on the staircase, which terrified me as much as the footsteps of the commander did Don Juan. The door at last opened; Albert de Morcerf entered first, and I began to hope my fears were vain, when, after him, another young man advanced, and the count exclaimed: 'Ah, here is the Baron Franz d'Épinay!' I summoned all my strength and courage to my support. Perhaps I turned pale and trembled, but certainly I smiled; and five minutes after I left, without having heard one word that had passed."

"Poor Maximilian!" murmured Valentine.

"Valentine, the time has arrived when you must answer me. And remember my life depends on your answer. What do you intend doing?" Valentine held down her head; she was overwhelmed.

"Listen," said Morrel; "it is not the first time you have contemplated our present position, which is a serious and urgent one; I do not think it is a moment to give way to useless sorrow; leave that for those who like to suffer at their leisure and indulge their grief in secret. There are such in the world, and God will doubtless reward them in heaven for their resignation on earth, but those who mean to contend must not lose one precious moment, but must return immediately the blow which fortune strikes. Do you intend to struggle against our ill-fortune? Tell me, Valentine for it is that I came to know."

Valentine trembled, and looked at him with amazement. The idea of resisting her father, her grandmother, and all the family, had never occurred to her.

"What do you say, Maximilian?" asked Valentine. "What do you mean by a struggle? Oh, it would be a sacrilege. What? I resist my father's order, and my dying grandmother's wish? Impossible!"

Morrel started.

"You are too noble not to understand me, and you understand me so well that you already yield, dear Maximilian. No, no; I shall need all my strength to struggle with myself and support my grief in secret, as you say. But to grieve my father—to disturb my grandmother's last moments—never!"

"You are right," said Morrel, calmly.

"In what a tone you speak!" cried Valentine.

"I speak as one who admires you, mademoiselle."

"Mademoiselle," cried Valentine; "mademoiselle! Oh, selfish man! he sees me in despair, and pretends he cannot understand me!"

"You mistake—I understand you perfectly. You will not oppose M. Villefort, you will not displease the marchioness, and tomorrow you will sign the contract which will bind you to your husband."

"But, *mon Dieu!* tell me, how can I do otherwise?"

"Do not appeal to me, mademoiselle; I shall be a bad judge in such a case; my selfishness will blind me," replied Morrel, whose low voice and clenched hands announced his growing desperation.

"What would you have proposed, Maximilian, had you found me willing to accede?"

"It is not for me to say."

"You are wrong; you must advise me what to do."

"Do you seriously ask my advice, Valentine?"

"Certainly, dear Maximilian, for if it is good, I will follow it; you know my devotion to you."

"Valentine," said Morrel pushing aside a loose plank, "give me your hand in token of forgiveness of my anger; my senses are confused, and during the last hour the most extravagant thoughts have passed through my brain. Oh, if you refuse my advice—"

"What do you advise?" said Valentine, raising her eyes to heaven and sighing.

"I am free," replied Maximilian, "and rich enough to support you. I swear to make you my lawful wife before my lips even shall have approached your forehead."

"You make me tremble!" said the young girl.

"Follow me," said Morrel; "I will take you to my sister, who is worthy also to be yours. We will embark for Algiers, for England, for America, or, if you prefer it, retire to the country and only return to Paris when our friends have reconciled your family."

Valentine shook her head.

"I feared it, Maximilian," said she; "it is the counsel of a madman, and I should be more mad than you, did I not stop you at once with the word 'Impossible, Morrel, impossible!'"

"You will then submit to what fate decrees for you without even attempting to contend with it?" said Morrel sorrowfully.

"Yes,—if I die!"

"Well, Valentine," resumed Maximilian, "I can only say again that you are right. Truly, it is I who am mad, and you prove to me that passion blinds the most well-meaning. I appreciate your calm reasoning. It is then understood that tomorrow you will be irrevocably promised to M. Franz d'Épinay, not only by that theatrical formality invented to heighten the effect of a comedy called the signature of the contract, but your own will?"

"Again you drive me to despair, Maximilian," said Valentine, "again you plunge the dagger into the wound! What would you do, tell me, if your sister listened to such a proposition?"

"Mademoiselle," replied Morrel with a bitter smile, "I am selfish—you have already said so—and as a selfish man I think not of what others would do in my situation, but of what I intend doing myself. I think only that I have known you not a whole year. From the day I first saw you, all my hopes of happiness have been in securing your affection. One day you acknowledged that you loved me, and since that day my hope of future happiness has rested on obtaining you, for to gain you would be life to me. Now, I think no more; I say only that fortune has turned against me—I had thought to gain heaven, and now I have lost it. It is an every-day occurrence for a gambler to lose not only what he possesses but also what he has not."

Morrel pronounced these words with perfect calmness; Valentine looked at him a moment with her large, scrutinizing eyes, endeavoring not to let Morrel discover the grief which struggled in her heart.

"But, in a word, what are you going to do?" asked she.

"I am going to have the honor of taking my leave of you, mademoiselle, solemnly assuring you that I wish your life may be so calm, so happy, and so fully occupied, that there may be no place for me even in your memory."

"Oh!" murmured Valentine.

"Adieu, Valentine, adieu!" said Morrel, bowing.

"Where are you going?" cried the young girl, extending her hand through the opening, and seizing Maximilian by his coat, for she understood from her own agitated feelings that her lover's calmness could not be real; "where are you going?"

"I am going, that I may not bring fresh trouble into your family: and to set an example which every honest and devoted man, situated as I am, may follow."

"Before you leave me, tell me what you are going to do, Maximilian." The young man smiled sorrowfully.

"Speak, speak!" said Valentine; "I entreat you."

"Has your resolution changed, Valentine?"

"It cannot change, unhappy man; you know it must not!" cried the young girl.

"Then adieu, Valentine!"

Valentine shook the gate with a strength of which she could not have been supposed to be possessed, as Morrel was going away, and passing both her hands through the opening, she clasped and wrung them. "I must know what you mean to do!" said she. "Where are you going?"

"Oh, fear not," said Maximilian, stopping at a short distance, "I do not intend to render another man responsible for the rigorous fate reserved for me. Another might threaten to seek M. Franz, to provoke him, and to fight with him; all that would be folly. What has M. Franz to do with it? He saw me this morning for the first time, and has already forgotten he has seen me. He did not even know I existed when it was arranged by your two families that you should be united. I have no enmity against M. Franz, and promise you the punishment shall not fall on him."

"On whom, then!—on me?"

"On you? Valentine! Oh, Heaven forbid! Woman is sacred; the woman one loves is holy."

"On yourself, then, unhappy man; on yourself?"

"I am the only guilty person, am I not?" said Maximilian.

"Maximilian!" said Valentine, "Maximilian, come back, I entreat you!"

He drew near with his sweet smile, and but for his paleness one might have thought him in his usual happy mood.

"Listen, my dear, my adored Valentine," said he in his melodious and grave tone; "those who, like us, have never had a thought for which we need blush before the world, such may read each other's hearts. I never was romantic, and am no melancholy hero. I imitate neither Manfred nor Anthony; but without words, protestations, or vows, my life has entwined itself with yours; you leave me, and you are right in doing so,—I repeat it, you are right; but in losing you, I lose my life. The moment you leave me, Valentine, I am alone in the world. My sister is happily married; her husband is only my brother-in-law, that is, a man whom the ties of social life alone attach to me; no one then longer needs my useless life. This is what I shall do; I will wait until the very moment you are married, for I will not lose the shadow of one of those unexpected chances which are sometimes reserved for us, since M. Franz may, after all, die before that time, a thunderbolt may fall even on the altar as you approach it,—nothing appears impossible to one condemned to die, and miracles appear quite reasonable when his escape from death is concerned. I will, then, wait until the last moment, and when my misery is certain, irremediable, hopeless, I will write a confidential letter to my brother-in-law, another to the prefect of police, to acquaint them with my intention, and at the corner of some wood, on the brink of some abyss, on the bank of some river, I will put an end to my existence, as certainly as I am the son of the most honest man who ever lived in France."

Valentine trembled convulsively; she loosened her hold of the gate, her arms fell by her side, and two large tears rolled down her cheeks. The young man stood before her, sorrowful and resolute.

"Oh, for pity's sake," said she, "you will live, will you not?"

"No, on my honor," said Maximilian; "but that will not affect you. You have done your duty, and your conscience will be at rest."

Valentine fell on her knees, and pressed her almost bursting heart. "Maximilian," said she, "Maximilian, my friend, my brother on earth, my true husband in heaven, I entreat you, do as I do, live in suffering; perhaps we may one day be united."

"Adieu, Valentine," repeated Morrel.

"My God," said Valentine, raising both her hands to heaven with a sublime expression, "I have done my utmost to remain a submissive daughter; I have begged, entreated, implored; he has regarded neither my prayers, my entreaties, nor my tears. It is done," cried she, wiping away her tears, and resuming her firmness, "I am resolved not to die of remorse, but rather of shame. Live, Maximilian, and I will be yours. Say when shall it be? Speak, command, I will obey."

Morrel, who had already gone some few steps away, again returned, and pale with joy extended both hands towards Valentine through the opening.

"Valentine," said he, "dear Valentine, you must not speak thus—rather let me die. Why should I obtain you by violence, if our love is mutual? Is it from mere humanity you bid me live? I would then rather die."

"Truly," murmured Valentine, "who on this earth cares for me, if he does not? Who has consoled me in my sorrow but he? On whom do my hopes rest? On whom does my bleeding heart repose? On him, on him, always on him! Yes, you are right, Maximilian, I will follow you. I will leave the paternal home, I will give up all. Oh, ungrateful girl that I am," cried Valentine, sobbing, "I will give up all, even my dear old grandfather, whom I had nearly forgotten."

"No," said Maximilian, "you shall not leave him. M. Noirtier has evinced, you say, a kind feeling towards me. Well, before you leave, tell him all; his consent would be your justification in God's sight. As soon as we are married, he shall come and live with us, instead of one child, he shall have two. You have told me how you talk to him and how he answers you; I shall very soon learn that language by signs, Valentine, and I promise you solemnly, that instead of despair, it is happiness that awaits us."

"Oh, see, Maximilian, see the power you have over me, you almost make me believe you; and yet, what you tell me is madness, for my father will curse me—he is inflexible—he will never pardon me. Now listen to me, Maximilian; if by artifice, by entreaty, by accident—in short, if by any means I can delay this marriage, will you wait?"

"Yes, I promise you, as faithfully as you have promised me that this horrible marriage shall not take place, and that if you are dragged before a magistrate or a priest, you will refuse."

"I promise you by all that is most sacred to me in the world, namely, by my mother."

"We will wait, then," said Morrel.

"Yes, we will wait," replied Valentine, who revived at these words; "there are so many things which may save unhappy beings such as we are."

"I rely on you, Valentine," said Morrel; "all you do will be well done; only if they disregard your prayers, if your father and Madame de Saint-Méran insist that M. d'Épinay should be called tomorrow to sign the contract—"

"Then you have my promise, Maximilian."

"Instead of signing—"

"I will go to you, and we will fly; but from this moment until then, let us not tempt Providence, let us not see each other. It is a miracle, it is a providence that we have not been discovered. If we were surprised, if it were known that we met thus, we should have no further resource."

"You are right, Valentine; but how shall I ascertain?"

"From the notary, M. Deschamps."

"I know him."

"And for myself—I will write to you, depend on me. I dread this marriage, Maximilian, as much as you."

"Thank you, my adored Valentine, thank you; that is enough. When once I know the hour, I will hasten to this spot, you can easily get over this fence with my assistance, a carriage will await us at the gate, in which you will accompany me to my sister's; there living, retired or mingling in society, as you wish, we shall be enabled to use our power to resist oppression, and not suffer ourselves to be put to death like sheep, which only defend themselves by sighs."

"Yes," said Valentine, "I will now acknowledge you are right, Maximilian; and now are you satisfied with your betrothal?" said the young girl sorrowfully.

"My adored Valentine, words cannot express one half of my satisfaction."

Valentine had approached, or rather, had placed her lips so near the fence, that they nearly touched those of Morrel, which were pressed against the other side of the cold and inexorable barrier.

"Adieu, then, till we meet again," said Valentine, tearing herself away. "I shall hear from you?"

"Yes."

"Thanks, thanks, dear love, adieu!"

The sound of a kiss was heard, and Valentine fled through the avenue. Morrel listened to catch the last sound of her dress brushing the branches, and of her footstep on the gravel, then raised his eyes with an ineffable smile of thankfulness to heaven for being permitted to be thus loved, and then also disappeared.

The young man returned home and waited all the evening and all the next day without getting any message. It was only on the following day, at about ten o'clock in the morning, as he was starting to call on M. Deschamps, the notary, that he received from the postman a small billet, which he knew to be from Valentine, although he had not before seen her writing. It was to this effect:

"Tears, entreaties, prayers, have availed me nothing. Yesterday, for two hours, I was at the church of Saint-Philippe-du-Roule, and for two hours I prayed most fervently. Heaven is as inflexible as man, and the signature of the contract is fixed for this evening at nine o'clock. I have but one promise and but one heart to give; that promise is pledged to you, that heart is also yours. This evening, then, at a quarter to nine at the gate.

"Your betrothed,

"Valentine de Villefort."

"P.S.—My poor grandmother gets worse and worse; yesterday her fever amounted to delirium; today her delirium is almost madness. You will be very kind to me, will you not, Morrel, to make me forget my sorrow in leaving her thus? I think it is kept a secret from grandpapa Noirtier, that the contract is to be signed this evening."

Morrel went also to the notary, who confirmed the news that the contract was to be signed that evening. Then he went to call on Monte Cristo and heard still more. Franz had been to announce the ceremony, and Madame de Villefort had also written to beg the count to excuse her not inviting him; the death of M. de Saint-Méran and the dangerous illness of his widow would cast a gloom over the meeting which she would regret should be shared by the count whom she wished every happiness.

The day before Franz had been presented to Madame de Saint-Méran, who had left her bed to receive him, but had been obliged to return to it immediately after.

It is easy to suppose that Morrel's agitation would not escape the count's penetrating eye. Monte Cristo was more affectionate than ever,—indeed, his manner was so kind that several times Morrel was on the point of telling him all. But he recalled the promise he had made to Valentine, and kept his secret.

The young man read Valentine's letter twenty times in the course of the day. It was her first, and on what an occasion! Each time he read it he renewed his vow to make her happy. How great is the power of a woman who has made so courageous a resolution! What devotion does she deserve from him for whom she has sacrificed everything! How ought she really to be supremely loved! She becomes at once a queen and a wife, and it is impossible to thank and love her sufficiently.

Morrel longed intensely for the moment when he should hear Valentine say, "Here I am, Maximilian; come and help me." He had arranged everything for her escape; two ladders were hidden in the clover-field; a cabriolet was ordered for Maximilian alone, without a servant, without lights; at the turning of the first street they would light the lamps, as it would be foolish to attract the notice of the police by too many precautions. Occasionally he shuddered; he thought of the moment when, from the top of that wall, he should protect the descent of his dear Valentine, pressing in his arms for the first time her of whom he had yet only kissed the delicate hand.

When the afternoon arrived and he felt that the hour was drawing near, he wished for solitude, his agitation was extreme; a simple question from a friend would have irritated him. He shut himself in his room, and tried to read, but his eye glanced over the page without understanding a word, and he threw away the book, and for the second time sat down to sketch his plan, the ladders and the fence.

At length the hour drew near. Never did a man deeply in love allow the clocks to go on peacefully. Morrel tormented his so effectually that they struck eight at half-past six. He then said, "It is time to start; the signature was indeed fixed to take place at nine o'clock, but perhaps Valentine will not wait for that." Consequently, Morrel, having left the Rue Meslay at half-past eight by his timepiece, entered the clover-field while the clock of Saint-Philippe-du-Roule was striking eight. The horse and cabriolet were concealed behind a small ruin, where Morrel had often waited.

The night gradually drew on, and the foliage in the garden assumed a deeper hue. Then Morrel came out from his hiding-place with a beating heart, and looked through the small opening in the gate; there was yet no one to be seen.

The clock struck half-past eight, and still another half-hour was passed in waiting, while Morrel walked to and fro, and gazed more and more frequently through the opening. The garden became darker still, but in the darkness he looked in vain for the white dress, and in the silence he vainly listened for the sound of footsteps. The house, which was discernible through the trees, remained in darkness, and gave no indication that so important an event as the signature of a marriage-contract was going on. Morrel looked at his watch, which wanted a quarter to ten; but soon the same clock he had already heard strike two or three times rectified the error by striking half-past nine.

This was already half an hour past the time Valentine had fixed. It was a terrible moment for the young man. The slightest rustling of the foliage, the least whistling of the wind, attracted his attention, and drew the perspiration to his brow; then he tremblingly fixed his ladder, and, not to lose a moment, placed his foot on the first step. Amidst all these alternations of hope and fear, the clock struck ten. "It is impossible," said Maximilian, "that the signing of a contract should occupy so long a time without unexpected interruptions. I have weighed all the chances, calculated the time required for all the forms; something must have happened."

And then he walked rapidly to and fro, and pressed his burning forehead against the fence. Had Valentine fainted? or had she been discovered and stopped in her flight? These were the only obstacles which appeared possible to the young man.

The idea that her strength had failed her in attempting to escape, and that she had fainted in one of the paths, was the one that most impressed itself upon his mind. "In that case," said he, "I should lose her, and by my own fault." He dwelt on this idea for a moment, then it appeared reality. He even thought he could perceive something on the ground at a distance; he ventured to call, and it seemed to him that the wind wafted back an almost inarticulate sigh.

At last the half-hour struck. It was impossible to wait longer, his temples throbbed violently, his eyes were growing dim; he passed one leg over the wall, and in a moment leaped down on the other side. He was on Villefort's premises—had arrived there by scaling the wall. What might be the consequences? However, he had not ventured thus far to draw back. He followed a short distance close under the wall, then crossed a path, hid entered a clump of trees. In a moment he had passed through them, and could see the house distinctly.

Then Morrel saw that he had been right in believing that the house was not illuminated. Instead of lights at every window, as is customary on days of ceremony, he saw only a gray mass, which was veiled also by a cloud, which at that moment obscured the moon's feeble light. A light moved rapidly from time to time past three windows of the second floor. These three windows were in Madame de Saint-Méran's room. Another remained motionless behind some red curtains which were in Madame de Villefort's bedroom. Morrel guessed all this. So many times, in order to follow Valentine in thought at every hour in the day, had he made her describe the whole house, that without having seen it he knew it all.

This darkness and silence alarmed Morrel still more than Valentine's absence had done. Almost mad with grief, and determined to venture everything in order to see Valentine once more, and be certain of the misfortune he feared, Morrel gained the edge of the clump of trees, and was going to pass as quickly as possible through the flower-garden, when the sound of a voice, still at some distance, but which was borne upon the wind, reached him. At this sound, as he was already partially exposed to view, he stepped back and concealed himself completely, remaining perfectly motionless.

He had formed his resolution. If it was Valentine alone, he would speak as she passed; if she was accompanied, and he could not speak, still he should see her, and know that she was safe; if they were strangers, he would listen to their conversation, and might understand something of this hitherto incomprehensible mystery.

The moon had just then escaped from behind the cloud which had concealed it, and Morrel saw Villefort come out upon the steps, followed by a gentleman in black. They descended, and advanced towards the clump of trees, and Morrel soon recognized the other gentleman as Doctor d'Avrigny.

The young man, seeing them approach, drew back mechanically, until he found himself stopped by a sycamore-tree in the centre of the clump; there he was compelled to remain. Soon the two gentlemen stopped also.

"Ah, my dear doctor," said the procureur, "Heaven declares itself against my house! What a dreadful death—what a blow! Seek not to console me; alas, nothing can alleviate so great a sorrow—the wound is too deep and too fresh! Dead, dead!"

The cold sweat sprang to the young man's brow, and his teeth chattered. Who could be dead in that house, which Villefort himself had called accursed?

"My dear M. de Villefort," replied the doctor, with a tone which redoubled the terror of the young man, "I have not led you here to console you; on the contrary—"

"What can you mean?" asked the procureur, alarmed.

"I mean that behind the misfortune which has just happened to you, there is another, perhaps, still greater."

"Can it be possible?" murmured Villefort, clasping his hands. "What are you going to tell me?"

"Are we quite alone, my friend?"

"Yes, quite; but why all these precautions?"

"Because I have a terrible secret to communicate to you," said the doctor. "Let us sit down."

Villefort fell, rather than seated himself. The doctor stood before him, with one hand placed on his shoulder. Morrel, horrified, supported his head with one hand, and with the other pressed his heart, lest its beatings should be heard. "Dead, dead!" repeated he within himself; and he felt as if he were also dying.

"Speak, doctor—I am listening," said Villefort; "strike—I am prepared for everything!"

"Madame de Saint-Méran was, doubtless, advancing in years, but she enjoyed excellent health." Morrel began again to breathe freely, which he had not done during the last ten minutes.

"Grief has consumed her," said Villefort—"yes, grief, doctor! After living forty years with the marquis—"

"It is not grief, my dear Villefort," said the doctor; "grief may kill, although it rarely does, and never in a day, never in an hour, never in ten minutes." Villefort answered nothing, he simply raised his head, which had been cast down before, and looked at the doctor with amazement.

"Were you present during the last struggle?" asked M. d'Avrigny.

"I was," replied the procureur; "you begged me not to leave."

"Did you notice the symptoms of the disease to which Madame de Saint-Méran has fallen a victim?"

"I did. Madame de Saint-Méran had three successive attacks, at intervals of some minutes, each one more serious than the former. When you arrived, Madame de Saint-Méran had already been panting for breath some minutes; she then had a fit, which I took to be simply a nervous attack, and it was only when I saw her raise herself in the bed, and her limbs and neck appear stiffened, that I became really alarmed. Then I understood from your countenance there was more to fear than I had thought. This crisis past, I endeavored to catch your eye, but could not. You held her hand—you were feeling her pulse—and the second fit came on before you had turned towards me. This was more terrible than the first; the same nervous movements were repeated, and the mouth contracted and turned purple."

"And at the third she expired."

"At the end of the first attack I discovered symptoms of tetanus; you confirmed my opinion."

"Yes, before others," replied the doctor; "but now we are alone—"

"What are you going to say? Oh, spare me!"

"That the symptoms of tetanus and poisoning by vegetable substances are the same."

M. de Villefort started from his seat, then in a moment fell down again, silent and motionless. Morrel knew not if he were dreaming or awake.

"Listen," said the doctor; "I know the full importance of the statement I have just made, and the disposition of the man to whom I have made it."

"Do you speak to me as a magistrate or as a friend?" asked Villefort.

"As a friend, and only as a friend, at this moment. The similarity in the symptoms of tetanus and poisoning by vegetable substances is so great, that were I obliged to affirm by oath what I have now stated, I should hesitate; I therefore repeat to you, I speak not to a magistrate, but to a friend. And to that friend I say, 'During the three-quarters of an hour that the struggle continued, I watched the convulsions and the death of Madame de Saint-Méran, and am thoroughly convinced that not only did her death proceed from poison, but I could also specify the poison.'"

"Can it be possible?"

"The symptoms are marked, do you see?—sleep broken by nervous spasms, excitation of the brain, torpor of the nerve centres. Madame de Saint-Méran succumbed to a powerful dose of brucine or of strychnine, which by some mistake, perhaps, has been given to her."

Villefort seized the doctor's hand.

"Oh, it is impossible," said he, "I must be dreaming! It is frightful to hear such things from such a man as you! Tell me, I entreat you, my dear doctor, that you may be deceived."

"Doubtless I may, but—"

"But?"

"But I do not think so."

"Have pity on me doctor! So many dreadful things have happened to me lately that I am on the verge of madness."

"Has anyone besides me seen Madame de Saint-Méran?"

"No."

"Has anything been sent for from a chemist's that I have not examined?"

"Nothing."

"Had Madame de Saint-Méran any enemies?"

"Not to my knowledge."

"Would her death affect anyone's interest?"

"It could not indeed, my daughter is her only heiress—Valentine alone. Oh, if such a thought could present itself, I would stab myself to punish my heart for having for one instant harbored it."

"Indeed, my dear friend," said M. d'Avrigny, "I would not accuse anyone; I speak only of an accident, you understand,—of a mistake,—but whether accident or mistake, the fact is there; it is on my conscience and compels me to speak aloud to you. Make inquiry."

"Of whom?—how?—of what?"

"May not Barrois, the old servant, have made a mistake, and have given Madame de Saint-Méran a dose prepared for his master?"

"For my father?"

"Yes."

"But how could a dose prepared for M. Noirtier poison Madame de Saint-Méran?"

"Nothing is more simple. You know poisons become remedies in certain diseases, of which paralysis is one. For instance, having tried every other remedy to restore movement and speech to M. Noirtier, I resolved to try one last means, and for three months I have been giving him brucine; so that in the last dose I ordered for him there were six grains. This quantity, which is perfectly safe to administer to the paralyzed frame of M. Noirtier, which has become gradually accustomed to it, would be sufficient to kill another person."

"My dear doctor, there is no communication between M. Noirtier's apartment and that of Madame de Saint-Méran, and Barrois never entered my mother-in-law's room. In short, doctor although I know you to be the most conscientious man in the world, and although I place the utmost reliance in you, I want, notwithstanding my conviction, to believe this axiom, *errare humanum est*."

"Is there one of my brethren in whom you have equal confidence with myself?"

"Why do you ask me that?—what do you wish?"

"Send for him; I will tell him what I have seen, and we will consult together, and examine the body."

"And you will find traces of poison?"

"No, I did not say of poison, but we can prove what was the state of the body; we shall discover the cause of her sudden death, and we shall say, 'Dear Villefort, if this thing has been caused by negligence, watch over your servants; if from hatred, watch your enemies.'"

"What do you propose to me, d'Avrigny?" said Villefort in despair; "so soon as another is admitted into our secret, an inquest will become necessary; and an inquest in my house—impossible! Still," continued the procureur, looking at the doctor with uneasiness, "if you wish it—if you demand it, why then it shall be done. But, doctor, you see me already so grieved—how can I introduce into my house so much scandal, after so much sorrow? My wife and my daughter would die of it! And I, doctor—you know a man does not arrive at the post I occupy—one has not been king's attorney twenty-five years without having amassed a tolerable number of enemies; mine are numerous. Let this affair be talked of, it will be a triumph for them, which will make them rejoice, and cover me with shame. Pardon me, doctor, these worldly ideas; were you a priest I should not dare tell you that, but you are a man, and you know mankind. Doctor, pray recall your words; you have said nothing, have you?"

"My dear M. de Villefort," replied the doctor, "my first duty is to humanity. I would have saved Madame de Saint-Méran, if science could have done it; but she is dead and my duty regards the living. Let us bury this terrible secret in the deepest recesses of our hearts; I am willing, if anyone should suspect this, that my silence on the subject should be imputed to my ignorance. Meanwhile, sir, watch always—watch carefully, for perhaps the evil may not stop here. And when you have found the culprit, if you find him, I will say to you, 'You are a magistrate, do as you will!'"

"I thank you, doctor," said Villefort with indescribable joy; "I never had a better friend than you." And, as if he feared Doctor d'Avrigny would recall his promise, he hurried him towards the house.

When they were gone, Morrel ventured out from under the trees, and the moon shone upon his face, which was so pale it might have been taken for that of a ghost.

"I am manifestly protected in a most wonderful, but most terrible manner," said he; "but Valentine, poor girl, how will she bear so much sorrow?"

As he thought thus, he looked alternately at the window with red curtains and the three windows with white curtains. The light had almost disappeared from the former; doubtless Madame de Villefort had just put out her lamp, and the nightlamp alone reflected its dull light on the window. At the extremity of the building, on the contrary, he saw one of the three windows open. A wax-light placed on the mantle-piece threw some of its pale rays without, and a shadow was seen for one moment on the balcony. Morrel shuddered; he thought he heard a sob.

It cannot be wondered at that his mind, generally so courageous, but now disturbed by the two strongest human passions, love and fear, was weakened even to the indulgence of superstitious thoughts. Although it was impossible that Valentine should see him, hidden as he was, he thought he heard the shadow at the window call him; his disturbed mind told him so. This double error became an irresistible reality, and by one of the incomprehensible transports of youth, he bounded from his hiding-place, and with two strides, at the risk of being seen, at the risk of alarming Valentine, at the risk of being discovered by some exclamation which might escape the young girl, he crossed the flower-garden, which by the light of the moon resembled a large white lake, and having passed the rows of orange-trees which extended in front of the house, he reached the step, ran quickly up and pushed the door, which opened without offering any resistance.

Valentine had not seen him. Her eyes, raised towards heaven, were watching a silvery cloud gliding over the azure, its form that of a shadow mounting towards heaven. Her poetic and excited mind pictured it as the soul of her grandmother.

Meanwhile, Morrel had traversed the anteroom and found the staircase, which, being carpeted, prevented his approach being heard, and he had regained that degree of confidence that the presence of M. de Villefort even would not have alarmed him.

He was quite prepared for any such encounter. He would at once approach Valentine's father and acknowledge all, begging Villefort to pardon and sanction the love which united two fond and loving hearts. Morrel was mad.

Happily he did not meet anyone. Now, especially, did he find the description Valentine had given of the interior of the house useful to him; he arrived safely at the top of the staircase, and while he was feeling his way, a sob indicated the direction he was to take. He turned back, a door partly open enabled him to see his road, and to hear the voice of one in sorrow. He pushed the door open and entered. At the other end of the room, under a white sheet which covered it, lay the corpse, still more alarming to Morrel since the account he had so unexpectedly overheard. By its side, on her knees, and with her head buried in the cushion of an easy-chair, was Valentine, trembling and sobbing, her hands extended above her head, clasped and stiff. She had turned from the window, which remained open, and was praying in accents that would have affected the most unfeeling; her words were rapid, incoherent, unintelligible, for the burning weight of grief almost stopped her utterance.

The moon shining through the open blinds made the lamp appear to burn paler, and cast a sepulchral hue over the whole scene. Morrel could not resist this; he was not exemplary for piety, he was not easily impressed, but Valentine suffering, weeping, wringing her hands before him, was more than he could bear in silence. He sighed, and whispered a name, and the head bathed in tears and pressed on the velvet cushion of the chair—a head like that of a Magdalen by Correggio—was raised and turned towards him. Valentine perceived him without betraying the least surprise. A heart overwhelmed with one great grief is insensible to minor emotions. Morrel held out his hand to her. Valentine, as her only apology for not having met him, pointed to the corpse under the sheet, and began to sob again.

Neither dared for some time to speak in that room. They hesitated to break the silence which death seemed to impose; at length Valentine ventured.

"My friend," said she, "how came you here? Alas, I would say you are welcome, had not death opened the way for you into this house."

"Valentine," said Morrel with a trembling voice, "I had waited since half-past eight, and did not see you come; I became uneasy, leaped the wall, found my way through the garden, when voices conversing about the fatal event—"

"What voices?" asked Valentine. Morrel shuddered as he thought of the conversation of the doctor and M. de Villefort, and he thought he could see through the sheet the extended hands, the stiff neck, and the purple lips.

"Your servants," said he, "who were repeating the whole of the sorrowful story; from them I learned it all."

"But it was risking the failure of our plan to come up here, love."

"Forgive me," replied Morrel; "I will go away."

"No," said Valentine, "you might meet someone; stay."

"But if anyone should come here—"

The young girl shook her head. "No one will come," said she; "do not fear, there is our safeguard," pointing to the bed.

"But what has become of M. d'Épinay?" replied Morrel.

"M. Franz arrived to sign the contract just as my dear grandmother was dying."

"Alas," said Morrel with a feeling of selfish joy; for he thought this death would cause the wedding to be postponed indefinitely.

"But what redoubles my sorrow," continued the young girl, as if this feeling was to receive its immediate punishment, "is that the poor old lady, on her death-bed, requested that the marriage might take place as soon as possible; she also, thinking to protect me, was acting against me."

"Hark!" said Morrel. They both listened; steps were distinctly heard in the corridor and on the stairs.

"It is my father, who has just left his study."

"To accompany the doctor to the door," added Morrel.

"How do you know it is the doctor?" asked Valentine, astonished.

"I imagined it must be," said Morrel.

Valentine looked at the young man; they heard the street door close, then M. de Villefort locked the garden door, and returned upstairs. He stopped a moment in the anteroom, as if hesitating whether to turn to his own apartment or into Madame de Saint-Méran's; Morrel concealed himself behind a door; Valentine remained motionless, grief seeming to deprive her of all fear. M. de Villefort passed on to his own room.

"Now," said Valentine, "you can neither go out by the front door nor by the garden."

Morrel looked at her with astonishment.

"There is but one way left you that is safe," said she; "it is through my grandfather's room." She rose. "Come," she added.

"Where?" asked Maximilian.

"To my grandfather's room."

"I in M. Noirtier's apartment?"

"Yes."

"Can you mean it, Valentine?"

"I have long wished it; he is my only remaining friend and we both need his help,—come."

"Be careful, Valentine," said Morrel, hesitating to comply with the young girl's wishes; "I now see my error—I acted like a madman in coming in here. Are you sure you are more reasonable?"

"Yes," said Valentine; "and I have but one scruple,—that of leaving my dear grandmother's remains, which I had undertaken to watch."

"Valentine," said Morrel, "death is in itself sacred."

"Yes," said Valentine; "besides, it will not be for long."

She then crossed the corridor, and led the way down a narrow staircase to M. Noirtier's room; Morrel followed her on tiptoe; at the door they found the old servant.

"Barrois," said Valentine, "shut the door, and let no one come in."

She passed first.

Noirtier, seated in his chair, and listening to every sound, was watching the door; he saw Valentine, and his eye brightened. There was something grave and solemn in the approach of the young girl which struck the old man, and immediately his bright eye began to interrogate.

"Dear grandfather." said she hurriedly, "you know poor grandmamma died an hour since, and now I have no friend in the world but you."

His expressive eyes evinced the greatest tenderness.

"To you alone, then, may I confide my sorrows and my hopes?"

The paralytic motioned "Yes."

Valentine took Maximilian's hand.

"Look attentively, then, at this gentleman."

The old man fixed his scrutinizing gaze with slight astonishment on Morrel.

"It is M. Maximilian Morrel," said she; "the son of that good merchant of Marseilles, whom you doubtless recollect."

"Yes," said the old man.

"He brings an irreproachable name, which Maximilian is likely to render glorious, since at thirty years of age he is a captain, an officer of the Legion of Honor."

The old man signified that he recollected him.

"Well, grandpapa," said Valentine, kneeling before him, and pointing to Maximilian, "I love him, and will be only his; were I compelled to marry another, I would destroy myself."

The eyes of the paralytic expressed a multitude of tumultuous thoughts.

"You like M. Maximilian Morrel, do you not, grandpapa?" asked Valentine.

"Yes."

"And you will protect us, who are your children, against the will of my father?"

Noirtier cast an intelligent glance at Morrel, as if to say, "perhaps I may."

Maximilian understood him.

"Mademoiselle," said he, "you have a sacred duty to fulfil in your deceased grandmother's room, will you allow me the honor of a few minutes' conversation with M. Noirtier?"

"That is it," said the old man's eye. Then he looked anxiously at Valentine.

"Do you fear he will not understand?"

"Yes."

"Oh, we have so often spoken of you, that he knows exactly how I talk to you." Then turning to Maximilian, with an adorable smile; although shaded by sorrow,— "He knows everything I know," said she.

Valentine arose, placed a chair for Morrel, requested Barrois not to admit anyone, and having tenderly embraced her grandfather, and sorrowfully taken leave of Morrel, she went away. To prove to Noirtier that he was in Valentine's confidence and knew all their secrets, Morrel took the dictionary, a pen, and some paper, and placed them all on a table where there was a light.

"But first," said Morrel, "allow me, sir, to tell you who I am, how much I love Mademoiselle Valentine, and what are my designs respecting her."

Noirtier made a sign that he would listen.

It was an imposing sight to witness this old man, apparently a mere useless burden, becoming the sole protector, support, and adviser of the lovers who were both young, beautiful, and strong. His remarkably noble and austere expression struck Morrel, who began his story with trembling. He related the manner in which he had become acquainted with Valentine, and how he had loved her, and that Valentine, in her solitude and her misfortune, had accepted the offer of his devotion. He told him his birth, his position, his fortune, and more than once, when he consulted the look of the paralytic, that look answered, "That is good, proceed."

"And now," said Morrel, when he had finished the first part of his recital, "now I have told you of my love and my hopes, may I inform you of my intentions?"

"Yes," signified the old man.

"This was our resolution; a cabriolet was in waiting at the gate, in which I intended to carry off Valentine to my sister's house, to marry her, and to wait respectfully M. de Villefort's pardon."

"No," said Noirtier.

"We must not do so?"

"No."

"You do not sanction our project?"

"No."

"There is another way," said Morrel. The old man's interrogative eye said, "Which?"

"I will go," continued Maximilian, "I will seek M. Franz d'Épinay—I am happy to be able to mention this in Mademoiselle de Villefort's absence—and will conduct myself toward him so as to compel him to challenge me." Noirtier's look continued to interrogate.

"You wish to know what I will do?"

"Yes."

"I will find him, as I told you. I will tell him the ties which bind me to Mademoiselle Valentine; if he be a sensible man, he will prove it by renouncing of his own accord the hand of his betrothed, and will secure my friendship, and love until death; if he refuse, either through interest or ridiculous pride, after I have proved to him that he would be forcing my wife from me, that Valentine loves me, and will have no other, I will fight with him, give him every advantage, and I shall kill him, or he will kill me; if I am victorious, he will not marry Valentine, and if I die, I am very sure Valentine will not marry him."

Noirtier watched, with indescribable pleasure, this noble and sincere countenance, on which every sentiment his tongue uttered was depicted, adding by the expression of his fine features all that coloring adds to a sound and faithful drawing.

Still, when Morrel had finished, he shut his eyes several times, which was his manner of saying "No."

"No?" said Morrel; "you disapprove of this second project, as you did of the first?"

"I do," signified the old man.

"But what then must be done?" asked Morrel. "Madame de Saint-Méran's last request was, that the marriage might not be delayed; must I let things take their course?" Noirtier did not move. "I understand," said Morrel; "I am to wait."

"Yes."

"But delay may ruin our plan, sir," replied the young man. "Alone, Valentine has no power; she will be compelled to submit. I am here almost miraculously, and can scarcely hope for so good an opportunity to occur again. Believe me, there are only the two plans I have proposed to you; forgive my vanity, and tell me which you prefer. Do you authorize Mademoiselle Valentine to intrust herself to my honor?"

"No."

"Do you prefer I should seek M. d'Épinay?"

"No."

"Whence then will come the help we need—from chance?" resumed Morrel.

"No."

"From you?"

"Yes."

"You thoroughly understand me, sir? Pardon my eagerness, for my life depends on your answer. Will our help come from you?"

"Yes."

"You are sure of it?"

"Yes." There was so much firmness in the look which gave this answer, no one could, at any rate, doubt his will, if they did his power.

"Oh, thank you a thousand times! But how, unless a miracle should restore your speech, your gesture, your movement, how can you, chained to that armchair, dumb and motionless, oppose this marriage?" A smile lit up the old man's face, a strange smile of the eyes in a paralyzed face.

"Then I must wait?" asked the young man.

"Yes."

"But the contract?" The same smile returned. "Will you assure me it shall not be signed?"

"Yes," said Noirtier.

"The contract shall not be signed!" cried Morrel. "Oh, pardon me, sir; I can scarcely realize so great a happiness. Will they not sign it?"

"No," said the paralytic. Notwithstanding that assurance, Morrel still hesitated. This promise of an impotent old man was so strange that, instead of being the result of the power of his will, it might emanate from enfeebled organs. Is it not natural that the madman, ignorant of his folly, should attempt things beyond his power? The weak man talks of burdens he can raise, the timid of giants he can confront, the poor of treasures he spends, the most humble peasant, in the height of his pride, calls himself Jupiter. Whether Noirtier understood the young man's indecision, or whether he had not full confidence in his docility, he looked uneasily at him.

"What do you wish, sir?" asked Morrel; "that I should renew my promise of remaining tranquil?" Noirtier's eye remained fixed and firm, as if to imply that a promise did not suffice; then it passed from his face to his hands.

"Shall I swear to you, sir?" asked Maximilian.

"Yes," said the paralytic with the same solemnity. Morrel understood that the old man attached great importance to an oath. He extended his hand.

"I swear to you, on my honor," said he, "to await your decision respecting the course I am to pursue with M. d'Épinay."

"That is right," said the old man.

"Now," said Morrel, "do you wish me to retire?"

"Yes."

"Without seeing Mademoiselle Valentine?"

"Yes."

Morrel made a sign that he was ready to obey. "But," said he, "first allow me to embrace you as your daughter did just now." Noirtier's expression could not be understood. The young man pressed his lips on the same spot, on the old man's forehead, where Valentine's had been. Then he bowed a second time and retired.

He found outside the door the old servant, to whom Valentine had given directions. Morrel was conducted along a dark passage, which led to a little door opening on the garden, soon found the spot where he had entered, with the assistance of the shrubs gained the top of the wall, and by his ladder was in an instant in the clover-field where his cabriolet was still waiting for him. He got in it, and thoroughly wearied by so many emotions, arrived about midnight in the Rue Meslay, threw himself on his bed and slept soundly.

Study Guide Questions

For Students:

1. What does Maximilian advise Valentine to do?
2. What is Madame de Saint-Méran's cause of death?
3. What is the promise Maximilian makes with M. Noirtier?

For Reading Club:

1. Do you think a modern-day girl would have reacted differently than Valentine?
2. Do you think Valentine should act upon Maximilian's advice? Why or why not?
3. What is the promise made by the two lovers. Do you think it is practical?

VOLUME FOUR

CHAPTER 74

The Villefort Family Vault

Two days after, a considerable crowd was assembled, towards ten o'clock in the morning, around the door of M. de Villefort's house, and a long file of mourning-coaches and private carriages extended along the Faubourg Saint-Honoré and the Rue de la Pépinière. Among them was one of a very singular form, which appeared to have come from a distance. It was a kind of covered wagon, painted black, and was one of the first to arrive. Inquiry was made, and it was ascertained that, by a strange coincidence, this carriage contained the corpse of the Marquis de Saint-Méran, and that those who had come thinking to attend one funeral would follow two. Their number was great. The Marquis de Saint-Méran, one of the most zealous and faithful dignitaries of Louis XVIII. and King Charles X., had preserved a great number of friends, and these, added to the personages whom the usages of society gave Villefort a claim on, formed a considerable body.

Due information was given to the authorities, and permission obtained that the two funerals should take place at the same time. A second hearse, decked with the same funereal pomp, was brought to M. de Villefort's door, and the coffin removed into it from the post-wagon. The two bodies were to be interred in the cemetery of Père-Lachaise, where M. de Villefort had long since had a tomb prepared for the reception of his family. The remains of poor Renée were already deposited there, and now, after ten years of separation, her father and mother were to be reunited with her.

The Parisians, always curious, always affected by funereal display, looked on with religious silence while the splendid procession accompanied to their last abode two of the number of the old aristocracy—the greatest protectors of commerce and sincere devotees to their principles.

In one of the mourning-coaches Beauchamp, Debray, and Château-Renaud were talking of the very sudden death of the marchioness.

"I saw Madame de Saint-Méran only last year at Marseilles, when I was coming back from Algiers," said Château-Renaud; "she looked like a woman destined to live to be a hundred years old, from her apparent sound health and great activity of mind and body. How old was she?"

"Franz assured me," replied Albert, "that she was sixty-six years old. But she has not died of old age, but of grief; it appears that since the death of the marquis, which affected her very deeply, she has not completely recovered her reason."

"But of what disease, then, did she die?" asked Debray.

"It is said to have been a congestion of the brain, or apoplexy, which is the same thing, is it not?"

"Nearly."

"It is difficult to believe that it was apoplexy," said Beauchamp. "Madame de Saint-Méran, whom I once saw, was short, of slender form, and of a much more nervous than sanguine temperament; grief could hardly produce apoplexy in such a constitution as that of Madame de Saint-Méran."

"At any rate," said Albert, "whatever disease or doctor may have killed her, M. de Villefort, or rather, Mademoiselle Valentine,—or, still rather, our friend Franz, inherits a magnificent fortune, amounting, I believe, to 80,000 livres per annum."

"And this fortune will be doubled at the death of the old Jacobin, Noirtier."

"That is a tenacious old grandfather," said Beauchamp. "*Tenacem propositi virum.* I think he must have made an agreement with death to outlive all his heirs, and he appears likely to succeed. He resembles the old Conventionalist of '93, who said to Napoleon, in 1814, 'You bend because your empire is a young stem, weakened by rapid growth. Take the Republic for a tutor; let us return with renewed strength to the battle-field, and I promise you 500,000 soldiers, another Marengo, and a second Austerlitz. Ideas do not become extinct, sire; they slumber sometimes, but only revive the stronger before they sleep entirely.'"

"Ideas and men appeared the same to him," said Albert. "One thing only puzzles me, namely, how Franz d'Épinay will like a grandfather who cannot be separated from his wife. But where is Franz?"

"In the first carriage, with M. de Villefort, who considers him already as one of the family."

Such was the conversation in almost all the carriages; these two sudden deaths, so quickly following each other, astonished everyone, but no one suspected the terrible secret which M. d'Avrigny had communicated, in his nocturnal walk to M. de Villefort.

They arrived in about an hour at the cemetery; the weather was mild, but dull, and in harmony with the funeral ceremony. Among the groups which flocked towards the family vault, Château-Renaud recognized Morrel, who had come alone in a cabriolet, and walked silently along the path bordered with yew-trees.

"You here?" said Château-Renaud, passing his arms through the young captain's; "are you a friend of Villefort's? How is it that I have never met you at his house?"

"I am no acquaintance of M. de Villefort's," answered Morrel, "but I was of Madame de Saint-Méran." Albert came up to them at this moment with Franz.

"The time and place are but ill-suited for an introduction." said Albert; "but we are not superstitious. M. Morrel, allow me to present to you M. Franz d'Épinay, a delightful travelling companion, with whom I made the tour of Italy. My dear Franz, M. Maximilian Morrel, an excellent friend I have acquired in your absence, and whose name you will hear me mention every time I make any allusion to affection, wit, or amiability."

Morrel hesitated for a moment; he feared it would be hypocritical to accost in a friendly manner the man whom he was tacitly opposing, but his oath and the gravity of the circumstances recurred to his memory; he struggled to conceal his emotion and bowed to Franz.

"Mademoiselle de Villefort is in deep sorrow, is she not?" said Debray to Franz.

"Extremely," replied he; "she looked so pale this morning, I scarcely knew her."

These apparently simple words pierced Morrel to the heart. This man had seen Valentine, and spoken to her! The young and high-spirited officer required all his strength of mind to resist breaking his oath. He took the arm of Château-Renaud, and turned towards the vault, where the attendants had already placed the two coffins.

"This is a magnificent habitation," said Beauchamp, looking towards the mausoleum; "a summer and winter palace. You will, in turn, enter it, my dear d'Épinay, for you will soon be numbered as one of the family. I, as a philosopher, should like a little country-house, a cottage down there under the trees, without so many free-stones over my poor body. In dying, I will say to those around me what Voltaire wrote to Piron: '*Eo rus*, and all will be over.' But come, Franz, take courage, your wife is an heiress."

"Indeed, Beauchamp, you are unbearable. Politics has made you laugh at everything, and political men have made you disbelieve everything. But when you have the honor of associating with ordinary men, and the pleasure of leaving politics for a moment, try to find your affectionate heart, which you leave with your stick when you go to the Chamber."

"But tell me," said Beauchamp, "what is life? Is it not a halt in Death's anteroom?"

"I am prejudiced against Beauchamp," said Albert, drawing Franz away, and leaving the former to finish his philosophical dissertation with Debray.

The Villefort vault formed a square of white stones, about twenty feet high; an interior partition separated the two families, and each apartment had its entrance door. Here were not, as in other tombs, ignoble drawers, one above another, where thrift bestows its dead and labels them like specimens in a museum; all that was visible within the bronze gates was a gloomy-looking room, separated by a wall from the vault itself. The two doors before mentioned were in the middle of this wall, and enclosed the Villefort and Saint-Méran coffins. There grief might freely expend itself without being disturbed by the trifling loungers who came from a picnic party to visit Père-Lachaise, or by lovers who make it their rendezvous.

The two coffins were placed on trestles previously prepared for their reception in the right-hand crypt belonging to the Saint-Méran family. Villefort, Franz, and a few near relatives alone entered the sanctuary.

As the religious ceremonies had all been performed at the door, and there was no address given, the party all separated; Château-Renaud, Albert, and Morrel, went one way, and Debray and Beauchamp the other. Franz remained with M. de Villefort; at the gate of the cemetery Morrel made an excuse to wait; he saw Franz and M. de Villefort get into the same mourning-coach, and thought this meeting forboded evil. He then returned to Paris, and although in the same carriage with Château-Renaud and Albert, he did not hear one word of their conversation.

As Franz was about to take leave of M. de Villefort, "When shall I see you again?" said the latter.

"At what time you please, sir," replied Franz.

"As soon as possible."

"I am at your command, sir; shall we return together?"

"If not unpleasant to you."

"On the contrary, I shall feel much pleasure."

Thus, the future father and son-in-law stepped into the same carriage, and Morrel, seeing them pass, became uneasy. Villefort and Franz returned to the Faubourg Saint-Honoré. The procureur, without going to see either his wife or his daughter, went at once to his study, and, offering the young man a chair:

"M. d'Épinay," said he, "allow me to remind you at this moment,—which is perhaps not so ill-chosen as at first sight may appear, for obedience to the wishes of the departed is the first offering which should be made at their tomb,—allow me then to remind you of the wish expressed by Madame de Saint-Méran on her death-bed, that Valentine's wedding might not be deferred. You know the affairs of the deceased are in perfect order, and her will bequeaths to Valentine the entire property of the Saint-Méran family; the notary showed me the documents yesterday, which will enable us to draw up the contract immediately. You may call on the notary, M. Deschamps, Place Beauveau, Faubourg Saint-Honoré, and you have my authority to inspect those deeds."

"Sir," replied M. d'Épinay, "it is not, perhaps, the moment for Mademoiselle Valentine, who is in deep distress, to think of a husband; indeed, I fear—"

"Valentine will have no greater pleasure than that of fulfilling her grandmother's last injunctions; there will be no obstacle from that quarter, I assure you."

"In that case," replied Franz, "as I shall raise none, you may make arrangements when you please; I have pledged my word, and shall feel pleasure and happiness in adhering to it."

"Then," said Villefort, "nothing further is required. The contract was to have been signed three days since; we shall find it all ready, and can sign it today."

"But the mourning?" said Franz, hesitating.

"Don't be uneasy on that score," replied Villefort; "no ceremony will be neglected in my house. Mademoiselle de Villefort may retire during the prescribed three months to her estate of Saint-Méran; I say hers, for she inherits it today. There, after a few days, if you like, the civil marriage shall be celebrated without pomp or ceremony. Madame de Saint-Méran wished her daughter should be married there. When that is over, you, sir, can return to Paris, while your wife passes the time of her mourning with her mother-in-law."

"As you please, sir," said Franz.

"Then," replied M. de Villefort, "have the kindness to wait half an hour; Valentine shall come down into the drawing-room. I will send for M. Deschamps; we will read and sign the contract before we separate, and this evening Madame de Villefort shall accompany Valentine to her estate, where we will rejoin them in a week."

"Sir," said Franz, "I have one request to make."

"What is it?"

"I wish Albert de Morcerf and Raoul de Château-Renaud to be present at this signature; you know they are my witnesses."

"Half an hour will suffice to apprise them; will you go for them yourself, or shall you send?"

"I prefer going, sir."

"I shall expect you, then, in half an hour, baron, and Valentine will be ready."

Franz bowed and left the room. Scarcely had the door closed, when M. de Villefort sent to tell Valentine to be ready in the drawing-room in half an hour, as he expected the notary and M. d'Épinay and his witnesses. The news caused a great sensation throughout the house; Madame de Villefort would not believe it, and Valentine was thunderstruck. She looked around for help, and would have gone down to her grandfather's room, but on the stairs she met M. de Villefort, who took her arm and led her into the drawing-room. In the anteroom, Valentine met Barrois, and looked despairingly at the old servant. A moment later, Madame de Villefort entered the drawing-room with her little Edward. It was evident that she had shared the grief of the family, for she was pale and looked fatigued. She sat down, took Edward on her knees, and from time to time pressed this child, on whom her affections appeared centred, almost convulsively to her bosom.

Two carriages were soon heard to enter the courtyard. One was the notary's; the other, that of Franz and his friends. In a moment the whole party was assembled. Valentine was so pale one might trace the blue veins from her temples, round her eyes and down her cheeks. Franz was deeply affected. Château-Renaud and Albert looked at each other with amazement; the ceremony which was just concluded had not appeared more sorrowful than did that which was about to begin. Madame de Villefort had placed herself in the shadow behind a velvet curtain, and as she constantly bent over her child, it was difficult to read the expression of her face. M. de Villefort was, as usual, unmoved.

The notary, after having, according to the customary method, arranged the papers on the table, taken his place in an armchair, and raised his spectacles, turned towards Franz:

"Are you M. Franz de Quesnel, baron d'Épinay?" asked he, although he knew it perfectly.

"Yes, sir," replied Franz. The notary bowed.

"I have, then, to inform you, sir, at the request of M. de Villefort, that your projected marriage with Mademoiselle de Villefort has changed the feeling of M. Noirtier towards his grandchild, and that he disinherits her entirely of the fortune he would have left her. Let me hasten to add," continued he, "that the testator, having only the right to alienate a part of his fortune, and having alienated it all, the will will not bear scrutiny, and is declared null and void."

"Yes." said Villefort; "but I warn M. d'Épinay, that during my life-time my father's will shall never be questioned, my position forbidding any doubt to be entertained."

"Sir," said Franz, "I regret much that such a question has been raised in the presence of Mademoiselle Valentine; I have never inquired the amount of her fortune, which, however limited it may be, exceeds mine. My family has sought consideration in this alliance with M. de Villefort; all I seek is happiness."

Valentine imperceptibly thanked him, while two silent tears rolled down her cheeks.

"Besides, sir," said Villefort, addressing himself to his future son-in-law, "excepting the loss of a portion of your hopes, this unexpected will need not personally wound you; M. Noirtier's weakness of mind sufficiently explains it. It is not because Mademoiselle Valentine is going to marry you that he is angry, but because she will marry, a union with any other would have caused him the same sorrow. Old age is selfish, sir, and Mademoiselle de Villefort has been a faithful companion to M. Noirtier, which she cannot be when she becomes the Baroness d'Épinay. My father's melancholy state prevents our speaking to him on any subjects, which the weakness of his mind would incapacitate him from understanding, and I am perfectly convinced that at the present time, although, he knows that his granddaughter is going to be married, M. Noirtier has even forgotten the name of his intended grandson." M. de Villefort had scarcely said this, when the door opened, and Barrois appeared.

"Gentlemen," said he, in a tone strangely firm for a servant speaking to his masters under such solemn circumstances,—"gentlemen, M. Noirtier de Villefort wishes to speak immediately to M. Franz de Quesnel, baron d'Épinay." He, as well as the notary, that there might be no mistake in the person, gave all his titles to the bridegroom elect.

Villefort started, Madame de Villefort let her son slip from her knees, Valentine rose, pale and dumb as a statue. Albert and Château-Renaud exchanged a second look, more full of amazement than the first. The notary looked at Villefort.

"It is impossible," said the procureur. "M. d'Épinay cannot leave the drawing-room at present."

"It is at this moment," replied Barrois with the same firmness, "that M. Noirtier, my master, wishes to speak on important subjects to M. Franz d'Épinay."

"Grandpapa Noirtier can speak now, then," said Edward, with his habitual quickness. However, his remark did not make Madame de Villefort even smile, so much was every mind engaged, and so solemn was the situation.

"Tell M. Nortier," resumed Villefort, "that what he demands is impossible."

"Then, M. Nortier gives notice to these gentlemen," replied Barrois, "that he will give orders to be carried to the drawing-room."

Astonishment was at its height. Something like a smile was perceptible on Madame de Villefort's countenance. Valentine instinctively raised her eyes, as if to thank heaven.

"Pray go, Valentine," said; M. de Villefort, "and see what this new fancy of your grandfather's is." Valentine rose quickly, and was hastening joyfully towards the door, when M. de Villefort altered his intention.

"Stop," said he; "I will go with you."

"Excuse me, sir," said Franz, "since M. Noirtier sent for me, I am ready to attend to his wish; besides, I shall be happy to pay my respects to him, not having yet had the honor of doing so."

"Pray, sir," said Villefort with marked uneasiness, "do not disturb yourself."

"Forgive me, sir," said Franz in a resolute tone. "I would not lose this opportunity of proving to M. Noirtier how wrong it would be of him to encourage feelings of dislike to me, which I am determined to conquer, whatever they may be, by my devotion."

And without listening to Villefort he arose, and followed Valentine, who was running downstairs with the joy of a shipwrecked mariner who finds a rock to cling to. M. de Villefort followed them. Château-Renaud and Morcerf exchanged a third look of still increasing wonder.

Study Guide Questions

For Students:

1. Who introduces M. Franz to M. Morrel and why?
2. What is going on in the Villefort Family Vault?
3. What is Madame de Saint-Méran's last wish?

For Reading Club:

1. Do you feel that the discussion about Franz and Valentine's marriage between M. Franz and M. de Villefort appears more like a business deal?
2. Do you think that Franz is after all a good man?
3. How does the chapter highlight the theme of patriarchy?

CHAPTER 75

A Signed Statement

Noirtier was prepared to receive them, dressed in black, and installed in his armchair. When the three persons he expected had entered, he looked at the door, which his valet immediately closed.

"Listen," whispered Villefort to Valentine, who could not conceal her joy; "if M. Noirtier wishes to communicate anything which would delay your marriage, I forbid you to understand him."

Valentine blushed, but did not answer. Villefort, approached Noirtier.

"Here is M. Franz d'Épinay," said he; "you requested to see him. We have all wished for this interview, and I trust it will convince you how ill-formed are your objections to Valentine's marriage."

Noirtier answered only by a look which made Villefort's blood run cold. He motioned to Valentine to approach. In a moment, thanks to her habit of conversing with her grandfather, she understood that he asked for a key. Then his eye was fixed on the drawer of a small chest between the windows. She opened the drawer, and found a key; and, understanding that was what he wanted, again watched his eyes, which turned toward an old secretaire which had been neglected for many years and was supposed to contain nothing but useless documents.

"Shall I open the secretaire?" asked Valentine.

"Yes," said the old man.

"And the drawers?"

"Yes."

"Those at the side?"

"No."

"The middle one?"

"Yes."

Valentine opened it and drew out a bundle of papers. "Is that what you wish for?" asked she.

"No."

She took successively all the other papers out till the drawer was empty. "But there are no more," said she. Noirtier's eye was fixed on the dictionary.

"Yes, I understand, grandfather," said the young girl.

She pointed to each letter of the alphabet. At the letter S the old man stopped her. She opened, and found the word "secret."

"Ah! is there a secret spring?" said Valentine.

"Yes," said Noirtier.

"And who knows it?" Noirtier looked at the door where the servant had gone out.

"Barrois?" said she.

"Yes."

"Shall I call him?"

"Yes."

Valentine went to the door, and called Barrois. Villefort's impatience during this scene made the perspiration roll from his forehead, and Franz was stupefied. The old servant came.

"Barrois," said Valentine, "my grandfather has told me to open that drawer in the secretaire, but there is a secret spring in it, which you know—will you open it?"

Barrois looked at the old man. "Obey," said Noirtier's intelligent eye. Barrois touched a spring, the false bottom came out, and they saw a bundle of papers tied with a black string.

"Is that what you wish for?" said Barrois.

"Yes."

"Shall I give these papers to M. de Villefort?"

"No."

"To Mademoiselle Valentine?"

"No."

"To M. Franz d'Épinay?"

"Yes."

Franz, astonished, advanced a step. "To me, sir?" said he.

"Yes."

Franz took them from Barrois and casting a glance at the cover, read:

"'To be given, after my death, to General Durand, who shall bequeath the packet to his son, with an injunction to preserve it as containing an important document.'

"Well, sir," asked Franz, "what do you wish me to do with this paper?"

"To preserve it, sealed up as it is, doubtless," said the procureur.

"No," replied Noirtier eagerly.

"Do you wish him to read it?" said Valentine.

"Yes," replied the old man.

"You understand, baron, my grandfather wishes you to read this paper," said Valentine.

"Then let us sit down," said Villefort impatiently, "for it will take some time."

"Sit down," said the old man. Villefort took a chair, but Valentine remained standing by her father's side, and Franz before him, holding the mysterious paper in his hand. "Read," said the old man. Franz untied it, and in the midst of the most profound silence read:

"'*Extract of the report of a meeting of the Bonapartist Club in the Rue Saint-Jacques, held February 5th, 1815.*'"

Franz stopped. "February 5th, 1815!" said he; "it is the day my father was murdered." Valentine and Villefort were dumb; the eye of the old man alone seemed to say clearly, "Go on."

"But it was on leaving this club," said he, "my father disappeared."

Noirtier's eye continued to say, "Read." He resumed:—

"'The undersigned Louis-Jacques Beaurepaire, lieutenant-colonel of artillery, Étienne Duchampy, general of brigade, and Claude Lecharpal, keeper of woods and forests, declare, that on the 4th of February, a letter arrived from the Island of Elba, recommending to the kindness and the confidence of the Bonapartist Club, General Flavien de Quesnel, who having served the emperor from 1804 to 1814 was supposed to be devoted to the interests of the Napoleon dynasty, notwithstanding the title of baron which Louis XVIII. had just granted to him with his estate of Épinay.

"'A note was in consequence addressed to General de Quesnel, begging him to be present at the meeting next day, the 5th. The note indicated neither the street nor the number of the house where the meeting was to be held; it bore no signature, but it announced to the general that someone would call for him if he would be ready at nine o'clock. The meetings were always held from that time till midnight. At nine o'clock the president of the club presented himself; the general was ready, the president informed him that one of the conditions of his introduction was that he should be eternally ignorant of the place of meeting, and that he would allow his eyes to be bandaged, swearing that he would not endeavor to take off the bandage. General de Quesnel accepted the condition, and promised on his honor not to seek to discover the road they took. The general's carriage was ready, but the president told him it was impossible for him to use it, since it was useless to blindfold the master if the coachman knew through what streets he went. "What must be done then?" asked the general.— "I have my carriage here," said the president.

"""Have you, then, so much confidence in your servant that you can intrust him with a secret you will not allow me to know?"

"""Our coachman is a member of the club," said the president; "we shall be driven by a State-Councillor."

"""Then we run another risk," said the general, laughing, "that of being upset." We insert this joke to prove that the general was not in the least compelled to attend the meeting, but that he came willingly. When they were seated in the carriage the president reminded the general of his promise to allow his eyes to be bandaged, to which he made no opposition. On the road the president thought he saw the general make an attempt to remove the handkerchief, and reminded him of his oath. "Sure enough," said the general. The carriage stopped at an alley leading out of the Rue Saint-Jacques. The general alighted, leaning on the arm of the president, of whose dignity he was not aware, considering him simply as a member of the club; they went through the alley, mounted a flight of stairs, and entered the assembly-room.

"'The deliberations had already begun. The members, apprised of the sort of presentation which was to be made that evening, were all in attendance. When in the middle of the room the general was invited to remove his bandage, he did so immediately, and was surprised to see so many well-known faces in a society of whose existence he had till then been ignorant. They questioned him as to his sentiments, but he contented himself with answering, that the letters from the Island of Elba ought to have informed them—'"

Franz interrupted himself by saying, "My father was a royalist; they need not have asked his sentiments, which were well known."

"And hence," said Villefort, "arose my affection for your father, my dear M. Franz. Opinions held in common are a ready bond of union."

"Read again," said the old man.

Franz continued:

"'The president then sought to make him speak more explicitly, but M. de Quesnel replied that he wished first to know what they wanted with him. He was then informed of the contents of the letter from the Island of Elba, in which he was recommended to the club as a man who would be likely to advance the interests of their party. One paragraph spoke of the return of Bonaparte and promised another letter and further details, on the arrival of the *Pharaon* belonging to the shipbuilder Morrel, of Marseilles, whose captain was entirely devoted to the emperor. During all this time, the general, on whom they thought to have relied as on a brother, manifested evidently signs of discontent and repugnance. When the reading was finished, he remained silent, with knitted brows.

"'"Well," asked the president, "what do you say to this letter, general?"

"'"I say that it is too soon after declaring myself for Louis XVIII. to break my vow in behalf of the ex-emperor." This answer was too clear to permit of any mistake as to his sentiments. "General," said the president, "we acknowledge no King Louis XVIII., or an ex-emperor, but his majesty the emperor and king, driven from France, which is his kingdom, by violence and treason."

"'"Excuse me, gentlemen," said the general; "you may not acknowledge Louis XVIII., but I do, as he has made me a baron and a field-marshal, and I shall never forget that for these two titles I am indebted to his happy return to France."

"'"Sir," said the president, rising with gravity, "be careful what you say; your words clearly show us that they are deceived concerning you in the Island of Elba, and have deceived us! The communication has been made to you in consequence of the confidence placed in you, and which does you honor. Now we discover our error; a title and promotion attach you to the government we wish to overturn. We will not constrain you to help us; we enroll no one against his conscience, but we will compel you to act generously, even if you are not disposed to do so."

"'"You would call acting generously, knowing your conspiracy and not informing against you, that is what I should call becoming your accomplice. You see I am more candid than you."'"

"Ah, my father!" said Franz, interrupting himself. "I understand now why they murdered him." Valentine could not help casting one glance towards the young man, whose filial enthusiasm it was delightful to behold. Villefort walked to and fro behind them. Noirtier watched the expression of each one, and preserved his dignified and commanding attitude. Franz returned to the manuscript, and continued:

"'"Sir," said the president, "you have been invited to join this assembly—you were not forced here; it was proposed to you to come blindfolded—you accepted. When you complied with this twofold request you well knew we did not wish to secure the throne of Louis XVIII., or we should not take so much care to avoid the vigilance of the police. It would be conceding too much to allow you to put on a mask to aid you in the discovery of our secret, and then to remove it that you may ruin those who have confided in you. No, no, you must first say if you declare yourself for the king of a day who now reigns, or for his majesty the emperor."

"'"I am a royalist," replied the general; "I have taken the oath of allegiance to Louis XVIII., and I will adhere to it." These words were followed by a general murmur, and it was evident that several of the members were discussing the propriety of making the general repent of his rashness.

"'The president again arose, and having imposed silence, said,—"Sir, you are too serious and too sensible a man not to understand the consequences of our present situation, and your candor has already dictated to us the conditions which remain for us to offer you." The general, putting his hand on his sword, exclaimed,—"If you talk of honor, do not begin by disavowing its laws, and impose nothing by violence."

"'"And you, sir," continued the president, with a calmness still more terrible than the general's anger, "I advise you not to touch your sword." The general looked around him with slight uneasiness; however he did not yield, but calling up all his fortitude, said,—"I will not swear."

"'"Then you must die," replied the president calmly. M. d'Épinay became very pale; he looked round him a second time, several members of the club were whispering, and getting their arms from under their cloaks. "General," said the president, "do not alarm yourself; you are among men of honor who will use every means to convince you before resorting to the last extremity, but as you have said, you are among conspirators, you are in possession of our secret, and you must restore it to us." A significant silence followed these words, and as the general did not reply,—"Close the doors," said the president to the door-keeper.

"'The same deadly silence succeeded these words. Then the general advanced, and making a violent effort to control his feelings,—"I have a son," said he, "and I ought to think of him, finding myself among assassins."

"'"General," said the chief of the assembly, "one man may insult fifty—it is the privilege of weakness. But he does wrong to use his privilege. Follow my advice, swear, and do not insult." The general, again daunted by the superiority of the chief, hesitated a moment; then advancing to the president's desk,—"What is the form, said he.

"'"It is this:—'I swear by my honor not to reveal to anyone what I have seen and heard on the 5th of February, 1815, between nine and ten o'clock in the evening; and I plead guilty of death should I ever violate this oath.'" The general appeared to be affected by a nervous tremor, which prevented his answering for some moments; then, overcoming his manifest repugnance, he pronounced the required oath, but in so low a tone as to be scarcely audible to the majority of the members, who insisted on his repeating it clearly and distinctly, which he did.

"'"Now am I at liberty to retire?" said the general. The president rose, appointed three members to accompany him, and got into the carriage with the general after bandaging his eyes. One of those three members was the coachman who had driven them there. The other members silently dispersed. "Where do you wish to be taken?"

asked the president.—"Anywhere out of your presence," replied M. d'Épinay. "Beware, sir," replied the president, "you are no longer in the assembly, and have only to do with individuals; do not insult them unless you wish to be held responsible." But instead of listening, M. d'Épinay went on,—"You are still as brave in your carriage as in your assembly because you are still four against one." The president stopped the coach. They were at that part of the Quai des Ormes where the steps lead down to the river. "Why do you stop here?" asked d'Épinay.

"""Because, sir," said the president, "you have insulted a man, and that man will not go one step farther without demanding honorable reparation."

"""Another method of assassination?" said the general, shrugging his shoulders.

"""Make no noise, sir, unless you wish me to consider you as one of the men of whom you spoke just now as cowards, who take their weakness for a shield. You are alone, one alone shall answer you; you have a sword by your side, I have one in my cane; you have no witness, one of these gentlemen will serve you. Now, if you please, remove your bandage." The general tore the handkerchief from his eyes. "At last," said he, "I shall know with whom I have to do." They opened the door and the four men alighted.'"

Franz again interrupted himself, and wiped the cold drops from his brow; there was something awful in hearing the son read aloud in trembling pallor these details of his father's death, which had hitherto been a mystery. Valentine clasped her hands as if in prayer. Noirtier looked at Villefort with an almost sublime expression of contempt and pride.

Franz continued:

"'It was, as we said, the fifth of February. For three days the mercury had been five or six degrees below freezing and the steps were covered with ice. The general was stout and tall, the president offered him the side of the railing to assist him in getting down. The two witnesses followed. It was a dark night. The ground from the steps to the river was covered with snow and hoarfrost, the water of the river looked black and deep. One of the seconds went for a lantern in a coal-barge near, and by its light they examined the weapons. The president's sword, which was simply, as he had said, one he carried in his cane, was five inches shorter than the general's, and had no guard. The general proposed to cast lots for the swords, but the president said it was he who had given the provocation, and when he had given it he had supposed each would use his own arms. The witnesses endeavored to insist, but the president bade them be silent. The lantern was placed on the ground, the two adversaries took their stations, and the duel began. The light made the two swords appear like flashes of lightning; as for the men, they were scarcely perceptible, the darkness was so great.

"'General d'Épinay passed for one of the best swordsmen in the army, but he was pressed so closely in the onset that he missed his aim and fell. The witnesses thought he was dead, but his adversary, who knew he had not struck him, offered him the assistance of his hand to rise. The circumstance irritated instead of calming the general, and he rushed on his adversary. But his opponent did not allow his guard to be broken. He received him on his sword and three times the general drew back on finding himself too closely engaged, and then returned to the charge. At the third he fell again. They thought he slipped, as at first, and the witnesses, seeing he did not move, approached and endeavored to raise him, but the one who passed his arm around the body found it was moistened with blood. The general, who had almost fainted, revived. "Ah," said he, "they have sent some fencing-master to fight with me." The president, without answering, approached the witness who held the lantern, and raising his sleeve, showed him two wounds he had received in his arm; then opening his coat, and unbuttoning his waistcoat, displayed his side, pierced with a third wound. Still he had not even uttered a sigh. General d'Épinay died five minutes after.'"

Franz read these last words in a voice so choked that they were hardly audible, and then stopped, passing his hand over his eyes as if to dispel a cloud; but after a moment's silence, he continued:

"'The president went up the steps, after pushing his sword into his cane; a track of blood on the snow marked his course. He had scarcely arrived at the top when he heard a heavy splash in the water—it was the general's body, which the witnesses had just thrown into the river after ascertaining that he was dead. The general fell, then, in a loyal duel, and not in ambush as it might have been reported. In proof of this we have signed this paper to establish the truth of the facts, lest the moment should arrive when either of the actors in this terrible scene should be accused of premeditated murder or of infringement of the laws of honor.

"'Signed, Beaurepaire, Duchampy, and Lecharpal.'"

When Franz had finished reading this account, so dreadful for a son; when Valentine, pale with emotion, had wiped away a tear; when Villefort, trembling, and crouched in a corner, had endeavored to lessen the storm by supplicating glances at the implacable old man,—

"Sir," said d'Épinay to Noirtier, "since you are well acquainted with all these details, which are attested by honorable signatures,—since you appear to take some interest in me, although you have only manifested it hitherto by causing me sorrow, refuse me not one final satisfaction—tell me the name of the president of the club, that I may at least know who killed my father."

Villefort mechanically felt for the handle of the door; Valentine, who understood sooner than anyone her grandfather's answer, and who had often seen two scars upon his right arm, drew back a few steps.

"Mademoiselle," said Franz, turning towards Valentine, "unite your efforts with mine to find out the name of the man who made me an orphan at two years of age." Valentine remained dumb and motionless.

"Hold, sir," said Villefort, "do not prolong this dreadful scene. The names have been purposely concealed; my father himself does not know who this president was, and if he knows, he cannot tell you; proper names are not in the dictionary."

"Oh, misery," cried Franz: "the only hope which sustained me and enabled me to read to the end was that of knowing, at least, the name of him who killed my father! Sir, sir," cried he, turning to Noirtier, "do what you can—make me understand in some way!"

"Yes," replied Noirtier.

"Oh, mademoiselle, mademoiselle!" cried Franz, "your grandfather says he can indicate the person. Help me,—lend me your assistance!"

Noirtier looked at the dictionary. Franz took it with a nervous trembling, and repeated the letters of the alphabet successively, until he came to M. At that letter the old man signified "Yes."

"M," repeated Franz. The young man's finger, glided over the words, but at each one Noirtier answered by a negative sign. Valentine hid her head between her hands. At length, Franz arrived at the word MYSELF.

"Yes!"

"You!" cried Franz, whose hair stood on end; "you, M. Noirtier—you killed my father?"

"Yes!" replied Noirtier, fixing a majestic look on the young man. Franz fell powerless on a chair; Villefort opened the door and escaped, for the idea had entered his mind to stifle the little remaining life in the heart of this terrible old man.

Study Guide Questions

For Students:

1. Why does everyone gather in M. Noirtier's room?
2. What does M. Noirtier give to M. Franz d'Epinay?
3. Who killed M. le Général d'Epinay and why?

For Reading Club:

1. What information is recorded in the secret papers given to M. Franz by M. Noirtier?
2. Discuss what you think M. Franz should do after he discovers who murdered his father.
3. Do you think the marriage between Valentine and M. Franz would have succeeded if M. Noirtier had not revealed the important facts about the family's past?

CHAPTER 76

Progress of Cavalcanti the Younger

Meanwhile M. Cavalcanti the elder had returned to his service, not in the army of his majesty the Emperor of Austria, but at the gaming-table of the baths of Lucca, of which he was one of the most assiduous courtiers. He had spent every farthing that had been allowed for his journey as a reward for the majestic and solemn manner in which he had maintained his assumed character of father.

M. Andrea at his departure inherited all the papers which proved that he had indeed the honor of being the son of the Marquis Bartolomeo and the Marchioness Oliva Corsinari. He was now fairly launched in that Parisian society which gives such ready access to foreigners, and treats them, not as they really are, but as they wish to be considered. Besides, what is required of a young man in Paris? To speak its language tolerably, to make a good appearance, to be a good gamester, and to pay in cash. They are certainly less particular with a foreigner than with a Frenchman. Andrea had, then, in a fortnight, attained a very fair position. He was called count, he was said to possess 50,000 livres per annum; and his father's immense riches, buried in the quarries of Saravezza, were a constant theme. A learned man, before whom the last circumstance was mentioned as a fact, declared he had seen the quarries in question, which gave great weight to assertions hitherto somewhat doubtful, but which now assumed the garb of reality.

Such was the state of society in Paris at the period we bring before our readers, when Monte Cristo went one evening to pay M. Danglars a visit. M. Danglars was out, but the count was asked to go and see the baroness, and he accepted the invitation. It was never without a nervous shudder, since the dinner at Auteuil, and the events which followed it, that Madame Danglars heard Monte Cristo's name announced. If he did not come, the painful sensation became most intense; if, on the contrary, he appeared, his noble countenance, his brilliant eyes, his amiability, his polite attention even towards Madame Danglars, soon dispelled every impression of fear. It appeared impossible to the baroness that a man of such delightfully pleasing manners should entertain evil designs against her; besides, the most corrupt minds only suspect evil when it would answer some interested end—useless injury is repugnant to every mind.

When Monte Cristo entered the boudoir, to which we have already once introduced our readers, and where the baroness was examining some drawings, which her daughter passed to her after having looked at them with M. Cavalcanti, his presence soon produced its usual effect, and it was with smiles that the baroness received the count, although she had been a little disconcerted at the announcement of his name. The latter took in the whole scene at a glance.

The baroness was partially reclining on a sofa, Eugénie sat near her, and Cavalcanti was standing. Cavalcanti, dressed in black, like one of Goethe's heroes, with varnished shoes and white silk open-worked stockings, passed a white and tolerably nice-looking hand through his light hair, and so displayed a sparkling diamond, that in spite of Monte Cristo's advice the vain young man had been unable to resist putting on his little finger. This movement was accompanied by killing glances at Mademoiselle Danglars, and by sighs launched in the same direction.

Mademoiselle Danglars was still the same—cold, beautiful, and satirical. Not one of these glances, nor one sigh, was lost on her; they might have been said to fall on the shield of Minerva, which some philosophers assert protected sometimes the breast of Sappho. Eugénie bowed coldly to the count, and availed herself of the first moment when the conversation became earnest to escape to her study, whence very soon two cheerful and noisy voices being heard in connection with occasional notes of the piano assured Monte Cristo that Mademoiselle Danglars preferred to his society and to that of M. Cavalcanti the company of Mademoiselle Louise d'Armilly, her singing teacher.

It was then, especially while conversing with Madame Danglars, and apparently absorbed by the charm of the conversation, that the count noticed M. Andrea Cavalcanti's solicitude, his manner of listening to the music at the door he dared not pass, and of manifesting his admiration.

The banker soon returned. His first look was certainly directed towards Monte Cristo, but the second was for Andrea. As for his wife, he bowed to her, as some husbands do to their wives, but in a way that bachelors will never comprehend, until a very extensive code is published on conjugal life.

"Have not the ladies invited you to join them at the piano?" said Danglars to Andrea.

"Alas, no, sir," replied Andrea with a sigh, still more remarkable than the former ones. Danglars immediately advanced towards the door and opened it.

The two young ladies were seen seated on the same chair, at the piano, accompanying themselves, each with one hand, a fancy to which they had accustomed themselves, and performed admirably. Mademoiselle d'Armilly, whom they then perceived through the open doorway, formed with Eugénie one of the *tableaux vivants* of which the Germans are so fond. She was somewhat beautiful, and exquisitely formed—a little fairy-like figure, with large curls falling on her neck, which was rather too long, as Perugino sometimes makes his Virgins, and her eyes dull from fatigue. She was said to have a weak chest, and like Antonia in the *Cremona Violin*, she would die one day while singing.

Monte Cristo cast one rapid and curious glance round this sanctum; it was the first time he had ever seen Mademoiselle d'Armilly, of whom he had heard much.

"Well," said the banker to his daughter, "are we then all to be excluded?"

He then led the young man into the study, and either by chance or manœuvre the door was partially closed after Andrea, so that from the place where they sat neither the Count nor the baroness could see anything; but as the banker had accompanied Andrea, Madame Danglars appeared to take no notice of it.

The count soon heard Andrea's voice, singing a Corsican song, accompanied by the piano. While the count smiled at hearing this song, which made him lose sight of Andrea in the recollection of Benedetto, Madame Danglars was boasting to Monte Cristo of her husband's strength of mind, who that very morning had lost three or four hundred thousand francs by a failure at Milan. The praise was well deserved, for had not the count heard it from the baroness, or by one of those means by which he knew everything, the baron's countenance would not have led him to suspect it.

"Hem," thought Monte Cristo, "he begins to conceal his losses; a month since he boasted of them."

Then aloud,—"Oh, madame, M. Danglars is so skilful, he will soon regain at the Bourse what he loses elsewhere."

"I see that you participate in a prevalent error," said Madame Danglars.

"What is it?" said Monte Cristo.

"That M. Danglars speculates, whereas he never does."

"Truly, madame, I recollect M. Debray told me—apropos, what has become of him? I have seen nothing of him the last three or four days."

"Nor I," said Madame Danglars; "but you began a sentence, sir, and did not finish."

"Which?"

"M. Debray had told you—"

"Ah, yes; he told me it was you who sacrificed to the demon of speculation."

"I was once very fond of it, but I do not indulge now."

"Then you are wrong, madame. Fortune is precarious; and if I were a woman and fate had made me a banker's wife, whatever might be my confidence in my husband's good fortune, still in speculation you know there is great risk. Well, I would secure for myself a fortune independent of him, even if I acquired it by placing my interests in hands unknown to him." Madame Danglars blushed, in spite of all her efforts.

"Stay," said Monte Cristo, as though he had not observed her confusion, "I have heard of a lucky hit that was made yesterday on the Neapolitan bonds."

"I have none—nor have I ever possessed any; but really we have talked long enough of money, count, we are like two stockbrokers; have you heard how fate is persecuting the poor Villeforts?"

"What has happened?" said the count, simulating total ignorance.

"You know the Marquis of Saint-Méran died a few days after he had set out on his journey to Paris, and the marchioness a few days after her arrival?"

"Yes," said Monte Cristo, "I have heard that; but, as Claudius said to Hamlet, 'it is a law of nature; their fathers died before them, and they mourned their loss; they will die before their children, who will, in their turn, grieve for them.'"

"But that is not all."

"Not all!"

"No; they were going to marry their daughter—"

"To M. Franz d'Épinay. Is it broken off?"

"Yesterday morning, it appears, Franz declined the honor."

"Indeed? And is the reason known?"

"No."

"How extraordinary! And how does M. de Villefort bear it?"

"As usual. Like a philosopher."

Danglars returned at this moment alone.

"Well," said the baroness, "do you leave M. Cavalcanti with your daughter?"

"And Mademoiselle d'Armilly," said the banker; "do you consider her no one?" Then, turning to Monte Cristo, he said, "Prince Cavalcanti is a charming young man, is he not? But is he really a prince?"

"I will not answer for it," said Monte Cristo. "His father was introduced to me as a marquis, so he ought to be a count; but I do not think he has much claim to that title."

"Why?" said the banker. "If he is a prince, he is wrong not to maintain his rank; I do not like anyone to deny his origin."

"Oh, you are a thorough democrat," said Monte Cristo, smiling.

"But do you see to what you are exposing yourself?" said the baroness. "If, perchance, M. de Morcerf came, he would find M. Cavalcanti in that room, where he, the betrothed of Eugénie, has never been admitted."

"You may well say, perchance," replied the banker; "for he comes so seldom, it would seem only chance that brings him."

"But should he come and find that young man with your daughter, he might be displeased."

"He? You are mistaken. M. Albert would not do us the honor to be jealous; he does not like Eugénie sufficiently. Besides, I care not for his displeasure."

"Still, situated as we are—"

"Yes, do you know how we are situated? At his mother's ball he danced once with Eugénie, and M. Cavalcanti three times, and he took no notice of it."

The valet announced the Vicomte Albert de Morcerf. The baroness rose hastily, and was going into the study, when Danglars stopped her.

"Let her alone," said he.

She looked at him in amazement. Monte Cristo appeared to be unconscious of what passed. Albert entered, looking very handsome and in high spirits. He bowed politely to the baroness, familiarly to Danglars, and affectionately to Monte Cristo. Then turning to the baroness: "May I ask how Mademoiselle Danglars is?" said he.

"She is quite well," replied Danglars quickly; "she is at the piano with M. Cavalcanti."

Albert retained his calm and indifferent manner; he might feel perhaps annoyed, but he knew Monte Cristo's eye was on him. "M. Cavalcanti has a fine tenor voice," said he, "and Mademoiselle Eugénie a splendid soprano, and then she plays the piano like Thalberg. The concert must be a delightful one."

"They suit each other remarkably well," said Danglars. Albert appeared not to notice this remark, which was, however, so rude that Madame Danglars blushed.

"I, too," said the young man, "am a musician—at least, my masters used to tell me so; but it is strange that my voice never would suit any other, and a soprano less than any."

Danglars smiled, and seemed to say, "It is of no consequence." Then, hoping doubtless to effect his purpose, he said,—"The prince and my daughter were universally admired yesterday. You were not of the party, M. de Morcerf?"

"What prince?" asked Albert.

"Prince Cavalcanti," said Danglars, who persisted in giving the young man that title.

"Pardon me," said Albert, "I was not aware that he was a prince. And Prince Cavalcanti sang with Mademoiselle Eugénie yesterday? It must have been charming, indeed. I regret not having heard them. But I was unable to accept your invitation, having promised to accompany my mother to a German concert given by the Baroness of Château-Renaud."

This was followed by rather an awkward silence.

"May I also be allowed," said Morcerf, "to pay my respects to Mademoiselle Danglars?"

"Wait a moment," said the banker, stopping the young man; "do you hear that delightful cavatina? Ta, ta, ta, ti, ta, ti, ta, ta; it is charming, let them finish—one moment. Bravo, bravi, brava!" The banker was enthusiastic in his applause.

"Indeed," said Albert, "it is exquisite; it is impossible to understand the music of his country better than Prince Cavalcanti does. You said prince, did you not? But he can easily become one, if he is not already; it is no uncommon thing in Italy. But to return to the charming musicians—you should give us a treat, Danglars, without telling them there is a stranger. Ask them to sing one more song; it is so delightful to hear music in the distance, when the musicians are unrestrained by observation."

Danglars was quite annoyed by the young man's indifference. He took Monte Cristo aside.

"What do you think of our lover?" said he.

"He appears cool. But, then your word is given."

"Yes, doubtless I have promised to give my daughter to a man who loves her, but not to one who does not. See him there, cold as marble and proud like his father. If he were rich, if he had Cavalcanti's fortune, that might be pardoned. *Ma foi*, I haven't consulted my daughter; but if she has good taste—"

"Oh," said Monte Cristo, "my fondness may blind me, but I assure you I consider Morcerf a charming young man who will render your daughter happy and will sooner or later attain a certain amount of distinction, and his father's position is good."

"Hem," said Danglars.

"Why do you doubt?"

"The past—that obscurity on the past."

"But that does not affect the son."

"Very true."

"Now, I beg of you, don't go off your head. It's a month now that you have been thinking of this marriage, and you must see that it throws some responsibility on me, for it was at my house you met this young Cavalcanti, whom I do not really know at all."

"But I do."

"Have you made inquiry?"

"Is there any need of that! Does not his appearance speak for him? And he is very rich."

"I am not so sure of that."

"And yet you said he had money."

"Fifty thousand livres—a mere trifle."

"He is well educated."

"Hem," said Monte Cristo in his turn.

"He is a musician."

"So are all Italians."

"Come, count, you do not do that young man justice."

"Well, I acknowledge it annoys me, knowing your connection with the Morcerf family, to see him throw himself in the way." Danglars burst out laughing.

"What a Puritan you are!" said he; "that happens every day."

"But you cannot break it off in this way; the Morcerfs are depending on this union."

"Indeed."

"Positively."

"Then let them explain themselves; you should give the father a hint, you are so intimate with the family."

"I?—where the devil did you find out that?"

"At their ball; it was apparent enough. Why, did not the countess, the proud Mercédès, the disdainful Catalane, who will scarcely open her lips to her oldest acquaintances, take your arm, lead you into the garden, into the private walks, and remain there for half an hour?"

"Ah, baron, baron," said Albert, "you are not listening—what barbarism in a megalomaniac like you!"

"Oh, don't worry about me, Sir Mocker," said Danglars; then turning to Monte Cristo he said:

"But will you undertake to speak to the father?"

"Willingly, if you wish it."

"But let it be done explicitly and positively. If he demands my daughter let him fix the day—declare his conditions; in short, let us either understand each other, or quarrel. You understand—no more delay."

"Yes, sir, I will give my attention to the subject."

"I do not say that I await with pleasure his decision, but I do await it. A banker must, you know, be a slave to his promise." And Danglars sighed as M. Cavalcanti had done half an hour before.

"Bravi! bravo! brava!" cried Morcerf, parodying the banker, as the selection came to an end. Danglars began to look suspiciously at Morcerf, when someone came and whispered a few words to him.

"I shall soon return," said the banker to Monte Cristo; "wait for me. I shall, perhaps, have something to say to you." And he went out.

The baroness took advantage of her husband's absence to push open the door of her daughter's study, and M. Andrea, who was sitting before the piano with Mademoiselle Eugénie, started up like a jack-in-the-box. Albert bowed with a smile to Mademoiselle Danglars, who did not appear in the least disturbed, and returned his bow with her usual coolness. Cavalcanti was evidently embarrassed; he bowed to Morcerf, who replied with the most impertinent look possible. Then Albert launched out in praise of Mademoiselle Danglars' voice, and on his regret, after what he had just heard, that he had been unable to be present the previous evening.

Cavalcanti, being left alone, turned to Monte Cristo.

"Come," said Madame Danglars, "leave music and compliments, and let us go and take tea."

"Come, Louise," said Mademoiselle Danglars to her friend.

They passed into the next drawing-room, where tea was prepared. Just as they were beginning, in the English fashion, to leave the spoons in their cups, the door again opened and Danglars entered, visibly agitated. Monte Cristo observed it particularly, and by a look asked the banker for an explanation.

"I have just received my courier from Greece," said Danglars.

"Ah, yes," said the count; "that was the reason of your running away from us."

"Yes."

"How is King Otho getting on?" asked Albert in the most sprightly tone.

Danglars cast another suspicious look towards him without answering, and Monte Cristo turned away to conceal the expression of pity which passed over his features, but which was gone in a moment.

"We shall go together, shall we not?" said Albert to the count.

"If you like," replied the latter.

Albert could not understand the banker's look, and turning to Monte Cristo, who understood it perfectly,—"Did you see," said he, "how he looked at me?"

"Yes," said the count; "but did you think there was anything particular in his look?"

"Indeed, I did; and what does he mean by his news from Greece?"

"How can I tell you?"

"Because I imagine you have correspondents in that country."

Monte Cristo smiled significantly.

"Stop," said Albert, "here he comes. I shall compliment Mademoiselle Danglars on her cameo, while the father talks to you."

"If you compliment her at all, let it be on her voice, at least," said Monte Cristo.

"No, everyone would do that."

"My dear viscount, you are dreadfully impertinent."

Albert advanced towards Eugénie, smiling.

Meanwhile, Danglars, stooping to Monte Cristo's ear, "Your advice was excellent," said he; "there is a whole history connected with the names Fernand and Yanina."

"Indeed?" said Monte Cristo.

"Yes, I will tell you all; but take away the young man; I cannot endure his presence."

"He is going with me. Shall I send the father to you?"

"Immediately."

"Very well." The count made a sign to Albert and they bowed to the ladies, and took their leave, Albert perfectly indifferent to Mademoiselle Danglars' contempt, Monte Cristo reiterating his advice to Madame Danglars on the prudence a banker's wife should exercise in providing for the future.

M. Cavalcanti remained master of the field.

Study Guide Questions

For Students:

1. What does Madame Danglars tell about the Villefort family to the Count?
2. Who is Mademoiselle d'Armilly?
3. Why is Danglars agitated upon receiving a courier from Greece?

For Reading Club:

1. Discuss the irony in Baron Danglars' statement when he says, "I do not like anyone to deny his origin."
2. Danglars finds Andrea a perfect match for his daughter but a month ago Albert was his perfect choice. Do you think greed rules the life of this man?
3. Why does Danglars ask the Count to talk to M. de Morcerf?

CHAPTER 77

Haydée

Scarcely had the count's horses cleared the angle of the boulevard, when Albert, turning towards the count, burst into a loud fit of laughter—much too loud in fact not to give the idea of its being rather forced and unnatural.

"Well," said he, "I will ask you the same question which Charles IX. put to Catherine de' Medici, after the massacre of Saint Bartholomew: 'How have I played my little part?'"

"To what do you allude?" asked Monte Cristo.

"To the installation of my rival at M. Danglars'."

"What rival?"

"*Ma foi!* what rival? Why, your protégé, M. Andrea Cavalcanti!"

"Ah, no joking, viscount, if you please; I do not patronize M. Andrea—at least, not as concerns M. Danglars."

"And you would be to blame for not assisting him, if the young man really needed your help in that quarter, but, happily for me, he can dispense with it."

"What, do you think he is paying his addresses?"

"I am certain of it; his languishing looks and modulated tones when addressing Mademoiselle Danglars fully proclaim his intentions. He aspires to the hand of the proud Eugénie."

"What does that signify, so long as they favor your suit?"

"But it is not the case, my dear count: on the contrary. I am repulsed on all sides."

"What!"

"It is so indeed; Mademoiselle Eugénie scarcely answers me, and Mademoiselle d'Armilly, her confidant, does not speak to me at all."

"But the father has the greatest regard possible for you," said Monte Cristo.

"He? Oh, no, he has plunged a thousand daggers into my heart, tragedy-weapons, I own, which instead of wounding sheathe their points in their own handles, but daggers which he nevertheless believed to be real and deadly."

"Jealousy indicates affection."

"True; but I am not jealous."

"He is."

"Of whom?—of Debray?"

"No, of you."

"Of me? I will engage to say that before a week is past the door will be closed against me."

"You are mistaken, my dear viscount."

"Prove it to me."

"Do you wish me to do so?"

"Yes."

"Well, I am charged with the commission of endeavoring to induce the Comte de Morcerf to make some definite arrangement with the baron."

"By whom are you charged?"

"By the baron himself."

"Oh," said Albert with all the cajolery of which he was capable. "You surely will not do that, my dear count?"

"Certainly I shall, Albert, as I have promised to do it."

"Well," said Albert, with a sigh, "it seems you are determined to marry me."

"I am determined to try and be on good terms with everybody, at all events," said Monte Cristo. "But apropos of Debray, how is it that I have not seen him lately at the baron's house?"

"There has been a misunderstanding."

"What, with the baroness?"

"No, with the baron."

"Has he perceived anything?"

"Ah, that is a good joke!"

"Do you think he suspects?" said Monte Cristo with charming artlessness.

"Where have you come from, my dear count?" said Albert.

"From Congo, if you will."

"It must be farther off than even that."

"But what do I know of your Parisian husbands?"

"Oh, my dear count, husbands are pretty much the same everywhere; an individual husband of any country is a pretty fair specimen of the whole race."

"But then, what can have led to the quarrel between Danglars and Debray? They seemed to understand each other so well," said Monte Cristo with renewed energy.

"Ah, now you are trying to penetrate into the mysteries of Isis, in which I am not initiated. When M. Andrea Cavalcanti has become one of the family, you can ask him that question."

The carriage stopped.

"Here we are," said Monte Cristo; "it is only half-past ten o'clock, come in."

"Certainly, I will."

"My carriage shall take you back."

"No, thank you; I gave orders for my *coupé* to follow me."

"There it is, then," said Monte Cristo, as he stepped out of the carriage. They both went into the house; the drawing-room was lighted up—they went in there. "You will make tea for us, Baptistin," said the count. Baptistin left the room without waiting to answer, and in two seconds reappeared, bringing on a tray, all that his master had ordered, ready prepared, and appearing to have sprung from the ground, like the repasts which we read of in fairy tales.

"Really, my dear count," said Morcerf, "what I admire in you is, not so much your riches, for perhaps there are people even wealthier than yourself, nor is it only your wit, for Beaumarchais might have possessed as much,—but it is your manner of being served, without any questions, in a moment, in a second; it is as if they guessed what you wanted by your manner of ringing, and made a point of keeping everything you can possibly desire in constant readiness."

"What you say is perhaps true; they know my habits. For instance, you shall see; how do you wish to occupy yourself during tea-time?"

"*Ma foi*, I should like to smoke."

Monte Cristo took the gong and struck it once. In about the space of a second a private door opened, and Ali appeared, bringing two chibouques filled with excellent latakia.

"It is quite wonderful," said Albert.

"Oh no, it is as simple as possible," replied Monte Cristo. "Ali knows I generally smoke while I am taking my tea or coffee; he has heard that I ordered tea, and he also knows that I brought you home with me; when I summoned him he naturally guessed the reason of my doing so, and as he comes from a country where hospitality is especially manifested through the medium of smoking, he naturally concludes that we shall smoke in company, and therefore brings two chibouques instead of one—and now the mystery is solved."

"Certainly you give a most commonplace air to your explanation, but it is not the less true that you—Ah, but what do I hear?" and Morcerf inclined his head towards the door, through which sounds seemed to issue resembling those of a guitar.

"*Ma foi*, my dear viscount, you are fated to hear music this evening; you have only escaped from Mademoiselle Danglars' piano, to be attacked by Haydée's guzla."

"Haydée—what an adorable name! Are there, then, really women who bear the name of Haydée anywhere but in Byron's poems?"

"Certainly there are. Haydée is a very uncommon name in France, but is common enough in Albania and Epirus; it is as if you said, for example, Chastity, Modesty, Innocence,—it is a kind of baptismal name, as you Parisians call it."

"Oh, that is charming," said Albert, "how I should like to hear my countrywomen called Mademoiselle Goodness, Mademoiselle Silence, Mademoiselle Christian Charity! Only think, then, if Mademoiselle Danglars, instead of being called Claire-Marie-Eugénie, had been named Mademoiselle Chastity-Modesty-Innocence Danglars; what a fine effect that would have produced on the announcement of her marriage!"

"Hush," said the count, "do not joke in so loud a tone; Haydée may hear you, perhaps."

"And you think she would be angry?"

"No, certainly not," said the count with a haughty expression.

"She is very amiable, then, is she not?" said Albert.

"It is not to be called amiability, it is her duty; a slave does not dictate to a master."

"Come; you are joking yourself now. Are there any more slaves to be had who bear this beautiful name?"

"Undoubtedly."

"Really, count, you do nothing, and have nothing like other people. The slave of the Count of Monte Cristo! Why, it is a rank of itself in France, and from the way in which you lavish money, it is a place that must be worth a hundred thousand francs a year."

"A hundred thousand francs! The poor girl originally possessed much more than that; she was born to treasures in comparison with which those recorded in the *Thousand and One Nights* would seem but poverty."

"She must be a princess then."

"You are right; and she is one of the greatest in her country too."

"I thought so. But how did it happen that such a great princess became a slave?"

"How was it that Dionysius the Tyrant became a schoolmaster? The fortune of war, my dear viscount,—the caprice of fortune; that is the way in which these things are to be accounted for."

"And is her name a secret?"

"As regards the generality of mankind it is; but not for you, my dear viscount, who are one of my most intimate friends, and on whose silence I feel I may rely, if I consider it necessary to enjoin it—may I not do so?"

"Certainly; on my word of honor."

"You know the history of the Pasha of Yanina, do you not?"

"Of Ali Tepelini?[6] Oh, yes; it was in his service that my father made his fortune."

"True, I had forgotten that."

"Well, what is Haydée to Ali Tepelini?"

"Merely his daughter."

"What? the daughter of Ali Pasha?"

"Of Ali Pasha and the beautiful Vasiliki."

"And your slave?"

"*Ma foi*, yes."

"But how did she become so?"

"Why, simply from the circumstance of my having bought her one day, as I was passing through the market at Constantinople."

"Wonderful! Really, my dear count, you seem to throw a sort of magic influence over all in which you are concerned; when I listen to you, existence no longer seems reality, but a waking dream. Now, I am perhaps going to make an imprudent and thoughtless request, but—"

"Say on."

"But, since you go out with Haydée, and sometimes even take her to the Opera—"

"Well?"

"I think I may venture to ask you this favor."

"You may venture to ask me anything."

"Well then, my dear count, present me to your princess."

"I will do so; but on two conditions."

"I accept them at once."

"The first is, that you will never tell anyone that I have granted the interview."

---

[6] Ali Pasha, "The Lion," was born at Tepelini, an Albanian village at the foot of the Klissoura Mountains, in 1741. By diplomacy and success in arms he became almost supreme ruler of Albania, Epirus, and adjacent territory. Having aroused the enmity of the Sultan, he was proscribed and put to death by treachery in 1822, at the age of eighty.—Ed.

"Very well," said Albert, extending his hand; "I swear I will not."

"The second is, that you will not tell her that your father ever served hers."

"I give you my oath that I will not."

"Enough, viscount; you will remember those two vows, will you not? But I know you to be a man of honor."

The count again struck the gong. Ali reappeared. "Tell Haydée," said he, "that I will take coffee with her, and give her to understand that I desire permission to present one of my friends to her."

Ali bowed and left the room.

"Now, understand me," said the count, "no direct questions, my dear Morcerf; if you wish to know anything, tell me, and I will ask her."

"Agreed."

Ali reappeared for the third time, and drew back the tapestried hanging which concealed the door, to signify to his master and Albert that they were at liberty to pass on.

"Let us go in," said Monte Cristo.

Albert passed his hand through his hair, and curled his moustache, then, having satisfied himself as to his personal appearance, followed the count into the room, the latter having previously resumed his hat and gloves. Ali was stationed as a kind of advanced guard, and the door was kept by the three French attendants, commanded by Myrtho.

Haydée was awaiting her visitors in the first room of her apartments, which was the drawing-room. Her large eyes were dilated with surprise and expectation, for it was the first time that any man, except Monte Cristo, had been accorded an entrance into her presence. She was sitting on a sofa placed in an angle of the room, with her legs crossed under her in the Eastern fashion, and seemed to have made for herself, as it were, a kind of nest in the rich Indian silks which enveloped her. Near her was the instrument on which she had just been playing; it was elegantly fashioned, and worthy of its mistress. On perceiving Monte Cristo, she arose and welcomed him with a smile peculiar to herself, expressive at once of the most implicit obedience and also of the deepest love. Monte Cristo advanced towards her and extended his hand, which she as usual raised to her lips.

Albert had proceeded no farther than the door, where he remained rooted to the spot, being completely fascinated by the sight of such surpassing beauty, beheld as it was for the first time, and of which an inhabitant of more northern climes could form no adequate idea.

"Whom do you bring?" asked the young girl in Romaic, of Monte Cristo; "is it a friend, a brother, a simple acquaintance, or an enemy."

"A friend," said Monte Cristo in the same language.

"What is his name?"

"Count Albert; it is the same man whom I rescued from the hands of the banditti at Rome."

"In what language would you like me to converse with him?"

Monte Cristo turned to Albert. "Do you know modern Greek," asked he.

"Alas! no," said Albert; "nor even ancient Greek, my dear count; never had Homer or Plato a more unworthy scholar than myself."

"Then," said Haydée, proving by her remark that she had quite understood Monte Cristo's question and Albert's answer, "then I will speak either in French or Italian, if my lord so wills it."

Monte Cristo reflected one instant. "You will speak in Italian," said he.

Then, turning towards Albert,—"It is a pity you do not understand either ancient or modern Greek, both of which Haydée speaks so fluently; the poor child will be obliged to talk to you in Italian, which will give you but a very false idea of her powers of conversation."

The count made a sign to Haydée to address his visitor. "Sir," she said to Morcerf, "you are most welcome as the friend of my lord and master." This was said in excellent Tuscan, and with that soft Roman accent which makes the language of Dante as sonorous as that of Homer. Then, turning to Ali, she directed him to bring coffee and pipes, and when he had left the room to execute the orders of his young mistress she beckoned Albert to approach nearer to her. Monte Cristo and Morcerf drew their seats towards a small table, on which were arranged music, drawings, and vases of flowers. Ali then entered bringing coffee and chibouques; as to M. Baptistin, this portion of the building was interdicted to him. Albert refused the pipe which the Nubian offered him.

"Oh, take it—take it," said the count; "Haydée is almost as civilized as a Parisian; the smell of a Havana is disagreeable to her, but the tobacco of the East is a most delicious perfume, you know."

Ali left the room. The cups of coffee were all prepared, with the addition of sugar, which had been brought for Albert. Monte Cristo and Haydée took the beverage in the original Arabian manner, that is to say, without sugar. Haydée took the porcelain cup in her little slender fingers and conveyed it to her mouth with all the innocent artlessness of a child when eating or drinking something which it likes. At this moment two women entered, bringing salvers filled with ices and sherbet, which they placed on two small tables appropriated to that purpose.

"My dear host, and you, signora," said Albert, in Italian, "excuse my apparent stupidity. I am quite bewildered, and it is natural that it should be so. Here I am in the heart of Paris; but a moment ago I heard the rumbling of the omnibuses and the tinkling of the bells of the lemonade-sellers, and now I feel as if I were suddenly transported to the East; not such as I have seen it, but such as my dreams have painted it. Oh, signora, if I could but speak Greek, your conversation, added to the fairy-scene which surrounds me, would furnish an evening of such delight as it would be impossible for me ever to forget."

"I speak sufficient Italian to enable me to converse with you, sir," said Haydée quietly; "and if you like what is Eastern, I will do my best to secure the gratification of your tastes while you are here."

"On what subject shall I converse with her?" said Albert, in a low tone to Monte Cristo.

"Just what you please; you may speak of her country and of her youthful reminiscences, or if you like it better you can talk of Rome, Naples, or Florence."

"Oh," said Albert, "it is of no use to be in the company of a Greek if one converses just in the same style as with a Parisian; let me speak to her of the East."

"Do so then, for of all themes which you could choose that will be the most agreeable to her taste."

Albert turned towards Haydée. "At what age did you leave Greece, signora?" asked he.

"I left it when I was but five years old," replied Haydée.

"And have you any recollection of your country?"

"When I shut my eyes and think, I seem to see it all again. The mind can see as well as the body. The body forgets sometimes; but the mind always remembers."

"And how far back into the past do your recollections extend?"

"I could scarcely walk when my mother, who was called Vasiliki, which means royal," said the young girl, tossing her head proudly, "took me by the hand, and after putting in our purse all the money we possessed, we went out, both covered with veils, to solicit alms for the prisoners, saying, 'He who giveth to the poor lendeth to the Lord.' Then when our purse was full we returned to the palace, and without saying a word to my father, we sent it to the convent, where it was divided amongst the prisoners."

"And how old were you at that time?"

"I was three years old," said Haydée.

"Then you remember everything that went on about you from the time when you were three years old?" said Albert.

"Everything."

"Count," said Albert, in a low tone to Monte Cristo, "do allow the signora to tell me something of her history. You prohibited my mentioning my father's name to her, but perhaps she will allude to him of her own accord in the course of the recital, and you have no idea how delighted I should be to hear our name pronounced by such beautiful lips."

Monte Cristo turned to Haydée, and with an expression of countenance which commanded her to pay the most implicit attention to his words, he said in Greek, "Πατρὸς μὲν ἄτην μήζε τὸ ὄνομα προδότου καὶ προδοσίαν εἰπὲ ἡμῖν,"—that is, "Tell us the fate of your father; but neither the name of the traitor nor the treason." Haydée sighed deeply, and a shade of sadness clouded her beautiful brow.

"What are you saying to her?" said Morcerf in an undertone.

"I again reminded her that you were a friend, and that she need not conceal anything from you."

"Then," said Albert, "this pious pilgrimage in behalf of the prisoners was your first remembrance; what is the next?"

"Oh, then I remember as if it were but yesterday sitting under the shade of some sycamore-trees, on the borders of a lake, in the waters of which the trembling foliage was reflected as in a mirror. Under the oldest and thickest of these trees, reclining on cushions, sat my father; my mother was at his feet, and I, childlike, amused myself by playing with his long white beard which descended to his girdle, or with the diamond-hilt of the scimitar attached to his girdle. Then from time to time there came to him an Albanian who said something to which I paid no attention, but which he always answered in the same tone of voice, either 'Kill,' or 'Pardon.'"

"It is very strange," said Albert, "to hear such words proceed from the mouth of anyone but an actress on the stage, and one needs constantly to be saying to one's self, 'This is no fiction, it is all reality,' in order to believe it. And how does France appear in your eyes, accustomed as they have been to gaze on such enchanted scenes?"

"I think it is a fine country," said Haydée, "but I see France as it really is, because I look on it with the eyes of a woman; whereas my own country, which I can only judge of from the impression produced on my childish mind, always seems enveloped in a vague atmosphere, which is luminous or otherwise, according as my remembrances of it are sad or joyous."

"So young," said Albert, forgetting at the moment the Count's command that he should ask no questions of the slave herself, "is it possible that you can have known what suffering is except by name?"

Haydée turned her eyes towards Monte Cristo, who, making at the same time some imperceptible sign, murmured:

"Είπέ—speak."

"Nothing is ever so firmly impressed on the mind as the memory of our early childhood, and with the exception of the two scenes I have just described to you, all my earliest reminiscences are fraught with deepest sadness."

"Speak, speak, signora," said Albert, "I am listening with the most intense delight and interest to all you say."

Haydée answered his remark with a melancholy smile. "You wish me, then, to relate the history of my past sorrows?" said she.

"I beg you to do so," replied Albert.

"Well, I was but four years old when one night I was suddenly awakened by my mother. We were in the palace of Yanina; she snatched me from the cushions on which I was sleeping, and on opening my eyes I saw hers filled with tears. She took me away without speaking. When I saw her weeping I began to cry too. 'Hush, child!' said she. At other times in spite of maternal endearments or threats, I had with a child's caprice been accustomed to indulge my feelings of sorrow or anger by crying as much as I felt inclined; but on this occasion there was an intonation of such extreme terror in my mother's voice when she enjoined me to silence, that I ceased crying as soon as her command was given. She bore me rapidly away.

"I saw then that we were descending a large staircase; around us were all my mother's servants carrying trunks, bags, ornaments, jewels, purses of gold, with which they were hurrying away in the greatest distraction.

"Behind the women came a guard of twenty men armed with long guns and pistols, and dressed in the costume which the Greeks have assumed since they have again become a nation. You may imagine there was something startling and ominous," said Haydée, shaking her head and turning pale at the mere remembrance of the scene, "in this long file of slaves and women only half-aroused from sleep, or at least so they appeared to me, who was myself scarcely awake. Here and there on the walls of the staircase, were reflected gigantic shadows, which trembled in the flickering light of the pine-torches till they seemed to reach to the vaulted roof above.

"'Quick!' said a voice at the end of the gallery. This voice made everyone bow before it, resembling in its effect the wind passing over a field of wheat, by its superior strength forcing every ear to yield obeisance. As for me, it made me tremble. This voice was that of my father. He came last, clothed in his splendid robes and holding in his hand the carbine which your emperor presented him. He was leaning on the shoulder of his favorite Selim, and he drove us all before him, as a shepherd would his straggling flock. My father," said Haydée, raising her head, "was that illustrious man known in Europe under the name of Ali Tepelini, pasha of Yanina, and before whom Turkey trembled."

Albert, without knowing why, started on hearing these words pronounced with such a haughty and dignified accent; it appeared to him as if there was something supernaturally gloomy and terrible in the expression which gleamed from the brilliant eyes of Haydée at this moment; she appeared like a Pythoness evoking a spectre, as she recalled to his mind the remembrance of the fearful death of this man, to the news of which all Europe had listened with horror.

"Soon," said Haydée, "we halted on our march, and found ourselves on the borders of a lake. My mother pressed me to her throbbing heart, and at the distance of a few paces I saw my father, who was glancing anxiously around. Four marble steps led down to the water's edge, and below them was a boat floating on the tide.

"From where we stood I could see in the middle of the lake a large blank mass; it was the kiosk to which we were going. This kiosk appeared to me to be at a considerable distance, perhaps on account of the darkness of the night, which prevented any object from being more than partially discerned. We stepped into the boat. I remember well that the oars made no noise whatever in striking the water, and when I leaned over to ascertain the cause I saw that they were muffled with the sashes of our Palikares.[7] Besides the rowers, the boat contained only the women, my father, mother, Selim, and myself. The Palikares had remained on the shore of the lake, ready to cover our retreat; they were kneeling on the lowest of the marble steps, and in that manner intended making a rampart of the three others, in case of pursuit. Our bark flew before the wind. 'Why does the boat go so fast?' asked I of my mother.

"'Silence, child! Hush, we are flying!' I did not understand. Why should my father fly?—he, the all-powerful—he, before whom others were accustomed to fly—he, who had taken for his device,

'They hate me; then they fear me!'

"It was, indeed, a flight which my father was trying to effect. I have been told since that the garrison of the castle of Yanina, fatigued with long service—"

Here Haydée cast a significant glance at Monte Cristo, whose eyes had been riveted on her countenance during the whole course of her narrative. The young girl

[7] Greek militiamen in the war for independence.—Ed.

then continued, speaking slowly, like a person who is either inventing or suppressing some feature of the history which he is relating.

"You were saying, signora," said Albert, who was paying the most implicit attention to the recital, "that the garrison of Yanina, fatigued with long service—"

"Had treated with the Seraskier[8] Kourchid, who had been sent by the sultan to gain possession of the person of my father; it was then that Ali Tepelini—after having sent to the sultan a French officer in whom he reposed great confidence—resolved to retire to the asylum which he had long before prepared for himself, and which he called *kataphygion*, or the refuge."

"And this officer," asked Albert, "do you remember his name, signora?"

Monte Cristo exchanged a rapid glance with the young girl, which was quite unperceived by Albert.

"No," said she, "I do not remember it just at this moment; but if it should occur to me presently, I will tell you."

Albert was on the point of pronouncing his father's name, when Monte Cristo gently held up his finger in token of reproach; the young man recollected his promise, and was silent.

"It was towards this kiosk that we were rowing. A ground floor, ornamented with arabesques, bathing its terraces in the water, and another floor, looking on the lake, was all which was visible to the eye. But beneath the ground floor, stretching out into the island, was a large subterranean cavern, to which my mother, myself, and the women were conducted. In this place were together 60,000 pouches and 200 barrels; the pouches contained 25,000,000 of money in gold, and the barrels were filled with 30,000 pounds of gunpowder.

"Near the barrels stood Selim, my father's favorite, whom I mentioned to you just now. He stood watch day and night with a lance provided with a lighted slowmatch in his hand, and he had orders to blow up everything—kiosk, guards, women, gold, and Ali Tepelini himself—at the first signal given by my father. I remember well that the slaves, convinced of the precarious tenure on which they held their lives, passed whole days and nights in praying, crying, and groaning. As for me, I can never forget the pale complexion and black eyes of the young soldier, and whenever the angel of death summons me to another world, I am quite sure I shall recognize Selim. I cannot tell you how long we remained in this state; at that period I did not even know what time meant. Sometimes, but very rarely, my father summoned me and my mother to the terrace of the palace; these were hours of recreation for me, as I never saw anything in

[8] A Turkish pasha in command of the troops of a province.—Ed.

the dismal cavern but the gloomy countenances of the slaves and Selim's fiery lance. My father was endeavoring to pierce with his eager looks the remotest verge of the horizon, examining attentively every black speck which appeared on the lake, while my mother, reclining by his side, rested her head on his shoulder, and I played at his feet, admiring everything I saw with that unsophisticated innocence of childhood which throws a charm round objects insignificant in themselves, but which in its eyes are invested with the greatest importance. The heights of Pindus towered above us; the castle of Yanina rose white and angular from the blue waters of the lake, and the immense masses of black vegetation which, viewed in the distance, gave the idea of lichens clinging to the rocks, were in reality gigantic fir-trees and myrtles.

"One morning my father sent for us; my mother had been crying all the night, and was very wretched; we found the pasha calm, but paler than usual. 'Take courage, Vasiliki,' said he; 'today arrives the firman of the master, and my fate will be decided. If my pardon be complete, we shall return triumphant to Yanina; if the news be inauspicious, we must fly this night.'—'But supposing our enemy should not allow us to do so?' said my mother. 'Oh, make yourself easy on that head,' said Ali, smiling; 'Selim and his flaming lance will settle that matter. They would be glad to see me dead, but they would not like themselves to die with me.'

"My mother only answered by sighs to consolations which she knew did not come from my father's heart. She prepared the iced water which he was in the habit of constantly drinking,—for since his sojourn at the kiosk he had been parched by the most violent fever,—after which she anointed his white beard with perfumed oil, and lighted his chibouque, which he sometimes smoked for hours together, quietly watching the wreaths of vapor that ascended in spiral clouds and gradually melted away in the surrounding atmosphere. Presently he made such a sudden movement that I was paralyzed with fear. Then, without taking his eyes from the object which had first attracted his attention, he asked for his telescope. My mother gave it him, and as she did so, looked whiter than the marble against which she leaned. I saw my father's hand tremble. 'A boat!—two!—three!' murmured my, father;—'four!' He then arose, seizing his arms and priming his pistols. 'Vasiliki,' said he to my mother, trembling perceptibly, 'the instant approaches which will decide everything. In the space of half an hour we shall know the emperor's answer. Go into the cavern with Haydée.'—'I will not quit you,' said Vasiliki; 'if you die, my lord, I will die with you.'—'Go to Selim!' cried my father. 'Adieu, my lord,' murmured my mother, determining quietly to await the approach of death. 'Take away Vasiliki!' said my father to his Palikares.

"As for me, I had been forgotten in the general confusion; I ran toward Ali Tepelini; he saw me hold out my arms to him, and he stooped down and pressed my forehead with his lips. Oh, how distinctly I remember that kiss!—it was the last he ever gave me, and I feel as if it were still warm on my forehead. On descending, we saw through the lattice-work several boats which were gradually becoming more distinct to our view. At first they appeared like black specks, and now they looked like birds skimming the surface of the waves. During this time, in the kiosk at my father's feet, were seated twenty Palikares, concealed from view by an angle of the wall and watching with eager eyes the arrival of the boats. They were armed with their long guns inlaid with mother-of-pearl and silver, and cartridges in great numbers were lying scattered on the floor. My father looked at his watch, and paced up and down with a countenance expressive of the greatest anguish. This was the scene which presented itself to my view as I quitted my father after that last kiss.

"My mother and I traversed the gloomy passage leading to the cavern. Selim was still at his post, and smiled sadly on us as we entered. We fetched our cushions from the other end of the cavern, and sat down by Selim. In great dangers the devoted ones cling to each other; and, young as I was, I quite understood that some imminent danger was hanging over our heads."

Albert had often heard—not from his father, for he never spoke on the subject, but from strangers—the description of the last moments of the vizier of Yanina; he had read different accounts of his death, but the story seemed to acquire fresh meaning from the voice and expression of the young girl, and her sympathetic accent and the melancholy expression of her countenance at once charmed and horrified him.

As to Haydée, these terrible reminiscences seemed to have overpowered her for a moment, for she ceased speaking, her head leaning on her hand like a beautiful flower bowing beneath the violence of the storm; and her eyes gazing on vacancy indicated that she was mentally contemplating the green summit of the Pindus and the blue waters of the lake of Yanina, which, like a magic mirror, seemed to reflect the sombre picture which she sketched. Monte Cristo looked at her with an indescribable expression of interest and pity.

"Go on, my child," said the count in the Romaic language.

Haydée looked up abruptly, as if the sonorous tones of Monte Cristo's voice had awakened her from a dream; and she resumed her narrative.

"It was about four o'clock in the afternoon, and although the day was brilliant out-of-doors, we were enveloped in the gloomy darkness of the cavern. One single, solitary light was burning there, and it appeared like a star set in a heaven of blackness; it was Selim's flaming lance. My mother was a Christian, and she prayed. Selim repeated from time to time the sacred words: 'God is great!' However, my mother had still some hope. As she was coming down, she thought she recognized the French officer who had been sent to Constantinople, and in whom my father placed so much confidence; for he knew that all the soldiers of the French emperor were naturally noble and generous. She advanced some steps towards the staircase, and listened. 'They are approaching,' said she; 'perhaps they bring us peace and liberty!'

"'What do you fear, Vasiliki?' said Selim, in a voice at once so gentle and yet so proud. 'If they do not bring us peace, we will give them war; if they do not bring life, we will give them death.' And he renewed the flame of his lance with a gesture which made one think of Dionysus of old Crete.[9] But I, being only a little child, was terrified by this undaunted courage, which appeared to me both ferocious and senseless, and I recoiled with horror from the idea of the frightful death amidst fire and flames which probably awaited us.

"My mother experienced the same sensations, for I felt her tremble. 'Mamma, mamma,' said I, 'are we really to be killed?' And at the sound of my voice the slaves redoubled their cries and prayers and lamentations. 'My child,' said Vasiliki, 'may God preserve you from ever wishing for that death which today you so much dread!' Then, whispering to Selim, she asked what were her master's orders. 'If he send me his poniard, it will signify that the emperor's intentions are not favorable, and I am to set fire to the powder; if, on the contrary, he send me his ring, it will be a sign that the emperor pardons him, and I am to extinguish the match and leave the magazine untouched.'—'My friend,' said my mother, 'when your master's orders arrive, if it is the poniard which he sends, instead of despatching us by that horrible death which we both so much dread, you will mercifully kill us with this same poniard, will you not?'—'Yes, Vasiliki,' replied Selim tranquilly.

"Suddenly we heard loud cries; and, listening, discerned that they were cries of joy. The name of the French officer who had been sent to Constantinople resounded on all sides amongst our Palikares; it was evident that he brought the answer of the emperor, and that it was favorable."

"And do you not remember the Frenchman's name?" said Morcerf, quite ready to aid the memory of the narrator. Monte Cristo made a sign to him to be silent.

"I do not recollect it," said Haydée.

"The noise increased; steps were heard approaching nearer and nearer; they were descending the steps leading to the cavern. Selim made ready his lance. Soon a figure appeared in the gray twilight at the entrance of the cave, formed by the reflection of the few rays of daylight which had found their way into this gloomy retreat. 'Who are

[9] The god of fruitfulness in Grecian mythology. In Crete he was supposed to be slain in winter with the decay of vegetation and to revive in the spring. Haydée's learned reference is to the behavior of an actor in the Dionysian festivals.—Ed.

you?' cried Selim. 'But whoever you may be, I charge you not to advance another step.'—'Long live the emperor!' said the figure. 'He grants a full pardon to the Vizier Ali, and not only gives him his life, but restores to him his fortune and his possessions.' My mother uttered a cry of joy, and clasped me to her bosom. 'Stop,' said Selim, seeing that she was about to go out; 'you see I have not yet received the ring,'—'True,' said my mother. And she fell on her knees, at the same time holding me up towards heaven, as if she desired, while praying to God in my behalf, to raise me actually to his presence."

And for the second time Haydée stopped, overcome by such violent emotion that the perspiration stood upon her pale brow, and her stifled voice seemed hardly able to find utterance, so parched and dry were her throat and lips.

Monte Cristo poured a little iced water into a glass, and presented it to her, saying with a mildness in which was also a shade of command,—"Courage."

Haydée dried her eyes, and continued:

"By this time our eyes, habituated to the darkness, had recognized the messenger of the pasha,—it was a friend. Selim had also recognized him, but the brave young man only acknowledged one duty, which was to obey. 'In whose name do you come?' said he to him. 'I come in the name of our master, Ali Tepelini.'—'If you come from Ali himself,' said Selim, 'you know what you were charged to remit to me?'—'Yes,' said the messenger, 'and I bring you his ring.' At these words he raised his hand above his head, to show the token; but it was too far off, and there was not light enough to enable Selim, where he was standing, to distinguish and recognize the object presented to his view. 'I do not see what you have in your hand,' said Selim. 'Approach then,' said the messenger, 'or I will come nearer to you, if you prefer it.'—'I will agree to neither one nor the other,' replied the young soldier; 'place the object which I desire to see in the ray of light which shines there, and retire while I examine it.'—'Be it so,' said the envoy; and he retired, after having first deposited the token agreed on in the place pointed out to him by Selim.

"Oh, how our hearts palpitated; for it did, indeed, seem to be a ring which was placed there. But was it my father's ring? that was the question. Selim, still holding in his hand the lighted match, walked towards the opening in the cavern, and, aided by the faint light which streamed in through the mouth of the cave, picked up the token.

"'It is well,' said he, kissing it; 'it is my master's ring!' And throwing the match on the ground, he trampled on it and extinguished it. The messenger uttered a cry of joy and clapped his hands. At this signal four soldiers of the Seraskier Kourchid suddenly appeared, and Selim fell, pierced by five blows. Each man had stabbed him separately, and, intoxicated by their crime, though still pale with fear, they sought all over the cavern to discover if there was any fear of fire, after which they amused themselves by rolling on the bags of gold. At this moment my mother seized me in her arms, and hurrying noiselessly along numerous turnings and windings known only to ourselves, she arrived at a private staircase of the kiosk, where was a scene of frightful tumult and confusion. The lower rooms were entirely filled with Kourchid's troops; that is to say, with our enemies. Just as my mother was on the point of pushing open a small door, we heard the voice of the pasha sounding in a loud and threatening tone. My mother applied her eye to the crack between the boards; I luckily found a small opening which afforded me a view of the apartment and what was passing within. 'What do you want?' said my father to some people who were holding a paper inscribed with characters of gold. 'What we want,' replied one, 'is to communicate to you the will of his highness. Do you see this firman?'—'I do,' said my father. 'Well, read it; he demands your head.'

"My father answered with a loud laugh, which was more frightful than even threats would have been, and he had not ceased when two reports of a pistol were heard; he had fired them himself, and had killed two men. The Palikares, who were prostrated at my father's feet, now sprang up and fired, and the room was filled with fire and smoke. At the same instant the firing began on the other side, and the balls penetrated the boards all round us. Oh, how noble did the grand vizier my father look at that moment, in the midst of the flying bullets, his scimitar in his hand, and his face blackened with the powder of his enemies! and how he terrified them, even then, and made them fly before him! 'Selim, Selim!' cried he, 'guardian of the fire, do your duty!'—'Selim is dead,' replied a voice which seemed to come from the depths of the earth, 'and you are lost, Ali!' At the same moment an explosion was heard, and the flooring of the room in which my father was sitting was suddenly torn up and shivered to atoms—the troops were firing from underneath. Three or four Palikares fell with their bodies literally ploughed with wounds.

"My father howled aloud, plunged his fingers into the holes which the balls had made, and tore up one of the planks entire. But immediately through this opening twenty more shots were fired, and the flame, rushing up like fire from the crater of a volcano, soon reached the tapestry, which it quickly devoured. In the midst of all this frightful tumult and these terrific cries, two reports, fearfully distinct, followed by two shrieks more heartrending than all, froze me with terror. These two shots had mortally wounded my father, and it was he who had given utterance to these frightful cries. However, he remained standing, clinging to a window. My mother tried to force the door, that she might go and die with him, but it was fastened on the inside. All around him were lying the Palikares, writhing in convulsive agonies, while two or three who were only slightly wounded were trying to escape by springing from the windows. At this crisis the whole flooring suddenly gave way, my father fell on one knee, and at the same moment twenty hands were thrust forth, armed with sabres, pistols, and poniards—twenty blows were instantaneously directed against one man, and my father disappeared in a whirlwind of fire and smoke kindled by these demons, and which seemed like hell itself opening beneath his feet. I felt myself fall to the ground, my mother had fainted."

Haydée's arms fell by her side, and she uttered a deep groan, at the same time looking towards the count as if to ask if he were satisfied with her obedience to his commands.

Monte Cristo arose and approached her, took her hand, and said to her in Romaic:

"Calm yourself, my dear child, and take courage in remembering that there is a God who will punish traitors."

"It is a frightful story, count," said Albert, terrified at the paleness of Haydée's countenance, "and I reproach myself now for having been so cruel and thoughtless in my request."

"Oh, it is nothing," said Monte Cristo. Then, patting the young girl on the head, he continued, "Haydée is very courageous, and she sometimes even finds consolation in the recital of her misfortunes."

"Because, my lord," said Haydée eagerly, "my miseries recall to me the remembrance of your goodness."

Albert looked at her with curiosity, for she had not yet related what he most desired to know,—how she had become the slave of the count. Haydée saw at a glance the same expression pervading the countenances of her two auditors; she continued:

"When my mother recovered her senses we were before the seraskier. 'Kill,' said she, 'but spare the honor of the widow of Ali.'—'It is not to me to whom you must address yourself,' said Kourchid.

"'To whom, then?'—'To your new master.'

"'Who and where is he?'—'He is here.'

"And Kourchid pointed out one who had more than any contributed to the death of my father," said Haydée, in a tone of chastened anger.

"Then," said Albert, "you became the property of this man?"

"No," replied Haydée, "he did not dare to keep us, so we were sold to some slave-merchants who were going to Constantinople. We traversed Greece, and arrived half dead at the imperial gates. They were surrounded by a crowd of people, who opened a way for us to pass, when suddenly my mother, having looked closely at an object which was attracting their attention, uttered a piercing cry and fell to the ground, pointing as she did so to a head which was placed over the gates, and beneath which were inscribed these words:

'*This is the head of Ali Tepelini, Pasha of Yanina.*'

"I cried bitterly, and tried to raise my mother from the earth, but she was dead! I was taken to the slave-market, and was purchased by a rich Armenian. He caused me to be instructed, gave me masters, and when I was thirteen years of age he sold me to the Sultan Mahmoud."

"Of whom I bought her," said Monte Cristo, "as I told you, Albert, with the emerald which formed a match to the one I had made into a box for the purpose of holding my hashish pills."

"Oh, you are good, you are great, my lord!" said Haydée, kissing the count's hand, "and I am very fortunate in belonging to such a master!"

Albert remained quite bewildered with all that he had seen and heard.

"Come, finish your cup of coffee," said Monte Cristo; "the history is ended."

Study Guide Questions

For Students:

1. Why does Albert call Andrea a rival?
2. Who is Ali Tebelen and what is his relationship with Haydée?
3. What is the favor that Albert asks of the Count concerning Haydée?

For Reading Club:

1. Albert is impressed by Haydée's Eastern beauty. Do you think external beauty still impacts one's opinion?
2. Discuss the relationship between Albert's father and Haydée's father.
3. Discuss how the Count comes in possession of Haydée.

CHAPTER 78

We hear From Yanina

If Valentine could have seen the trembling step and agitated countenance of Franz when he quitted the chamber of M. Noirtier, even she would have been constrained to pity him. Villefort had only just given utterance to a few incoherent sentences, and then retired to his study, where he received about two hours afterwards the following letter:

> "After all the disclosures which were made this morning, M. Noirtier de Villefort must see the utter impossibility of any alliance being formed between his family and that of M. Franz d'Épinay. M. d'Épinay must say that he is shocked and astonished that M. de Villefort, who appeared to be aware of all the circumstances detailed this morning, should not have anticipated him in this announcement."

No one who had seen the magistrate at this moment, so thoroughly unnerved by the recent inauspicious combination of circumstances, would have supposed for an instant that he had anticipated the annoyance; although it certainly never had occurred to him that his father would carry candor, or rather rudeness, so far as to relate such a history. And in justice to Villefort, it must be understood that M. Noirtier, who never cared for the opinion of his son on any subject, had always omitted to explain the affair to Villefort, so that he had all his life entertained the belief that General de Quesnel, or the Baron d'Épinay, as he was alternately styled, according as the speaker wished to identify him by his own family name, or by the title which had been conferred on him, fell the victim of assassination, and not that he was killed fairly in a duel. This harsh letter, coming as it did from a man generally so polite and respectful, struck a mortal blow at the pride of Villefort.

Hardly had he read the letter, when his wife entered. The sudden departure of Franz, after being summoned by M. Noirtier, had so much astonished everyone, that the position of Madame de Villefort, left alone with the notary and the witnesses, became every moment more embarrassing. Determined to bear it no longer, she arose and left the room; saying she would go and make some inquiries into the cause of his sudden disappearance.

M. de Villefort's communications on the subject were very limited and concise; he told her, in fact, that an explanation had taken place between M. Noirtier, M. d'Épinay, and himself, and that the marriage of Valentine and Franz would consequently be broken off. This was an awkward and unpleasant thing to have to report to those who were waiting. She therefore contented herself with saying that M. Noirtier having at the commencement of the discussion been attacked by a sort of apoplectic fit, the affair would necessarily be deferred for some days longer. This news, false as it was following so singularly in the train of the two similar misfortunes which had so recently occurred, evidently astonished the auditors, and they retired without a word.

During this time Valentine, at once terrified and happy, after having embraced and thanked the feeble old man for thus breaking with a single blow the chain which she had been accustomed to consider as irrefragable, asked leave to retire to her own room, in order to recover her composure. Noirtier looked the permission which she solicited. But instead of going to her own room, Valentine, having once gained her liberty, entered the gallery, and, opening a small door at the end of it, found herself at once in the garden.

In the midst of all the strange events which had crowded one on the other, an indefinable sentiment of dread had taken possession of Valentine's mind. She expected every moment that she should see Morrel appear, pale and trembling, to forbid the signing of the contract, like the Laird of Ravenswood in *The Bride of Lammermoor.*

It was high time for her to make her appearance at the gate, for Maximilian had long awaited her coming. He had half guessed what was going on when he saw Franz quit the cemetery with M. de Villefort. He followed M. d'Épinay, saw him enter, afterwards go out, and then re-enter with Albert and Château-Renaud. He had no longer any doubts as to the nature of the conference; he therefore quickly went to the gate in the clover-patch, prepared to hear the result of the proceedings, and very certain that Valentine would hasten to him the first moment she should be set at liberty. He was not mistaken; peering through the crevices of the wooden partition, he soon discovered the young girl, who cast aside all her usual precautions and walked at once to the barrier. The first glance which Maximilian directed towards her entirely reassured him, and the first words she spoke made his heart bound with delight.

"We are saved!" said Valentine.

"Saved?" repeated Morrel, not being able to conceive such intense happiness; "by whom?"

"By my grandfather. Oh, Morrel, pray love him for all his goodness to us!"

Morrel swore to love him with all his soul; and at that moment he could safely promise to do so, for he felt as though it were not enough to love him merely as a friend or even as a father, he worshiped him as a god.

"But tell me, Valentine, how has it all been effected? What strange means has he used to compass this blessed end?"

Valentine was on the point of relating all that had passed, but she suddenly remembered that in doing so she must reveal a terrible secret which concerned others as well as her grandfather, and she said:

"At some future time I will tell you all about it."

"But when will that be?"

"When I am your wife."

The conversation had now turned upon a topic so pleasing to Morrel, that he was ready to accede to anything that Valentine thought fit to propose, and he likewise felt that a piece of intelligence such as he just heard ought to be more than sufficient to content him for one day. However, he would not leave without the promise of seeing Valentine again the next night. Valentine promised all that Morrel required of her, and certainly it was less difficult now for her to believe that she should marry Maximilian than it was an hour ago to assure herself that she should not marry Franz.

During the time occupied by the interview we have just detailed, Madame de Villefort had gone to visit M. Noirtier. The old man looked at her with that stern and forbidding expression with which he was accustomed to receive her.

"Sir," said she, "it is superfluous for me to tell you that Valentine's marriage is broken off, since it was here that the affair was concluded."

Noirtier's countenance remained immovable.

"But one thing I can tell you, of which I do not think you are aware; that is, that I have always been opposed to this marriage, and that the contract was entered into entirely without my consent or approbation."

Noirtier regarded his daughter-in-law with the look of a man desiring an explanation.

"Now that this marriage, which I know you so much disliked, is done away with, I come to you on an errand which neither M. de Villefort nor Valentine could consistently undertake."

Noirtier's eyes demanded the nature of her mission.

"I come to entreat you, sir," continued Madame de Villefort, "as the only one who has the right of doing so, inasmuch as I am the only one who will receive no personal benefit from the transaction,—I come to entreat you to restore, not your love, for that she has always possessed, but to restore your fortune to your granddaughter."

There was a doubtful expression in Noirtier's eyes; he was evidently trying to discover the motive of this proceeding, and he could not succeed in doing so.

"May I hope, sir," said Madame de Villefort, "that your intentions accord with my request?"

Noirtier made a sign that they did.

"In that case, sir," rejoined Madame de Villefort, "I will leave you overwhelmed with gratitude and happiness at your prompt acquiescence to my wishes." She then bowed to M. Noirtier and retired.

The next day M. Noirtier sent for the notary; the first will was torn up and a second made, in which he left the whole of his fortune to Valentine, on condition that she should never be separated from him. It was then generally reported that Mademoiselle de Villefort, the heiress of the marquis and marchioness of Saint-Méran, had regained the good graces of her grandfather, and that she would ultimately be in possession of an income of 300,000 livres.

While all the proceedings relative to the dissolution of the marriage-contract were being carried on at the house of M. de Villefort, Monte Cristo had paid his visit to the Count of Morcerf, who, in order to lose no time in responding to M. Danglars' wishes, and at the same time to pay all due deference to his position in society, donned his uniform of lieutenant-general, which he ornamented with all his crosses, and thus attired, ordered his finest horses and drove to the Rue de la Chaussée d'Antin.

Danglars was balancing his monthly accounts, and it was perhaps not the most favorable moment for finding him in his best humor. At the first sight of his old friend, Danglars assumed his majestic air, and settled himself in his easy-chair.

Morcerf, usually so stiff and formal, accosted the banker in an affable and smiling manner, and, feeling sure that the overture he was about to make would be well received, he did not consider it necessary to adopt any manœuvres in order to gain his end, but went at once straight to the point.

"Well, baron," said he, "here I am at last; some time has elapsed since our plans were formed, and they are not yet executed."

Morcerf paused at these words, quietly waiting till the cloud should have dispersed which had gathered on the brow of Danglars, and which he attributed to his silence; but, on the contrary, to his great surprise, it grew darker and darker.

"To what do you allude, monsieur?" said Danglars; as if he were trying in vain to guess at the possible meaning of the general's words.

"Ah," said Morcerf, "I see you are a stickler for forms, my dear sir, and you would remind me that the ceremonial rites should not be omitted. *Ma foi*, I beg your pardon, but as I have but one son, and it is the first time I have ever thought of marrying him, I am still serving my apprenticeship, you know; come, I will reform."

And Morcerf with a forced smile arose, and, making a low bow to M. Danglars, said:

"Baron, I have the honor of asking of you the hand of Mademoiselle Eugénie Danglars for my son, the Vicomte Albert de Morcerf."

But Danglars, instead of receiving this address in the favorable manner which Morcerf had expected, knit his brow, and without inviting the count, who was still standing, to take a seat, he said:

"Monsieur, it will be necessary to reflect before I give you an answer."

"To reflect?" said Morcerf, more and more astonished; "have you not had enough time for reflection during the eight years which have elapsed since this marriage was first discussed between us?"

"Count," said the banker, "things are constantly occurring in the world to induce us to lay aside our most established opinions, or at all events to cause us to remodel them according to the change of circumstances, which may have placed affairs in a totally different light to that in which we at first viewed them."

"I do not understand you, baron," said Morcerf.

"What I mean to say is this, sir,—that during the last fortnight unforeseen circumstances have occurred—"

"Excuse me," said Morcerf, "but is it a play we are acting?"

"A play?"

"Yes, for it is like one; pray let us come more to the point, and endeavor thoroughly to understand each other."

"That is quite my desire."

"You have seen M. de Monte Cristo have you not?"

"I see him very often," said Danglars, drawing himself up; "he is a particular friend of mine."

"Well, in one of your late conversations with him, you said that I appeared to be forgetful and irresolute concerning this marriage, did you not?"

"I did say so."

"Well, here I am, proving at once that I am really neither the one nor the other, by entreating you to keep your promise on that score."

Danglars did not answer.

"Have you so soon changed your mind," added Morcerf, "or have you only provoked my request that you may have the pleasure of seeing me humbled?"

Danglars, seeing that if he continued the conversation in the same tone in which he had begun it, the whole thing might turn out to his own disadvantage, turned to Morcerf, and said:

"Count, you must doubtless be surprised at my reserve, and I assure you it costs me much to act in such a manner towards you; but, believe me when I say that imperative necessity has imposed the painful task upon me."

"These are all so many empty words, my dear sir," said Morcerf: "they might satisfy a new acquaintance, but the Comte de Morcerf does not rank in that list; and when a man like him comes to another, recalls to him his plighted word, and this man fails to redeem the pledge, he has at least a right to exact from him a good reason for so doing."

Danglars was a coward, but did not wish to appear so; he was piqued at the tone which Morcerf had just assumed.

"I am not without a good reason for my conduct," replied the banker.

"What do you mean to say?"

"I mean to say that I have a good reason, but that it is difficult to explain."

"You must be aware, at all events, that it is impossible for me to understand motives before they are explained to me; but one thing at least is clear, which is, that you decline allying yourself with my family."

"No, sir," said Danglars; "I merely suspend my decision, that is all."

"And do you really flatter yourself that I shall yield to all your caprices, and quietly and humbly await the time of again being received into your good graces?"

"Then, count, if you will not wait, we must look upon these projects as if they had never been entertained."

The count bit his lips till the blood almost started, to prevent the ebullition of anger which his proud and irritable temper scarcely allowed him to restrain; understanding, however, that in the present state of things the laugh would decidedly be against him, he turned from the door, towards which he had been directing his steps, and again confronted the banker. A cloud settled on his brow, evincing decided anxiety and uneasiness, instead of the expression of offended pride which had lately reigned there.

"My dear Danglars," said Morcerf, "we have been acquainted for many years, and consequently we ought to make some allowance for each other's failings. You owe me an explanation, and really it is but fair that I should know what circumstance has occurred to deprive my son of your favor."

"It is from no personal ill-feeling towards the viscount, that is all I can say, sir," replied Danglars, who resumed his insolent manner as soon as he perceived that Morcerf was a little softened and calmed down.

"And towards whom do you bear this personal ill-feeling, then?" said Morcerf, turning pale with anger. The expression of the count's face had not remained unperceived by the banker; he fixed on him a look of greater assurance than before, and said:

"You may, perhaps, be better satisfied that I should not go farther into particulars."

A tremor of suppressed rage shook the whole frame of the count, and making a violent effort over himself, he said: "I have a right to insist on your giving me an explanation. Is it Madame de Morcerf who has displeased you? Is it my fortune which you find insufficient? Is it because my opinions differ from yours?"

"Nothing of the kind, sir," replied Danglars: "if such had been the case, I only should have been to blame, inasmuch as I was aware of all these things when I made the engagement. No, do not seek any longer to discover the reason. I really am quite ashamed to have been the cause of your undergoing such severe self-examination; let us drop the subject, and adopt the middle course of delay, which implies neither a rupture nor an engagement. *Ma foi*, there is no hurry. My daughter is only seventeen years old, and your son twenty-one. While we wait, time will be progressing, events will succeed each other; things which in the evening look dark and obscure, appear but too clearly in the light of morning, and sometimes the utterance of one word, or the lapse of a single day, will reveal the most cruel calumnies."

"Calumnies, did you say, sir?" cried Morcerf, turning livid with rage. "Does anyone dare to slander me?"

"Monsieur, I told you that I considered it best to avoid all explanation."

"Then, sir, I am patiently to submit to your refusal?"

"Yes, sir, although I assure you the refusal is as painful for me to give as it is for you to receive, for I had reckoned on the honor of your alliance, and the breaking off of a marriage contract always injures the lady more than the gentleman."

"Enough, sir," said Morcerf, "we will speak no more on the subject."

And clutching his gloves in anger, he left the apartment. Danglars observed that during the whole conversation Morcerf had never once dared to ask if it was on his own account that Danglars recalled his word.

That evening he had a long conference with several friends; and M. Cavalcanti, who had remained in the drawing-room with the ladies, was the last to leave the banker's house.

The next morning, as soon as he awoke, Danglars asked for the newspapers; they were brought to him; he laid aside three or four, and at last fixed on *l'Impartial*, the paper of which Beauchamp was the chief editor. He hastily tore off the cover, opened the journal with nervous precipitation, passed contemptuously over the Paris jottings, and arriving at the miscellaneous intelligence, stopped with a malicious smile, at a paragraph headed

We hear from Yanina.

"Very good," observed Danglars, after having read the paragraph; "here is a little article on Colonel Fernand, which, if I am not mistaken, would render the explanation which the Comte de Morcerf required of me perfectly unnecessary."

At the same moment, that is, at nine o'clock in the morning, Albert de Morcerf, dressed in a black coat buttoned up to his chin, might have been seen walking with a quick and agitated step in the direction of Monte Cristo's house in the Champs-Élysées. When he presented himself at the gate the porter informed him that the Count had gone out about half an hour previously.

"Did he take Baptistin with him?"

"No, my lord."

"Call him, then; I wish to speak to him."

The concierge went to seek the valet de chambre, and returned with him in an instant.

"My good friend," said Albert, "I beg pardon for my intrusion, but I was anxious to know from your own mouth if your master was really out or not."

"He is really out, sir," replied Baptistin.

"Out, even to me?"

"I know how happy my master always is to receive the vicomte," said Baptistin; "and I should therefore never think of including him in any general order."

"You are right; and now I wish to see him on an affair of great importance. Do you think it will be long before he comes in?"

"No, I think not, for he ordered his breakfast at ten o'clock."

"Well, I will go and take a turn in the Champs-Élysées, and at ten o'clock I will return here; meanwhile, if the count should come in, will you beg him not to go out again without seeing me?"

"You may depend on my doing so, sir," said Baptistin.

Albert left the cab in which he had come at the count's door, intending to take a turn on foot. As he was passing the Allée des Veuves, he thought he saw the count's horses standing at Gosset's shooting-gallery; he approached, and soon recognized the coachman.

"Is the count shooting in the gallery?" said Morcerf.

"Yes, sir," replied the coachman. While he was speaking, Albert had heard the report of two or three pistol-shots. He entered, and on his way met the waiter.

"Excuse me, my lord," said the lad; "but will you have the kindness to wait a moment?"

"What for, Philip?" asked Albert, who, being a constant visitor there, did not understand this opposition to his entrance.

"Because the person who is now in the gallery prefers being alone, and never practices in the presence of anyone."

"Not even before you, Philip? Then who loads his pistol?"

"His servant."

"A Nubian?"

"A negro."

"It is he, then."

"Do you know this gentleman?"

"Yes, and I am come to look for him; he is a friend of mine."

"Oh, that is quite another thing, then. I will go immediately and inform him of your arrival."

And Philip, urged by his own curiosity, entered the gallery; a second afterwards, Monte Cristo appeared on the threshold.

"I ask your pardon, my dear count," said Albert, "for following you here, and I must first tell you that it was not the fault of your servants that I did so; I alone am to blame for the indiscretion. I went to your house, and they told me you were out, but that they expected you home at ten o'clock to breakfast. I was walking about in order to pass away the time till ten o'clock, when I caught sight of your carriage and horses."

"What you have just said induces me to hope that you intend breakfasting with me."

"No, thank you, I am thinking of other things besides breakfast just now; perhaps we may take that meal at a later hour and in worse company."

"What on earth are you talking of?"

"I am to fight today."

"For what?"

"For the sake of fighting!"

"Yes, I understand that, but what is the quarrel? People fight for all sorts of reasons, you know."

"I fight in the cause of honor."

"Ah, that is something serious."

"So serious, that I come to beg you to render me a service."

"What is it?"

"To be my second."

"That is a serious matter, and we will not discuss it here; let us speak of nothing till we get home. Ali, bring me some water."

The count turned up his sleeves, and passed into the little vestibule where the gentlemen were accustomed to wash their hands after shooting.

"Come in, my lord," said Philip in a low tone, "and I will show you something droll." Morcerf entered, and in place of the usual target, he saw some playing-cards fixed against the wall. At a distance Albert thought it was a complete suit, for he counted from the ace to the ten.

"Ah, ha," said Albert, "I see you were preparing for a game of cards."

"No," said the count, "I was making a suit."

"How?" said Albert.

"Those are really aces and twos which you see, but my shots have turned them into threes, fives, sevens, eights, nines, and tens."

Albert approached. In fact, the bullets had actually pierced the cards in the exact places which the painted signs would otherwise have occupied, the lines and distances being as regularly kept as if they had been ruled with pencil. In going up to the target Morcerf picked up two or three swallows that had been rash enough to come within the range of the count's pistol.

"*Diable!*" said Morcerf.

"What would you have, my dear viscount?" said Monte Cristo, wiping his hands on the towel which Ali had brought him; "I must occupy my leisure moments in some way or other. But come, I am waiting for you."

Both men entered Monte Cristo's carriage, which in the course of a few minutes deposited them safely at No. 30. Monte Cristo took Albert into his study, and pointing to a seat, placed another for himself. "Now let us talk the matter over quietly," said the count.

"You see I am perfectly composed," said Albert.

"With whom are you going to fight?"

"With Beauchamp."

"One of your friends!"

"Of course; it is always with friends that one fights."

"I suppose you have some cause of quarrel?"

"I have."

"What has he done to you?"

"There appeared in his journal last night—but wait, and read for yourself." And Albert handed over the paper to the count, who read as follows:

> "A correspondent at Yanina informs us of a fact of which until now we had remained in ignorance. The castle which formed the protection of the town was given up to the Turks by a French officer named Fernand, in whom the grand vizier, Ali Tepelini, had reposed the greatest confidence."

"Well," said Monte Cristo, "what do you see in that to annoy you?"

"What do I see in it?"

"Yes; what does it signify to you if the castle of Yanina was given up by a French officer?"

"It signifies to my father, the Count of Morcerf, whose Christian name is Fernand!"

"Did your father serve under Ali Pasha?"

"Yes; that is to say, he fought for the independence of the Greeks, and hence arises the calumny."

"Oh, my dear viscount, do talk reason!"

"I do not desire to do otherwise."

"Now, just tell me who the devil should know in France that the officer Fernand and the Count of Morcerf are one and the same person? and who cares now about Yanina, which was taken as long ago as the year 1822 or 1823?"

"That just shows the meanness of this slander. They have allowed all this time to elapse, and then all of a sudden rake up events which have been forgotten to furnish materials for scandal, in order to tarnish the lustre of our high position. I inherit my father's name, and I do not choose that the shadow of disgrace should darken it. I am going to Beauchamp, in whose journal this paragraph appears, and I shall insist on his retracting the assertion before two witnesses."

"Beauchamp will never retract."

"Then we must fight."

"No you will not, for he will tell you, what is very true, that perhaps there were fifty officers in the Greek army bearing the same name."

"We will fight, nevertheless. I will efface that blot on my father's character. My father, who was such a brave soldier, whose career was so brilliant—"

"Oh, well, he will add, 'We are warranted in believing that this Fernand is not the illustrious Count of Morcerf, who also bears the same Christian name.'"

"I am determined not to be content with anything short of an entire retractation."

"And you intend to make him do it in the presence of two witnesses, do you?"

"Yes."

"You do wrong."

"Which means, I suppose, that you refuse the service which I asked of you?"

"You know my theory regarding duels; I told you my opinion on that subject, if you remember, when we were at Rome."

"Nevertheless, my dear count, I found you this morning engaged in an occupation but little consistent with the notions you profess to entertain."

"Because, my dear fellow, you understand one must never be eccentric. If one's lot is cast among fools, it is necessary to study folly. I shall perhaps find myself one day called out by some harebrained scamp, who has no more real cause of quarrel with me than you have with Beauchamp; he may take me to task for some foolish trifle or other, he will bring his witnesses, or will insult me in some public place, and I am expected to kill him for all that."

"You admit that you would fight, then? Well, if so, why do you object to my doing so?"

"I do not say that you ought not to fight, I only say that a duel is a serious thing, and ought not to be undertaken without due reflection."

"Did he reflect before he insulted my father?"

"If he spoke hastily, and owns that he did so, you ought to be satisfied."

"Ah, my dear count, you are far too indulgent."

"And you are far too exacting. Supposing, for instance, and do not be angry at what I am going to say—"

"Well."

"Supposing the assertion to be really true?"

"A son ought not to submit to such a stain on his father's honor."

"*Ma foi!* we live in times when there is much to which we must submit."

"That is precisely the fault of the age."

"And do you undertake to reform it?"

"Yes, as far as I am personally concerned."

"Well, you are indeed exacting, my dear fellow!"

"Yes, I own it."

"Are you quite impervious to good advice?"

"Not when it comes from a friend."

"And do you account me that title?"

"Certainly I do."

"Well, then, before going to Beauchamp with your witnesses, seek further information on the subject."

"From whom?"

"From Haydée."

"Why, what can be the use of mixing a woman up in the affair?—what can she do in it?"

"She can declare to you, for example, that your father had no hand whatever in the defeat and death of the vizier; or if by chance he had, indeed, the misfortune to—"

"I have told you, my dear count, that I would not for one moment admit of such a proposition."

"You reject this means of information, then?"

"I do—most decidedly."

"Then let me offer one more word of advice."

"Do so, then, but let it be the last."

"You do not wish to hear it, perhaps?"

"On the contrary, I request it."

"Do not take any witnesses with you when you go to Beauchamp—visit him alone."

"That would be contrary to all custom."

"Your case is not an ordinary one."

"And what is your reason for advising me to go alone?"

"Because then the affair will rest between you and Beauchamp."

"Explain yourself."

"I will do so. If Beauchamp be disposed to retract, you ought at least to give him the opportunity of doing it of his own free will,—the satisfaction to you will be the same. If, on the contrary, he refuses to do so, it will then be quite time enough to admit two strangers into your secret."

"They will not be strangers, they will be friends."

"Ah, but the friends of today are the enemies of tomorrow; Beauchamp, for instance."

"So you recommend—"

"I recommend you to be prudent."

"Then you advise me to go alone to Beauchamp?"

"I do, and I will tell you why. When you wish to obtain some concession from a man's self-love, you must avoid even the appearance of wishing to wound it."

"I believe you are right."

"I am glad of it."

"Then I will go alone."

"Go; but you would do better still by not going at all."

"That is impossible."

"Do so, then; it will be a wiser plan than the first which you proposed."

"But if, in spite of all my precautions, I am at last obliged to fight, will you not be my second?"

"My dear viscount," said Monte Cristo gravely, "you must have seen before today that at all times and in all places I have been at your disposal, but the service which you have just demanded of me is one which it is out of my power to render you."

"Why?"

"Perhaps you may know at some future period, and in the mean time I request you to excuse my declining to put you in possession of my reasons."

"Well, I will have Franz and Château-Renaud; they will be the very men for it."

"Do so, then."

"But if I do fight, you will surely not object to giving me a lesson or two in shooting and fencing?"

"That, too, is impossible."

"What a singular being you are!—you will not interfere in anything."

"You are right—that is the principle on which I wish to act."

"We will say no more about it, then. Good-bye, count."

Morcerf took his hat, and left the room. He found his carriage at the door, and doing his utmost to restrain his anger he went at once to find Beauchamp, who was in his office. It was a gloomy, dusty-looking apartment, such as journalists' offices have always been from time immemorial. The servant announced M. Albert de Morcerf. Beauchamp repeated the name to himself, as though he could scarcely believe that he had heard aright, and then gave orders for him to be admitted. Albert entered.

Beauchamp uttered an exclamation of surprise on seeing his friend leap over and trample under foot all the newspapers which were strewed about the room.

"This way, this way, my dear Albert!" said he, holding out his hand to the young man. "Are you out of your senses, or do you come peaceably to take breakfast with me? Try and find a seat—there is one by that geranium, which is the only thing in the room to remind me that there are other leaves in the world besides leaves of paper."

"Beauchamp," said Albert, "it is of your journal that I come to speak."

"Indeed? What do you wish to say about it?"

"I desire that a statement contained in it should be rectified."

"To what do you refer? But pray sit down."

"Thank you," said Albert, with a cold and formal bow.

"Will you now have the kindness to explain the nature of the statement which has displeased you?"

"An announcement has been made which implicates the honor of a member of my family."

"What is it?" said Beauchamp, much surprised; "surely you must be mistaken."

"The story sent you from Yanina."

"Yanina?"

"Yes; really you appear to be totally ignorant of the cause which brings me here."

"Such is really the case, I assure you, upon my honor! Baptiste, give me yesterday's paper," cried Beauchamp.

"Here, I have brought mine with me," replied Albert.

Beauchamp took the paper, and read the article to which Albert pointed in an undertone.

"You see it is a serious annoyance," said Morcerf, when Beauchamp had finished the perusal of the paragraph.

"Is the officer referred to a relation of yours, then?" demanded the journalist.

"Yes," said Albert, blushing.

"Well, what do you wish me to do for you?" said Beauchamp mildly.

"My dear Beauchamp, I wish you to contradict this statement." Beauchamp looked at Albert with a benevolent expression.

"Come," said he, "this matter will want a good deal of talking over; a retractation is always a serious thing, you know. Sit down, and I will read it again."

Albert resumed his seat, and Beauchamp read, with more attention than at first, the lines denounced by his friend.

"Well," said Albert in a determined tone, "you see that your paper has insulted a member of my family, and I insist on a retractation being made."

"You insist?"

"Yes, I insist."

"Permit me to remind you that you are not in the Chamber, my dear viscount."

"Nor do I wish to be there," replied the young man, rising. "I repeat that I am determined to have the announcement of yesterday contradicted. You have known me long enough," continued Albert, biting his lips convulsively, for he saw that Beauchamp's anger was beginning to rise,—"you have been my friend, and therefore sufficiently intimate with me to be aware that I am likely to maintain my resolution on this point."

"If I have been your friend, Morcerf, your present manner of speaking would almost lead me to forget that I ever bore that title. But wait a moment, do not let us get angry, or at least not yet. You are irritated and vexed—tell me how this Fernand is related to you?"

"He is merely my father," said Albert—"M. Fernand Mondego, Count of Morcerf, an old soldier who has fought in twenty battles and whose honorable scars they would denounce as badges of disgrace."

"Is it your father?" said Beauchamp; "that is quite another thing. Then I can well understand your indignation, my dear Albert. I will look at it again;" and he read the paragraph for the third time, laying a stress on each word as he proceeded. "But the paper nowhere identifies this Fernand with your father."

"No; but the connection will be seen by others, and therefore I will have the article contradicted."

At the words *I will*, Beauchamp steadily raised his eyes to Albert's countenance, and then as gradually lowering them, he remained thoughtful for a few moments.

"You will retract this assertion, will you not, Beauchamp?" said Albert with increased though stifled anger.

"Yes," replied Beauchamp.

"Immediately?" said Albert.

"When I am convinced that the statement is false."

"What?"

"The thing is worth looking into, and I will take pains to investigate the matter thoroughly."

"But what is there to investigate, sir?" said Albert, enraged beyond measure at Beauchamp's last remark. "If you do not believe that it is my father, say so immediately; and if, on the contrary, you believe it to be him, state your reasons for doing so."

Beauchamp looked at Albert with the smile which was so peculiar to him, and which in its numerous modifications served to express every varied emotion of his mind.

"Sir," replied he, "if you came to me with the idea of demanding satisfaction, you should have gone at once to the point, and not have entertained me with the idle conversation to which I have been patiently listening for the last half hour. Am I to put this construction on your visit?"

"Yes, if you will not consent to retract that infamous calumny."

"Wait a moment—no threats, if you please, M. Fernand Mondego, Vicomte de Morcerf; I never allow them from my enemies, and therefore shall not put up with them from my friends. You insist on my contradicting the article relating to General Fernand, an article with which, I assure you on my word of honor, I had nothing whatever to do?"

"Yes, I insist on it," said Albert, whose mind was beginning to get bewildered with the excitement of his feelings.

"And if I refuse to retract, you wish to fight, do you?" said Beauchamp in a calm tone.

"Yes," replied Albert, raising his voice.

"Well," said Beauchamp, "here is my answer, my dear sir. The article was not inserted by me—I was not even aware of it; but you have, by the step you have taken, called my attention to the paragraph in question, and it will remain until it shall be either contradicted or confirmed by someone who has a right to do so."

"Sir," said Albert, rising, "I will do myself the honor of sending my seconds to you, and you will be kind enough to arrange with them the place of meeting and the weapons."

"Certainly, my dear sir."

"And this evening, if you please, or tomorrow at the latest, we will meet."

"No, no, I will be on the ground at the proper time; but in my opinion (and I have a right to dictate the preliminaries, as it is I who have received the provocation)—in my opinion the time ought not to be yet. I know you to be well skilled in the management of the sword, while I am only moderately so; I know, too, that you are a good marksman—there we are about equal. I know that a duel between us two would be a serious affair, because you are brave, and I am brave also. I do not therefore wish either to kill you, or to be killed myself without a cause. Now, I am going to put a question to you, and one very much to the purpose too. Do you insist on this retractation so far as to kill me if I do not make it, although I have repeated more than once, and affirmed on my honor, that I was ignorant of the thing with which you charge me, and although I still declare that it is impossible for anyone but you to recognize the Count of Morcerf under the name of Fernand?"

"I maintain my original resolution."

"Very well, my dear sir; then I consent to cut throats with you. But I require three weeks' preparation; at the end of that time I shall come and say to you, 'The assertion is false, and I retract it,' or 'The assertion is true,' when I shall immediately draw the sword from its sheath, or the pistols from the case, whichever you please."

"Three weeks!" cried Albert; "they will pass as slowly as three centuries when I am all the time suffering dishonor."

"Had you continued to remain on amicable terms with me, I should have said, 'Patience, my friend;' but you have constituted yourself my enemy, therefore I say, 'What does that signify to me, sir?'"

"Well, let it be three weeks then," said Morcerf; "but remember, at the expiration of that time no delay or subterfuge will justify you in—"

"M. Albert de Morcerf," said Beauchamp, rising in his turn, "I cannot throw you out of window for three weeks—that is to say, for twenty-four days to come—nor have you any right to split my skull open till that time has elapsed. Today is the 29th of August; the 21st of September will, therefore, be the conclusion of the term agreed on, and till that time arrives—and it is the advice of a gentleman which I am about to give you—till then we will refrain from growling and barking like two dogs chained within sight of each other."

When he had concluded his speech, Beauchamp bowed coldly to Albert, turned his back upon him, and went to the press-room. Albert vented his anger on a pile of newspapers, which he sent flying all over the office by switching them violently with his stick; after which ebullition he departed—not, however, without walking several times to the door of the press-room, as if he had half a mind to enter.

While Albert was lashing the front of his carriage in the same manner that he had the newspapers which were the innocent agents of his discomfiture, as he was crossing the barrier he perceived Morrel, who was walking with a quick step and a bright eye. He was passing the Chinese Baths, and appeared to have come from the direction of the Porte Saint-Martin, and to be going towards the Madeleine.

"Ah," said Morcerf, "there goes a happy man!" And it so happened Albert was not mistaken in his opinion.

Study Guide Questions

For Students:

1. What is included in the letter received by M. de Villefort?
2. On what condition does M. Noirtier leave his fortune for Valentine?
3. What does Beauchamp print in the paper and why does it offend Albert?

For Reading Club:

1. Discuss how is Yanina important to the events that take place in this chapter.
2. Do you think Albert is right in fighting for honor?
3. Discuss the statement with reference to contemporary society, "we live in times when there is much to which we must submit."

CHAPTER 79

The Lemonade

Morrel was, in fact, very happy. M. Noirtier had just sent for him, and he was in such haste to know the reason of his doing so that he had not stopped to take a cab, placing infinitely more dependence on his own two legs than on the four legs of a cab-horse. He had therefore set off at a furious rate from the Rue Meslay, and was hastening with rapid strides in the direction of the Faubourg Saint-Honoré.

Morrel advanced with a firm, manly tread, and poor Barrois followed him as he best might. Morrel was only thirty-one, Barrois was sixty years of age; Morrel was deeply in love, and Barrois was dying with heat and exertion. These two men, thus opposed in age and interests, resembled two parts of a triangle, presenting the extremes of separation, yet nevertheless possessing their point of union. This point of union was Noirtier, and it was he who had just sent for Morrel, with the request that the latter would lose no time in coming to him—a command which Morrel obeyed to the letter, to the great discomfiture of Barrois. On arriving at the house, Morrel was not even out of breath, for love lends wings to our desires; but Barrois, who had long forgotten what it was to love, was sorely fatigued by the expedition he had been constrained to use.

The old servant introduced Morrel by a private entrance, closed the door of the study, and soon the rustling of a dress announced the arrival of Valentine. She looked marvellously beautiful in her deep mourning dress, and Morrel experienced such intense delight in gazing upon her that he felt as if he could almost have dispensed with the conversation of her grandfather.

But the easy-chair of the old man was heard rolling along the floor, and he soon made his appearance in the room. Noirtier acknowledged by a look of extreme kindness and benevolence the thanks which Morrel lavished on him for his timely intervention on behalf of Valentine and himself—an intervention which had saved them from despair. Morrel then cast on the invalid an interrogative look as to the new favor which he designed to bestow on him. Valentine was sitting at a little distance from them, timidly awaiting the moment when she should be obliged to speak. Noirtier fixed his eyes on her.

"Am I to say what you told me?" asked Valentine. Noirtier made a sign that she was to do so.

"Monsieur Morrel," said Valentine to the young man, who was regarding her with the most intense interest, "my grandfather, M. Noirtier, had a thousand things to say, which he told me three days ago; and now, he has sent for you, that I may repeat them to you. I will repeat them, then; and since he has chosen me as his interpreter, I will be faithful to the trust, and will not alter a word of his intentions."

"Oh, I am listening with the greatest impatience," replied the young man; "speak, I beg of you."

Valentine cast down her eyes; this was a good omen for Morrel, for he knew that nothing but happiness could have the power of thus overcoming Valentine.

"My grandfather intends leaving this house," said she, "and Barrois is looking out for suitable apartments for him in another."

"But you, Mademoiselle de Villefort,—you, who are necessary to M. Noirtier's happiness—"

"I?" interrupted Valentine; "I shall not leave my grandfather,—that is an understood thing between us. My apartment will be close to his. Now, M. de Villefort must either give his consent to this plan or his refusal; in the first case, I shall leave directly, and in the second, I shall wait till I am of age, which will be in about ten months. Then I shall be free, I shall have an independent fortune, and"—

"And what?" demanded Morrel.

"And with my grandfather's consent I shall fulfil the promise which I have made you."

Valentine pronounced these last few words in such a low tone, that nothing but Morrel's intense interest in what she was saying could have enabled him to hear them.

"Have I not explained your wishes, grandpapa?" said Valentine, addressing Noirtier.

"Yes," looked the old man.

"Once under my grandfather's roof, M. Morrel can visit me in the presence of my good and worthy protector, if we still feel that the union we contemplated will be likely to insure our future comfort and happiness; in that case I shall expect M. Morrel to come and claim me at my own hands. But, alas, I have heard it said that hearts inflamed by obstacles to their desire grew cold in time of security; I trust we shall never find it so in our experience!"

"Oh," cried Morrel, almost tempted to throw himself on his knees before Noirtier and Valentine, and to adore them as two superior beings, "what have I ever done in my life to merit such unbounded happiness?"

"Until that time," continued the young girl in a calm and self-possessed tone of voice, "we will conform to circumstances, and be guided by the wishes of our friends, so long as those wishes do not tend finally to separate us; in a word, and I repeat it, because it expresses all I wish to convey,—we will wait."

"And I swear to make all the sacrifices which this word imposes, sir," said Morrel, "not only with resignation, but with cheerfulness."

"Therefore," continued Valentine, looking playfully at Maximilian, "no more inconsiderate actions—no more rash projects; for you surely would not wish to compromise one who from this day regards herself as destined, honorably and happily, to bear your name?"

Morrel looked obedience to her commands. Noirtier regarded the lovers with a look of ineffable tenderness, while Barrois, who had remained in the room in the character of a man privileged to know everything that passed, smiled on the youthful couple as he wiped the perspiration from his bald forehead.

"How hot you look, my good Barrois," said Valentine.

"Ah, I have been running very fast, mademoiselle, but I must do M. Morrel the justice to say that he ran still faster."

Noirtier directed their attention to a waiter, on which was placed a decanter containing lemonade and a glass. The decanter was nearly full, with the exception of a little, which had been already drunk by M. Noirtier.

"Come, Barrois," said the young girl, "take some of this lemonade; I see you are coveting a good draught of it."

"The fact is, mademoiselle," said Barrois, "I am dying with thirst, and since you are so kind as to offer it me, I cannot say I should at all object to drinking your health in a glass of it."

"Take some, then, and come back immediately."

Barrois took away the waiter, and hardly was he outside the door, which in his haste he forgot to shut, than they saw him throw back his head and empty to the very dregs the glass which Valentine had filled. Valentine and Morrel were exchanging their adieux in the presence of Noirtier when a ring was heard at the door-bell. It was the signal of a visit. Valentine looked at her watch.

"It is past noon," said she, "and today is Saturday; I dare say it is the doctor, grandpapa."

Noirtier looked his conviction that she was right in her supposition.

"He will come in here, and M. Morrel had better go,—do you not think so, grandpapa?"

"Yes," signed the old man.

"Barrois," cried Valentine, "Barrois!"

"I am coming, mademoiselle," replied he.

"Barrois will open the door for you," said Valentine, addressing Morrel. "And now remember one thing, Monsieur Officer, that my grandfather commands you not to take any rash or ill-advised step which would be likely to compromise our happiness."

"I promised him to wait," replied Morrel; "and I will wait."

At this moment Barrois entered. "Who rang?" asked Valentine.

"Doctor d'Avrigny," said Barrois, staggering as if he would fall.

"What is the matter, Barrois?" said Valentine. The old man did not answer, but looked at his master with wild staring eyes, while with his cramped hand he grasped a piece of furniture to enable him to stand upright.

"He is going to fall!" cried Morrel.

The rigors which had attacked Barrois gradually increased, the features of the face became quite altered, and the convulsive movement of the muscles appeared to indicate the approach of a most serious nervous disorder. Noirtier, seeing Barrois in this pitiable condition, showed by his looks all the various emotions of sorrow and sympathy which can animate the heart of man. Barrois made some steps towards his master.

"Ah, sir," said he, "tell me what is the matter with me. I am suffering—I cannot see. A thousand fiery darts are piercing my brain. Ah, don't touch me, pray don't."

By this time his haggard eyes had the appearance of being ready to start from their sockets; his head fell back, and the lower extremities of the body began to stiffen. Valentine uttered a cry of horror; Morrel took her in his arms, as if to defend her from some unknown danger.

"M. d'Avrigny, M. d'Avrigny," cried she, in a stifled voice. "Help, help!"

Barrois turned round and with a great effort stumbled a few steps, then fell at the feet of Noirtier, and resting his hand on the knee of the invalid, exclaimed:

"My master, my good master!"

At this moment M. de Villefort, attracted by the noise, appeared on the threshold. Morrel relaxed his hold of Valentine, and retreating to a distant corner of the room remained half hidden behind a curtain. Pale as if he had been gazing on a serpent, he fixed his terrified eye on the agonized sufferer.

Noirtier, burning with impatience and terror, was in despair at his utter inability to help his old domestic, whom he regarded more in the light of a friend than a servant. One might by the fearful swelling of the veins of his forehead and the contraction of the muscles round the eye, trace the terrible conflict which was going on between the living energetic mind and the inanimate and helpless body.

Barrois, his features convulsed, his eyes suffused with blood, and his head thrown back, was lying at full length, beating the floor with his hands, while his legs had become so stiff, that they looked as if they would break rather than bend. A slight appearance of foam was visible around the mouth, and he breathed painfully, and with extreme difficulty.

Villefort seemed stupefied with astonishment, and remained gazing intently on the scene before him without uttering a word. He had not seen Morrel. After a moment of dumb contemplation, during which his face became pale and his hair seemed to stand on end, he sprang towards the door, crying out:

"Doctor, doctor! come instantly, pray come!"

"Madame, madame!" cried Valentine, calling her step-mother, and running upstairs to meet her; "come quick, quick!—and bring your bottle of smelling-salts with you."

"What is the matter?" said Madame de Villefort in a harsh and constrained tone.

"Oh! come! come!"

"But where is the doctor?" exclaimed Villefort; "where is he?"

Madame de Villefort now deliberately descended the staircase. In one hand she held her handkerchief, with which she appeared to be wiping her face, and in the other a bottle of English smelling-salts. Her first look on entering the room was at Noirtier, whose face, independent of the emotion which such a scene could not fail of producing, proclaimed him to be in possession of his usual health; her second glance was at the dying man. She turned pale, and her eye passed quickly from the servant and rested on the master.

"In the name of heaven, madame," said Villefort, "where is the doctor? He was with you just now. You see this is a fit of apoplexy, and he might be saved if he could but be bled!"

"Has he eaten anything lately?" asked Madame de Villefort, eluding her husband's question.

"Madame," replied Valentine, "he has not even breakfasted. He has been running very fast on an errand with which my grandfather charged him, and when he returned, took nothing but a glass of lemonade."

"Ah," said Madame de Villefort, "why did he not take wine? Lemonade was a very bad thing for him."

"Grandpapa's bottle of lemonade was standing just by his side; poor Barrois was very thirsty, and was thankful to drink anything he could find."

Madame de Villefort started. Noirtier looked at her with a glance of the most profound scrutiny.

"He has such a short neck," said she.

"Madame," said Villefort, "I ask where is M. d'Avrigny? In God's name answer me!"

"He is with Edward, who is not quite well," replied Madame de Villefort, no longer being able to avoid answering.

Villefort rushed upstairs to fetch him.

"Take this," said Madame de Villefort, giving her smelling-bottle to Valentine. "They will, no doubt, bleed him; therefore I will retire, for I cannot endure the sight of blood;" and she followed her husband upstairs. Morrel now emerged from his hiding-place, where he had remained quite unperceived, so great had been the general confusion.

"Go away as quick as you can, Maximilian," said Valentine, "and stay till I send for you. Go."

Morrel looked towards Noirtier for permission to retire. The old man, who had preserved all his usual coolness, made a sign to him to do so. The young man pressed Valentine's hand to his lips, and then left the house by a back staircase.

At the same moment that he quitted the room, Villefort and the doctor entered by an opposite door. Barrois was now showing signs of returning consciousness. The crisis seemed past, a low moaning was heard, and he raised himself on one knee. D'Avrigny and Villefort laid him on a couch.

"What do you prescribe, doctor?" demanded Villefort.

"Give me some water and ether. You have some in the house, have you not?"

"Yes."

"Send for some oil of turpentine and tartar emetic."

Villefort immediately despatched a messenger. "And now let everyone retire."

"Must I go too?" asked Valentine timidly.

"Yes, mademoiselle, you especially," replied the doctor abruptly.

Valentine looked at M. d'Avrigny with astonishment, kissed her grandfather on the forehead, and left the room. The doctor closed the door after her with a gloomy air.

"Look, look, doctor," said Villefort, "he is quite coming round again; I really do not think, after all, it is anything of consequence."

M. d'Avrigny answered by a melancholy smile.

"How do you feel, Barrois?" asked he.

"A little better, sir."

"Will you drink some of this ether and water?"

"I will try; but don't touch me."

"Why not?"

"Because I feel that if you were only to touch me with the tip of your finger the fit would return."

"Drink."

Barrois took the glass, and, raising it to his purple lips, took about half of the liquid offered him.

"Where do you suffer?" asked the doctor.

"Everywhere. I feel cramps over my whole body."

"Do you find any dazzling sensation before the eyes?"

"Yes."

"Any noise in the ears?"

"Frightful."

"When did you first feel that?"

"Just now."

"Suddenly?"

"Yes, like a clap of thunder."

"Did you feel nothing of it yesterday or the day before?"

"Nothing."

"No drowsiness?"

"None."

"What have you eaten today?"

"I have eaten nothing; I only drank a glass of my master's lemonade—that's all." And Barrois turned towards Noirtier, who, immovably fixed in his armchair, was contemplating this terrible scene without allowing a word or a movement to escape him.

"Where is this lemonade?" asked the doctor eagerly.

"Downstairs in the decanter."

"Whereabouts downstairs?"

"In the kitchen."

"Shall I go and fetch it, doctor?" inquired Villefort.

"No, stay here and try to make Barrois drink the rest of this glass of ether and water. I will go myself and fetch the lemonade."

D'Avrigny bounded towards the door, flew down the back staircase, and almost knocked down Madame de Villefort, in his haste, who was herself going down to the kitchen. She cried out, but d'Avrigny paid no attention to her; possessed with but one idea, he cleared the last four steps with a bound, and rushed into the kitchen, where he saw the decanter about three parts empty still standing on the waiter, where it had been left. He darted upon it as an eagle would seize upon its prey. Panting with loss of breath, he returned to the room he had just left. Madame de Villefort was slowly ascending the steps which led to her room.

"Is this the decanter you spoke of?" asked d'Avrigny.

"Yes, doctor."

"Is this the same lemonade of which you partook?"

"I believe so."

"What did it taste like?"

"It had a bitter taste."

The doctor poured some drops of the lemonade into the palm of his hand, put his lips to it, and after having rinsed his mouth as a man does when he is tasting wine, he spat the liquor into the fireplace.

"It is no doubt the same," said he. "Did you drink some too, M. Noirtier?"

"Yes."

"And did you also discover a bitter taste?"

"Yes."

"Oh, doctor," cried Barrois, "the fit is coming on again. Oh, do something for me." The doctor flew to his patient.

"That emetic, Villefort—see if it is coming."

Villefort sprang into the passage, exclaiming, "The emetic! the emetic!—is it come yet?" No one answered. The most profound terror reigned throughout the house.

"If I had anything by means of which I could inflate the lungs," said d'Avrigny, looking around him, "perhaps I might prevent suffocation. But there is nothing which would do!—nothing!"

"Oh, sir," cried Barrois, "are you going to let me die without help? Oh, I am dying! Oh, save me!"

"A pen, a pen!" said the doctor. There was one lying on the table; he endeavored to introduce it into the mouth of the patient, who, in the midst of his convulsions, was making vain attempts to vomit; but the jaws were so clenched that the pen could not pass them. This second attack was much more violent than the first, and he had slipped from the couch to the ground, where he was writhing in agony. The doctor left him in this paroxysm, knowing that he could do nothing to alleviate it, and, going up to Noirtier, said abruptly:

"How do you find yourself?—well?"

"Yes."

"Have you any weight on the chest; or does your stomach feel light and comfortable—eh?"

"Yes."

"Then you feel pretty much as you generally do after you have had the dose which I am accustomed to give you every Sunday?"

"Yes."

"Did Barrois make your lemonade?"

"Yes."

"Was it you who asked him to drink some of it?"

"No."

"Was it M. de Villefort?"

"No."

"Madame?"

"No."

"It was your granddaughter, then, was it not?"

"Yes."

A groan from Barrois, accompanied by a yawn which seemed to crack the very jawbones, attracted the attention of M. d'Avrigny; he left M. Noirtier, and returned to the sick man.

"Barrois," said the doctor, "can you speak?" Barrois muttered a few unintelligible words. "Try and make an effort to do so, my good man." said d'Avrigny. Barrois reopened his bloodshot eyes.

"Who made the lemonade?"

"I did."

"Did you bring it to your master directly it was made?"

"No."

"You left it somewhere, then, in the meantime?"

"Yes; I left it in the pantry, because I was called away."

"Who brought it into this room, then?"

"Mademoiselle Valentine." D'Avrigny struck his forehead with his hand.

"Gracious heaven," exclaimed he.

"Doctor, doctor!" cried Barrois, who felt another fit coming.

"Will they never bring that emetic?" asked the doctor.

"Here is a glass with one already prepared," said Villefort, entering the room.

"Who prepared it?"

"The chemist who came here with me."

"Drink it," said the doctor to Barrois.

"Impossible, doctor; it is too late; my throat is closing up. I am choking! Oh, my heart! Ah, my head!—Oh, what agony!—Shall I suffer like this long?"

"No, no, friend," replied the doctor, "you will soon cease to suffer."

"Ah, I understand you," said the unhappy man. "My God, have mercy upon me!" and, uttering a fearful cry, Barrois fell back as if he had been struck by lightning. D'Avrigny put his hand to his heart, and placed a glass before his lips.

"Well?" said Villefort.

"Go to the kitchen and get me some syrup of violets."

Villefort went immediately.

"Do not be alarmed, M. Noirtier," said d'Avrigny; "I am going to take my patient into the next room to bleed him; this sort of attack is very frightful to witness."

And taking Barrois under the arms, he dragged him into an adjoining room; but almost immediately he returned to fetch the lemonade. Noirtier closed his right eye.

"You want Valentine, do you not? I will tell them to send her to you."

Villefort returned, and d'Avrigny met him in the passage.

"Well, how is he now?" asked he.

"Come in here," said d'Avrigny, and he took him into the chamber where the sick man lay.

"Is he still in a fit?" said the procureur.

"He is dead."

Villefort drew back a few steps, and, clasping his hands, exclaimed, with real amazement and sympathy, "Dead?—and so soon too!"

"Yes, it is very soon," said the doctor, looking at the corpse before him; "but that ought not to astonish you; Monsieur and Madame de Saint-Méran died as soon. People die very suddenly in your house, M. de Villefort."

"What?" cried the magistrate, with an accent of horror and consternation, "are you still harping on that terrible idea?"

"Still, sir; and I shall always do so," replied d'Avrigny, "for it has never for one instant ceased to retain possession of my mind; and that you may be quite sure I am not mistaken this time, listen well to what I am going to say, M. de Villefort."

The magistrate trembled convulsively.

"There is a poison which destroys life almost without leaving any perceptible traces. I know it well; I have studied it in all its forms and in the effects which it produces. I recognized the presence of this poison in the case of poor Barrois as well as in that of Madame de Saint-Méran. There is a way of detecting its presence. It restores the blue color of litmus-paper reddened by an acid, and it turns syrup of violets green. We have no litmus-paper, but, see, here they come with the syrup of violets."

The doctor was right; steps were heard in the passage. M. d'Avrigny opened the door, and took from the hands of the chambermaid a cup which contained two or three spoonfuls of the syrup, he then carefully closed the door.

"Look," said he to the procureur, whose heart beat so loudly that it might almost be heard, "here is in this cup some syrup of violets, and this decanter contains the remainder of the lemonade of which M. Noirtier and Barrois partook. If the lemonade be pure and inoffensive, the syrup will retain its color; if, on the contrary, the lemonade be drugged with poison, the syrup will become green. Look closely!"

The doctor then slowly poured some drops of the lemonade from the decanter into the cup, and in an instant a light cloudy sediment began to form at the bottom of the cup; this sediment first took a blue shade, then from the color of sapphire it passed to that of opal, and from opal to emerald. Arrived at this last hue, it changed no more. The result of the experiment left no doubt whatever on the mind.

"The unfortunate Barrois has been poisoned," said d'Avrigny, "and I will maintain this assertion before God and man."

Villefort said nothing, but he clasped his hands, opened his haggard eyes, and, overcome with his emotion, sank into a chair.

Study Guide Questions

For Students:

1. What does Valentine tell M. Morrel?
2. What happens to Barrois?
3. How does D'Avrigny trace the poison in lemonade?

For Reading Club:

1. Discuss the statement, "hearts inflamed by obstacles to their desire grow cold in time of security."
2. Discuss how is the lemonade connected with the events that take place in this chapter.
3. D'Avrigny tells Villefort that people die very soon in his house. What do you think is actually happening in his house?

CHAPTER 80

The Accusation

M. d'Avrigny soon restored the magistrate to consciousness, who had looked like a second corpse in that chamber of death.

"Oh, death is in my house!" cried Villefort.

"Say, rather, crime!" replied the doctor.

"M. d'Avrigny," cried Villefort, "I cannot tell you all I feel at this moment,—terror, grief, madness."

"Yes," said M. d'Avrigny, with an imposing calmness, "but I think it is now time to act. I think it is time to stop this torrent of mortality. I can no longer bear to be in possession of these secrets without the hope of seeing the victims and society generally revenged."

Villefort cast a gloomy look around him. "In my house," murmured he, "in my house!"

"Come, magistrate," said M. d'Avrigny, "show yourself a man; as an interpreter of the law, do honor to your profession by sacrificing your selfish interests to it."

"You make me shudder, doctor. Do you talk of a sacrifice?"

"I do."

"Do you then suspect anyone?"

"I suspect no one; death raps at your door—it enters—it goes, not blindfolded, but circumspectly, from room to room. Well, I follow its course, I track its passage; I adopt the wisdom of the ancients, and feel my way, for my friendship for your family and my respect for you are as a twofold bandage over my eyes; well—"

"Oh, speak, speak, doctor; I shall have courage."

"Well, sir, you have in your establishment, or in your family, perhaps, one of the frightful monstrosities of which each century produces only one. Locusta and

Agrippina, living at the same time, were an exception, and proved the determination of Providence to effect the entire ruin of the Roman empire, sullied by so many crimes. Brunhilda and Fredegund were the results of the painful struggle of civilization in its infancy, when man was learning to control mind, were it even by an emissary from the realms of darkness. All these women had been, or were, beautiful. The same flower of innocence had flourished, or was still flourishing, on their brow, that is seen on the brow of the culprit in your house."

Villefort shrieked, clasped his hands, and looked at the doctor with a supplicating air. But the latter went on without pity:

"'Seek whom the crime will profit,' says an axiom of jurisprudence."

"Doctor," cried Villefort, "alas, doctor, how often has man's justice been deceived by those fatal words. I know not why, but I feel that this crime—"

"You acknowledge, then, the existence of the crime?"

"Yes, I see too plainly that it does exist. But it seems that it is intended to affect me personally. I fear an attack myself, after all these disasters."

"Oh, man!" murmured d'Avrigny, "the most selfish of all animals, the most personal of all creatures, who believes the earth turns, the sun shines, and death strikes for him alone,—an ant cursing God from the top of a blade of grass! And have those who have lost their lives lost nothing?—M. de Saint-Méran, Madame de Saint-Méran, M. Noirtier—"

"How? M. Noirtier?"

"Yes; think you it was the poor servant's life was coveted? No, no; like Shakespeare's Polonius, he died for another. It was Noirtier the lemonade was intended for—it is Noirtier, logically speaking, who drank it. The other drank it only by accident, and, although Barrois is dead, it was Noirtier whose death was wished for."

"But why did it not kill my father?"

"I told you one evening in the garden after Madame de Saint-Méran's death—because his system is accustomed to that very poison, and the dose was trifling to him, which would be fatal to another; because no one knows, not even the assassin, that, for the last twelve months, I have given M. Noirtier brucine for his paralytic affection, while the assassin is not ignorant, for he has proved that brucine is a violent poison."

"Oh, have pity—have pity!" murmured Villefort, wringing his hands.

"Follow the culprit's steps; he first kills M. de Saint-Méran—"

"Oh, doctor!"

"I would swear to it; what I heard of his symptoms agrees too well with what I have seen in the other cases." Villefort ceased to contend; he only groaned. "He first kills M. de Saint-Méran," repeated the doctor, "then Madame de Saint-Méran,—a double fortune to inherit." Villefort wiped the perspiration from his forehead. "Listen attentively."

"Alas," stammered Villefort, "I do not lose a single word."

"M. Noirtier," resumed M. d'Avrigny in the same pitiless tone,—"M. Noirtier had once made a will against you—against your family—in favor of the poor, in fact; M. Noirtier is spared, because nothing is expected from him. But he has no sooner destroyed his first will and made a second, than, for fear he should make a third, he is struck down. The will was made the day before yesterday, I believe; you see there has been no time lost."

"Oh, mercy, M. d'Avrigny!"

"No mercy, sir! The physician has a sacred mission on earth; and to fulfil it he begins at the source of life, and goes down to the mysterious darkness of the tomb. When crime has been committed, and God, doubtless in anger, turns away his face, it is for the physician to bring the culprit to justice."

"Have mercy on my child, sir," murmured Villefort.

"You see it is yourself who have first named her—you, her father."

"Have pity on Valentine! Listen, it is impossible. I would as willingly accuse myself! Valentine, whose heart is pure as a diamond or a lily!"

"No pity, procureur; the crime is fragrant. Mademoiselle herself packed all the medicines which were sent to M. de Saint-Méran; and M. de Saint-Méran is dead. Mademoiselle de Villefort prepared all the cooling draughts which Madame de Saint-Méran took, and Madame de Saint-Méran is dead. Mademoiselle de Villefort took from the hands of Barrois, who was sent out, the lemonade which M. Noirtier had every morning, and he has escaped by a miracle. Mademoiselle de Villefort is the culprit—she is the poisoner! To you, as the king's attorney, I denounce Mademoiselle de Villefort, do your duty."

"Doctor, I resist no longer—I can no longer defend myself—I believe you; but, for pity's sake, spare my life, my honor!"

"M. de Villefort," replied the doctor, with increased vehemence, "there are occasions when I dispense with all foolish human circumspection. If your daughter had committed only one crime, and I saw her meditating another, I would say 'Warn her, punish her, let her pass the remainder of her life in a convent, weeping and praying.' If she had committed two crimes, I would say, 'Here, M. de Villefort, is a poison that the prisoner is not acquainted with,—one that has no known antidote, quick as thought, rapid as lightning, mortal as the thunderbolt; give her that poison, recommending her soul to God, and save your honor and your life, for it is yours she aims at; and I can picture her approaching your pillow with her hypocritical smiles and her sweet exhortations. Woe to you, M. de Villefort, if you do not strike first!' This is what I would say had she only killed two persons but she has seen three deaths,—has contemplated three murdered persons,—has knelt by three corpses! To the scaffold with the poisoner—to the scaffold! Do you talk of your honor? Do what I tell you, and immortality awaits you!"

Villefort fell on his knees.

"Listen," said he; "I have not the strength of mind you have, or rather that which you would not have, if instead of my daughter Valentine your daughter Madeleine were concerned." The doctor turned pale. "Doctor, every son of woman is born to suffer and to die; I am content to suffer and to await death."

"Beware," said M. d'Avrigny, "it may come slowly; you will see it approach after having struck your father, your wife, perhaps your son."

Villefort, suffocating, pressed the doctor's arm.

"Listen," cried he; "pity me—help me! No, my daughter is not guilty. If you drag us both before a tribunal I will still say, 'No, my daughter is not guilty;—there is no crime in my house. I will not acknowledge a crime in my house; for when crime enters a dwelling, it is like death—it does not come alone.' Listen. What does it signify to you if I am murdered? Are you my friend? Are you a man? Have you a heart? No, you are a physician! Well, I tell you I will not drag my daughter before a tribunal, and give her up to the executioner! The bare idea would kill me—would drive me like a madman to dig my heart out with my finger-nails! And if you were mistaken, doctor—if it were not my daughter—if I should come one day, pale as a spectre, and say to you, 'Assassin, you have killed my child!'—hold—if that should happen, although I am a Christian, M. d'Avrigny, I should kill myself."

"Well," said the doctor, after a moment's silence, "I will wait."

Villefort looked at him as if he had doubted his words.

"Only," continued M. d'Avrigny, with a slow and solemn tone, "if anyone falls ill in your house, if you feel yourself attacked, do not send for me, for I will come no more. I will consent to share this dreadful secret with you, but I will not allow shame and remorse to grow and increase in my conscience, as crime and misery will in your house."

"Then you abandon me, doctor?"

"Yes, for I can follow you no farther, and I only stop at the foot of the scaffold. Some further discovery will be made, which will bring this dreadful tragedy to a close. Adieu."

"I entreat you, doctor!"

"All the horrors that disturb my thoughts make your house odious and fatal. Adieu, sir."

"One word—one single word more, doctor! You go, leaving me in all the horror of my situation, after increasing it by what you have revealed to me. But what will be reported of the sudden death of the poor old servant?"

"True," said M. d'Avrigny; "we will return."

The doctor went out first, followed by M. de Villefort. The terrified servants were on the stairs and in the passage where the doctor would pass.

"Sir," said d'Avrigny to Villefort, so loud that all might hear, "poor Barrois has led too sedentary a life of late; accustomed formerly to ride on horseback, or in the carriage, to the four corners of Europe, the monotonous walk around that armchair has killed him—his blood has thickened. He was stout, had a short, thick neck; he was attacked with apoplexy, and I was called in too late. By the way," added he in a low tone, "take care to throw away that cup of syrup of violets in the ashes."

The doctor, without shaking hands with Villefort, without adding a word to what he had said, went out, amid the tears and lamentations of the whole household. The same evening all Villefort's servants, who had assembled in the kitchen, and had a long consultation, came to tell Madame de Villefort that they wished to leave. No entreaty, no proposition of increased wages, could induce them to remain; to every argument they replied, "We must go, for death is in this house."

They all left, in spite of prayers and entreaties, testifying their regret at leaving so good a master and mistress, and especially Mademoiselle Valentine, so good, so kind, and so gentle.

Villefort looked at Valentine as they said this. She was in tears, and, strange as it was, in spite of the emotions he felt at the sight of these tears, he looked also at Madame de Villefort, and it appeared to him as if a slight gloomy smile had passed over her thin lips, like a meteor seen passing inauspiciously between two clouds in a stormy sky.

Study Guide Questions

For Students:

1. What is the crime that Villefort and D'Avrigny refer to?
2. Whom does D'Avrigny accuse of killing M. Noirtier?
3. Why does D'Avrigny ask Villefort not to call him again if anybody falls ill?

For Reading Club:

1. Discuss the accusation in the chapter.
2. Discuss Villefort's character as a father.
3. Do you think that Barrois' death symbolically shows that the poor are collateral damage in a fight among the rich?

CHAPTER 81

The Room of the Retired Baker

The evening of the day on which the Count of Morcerf had left Danglars' house with feelings of shame and anger at the rejection of the projected alliance, M. Andrea Cavalcanti, with curled hair, moustaches in perfect order, and white gloves which fitted admirably, had entered the courtyard of the banker's house in Rue de la Chaussée d'Antin. He had not been more than ten minutes in the drawing-room before he drew Danglars aside into the recess of a bow-window, and, after an ingenious preamble, related to him all his anxieties and cares since his noble father's departure. He acknowledged the extreme kindness which had been shown him by the banker's family, in which he had been received as a son, and where, besides, his warmest affections had found an object on which to centre in Mademoiselle Danglars.

Danglars listened with the most profound attention; he had expected this declaration for the last two or three days, and when at last it came his eyes glistened as much as they had lowered on listening to Morcerf. He would not, however, yield immediately to the young man's request, but made a few conscientious objections.

"Are you not rather young, M. Andrea, to think of marrying?"

"I think not, sir," replied M. Cavalcanti; "in Italy the nobility generally marry young. Life is so uncertain, that we ought to secure happiness while it is within our reach."

"Well, sir," said Danglars, "in case your proposals, which do me honor, are accepted by my wife and daughter, by whom shall the preliminary arrangements be settled? So important a negotiation should, I think, be conducted by the respective fathers of the young people."

"Sir, my father is a man of great foresight and prudence. Thinking that I might wish to settle in France, he left me at his departure, together with the papers establishing my identity, a letter promising, if he approved of my choice, 150,000 livres per annum from the day I was married. So far as I can judge, I suppose this to be a quarter of my father's revenue."

"I," said Danglars, "have always intended giving my daughter 500,000 francs as her dowry; she is, besides, my sole heiress."

"All would then be easily arranged if the baroness and her daughter are willing. We should command an annuity of 175,000 livres. Supposing, also, I should persuade the marquis to give me my capital, which is not likely, but still is possible, we would place these two or three millions in your hands, whose talent might make it realize ten per cent."

"I never give more than four per cent, and generally only three and a half; but to my son-in-law I would give five, and we would share the profits."

"Very good, father-in-law," said Cavalcanti, yielding to his low-born nature, which would escape sometimes through the aristocratic gloss with which he sought to conceal it. Correcting himself immediately, he said, "Excuse me, sir; hope alone makes me almost mad,—what will not reality do?"

"But," said Danglars, who, on his part, did not perceive how soon the conversation, which was at first disinterested, was turning to a business transaction, "there is, doubtless, a part of your fortune your father could not refuse you?"

"Which?" asked the young man.

"That you inherit from your mother."

"Truly, from my mother, Leonora Corsinari."

"How much may it amount to?"

"Indeed, sir," said Andrea, "I assure you I have never given the subject a thought, but I suppose it must have been at least two millions."

Danglars felt as much overcome with joy as the miser who finds a lost treasure, or as the shipwrecked mariner who feels himself on solid ground instead of in the abyss which he expected would swallow him up.

"Well, sir," said Andrea, bowing to the banker respectfully, "may I hope?"

"You may not only hope," said Danglars, "but consider it a settled thing, if no obstacle arises on your part."

"I am, indeed, rejoiced," said Andrea.

"But," said Danglars thoughtfully, "how is it that your patron, M. de Monte Cristo, did not make his proposal for you?"

Andrea blushed imperceptibly.

"I have just left the count, sir," said he; "he is, doubtless, a delightful man but inconceivably peculiar in his ideas. He esteems me highly. He even told me he had not the slightest doubt that my father would give me the capital instead of the interest of my property. He has promised to use his influence to obtain it for me; but he also declared that he never had taken on himself the responsibility of making proposals for another, and he never would. I must, however, do him the justice to add that he assured me if ever he had regretted the repugnance he felt to such a step it was on this occasion, because he thought the projected union would be a happy and suitable one. Besides, if he will do nothing officially, he will answer any questions you propose to him. And now," continued he, with one of his most charming smiles, "having finished talking to the father-in-law, I must address myself to the banker."

"And what may you have to say to him?" said Danglars, laughing in his turn.

"That the day after tomorrow I shall have to draw upon you for about four thousand francs; but the count, expecting my bachelor's revenue could not suffice for the coming month's outlay, has offered me a draft for twenty thousand francs. It bears his signature, as you see, which is all-sufficient."

"Bring me a million such as that," said Danglars, "I shall be well pleased," putting the draft in his pocket. "Fix your own hour for tomorrow, and my cashier shall call on you with a check for eighty thousand francs."

"At ten o'clock then, if you please; I should like it early, as I am going into the country tomorrow."

"Very well, at ten o'clock; you are still at the Hôtel des Princes?"

"Yes."

The following morning, with the banker's usual punctuality, the eighty thousand francs were placed in the young man's hands, as he was on the point of starting, after having left two hundred francs for Caderousse. He went out chiefly to avoid this dangerous enemy, and returned as late as possible in the evening.

But scarcely had he stepped out of his carriage when the porter met him with a parcel in his hand.

"Sir," said he, "that man has been here."

"What man?" said Andrea carelessly, apparently forgetting him whom he but too well recollected.

"Him to whom your excellency pays that little annuity."

"Oh," said Andrea, "my father's old servant. Well, you gave him the two hundred francs I had left for him?"

"Yes, your excellency." Andrea had expressed a wish to be thus addressed. "But," continued the porter, "he would not take them."

Andrea turned pale, but as it was dark his pallor was not perceptible. "What? he would not take them?" said he with slight emotion.

"No, he wished to speak to your excellency; I told him you were gone out, and after some dispute he believed me and gave me this letter, which he had brought with him already sealed."

"Give it me," said Andrea, and he read by the light of his carriage-lamp:

"'You know where I live; I expect you tomorrow morning at nine o'clock.'"

Andrea examined it carefully, to ascertain if the letter had been opened, or if any indiscreet eyes had seen its contents; but it was so carefully folded, that no one could have read it, and the seal was perfect.

"Very well," said he. "Poor man, he is a worthy creature." He left the porter to ponder on these words, not knowing which most to admire, the master or the servant.

"Take out the horses quickly, and come up to me," said Andrea to his groom. In two seconds the young man had reached his room and burnt Caderousse's letter. The servant entered just as he had finished.

"You are about my height, Pierre," said he.

"I have that honor, your excellency."

"You had a new livery yesterday?"

"Yes, sir."

"I have an engagement with a pretty little girl for this evening, and do not wish to be known; lend me your livery till tomorrow. I may sleep, perhaps, at an inn."

Pierre obeyed. Five minutes after, Andrea left the hotel, completely disguised, took a cabriolet, and ordered the driver to take him to the Cheval Rouge, at Picpus. The next morning he left that inn as he had left the Hôtel des Princes, without being noticed, walked down the Faubourg Saint-Antoine, along the boulevard to Rue Ménilmontant, and stopping at the door of the third house on the left looked for someone of whom to make inquiry in the porter's absence.

"For whom are you looking, my fine fellow?" asked the fruiteress on the opposite side.

"Monsieur Pailletin, if you please, my good woman," replied Andrea.

"A retired baker?" asked the fruiteress.

"Exactly."

"He lives at the end of the yard, on the left, on the third story."

Andrea went as she directed him, and on the third floor he found a hare's paw, which, by the hasty ringing of the bell, it was evident he pulled with considerable ill-temper. A moment after Caderousse's face appeared at the grating in the door.

"Ah! you are punctual," said he, as he drew back the door.

"Confound you and your punctuality!" said Andrea, throwing himself into a chair in a manner which implied that he would rather have flung it at the head of his host.

"Come, come, my little fellow, don't be angry. See, I have thought about you—look at the good breakfast we are going to have; nothing but what you are fond of."

Andrea, indeed, inhaled the scent of something cooking which was not unwelcome to him, hungry as he was; it was that mixture of fat and garlic peculiar to Provençal kitchens of an inferior order, added to that of dried fish, and above all, the pungent smell of musk and cloves. These odors escaped from two deep dishes which were covered and placed on a stove, and from a copper pan placed in an old iron pot. In an adjoining room Andrea saw also a tolerably clean table prepared for two, two bottles of wine sealed, the one with green, the other with yellow, a supply of brandy in a decanter, and a measure of fruit in a cabbage-leaf, cleverly arranged on an earthenware plate.

"What do you think of it, my little fellow?" said Caderousse. "Ay, that smells good! You know I used to be a good cook; do you recollect how you used to lick your fingers? You were among the first who tasted any of my dishes, and I think you relished them tolerably." While speaking, Caderousse went on peeling a fresh supply of onions.

"But," said Andrea, ill-temperedly, "by my faith, if it was only to breakfast with you, that you disturbed me, I wish the devil had taken you!"

"My boy," said Caderousse sententiously, "one can talk while eating. And then, you ungrateful being, you are not pleased to see an old friend? I am weeping with joy."

He was truly crying, but it would have been difficult to say whether joy or the onions produced the greatest effect on the lachrymal glands of the old innkeeper of the Pont-du-Gard.

"Hold your tongue, hypocrite," said Andrea; "you love me!"

"Yes, I do, or may the devil take me. I know it is a weakness," said Caderousse, "but it overpowers me."

"And yet it has not prevented your sending for me to play me some trick."

"Come," said Caderousse, wiping his large knife on his apron, "if I did not like you, do you think I should endure the wretched life you lead me? Think for a moment. You have your servant's clothes on—you therefore keep a servant; I have none, and am obliged to prepare my own meals. You abuse my cookery because you dine at the table d'hôte of the Hôtel des Princes, or the Café de Paris. Well, I too could keep a servant; I too could have a tilbury; I too could dine where I like; but why do I not? Because I would not annoy my little Benedetto. Come, just acknowledge that I could, eh?"

This address was accompanied by a look which was by no means difficult to understand.

"Well," said Andrea, "admitting your love, why do you want me to breakfast with you?"

"That I may have the pleasure of seeing you, my little fellow."

"What is the use of seeing me after we have made all our arrangements?"

"Eh, dear friend," said Caderousse, "are wills ever made without codicils? But you first came to breakfast, did you not? Well, sit down, and let us begin with these pilchards, and this fresh butter; which I have put on some vine-leaves to please you, wicked one. Ah, yes; you look at my room, my four straw chairs, my images, three francs each. But what do you expect? This is not the Hôtel des Princes."

"Come, you are growing discontented, you are no longer happy; you, who only wish to live like a retired baker."

Caderousse sighed.

"Well, what have you to say? you have seen your dream realized."

"I can still say it is a dream; a retired baker, my poor Benedetto, is rich—he has an annuity."

"Well, you have an annuity."

"I have?"

"Yes, since I bring you your two hundred francs."

Caderousse shrugged his shoulders.

"It is humiliating," said he, "thus to receive money given grudgingly,—an uncertain supply which may soon fail. You see I am obliged to economize, in case your prosperity should cease. Well, my friend, fortune is inconstant, as the chaplain of the regiment said. I know your prosperity is great, you rascal; you are to marry the daughter of Danglars."

"What? of Danglars?"

"Yes, to be sure; must I say Baron Danglars? I might as well say Count Benedetto. He was an old friend of mine and if he had not so bad a memory he ought to invite me to your wedding, seeing he came to mine. Yes, yes, to mine; gad, he was not so proud then,—he was an under-clerk to the good M. Morrel. I have dined many times with him and the Count of Morcerf, so you see I have some high connections and were I to cultivate them a little, we might meet in the same drawing-rooms."

"Come, your jealousy represents everything to you in the wrong light."

"That is all very fine, Benedetto mio, but I know what I am saying. Perhaps I may one day put on my best coat, and presenting myself at the great gate, introduce myself. Meanwhile let us sit down and eat."

Caderousse set the example and attacked the breakfast with good appetite, praising each dish he set before his visitor. The latter seemed to have resigned himself; he drew the corks, and partook largely of the fish with the garlic and fat.

"Ah, mate," said Caderousse, "you are getting on better terms with your old landlord!"

"Faith, yes," replied Andrea, whose hunger prevailed over every other feeling.

"So you like it, you rogue?"

"So much that I wonder how a man who can cook thus can complain of hard living."

"Do you see," said Caderousse, "all my happiness is marred by one thought?"

"What is that?"

"That I am dependent on another, I who have always gained my own livelihood honestly."

"Do not let that disturb you, I have enough for two."

"No, truly; you may believe me if you will; at the end of every month I am tormented by remorse."

"Good Caderousse!"

"So much so, that yesterday I would not take the two hundred francs."

"Yes, you wished to speak to me; but was it indeed remorse, tell me?"

"True remorse; and, besides, an idea had struck me."

Andrea shuddered; he always did so at Caderousse's ideas.

"It is miserable—do you see?—always to wait till the end of the month."

"Oh," said Andrea philosophically, determined to watch his companion narrowly, "does not life pass in waiting? Do I, for instance, fare better? Well, I wait patiently, do I not?"

"Yes; because instead of expecting two hundred wretched francs, you expect five or six thousand, perhaps ten, perhaps even twelve, for you take care not to let anyone know the utmost. Down there, you always had little presents and Christmas-boxes, which you tried to hide from your poor friend Caderousse. Fortunately he is a cunning fellow, that friend Caderousse."

"There you are beginning again to ramble, to talk again and again of the past! But what is the use of teasing me with going all over that again?"

"Ah, you are only one-and-twenty, and can forget the past; I am fifty, and am obliged to recollect it. But let us return to business."

"Yes."

"I was going to say, if I were in your place—"

"Well."

"I would realize—"

"How would you realize?"

"I would ask for six months' in advance, under pretence of being able to purchase a farm, then with my six months I would decamp."

"Well, well," said Andrea, "that isn't a bad idea."

"My dear friend," said Caderousse, "eat of my bread, and take my advice; you will be none the worse off, physically or morally."

"But," said Andrea, "why do you not act on the advice you gave me? Why do you not realize a six months', a year's advance even, and retire to Brussels? Instead of living the retired baker, you might live as a bankrupt, using his privileges; that would be very good."

"But how the devil would you have me retire on twelve hundred francs?"

"Ah, Caderousse," said Andrea, "how covetous you are! Two months ago you were dying with hunger."

"The appetite grows by what it feeds on," said Caderousse, grinning and showing his teeth, like a monkey laughing or a tiger growling. "And," added he, biting off with his large white teeth an enormous mouthful of bread, "I have formed a plan."

Caderousse's plans alarmed Andrea still more than his ideas; ideas were but the germ, the plan was reality.

"Let me see your plan; I dare say it is a pretty one."

"Why not? Who formed the plan by which we left the establishment of M—! eh? was it not I? and it was no bad one I believe, since here we are!"

"I do not say," replied Andrea, "that you never make a good one; but let us see your plan."

"Well," pursued Caderousse, "can you without expending one sou, put me in the way of getting fifteen thousand francs? No, fifteen thousand are not enough,—I cannot again become an honest man with less than thirty thousand francs."

"No," replied Andrea, dryly, "no, I cannot."

"I do not think you understand me," replied Caderousse, calmly; "I said without your laying out a sou."

"Do you want me to commit a robbery, to spoil all my good fortune—and yours with mine—and both of us to be dragged down there again?"

"It would make very little difference to me," said Caderousse, "if I were retaken, I am a poor creature to live alone, and sometimes pine for my old comrades; not like you, heartless creature, who would be glad never to see them again."

Andrea did more than tremble this time, he turned pale.

"Come, Caderousse, no nonsense!" said he.

"Don't alarm yourself, my little Benedetto, but just point out to me some means of gaining those thirty thousand francs without your assistance, and I will contrive it."

"Well, I'll see—I'll try to contrive some way," said Andrea.

"Meanwhile you will raise my monthly allowance to five hundred francs, my little fellow? I have a fancy, and mean to get a housekeeper."

"Well, you shall have your five hundred francs," said Andrea; "but it is very hard for me, my poor Caderousse—you take advantage—"

"Bah," said Caderousse, "when you have access to countless stores."

One would have said Andrea anticipated his companion's words, so did his eye flash like lightning, but it was but for a moment.

"True," he replied, "and my protector is very kind."

"That dear protector," said Caderousse; "and how much does he give you monthly?"

"Five thousand francs."

"As many thousands as you give me hundreds! Truly, it is only bastards who are thus fortunate. Five thousand francs per month! What the devil can you do with all that?"

"Oh, it is no trouble to spend that; and I am like you, I want capital."

"Capital?—yes—I understand—everyone would like capital."

"Well, and I shall get it."

"Who will give it to you—your prince?"

"Yes, my prince. But unfortunately I must wait."

"You must wait for what?" asked Caderousse.

"For his death."

"The death of your prince?"

"Yes."

"How so?"

"Because he has made his will in my favor."

"Indeed?"

"On my honor."

"For how much?"

"For five hundred thousand."

"Only that? It's little enough."

"But so it is."

"No, it cannot be!"

"Are you my friend, Caderousse?"

"Yes, in life or death."

"Well, I will tell you a secret."

"What is it?"

"But remember—"

"Ah! *pardieu!* mute as a carp."

"Well, I think—"

Andrea stopped and looked around.

"You think? Do not fear; *pardieu!* we are alone."

"I think I have discovered my father."

"Your true father?"

"Yes."

"Not old Cavalcanti?"

"No, for he has gone again; the true one, as you say."

"And that father is—"

"Well, Caderousse, it is Monte Cristo."

"Bah!"

"Yes, you understand, that explains all. He cannot acknowledge me openly, it appears, but he does it through M. Cavalcanti, and gives him fifty thousand francs for it."

"Fifty thousand francs for being your father? I would have done it for half that, for twenty thousand, for fifteen thousand; why did you not think of me, ungrateful man?"

"Did I know anything about it, when it was all done when I was down there?"

"Ah, truly? And you say that by his will—"

"He leaves me five hundred thousand livres."

"Are you sure of it?"

"He showed it me; but that is not all—there is a codicil, as I said just now."

"Probably."

"And in that codicil he acknowledges me."

"Oh, the good father, the brave father, the very honest father!" said Caderousse, twirling a plate in the air between his two hands.

"Now, say if I conceal anything from you?"

"No, and your confidence makes you honorable in my opinion; and your princely father, is he rich, very rich?"

"Yes, he is that; he does not himself know the amount of his fortune."

"Is it possible?"

"It is evident enough to me, who am always at his house. The other day a banker's clerk brought him fifty thousand francs in a portfolio about the size of your plate; yesterday his banker brought him a hundred thousand francs in gold."

Caderousse was filled with wonder; the young man's words sounded to him like metal, and he thought he could hear the rushing of cascades of louis.

"And you go into that house?" cried he briskly.

"When I like."

Caderousse was thoughtful for a moment. It was easy to perceive he was revolving some unfortunate idea in his mind. Then suddenly,—

"How I should like to see all that," cried he; "how beautiful it must be!"

"It is, in fact, magnificent," said Andrea.

"And does he not live in the Champs-Élysées?"

"Yes, No. 30."

"Ah," said Caderousse, "No. 30."

"Yes, a fine house standing alone, between a courtyard and a garden,—you must know it."

"Possibly; but it is not the exterior I care for, it is the interior. What beautiful furniture there must be in it!"

"Have you ever seen the Tuileries?"

"No."

"Well, it surpasses that."

"It must be worth one's while to stoop, Andrea, when that good M. Monte Cristo lets fall his purse."

"It is not worthwhile to wait for that," said Andrea; "money is as plentiful in that house as fruit in an orchard."

"But you should take me there one day with you."

"How can I? On what plea?"

"You are right; but you have made my mouth water. I must absolutely see it; I shall find a way."

"No nonsense, Caderousse!"

"I will offer myself as floor-polisher."

"The rooms are all carpeted."

"Well, then, I must be contented to imagine it."

"That is the best plan, believe me."

"Try, at least, to give me an idea of what it is."

"How can I?"

"Nothing is easier. Is it large?"

"Middling."

"How is it arranged?"

"Faith, I should require pen, ink, and paper to make a plan."

"They are all here," said Caderousse, briskly. He fetched from an old secretaire a sheet of white paper and pen and ink. "Here," said Caderousse, "draw me all that on the paper, my boy."

Andrea took the pen with an imperceptible smile and began.

"The house, as I said, is between the court and the garden; in this way, do you see?" Andrea drew the garden, the court and the house.

"High walls?"

"Not more than eight or ten feet."

"That is not prudent," said Caderousse.

"In the court are orange-trees in pots, turf, and clumps of flowers."

"And no steel-traps?"

"No."

"The stables?"

"Are on either side of the gate, which you see there." And Andrea continued his plan.

"Let us see the ground floor," said Caderousse.

"On the ground floor, dining-room, two drawing-rooms, billiard-room, staircase in the hall, and a little back staircase."

"Windows?"

"Magnificent windows, so beautiful, so large, that I believe a man of your size should pass through each frame."

"Why the devil have they any stairs with such windows?"

"Luxury has everything."

"But shutters?"

"Yes, but they are never used. That Count of Monte Cristo is an original, who loves to look at the sky even at night."

"And where do the servants sleep?"

"Oh, they have a house to themselves. Picture to yourself a pretty coach-house at the right-hand side where the ladders are kept. Well, over that coach-house are the servants' rooms, with bells corresponding with the different apartments."

"Ah, *diable!* bells did you say?"

"What do you mean?"

"Oh, nothing! I only say they cost a load of money to hang, and what is the use of them, I should like to know?"

"There used to be a dog let loose in the yard at night, but it has been taken to the house at Auteuil, to that you went to, you know."

"Yes."

"I was saying to him only yesterday, 'You are imprudent, Monsieur Count; for when you go to Auteuil and take your servants the house is left unprotected.' 'Well,' said he, 'what next?' 'Well, next, some day you will be robbed.'"

"What did he answer?"

"He quietly said, 'What do I care if I am?'"

"Andrea, he has some secretaire with a spring."

"How do you know?"

"Yes, which catches the thief in a trap and plays a tune. I was told there were such at the last exhibition."

"He has simply a mahogany secretaire, in which the key is always kept."

"And he is not robbed?"

"No; his servants are all devoted to him."

"There ought to be some money in that secretaire?"

"There may be. No one knows what there is."

"And where is it?"

"On the first floor."

"Sketch me the plan of that floor, as you have done of the ground floor, my boy."

"That is very simple." Andrea took the pen. "On the first story, do you see, there is the anteroom and the drawing-room; to the right of the drawing-room, a library and a study; to the left, a bedroom and a dressing-room. The famous secretaire is in the dressing-room."

"Is there a window in the dressing-room?"

"Two,—one here and one there." Andrea sketched two windows in the room, which formed an angle on the plan, and appeared as a small square added to the rectangle of the bedroom. Caderousse became thoughtful.

"Does he often go to Auteuil?" added he.

"Two or three times a week. Tomorrow, for instance, he is going to spend the day and night there."

"Are you sure of it?"

"He has invited me to dine there."

"There's a life for you," said Caderousse; "a town house and a country house."

"That is what it is to be rich."

"And shall you dine there?"

"Probably."

"When you dine there, do you sleep there?"

"If I like; I am at home there."

Caderousse looked at the young man, as if to get at the truth from the bottom of his heart. But Andrea drew a cigar-case from his pocket, took a Havana, quietly lit it, and began smoking.

"When do you want your twelve hundred francs?" said he to Caderousse.

"Now, if you have them." Andrea took five-and-twenty louis from his pocket.

"Yellow boys?" said Caderousse; "no, I thank you."

"Oh, you despise them."

"On the contrary, I esteem them, but will not have them."

"You can change them, idiot; gold is worth five sous."

"Exactly; and he who changes them will follow friend Caderousse, lay hands on him, and demand what farmers pay him their rent in gold. No nonsense, my good fellow; silver simply, round coins with the head of some monarch or other on them. Anybody may possess a five-franc piece."

"But do you suppose I carry five hundred francs about with me? I should want a porter."

"Well, leave them with your porter; he is to be trusted. I will call for them."

"Today?"

"No, tomorrow; I shall not have time today."

"Well, tomorrow I will leave them when I go to Auteuil."

"May I depend on it?"

"Certainly."

"Because I shall secure my housekeeper on the strength of it."

"Now see here, will that be all? Eh? And will you not torment me any more?"

"Never."

Caderousse had become so gloomy that Andrea feared he should be obliged to notice the change. He redoubled his gayety and carelessness.

"How sprightly you are," said Caderousse; "One would say you were already in possession of your property."

"No, unfortunately; but when I do obtain it—"

"Well?"

"I shall remember old friends, I can tell you that."

"Yes, since you have such a good memory."

"What do you want? It looks as if you were trying to fleece me?"

"I? What an idea! I, who am going to give you another piece of good advice."

"What is it?"

"To leave behind you the diamond you have on your finger. We shall both get into trouble. You will ruin both yourself and me by your folly."

"How so?" said Andrea.

"How? You put on a livery, you disguise yourself as a servant, and yet keep a diamond on your finger worth four or five thousand francs."

"You guess well."

"I know something of diamonds; I have had some."

"You do well to boast of it," said Andrea, who, without becoming angry, as Caderousse feared, at this new extortion, quietly resigned the ring. Caderousse looked so closely at it that Andrea well knew that he was examining to see if all the edges were perfect.

"It is a false diamond," said Caderousse.

"You are joking now," replied Andrea.

"Do not be angry, we can try it." Caderousse went to the window, touched the glass with it, and found it would cut.

"*Confiteor!*" said Caderousse, putting the diamond on his little finger; "I was mistaken; but those thieves of jewellers imitate so well that it is no longer worthwhile to rob a jeweller's shop—it is another branch of industry paralyzed."

"Have you finished?" said Andrea,—"do you want anything more?—will you have my waistcoat or my hat? Make free, now you have begun."

"No; you are, after all, a good companion; I will not detain you, and will try to cure myself of my ambition."

"But take care the same thing does not happen to you in selling the diamond you feared with the gold."

"I shall not sell it—do not fear."

"Not at least till the day after tomorrow," thought the young man.

"Happy rogue," said Caderousse; "you are going to find your servants, your horses, your carriage, and your betrothed!"

"Yes," said Andrea.

"Well, I hope you will make a handsome wedding-present the day you marry Mademoiselle Danglars."

"I have already told you it is a fancy you have taken in your head."

"What fortune has she?"

"But I tell you—"

"A million?"

Andrea shrugged his shoulders.

"Let it be a million," said Caderousse; "you can never have so much as I wish you."

"Thank you," said the young man.

"Oh, I wish it you with all my heart!" added Caderousse with his hoarse laugh. "Stop, let me show you the way."

"It is not worthwhile."

"Yes, it is."

"Why?"

"Because there is a little secret, a precaution I thought it desirable to take, one of Huret & Fichet's locks, revised and improved by Gaspard Caderousse; I will manufacture you a similar one when you are a capitalist."

"Thank you," said Andrea; "I will let you know a week beforehand."

They parted. Caderousse remained on the landing until he had not only seen Andrea go down the three stories, but also cross the court. Then he returned hastily, shut his door carefully, and began to study, like a clever architect, the plan Andrea had left him.

"Dear Benedetto," said he, "I think he will not be sorry to inherit his fortune, and he who hastens the day when he can touch his five hundred thousand will not be his worst friend."

Study Guide Questions

For Students:

1. Who sends a proposal to Mademoiselle Danglars?
2. Why does Danglars send 80 thousand francs to Andrea?
3. What is written in the letter that Caderousse leaves for Andrea?

For Reading Club:

1. Do you think that Andrea has any other way to deal with Caderousse's blackmail?
2. Discuss the statement, "The appetite grows by what it feeds on."
3. Discuss Caderousse as a man of contemporary society. Why do you think he acquires all the information about the Count's house?

CHAPTER 82

The Burglary

The day following that on which the conversation we have related took place, the Count of Monte Cristo set out for Auteuil, accompanied by Ali and several attendants, and also taking with him some horses whose qualities he was desirous of ascertaining. He was induced to undertake this journey, of which the day before he had not even thought and which had not occurred to Andrea either, by the arrival of Bertuccio from Normandy with intelligence respecting the house and sloop. The house was ready, and the sloop which had arrived a week before lay at anchor in a small creek with her crew of six men, who had observed all the requisite formalities and were ready again to put to sea.

The count praised Bertuccio's zeal, and ordered him to prepare for a speedy departure, as his stay in France would not be prolonged more than a month.

"Now," said he, "I may require to go in one night from Paris to Tréport; let eight fresh horses be in readiness on the road, which will enable me to go fifty leagues in ten hours."

"Your highness had already expressed that wish," said Bertuccio, "and the horses are ready. I have bought them, and stationed them myself at the most desirable posts, that is, in villages, where no one generally stops."

"That's well," said Monte Cristo; "I remain here a day or two—arrange accordingly."

As Bertuccio was leaving the room to give the requisite orders, Baptistin opened the door: he held a letter on a silver waiter.

"What are you doing here?" asked the count, seeing him covered with dust; "I did not send for you, I think?"

Baptistin, without answering, approached the count, and presented the letter. "Important and urgent," said he.

The count opened the letter, and read:

> "'M. de Monte Cristo is apprised that this night a man will enter his house in the Champs-Élysées with the intention of carrying off some papers supposed to be in the secretaire in the dressing-room. The count's well-known courage will render unnecessary the aid of the police, whose interference might seriously affect him who sends this advice. The count, by any opening from the bedroom, or by concealing himself in the dressing-room, would be able to defend his property himself. Many attendants or apparent precautions would prevent the villain from the attempt, and M. de Monte Cristo would lose the opportunity of discovering an enemy whom chance has revealed to him who now sends this warning to the count,—a warning he might not be able to send another time, if this first attempt should fail and another be made.'"

The count's first idea was that this was an artifice—a gross deception, to draw his attention from a minor danger in order to expose him to a greater. He was on the point of sending the letter to the commissary of police, notwithstanding the advice of his anonymous friend, or perhaps because of that advice, when suddenly the idea occurred to him that it might be some personal enemy, whom he alone should recognize and over whom, if such were the case, he alone would gain any advantage, as Fiesco[10] had done over the Moor who would have killed him. We know the count's vigorous and daring mind, denying anything to be impossible, with that energy which marks the great man.

From his past life, from his resolution to shrink from nothing, the count had acquired an inconceivable relish for the contests in which he had engaged, sometimes against nature, that is to say, against God, and sometimes against the world, that is, against the devil.

"They do not want my papers," said Monte Cristo, "they want to kill me; they are no robbers, but assassins. I will not allow the prefect of police to interfere with my private affairs. I am rich enough, forsooth, to distribute his authority on this occasion."

The count recalled Baptistin, who had left the room after delivering the letter.

"Return to Paris," said he; "assemble the servants who remain there. I want all my household at Auteuil."

---

[10] The Genoese conspirator.

"But will no one remain in the house, my lord?" asked Baptistin.

"Yes, the porter."

"My lord will remember that the lodge is at a distance from the house."

"Well?"

"The house might be stripped without his hearing the least noise."

"By whom?"

"By thieves."

"You are a fool, M. Baptistin. Thieves might strip the house—it would annoy me less than to be disobeyed." Baptistin bowed.

"You understand me?" said the count. "Bring your comrades here, one and all; but let everything remain as usual, only close the shutters of the ground floor."

"And those of the first floor?"

"You know they are never closed. Go!"

The count signified his intention of dining alone, and that no one but Ali should attend him. Having dined with his usual tranquillity and moderation, the count, making a signal to Ali to follow him, went out by the side-gate and on reaching the Bois de Boulogne turned, apparently without design towards Paris and at twilight; found himself opposite his house in the Champs-Élysées. All was dark; one solitary, feeble light was burning in the porter's lodge, about forty paces distant from the house, as Baptistin had said.

Monte Cristo leaned against a tree, and with that scrutinizing glance which was so rarely deceived, looked up and down the avenue, examined the passers-by, and carefully looked down the neighboring streets, to see that no one was concealed. Ten minutes passed thus, and he was convinced that no one was watching him. He hastened to the side-door with Ali, entered hurriedly, and by the servants' staircase, of which he had the key, gained his bedroom without opening or disarranging a single curtain, without even the porter having the slightest suspicion that the house, which he supposed empty, contained its chief occupant.

Arrived in his bedroom, the count motioned to Ali to stop; then he passed into the dressing-room, which he examined. Everything appeared as usual—the precious secretaire in its place, and the key in the secretaire. He double locked it, took the key, returned to the bedroom door, removed the double staple of the bolt, and went in. Meanwhile Ali had procured the arms the count required—namely, a short carbine and a pair of double-barrelled pistols, with which as sure an aim might be taken as with a single-barrelled one. Thus armed, the count held the lives of five men in his hands. It was about half-past nine.

The count and Ali ate in haste a crust of bread and drank a glass of Spanish wine; then Monte Cristo slipped aside one of the movable panels, which enabled him to see into the adjoining room. He had within his reach his pistols and carbine, and Ali, standing near him, held one of the small Arabian hatchets, whose form has not varied since the Crusades. Through one of the windows of the bedroom, on a line with that in the dressing-room, the count could see into the street.

Two hours passed thus. It was intensely dark; still Ali, thanks to his wild nature, and the count, thanks doubtless to his long confinement, could distinguish in the darkness the slightest movement of the trees. The little light in the lodge had long been extinct. It might be expected that the attack, if indeed an attack was projected, would be made from the staircase of the ground floor, and not from a window; in Monte Cristo's opinion, the villains sought his life, not his money. It would be his bedroom they would attack, and they must reach it by the back staircase, or by the window in the dressing-room.

The clock of the Invalides struck a quarter to twelve; the west wind bore on its moistened gusts the doleful vibration of the three strokes.

As the last stroke died away, the count thought he heard a slight noise in the dressing-room; this first sound, or rather this first grinding, was followed by a second, then a third; at the fourth, the count knew what to expect. A firm and well-practised hand was engaged in cutting the four sides of a pane of glass with a diamond. The count felt his heart beat more rapidly.

Inured as men may be to danger, forewarned as they may be of peril, they understand, by the fluttering of the heart and the shuddering of the frame, the enormous difference between a dream and a reality, between the project and the execution. However, Monte Cristo only made a sign to apprise Ali, who, understanding that danger was approaching from the other side, drew nearer to his master. Monte Cristo was eager to ascertain the strength and number of his enemies.

The window whence the noise proceeded was opposite the opening by which the count could see into the dressing-room. He fixed his eyes on that window—he distinguished a shadow in the darkness; then one of the panes became quite opaque, as if a sheet of paper were stuck on the outside, then the square cracked without falling. Through the opening an arm was passed to find the fastening, then a second; the window turned on its hinges, and a man entered. He was alone.

"That's a daring rascal," whispered the count.

At that moment Ali touched him slightly on the shoulder. He turned; Ali pointed to the window of the room in which they were, facing the street.

"I see!" said he, "there are two of them; one does the work while the other stands guard." He made a sign to Ali not to lose sight of the man in the street, and turned to the one in the dressing-room.

The glass-cutter had entered, and was feeling his way, his arms stretched out before him. At last he appeared to have made himself familiar with his surroundings. There were two doors; he bolted them both.

When he drew near to the bedroom door, Monte Cristo expected that he was coming in, and raised one of his pistols; but he simply heard the sound of the bolts sliding in their copper rings. It was only a precaution. The nocturnal visitor, ignorant of the fact that the count had removed the staples, might now think himself at home, and pursue his purpose with full security. Alone and free to act as he wished, the man then drew from his pocket something which the count could not discern, placed it on a stand, then went straight to the secretaire, felt the lock, and contrary to his expectation found that the key was missing. But the glass-cutter was a prudent man who had provided for all emergencies. The count soon heard the rattling of a bunch of skeleton keys, such as the locksmith brings when called to force a lock, and which thieves call nightingales, doubtless from the music of their nightly song when they grind against the bolt.

"Ah, ha," whispered Monte Cristo with a smile of disappointment, "he is only a thief."

But the man in the dark could not find the right key. He reached the instrument he had placed on the stand, touched a spring, and immediately a pale light, just bright enough to render objects distinct, was reflected on his hands and countenance.

"By heavens," exclaimed Monte Cristo, starting back, "it is—"

Ali raised his hatchet.

"Don't stir," whispered Monte Cristo, "and put down your hatchet; we shall require no arms."

Then he added some words in a low tone, for the exclamation which surprise had drawn from the count, faint as it had been, had startled the man who remained in the pose of the old knife-grinder.

It was an order the count had just given, for immediately Ali went noiselessly, and returned, bearing a black dress and a three-cornered hat. Meanwhile Monte Cristo had rapidly taken off his greatcoat, waistcoat, and shirt, and one might distinguish by the glimmering through the open panel that he wore a pliant tunic of steel mail, of which the last in France, where daggers are no longer dreaded, was worn by King Louis XVI., who feared the dagger at his breast, and whose head was cleft with a hatchet. The tunic soon disappeared under a long cassock, as did his hair under a priest's wig; the three-cornered hat over this effectually transformed the count into an abbé.

The man, hearing nothing more, stood erect, and while Monte Cristo was completing his disguise had advanced straight to the secretaire, whose lock was beginning to crack under his nightingale.

"Try again," whispered the count, who depended on the secret spring, which was unknown to the picklock, clever as he might be—"try again, you have a few minutes' work there."

And he advanced to the window. The man whom he had seen seated on a fence had got down, and was still pacing the street; but, strange as it appeared, he cared not for those who might pass from the avenue of the Champs-Élysées or by the Faubourg Saint-Honoré; his attention was engrossed with what was passing at the count's, and his only aim appeared to be to discern every movement in the dressing-room.

Monte Cristo suddenly struck his finger on his forehead and a smile passed over his lips; then drawing near to Ali, he whispered:

"Remain here, concealed in the dark, and whatever noise you hear, whatever passes, only come in or show yourself if I call you."

Ali bowed in token of strict obedience. Monte Cristo then drew a lighted taper from a closet, and when the thief was deeply engaged with his lock, silently opened the door, taking care that the light should shine directly on his face. The door opened so quietly that the thief heard no sound; but, to his astonishment, the room was suddenly illuminated. He turned.

"Ah, good-evening, my dear M. Caderousse," said Monte Cristo; "what are you doing here, at such an hour?"

"The Abbé Busoni!" exclaimed Caderousse; and, not knowing how this strange apparition could have entered when he had bolted the doors, he let fall his bunch of keys, and remained motionless and stupefied. The count placed himself between Caderousse and the window, thus cutting off from the thief his only chance of retreat.

"The Abbé Busoni!" repeated Caderousse, fixing his haggard gaze on the count.

"Yes, undoubtedly, the Abbé Busoni himself," replied Monte Cristo. "And I am very glad you recognize me, dear M. Caderousse; it proves you have a good memory, for it must be about ten years since we last met."

This calmness of Busoni, combined with his irony and boldness, staggered Caderousse.

"The abbé, the abbé!" murmured he, clenching his fists, and his teeth chattering.

"So you would rob the Count of Monte Cristo?" continued the false abbé.

"Reverend sir," murmured Caderousse, seeking to regain the window, which the count pitilessly blocked—"reverend sir, I don't know—believe me—I take my oath—"

"A pane of glass out," continued the count, "a dark lantern, a bunch of false keys, a secretaire half forced—it is tolerably evident—"

Caderousse was choking; he looked around for some corner to hide in, some way of escape.

"Come, come," continued the count, "I see you are still the same,—an assassin."

"Reverend sir, since you know everything, you know it was not I—it was La Carconte; that was proved at the trial, since I was only condemned to the galleys."

"Is your time, then, expired, since I find you in a fair way to return there?"

"No, reverend sir; I have been liberated by someone."

"That someone has done society a great kindness."

"Ah," said Caderousse, "I had promised—"

"And you are breaking your promise!" interrupted Monte Cristo.

"Alas, yes!" said Caderousse very uneasily.

"A bad relapse, that will lead you, if I mistake not, to the Place de Grève. So much the worse, so much the worse—*diavolo!* as they say in my country."

"Reverend sir, I am impelled—"

"Every criminal says the same thing."

"Poverty—"

"Pshaw!" said Busoni disdainfully; "poverty may make a man beg, steal a loaf of bread at a baker's door, but not cause him to open a secretaire in a house supposed to be inhabited. And when the jeweller Johannes had just paid you 45,000 francs for the diamond I had given you, and you killed him to get the diamond and the money both, was that also poverty?"

"Pardon, reverend sir," said Caderousse; "you have saved my life once, save me again!"

"That is but poor encouragement."

"Are you alone, reverend sir, or have you there soldiers ready to seize me?"

"I am alone," said the abbé, "and I will again have pity on you, and will let you escape, at the risk of the fresh miseries my weakness may lead to, if you tell me the truth."

"Ah, reverend sir," cried Caderousse, clasping his hands, and drawing nearer to Monte Cristo, "I may indeed say you are my deliverer!"

"You mean to say you have been freed from confinement?"

"Yes, that is true, reverend sir."

"Who was your liberator?"

"An Englishman."

"What was his name?"

"Lord Wilmore."

"I know him; I shall know if you lie."

"Ah, reverend sir, I tell you the simple truth."

"Was this Englishman protecting you?"

"No, not me, but a young Corsican, my companion."

"What was this young Corsican's name?"

"Benedetto."

"Is that his Christian name?"

"He had no other; he was a foundling."

"Then this young man escaped with you?"

"He did."

"In what way?"

"We were working at Saint-Mandrier, near Toulon. Do you know Saint-Mandrier?"

"I do."

"In the hour of rest, between noon and one o'clock—"

"Galley-slaves having a nap after dinner! We may well pity the poor fellows!" said the abbé.

"Nay," said Caderousse, "one can't always work—one is not a dog."

"So much the better for the dogs," said Monte Cristo.

"While the rest slept, then, we went away a short distance; we severed our fetters with a file the Englishman had given us, and swam away."

"And what is become of this Benedetto?"

"I don't know."

"You ought to know."

"No, in truth; we parted at Hyères." And, to give more weight to his protestation, Caderousse advanced another step towards the abbé, who remained motionless in his place, as calm as ever, and pursuing his interrogation.

"You lie," said the Abbé Busoni, with a tone of irresistible authority.

"Reverend sir!"

"You lie! This man is still your friend, and you, perhaps, make use of him as your accomplice."

"Oh, reverend sir!"

"Since you left Toulon what have you lived on? Answer me!"

"On what I could get."

"You lie," repeated the abbé a third time, with a still more imperative tone. Caderousse, terrified, looked at the count. "You have lived on the money he has given you."

"True," said Caderousse; "Benedetto has become the son of a great lord."

"How can he be the son of a great lord?"

"A natural son."

"And what is that great lord's name?"

"The Count of Monte Cristo, the very same in whose house we are."

"Benedetto the count's son?" replied Monte Cristo, astonished in his turn.

"Well, I should think so, since the count has found him a false father—since the count gives him four thousand francs a month, and leaves him 500,000 francs in his will."

"Ah, yes," said the factitious abbé, who began to understand; "and what name does the young man bear meanwhile?"

"Andrea Cavalcanti."

"Is it, then, that young man whom my friend the Count of Monte Cristo has received into his house, and who is going to marry Mademoiselle Danglars?"

"Exactly."

"And you suffer that, you wretch!—you, who know his life and his crime?"

"Why should I stand in a comrade's way?" said Caderousse.

"You are right; it is not you who should apprise M. Danglars, it is I."

"Do not do so, reverend sir."

"Why not?"

"Because you would bring us to ruin."

"And you think that to save such villains as you I will become an abettor of their plot, an accomplice in their crimes?"

"Reverend sir," said Caderousse, drawing still nearer.

"I will expose all."

"To whom?"

"To M. Danglars."

"By Heaven!" cried Caderousse, drawing from his waistcoat an open knife, and striking the count in the breast, "you shall disclose nothing, reverend sir!"

To Caderousse's great astonishment, the knife, instead of piercing the count's breast, flew back blunted. At the same moment the count seized with his left hand the assassin's wrist, and wrung it with such strength that the knife fell from his stiffened fingers, and Caderousse uttered a cry of pain. But the count, disregarding his cry, continued to wring the bandit's wrist, until, his arm being dislocated, he fell first on his knees, then flat on the floor.

The count then placed his foot on his head, saying, "I know not what restrains me from crushing thy skull, rascal."

"Ah, mercy—mercy!" cried Caderousse.

The count withdrew his foot.

"Rise!" said he. Caderousse rose.

"What a wrist you have, reverend sir!" said Caderousse, stroking his arm, all bruised by the fleshy pincers which had held it; "what a wrist!"

"Silence! God gives me strength to overcome a wild beast like you; in the name of that God I act,—remember that, wretch,—and to spare thee at this moment is still serving him."

"Oh!" said Caderousse, groaning with pain.

"Take this pen and paper, and write what I dictate."

"I don't know how to write, reverend sir."

"You lie! Take this pen, and write!"

Caderousse, awed by the superior power of the abbé, sat down and wrote:

> "Sir,—The man whom you are receiving at your house, and to whom you intend to marry your daughter, is a felon who escaped with me from confinement at Toulon. He was No. 59, and I No. 58. He was called Benedetto, but he is ignorant of his real name, having never known his parents."

"Sign it!" continued the count.

"But would you ruin me?"

"If I sought your ruin, fool, I should drag you to the first guard-house; besides, when that note is delivered, in all probability you will have no more to fear. Sign it, then!"

Caderousse signed it.

"The address, 'To monsieur the Baron Danglars, banker, Rue de la Chaussée d'Antin.'"

Caderousse wrote the address. The abbé took the note.

"Now," said he, "that suffices—begone!"

"Which way?"

"The way you came."

"You wish me to get out at that window?"

"You got in very well."

"Oh, you have some design against me, reverend sir."

"Idiot! what design can I have?"

"Why, then, not let me out by the door?"

"What would be the advantage of waking the porter?"

"Ah, reverend sir, tell me, do you wish me dead?"

"I wish what God wills."

"But swear that you will not strike me as I go down."

"Cowardly fool!"

"What do you intend doing with me?"

"I ask you what can I do? I have tried to make you a happy man, and you have turned out a murderer."

"Oh, monsieur," said Caderousse, "make one more attempt—try me once more!"

"I will," said the count. "Listen—you know if I may be relied on."

"Yes," said Caderousse.

"If you arrive safely at home—"

"What have I to fear, except from you?"

"If you reach your home safely, leave Paris, leave France, and wherever you may be, so long as you conduct yourself well, I will send you a small annuity; for, if you return home safely, then—"

"Then?" asked Caderousse, shuddering.

"Then I shall believe God has forgiven you, and I will forgive you too."

"As true as I am a Christian," stammered Caderousse, "you will make me die of fright!"

"Now begone," said the count, pointing to the window.

Caderousse, scarcely yet relying on this promise, put his legs out of the window and stood on the ladder.

"Now go down," said the abbé, folding his arms. Understanding he had nothing more to fear from him, Caderousse began to go down. Then the count brought the taper to the window, that it might be seen in the Champs-Élysées that a man was getting out of the window while another held a light.

"What are you doing, reverend sir? Suppose a watchman should pass?" And he blew out the light. He then descended, but it was only when he felt his foot touch the ground that he was satisfied of his safety.

Monte Cristo returned to his bedroom, and, glancing rapidly from the garden to the street, he saw first Caderousse, who after walking to the end of the garden, fixed his ladder against the wall at a different part from where he came in. The count then looking over into the street, saw the man who appeared to be waiting run in the same direction, and place himself against the angle of the wall where Caderousse would come over. Caderousse climbed the ladder slowly, and looked over the coping to see if the street was quiet. No one could be seen or heard. The clock of the Invalides struck one. Then Caderousse sat astride the coping, and drawing up his ladder passed it over the wall; then he began to descend, or rather to slide down by the two stanchions, which he did with an ease which proved how accustomed he was to the exercise. But, once started, he could not stop. In vain did he see a man start from the shadow when he was halfway down—in vain did he see an arm raised as he touched the ground.

Before he could defend himself that arm struck him so violently in the back that he let go the ladder, crying, "Help!" A second blow struck him almost immediately in the side, and he fell, calling, "Help, murder!" Then, as he rolled on the ground, his adversary seized him by the hair, and struck him a third blow in the chest.

This time Caderousse endeavored to call again, but he could only utter a groan, and he shuddered as the blood flowed from his three wounds. The assassin, finding that he no longer cried out, lifted his head up by the hair; his eyes were closed, and the mouth was distorted. The murderer, supposing him dead, let fall his head and disappeared.

Then Caderousse, feeling that he was leaving him, raised himself on his elbow, and with a dying voice cried with great effort:

"Murder! I am dying! Help, reverend sir,—help!"

This mournful appeal pierced the darkness. The door of the back-staircase opened, then the side-gate of the garden, and Ali and his master were on the spot with lights.

Study Guide Questions

For Students:

1. What information is given in the letter that the Count receives?
2. Who transforms himself into an abbé and why?
3. What is written in the note that the Count makes Caderousse write?

For Reading Club:

1. Why do you think the Count never closes the shutters?
2. Do you think Caderousse is stealing because he is poor?
3. What happens to Caderousse and what does it tell you about divine justice?

CHAPTER 83

The Hand of God

Caderousse continued to call piteously, "Help, reverend sir, help!"

"What is the matter?" asked Monte Cristo.

"Help," cried Caderousse; "I am murdered!"

"We are here;—take courage."

"Ah, it's all over! You are come too late—you are come to see me die. What blows, what blood!"

He fainted. Ali and his master conveyed the wounded man into a room. Monte Cristo motioned to Ali to undress him, and he then examined his dreadful wounds.

"My God!" he exclaimed, "thy vengeance is sometimes delayed, but only that it may fall the more effectually." Ali looked at his master for further instructions. "Bring here immediately the king's attorney, M. de Villefort, who lives in the Faubourg Saint-Honoré. As you pass the lodge, wake the porter, and send him for a surgeon."

Ali obeyed, leaving the abbé alone with Caderousse, who had not yet revived.

When the wretched man again opened his eyes, the count looked at him with a mournful expression of pity, and his lips moved as if in prayer. "A surgeon, reverend sir—a surgeon!" said Caderousse.

"I have sent for one," replied the abbé.

"I know he cannot save my life, but he may strengthen me to give my evidence."

"Against whom?"

"Against my murderer."

"Did you recognize him?"

"Yes; it was Benedetto."

"The young Corsican?"

"Himself."

"Your comrade?"

"Yes. After giving me the plan of this house, doubtless hoping I should kill the count and he thus become his heir, or that the count would kill me and I should be out of his way, he waylaid me, and has murdered me."

"I have also sent for the procureur."

"He will not come in time; I feel my life fast ebbing."

"Wait a moment," said Monte Cristo. He left the room, and returned in five minutes with a phial. The dying man's eyes were all the time riveted on the door, through which he hoped succor would arrive.

"Hasten, reverend sir, hasten! I shall faint again!" Monte Cristo approached, and dropped on his purple lips three or four drops of the contents of the phial. Caderousse drew a deep breath. "Oh," said he, "that is life to me; more, more!"

"Two drops more would kill you," replied the abbé.

"Oh, send for someone to whom I can denounce the wretch!"

"Shall I write your deposition? You can sign it."

"Yes, yes," said Caderousse; and his eyes glistened at the thought of this posthumous revenge. Monte Cristo wrote:

> "I die, murdered by the Corsican Benedetto, my comrade in the galleys at Toulon, No. 59."

"Quick, quick!" said Caderousse, "or I shall be unable to sign it."

Monte Cristo gave the pen to Caderousse, who collected all his strength, signed it, and fell back on his bed, saying:

"You will relate all the rest, reverend sir; you will say he calls himself Andrea Cavalcanti. He lodges at the Hôtel des Princes. Oh, I am dying!" He again fainted. The abbé made him smell the contents of the phial, and he again opened his eyes. His desire for revenge had not forsaken him.

"Ah, you will tell all I have said, will you not, reverend sir?"

"Yes, and much more."

"What more will you say?"

"I will say he had doubtless given you the plan of this house, in the hope the count would kill you. I will say, likewise, he had apprised the count, by a note, of your intention, and, the count being absent, I read the note and sat up to await you."

"And he will be guillotined, will he not?" said Caderousse. "Promise me that, and I will die with that hope."

"I will say," continued the count, "that he followed and watched you the whole time, and when he saw you leave the house, ran to the angle of the wall to conceal himself."

"Did you see all that?"

"Remember my words: 'If you return home safely, I shall believe God has forgiven you, and I will forgive you also.'"

"And you did not warn me!" cried Caderousse, raising himself on his elbows. "You knew I should be killed on leaving this house, and did not warn me!"

"No; for I saw God's justice placed in the hands of Benedetto, and should have thought it sacrilege to oppose the designs of Providence."

"God's justice! Speak not of it, reverend sir. If God were just, you know how many would be punished who now escape."

"Patience," said the abbé, in a tone which made the dying man shudder; "have patience!"

Caderousse looked at him with amazement.

"Besides," said the abbé, "God is merciful to all, as he has been to you; he is first a father, then a judge."

"Do you then believe in God?" said Caderousse.

"Had I been so unhappy as not to believe in him until now," said Monte Cristo, "I must believe on seeing you."

Caderousse raised his clenched hands towards heaven.

"Listen," said the abbé, extending his hand over the wounded man, as if to command him to believe; "this is what the God in whom, on your death-bed, you refuse to believe, has done for you—he gave you health, strength, regular employment, even friends—a life, in fact, which a man might enjoy with a calm conscience. Instead of improving these gifts, rarely granted so abundantly, this has been your course—you have given yourself up to sloth and drunkenness, and in a fit of intoxication have ruined your best friend."

"Help!" cried Caderousse; "I require a surgeon, not a priest; perhaps I am not mortally wounded—I may not die; perhaps they can yet save my life."

"Your wounds are so far mortal that, without the three drops I gave you, you would now be dead. Listen, then."

"Ah," murmured Caderousse, "what a strange priest you are; you drive the dying to despair, instead of consoling them."

"Listen," continued the abbé. "When you had betrayed your friend, God began not to strike, but to warn you. Poverty overtook you. You had already passed half your life in coveting that which you might have honorably acquired; and already you contemplated crime under the excuse of want, when God worked a miracle in your behalf, sending you, by my hands, a fortune—brilliant, indeed, for you, who had never possessed any. But this unexpected, unhoped-for, unheard-of fortune sufficed you no longer when you once possessed it; you wished to double it, and how?—by a murder! You succeeded, and then God snatched it from you, and brought you to justice."

"It was not I who wished to kill the Jew," said Caderousse; "it was La Carconte."

"Yes," said Monte Cristo, "and God,—I cannot say in justice, for his justice would have slain you,—but God, in his mercy, spared your life."

"*Pardieu!* to transport me for life, how merciful!"

"You thought it a mercy then, miserable wretch! The coward who feared death rejoiced at perpetual disgrace; for like all galley-slaves, you said, 'I may escape from prison, I cannot from the grave.' And you said truly; the way was opened for you unexpectedly. An Englishman visited Toulon, who had vowed to rescue two men from infamy, and his choice fell on you and your companion. You received a second fortune, money and tranquillity were restored to you, and you, who had been condemned to a felon's life, might live as other men. Then, wretched creature, then you tempted God a third time. 'I have not enough,' you said, when you had more than you before possessed, and you committed a third crime, without reason, without excuse. God is wearied; he has punished you."

Caderousse was fast sinking. "Give me drink," said he: "I thirst—I burn!" Monte Cristo gave him a glass of water. "And yet that villain, Benedetto, will escape!"

"No one, I tell you, will escape; Benedetto will be punished."

"Then, you, too, will be punished, for you did not do your duty as a priest—you should have prevented Benedetto from killing me."

"I?" said the count, with a smile which petrified the dying man, "when you had just broken your knife against the coat of mail which protected my breast! Yet perhaps if I had found you humble and penitent, I might have prevented Benedetto from killing you; but I found you proud and blood-thirsty, and I left you in the hands of God."

"I do not believe there is a God," howled Caderousse; "you do not believe it; you lie—you lie!"

"Silence," said the abbé; "you will force the last drop of blood from your veins. What! you do not believe in God when he is striking you dead? you will not believe in him, who requires but a prayer, a word, a tear, and he will forgive? God, who might have directed the assassin's dagger so as to end your career in a moment, has given you this quarter of an hour for repentance. Reflect, then, wretched man, and repent."

"No," said Caderousse, "no; I will not repent. There is no God; there is no Providence—all comes by chance."

"There is a Providence; there is a God," said Monte Cristo, "of whom you are a striking proof, as you lie in utter despair, denying him, while I stand before you, rich, happy, safe and entreating that God in whom you endeavor not to believe, while in your heart you still believe in him."

"But who are you, then?" asked Caderousse, fixing his dying eyes on the count.

"Look well at me!" said Monte Cristo, putting the light near his face.

"Well, the abbé—the Abbé Busoni." Monte Cristo took off the wig which disfigured him, and let fall his black hair, which added so much to the beauty of his pallid features.

"Oh?" said Caderousse, thunderstruck, "but for that black hair, I should say you were the Englishman, Lord Wilmore."

"I am neither the Abbé Busoni nor Lord Wilmore," said Monte Cristo; "think again,—do you not recollect me?"

There was a magic effect in the count's words, which once more revived the exhausted powers of the miserable man.

"Yes, indeed," said he; "I think I have seen you and known you formerly."

"Yes, Caderousse, you have seen me; you knew me once."

"Who, then, are you? and why, if you knew me, do you let me die?"

"Because nothing can save you; your wounds are mortal. Had it been possible to save you, I should have considered it another proof of God's mercy, and I would again have endeavored to restore you, I swear by my father's tomb."

"By your father's tomb!" said Caderousse, supported by a supernatural power, and half-raising himself to see more distinctly the man who had just taken the oath which all men hold sacred; "who, then, are you?"

The count had watched the approach of death. He knew this was the last struggle. He approached the dying man, and, leaning over him with a calm and melancholy look, he whispered, "I am—I am—"

And his almost closed lips uttered a name so low that the count himself appeared afraid to hear it. Caderousse, who had raised himself on his knees, and stretched out his arm, tried to draw back, then clasping his hands, and raising them with a desperate effort, "Oh, my God, my God!" said he, "pardon me for having denied thee; thou dost exist, thou art indeed man's father in heaven, and his judge on earth. My God, my Lord, I have long despised thee! Pardon me, my God; receive me, Oh, my Lord!"

Caderousse sighed deeply, and fell back with a groan. The blood no longer flowed from his wounds. He was dead.

"*One!*" said the count mysteriously, his eyes fixed on the corpse, disfigured by so awful a death.

Ten minutes afterwards the surgeon and the procureur arrived, the one accompanied by the porter, the other by Ali, and were received by the Abbé Busoni, who was praying by the side of the corpse.

Study Guide Questions

For Students:

1. Who tries to kill Caderousse?
2. What does Caderousse sign?
3. The chapter reveals the identity of Abbé Busoni and Lord Wilmore. Who are they?

For Reading Club:

1. Caderousse and the Count have different opinions about God's justice. With whom do you agree and why?
2. How do you think the chapter highlights divine justice?
3. What does Caderousse realize when he is about to die?

CHAPTER 84

Beauchamp

The daring attempt to rob the count was the topic of conversation throughout Paris for the next fortnight. The dying man had signed a deposition declaring Benedetto to be the assassin. The police had orders to make the strictest search for the murderer. Caderousse's knife, dark lantern, bunch of keys, and clothing, excepting the waistcoat, which could not be found, were deposited at the registry; the corpse was conveyed to the morgue. The count told everyone that this adventure had happened during his absence at Auteuil, and that he only knew what was related by the Abbé Busoni, who that evening, by mere chance, had requested to pass the night in his house, to examine some valuable books in his library.

Bertuccio alone turned pale whenever Benedetto's name was mentioned in his presence, but there was no reason why anyone should notice his doing so.

Villefort, being called on to prove the crime, was preparing his brief with the same ardor that he was accustomed to exercise when required to speak in criminal cases.

But three weeks had already passed, and the most diligent search had been unsuccessful; the attempted robbery and the murder of the robber by his comrade were almost forgotten in anticipation of the approaching marriage of Mademoiselle Danglars to the Count Andrea Cavalcanti. It was expected that this wedding would shortly take place, as the young man was received at the banker's as the betrothed.

Letters had been despatched to M. Cavalcanti, as the count's father, who highly approved of the union, regretted his inability to leave Parma at that time, and promised a wedding gift of a hundred and fifty thousand livres. It was agreed that the three millions should be intrusted to Danglars to invest; some persons had warned the young man of the circumstances of his future father-in-law, who had of late sustained repeated losses; but with sublime disinterestedness and confidence the young man refused to listen, or to express a single doubt to the baron.

The baron adored Count Andrea Cavalcanti; not so Mademoiselle Eugénie Danglars. With an instinctive hatred of matrimony, she suffered Andrea's attentions in order to get rid of Morcerf; but when Andrea urged his suit, she betrayed an entire dislike to him. The baron might possibly have perceived it, but, attributing it to a caprice, feigned ignorance.

The delay demanded by Beauchamp had nearly expired. Morcerf appreciated the advice of Monte Cristo to let things die away of their own accord. No one had taken up the remark about the general, and no one had recognized in the officer who betrayed the castle of Yanina the noble count in the House of Peers.

Albert, however, felt no less insulted; the few lines which had irritated him were certainly intended as an insult. Besides, the manner in which Beauchamp had closed the conference left a bitter recollection in his heart. He cherished the thought of the duel, hoping to conceal its true cause even from his seconds. Beauchamp had not been seen since the day he visited Albert, and those of whom the latter inquired always told him he was out on a journey which would detain him some days. Where he was no one knew.

One morning Albert was awakened by his valet de chambre, who announced Beauchamp. Albert rubbed his eyes, ordered his servant to introduce him into the small smoking-room on the ground floor, dressed himself quickly, and went down.

He found Beauchamp pacing the room; on perceiving him Beauchamp stopped.

"Your arrival here, without waiting my visit at your house today, looks well, sir," said Albert. "Tell me, may I shake hands with you, saying, 'Beauchamp, acknowledge you have injured me, and retain my friendship,' or must I simply propose to you a choice of arms?"

"Albert," said Beauchamp, with a look of sorrow which stupefied the young man, "let us first sit down and talk."

"Rather, sir, before we sit down, I must demand your answer."

"Albert," said the journalist, "these are questions which it is difficult to answer."

"I will facilitate it by repeating the question, 'Will you, or will you not, retract?'"

"Morcerf, it is not enough to answer 'yes' or 'no' to questions which concern the honor, the social interest, and the life of such a man as Lieutenant-général the Count of Morcerf, peer of France."

"What must then be done?"

"What I have done, Albert. I reasoned thus—money, time, and fatigue are nothing compared with the reputation and interests of a whole family; probabilities will not suffice, only facts will justify a deadly combat with a friend. If I strike with the sword, or discharge the contents of a pistol at man with whom, for three years, I have been on terms of intimacy, I must, at least, know why I do so; I must meet him with a heart at ease, and that quiet conscience which a man needs when his own arm must save his life."

"Well," said Morcerf, impatiently, "what does all this mean?"

"It means that I have just returned from Yanina."

"From Yanina?"

"Yes."

"Impossible!"

"Here is my passport; examine the visa—Geneva, Milan, Venice, Trieste, Delvino, Yanina. Will you believe the government of a republic, a kingdom, and an empire?" Albert cast his eyes on the passport, then raised them in astonishment to Beauchamp.

"You have been to Yanina?" said he.

"Albert, had you been a stranger, a foreigner, a simple lord, like that Englishman who came to demand satisfaction three or four months since, and whom I killed to get rid of, I should not have taken this trouble; but I thought this mark of consideration due to you. I took a week to go, another to return, four days of quarantine, and forty-eight hours to stay there; that makes three weeks. I returned last night, and here I am."

"What circumlocution! How long you are before you tell me what I most wish to know?"

"Because, in truth, Albert—"

"You hesitate?"

"Yes,—I fear."

"You fear to acknowledge that your correspondent has deceived you? Oh, no self-love, Beauchamp. Acknowledge it, Beauchamp; your courage cannot be doubted."

"Not so," murmured the journalist; "on the contrary—"

Albert turned frightfully pale; he endeavored to speak, but the words died on his lips.

"My friend," said Beauchamp, in the most affectionate tone, "I should gladly make an apology; but, alas!—"

"But what?"

"The paragraph was correct, my friend."

"What? That French officer—"

"Yes."

"Fernand?"

"Yes."

"The traitor who surrendered the castle of the man in whose service he was—"

"Pardon me, my friend, that man was your father!"

Albert advanced furiously towards Beauchamp, but the latter restrained him more by a mild look than by his extended hand.

"My friend," said he, "here is a proof of it."

Albert opened the paper, it was an attestation of four notable inhabitants of Yanina, proving that Colonel Fernand Mondego, in the service of Ali Tepelini, had surrendered the castle for two million crowns. The signatures were perfectly legal. Albert tottered and fell overpowered in a chair. It could no longer be doubted; the family name was fully given. After a moment's mournful silence, his heart overflowed, and he gave way to a flood of tears. Beauchamp, who had watched with sincere pity the young man's paroxysm of grief, approached him.

"Now, Albert," said he, "you understand me—do you not? I wished to see all, and to judge of everything for myself, hoping the explanation would be in your father's favor, and that I might do him justice. But, on the contrary, the particulars which are given prove that Fernand Mondego, raised by Ali Pasha to the rank of governor-general, is no other than Count Fernand of Morcerf; then, recollecting the honor you had done me, in admitting me to your friendship, I hastened to you."

Albert, still extended on the chair, covered his face with both hands, as if to prevent the light from reaching him.

"I hastened to you," continued Beauchamp, "to tell you, Albert, that in this changing age, the faults of a father cannot revert upon his children. Few have passed through this revolutionary period, in the midst of which we were born, without some stain of infamy or blood to soil the uniform of the soldier, or the gown of the magistrate. Now I have these proofs, Albert, and I am in your confidence, no human power can force me to a duel which your own conscience would reproach you with as criminal, but I come to offer you what you can no longer demand of me. Do you wish these proofs, these attestations, which I alone possess, to be destroyed? Do you wish this frightful secret to remain with us? Confided to me, it shall never escape my lips; say, Albert, my friend, do you wish it?"

Albert threw himself on Beauchamp's neck.

"Ah, noble fellow!" cried he.

"Take these," said Beauchamp, presenting the papers to Albert.

Albert seized them with a convulsive hand, tore them in pieces, and trembling lest the least vestige should escape and one day appear to confront him, he approached the wax-light, always kept burning for cigars, and burned every fragment.

"Dear, excellent friend," murmured Albert, still burning the papers.

"Let all be forgotten as a sorrowful dream," said Beauchamp; "let it vanish as the last sparks from the blackened paper, and disappear as the smoke from those silent ashes."

"Yes, yes," said Albert, "and may there remain only the eternal friendship which I promised to my deliverer, which shall be transmitted to our children's children, and shall always remind me that I owe my life and the honor of my name to you,—for had this been known, oh, Beauchamp, I should have destroyed myself; or,—no, my poor mother! I could not have killed her by the same blow,—I should have fled from my country."

"Dear Albert," said Beauchamp. But this sudden and factitious joy soon forsook the young man, and was succeeded by a still greater grief.

"Well," said Beauchamp, "what still oppresses you, my friend?"

"I am broken-hearted," said Albert. "Listen, Beauchamp! I cannot thus, in a moment relinquish the respect, the confidence, and pride with which a father's untarnished name inspires a son. Oh, Beauchamp, Beauchamp, how shall I now approach mine? Shall I draw back my forehead from his embrace, or withhold my hand from his? I am the most wretched of men. Ah, my mother, my poor mother!" said Albert, gazing through his tears at his mother's portrait; "if you know this, how much must you suffer!"

"Come," said Beauchamp, taking both his hands, "take courage, my friend."

"But how came that first note to be inserted in your journal? Some unknown enemy—an invisible foe—has done this."

"The more must you fortify yourself, Albert. Let no trace of emotion be visible on your countenance, bear your grief as the cloud bears within it ruin and death—a fatal secret, known only when the storm bursts. Go, my friend, reserve your strength for the moment when the crash shall come."

"You think, then, all is not over yet?" said Albert, horror-stricken.

"I think nothing, my friend; but all things are possible. By the way—"

"What?" said Albert, seeing that Beauchamp hesitated.

"Are you going to marry Mademoiselle Danglars?"

"Why do you ask me now?"

"Because the rupture or fulfilment of this engagement is connected with the person of whom we were speaking."

"How?" said Albert, whose brow reddened; "you think M. Danglars—"

"I ask you only how your engagement stands? Pray put no construction on my words I do not mean they should convey, and give them no undue weight."

"No." said Albert, "the engagement is broken off."

"Well," said Beauchamp. Then, seeing the young man was about to relapse into melancholy, "Let us go out, Albert," said he; "a ride in the wood in the phaeton, or on horseback, will refresh you; we will then return to breakfast, and you shall attend to your affairs, and I to mine."

"Willingly," said Albert; "but let us walk. I think a little exertion would do me good."

The two friends walked out on the fortress. When they arrived at the Madeleine:

"Since we are out," said Beauchamp, "let us call on M. de Monte Cristo; he is admirably adapted to revive one's spirits, because he never interrogates, and in my opinion those who ask no questions are the best comforters."

"Gladly," said Albert; "let us call—I love him."

Study Guide Questions

For Students:

1. Whose wedding preparations are in progress at the beginning of this chapter?
2. Who is Beauchamp?
3. What important information does Beauchamp collect from Yanina?

For Reading Club:

1. Discuss Beauchamp as a friend.
2. Discuss how a dishonorable father can impact the reputation of a son in contemporary society.
3. Discuss the statement, "those who ask no questions are the best comforters."

CHAPTER 85

The Journey

Monte Cristo uttered a joyful exclamation on seeing the young men together. "Ah, ha!" said he, "I hope all is over, explained and settled."

"Yes," said Beauchamp; "the absurd reports have died away, and should they be renewed, I would be the first to oppose them; so let us speak no more of it."

"Albert will tell you," replied the count "that I gave him the same advice. Look," added he. "I am finishing the most execrable morning's work."

"What is it?" said Albert; "arranging your papers, apparently."

"My papers, thank God, no,—my papers are all in capital order, because I have none; but M. Cavalcanti's."

"M. Cavalcanti's?" asked Beauchamp.

"Yes; do you not know that this is a young man whom the count is introducing?" said Morcerf.

"Let us not misunderstand each other," replied Monte Cristo; "I introduce no one, and certainly not M. Cavalcanti."

"And who," said Albert with a forced smile, "is to marry Mademoiselle Danglars instead of me, which grieves me cruelly."

"What? Cavalcanti is going to marry Mademoiselle Danglars?" asked Beauchamp.

"Certainly! do you come from the end of the world?" said Monte Cristo; "you, a journalist, the husband of renown? It is the talk of all Paris."

"And you, count, have made this match?" asked Beauchamp.

"I? Silence, purveyor of gossip, do not spread that report. I make a match? No, you do not know me; I have done all in my power to oppose it."

"Ah, I understand," said Beauchamp, "on our friend Albert's account."

"On my account?" said the young man; "oh, no, indeed, the count will do me the justice to assert that I have, on the contrary, always entreated him to break off my engagement, and happily it is ended. The count pretends I have not him to thank;—so be it—I will erect an altar *Deo ignoto.*"

"Listen," said Monte Cristo; "I have had little to do with it, for I am at variance both with the father-in-law and the young man; there is only Mademoiselle Eugénie, who appears but little charmed with the thoughts of matrimony, and who, seeing how little I was disposed to persuade her to renounce her dear liberty, retains any affection for me."

"And do you say this wedding is at hand?"

"Oh, yes, in spite of all I could say. I do not know the young man; he is said to be of good family and rich, but I never trust to vague assertions. I have warned M. Danglars of it till I am tired, but he is fascinated with his Luccanese. I have even informed him of a circumstance I consider very serious; the young man was either charmed by his nurse, stolen by gypsies, or lost by his tutor, I scarcely know which. But I do know his father lost sight of him for more than ten years; what he did during these ten years, God only knows. Well, all that was useless. They have commissioned me to write to the major to demand papers, and here they are. I send them, but like Pilate—washing my hands."

"And what does Mademoiselle d'Armilly say to you for robbing her of her pupil?"

"Oh, well, I don't know; but I understand that she is going to Italy. Madame Danglars asked me for letters of recommendation for the *impresari*; I gave her a few lines for the director of the Valle Theatre, who is under some obligation to me. But what is the matter, Albert? you look dull; are you, after all, unconsciously in love with Mademoiselle Eugénie?"

"I am not aware of it," said Albert, smiling sorrowfully. Beauchamp turned to look at some paintings.

"But," continued Monte Cristo, "you are not in your usual spirits?"

"I have a dreadful headache," said Albert.

"Well, my dear viscount," said Monte Cristo, "I have an infallible remedy to propose to you."

"What is that?" asked the young man.

"A change."

"Indeed?" said Albert.

"Yes; and as I am just now excessively annoyed, I shall go from home. Shall we go together?"

"You annoyed, count?" said Beauchamp; "and by what?"

"Ah, you think very lightly of it; I should like to see you with a brief preparing in your house."

"What brief?"

"The one M. de Villefort is preparing against my amiable assassin—some brigand escaped from the gallows apparently."

"True," said Beauchamp; "I saw it in the paper. Who is this Caderousse?"

"Some Provençal, it appears. M. de Villefort heard of him at Marseilles, and M. Danglars recollects having seen him. Consequently, the procureur is very active in the affair, and the prefect of police very much interested; and, thanks to that interest, for which I am very grateful, they send me all the robbers of Paris and the neighborhood, under pretence of their being Caderousse's murderers, so that in three months, if this continues, every robber and assassin in France will have the plan of my house at his fingers' ends. I am resolved to desert them and go to some remote corner of the earth, and shall be happy if you will accompany me, viscount."

"Willingly."

"Then it is settled?"

"Yes, but where?"

"I have told you, where the air is pure, where every sound soothes, where one is sure to be humbled, however proud may be his nature. I love that humiliation, I, who am master of the universe, as was Augustus."

"But where are you really going?"

"To sea, viscount; you know I am a sailor. I was rocked when an infant in the arms of old Ocean, and on the bosom of the beautiful Amphitrite; I have sported with the green mantle of the one and the azure robe of the other; I love the sea as a mistress, and pine if I do not often see her."

"Let us go, count."

"To sea?"

"Yes."

"You accept my proposal?"

"I do."

"Well, viscount, there will be in my courtyard this evening a good travelling britzka, with four post-horses, in which one may rest as in a bed. M. Beauchamp, it holds four very well, will you accompany us?"

"Thank you, I have just returned from sea."

"What? you have been to sea?"

"Yes; I have just made a little excursion to the Borromean Islands[11]."

"What of that? come with us," said Albert.

"No, dear Morcerf; you know I only refuse when the thing is impossible. Besides, it is important," added he in a low tone, "that I should remain in Paris just now to watch the paper."

"Ah, you are a good and an excellent friend," said Albert; "yes, you are right; watch, watch, Beauchamp, and try to discover the enemy who made this disclosure."

Albert and Beauchamp parted, the last pressure of their hands expressing what their tongues could not before a stranger.

"Beauchamp is a worthy fellow," said Monte Cristo, when the journalist was gone; "is he not, Albert?"

"Yes, and a sincere friend; I love him devotedly. But now we are alone,—although it is immaterial to me,—where are we going?"

"Into Normandy, if you like."

"Delightful; shall we be quite retired? have no society, no neighbors?"

"Our companions will be riding-horses, dogs to hunt with, and a fishing-boat."

"Exactly what I wish for; I will apprise my mother of my intention, and return to you."

"But shall you be allowed to go into Normandy?"

"I may go where I please."

"Yes, I am aware you may go alone, since I once met you in Italy—but to accompany the mysterious Monte Cristo?"

"You forget, count, that I have often told you of the deep interest my mother takes in you."

"'Woman is fickle.' said Francis I.; 'woman is like a wave of the sea,' said Shakespeare; both the great king and the great poet ought to have known woman's nature well."

"Woman's, yes; my mother is not woman, but *a* woman."

"As I am only a humble foreigner, you must pardon me if I do not understand all the subtle refinements of your language."

"What I mean to say is, that my mother is not quick to give her confidence, but when she does she never changes."

"Ah, yes, indeed," said Monte Cristo with a sigh; "and do you think she is in the least interested in me?"

---

[11] Lake Maggiore.

"I repeat it, you must really be a very strange and superior man, for my mother is so absorbed by the interest you have excited, that when I am with her she speaks of no one else."

"And does she try to make you dislike me?"

"On the contrary, she often says, 'Morcerf, I believe the count has a noble nature; try to gain his esteem.'"

"Indeed?" said Monte Cristo, sighing.

"You see, then," said Albert, "that instead of opposing, she will encourage me."

"Adieu, then, until five o'clock; be punctual, and we shall arrive at twelve or one."

"At Tréport?"

"Yes; or in the neighborhood."

"But can we travel forty-eight leagues in eight hours?"

"Easily," said Monte Cristo.

"You are certainly a prodigy; you will soon not only surpass the railway, which would not be very difficult in France, but even the telegraph."

"But, viscount, since we cannot perform the journey in less than seven or eight hours, do not keep me waiting."

"Do not fear, I have little to prepare."

Monte Cristo smiled as he nodded to Albert, then remained a moment absorbed in deep meditation. But passing his hand across his forehead as if to dispel his reverie, he rang the bell twice and Bertuccio entered.

"Bertuccio," said he, "I intend going this evening to Normandy, instead of tomorrow or the next day. You will have sufficient time before five o'clock; despatch a messenger to apprise the grooms at the first station. M. de Morcerf will accompany me."

Bertuccio obeyed and despatched a courier to Pontoise to say the travelling-carriage would arrive at six o'clock. From Pontoise another express was sent to the next stage, and in six hours all the horses stationed on the road were ready.

Before his departure, the count went to Haydée's apartments, told her his intention, and resigned everything to her care.

Albert was punctual. The journey soon became interesting from its rapidity, of which Morcerf had formed no previous idea.

"Truly," said Monte Cristo, "with your post-horses going at the rate of two leagues an hour, and that absurd law that one traveller shall not pass another without permission, so that an invalid or ill-tempered traveller may detain those who are well and active, it is impossible to move; I escape this annoyance by travelling with my own postilion and horses; do I not, Ali?"

The count put his head out of the window and whistled, and the horses appeared to fly. The carriage rolled with a thundering noise over the pavement, and everyone turned to notice the dazzling meteor. Ali, smiling, repeated the sound, grasped the reins with a firm hand, and spurred his horses, whose beautiful manes floated in the breeze. This child of the desert was in his element, and with his black face and sparkling eyes appeared, in the cloud of dust he raised, like the genius of the simoom and the god of the hurricane.

"I never knew till now the delight of speed," said Morcerf, and the last cloud disappeared from his brow; "but where the devil do you get such horses? Are they made to order?"

"Precisely," said the count; "six years since I bought a horse in Hungary remarkable for its swiftness. The thirty-two that we shall use tonight are its progeny; they are all entirely black, with the exception of a star upon the forehead."

"That is perfectly admirable; but what do you do, count, with all these horses?"

"You see, I travel with them."

"But you are not always travelling."

"When I no longer require them, Bertuccio will sell them, and he expects to realize thirty or forty thousand francs by the sale."

"But no monarch in Europe will be wealthy enough to purchase them."

"Then he will sell them to some Eastern vizier, who will empty his coffers to purchase them, and refill them by applying the bastinado to his subjects."

"Count, may I suggest one idea to you?"

"Certainly."

"It is that, next to you, Bertuccio must be the richest gentleman in Europe."

"You are mistaken, viscount; I believe he has not a franc in his possession."

"Then he must be a wonder. My dear count, if you tell me many more marvellous things, I warn you I shall not believe them."

"I countenance nothing that is marvellous, M. Albert. Tell me, why does a steward rob his master?"

"Because, I suppose, it is his nature to do so, for the love of robbing."

"You are mistaken; it is because he has a wife and family, and ambitious desires for himself and them. Also because he is not sure of always retaining his situation, and wishes to provide for the future. Now, M. Bertuccio is alone in the world; he uses my property without accounting for the use he makes of it; he is sure never to leave my service."

"Why?"

"Because I should never get a better."

"Probabilities are deceptive."

"But I deal in certainties; he is the best servant over whom one has the power of life and death."

"Do you possess that right over Bertuccio?"

"Yes."

There are words which close a conversation with an iron door; such was the count's "yes."

The whole journey was performed with equal rapidity; the thirty-two horses, dispersed over seven stages, brought them to their destination in eight hours. At midnight they arrived at the gate of a beautiful park. The porter was in attendance; he had been apprised by the groom of the last stage of the count's approach. At half past two in the morning Morcerf was conducted to his apartments, where a bath and supper were prepared. The servant who had travelled at the back of the carriage waited on him; Baptistin, who rode in front, attended the count.

Albert bathed, took his supper, and went to bed. All night he was lulled by the melancholy noise of the surf. On rising, he went to his window, which opened on a terrace, having the sea in front, and at the back a pretty park bounded by a small forest.

In a creek lay a little sloop, with a narrow keel and high masts, bearing on its flag the Monte Cristo arms which were a mountain *or*, on a sea *azure*, with a cross *gules* in chief which might be an allusion to his name that recalled Calvary, the mount rendered by our Lord's passion more precious than gold, and to the degrading cross which his blood had rendered holy; or it might be some personal remembrance of suffering and regeneration buried in the night of this mysterious personage's past life.

Around the schooner lay a number of small fishing-boats belonging to the fishermen of the neighboring village, like humble subjects awaiting orders from their queen. There, as in every spot where Monte Cristo stopped, if but for two days, luxury abounded and life went on with the utmost ease.

Albert found in his anteroom two guns, with all the accoutrements for hunting; a lofty room on the ground floor containing all the ingenious instruments the English—eminent in piscatory pursuits, since they are patient and sluggish—have invented for fishing. The day passed in pursuing those exercises in which Monte Cristo excelled. They killed a dozen pheasants in the park, as many trout in the stream, dined in a summer-house overlooking the ocean, and took tea in the library.

Towards the evening of the third day. Albert, completely exhausted with the exercise which invigorated Monte Cristo, was sleeping in an armchair near the window, while the count was designing with his architect the plan of a conservatory in his house, when the sound of a horse at full speed on the high road made Albert look up. He was disagreeably surprised to see his own valet de chambre, whom he had not brought, that he might not inconvenience Monte Cristo.

"Florentin here!" cried he, starting up; "is my mother ill?" And he hastened to the door. Monte Cristo watched and saw him approach the valet, who drew a small sealed parcel from his pocket, containing a newspaper and a letter.

"From whom is this?" said he eagerly.

"From M. Beauchamp," replied Florentin.

"Did he send you?"

"Yes, sir; he sent for me to his house, gave me money for my journey, procured a horse, and made me promise not to stop till I had reached you, I have come in fifteen hours."

Albert opened the letter with fear, uttered a shriek on reading the first line, and seized the paper. His sight was dimmed, his legs sank under him, and he would have fallen had not Florentin supported him.

"Poor young man," said Monte Cristo in a low voice; "it is then true that the sin of the father shall fall on the children to the third and fourth generation."

Meanwhile Albert had revived, and, continuing to read, he threw back his head, saying:

"Florentin, is your horse fit to return immediately?"

"It is a poor, lame post-horse."

"In what state was the house when you left?"

"All was quiet, but on returning from M. Beauchamp's, I found madame in tears; she had sent for me to know when you would return. I told her my orders from M. Beauchamp; she first extended her arms to prevent me, but after a moment's reflection, 'Yes, go, Florentin,' said she, 'and may he come quickly.'"

"Yes, my mother," said Albert, "I will return, and woe to the infamous wretch! But first of all I must get there."

He went back to the room where he had left Monte Cristo. Five minutes had sufficed to make a complete transformation in his appearance. His voice had become rough and hoarse; his face was furrowed with wrinkles; his eyes burned under the blue-veined lids, and he tottered like a drunken man.

"Count," said he, "I thank you for your hospitality, which I would gladly have enjoyed longer; but I must return to Paris."

"What has happened?"

"A great misfortune, more important to me than life. Don't question me, I beg of you, but lend me a horse."

"My stables are at your command, viscount; but you will kill yourself by riding on horseback. Take a post-chaise or a carriage."

"No, it would delay me, and I need the fatigue you warn me of; it will do me good."

Albert reeled as if he had been shot, and fell on a chair near the door. Monte Cristo did not see this second manifestation of physical exhaustion; he was at the window, calling:

"Ali, a horse for M. de Morcerf—quick! he is in a hurry!"

These words restored Albert; he darted from the room, followed by the count.

"Thank you!" cried he, throwing himself on his horse.

"Return as soon as you can, Florentin. Must I use any password to procure a horse?"

"Only dismount; another will be immediately saddled."

Albert hesitated a moment. "You may think my departure strange and foolish," said the young man; "you do not know how a paragraph in a newspaper may exasperate one. Read that," said he, "when I am gone, that you may not be witness of my anger."

While the count picked up the paper he put spurs to his horse, which leaped in astonishment at such an unusual stimulus, and shot away with the rapidity of an arrow. The count watched him with a feeling of compassion, and when he had completely disappeared, read as follows:

"The French officer in the service of Ali Pasha of Yanina alluded to three weeks since in *l'Impartial*, who not only surrendered the castle of Yanina, but sold his benefactor to the Turks, styled himself truly at that time Fernand, as our esteemed contemporary states; but he has since added to his Christian name a title of nobility and a family name. He now calls himself the Count of Morcerf, and ranks among the peers."

Thus the terrible secret, which Beauchamp had so generously destroyed, appeared again like an armed phantom; and another paper, deriving its information from some malicious source, had published two days after Albert's departure for Normandy the few lines which had rendered the unfortunate young man almost crazy.

Study Guide Questions

For Students:

1. Why do Albert and Beauchamp go to meet the Count?
2. Where do Albert and the Count go for a change?
3. Who sends a letter to Albert?

For Reading Club:

1. Discuss the statement, “the sin of the father shall fall on the children to the third and fourth generation.” Do you think it stands true in contemporary society?
2. Discuss the content of the paper sent by Beauchamp.
3. How do you think media (print media or electronic media) still impacts the reputation of people?

CHAPTER 86

The Trial

At eight o'clock in the morning Albert had arrived at Beauchamp's door. The valet de chambre had received orders to usher him in at once. Beauchamp was in his bath.

"Here I am," Albert said.

"Well, my poor friend," replied Beauchamp, "I expected you."

"I need not say I think you are too faithful and too kind to have spoken of that painful circumstance. Your having sent for me is another proof of your affection. So, without losing time, tell me, have you the slightest idea whence this terrible blow proceeds?"

"I think I have some clew."

"But first tell me all the particulars of this shameful plot."

Beauchamp proceeded to relate to the young man, who was overwhelmed with shame and grief, the following facts. Two days previously, the article had appeared in another paper besides *l'Impartial*, and, what was more serious, one that was well known as a government paper. Beauchamp was breakfasting when he read the paragraph. He sent immediately for a cabriolet, and hastened to the publisher's office. Although professing diametrically opposite principles from those of the editor of the other paper, Beauchamp—as it sometimes, we may say often, happens—was his intimate friend. The editor was reading, with apparent delight, a leading article in the same paper on beet-sugar, probably a composition of his own.

"Ah, *pardieu!*" said Beauchamp, "with the paper in your hand, my friend, I need not tell you the cause of my visit."

"Are you interested in the sugar question?" asked the editor of the ministerial paper.

"No," replied Beauchamp, "I have not considered the question; a totally different subject interests me."

"What is it?"

"The article relative to Morcerf."

"Indeed? Is it not a curious affair?"

"So curious, that I think you are running a great risk of a prosecution for defamation of character."

"Not at all; we have received with the information all the requisite proofs, and we are quite sure M. de Morcerf will not raise his voice against us; besides, it is rendering a service to one's country to denounce these wretched criminals who are unworthy of the honor bestowed on them."

Beauchamp was thunderstruck.

"Who, then, has so correctly informed you?" asked he; "for my paper, which gave the first information on the subject, has been obliged to stop for want of proof; and yet we are more interested than you in exposing M. de Morcerf, as he is a peer of France, and we are of the opposition."

"Oh, that is very simple; we have not sought to scandalize. This news was brought to us. A man arrived yesterday from Yanina, bringing a formidable array of documents; and when we hesitated to publish the accusatory article, he told us it should be inserted in some other paper."

Beauchamp understood that nothing remained but to submit, and left the office to despatch a courier to Morcerf. But he had been unable to send to Albert the following particulars, as the events had transpired after the messenger's departure; namely, that the same day a great agitation was manifest in the House of Peers among the usually calm members of that dignified assembly. Everyone had arrived almost before the usual hour, and was conversing on the melancholy event which was to attract the attention of the public towards one of their most illustrious colleagues. Some were perusing the article, others making comments and recalling circumstances which substantiated the charges still more.

The Count of Morcerf was no favorite with his colleagues. Like all upstarts, he had had recourse to a great deal of haughtiness to maintain his position. The true nobility laughed at him, the talented repelled him, and the honorable instinctively despised him. He was, in fact, in the unhappy position of the victim marked for sacrifice; the finger of God once pointed at him, everyone was prepared to raise the hue and cry.

The Count of Morcerf alone was ignorant of the news. He did not take in the paper containing the defamatory article, and had passed the morning in writing letters and in trying a horse. He arrived at his usual hour, with a proud look and insolent demeanor; he alighted, passed through the corridors, and entered the house without observing the hesitation of the door-keepers or the coolness of his colleagues.

Business had already been going on for half an hour when he entered. Everyone held the accusing paper, but, as usual, no one liked to take upon himself the responsibility of the attack. At length an honorable peer, Morcerf's acknowledged enemy, ascended the tribune with that solemnity which announced that the expected moment had arrived. There was an impressive silence; Morcerf alone knew not why such profound attention was given to an orator who was not always listened to with so much complacency.

The count did not notice the introduction, in which the speaker announced that his communication would be of that vital importance that it demanded the undivided attention of the House; but at the mention of Yanina and Colonel Fernand, he turned so frightfully pale that every member shuddered and fixed his eyes upon him. Moral wounds have this peculiarity,—they may be hidden, but they never close; always painful, always ready to bleed when touched, they remain fresh and open in the heart.

The article having been read during the painful hush that followed, a universal shudder pervaded the assembly, and immediately the closest attention was given to the orator as he resumed his remarks. He stated his scruples and the difficulties of the case; it was the honor of M. de Morcerf, and that of the whole House, he proposed to defend, by provoking a debate on personal questions, which are always such painful themes of discussion. He concluded by calling for an investigation, which might dispose of the calumnious report before it had time to spread, and restore M. de Morcerf to the position he had long held in public opinion.

Morcerf was so completely overwhelmed by this great and unexpected calamity that he could scarcely stammer a few words as he looked around on the assembly. This timidity, which might proceed from the astonishment of innocence as well as the shame of guilt, conciliated some in his favor; for men who are truly generous are always ready to compassionate when the misfortune of their enemy surpasses the limits of their hatred.

The president put it to the vote, and it was decided that the investigation should take place. The count was asked what time he required to prepare his defence. Morcerf's courage had revived when he found himself alive after this horrible blow.

"My lords," answered he, "it is not by time I could repel the attack made on me by enemies unknown to me, and, doubtless, hidden in obscurity; it is immediately, and by a thunderbolt, that I must repel the flash of lightning which, for a moment, startled me. Oh, that I could, instead of taking up this defence, shed my last drop of blood to prove to my noble colleagues that I am their equal in worth."

These words made a favorable impression on behalf of the accused.

"I demand, then, that the examination shall take place as soon as possible, and I will furnish the house with all necessary information."

"What day do you fix?" asked the president.

"Today I am at your service," replied the count.

The president rang the bell. "Does the House approve that the examination should take place today?"

"Yes," was the unanimous answer.

A committee of twelve members was chosen to examine the proofs brought forward by Morcerf. The investigation would begin at eight o'clock that evening in the committee-room, and if postponement were necessary, the proceedings would be resumed each evening at the same hour. Morcerf asked leave to retire; he had to collect the documents he had long been preparing against this storm, which his sagacity had foreseen.

Beauchamp related to the young man all the facts we have just narrated; his story, however, had over ours all the advantage of the animation of living things over the coldness of dead things.

Albert listened, trembling now with hope, then with anger, and then again with shame, for from Beauchamp's confidence he knew his father was guilty, and he asked himself how, since he was guilty, he could prove his innocence. Beauchamp hesitated to continue his narrative.

"What next?" asked Albert.

"What next? My friend, you impose a painful task on me. Must you know all?"

"Absolutely; and rather from your lips than another's."

"Muster up all your courage, then, for never have you required it more."

Albert passed his hand over his forehead, as if to try his strength, as a man who is preparing to defend his life proves his shield and bends his sword. He thought himself strong enough, for he mistook fever for energy. "Go on," said he.

"The evening arrived; all Paris was in expectation. Many said your father had only to show himself to crush the charge against him; many others said he would not appear; while some asserted that they had seen him start for Brussels; and others went to the police-office to inquire if he had taken out a passport. I used all my influence with one of the committee, a young peer of my acquaintance, to get admission to one of the galleries. He called for me at seven o'clock, and, before anyone had arrived, asked one of the door-keepers to place me in a box. I was concealed by a column, and might witness the whole of the terrible scene which was about to take place. At eight o'clock all were in their places, and M. de Morcerf entered at the last stroke. He held some papers in his hand; his countenance was calm, and his step firm, and he was dressed with great care in his military uniform, which was buttoned completely up to the chin. His presence produced a good effect. The committee was made up of Liberals, several of whom came forward to shake hands with him."

Albert felt his heart bursting at these particulars, but gratitude mingled with his sorrow: he would gladly have embraced those who had given his father this proof of esteem at a moment when his honor was so powerfully attacked.

"At this moment one of the door-keepers brought in a letter for the president. 'You are at liberty to speak, M. de Morcerf,' said the president, as he unsealed the letter; and the count began his defence, I assure you, Albert, in a most eloquent and skilful manner. He produced documents proving that the Vizier of Yanina had up to the last moment honored him with his entire confidence, since he had interested him with a negotiation of life and death with the emperor. He produced the ring, his mark of authority, with which Ali Pasha generally sealed his letters, and which the latter had given him, that he might, on his return at any hour of the day or night, gain access to the presence, even in the harem. Unfortunately, the negotiation failed, and when he returned to defend his benefactor, he was dead. 'But,' said the count, 'so great was Ali Pasha's confidence, that on his death-bed he resigned his favorite mistress and her daughter to my care.'"

Albert started on hearing these words; the history of Haydée recurred to him, and he remembered what she had said of that message and the ring, and the manner in which she had been sold and made a slave.

"And what effect did this discourse produce?" anxiously inquired Albert.

"I acknowledge it affected me, and, indeed, all the committee also," said Beauchamp.

"Meanwhile, the president carelessly opened the letter which had been brought to him; but the first lines aroused his attention; he read them again and again, and fixing his eyes on M. de Morcerf, 'Count,' said he, 'you have said that the Vizier of Yanina confided his wife and daughter to your care?'—'Yes, sir,' replied Morcerf; 'but in that, like all the rest, misfortune pursued me. On my return, Vasiliki and her daughter Haydée had disappeared.'—'Did you know them?'—'My intimacy with the pasha and his unlimited confidence had gained me an introduction to them, and I had seen them above twenty times.'

"'Have you any idea what became of them?'—'Yes, sir; I heard they had fallen victims to their sorrow, and, perhaps, to their poverty. I was not rich; my life was in constant danger; I could not seek them, to my great regret.' The president frowned imperceptibly. 'Gentlemen,' said he, 'you have heard the Comte de Morcerf's defence. Can you, sir, produce any witnesses to the truth of what you have asserted?'—'Alas, no, monsieur,' replied the count; 'all those who surrounded the vizier, or who knew me at his court, are either dead or gone away, I know not where. I believe that I alone, of all my countrymen, survived that dreadful war. I have only the letters of Ali Tepelini, which I have placed before you; the ring, a token of his good-will, which is here; and, lastly, the most convincing proof I can offer, after an anonymous attack, and that is the absence of any witness against my veracity and the purity of my military life.'

"A murmur of approbation ran through the assembly; and at this moment, Albert, had nothing more transpired, your father's cause had been gained. It only remained to put it to the vote, when the president resumed: 'Gentlemen and you, monsieur,—you will not be displeased, I presume, to listen to one who calls himself a very important witness, and who has just presented himself. He is, doubtless, come to prove the perfect innocence of our colleague. Here is a letter I have just received on the subject; shall it be read, or shall it be passed over? and shall we take no notice of this incident?' M. de Morcerf turned pale, and clenched his hands on the papers he held. The committee decided to hear the letter; the count was thoughtful and silent. The president read:

"'Mr. President,—I can furnish the committee of inquiry into the conduct of the Lieutenant-General the Count of Morcerf in Epirus and in Macedonia with important particulars.'

"The president paused, and the count turned pale. The president looked at his auditors. 'Proceed,' was heard on all sides. The president resumed:

"'I was on the spot at the death of Ali Pasha. I was present during his last moments. I know what is become of Vasiliki and Haydée. I am at the command of the committee, and even claim the honor of being heard. I shall be in the lobby when this note is delivered to you.'

"'And who is this witness, or rather this enemy?' asked the count, in a tone in which there was a visible alteration. 'We shall know, sir,' replied the president. 'Is the committee willing to hear this witness?'—'Yes, yes,' they all said at once. The door-keeper was called. 'Is there anyone in the lobby?' said the president.

"'Yes, sir.'—'Who is it?'—'A woman, accompanied by a servant.' Everyone looked at his neighbor. 'Bring her in,' said the president. Five minutes after the door-keeper again appeared; all eyes were fixed on the door, and I," said Beauchamp, "shared the general expectation and anxiety. Behind the door-keeper walked a woman enveloped in a large veil, which completely concealed her. It was evident, from her figure and the perfumes she had about her, that she was young and fastidious in her tastes, but that was all. The president requested her to throw aside her veil, and it was then seen that she was dressed in the Grecian costume, and was remarkably beautiful."

"Ah," said Albert, "it was she."

"Who?"

"Haydée."

"Who told you that?"

"Alas, I guess it. But go on, Beauchamp. You see I am calm and strong. And yet we must be drawing near the disclosure."

"M. de Morcerf," continued Beauchamp, "looked at this woman with surprise and terror. Her lips were about to pass his sentence of life or death. To the committee the adventure was so extraordinary and curious, that the interest they had felt for the count's safety became now quite a secondary matter. The president himself advanced to place a seat for the young lady; but she declined availing herself of it. As for the count, he had fallen on his chair; it was evident that his legs refused to support him.

"'Madame,' said the president, 'you have engaged to furnish the committee with some important particulars respecting the affair at Yanina, and you have stated that you were an eyewitness of the event.'—'I was, indeed,' said the stranger, with a tone of sweet melancholy, and with the sonorous voice peculiar to the East.

"'But allow me to say that you must have been very young then.'—'I was four years old; but as those events deeply concerned me, not a single detail has escaped my memory.'—'In what manner could these events concern you? and who are you, that they should have made so deep an impression on you?'—'On them depended my father's life,' replied she. 'I am Haydée, the daughter of Ali Tepelini, pasha of Yanina, and of Vasiliki, his beloved wife.'

"The blush of mingled pride and modesty which suddenly suffused the cheeks of the young woman, the brilliancy of her eye, and her highly important communication, produced an indescribable effect on the assembly. As for the count, he could not have been more overwhelmed if a thunderbolt had fallen at his feet and opened an immense gulf before him.

"'Madame,' replied the president, bowing with profound respect, 'allow me to ask one question; it shall be the last: Can you prove the authenticity of what you have now stated?'

"'I can, sir,' said Haydée, drawing from under her veil a satin satchel highly perfumed; 'for here is the register of my birth, signed by my father and his principal officers, and that of my baptism, my father having consented to my being brought up in my mother's faith,—this latter has been sealed by the grand primate of Macedonia and Epirus; and lastly (and perhaps the most important), the record of the sale of my person and that of my mother to the Armenian merchant El-Kobbir, by the French officer, who, in his infamous bargain with the Porte, had reserved as his part of the booty the wife and daughter of his benefactor, whom he sold for the sum of four hundred thousand francs.' A greenish pallor spread over the count's cheeks, and his eyes became bloodshot at these terrible imputations, which were listened to by the assembly with ominous silence.

"Haydée, still calm, but with a calmness more dreadful than the anger of another would have been, handed to the president the record of her sale, written in Arabic. It had been supposed some of the papers might be in the Arabian, Romaic, or Turkish language, and the interpreter of the House was in attendance. One of the noble peers, who was familiar with the Arabic language, having studied it during the famous Egyptian campaign, followed with his eye as the translator read aloud:

"'I, El-Kobbir, a slave-merchant, and purveyor of the harem of his highness, acknowledge having received for transmission to the sublime emperor, from the French lord, the Count of Monte Cristo, an emerald valued at eight hundred thousand francs; as the ransom of a young Christian slave of eleven years of age, named Haydée, the acknowledged daughter of the late lord Ali Tepelini, pasha of Yanina, and of Vasiliki, his favorite; she having been sold to me seven years previously, with her mother, who had died on arriving at Constantinople, by a French colonel in the service of the Vizier Ali Tepelini, named Fernand Mondego. The above-mentioned purchase was made on his highness's account, whose mandate I had, for the sum of four hundred thousand francs.

"'Given at Constantinople, by authority of his highness, in the year 1247 of the Hegira.

"'Signed, El-Kobbir.'

"'That this record should have all due authority, it shall bear the imperial seal, which the vendor is bound to have affixed to it.'

"Near the merchant's signature there was, indeed, the seal of the sublime emperor. A dreadful silence followed the reading of this document; the count could only stare, and his gaze, fixed as if unconsciously on Haydée, seemed one of fire and blood. 'Madame,' said the president, 'may reference be made to the Count of Monte Cristo, who is now, I believe, in Paris?'

"'Sir,' replied Haydée, 'the Count of Monte Cristo, my foster-father, has been in Normandy the last three days.'

"'Who, then, has counselled you to take this step, one for which the court is deeply indebted to you, and which is perfectly natural, considering your birth and your misfortunes?'—'Sir,' replied Haydée, 'I have been led to take this step from a feeling of respect and grief. Although a Christian, may God forgive me, I have always sought to revenge my illustrious father. Since I set my foot in France, and knew the traitor lived in Paris, I have watched carefully. I live retired in the house of my noble protector, but I do it from choice. I love retirement and silence, because I can live with my thoughts and recollections of past days. But the Count of Monte Cristo surrounds me with every paternal care, and I am ignorant of nothing which passes in the world. I learn all in the silence of my apartments,—for instance, I see all the newspapers, every periodical, as well as every new piece of music; and by thus watching the course of the life of others, I learned what had transpired this morning in the House of Peers, and what was to take place this evening; then I wrote.'

"'Then,' remarked the president, 'the Count of Monte Cristo knows nothing of your present proceedings?'—'He is quite unaware of them, and I have but one fear, which is that he should disapprove of what I have done. But it is a glorious day for me,' continued the young girl, raising her ardent gaze to heaven, 'that on which I find at last an opportunity of avenging my father!'

"The count had not uttered one word the whole of this time. His colleagues looked at him, and doubtless pitied his prospects, blighted under the perfumed breath of a woman. His misery was depicted in sinister lines on his countenance. 'M. de Morcerf,' said the president, 'do you recognize this lady as the daughter of Ali Tepelini, pasha of Yanina?'—'No,' said Morcerf, attempting to rise, 'it is a base plot, contrived by my enemies.' Haydée, whose eyes had been fixed on the door, as if expecting someone, turned hastily, and, seeing the count standing, shrieked, 'You do not know me?' said she. 'Well, I fortunately recognize you! You are Fernand Mondego, the French officer who led the troops of my noble father! It is you who surrendered the castle of Yanina! It is you who, sent by him to Constantinople, to treat with the emperor for the life or death of your benefactor, brought back a false mandate granting full pardon! It is you who, with that mandate, obtained the pasha's ring, which gave you authority over Selim, the fire-keeper! It is you who stabbed Selim. It is you who sold us, my mother and me, to the merchant, El-Kobbir! Assassin, assassin, assassin, you have still on your brow your master's blood! Look, gentlemen, all!'

"These words had been pronounced with such enthusiasm and evident truth, that every eye was fixed on the count's forehead, and he himself passed his hand across it, as if he felt Ali's blood still lingering there. 'You positively recognize M. de Morcerf as the officer, Fernand Mondego?'—'Indeed I do!' cried Haydée. 'Oh, my mother, it was you who said, "You were free, you had a beloved father, you were destined to be almost a queen. Look well at that man; it is he who raised your father's head on the point of a spear; it is he who sold us; it is he who forsook us! Look well at his right hand, on which he has a large wound; if you forgot his features, you would know him by that hand, into which fell, one by one, the gold pieces of the merchant El-Kobbir!" I know him! Ah, let him say now if he does not recognize me!' Each word fell like a dagger on Morcerf, and deprived him of a portion of his energy; as she uttered the last, he hid his mutilated hand hastily in his bosom, and fell back on his seat, overwhelmed by wretchedness and despair. This scene completely changed the opinion of the assembly respecting the accused count.

"'Count of Morcerf,' said the president, 'do not allow yourself to be cast down; answer. The justice of the court is supreme and impartial as that of God; it will not suffer you to be trampled on by your enemies without giving you an opportunity of defending yourself. Shall further inquiries be made? Shall two members of the House be sent to Yanina? Speak!' Morcerf did not reply. Then all the members looked at each other with terror. They knew the count's energetic and violent temper; it must be, indeed, a dreadful blow which would deprive him of courage to defend himself. They expected that his stupefied silence would be followed by a fiery outburst. 'Well,' asked the president, 'what is your decision?'

"'I have no reply to make,' said the count in a low tone.

"'Has the daughter of Ali Tepelini spoken the truth?' said the president. 'Is she, then, the terrible witness to whose charge you dare not plead "Not guilty"? Have you really committed the crimes of which you are accused?' The count looked around him with an expression which might have softened tigers, but which could not disarm his judges. Then he raised his eyes towards the ceiling, but withdrew then, immediately, as if he feared the roof would open and reveal to his distressed view that second tribunal called heaven, and that other judge named God. Then, with a hasty movement, he tore open his coat, which seemed to stifle him, and flew from the room like a madman; his footstep was heard one moment in the corridor, then the rattling of his carriage-wheels as he was driven rapidly away. 'Gentlemen,' said the president, when silence was restored, 'is the Count of Morcerf convicted of felony, treason, and conduct unbecoming a member of this House?'—'Yes,' replied all the members of the committee of inquiry with a unanimous voice.

"Haydée had remained until the close of the meeting. She heard the count's sentence pronounced without betraying an expression of joy or pity; then drawing her veil over her face she bowed majestically to the councillors, and left with that dignified step which Virgil attributes to his goddesses."

Study Guide Questions

For Students:

1. How does M. de Morcerf come to know of his disgrace?
2. Who is the witness that comes to Morcerf's trial?
3. What is the outcome of the trial?

For Reading Club:

1. Morcerf's tale of corruption is very old but it affects his life years later. Do you think it often happens in real life that a sin from long ago comes back to haunt one's life?
2. What is included in the letter that the president receives?
3. Discuss the evidence provided by Haydée against Morcerf.

CHAPTER 87

The Challenge

Then," continued Beauchamp, "I took advantage of the silence and the darkness to leave the house without being seen. The usher who had introduced me was waiting for me at the door, and he conducted me through the corridors to a private entrance opening into the Rue de Vaugirard. I left with mingled feelings of sorrow and delight. Excuse me, Albert,—sorrow on your account, and delight with that noble girl, thus pursuing paternal vengeance. Yes, Albert, from whatever source the blow may have proceeded—it may be from an enemy, but that enemy is only the agent of Providence."

Albert held his head between his hands; he raised his face, red with shame and bathed in tears, and seizing Beauchamp's arm:

"My friend," said he, "my life is ended. I cannot calmly say with you, 'Providence has struck the blow;' but I must discover who pursues me with this hatred, and when I have found him I shall kill him, or he will kill me. I rely on your friendship to assist me, Beauchamp, if contempt has not banished it from your heart."

"Contempt, my friend? How does this misfortune affect you? No, happily that unjust prejudice is forgotten which made the son responsible for the father's actions. Review your life, Albert; although it is only just beginning, did a lovely summer's day ever dawn with greater purity than has marked the commencement of your career? No, Albert, take my advice. You are young and rich—leave Paris—all is soon forgotten in this great Babylon of excitement and changing tastes. You will return after three or four years with a Russian princess for a bride, and no one will think more of what occurred yesterday than if it had happened sixteen years ago."

"Thank you, my dear Beauchamp, thank you for the excellent feeling which prompts your advice; but it cannot be. I have told you my wish, or rather my determination. You understand that, interested as I am in this affair, I cannot see it in the same light as you do. What appears to you to emanate from a celestial source, seems to me to proceed from one far less pure. Providence appears to me to have no share in this affair; and happily so, for instead of the invisible, impalpable agent of celestial rewards and punishments, I shall find one both palpable and visible, on whom I shall revenge myself, I assure you, for all I have suffered during the last month. Now, I repeat, Beauchamp, I wish to return to human and material existence, and if you are still the friend you profess to be, help me to discover the hand that struck the blow."

"Be it so," said Beauchamp; "if you must have me descend to earth, I submit; and if you will seek your enemy, I will assist you, and I will engage to find him, my honor being almost as deeply interested as yours."

"Well, then, you understand, Beauchamp, that we begin our search immediately. Each moment's delay is an eternity for me. The calumniator is not yet punished, and he may hope that he will not be; but, on my honor, if he thinks so, he deceives himself."

"Well, listen, Morcerf."

"Ah, Beauchamp, I see you know something already; you will restore me to life."

"I do not say there is any truth in what I am going to tell you, but it is, at least, a ray of light in a dark night; by following it we may, perhaps, discover something more certain."

"Tell me; satisfy my impatience."

"Well, I will tell you what I did not like to mention on my return from Yanina."

"Say on."

"I went, of course, to the chief banker of the town to make inquiries. At the first word, before I had even mentioned your father's name"—

"'Ah,' said he. 'I guess what brings you here.'

"'How, and why?'

"'Because a fortnight since I was questioned on the same subject.'

"'By whom?'

"'By a banker of Paris, my correspondent.'

"'Whose name is—'

"'Danglars.'"

"He!" cried Albert; "yes, it is indeed he who has so long pursued my father with jealous hatred. He, the man who would be popular, cannot forgive the Count of Morcerf for being created a peer; and this marriage broken off without a reason being assigned—yes, it is all from the same cause."

"Make inquiries, Albert, but do not be angry without reason; make inquiries, and if it be true—"

"Oh, yes, if it be true," cried the young man, "he shall pay me all I have suffered."

"Beware, Morcerf, he is already an old man."

"I will respect his age as he has respected the honor of my family; if my father had offended him, why did he not attack him personally? Oh, no, he was afraid to encounter him face to face."

"I do not condemn you, Albert; I only restrain you. Act prudently."

"Oh, do not fear; besides, you will accompany me. Beauchamp, solemn transactions should be sanctioned by a witness. Before this day closes, if M. Danglars is guilty, he shall cease to live, or I shall die. *Pardieu*, Beauchamp, mine shall be a splendid funeral!"

"When such resolutions are made, Albert, they should be promptly executed. Do you wish to go to M. Danglars? Let us go immediately."

They sent for a cabriolet. On entering the banker's mansion, they perceived the phaeton and servant of M. Andrea Cavalcanti.

"Ah! *parbleu!* that's good," said Albert, with a gloomy tone. "If M. Danglars will not fight with me, I will kill his son-in-law; Cavalcanti will certainly fight."

The servant announced the young man; but the banker, recollecting what had transpired the day before, did not wish him admitted. It was, however, too late; Albert had followed the footman, and, hearing the order given, forced the door open, and followed by Beauchamp found himself in the banker's study.

"Sir," cried the latter, "am I no longer at liberty to receive whom I choose in my house? You appear to forget yourself sadly."

"No, sir," said Albert, coldly; "there are circumstances in which one cannot, except through cowardice,—I offer you that refuge,—refuse to admit certain persons at least."

"What is your errand, then, with me, sir?"

"I mean," said Albert, drawing near, and without apparently noticing Cavalcanti, who stood with his back towards the fireplace—"I mean to propose a meeting in some retired corner where no one will interrupt us for ten minutes; that will be sufficient—where two men having met, one of them will remain on the ground."

Danglars turned pale; Cavalcanti moved a step forward, and Albert turned towards him.

"And you, too," said he, "come, if you like, monsieur; you have a claim, being almost one of the family, and I will give as many rendezvous of that kind as I can find persons willing to accept them."

Cavalcanti looked at Danglars with a stupefied air, and the latter, making an effort, arose and stepped between the two young men. Albert's attack on Andrea had placed him on a different footing, and he hoped this visit had another cause than that he had at first supposed.

"Indeed, sir," said he to Albert, "if you are come to quarrel with this gentleman because I have preferred him to you, I shall resign the case to the king's attorney."

"You mistake, sir," said Morcerf with a gloomy smile; "I am not referring in the least to matrimony, and I only addressed myself to M. Cavalcanti because he appeared disposed to interfere between us. In one respect you are right, for I am ready to quarrel with everyone today; but you have the first claim, M. Danglars."

"Sir," replied Danglars, pale with anger and fear, "I warn you, when I have the misfortune to meet with a mad dog, I kill it; and far from thinking myself guilty of a crime, I believe I do society a kindness. Now, if you are mad and try to bite me, I will kill you without pity. Is it my fault that your father has dishonored himself?"

"Yes, miserable wretch!" cried Morcerf, "it is your fault."

Danglars retreated a few steps. "My fault?" said he; "you must be mad! What do I know of the Grecian affair? Have I travelled in that country? Did I advise your father to sell the castle of Yanina—to betray—"

"Silence!" said Albert, with a thundering voice. "No; it is not you who have directly made this exposure and brought this sorrow on us, but you hypocritically provoked it."

"I?"

"Yes; you! How came it known?"

"I suppose you read it in the paper in the account from Yanina?"

"Who wrote to Yanina?"

"To Yanina?"

"Yes. Who wrote for particulars concerning my father?"

"I imagine anyone may write to Yanina."

"But one person only wrote!"

"One only?"

"Yes; and that was you!"

"I, doubtless, wrote. It appears to me that when about to marry your daughter to a young man, it is right to make some inquiries respecting his family; it is not only a right, but a duty."

"You wrote, sir, knowing what answer you would receive."

"I, indeed? I assure you," cried Danglars, with a confidence and security proceeding less from fear than from the interest he really felt for the young man, "I solemnly declare to you, that I should never have thought of writing to Yanina, did I know anything of Ali Pasha's misfortunes."

"Who, then, urged you to write? Tell me."

"*Pardieu!* it was the most simple thing in the world. I was speaking of your father's past history. I said the origin of his fortune remained obscure. The person to whom I addressed my scruples asked me where your father had acquired his property? I answered, 'In Greece.'—'Then,' said he, 'write to Yanina.'"

"And who thus advised you?"

"No other than your friend, Monte Cristo."

"The Count of Monte Cristo told you to write to Yanina?"

"Yes; and I wrote, and will show you my correspondence, if you like."

Albert and Beauchamp looked at each other.

"Sir," said Beauchamp, who had not yet spoken, "you appear to accuse the count, who is absent from Paris at this moment, and cannot justify himself."

"I accuse no one, sir," said Danglars; "I relate, and I will repeat before the count what I have said to you."

"Does the count know what answer you received?"

"Yes; I showed it to him."

"Did he know my father's Christian name was Fernand, and his family name Mondego?"

"Yes, I had told him that long since, and I did only what any other would have done in my circumstances, and perhaps less. When, the day after the arrival of this answer, your father came by the advice of Monte Cristo to ask my daughter's hand for you, I decidedly refused him, but without any explanation or exposure. In short, why should I have any more to do with the affair? How did the honor or disgrace of M. de Morcerf affect me? It neither increased nor decreased my income."

Albert felt the blood mounting to his brow; there was no doubt upon the subject. Danglars defended himself with the baseness, but at the same time with the assurance, of a man who speaks the truth, at least in part, if not wholly—not for conscience' sake, but through fear. Besides, what was Morcerf seeking? It was not whether Danglars or Monte Cristo was more or less guilty; it was a man who would answer for the offence, whether trifling or serious; it was a man who would fight, and it was evident Danglars would not fight.

In addition to this, everything forgotten or unperceived before presented itself now to his recollection. Monte Cristo knew everything, as he had bought the daughter of Ali Pasha; and, knowing everything, he had advised Danglars to write to Yanina. The answer known, he had yielded to Albert's wish to be introduced to Haydée, and allowed the conversation to turn on the death of Ali, and had not opposed Haydée's recital (but having, doubtless, warned the young girl, in the few Romaic words he spoke to her, not to implicate Morcerf's father). Besides, had he not begged of Morcerf not to mention his father's name before Haydée? Lastly, he had taken Albert to Normandy when he knew the final blow was near. There could be no doubt that all had been calculated and previously arranged; Monte Cristo then was in league with his father's enemies. Albert took Beauchamp aside, and communicated these ideas to him.

"You are right," said the latter; "M. Danglars has only been a secondary agent in this sad affair, and it is of M. de Monte Cristo that you must demand an explanation."

Albert turned.

"Sir," said he to Danglars, "understand that I do not take a final leave of you; I must ascertain if your insinuations are just, and am going now to inquire of the Count of Monte Cristo."

He bowed to the banker, and went out with Beauchamp, without appearing to notice Cavalcanti. Danglars accompanied him to the door, where he again assured Albert that no motive of personal hatred had influenced him against the Count of Morcerf.

Study Guide Questions

For Students:

1. What does Beauchamp tell Albert about his tour to Yanina?
2. Why does Albert go to Danglars' house?
3. Who urged Danglars to write to Yanina?

For Reading Club:

1. What do you think of Beauchamp's advice?
2. Do you think Albert is right in considering revenge?
3. What does Albert realize about the Count of Monte Cristo?

CHAPTER 88

The Insult

At the banker's door Beauchamp stopped Morcerf.

"Listen," said he; "just now I told you it was of M. de Monte Cristo you must demand an explanation."

"Yes; and we are going to his house."

"Reflect, Morcerf, one moment before you go."

"On what shall I reflect?"

"On the importance of the step you are taking."

"Is it more serious than going to M. Danglars?"

"Yes; M. Danglars is a money-lover, and those who love money, you know, think too much of what they risk to be easily induced to fight a duel. The other is, on the contrary, to all appearance a true nobleman; but do you not fear to find him a bully?"

"I only fear one thing; namely, to find a man who will not fight."

"Do not be alarmed," said Beauchamp; "he will meet you. My only fear is that he will be too strong for you."

"My friend," said Morcerf, with a sweet smile, "that is what I wish. The happiest thing that could occur to me, would be to die in my father's stead; that would save us all."

"Your mother would die of grief."

"My poor mother!" said Albert, passing his hand across his eyes, "I know she would; but better so than die of shame."

"Are you quite decided, Albert?"

"Yes; let us go."

"But do you think we shall find the count at home?"

"He intended returning some hours after me, and doubtless he is now at home."

They ordered the driver to take them to No. 30 Champs-Élysées. Beauchamp wished to go in alone, but Albert observed that as this was an unusual circumstance he might be allowed to deviate from the usual etiquette of duels. The cause which the young man espoused was one so sacred that Beauchamp had only to comply with all his wishes; he yielded and contented himself with following Morcerf. Albert sprang from the porter's lodge to the steps. He was received by Baptistin. The count had, indeed, just arrived, but he was in his bath, and had forbidden that anyone should be admitted.

"But after his bath?" asked Morcerf.

"My master will go to dinner."

"And after dinner?"

"He will sleep an hour."

"Then?"

"He is going to the Opera."

"Are you sure of it?" asked Albert.

"Quite, sir; my master has ordered his horses at eight o'clock precisely."

"Very good," replied Albert; "that is all I wished to know."

Then, turning towards Beauchamp, "If you have anything to attend to, Beauchamp, do it directly; if you have any appointment for this evening, defer it till tomorrow. I depend on you to accompany me to the Opera; and if you can, bring Château-Renaud with you."

Beauchamp availed himself of Albert's permission, and left him, promising to call for him at a quarter before eight. On his return home, Albert expressed his wish to Franz Debray, and Morrel, to see them at the Opera that evening. Then he went to see his mother, who since the events of the day before had refused to see anyone, and had kept her room. He found her in bed, overwhelmed with grief at this public humiliation.

The sight of Albert produced the effect which might naturally be expected on Mercédès; she pressed her son's hand and sobbed aloud, but her tears relieved her. Albert stood one moment speechless by the side of his mother's bed. It was evident from his pale face and knit brows that his resolution to revenge himself was growing weaker.

"My dear mother," said he, "do you know if M. de Morcerf has any enemy?"

Mercédès started; she noticed that the young man did not say "my father."

"My son," she said, "persons in the count's situation have many secret enemies. Those who are known are not the most dangerous."

"I know it, and appeal to your penetration. You are of so superior a mind, nothing escapes you."

"Why do you say so?"

"Because, for instance, you noticed on the evening of the ball we gave, that M. de Monte Cristo would eat nothing in our house."

Mercédès raised herself on her feverish arm.

"M. de Monte Cristo!" she exclaimed; "and how is he connected with the question you asked me?"

"You know, mother, M. de Monte Cristo is almost an Oriental, and it is customary with the Orientals to secure full liberty for revenge by not eating or drinking in the houses of their enemies."

"Do you say M. de Monte Cristo is our enemy?" replied Mercédès, becoming paler than the sheet which covered her. "Who told you so? Why, you are mad, Albert! M. de Monte Cristo has only shown us kindness. M. de Monte Cristo saved your life; you yourself presented him to us. Oh, I entreat you, my son, if you had entertained such an idea, dispel it; and my counsel to you—nay, my prayer—is to retain his friendship."

"Mother," replied the young man, "you have special reasons for telling me to conciliate that man."

"I?" said Mercédès, blushing as rapidly as she had turned pale, and again becoming paler than ever.

"Yes, doubtless; and is it not that he may never do us any harm?"

Mercédès shuddered, and, fixing on her son a scrutinizing gaze, "You speak strangely," said she to Albert, "and you appear to have some singular prejudices. What has the count done? Three days since you were with him in Normandy; only three days since we looked on him as our best friend."

An ironical smile passed over Albert's lips. Mercédès saw it and with the double instinct of woman and mother guessed all; but as she was prudent and strong-minded she concealed both her sorrows and her fears. Albert was silent; an instant after, the countess resumed:

"You came to inquire after my health; I will candidly acknowledge that I am not well. You should install yourself here, and cheer my solitude. I do not wish to be left alone."

"Mother," said the young man, "you know how gladly I would obey your wish, but an urgent and important affair obliges me to leave you for the whole evening."

"Well," replied Mercédès, sighing, "go, Albert; I will not make you a slave to your filial piety."

Albert pretended he did not hear, bowed to his mother, and quitted her. Scarcely had he shut her door, when Mercédès called a confidential servant, and ordered him to follow Albert wherever he should go that evening, and to come and tell her immediately what he observed. Then she rang for her lady's maid, and, weak as she was, she dressed, in order to be ready for whatever might happen. The footman's mission was an easy one. Albert went to his room, and dressed with unusual care. At ten minutes to eight Beauchamp arrived; he had seen Château-Renaud, who had promised to be in the orchestra before the curtain was raised. Both got into Albert's *coupé*; and, as the young man had no reason to conceal where he was going, he called aloud, "To the Opera." In his impatience he arrived before the beginning of the performance.

Château-Renaud was at his post; apprised by Beauchamp of the circumstances, he required no explanation from Albert. The conduct of the son in seeking to avenge his father was so natural that Château-Renaud did not seek to dissuade him, and was content with renewing his assurances of devotion. Debray was not yet come, but Albert knew that he seldom lost a scene at the Opera.

Albert wandered about the theatre until the curtain was drawn up. He hoped to meet with M. de Monte Cristo either in the lobby or on the stairs. The bell summoned him to his seat, and he entered the orchestra with Château-Renaud and Beauchamp. But his eyes scarcely quitted the box between the columns, which remained obstinately closed during the whole of the first act. At last, as Albert was looking at his watch for about the hundredth time, at the beginning of the second act the door opened, and Monte Cristo entered, dressed in black, and, leaning over the front of the box, looked around the pit. Morrel followed him, and looked also for his sister and brother in-law; he soon discovered them in another box, and kissed his hand to them.

The count, in his survey of the pit, encountered a pale face and threatening eyes, which evidently sought to gain his attention. He recognized Albert, but thought it better not to notice him, as he looked so angry and discomposed. Without communicating his thoughts to his companion, he sat down, drew out his opera-glass, and looked another way. Although apparently not noticing Albert, he did not, however, lose sight of him, and when the curtain fell at the end of the second act, he saw him leave the orchestra with his two friends. Then his head was seen passing at the back of the boxes, and the count knew that the approaching storm was intended to fall on him. He was at the moment conversing cheerfully with Morrel, but he was well prepared for what might happen.

The door opened, and Monte Cristo, turning round, saw Albert, pale and trembling, followed by Beauchamp and Château-Renaud.

"Well," cried he, with that benevolent politeness which distinguished his salutation from the common civilities of the world, "my cavalier has attained his object. Good-evening, M. de Morcerf."

The countenance of this man, who possessed such extraordinary control over his feelings, expressed the most perfect cordiality. Morrel only then recollected the letter he had received from the viscount, in which, without assigning any reason, he begged him to go to the Opera, but he understood that something terrible was brooding.

"We are not come here, sir, to exchange hypocritical expressions of politeness, or false professions of friendship," said Albert, "but to demand an explanation."

The young man's trembling voice was scarcely audible.

"An explanation at the Opera?" said the count, with that calm tone and penetrating eye which characterize the man who knows his cause is good. "Little acquainted as I am with the habits of Parisians, I should not have thought this the place for such a demand."

"Still, if people will shut themselves up," said Albert, "and cannot be seen because they are bathing, dining, or asleep, we must avail ourselves of the opportunity whenever they are to be seen."

"I am not difficult of access, sir; for yesterday, if my memory does not deceive me, you were at my house."

"Yesterday I was at your house, sir," said the young man; "because then I knew not who you were."

In pronouncing these words Albert had raised his voice so as to be heard by those in the adjoining boxes and in the lobby. Thus the attention of many was attracted by this altercation.

"Where are you come from, sir?" said Monte Cristo "You do not appear to be in the possession of your senses."

"Provided I understand your perfidy, sir, and succeed in making you understand that I will be revenged, I shall be reasonable enough," said Albert furiously.

"I do not understand you, sir," replied Monte Cristo; "and if I did, your tone is too high. I am at home here, and I alone have a right to raise my voice above another's. Leave the box, sir!"

Monte Cristo pointed towards the door with the most commanding dignity.

"Ah, I shall know how to make you leave your home!" replied Albert, clasping in his convulsed grasp the glove, which Monte Cristo did not lose sight of.

"Well, well," said Monte Cristo quietly, "I see you wish to quarrel with me; but I would give you one piece of advice, which you will do well to keep in mind. It is in poor taste to make a display of a challenge. Display is not becoming to everyone, M. de Morcerf."

At this name a murmur of astonishment passed around the group of spectators of this scene. They had talked of no one but Morcerf the whole day. Albert understood the allusion in a moment, and was about to throw his glove at the count, when Morrel seized his hand, while Beauchamp and Château-Renaud, fearing the scene would surpass the limits of a challenge, held him back. But Monte Cristo, without rising, and leaning forward in his chair, merely stretched out his arm and, taking the damp, crushed glove from the clenched hand of the young man:

"Sir," said he in a solemn tone, "I consider your glove thrown, and will return it to you wrapped around a bullet. Now leave me or I will summon my servants to throw you out at the door."

Wild, almost unconscious, and with eyes inflamed, Albert stepped back, and Morrel closed the door. Monte Cristo took up his glass again as if nothing had happened; his face was like marble, and his heart was like bronze. Morrel whispered, "What have you done to him?"

"I? Nothing—at least personally," said Monte Cristo.

"But there must be some cause for this strange scene."

"The Count of Morcerf's adventure exasperates the young man."

"Have you anything to do with it?"

"It was through Haydée that the Chamber was informed of his father's treason."

"Indeed?" said Morrel. "I had been told, but would not credit it, that the Grecian slave I have seen with you here in this very box was the daughter of Ali Pasha."

"It is true, nevertheless."

"Then," said Morrel, "I understand it all, and this scene was premeditated."

"How so?"

"Yes. Albert wrote to request me to come to the Opera, doubtless that I might be a witness to the insult he meant to offer you."

"Probably," said Monte Cristo with his imperturbable tranquillity.

"But what shall you do with him?"

"With whom?"

"With Albert."

"What shall I do with Albert? As certainly, Maximilian, as I now press your hand, I shall kill him before ten o'clock tomorrow morning." Morrel, in his turn, took Monte Cristo's hand in both of his, and he shuddered to feel how cold and steady it was.

"Ah, count," said he, "his father loves him so much!"

"Do not speak to me of that," said Monte Cristo, with the first movement of anger he had betrayed; "I will make him suffer."

Morrel, amazed, let fall Monte Cristo's hand. "Count, count!" said he.

"Dear Maximilian," interrupted the count, "listen how adorably Duprez is singing that line,—

'O Mathilde! idole de mon âme!'

"I was the first to discover Duprez at Naples, and the first to applaud him. Bravo, bravo!"

Morrel saw it was useless to say more, and refrained. The curtain, which had risen at the close of the scene with Albert, again fell, and a rap was heard at the door.

"Come in," said Monte Cristo with a voice that betrayed not the least emotion; and immediately Beauchamp appeared. "Good-evening, M. Beauchamp," said Monte Cristo, as if this was the first time he had seen the journalist that evening; "be seated."

Beauchamp bowed, and, sitting down, "Sir," said he, "I just now accompanied M. de Morcerf, as you saw."

"And that means," replied Monte Cristo, laughing, "that you had, probably, just dined together. I am happy to see, M. Beauchamp, that you are more sober than he was."

"Sir," said M. Beauchamp, "Albert was wrong, I acknowledge, to betray so much anger, and I come, on my own account, to apologize for him. And having done so, entirely on my own account, be it understood, I would add that I believe you too gentlemanly to refuse giving him some explanation concerning your connection with Yanina. Then I will add two words about the young Greek girl."

Monte Cristo motioned him to be silent. "Come," said he, laughing, "there are all my hopes about to be destroyed."

"How so?" asked Beauchamp.

"Doubtless you wish to make me appear a very eccentric character. I am, in your opinion, a Lara, a Manfred, a Lord Ruthven; then, just as I am arriving at the climax, you defeat your own end, and seek to make an ordinary man of me. You bring me down to your own level, and demand explanations! Indeed, M. Beauchamp, it is quite laughable."

"Yet," replied Beauchamp haughtily, "there are occasions when probity commands—"

"M. Beauchamp," interposed this strange man, "the Count of Monte Cristo bows to none but the Count of Monte Cristo himself. Say no more, I entreat you. I do what I please, M. Beauchamp, and it is always well done."

"Sir," replied the young man, "honest men are not to be paid with such coin. I require honorable guaranties."

"I am, sir, a living guaranty," replied Monte Cristo, motionless, but with a threatening look; "we have both blood in our veins which we wish to shed—that is our mutual guaranty. Tell the viscount so, and that tomorrow, before ten o'clock, I shall see what color his is."

"Then I have only to make arrangements for the duel," said Beauchamp.

"It is quite immaterial to me," said Monte Cristo, "and it was very unnecessary to disturb me at the Opera for such a trifle. In France people fight with the sword or pistol, in the colonies with the carbine, in Arabia with the dagger. Tell your client that, although I am the insulted party, in order to carry out my eccentricity, I leave him the choice of arms, and will accept without discussion, without dispute, anything, even combat by drawing lots, which is always stupid, but with me different from other people, as I am sure to gain."

"Sure to gain!" repeated Beauchamp, looking with amazement at the count.

"Certainly," said Monte Cristo, slightly shrugging his shoulders; "otherwise I would not fight with M. de Morcerf. I shall kill him—I cannot help it. Only by a single line this evening at my house let me know the arms and the hour; I do not like to be kept waiting."

"Pistols, then, at eight o'clock, in the Bois de Vincennes," said Beauchamp, quite disconcerted, not knowing if he was dealing with an arrogant braggadocio or a supernatural being.

"Very well, sir," said Monte Cristo. "Now all that is settled, do let me see the performance, and tell your friend Albert not to come any more this evening; he will hurt himself with all his ill-chosen barbarisms: let him go home and go to sleep."

Beauchamp left the box, perfectly amazed.

"Now," said Monte Cristo, turning towards Morrel, "I may depend upon you, may I not?"

"Certainly," said Morrel, "I am at your service, count; still—"

"What?"

"It is desirable I should know the real cause."

"That is to say, you would rather not?"

"No."

"The young man himself is acting blindfolded, and knows not the true cause, which is known only to God and to me; but I give you my word, Morrel, that God, who does know it, will be on our side."

"Enough," said Morrel; "who is your second witness?"

"I know no one in Paris, Morrel, on whom I could confer that honor besides you and your brother Emmanuel. Do you think Emmanuel would oblige me?"

"I will answer for him, count."

"Well? that is all I require. Tomorrow morning, at seven o'clock, you will be with me, will you not?"

"We will."

"Hush, the curtain is rising. Listen! I never lose a note of this opera if I can avoid it; the music of *William Tell* is so sweet."

Study Guide Questions

For Students:

1. Why does Albert decide to go to the Count's house?
2. Why is Mercédès grieving?
3. Why does Albert go to the opera?

For Reading Club:

1. Discuss what happens in the Count's box in the opera.
2. Do you think that the Count owes Albert an explanation? Why or why not?
3. Who will fight in a duel and why? Also, what are your opinions on the custom of the duel?

CHAPTER 89

The Night

Monte Cristo waited, according to his usual custom, until Duprez had sung his famous "*Suivez-moi!*" then he rose and went out. Morrel took leave of him at the door, renewing his promise to be with him the next morning at seven o'clock, and to bring Emmanuel. Then he stepped into his *coupé*, calm and smiling, and was at home in five minutes. No one who knew the count could mistake his expression when, on entering, he said:

"Ali, bring me my pistols with the ivory cross."

Ali brought the box to his master, who examined the weapons with a solicitude very natural to a man who is about to intrust his life to a little powder and shot. These were pistols of an especial pattern, which Monte Cristo had had made for target practice in his own room. A cap was sufficient to drive out the bullet, and from the adjoining room no one would have suspected that the count was, as sportsmen would say, keeping his hand in.

He was just taking one up and looking for the point to aim at on a little iron plate which served him as a target, when his study door opened, and Baptistin entered. Before he had spoken a word, the count saw in the next room a veiled woman, who had followed closely after Baptistin, and now, seeing the count with a pistol in his hand and swords on the table, rushed in. Baptistin looked at his master, who made a sign to him, and he went out, closing the door after him.

"Who are you, madame?" said the count to the veiled woman.

The stranger cast one look around her, to be certain that they were quite alone; then bending as if she would have knelt, and joining her hands, she said with an accent of despair:

"Edmond, you will not kill my son!"

The count retreated a step, uttered a slight exclamation, and let fall the pistol he held.

"What name did you pronounce then, Madame de Morcerf?" said he.

"Yours!" cried she, throwing back her veil,—"yours, which I alone, perhaps, have not forgotten. Edmond, it is not Madame de Morcerf who is come to you, it is Mercédès."

"Mercédès is dead, madame," said Monte Cristo; "I know no one now of that name."

"Mercédès lives, sir, and she remembers, for she alone recognized you when she saw you, and even before she saw you, by your voice, Edmond,—by the simple sound of your voice; and from that moment she has followed your steps, watched you, feared you, and she needs not to inquire what hand has dealt the blow which now strikes M. de Morcerf."

"Fernand, do you mean?" replied Monte Cristo, with bitter irony; "since we are recalling names, let us remember them all." Monte Cristo had pronounced the name of Fernand with such an expression of hatred that Mercédès felt a thrill of horror run through every vein.

"You see, Edmond, I am not mistaken, and have cause to say, 'Spare my son!'"

"And who told you, madame, that I have any hostile intentions against your son?"

"No one, in truth; but a mother has twofold sight. I guessed all; I followed him this evening to the Opera, and, concealed in a parquet box, have seen all."

"If you have seen all, madame, you know that the son of Fernand has publicly insulted me," said Monte Cristo with awful calmness.

"Oh, for pity's sake!"

"You have seen that he would have thrown his glove in my face if Morrel, one of my friends, had not stopped him."

"Listen to me, my son has also guessed who you are,—he attributes his father's misfortunes to you."

"Madame, you are mistaken, they are not misfortunes,—it is a punishment. It is not I who strike M. de Morcerf; it is Providence which punishes him."

"And why do you represent Providence?" cried Mercédès. "Why do you remember when it forgets? What are Yanina and its vizier to you, Edmond? What injury has Fernand Mondego done you in betraying Ali Tepelini?"

"Ah, madame," replied Monte Cristo, "all this is an affair between the French captain and the daughter of Vasiliki. It does not concern me, you are right; and if I have sworn to revenge myself, it is not on the French captain, or the Count of Morcerf, but on the fisherman Fernand, the husband of Mercédès the Catalane."

"Ah, sir!" cried the countess, "how terrible a vengeance for a fault which fatality made me commit!—for I am the only culprit, Edmond, and if you owe revenge to anyone, it is to me, who had not fortitude to bear your absence and my solitude."

"But," exclaimed Monte Cristo, "why was I absent? And why were you alone?"

"Because you had been arrested, Edmond, and were a prisoner."

"And why was I arrested? Why was I a prisoner?"

"I do not know," said Mercédès.

"You do not, madame; at least, I hope not. But I will tell you. I was arrested and became a prisoner because, under the arbor of La Réserve, the day before I was to marry you, a man named Danglars wrote this letter, which the fisherman Fernand himself posted."

Monte Cristo went to a secretaire, opened a drawer by a spring, from which he took a paper which had lost its original color, and the ink of which had become of a rusty hue—this he placed in the hands of Mercédès. It was Danglars' letter to the king's attorney, which the Count of Monte Cristo, disguised as a clerk from the house of Thomson & French, had taken from the file against Edmond Dantès, on the day he had paid the two hundred thousand francs to M. de Boville. Mercédès read with terror the following lines:

> "The king's attorney is informed by a friend to the throne and religion that one Edmond Dantès, second in command on board the *Pharaon*, this day arrived from Smyrna, after having touched at Naples and Porto-Ferrajo, is the bearer of a letter from Murat to the usurper, and of another letter from the usurper to the Bonapartist club in Paris. Ample corroboration of this statement may be obtained by arresting the above-mentioned Edmond Dantès, who either carries the letter for Paris about with him, or has it at his father's abode. Should it not be found in possession of either father or son, then it will assuredly be discovered in the cabin belonging to the said Dantès on board the *Pharaon*."

"How dreadful!" said Mercédès, passing her hand across her brow, moist with perspiration; "and that letter—"

"I bought it for two hundred thousand francs, madame," said Monte Cristo; "but that is a trifle, since it enables me to justify myself to you."

"And the result of that letter—"

"You well know, madame, was my arrest; but you do not know how long that arrest lasted. You do not know that I remained for fourteen years within a quarter of a league of you, in a dungeon in the Château d'If. You do not know that every day of those fourteen years I renewed the vow of vengeance which I had made the first day; and yet I was not aware that you had married Fernand, my calumniator, and that my father had died of hunger!"

"Can it be?" cried Mercédès, shuddering.

"That is what I heard on leaving my prison fourteen years after I had entered it; and that is why, on account of the living Mercédès and my deceased father, I have sworn to revenge myself on Fernand, and—I have revenged myself."

"And you are sure the unhappy Fernand did that?"

"I am satisfied, madame, that he did what I have told you; besides, that is not much more odious than that a Frenchman by adoption should pass over to the English; that a Spaniard by birth should have fought against the Spaniards; that a stipendiary of Ali should have betrayed and murdered Ali. Compared with such things, what is the letter you have just read?—a lover's deception, which the woman who has married that man ought certainly to forgive; but not so the lover who was to have married her. Well, the French did not avenge themselves on the traitor, the Spaniards did not shoot the traitor, Ali in his tomb left the traitor unpunished; but I, betrayed, sacrificed, buried, have risen from my tomb, by the grace of God, to punish that man. He sends me for that purpose, and here I am."

The poor woman's head and arms fell; her legs bent under her, and she fell on her knees.

"Forgive, Edmond, forgive for my sake, who love you still!"

The dignity of the wife checked the fervor of the lover and the mother. Her forehead almost touched the carpet, when the count sprang forward and raised her. Then seated on a chair, she looked at the manly countenance of Monte Cristo, on which grief and hatred still impressed a threatening expression.

"Not crush that accursed race?" murmured he; "abandon my purpose at the moment of its accomplishment? Impossible, madame, impossible!"

"Edmond," said the poor mother, who tried every means, "when I call you Edmond, why do you not call me Mercédès?"

"Mercédès!" repeated Monte Cristo; "Mercédès! Well yes, you are right; that name has still its charms, and this is the first time for a long period that I have pronounced it so distinctly. Oh, Mercédès, I have uttered your name with the sigh of melancholy, with the groan of sorrow, with the last effort of despair; I have uttered it when frozen with cold, crouched on the straw in my dungeon; I have uttered it, consumed with heat, rolling on the stone floor of my prison. Mercédès, I must revenge myself, for I suffered fourteen years,—fourteen years I wept, I cursed; now I tell you, Mercédès, I must revenge myself."

The count, fearing to yield to the entreaties of her he had so ardently loved, called his sufferings to the assistance of his hatred.

"Revenge yourself, then, Edmond," cried the poor mother; "but let your vengeance fall on the culprits,—on him, on me, but not on my son!"

"It is written in the good book," said Monte Cristo, "that the sins of the fathers shall fall upon their children to the third and fourth generation. Since God himself dictated those words to his prophet, why should I seek to make myself better than God?"

"Edmond," continued Mercédès, with her arms extended towards the count, "since I first knew you, I have adored your name, have respected your memory. Edmond, my friend, do not compel me to tarnish that noble and pure image reflected incessantly on the mirror of my heart. Edmond, if you knew all the prayers I have addressed to God for you while I thought you were living and since I have thought you must be dead! Yes, dead, alas! I imagined your dead body buried at the foot of some gloomy tower, or cast to the bottom of a pit by hateful jailers, and I wept! What could I do for you, Edmond, besides pray and weep? Listen; for ten years I dreamed each night the same dream. I had been told that you had endeavored to escape; that you had taken the place of another prisoner; that you had slipped into the winding sheet of a dead body; that you had been thrown alive from the top of the Château d'If, and that the cry you uttered as you dashed upon the rocks first revealed to your jailers that they were your murderers. Well, Edmond, I swear to you, by the head of that son for whom I entreat your pity,—Edmond, for ten years I saw every night every detail of that frightful tragedy, and for ten years I heard every night the cry which awoke me, shuddering and cold. And I, too, Edmond—oh! believe me—guilty as I was—oh, yes, I, too, have suffered much!"

"Have you known what it is to have your father starve to death in your absence?" cried Monte Cristo, thrusting his hands into his hair; "have you seen the woman you loved giving her hand to your rival, while you were perishing at the bottom of a dungeon?"

"No," interrupted Mercédès, "but I have seen him whom I loved on the point of murdering my son."

Mercédès uttered these words with such deep anguish, with an accent of such intense despair, that Monte Cristo could not restrain a sob. The lion was daunted; the avenger was conquered.

"What do you ask of me?" said he,—"your son's life? Well, he shall live!"

Mercédès uttered a cry which made the tears start from Monte Cristo's eyes; but these tears disappeared almost instantaneously, for, doubtless, God had sent some angel to collect them—far more precious were they in his eyes than the richest pearls of Guzerat and Ophir.

"Oh," said she, seizing the count's hand and raising it to her lips; "oh, thank you, thank you, Edmond! Now you are exactly what I dreamt you were,—the man I always loved. Oh, now I may say so!"

"So much the better," replied Monte Cristo; "as that poor Edmond will not have long to be loved by you. Death is about to return to the tomb, the phantom to retire in darkness."

"What do you say, Edmond?"

"I say, since you command me, Mercédès, I must die."

"Die? and why so? Who talks of dying? Whence have you these ideas of death?"

"You do not suppose that, publicly outraged in the face of a whole theatre, in the presence of your friends and those of your son—challenged by a boy who will glory in my forgiveness as if it were a victory—you do not suppose that I can for one moment wish to live. What I most loved after you, Mercédès, was myself, my dignity, and that strength which rendered me superior to other men; that strength was my life. With one word you have crushed it, and I die."

"But the duel will not take place, Edmond, since you forgive?"

"It will take place," said Monte Cristo, in a most solemn tone; "but instead of your son's blood to stain the ground, mine will flow."

Mercédès shrieked, and sprang towards Monte Cristo, but, suddenly stopping, "Edmond," said she, "there is a God above us, since you live and since I have seen you again; I trust to him from my heart. While waiting his assistance I trust to your word; you have said that my son should live, have you not?"

"Yes, madame, he shall live," said Monte Cristo, surprised that without more emotion Mercédès had accepted the heroic sacrifice he made for her. Mercédès extended her hand to the count.

"Edmond," said she, and her eyes were wet with tears while looking at him to whom she spoke, "how noble it is of you, how great the action you have just performed, how sublime to have taken pity on a poor woman who appealed to you with every chance against her, Alas, I am grown old with grief more than with years, and cannot now remind my Edmond by a smile, or by a look, of that Mercédès whom he once spent so many hours in contemplating. Ah, believe me, Edmond, as I told you, I too have suffered much; I repeat, it is melancholy to pass one's life without having one joy to recall, without preserving a single hope; but that proves that all is not yet over. No, it is not finished; I feel it by what remains in my heart. Oh, I repeat it, Edmond; what you have just done is beautiful—it is grand; it is sublime."

"Do you say so now, Mercédès?—then what would you say if you knew the extent of the sacrifice I make to you? Suppose that the Supreme Being, after having created the world and fertilized chaos, had paused in the work to spare an angel the tears that might one day flow for mortal sins from her immortal eyes; suppose that when everything was in readiness and the moment had come for God to look upon his work and see that it was good—suppose he had snuffed out the sun and tossed the world back into eternal night—then—even then, Mercédès, you could not imagine what I lose in sacrificing my life at this moment."

Mercédès looked at the count in a way which expressed at the same time her astonishment, her admiration, and her gratitude. Monte Cristo pressed his forehead on his burning hands, as if his brain could no longer bear alone the weight of its thoughts.

"Edmond," said Mercédès, "I have but one word more to say to you."

The count smiled bitterly.

"Edmond," continued she, "you will see that if my face is pale, if my eyes are dull, if my beauty is gone; if Mercédès, in short, no longer resembles her former self in her features, you will see that her heart is still the same. Adieu, then, Edmond; I have nothing more to ask of heaven—I have seen you again, and have found you as noble and as great as formerly you were. Adieu, Edmond, adieu, and thank you."

But the count did not answer. Mercédès opened the door of the study and had disappeared before he had recovered from the painful and profound reverie into which his thwarted vengeance had plunged him.

The clock of the Invalides struck one when the carriage which conveyed Madame de Morcerf rolled away on the pavement of the Champs-Élysées, and made Monte Cristo raise his head.

"What a fool I was," said he, "not to tear my heart out on the day when I resolved to avenge myself!"

Study Guide Questions

For Students:

1. Who is the veiled woman that comes to meet the Count before the duel?
2. Who according to the Count has punished Fernand?
3. What does the Count show Mercédès to justify his stance?

For Reading Club:

1. Since when do you think Mercédès knows that the Count is in fact Edmond Dantès?
2. Discuss your favorite scene from the meeting of the Count and Mercédès.
3. Discuss Mercédès as a lover, wife, and mother.

CHAPTER 90

The Meeting

After Mercédès had left Monte Cristo, he fell into profound gloom. Around him and within him the flight of thought seemed to have stopped; his energetic mind slumbered, as the body does after extreme fatigue.

"What?" said he to himself, while the lamp and the wax lights were nearly burnt out, and the servants were waiting impatiently in the anteroom; "what? this edifice which I have been so long preparing, which I have reared with so much care and toil, is to be crushed by a single touch, a word, a breath! Yes, this self, of whom I thought so much, of whom I was so proud, who had appeared so worthless in the dungeons of the Château d'If, and whom I had succeeded in making so great, will be but a lump of clay tomorrow. Alas, it is not the death of the body I regret; for is not the destruction of the vital principle, the repose to which everything is tending, to which every unhappy being aspires,—is not this the repose of matter after which I so long sighed, and which I was seeking to attain by the painful process of starvation when Faria appeared in my dungeon? What is death for me? One step farther into rest,—two, perhaps, into silence. No, it is not existence, then, that I regret, but the ruin of projects so slowly carried out, so laboriously framed. Providence is now opposed to them, when I most thought it would be propitious. It is not God's will that they should be accomplished. This burden, almost as heavy as a world, which I had raised, and I had thought to bear to the end, was too great for my strength, and I was compelled to lay it down in the middle of my career. Oh, shall I then, again become a fatalist, whom fourteen years of despair and ten of hope had rendered a believer in Providence?

"And all this—all this, because my heart, which I thought dead, was only sleeping; because it has awakened and has begun to beat again, because I have yielded to the pain of the emotion excited in my breast by a woman's voice.

"Yet," continued the count, becoming each moment more absorbed in the anticipation of the dreadful sacrifice for the morrow, which Mercédès had accepted, "yet, it is impossible that so noble-minded a woman should thus through selfishness consent to my death when I am in the prime of life and strength; it is impossible that she can carry to such a point maternal love, or rather delirium. There are virtues which become crimes by exaggeration. No, she must have conceived some pathetic scene; she will come and throw herself between us; and what would be sublime here will there appear ridiculous."

The blush of pride mounted to the count's forehead as this thought passed through his mind.

"Ridiculous?" repeated he; "and the ridicule will fall on me. I ridiculous? No, I would rather die."

By thus exaggerating to his own mind the anticipated ill-fortune of the next day, to which he had condemned himself by promising Mercédès to spare her son, the count at last exclaimed:

"Folly, folly, folly!—to carry generosity so far as to put myself up as a mark for that young man to aim at. He will never believe that my death was suicide; and yet it is important for the honor of my memory,—and this surely is not vanity, but a justifiable pride,—it is important the world should know that I have consented, by my free will, to stop my arm, already raised to strike, and that with the arm which has been so powerful against others I have struck myself. It must be; it shall be."

Seizing a pen, he drew a paper from a secret drawer in his desk, and wrote at the bottom of the document (which was no other than his will, made since his arrival in Paris) a sort of codicil, clearly explaining the nature of his death.

"I do this, Oh, my God," said he, with his eyes raised to heaven, "as much for thy honor as for mine. I have during ten years considered myself the agent of thy vengeance, and other wretches, like Morcerf, Danglars, Villefort, even Morcerf himself, must not imagine that chance has freed them from their enemy. Let them know, on the contrary, that their punishment, which had been decreed by Providence, is only delayed by my present determination, and although they escape it in this world, it awaits them in another, and that they are only exchanging time for eternity."

While he was thus agitated by gloomy uncertainties,—wretched waking dreams of grief,—the first rays of morning pierced his windows, and shone upon the pale blue paper on which he had just inscribed his justification of Providence.

It was just five o'clock in the morning when a slight noise like a stifled sigh reached his ear. He turned his head, looked around him, and saw no one; but the sound was repeated distinctly enough to convince him of its reality.

He arose, and quietly opening the door of the drawing-room, saw Haydée, who had fallen on a chair, with her arms hanging down and her beautiful head thrown back. She had been standing at the door, to prevent his going out without seeing her, until sleep, which the young cannot resist, had overpowered her frame, wearied as she was with watching. The noise of the door did not awaken her, and Monte Cristo gazed at her with affectionate regret.

"She remembered that she had a son," said he; "and I forgot I had a daughter." Then, shaking his head sorrowfully, "Poor Haydée," said he; "she wished to see me, to speak to me; she has feared or guessed something. Oh, I cannot go without taking leave of her; I cannot die without confiding her to someone."

He quietly regained his seat, and wrote under the other lines:

> "I bequeath to Maximilian Morrel, captain of Spahis,—and son of my former patron, Pierre Morrel, shipowner at Marseilles,—the sum of twenty millions, a part of which may be offered to his sister Julie and brother-in-law Emmanuel, if he does not fear this increase of fortune may mar their happiness. These twenty millions are concealed in my grotto at Monte Cristo, of which Bertuccio knows the secret. If his heart is free, and he will marry Haydée, the daughter of Ali Pasha of Yanina, whom I have brought up with the love of a father, and who has shown the love and tenderness of a daughter for me, he will thus accomplish my last wish. This will has already constituted Haydée heiress of the rest of my fortune, consisting of lands, funds in England, Austria, and Holland, furniture in my different palaces and houses, and which without the twenty millions and the legacies to my servants, may still amount to sixty millions."

He was finishing the last line when a cry behind him made him start, and the pen fell from his hand.

"Haydée," said he, "did you read it?"

"Oh, my lord," said she, "why are you writing thus at such an hour? Why are you bequeathing all your fortune to me? Are you going to leave me?"

"I am going on a journey, dear child," said Monte Cristo, with an expression of infinite tenderness and melancholy; "and if any misfortune should happen to me—"

The count stopped.

"Well?" asked the young girl, with an authoritative tone the count had never observed before, and which startled him.

"Well, if any misfortune happen to me," replied Monte Cristo, "I wish my daughter to be happy." Haydée smiled sorrowfully, and shook her head.

"Do you think of dying, my lord?" said she.

"The wise man, my child, has said, 'It is good to think of death.'"

"Well, if you die," said she, "bequeath your fortune to others, for if you die I shall require nothing;" and, taking the paper, she tore it in four pieces, and threw it into the middle of the room. Then, the effort having exhausted her strength, she fell, not asleep this time, but fainting on the floor.

The count leaned over her and raised her in his arms; and seeing that sweet pale face, those lovely eyes closed, that beautiful form motionless and to all appearance lifeless, the idea occurred to him for the first time, that perhaps she loved him otherwise than as a daughter loves a father.

"Alas," murmured he, with intense suffering, "I might, then, have been happy yet."

Then he carried Haydée to her room, resigned her to the care of her attendants, and returning to his study, which he shut quickly this time, he again copied the destroyed will. As he was finishing, the sound of a cabriolet entering the yard was heard. Monte Cristo approached the window, and saw Maximilian and Emmanuel alight. "Good," said he; "it was time,"—and he sealed his will with three seals.

A moment afterwards he heard a noise in the drawing-room, and went to open the door himself. Morrel was there; he had come twenty minutes before the time appointed.

"I am perhaps come too soon, count," said he, "but I frankly acknowledge that I have not closed my eyes all night, nor has anyone in my house. I need to see you strong in your courageous assurance, to recover myself."

Monte Cristo could not resist this proof of affection; he not only extended his hand to the young man, but flew to him with open arms.

"Morrel," said he, "it is a happy day for me, to feel that I am beloved by such a man as you. Good-morning, Emmanuel; you will come with me then, Maximilian?"

"Did you doubt it?" said the young captain.

"But if I were wrong—"

"I watched you during the whole scene of that challenge yesterday; I have been thinking of your firmness all night, and I said to myself that justice must be on your side, or man's countenance is no longer to be relied on."

"But, Morrel, Albert is your friend?"

"Simply an acquaintance, sir."

"You met on the same day you first saw me?"

"Yes, that is true; but I should not have recollected it if you had not reminded me."

"Thank you, Morrel." Then ringing the bell once, "Look." said he to Ali, who came immediately, "take that to my solicitor. It is my will, Morrel. When I am dead, you will go and examine it."

"What?" said Morrel, "you dead?"

"Yes; must I not be prepared for everything, dear friend? But what did you do yesterday after you left me?"

"I went to Tortoni's, where, as I expected, I found Beauchamp and Château-Renaud. I own I was seeking them."

"Why, when all was arranged?"

"Listen, count; the affair is serious and unavoidable."

"Did you doubt it!"

"No; the offence was public, and everyone is already talking of it."

"Well?"

"Well, I hoped to get an exchange of arms,—to substitute the sword for the pistol; the pistol is blind."

"Have you succeeded?" asked Monte Cristo quickly, with an imperceptible gleam of hope.

"No; for your skill with the sword is so well known."

"Ah?—who has betrayed me?"

"The skilful swordsman whom you have conquered."

"And you failed?"

"They positively refused."

"Morrel," said the count, "have you ever seen me fire a pistol?"

"Never."

"Well, we have time; look." Monte Cristo took the pistols he held in his hand when Mercédès entered, and fixing an ace of clubs against the iron plate, with four shots he successively shot off the four sides of the club. At each shot Morrel turned pale. He examined the bullets with which Monte Cristo performed this dexterous feat, and saw that they were no larger than buckshot.

"It is astonishing," said he. "Look, Emmanuel." Then turning towards Monte Cristo, "Count," said he, "in the name of all that is dear to you, I entreat you not to kill Albert!—the unhappy youth has a mother."

"You are right," said Monte Cristo; "and I have none." These words were uttered in a tone which made Morrel shudder.

"You are the offended party, count."

"Doubtless; what does that imply?"

"That you will fire first."

"I fire first?"

"Oh, I obtained, or rather claimed that; we had conceded enough for them to yield us that."

"And at what distance?"

"Twenty paces." A smile of terrible import passed over the count's lips.

"Morrel," said he, "do not forget what you have just seen."

"The only chance for Albert's safety, then, will arise from your emotion."

"I suffer from emotion?" said Monte Cristo.

"Or from your generosity, my friend; to so good a marksman as you are, I may say what would appear absurd to another."

"What is that?"

"Break his arm—wound him—but do not kill him."

"I will tell you, Morrel," said the count, "that I do not need entreating to spare the life of M. de Morcerf; he shall be so well spared, that he will return quietly with his two friends, while I—"

"And you?"

"That will be another thing; I shall be brought home."

"No, no," cried Maximilian, quite unable to restrain his feelings.

"As I told you, my dear Morrel, M. de Morcerf will kill me."

Morrel looked at him in utter amazement. "But what has happened, then, since last evening, count?"

"The same thing that happened to Brutus the night before the battle of Philippi; I have seen a ghost."

"And that ghost—"

"Told me, Morrel, that I had lived long enough."

Maximilian and Emmanuel looked at each other. Monte Cristo drew out his watch. "Let us go," said he; "it is five minutes past seven, and the appointment was for eight o'clock."

A carriage was in readiness at the door. Monte Cristo stepped into it with his two friends. He had stopped a moment in the passage to listen at a door, and Maximilian and Emmanuel, who had considerately passed forward a few steps, thought they heard him answer by a sigh to a sob from within. As the clock struck eight they drove up to the place of meeting.

"We are first," said Morrel, looking out of the window.

"Excuse me, sir," said Baptistin, who had followed his master with indescribable terror, "but I think I see a carriage down there under the trees."

Monte Cristo sprang lightly from the carriage, and offered his hand to assist Emmanuel and Maximilian. The latter retained the count's hand between his.

"I like," said he, "to feel a hand like this, when its owner relies on the goodness of his cause."

"It seems to me," said Emmanuel, "that I see two young men down there, who are evidently, waiting."

Monte Cristo drew Morrel a step or two behind his brother-in-law.

"Maximilian," said he, "are your affections disengaged?" Morrel looked at Monte Cristo with astonishment. "I do not seek your confidence, my dear friend. I only ask you a simple question; answer it;—that is all I require."

"I love a young girl, count."

"Do you love her much?"

"More than my life."

"Another hope defeated!" said the count. Then, with a sigh, "Poor Haydée!" murmured he.

"To tell the truth, count, if I knew less of you, I should think that you were less brave than you are."

"Because I sigh when thinking of someone I am leaving? Come, Morrel, it is not like a soldier to be so bad a judge of courage. Do I regret life? What is it to me, who have passed twenty years between life and death? Moreover, do not alarm yourself, Morrel; this weakness, if it is such, is betrayed to you alone. I know the world is a drawing-room, from which we must retire politely and honestly; that is, with a bow, and our debts of honor paid."

"That is to the purpose. Have you brought your arms?"

"I?—what for? I hope these gentlemen have theirs."

"I will inquire," said Morrel.

"Do; but make no treaty—you understand me?"

"You need not fear." Morrel advanced towards Beauchamp and Château-Renaud, who, seeing his intention, came to meet him. The three young men bowed to each other courteously, if not affably.

"Excuse me, gentlemen," said Morrel, "but I do not see M. de Morcerf."

"He sent us word this morning," replied Château-Renaud, "that he would meet us on the ground."

"Ah," said Morrel. Beauchamp pulled out his watch.

"It is only five minutes past eight," said he to Morrel; "there is not much time lost yet."

"Oh, I made no allusion of that kind," replied Morrel.

"There is a carriage coming," said Château-Renaud. It advanced rapidly along one of the avenues leading towards the open space where they were assembled.

"You are doubtless provided with pistols, gentlemen? M. de Monte Cristo yields his right of using his."

"We had anticipated this kindness on the part of the count," said Beauchamp, "and I have brought some weapons which I bought eight or ten days since, thinking to want them on a similar occasion. They are quite new, and have not yet been used. Will you examine them."

"Oh, M. Beauchamp, if you assure me that M. de Morcerf does not know these pistols, you may readily believe that your word will be quite sufficient."

"Gentlemen," said Château-Renaud, "it is not Morcerf coming in that carriage;—faith, it is Franz and Debray!"

The two young men he announced were indeed approaching. "What chance brings you here, gentlemen?" said Château-Renaud, shaking hands with each of them.

"Because," said Debray, "Albert sent this morning to request us to come." Beauchamp and Château-Renaud exchanged looks of astonishment. "I think I understand his reason," said Morrel.

"What is it?"

"Yesterday afternoon I received a letter from M. de Morcerf, begging me to attend the Opera."

"And I," said Debray.

"And I also," said Franz.

"And we, too," added Beauchamp and Château-Renaud.

"Having wished you all to witness the challenge, he now wishes you to be present at the combat."

"Exactly so," said the young men; "you have probably guessed right."

"But, after all these arrangements, he does not come himself," said Château-Renaud. "Albert is ten minutes after time."

"There he comes," said Beauchamp, "on horseback, at full gallop, followed by a servant."

"How imprudent," said Château-Renaud, "to come on horseback to fight a duel with pistols, after all the instructions I had given him."

"And besides," said Beauchamp, "with a collar above his cravat, an open coat and white waistcoat! Why has he not painted a spot upon his heart?—it would have been more simple."

Meanwhile Albert had arrived within ten paces of the group formed by the five young men. He jumped from his horse, threw the bridle on his servant's arms, and joined them. He was pale, and his eyes were red and swollen; it was evident that he had not slept. A shade of melancholy gravity overspread his countenance, which was not natural to him.

"I thank you, gentlemen," said he, "for having complied with my request; I feel extremely grateful for this mark of friendship." Morrel had stepped back as Morcerf approached, and remained at a short distance. "And to you also, M. Morrel, my thanks are due. Come, there cannot be too many."

"Sir," said Maximilian, "you are not perhaps aware that I am M. de Monte Cristo's friend?"

"I was not sure, but I thought it might be so. So much the better; the more honorable men there are here the better I shall be satisfied."

"M. Morrel," said Château-Renaud, "will you apprise the Count of Monte Cristo that M. de Morcerf is arrived, and we are at his disposal?"

Morrel was preparing to fulfil his commission. Beauchamp had meanwhile drawn the box of pistols from the carriage.

"Stop, gentlemen," said Albert; "I have two words to say to the Count of Monte Cristo."

"In private?" asked Morrel.

"No, sir; before all who are here."

Albert's witnesses looked at each other. Franz and Debray exchanged some words in a whisper, and Morrel, rejoiced at this unexpected incident, went to fetch the count, who was walking in a retired path with Emmanuel.

"What does he want with me?" said Monte Cristo.

"I do not know, but he wishes to speak to you."

"Ah?" said Monte Cristo, "I trust he is not going to tempt me by some fresh insult!"

"I do not think that such is his intention," said Morrel.

The count advanced, accompanied by Maximilian and Emmanuel. His calm and serene look formed a singular contrast to Albert's grief-stricken face, who approached also, followed by the other four young men.

When at three paces distant from each other, Albert and the count stopped.

"Approach, gentlemen," said Albert; "I wish you not to lose one word of what I am about to have the honor of saying to the Count of Monte Cristo, for it must be repeated by you to all who will listen to it, strange as it may appear to you."

"Proceed, sir," said the count.

"Sir," said Albert, at first with a tremulous voice, but which gradually became firmer, "I reproached you with exposing the conduct of M. de Morcerf in Epirus, for guilty as I knew he was, I thought you had no right to punish him; but I have since learned that you had that right. It is not Fernand Mondego's treachery towards Ali Pasha which induces me so readily to excuse you, but the treachery of the fisherman Fernand towards you, and the almost unheard-of miseries which were its consequences; and I say, and proclaim it publicly, that you were justified in revenging yourself on my father, and I, his son, thank you for not using greater severity."

Had a thunderbolt fallen in the midst of the spectators of this unexpected scene, it would not have surprised them more than did Albert's declaration. As for Monte Cristo, his eyes slowly rose towards heaven with an expression of infinite gratitude. He could not understand how Albert's fiery nature, of which he had seen so much among the Roman bandits, had suddenly stooped to this humiliation. He recognized the influence of Mercédès, and saw why her noble heart had not opposed the sacrifice she knew beforehand would be useless.

"Now, sir," said Albert, "if you think my apology sufficient, pray give me your hand. Next to the merit of infallibility which you appear to possess, I rank that of candidly acknowledging a fault. But this confession concerns me only. I acted well as a man, but you have acted better than man. An angel alone could have saved one of us from death—that angel came from heaven, if not to make us friends (which, alas, fatality renders impossible), at least to make us esteem each other."

Monte Cristo, with moistened eye, heaving breast, and lips half open, extended to Albert a hand which the latter pressed with a sentiment resembling respectful fear.

"Gentlemen," said he, "M. de Monte Cristo receives my apology. I had acted hastily towards him. Hasty actions are generally bad ones. Now my fault is repaired. I hope the world will not call me cowardly for acting as my conscience dictated. But if anyone should entertain a false opinion of me," added he, drawing himself up as if he would challenge both friends and enemies, "I shall endeavor to correct his mistake."

"What happened during the night?" asked Beauchamp of Château-Renaud; "we appear to make a very sorry figure here."

"In truth, what Albert has just done is either very despicable or very noble," replied the baron.

"What can it mean?" said Debray to Franz.

"The Count of Monte Cristo acts dishonorably to M. de Morcerf, and is justified by his son! Had I ten Yaninas in my family, I should only consider myself the more bound to fight ten times."

As for Monte Cristo, his head was bent down, his arms were powerless. Bowing under the weight of twenty-four years' reminiscences, he thought not of Albert, of Beauchamp, of Château-Renaud, or of any of that group; but he thought of that courageous woman who had come to plead for her son's life, to whom he had offered his, and who had now saved it by the revelation of a dreadful family secret, capable of destroying forever in that young man's heart every feeling of filial piety.

"Providence still," murmured he; "now only am I fully convinced of being the emissary of God!"

Study Guide Questions

For Students:

1. What does the Count tell Haydée?
2. Why does the Count write his will?
3. What does the Count tell Morrel about the result of the duel?

For Reading Club:

1. What does the Count mention in his letter?
2. Do you think the Count is right in obeying Mercédès? How do you think it reveals the theme of love vs duty?
3. Discuss what happens in the Meeting.

CHAPTER 91

Mother and Son

The Count of Monte Cristo bowed to the five young men with a melancholy and dignified smile, and got into his carriage with Maximilian and Emmanuel. Albert, Beauchamp, and Château-Renaud remained alone. Albert looked at his two friends, not timidly, but in a way that appeared to ask their opinion of what he had just done.

"Indeed, my dear friend," said Beauchamp first, who had either the most feeling or the least dissimulation, "allow me to congratulate you; this is a very unhoped-for conclusion of a very disagreeable affair."

Albert remained silent and wrapped in thought. Château-Renaud contented himself with tapping his boot with his flexible cane.

"Are we not going?" said he, after this embarrassing silence.

"When you please," replied Beauchamp; "allow me only to compliment M. de Morcerf, who has given proof today of rare chivalric generosity."

"Oh, yes," said Château-Renaud.

"It is magnificent," continued Beauchamp, "to be able to exercise so much self-control!"

"Assuredly; as for me, I should have been incapable of it," said Château-Renaud, with most significant coolness.

"Gentlemen," interrupted Albert, "I think you did not understand that something very serious had passed between M. de Monte Cristo and myself."

"Possibly, possibly," said Beauchamp immediately; "but every simpleton would not be able to understand your heroism, and sooner or later you will find yourself compelled to explain it to them more energetically than would be convenient to your bodily health and the duration of your life. May I give you a friendly counsel? Set out for Naples, the Hague, or St. Petersburg—calm countries, where the point of honor is better understood than among our hot-headed Parisians. Seek quietude and oblivion, so that you may return peaceably to France after a few years. Am I not right, M. de Château-Renaud?"

"That is quite my opinion," said the gentleman; "nothing induces serious duels so much as a duel forsworn."

"Thank you, gentlemen," replied Albert, with a smile of indifference; "I shall follow your advice—not because you give it, but because I had before intended to quit France. I thank you equally for the service you have rendered me in being my seconds. It is deeply engraved on my heart, and, after what you have just said, I remember that only."

Château-Renaud and Beauchamp looked at each other; the impression was the same on both of them, and the tone in which Morcerf had just expressed his thanks was so determined that the position would have become embarrassing for all if the conversation had continued.

"Good-bye, Albert," said Beauchamp suddenly, carelessly extending his hand to the young man. The latter did not appear to arouse from his lethargy; in fact, he did not notice the offered hand.

"Good-bye," said Château-Renaud in his turn, keeping his little cane in his left hand, and saluting with his right.

Albert's lips scarcely whispered "Good-bye," but his look was more explicit; it expressed a whole poem of restrained anger, proud disdain, and generous indignation. He preserved his melancholy and motionless position for some time after his two friends had regained their carriage; then suddenly unfastening his horse from the little tree to which his servant had tied it, he mounted and galloped off in the direction of Paris.

In a quarter of an hour he was entering the house in the Rue du Helder. As he alighted, he thought he saw his father's pale face behind the curtain of the count's bedroom. Albert turned away his head with a sigh, and went to his own apartments. He cast one lingering look on all the luxuries which had rendered life so easy and so happy since his infancy; he looked at the pictures, whose faces seemed to smile, and the landscapes, which appeared painted in brighter colors. Then he took away his mother's portrait, with its oaken frame, leaving the gilt frame from which he took it black and empty. Then he arranged all his beautiful Turkish arms, his fine English guns, his Japanese china, his cups mounted in silver, his artistic bronzes by Feuchères or Barye; examined the cupboards, and placed the key in each; threw into a drawer of his secretaire, which he left open, all the pocket-money he had about him, and with it the thousand fancy jewels from his vases and his jewel-boxes; then he made an exact inventory of everything, and placed it in the most conspicuous part of the table, after putting aside the books and papers which had collected there.

At the beginning of this work, his servant, notwithstanding orders to the contrary, came to his room.

"What do you want?" asked he, with a more sorrowful than angry tone.

"Pardon me, sir," replied the valet; "you had forbidden me to disturb you, but the Count of Morcerf has called me."

"Well!" said Albert.

"I did not like to go to him without first seeing you."

"Why?"

"Because the count is doubtless aware that I accompanied you to the meeting this morning."

"It is probable," said Albert.

"And since he has sent for me, it is doubtless to question me on what happened there. What must I answer?"

"The truth."

"Then I shall say the duel did not take place?"

"You will say I apologized to the Count of Monte Cristo. Go."

The valet bowed and retired, and Albert returned to his inventory. As he was finishing this work, the sound of horses prancing in the yard, and the wheels of a carriage shaking his window, attracted his attention. He approached the window, and saw his father get into it, and drive away. The door was scarcely closed when Albert bent his steps to his mother's room; and, no one being there to announce him, he advanced to her bedchamber, and distressed by what he saw and guessed, stopped for one moment at the door.

As if the same idea had animated these two beings, Mercédès was doing the same in her apartments that he had just done in his. Everything was in order,—laces, dresses, jewels, linen, money, all were arranged in the drawers, and the countess was carefully collecting the keys. Albert saw all these preparations and understood them, and exclaiming, "My mother!" he threw his arms around her neck.

The artist who could have depicted the expression of these two countenances would certainly have made of them a beautiful picture. All these proofs of an energetic resolution, which Albert did not fear on his own account, alarmed him for his mother. "What are you doing?" asked he.

"What were you doing?" replied she.

"Oh, my mother!" exclaimed Albert, so overcome he could scarcely speak; "it is not the same with you and me—you cannot have made the same resolution I have, for I have come to warn you that I bid adieu to your house, and—and to you."

"I also," replied Mercédès, "am going, and I acknowledge I had depended on your accompanying me; have I deceived myself?"

"Mother," said Albert with firmness. "I cannot make you share the fate I have planned for myself. I must live henceforth without rank and fortune, and to begin this hard apprenticeship I must borrow from a friend the loaf I shall eat until I have earned one. So, my dear mother, I am going at once to ask Franz to lend me the small sum I shall require to supply my present wants."

"You, my poor child, suffer poverty and hunger? Oh, do not say so; it will break my resolutions."

"But not mine, mother," replied Albert. "I am young and strong; I believe I am courageous, and since yesterday I have learned the power of will. Alas, my dear mother, some have suffered so much, and yet live, and have raised a new fortune on the ruin of all the promises of happiness which heaven had made them—on the fragments of all the hope which God had given them! I have seen that, mother; I know that from the gulf in which their enemies have plunged them they have risen with so much vigor and glory that in their turn they have ruled their former conquerors, and have punished them. No, mother; from this moment I have done with the past, and accept nothing from it—not even a name, because you can understand that your son cannot bear the name of a man who ought to blush for it before another."

"Albert, my child," said Mercédès, "if I had a stronger heart, that is the counsel I would have given you; your conscience has spoken when my voice became too weak; listen to its dictates. You had friends, Albert; break off their acquaintance. But do not despair; you have life before you, my dear Albert, for you are yet scarcely twenty-two years old; and as a pure heart like yours wants a spotless name, take my father's—it was Herrera. I am sure, my dear Albert, whatever may be your career, you will soon render that name illustrious. Then, my son, return to the world still more brilliant because of your former sorrows; and if I am wrong, still let me cherish these hopes, for I have no future to look forward to. For me the grave opens when I pass the threshold of this house."

"I will fulfil all your wishes, my dear mother," said the young man. "Yes, I share your hopes; the anger of Heaven will not pursue us, since you are pure and I am innocent. But, since our resolution is formed, let us act promptly. M. de Morcerf went out about half an hour ago; the opportunity is favorable to avoid an explanation."

"I am ready, my son," said Mercédès.

Albert ran to fetch a carriage. He recollected that there was a small furnished house to let in the Rue des Saints-Pères, where his mother would find a humble but decent lodging, and thither he intended conducting the countess. As the carriage stopped at the door, and Albert was alighting, a man approached and gave him a letter.

Albert recognized the bearer. "From the count," said Bertuccio. Albert took the letter, opened, and read it, then looked round for Bertuccio, but he was gone.

He returned to Mercédès with tears in his eyes and heaving breast, and without uttering a word he gave her the letter. Mercédès read:

"Albert,—While showing you that I have discovered your plans, I hope also to convince you of my delicacy. You are free, you leave the count's house, and you take your mother to your home; but reflect, Albert, you owe her more than your poor noble heart can pay her. Keep the struggle for yourself, bear all the suffering, but spare her the trial of poverty which must accompany your first efforts; for she deserves not even the shadow of the misfortune which has this day fallen on her, and Providence is not willing that the innocent should suffer for the guilty. I know you are going to leave the Rue du Helder without taking anything with you. Do not seek to know how I discovered it; I know it—that is sufficient.

"Now, listen, Albert. Twenty-four years ago I returned, proud and joyful, to my country. I had a betrothed, Albert, a lovely girl whom I adored, and I was bringing to my betrothed a hundred and fifty louis, painfully amassed by ceaseless toil. This money was for her; I destined it for her, and, knowing the treachery of the sea I buried our treasure in the little garden of the house my father lived in at Marseilles, on the Allées de Meilhan. Your mother, Albert, knows that poor house well. A short time since I passed through Marseilles, and went to see the old place, which revived so many painful recollections; and in the evening I took a spade and dug in the corner of the garden where I had concealed my treasure. The iron box was there—no one had touched it—under a beautiful fig-tree my father had planted the day I was born, which overshadowed the spot. Well, Albert, this money, which was formerly designed to promote the comfort and tranquillity of the woman I adored, may now, through strange and painful circumstances, be devoted to the same purpose.

"Oh, feel for me, who could offer millions to that poor woman, but who return her only the piece of black bread forgotten under my poor roof since the day I was torn from her I loved. You are a generous man, Albert, but perhaps you may be blinded by pride or resentment; if you refuse me, if you ask another for what I have a right to offer you, I will say it is ungenerous of you to refuse the life of your mother at the hands of a man whose father was allowed by your father to die in all the horrors of poverty and despair."

Albert stood pale and motionless to hear what his mother would decide after she had finished reading this letter. Mercédès turned her eyes with an ineffable look towards heaven.

"I accept it," said she; "he has a right to pay the dowry, which I shall take with me to some convent!"

Putting the letter in her bosom, she took her son's arm, and with a firmer step than she even herself expected she went downstairs.

Study Guide Questions

For Students:

1. How do Albert's friends react to his decision?
2. What do the mother and the son decide to do?
3. What does Mercédès decide to do after reading the Count's letter?

For Reading Club:

1. What do you think of Albert's decision of leaving everything behind for the sake of honor?
2. If Mercédès had no son, do you think she would have been able to leave her husband?
3. Discuss the letter sent by the Count. What does it reveal about his character?

CHAPTER 92

The Suicide

Meanwhile Monte Cristo had also returned to town with Emmanuel and Maximilian. Their return was cheerful. Emmanuel did not conceal his joy at the peaceful termination of the affair, and was loud in his expressions of delight. Morrel, in a corner of the carriage, allowed his brother-in-law's gayety to expend itself in words, while he felt equal inward joy, which, however, betrayed itself only in his countenance.

At the Barrière du Trône they met Bertuccio, who was waiting there, motionless as a sentinel at his post. Monte Cristo put his head out of the window, exchanged a few words with him in a low tone, and the steward disappeared.

"Count," said Emmanuel, when they were at the end of the Place Royale, "put me down at my door, that my wife may not have a single moment of needless anxiety on my account or yours."

"If it were not ridiculous to make a display of our triumph, said Morrel, I would invite the count to our house; besides that, he doubtless has some trembling heart to comfort. So we will take leave of our friend, and let him hasten home."

"Stop a moment," said Monte Cristo; "do not let me lose both my companions. Return, Emmanuel, to your charming wife, and present my best compliments to her; and do you, Morrel, accompany me to the Champs-Élysées."

"Willingly," said Maximilian; "particularly as I have business in that quarter."

"Shall we wait breakfast for you?" asked Emmanuel.

"No," replied the young man. The door was closed, and the carriage proceeded. "See what good fortune I brought you!" said Morrel, when he was alone with the count. "Have you not thought so?"

"Yes," said Monte Cristo; "for that reason I wished to keep you near me."

"It is miraculous!" continued Morrel, answering his own thoughts.

"What?" said Monte Cristo.

"What has just happened."

"Yes," said the Count, "you are right—it is miraculous."

"For Albert is brave," resumed Morrel.

"Very brave," said Monte Cristo; "I have seen him sleep with a sword suspended over his head."

"And I know he has fought two duels," said Morrel. "How can you reconcile that with his conduct this morning?"

"All owing to your influence," replied Monte Cristo, smiling.

"It is well for Albert he is not in the army," said Morrel.

"Why?"

"An apology on the ground!" said the young captain, shaking his head.

"Come," said the count mildly, "do not entertain the prejudices of ordinary men, Morrel! Acknowledge, that if Albert is brave, he cannot be a coward; he must then have had some reason for acting as he did this morning, and confess that his conduct is more heroic than otherwise."

"Doubtless, doubtless," said Morrel; "but I shall say, like the Spaniard, 'He has not been so brave today as he was yesterday.'"

"You will breakfast with me, will you not, Morrel?" said the count, to turn the conversation.

"No; I must leave you at ten o'clock."

"Your engagement was for breakfast, then?" said the count.

Morrel smiled, and shook his head.

"Still you must breakfast somewhere."

"But if I am not hungry?" said the young man.

"Oh," said the count, "I only know two things which destroy the appetite,—grief—and as I am happy to see you very cheerful, it is not that—and love. Now after what you told me this morning of your heart, I may believe—"

"Well, count," replied Morrel gayly, "I will not dispute it."

"But you will not make me your confidant, Maximilian?" said the count, in a tone which showed how gladly he would have been admitted to the secret.

"I showed you this morning that I had a heart, did I not, count?" Monte Cristo only answered by extending his hand to the young man. "Well," continued the latter, "since that heart is no longer with you in the Bois de Vincennes, it is elsewhere, and I must go and find it."

"Go," said the count deliberately; "go, dear friend, but promise me if you meet with any obstacle to remember that I have some power in this world, that I am happy to use that power in the behalf of those I love, and that I love you, Morrel."

"I will remember it," said the young man, "as selfish children recollect their parents when they want their aid. When I need your assistance, and the moment arrives, I will come to you, count."

"Well, I rely upon your promise. Good-bye, then."

"Good-bye, till we meet again."

They had arrived in the Champs-Élysées. Monte Cristo opened the carriage-door, Morrel sprang out on the pavement, Bertuccio was waiting on the steps. Morrel disappeared down the Avenue de Marigny, and Monte Cristo hastened to join Bertuccio.

"Well?" asked he.

"She is going to leave her house," said the steward.

"And her son?"

"Florentin, his valet, thinks he is going to do the same."

"Come this way." Monte Cristo took Bertuccio into his study, wrote the letter we have seen, and gave it to the steward. "Go," said he quickly. "But first, let Haydée be informed that I have returned."

"Here I am," said the young girl, who at the sound of the carriage had run downstairs and whose face was radiant with joy at seeing the count return safely. Bertuccio left. Every transport of a daughter finding a father, all the delight of a mistress seeing an adored lover, were felt by Haydée during the first moments of this meeting, which she had so eagerly expected. Doubtless, although less evident, Monte Cristo's joy was not less intense. Joy to hearts which have suffered long is like the dew on the ground after a long drought; both the heart and the ground absorb that beneficent moisture falling on them, and nothing is outwardly apparent.

Monte Cristo was beginning to think, what he had not for a long time dared to believe, that there were two Mercédès in the world, and he might yet be happy. His eye, elate with happiness, was reading eagerly the tearful gaze of Haydée, when suddenly the door opened. The count knit his brow.

"M. de Morcerf!" said Baptistin, as if that name sufficed for his excuse. In fact, the count's face brightened.

"Which," asked he, "the viscount or the count?"

"The count."

"Oh," exclaimed Haydée, "is it not yet over?"

"I know not if it is finished, my beloved child," said Monte Cristo, taking the young girl's hands; "but I do know you have nothing more to fear."

"But it is the wretched—"

"That man cannot injure me, Haydée," said Monte Cristo; "it was his son alone that there was cause to fear."

"And what I have suffered," said the young girl, "you shall never know, my lord."

Monte Cristo smiled. "By my father's tomb," said he, extending his hand over the head of the young girl, "I swear to you, Haydée, that if any misfortune happens, it will not be to me."

"I believe you, my lord, as implicitly as if God had spoken to me," said the young girl, presenting her forehead to him. Monte Cristo pressed on that pure beautiful forehead a kiss which made two hearts throb at once, the one violently, the other secretly.

"Oh," murmured the count, "shall I then be permitted to love again? Ask M. de Morcerf into the drawing-room," said he to Baptistin, while he led the beautiful Greek girl to a private staircase.

We must explain this visit, which although expected by Monte Cristo, is unexpected to our readers. While Mercédès, as we have said, was making a similar inventory of her property to Albert's, while she was arranging her jewels, shutting her drawers, collecting her keys, to leave everything in perfect order, she did not perceive a pale and sinister face at a glass door which threw light into the passage, from which everything could be both seen and heard. He who was thus looking, without being heard or seen, probably heard and saw all that passed in Madame de Morcerf's apartments. From that glass door the pale-faced man went to the count's bedroom and raised with a constricted hand the curtain of a window overlooking the courtyard. He remained there ten minutes, motionless and dumb, listening to the beating of his own heart. For him those ten minutes were very long. It was then Albert, returning from his meeting with the count, perceived his father watching for his arrival behind a curtain, and turned aside. The count's eye expanded; he knew Albert had insulted the count dreadfully, and that in every country in the world such an insult would lead to a deadly duel. Albert returned safely—then the count was revenged.

An indescribable ray of joy illumined that wretched countenance like the last ray of the sun before it disappears behind the clouds which bear the aspect, not of a downy couch, but of a tomb. But as we have said, he waited in vain for his son to come to his apartment with the account of his triumph. He easily understood why his son did not come to see him before he went to avenge his father's honor; but when that was done, why did not his son come and throw himself into his arms?

It was then, when the count could not see Albert, that he sent for his servant, who he knew was authorized not to conceal anything from him. Ten minutes afterwards, General Morcerf was seen on the steps in a black coat with a military collar, black pantaloons, and black gloves. He had apparently given previous orders, for as he reached the bottom step his carriage came from the coach-house ready for him. The valet threw into the carriage his military cloak, in which two swords were wrapped, and, shutting the door, he took his seat by the side of the coachman. The coachman stooped down for his orders.

"To the Champs-Élysées," said the general; "the Count of Monte Cristo's. Hurry!"

The horses bounded beneath the whip; and in five minutes they stopped before the count's door. M. de Morcerf opened the door himself, and as the carriage rolled away he passed up the walk, rang, and entered the open door with his servant.

A moment afterwards, Baptistin announced the Count of Morcerf to Monte Cristo, and the latter, leading Haydée aside, ordered that Morcerf be asked into the drawing-room. The general was pacing the room the third time when, in turning, he perceived Monte Cristo at the door.

"Ah, it is M. de Morcerf," said Monte Cristo quietly; "I thought I had not heard aright."

"Yes, it is I," said the count, whom a frightful contraction of the lips prevented from articulating freely.

"May I know the cause which procures me the pleasure of seeing M. de Morcerf so early?"

"Had you not a meeting with my son this morning?" asked the general.

"I had," replied the count.

"And I know my son had good reasons to wish to fight with you, and to endeavor to kill you."

"Yes, sir, he had very good ones; but you see that in spite of them he has not killed me, and did not even fight."

"Yet he considered you the cause of his father's dishonor, the cause of the fearful ruin which has fallen on my house."

"It is true, sir," said Monte Cristo with his dreadful calmness; "a secondary cause, but not the principal."

"Doubtless you made, then, some apology or explanation?"

"I explained nothing, and it is he who apologized to me."

"But to what do you attribute this conduct?"

"To the conviction, probably, that there was one more guilty than I."

"And who was that?"

"His father."

"That may be," said the count, turning pale; "but you know the guilty do not like to find themselves convicted."

"I know it, and I expected this result."

"You expected my son would be a coward?" cried the count.

"M. Albert de Morcerf is no coward!" said Monte Cristo.

"A man who holds a sword in his hand, and sees a mortal enemy within reach of that sword, and does not fight, is a coward! Why is he not here that I may tell him so?"

"Sir," replied Monte Cristo coldly, "I did not expect that you had come here to relate to me your little family affairs. Go and tell M. Albert that, and he may know what to answer you."

"Oh, no, no," said the general, smiling faintly, "I did not come for that purpose; you are right. I came to tell you that I also look upon you as my enemy. I came to tell you that I hate you instinctively; that it seems as if I had always known you, and always hated you; and, in short, since the young people of the present day will not fight, it remains for us to do so. Do you think so, sir?"

"Certainly. And when I told you I had foreseen the result, it is the honor of your visit I alluded to."

"So much the better. Are you prepared?"

"Yes, sir."

"You know that we shall fight till one of us is dead," said the general, whose teeth were clenched with rage.

"Until one of us dies," repeated Monte Cristo, moving his head slightly up and down.

"Let us start, then; we need no witnesses."

"Very true," said Monte Cristo; "it is unnecessary, we know each other so well!"

"On the contrary," said the count, "we know so little of each other."

"Indeed?" said Monte Cristo, with the same indomitable coolness; "let us see. Are you not the soldier Fernand who deserted on the eve of the battle of Waterloo? Are you not the Lieutenant Fernand who served as guide and spy to the French army in Spain? Are you not the Captain Fernand who betrayed, sold, and murdered his benefactor, Ali? And have not all these Fernands, united, made Lieutenant-General, the Count of Morcerf, peer of France?"

"Oh," cried the general, as if branded with a hot iron, "wretch,—to reproach me with my shame when about, perhaps, to kill me! No, I did not say I was a stranger to you. I know well, demon, that you have penetrated into the darkness of the past, and that you have read, by the light of what torch I know not, every page of my life; but perhaps I may be more honorable in my shame than you under your pompous coverings. No—no, I am aware you know me; but I know you only as an adventurer sewn up in gold and jewellery. You call yourself, in Paris, the Count of Monte Cristo; in Italy, Sinbad the Sailor; in Malta, I forget what. But it is your real name I want to know, in the midst of your hundred names, that I may pronounce it when we meet to fight, at the moment when I plunge my sword through your heart."

The Count of Monte Cristo turned dreadfully pale; his eye seemed to burn with a devouring fire. He leaped towards a dressing-room near his bedroom, and in less than a moment, tearing off his cravat, his coat and waistcoat, he put on a sailor's jacket and hat, from beneath which rolled his long black hair. He returned thus, formidable and implacable, advancing with his arms crossed on his breast, towards the general, who could not understand why he had disappeared, but who on seeing him again, and feeling his teeth chatter and his legs sink under him, drew back, and only stopped when he found a table to support his clenched hand.

"Fernand," cried he, "of my hundred names I need only tell you one, to overwhelm you! But you guess it now, do you not?—or, rather, you remember it? For, notwithstanding all my sorrows and my tortures, I show you today a face which the happiness of revenge makes young again—a face you must often have seen in your dreams since your marriage with Mercédès, my betrothed!"

The general, with his head thrown back, hands extended, gaze fixed, looked silently at this dreadful apparition; then seeking the wall to support him, he glided along close to it until he reached the door, through which he went out backwards, uttering this single mournful, lamentable, distressing cry:

"Edmond Dantès!"

Then, with sighs which were unlike any human sound, he dragged himself to the door, reeled across the courtyard, and falling into the arms of his valet, he said in a voice scarcely intelligible,—"Home, home."

The fresh air and the shame he felt at having exposed himself before his servants, partly recalled his senses, but the ride was short, and as he drew near his house all his wretchedness revived. He stopped at a short distance from the house and alighted. The door was wide open, a hackney-coach was standing in the middle of the yard—a strange sight before so noble a mansion; the count looked at it with terror, but without daring to inquire its meaning, he rushed towards his apartment.

Two persons were coming down the stairs; he had only time to creep into an alcove to avoid them. It was Mercédès leaning on her son's arm and leaving the house. They passed close by the unhappy being, who, concealed behind the damask curtain, almost felt Mercédès dress brush past him, and his son's warm breath, pronouncing these words:

"Courage, mother! Come, this is no longer our home!"

The words died away, the steps were lost in the distance. The general drew himself up, clinging to the curtain; he uttered the most dreadful sob which ever escaped from the bosom of a father abandoned at the same time by his wife and son. He soon heard the clatter of the iron step of the hackney-coach, then the coachman's voice, and then the rolling of the heavy vehicle shook the windows. He darted to his bedroom to see once more all he had loved in the world; but the hackney-coach drove on and the head of neither Mercédès nor her son appeared at the window to take a last look at the house or the deserted father and husband.

And at the very moment when the wheels of that coach crossed the gateway a report was heard, and a thick smoke escaped through one of the panes of the window, which was broken by the explosion.

Study Guide Questions

For Students:

1. How do Maximillian and Emmanuel react to Albert's decision?
2. Why does Fernand come to meet the Count?
3. Who commits suicide at the end of the chapter and why?

For Reading Club:

1. Discuss the theme of friendship considering the relationship between Maximillian Morrel and Edmond Dantès.
2. Briefly discuss Fernand's meeting with the Count.
3. How does the Count reveal his true identity before Fernand?

CHAPTER 93

Valentine

We may easily conceive where Morrel's appointment was. On leaving Monte Cristo he walked slowly towards Villefort's; we say slowly, for Morrel had more than half an hour to spare to go five hundred steps, but he had hastened to take leave of Monte Cristo because he wished to be alone with his thoughts. He knew his time well—the hour when Valentine was giving Noirtier his breakfast, and was sure not to be disturbed in the performance of this pious duty. Noirtier and Valentine had given him leave to go twice a week, and he was now availing himself of that permission.

He arrived; Valentine was expecting him. Uneasy and almost crazed, she seized his hand and led him to her grandfather. This uneasiness, amounting almost to frenzy, arose from the report Morcerf's adventure had made in the world, for the affair at the Opera was generally known. No one at Villefort's doubted that a duel would ensue from it. Valentine, with her woman's instinct, guessed that Morrel would be Monte Cristo's second, and from the young man's well-known courage and his great affection for the count, she feared that he would not content himself with the passive part assigned to him. We may easily understand how eagerly the particulars were asked for, given, and received; and Morrel could read an indescribable joy in the eyes of his beloved, when she knew that the termination of this affair was as happy as it was unexpected.

"Now," said Valentine, motioning to Morrel to sit down near her grandfather, while she took her seat on his footstool,—"now let us talk about our own affairs. You know, Maximilian, grandpapa once thought of leaving this house, and taking an apartment away from M. de Villefort's."

"Yes," said Maximilian, "I recollect the project, of which I highly approved."

"Well," said Valentine, "you may approve again, for grandpapa is again thinking of it."

"Bravo," said Maximilian.

"And do you know," said Valentine, "what reason grandpapa gives for leaving this house." Noirtier looked at Valentine to impose silence, but she did not notice him; her looks, her eyes, her smile, were all for Morrel.

"Oh, whatever may be M. Noirtier's reason," answered Morrel, "I can readily believe it to be a good one."

"An excellent one," said Valentine. "He pretends the air of the Faubourg Saint-Honoré is not good for me."

"Indeed?" said Morrel; "in that M. Noirtier may be right; you have not seemed to be well for the last fortnight."

"Not very," said Valentine. "And grandpapa has become my physician, and I have the greatest confidence in him, because he knows everything."

"Do you then really suffer?" asked Morrel quickly.

"Oh, it must not be called suffering; I feel a general uneasiness, that is all. I have lost my appetite, and my stomach feels as if it were struggling to get accustomed to something." Noirtier did not lose a word of what Valentine said.

"And what treatment do you adopt for this singular complaint?"

"A very simple one," said Valentine. "I swallow every morning a spoonful of the mixture prepared for my grandfather. When I say one spoonful, I began by one—now I take four. Grandpapa says it is a panacea." Valentine smiled, but it was evident that she suffered.

Maximilian, in his devotedness, gazed silently at her. She was very beautiful, but her usual pallor had increased; her eyes were more brilliant than ever, and her hands, which were generally white like mother-of-pearl, now more resembled wax, to which time was adding a yellowish hue.

From Valentine the young man looked towards Noirtier. The latter watched with strange and deep interest the young girl, absorbed by her affection, and he also, like Morrel, followed those traces of inward suffering which was so little perceptible to a common observer that they escaped the notice of everyone but the grandfather and the lover.

"But," said Morrel, "I thought this mixture, of which you now take four spoonfuls, was prepared for M. Noirtier?"

"I know it is very bitter," said Valentine; "so bitter, that all I drink afterwards appears to have the same taste." Noirtier looked inquiringly at his granddaughter. "Yes, grandpapa," said Valentine; "it is so. Just now, before I came down to you, I drank a glass of sugared water; I left half, because it seemed so bitter." Noirtier turned pale, and made a sign that he wished to speak.

Valentine rose to fetch the dictionary. Noirtier watched her with evident anguish. In fact, the blood was rushing to the young girl's head already, her cheeks were becoming red.

"Oh," cried she, without losing any of her cheerfulness, "this is singular! I can't see! Did the sun shine in my eyes?" And she leaned against the window.

"The sun is not shining," said Morrel, more alarmed by Noirtier's expression than by Valentine's indisposition. He ran towards her. The young girl smiled.

"Cheer up," said she to Noirtier. "Do not be alarmed, Maximilian; it is nothing, and has already passed away. But listen! Do I not hear a carriage in the courtyard?" She opened Noirtier's door, ran to a window in the passage, and returned hastily. "Yes," said she, "it is Madame Danglars and her daughter, who have come to call on us. Good-bye;—I must run away, for they would send here for me, or, rather, farewell till I see you again. Stay with grandpapa, Maximilian; I promise you not to persuade them to stay."

Morrel watched her as she left the room; he heard her ascend the little staircase which led both to Madame de Villefort's apartments and to hers. As soon as she was gone, Noirtier made a sign to Morrel to take the dictionary. Morrel obeyed; guided by Valentine, he had learned how to understand the old man quickly. Accustomed, however, as he was to the work, he had to repeat most of the letters of the alphabet and to find every word in the dictionary, so that it was ten minutes before the thought of the old man was translated by these words,

"Fetch the glass of water and the decanter from Valentine's room."

Morrel rang immediately for the servant who had taken Barrois's situation, and in Noirtier's name gave that order. The servant soon returned. The decanter and the glass were completely empty. Noirtier made a sign that he wished to speak.

"Why are the glass and decanter empty?" asked he; "Valentine said she only drank half the glassful."

The translation of this new question occupied another five minutes.

"I do not know," said the servant, "but the housemaid is in Mademoiselle Valentine's room: perhaps she has emptied them."

"Ask her," said Morrel, translating Noirtier's thought this time by his look. The servant went out, but returned almost immediately. "Mademoiselle Valentine passed through the room to go to Madame de Villefort's," said he; "and in passing, as she was thirsty, she drank what remained in the glass; as for the decanter, Master Edward had emptied that to make a pond for his ducks."

Noirtier raised his eyes to heaven, as a gambler does who stakes his all on one stroke. From that moment the old man's eyes were fixed on the door, and did not quit it.

It was indeed Madame Danglars and her daughter whom Valentine had seen; they had been ushered into Madame de Villefort's room, who had said she would receive them there. That is why Valentine passed through her room, which was on a level with Valentine's, and only separated from it by Edward's. The two ladies entered the drawing-room with that sort of official stiffness which preludes a formal communication. Among worldly people manner is contagious. Madame de Villefort received them with equal solemnity. Valentine entered at this moment, and the formalities were resumed.

"My dear friend," said the baroness, while the two young people were shaking hands, "I and Eugénie are come to be the first to announce to you the approaching marriage of my daughter with Prince Cavalcanti." Danglars kept up the title of prince. The popular banker found that it answered better than count.

"Allow me to present you my sincere congratulations," replied Madame de Villefort. "Prince Cavalcanti appears to be a young man of rare qualities."

"Listen," said the baroness, smiling; "speaking to you as a friend I can say that the prince does not yet appear all he will be. He has about him a little of that foreign manner by which French persons recognize, at first sight, the Italian or German nobleman. Besides, he gives evidence of great kindness of disposition, much keenness of wit, and as to suitability, M. Danglars assures me that his fortune is majestic—that is his word."

"And then," said Eugénie, while turning over the leaves of Madame de Villefort's album, "add that you have taken a great fancy to the young man."

"And," said Madame de Villefort, "I need not ask you if you share that fancy."

"I?" replied Eugénie with her usual candor. "Oh, not the least in the world, madame! My wish was not to confine myself to domestic cares, or the caprices of any man, but to be an artist, and consequently free in heart, in person, and in thought."

Eugénie pronounced these words with so firm a tone that the color mounted to Valentine's cheeks. The timid girl could not understand that vigorous nature which appeared to have none of the timidities of woman.

"At any rate," said she, "since I am to be married whether I will or not, I ought to be thankful to Providence for having released me from my engagement with M. Albert de Morcerf, or I should this day have been the wife of a dishonored man."

"It is true," said the baroness, with that strange simplicity sometimes met with among fashionable ladies, and of which plebeian intercourse can never entirely deprive them,—"it is very true that had not the Morcerfs hesitated, my daughter would have married Monsieur Albert. The general depended much on it; he even came to force M. Danglars. We have had a narrow escape."

"But," said Valentine, timidly, "does all the father's shame revert upon the son? Monsieur Albert appears to me quite innocent of the treason charged against the general."

"Excuse me," said the implacable young girl, "Monsieur Albert claims and well deserves his share. It appears that after having challenged M. de Monte Cristo at the Opera yesterday, he apologized on the ground today."

"Impossible," said Madame de Villefort.

"Ah, my dear friend," said Madame Danglars, with the same simplicity we before noticed, "it is a fact. I heard it from M. Debray, who was present at the explanation."

Valentine also knew the truth, but she did not answer. A single word had reminded her that Morrel was expecting her in M. Noirtier's room. Deeply engaged with a sort of inward contemplation, Valentine had ceased for a moment to join in the conversation. She would, indeed, have found it impossible to repeat what had been said the last few minutes, when suddenly Madame Danglars' hand, pressed on her arm, aroused her from her lethargy.

"What is it?" said she, starting at Madame Danglars' touch as she would have done from an electric shock.

"It is, my dear Valentine," said the baroness, "that you are, doubtless, suffering."

"I?" said the young girl, passing her hand across her burning forehead.

"Yes, look at yourself in that glass; you have turned pale and then red successively, three or four times in one minute."

"Indeed," cried Eugénie, "you are very pale!"

"Oh, do not be alarmed; I have been so for many days." Artless as she was, the young girl knew that this was an opportunity to leave, and besides, Madame de Villefort came to her assistance.

"Retire, Valentine," said she; "you are really suffering, and these ladies will excuse you; drink a glass of pure water, it will restore you."

Valentine kissed Eugénie, bowed to Madame Danglars, who had already risen to take her leave, and went out.

"That poor child," said Madame de Villefort when Valentine was gone, "she makes me very uneasy, and I should not be astonished if she had some serious illness."

Meanwhile, Valentine, in a sort of excitement which she could not quite understand, had crossed Edward's room without noticing some trick of the child, and through her own had reached the little staircase.

She was within three steps of the bottom; she already heard Morrel's voice, when suddenly a cloud passed over her eyes, her stiffened foot missed the step, her hands had no power to hold the baluster, and falling against the wall she lost her balance wholly and toppled to the floor. Morrel bounded to the door, opened it, and found Valentine stretched out at the bottom of the stairs. Quick as a flash, he raised her in his arms and placed her in a chair. Valentine opened her eyes.

"Oh, what a clumsy thing I am," said she with feverish volubility; "I don't know my way. I forgot there were three more steps before the landing."

"You have hurt yourself, perhaps," said Morrel. "What can I do for you, Valentine?"

Valentine looked around her; she saw the deepest terror depicted in Noirtier's eyes.

"Don't worry, dear grandpapa," said she, endeavoring to smile; "it is nothing—it is nothing; I was giddy, that is all."

"Another attack of giddiness," said Morrel, clasping his hands. "Oh, attend to it, Valentine, I entreat you."

"But no," said Valentine,—"no, I tell you it is all past, and it was nothing. Now, let me tell you some news; Eugénie is to be married in a week, and in three days there is to be a grand feast, a betrothal festival. We are all invited, my father, Madame de Villefort, and I—at least, I understood it so."

"When will it be our turn to think of these things? Oh, Valentine, you who have so much influence over your grandpapa, try to make him answer—Soon."

"And do you," said Valentine, "depend on me to stimulate the tardiness and arouse the memory of grandpapa?"

"Yes," cried Morrel, "make haste. So long as you are not mine, Valentine, I shall always think I may lose you."

"Oh," replied Valentine with a convulsive movement, "oh, indeed, Maximilian, you are too timid for an officer, for a soldier who, they say, never knows fear. Ha, ha, ha!"

She burst into a forced and melancholy laugh, her arms stiffened and twisted, her head fell back on her chair, and she remained motionless. The cry of terror which was stopped on Noirtier's lips, seemed to start from his eyes. Morrel understood it; he knew he must call assistance. The young man rang the bell violently; the housemaid who had been in Mademoiselle Valentine's room, and the servant who had replaced Barrois, ran in at the same moment. Valentine was so pale, so cold, so inanimate that without listening to what was said to them they were seized with the fear which pervaded that house, and they flew into the passage crying for help. Madame Danglars and Eugénie were going out at that moment; they heard the cause of the disturbance.

"I told you so!" exclaimed Madame de Villefort. "Poor child!"

Study Guide Questions

For Students:

1. Who comes to meet Valentine?
2. Why is Valentine sick?
3. What is the announcement made by Madame Danglars?

For Reading Club:

1. How does the chapter comment on the theme of family?
2. Compare and contrast the personality of Valentine with Eugénie. Who do you like the most and why?
3. Do you think the chapter alludes to some tragedy that may befall Valentine and Morrel? Why or why not?

CHAPTER 94

Maximilian's Avowal

At the same moment M. de Villefort's voice was heard calling from his study, "What is the matter?"

Morrel looked at Noirtier who had recovered his self-command, and with a glance indicated the closet where once before under somewhat similar circumstances, he had taken refuge. He had only time to get his hat and throw himself breathless into the closet when the procureur's footstep was heard in the passage.

Villefort sprang into the room, ran to Valentine, and took her in his arms.

"A physician, a physician,—M. d'Avrigny!" cried Villefort; "or rather I will go for him myself."

He flew from the apartment, and Morrel at the same moment darted out at the other door. He had been struck to the heart by a frightful recollection—the conversation he had heard between the doctor and Villefort the night of Madame de Saint-Méran's death, recurred to him; these symptoms, to a less alarming extent, were the same which had preceded the death of Barrois. At the same time Monte Cristo's voice seemed to resound in his ear with the words he had heard only two hours before, "Whatever you want, Morrel, come to me; I have great power."

More rapidly than thought, he darted down the Rue Matignon, and thence to the Avenue des Champs-Élysées.

Meanwhile M. de Villefort arrived in a hired cabriolet at M. d'Avrigny's door. He rang so violently that the porter was alarmed. Villefort ran upstairs without saying a word. The porter knew him, and let him pass, only calling to him:

"In his study, Monsieur Procureur—in his study!" Villefort pushed, or rather forced, the door open.

"Ah," said the doctor, "is it you?"

"Yes," said Villefort, closing the door after him, "it is I, who am come in my turn to ask you if we are quite alone. Doctor, my house is accursed!"

"What?" said the latter with apparent coolness, but with deep emotion, "have you another invalid?"

"Yes, doctor," cried Villefort, clutching his hair, "yes!"

D'Avrigny's look implied, "I told you it would be so." Then he slowly uttered these words, "Who is now dying in your house? What new victim is going to accuse you of weakness before God?"

A mournful sob burst from Villefort's heart; he approached the doctor, and seizing his arm,—"Valentine," said he, "it is Valentine's turn!"

"Your daughter!" cried d'Avrigny with grief and surprise.

"You see you were deceived," murmured the magistrate; "come and see her, and on her bed of agony entreat her pardon for having suspected her."

"Each time you have applied to me," said the doctor, "it has been too late; still I will go. But let us make haste, sir; with the enemies you have to do with there is no time to be lost."

"Oh, this time, doctor, you shall not have to reproach me with weakness. This time I will know the assassin, and will pursue him."

"Let us try first to save the victim before we think of revenging her," said d'Avrigny. "Come."

The same cabriolet which had brought Villefort took them back at full speed, and at this moment Morrel rapped at Monte Cristo's door.

The count was in his study and was reading with an angry look something which Bertuccio had brought in haste. Hearing the name of Morrel, who had left him only two hours before, the count raised his head, arose, and sprang to meet him.

"What is the matter, Maximilian?" asked he; "you are pale, and the perspiration rolls from your forehead." Morrel fell into a chair.

"Yes," said he, "I came quickly; I wanted to speak to you."

"Are all your family well?" asked the count, with an affectionate benevolence, whose sincerity no one could for a moment doubt.

"Thank you, count—thank you," said the young man, evidently embarrassed how to begin the conversation; "yes, everyone in my family is well."

"So much the better; yet you have something to tell me?" replied the count with increased anxiety.

"Yes," said Morrel, "it is true; I have but now left a house where death has just entered, to run to you."

"Are you then come from M. de Morcerf's?" asked Monte Cristo.

"No," said Morrel; "is someone dead in his house?"

"The general has just blown his brains out," replied Monte Cristo with great coolness.

"Oh, what a dreadful event!" cried Maximilian.

"Not for the countess, or for Albert," said Monte Cristo; "a dead father or husband is better than a dishonored one,—blood washes out shame."

"Poor countess," said Maximilian, "I pity her very much; she is so noble a woman!"

"Pity Albert also, Maximilian; for believe me he is the worthy son of the countess. But let us return to yourself. You have hastened to me—can I have the happiness of being useful to you?"

"Yes, I need your help: that is I thought like a madman that you could lend me your assistance in a case where God alone can succor me."

"Tell me what it is," replied Monte Cristo.

"Oh," said Morrel, "I know not, indeed, if I may reveal this secret to mortal ears, but fatality impels me, necessity constrains me, count—" Morrel hesitated.

"Do you think I love you?" said Monte Cristo, taking the young man's hand affectionately in his.

"Oh, you encourage me, and something tells me there," placing his hand on his heart, "that I ought to have no secret from you."

"You are right, Morrel; God is speaking to your heart, and your heart speaks to you. Tell me what it says."

"Count, will you allow me to send Baptistin to inquire after someone you know?"

"I am at your service, and still more my servants."

"Oh, I cannot live if she is not better."

"Shall I ring for Baptistin?"

"No, I will go and speak to him myself." Morrel went out, called Baptistin, and whispered a few words to him. The valet ran directly.

"Well, have you sent?" asked Monte Cristo, seeing Morrel return.

"Yes, and now I shall be more calm."

"You know I am waiting," said Monte Cristo, smiling.

"Yes, and I will tell you. One evening I was in a garden; a clump of trees concealed me; no one suspected I was there. Two persons passed near me—allow me to conceal their names for the present; they were speaking in an undertone, and yet I was so interested in what they said that I did not lose a single word."

"This is a gloomy introduction, if I may judge from your pallor and shuddering, Morrel."

"Oh, yes, very gloomy, my friend. Someone had just died in the house to which that garden belonged. One of the persons whose conversation I overheard was the master of the house; the other, the physician. The former was confiding to the latter his grief and fear, for it was the second time within a month that death had suddenly and unexpectedly entered that house which was apparently destined to destruction by some exterminating angel, as an object of God's anger."

"Ah, indeed?" said Monte Cristo, looking earnestly at the young man, and by an imperceptible movement turning his chair, so that he remained in the shade while the light fell full on Maximilian's face.

"Yes," continued Morrel, "death had entered that house twice within one month."

"And what did the doctor answer?" asked Monte Cristo.

"He replied—he replied, that the death was not a natural one, and must be attributed"—

"To what?"

"To poison."

"Indeed!" said Monte Cristo with a slight cough which in moments of extreme emotion helped him to disguise a blush, or his pallor, or the intense interest with which he listened; "indeed, Maximilian, did you hear that?"

"Yes, my dear count, I heard it; and the doctor added that if another death occurred in a similar way he must appeal to justice."

Monte Cristo listened, or appeared to do so, with the greatest calmness.

"Well," said Maximilian, "death came a third time, and neither the master of the house nor the doctor said a word. Death is now, perhaps, striking a fourth blow. Count, what am I bound to do, being in possession of this secret?"

"My dear friend," said Monte Cristo, "you appear to be relating an adventure which we all know by heart. I know the house where you heard it, or one very similar to it; a house with a garden, a master, a physician, and where there have been three unexpected and sudden deaths. Well, I have not intercepted your confidence, and yet I know all that as well as you, and I have no conscientious scruples. No, it does not concern me. You say an exterminating angel appears to have devoted that house to God's anger—well, who says your supposition is not reality? Do not notice things which those whose interest it is to see them pass over. If it is God's justice, instead of his anger, which is walking through that house, Maximilian, turn away your face and let his justice accomplish its purpose."

Morrel shuddered. There was something mournful, solemn, and terrible in the count's manner.

"Besides," continued he, in so changed a tone that no one would have supposed it was the same person speaking—"besides, who says that it will begin again?"

"It has returned, count," exclaimed Morrel; "that is why I hastened to you."

"Well, what do you wish me to do? Do you wish me, for instance, to give information to the procureur?" Monte Cristo uttered the last words with so much meaning that Morrel, starting up, cried out:

"You know of whom I speak, count, do you not?"

"Perfectly well, my good friend; and I will prove it to you by putting the dots to the *i*, or rather by naming the persons. You were walking one evening in M. de Villefort's garden; from what you relate, I suppose it to have been the evening of Madame de Saint-Méran's death. You heard M. de Villefort talking to M. d'Avrigny about the death of M. de Saint-Méran, and that no less surprising, of the countess. M. d'Avrigny said he believed they both proceeded from poison; and you, honest man, have ever since been asking your heart and sounding your conscience to know if you ought to expose or conceal this secret. We are no longer in the Middle Ages; there is no longer a Vehmgericht, or Free Tribunals; what do you want to ask these people? 'Conscience, what hast thou to do with me?' as Sterne said. My dear fellow, let them sleep on, if they are asleep; let them grow pale in their drowsiness, if they are disposed to do so, and pray do you remain in peace, who have no remorse to disturb you."

Deep grief was depicted on Morrel's features; he seized Monte Cristo's hand. "But it is beginning again, I say!"

"Well," said the Count, astonished at his perseverance, which he could not understand, and looking still more earnestly at Maximilian, "let it begin again,—it is like the house of the Atreidae;[12] God has condemned them, and they must submit to their punishment. They will all disappear, like the fabrics children build with cards, and which fall, one by one, under the breath of their builder, even if there are two hundred of them. Three months since it was M. de Saint-Méran; Madame de Saint-Méran two months since; the other day it was Barrois; today, the old Noirtier, or young Valentine."

"You knew it?" cried Morrel, in such a paroxysm of terror that Monte Cristo started,—he whom the falling heavens would have found unmoved; "you knew it, and said nothing?"

---

[12] In the old Greek legend the Atreidae, or children of Atreus, were doomed to punishment because of the abominable crime of their father. The Agamemnon of Aeschylus is based on this legend.

"And what is it to me?" replied Monte Cristo, shrugging his shoulders; "do I know those people? and must I lose the one to save the other? Faith, no, for between the culprit and the victim I have no choice."

"But I," cried Morrel, groaning with sorrow, "I love her!"

"You love?—whom?" cried Monte Cristo, starting to his feet, and seizing the two hands which Morrel was raising towards heaven.

"I love most fondly—I love madly—I love as a man who would give his life-blood to spare her a tear—I love Valentine de Villefort, who is being murdered at this moment! Do you understand me? I love her; and I ask God and you how I can save her?"

Monte Cristo uttered a cry which those only can conceive who have heard the roar of a wounded lion. "Unhappy man," cried he, wringing his hands in his turn; "you love Valentine,—that daughter of an accursed race!"

Never had Morrel witnessed such an expression—never had so terrible an eye flashed before his face—never had the genius of terror he had so often seen, either on the battle-field or in the murderous nights of Algeria, shaken around him more dreadful fire. He drew back terrified.

As for Monte Cristo, after this ebullition he closed his eyes as if dazzled by internal light. In a moment he restrained himself so powerfully that the tempestuous heaving of his breast subsided, as turbulent and foaming waves yield to the sun's genial influence when the cloud has passed. This silence, self-control, and struggle lasted about twenty seconds, then the count raised his pallid face.

"See," said he, "my dear friend, how God punishes the most thoughtless and unfeeling men for their indifference, by presenting dreadful scenes to their view. I, who was looking on, an eager and curious spectator,—I, who was watching the working of this mournful tragedy,—I, who like a wicked angel was laughing at the evil men committed protected by secrecy (a secret is easily kept by the rich and powerful), I am in my turn bitten by the serpent whose tortuous course I was watching, and bitten to the heart!"

Morrel groaned.

"Come, come," continued the count, "complaints are unavailing, be a man, be strong, be full of hope, for I am here and will watch over you."

Morrel shook his head sorrowfully.

"I tell you to hope. Do you understand me?" cried Monte Cristo. "Remember that I never uttered a falsehood and am never deceived. It is twelve o'clock, Maximilian; thank heaven that you came at noon rather than in the evening, or tomorrow morning. Listen, Morrel—it is noon; if Valentine is not now dead, she will not die."

"How so?" cried Morrel, "when I left her dying?"

Monte Cristo pressed his hands to his forehead. What was passing in that brain, so loaded with dreadful secrets? What does the angel of light or the angel of darkness say to that mind, at once implacable and generous? God only knows.

Monte Cristo raised his head once more, and this time he was calm as a child awaking from its sleep.

"Maximilian," said he, "return home. I command you not to stir—attempt nothing, not to let your countenance betray a thought, and I will send you tidings. Go."

"Oh, count, you overwhelm me with that coolness. Have you, then, power against death? Are you superhuman? Are you an angel?" And the young man, who had never shrunk from danger, shrank before Monte Cristo with indescribable terror. But Monte Cristo looked at him with so melancholy and sweet a smile, that Maximilian felt the tears filling his eyes.

"I can do much for you, my friend," replied the count. "Go; I must be alone."

Morrel, subdued by the extraordinary ascendancy Monte Cristo exercised over everything around him, did not endeavor to resist it. He pressed the count's hand and left. He stopped one moment at the door for Baptistin, whom he saw in the Rue Matignon, and who was running.

Meanwhile, Villefort and d'Avrigny had made all possible haste, Valentine had not revived from her fainting fit on their arrival, and the doctor examined the invalid with all the care the circumstances demanded, and with an interest which the knowledge of the secret intensified twofold. Villefort, closely watching his countenance and his lips, awaited the result of the examination. Noirtier, paler than even the young girl, more eager than Villefort for the decision, was watching also intently and affectionately.

At last d'Avrigny slowly uttered these words: "She is still alive!"

"Still?" cried Villefort; "oh, doctor, what a dreadful word is that."

"Yes," said the physician, "I repeat it; she is still alive, and I am astonished at it."

"But is she safe?" asked the father.

"Yes, since she lives."

At that moment d'Avrigny's glance met Noirtier's eye. It glistened with such extraordinary joy, so rich and full of thought, that the physician was struck. He placed the young girl again on the chair,—her lips were scarcely discernible, they were so pale and white, as well as her whole face,—and remained motionless, looking at Noirtier, who appeared to anticipate and commend all he did.

"Sir," said d'Avrigny to Villefort, "call Mademoiselle Valentine's maid, if you please."

Villefort went himself to find her; and d'Avrigny approached Noirtier.

"Have you something to tell me?" asked he. The old man winked his eyes expressively, which we may remember was his only way of expressing his approval.

"Privately?"

"Yes."

"Well, I will remain with you." At this moment Villefort returned, followed by the lady's maid; and after her came Madame de Villefort.

"What is the matter, then, with this dear child? she has just left me, and she complained of being indisposed, but I did not think seriously of it."

The young woman with tears in her eyes and every mark of affection of a true mother, approached Valentine and took her hand. D'Avrigny continued to look at Noirtier; he saw the eyes of the old man dilate and become round, his cheeks turn pale and tremble; the perspiration stood in drops upon his forehead.

"Ah," said he, involuntarily following Noirtier's eyes, which were fixed on Madame de Villefort, who repeated:

"This poor child would be better in bed. Come, Fanny, we will put her to bed."

M. d'Avrigny, who saw that would be a means of his remaining alone with Noirtier, expressed his opinion that it was the best thing that could be done; but he forbade that anything should be given to her except what he ordered.

They carried Valentine away; she had revived, but could scarcely move or speak, so shaken was her frame by the attack. She had, however, just power to give one parting look to her grandfather, who in losing her seemed to be resigning his very soul. D'Avrigny followed the invalid, wrote a prescription, ordered Villefort to take a cabriolet, go in person to a chemist's to get the prescribed medicine, bring it himself, and wait for him in his daughter's room. Then, having renewed his injunction not to give Valentine anything, he went down again to Noirtier, shut the doors carefully, and after convincing himself that no one was listening:

"Do you," said he, "know anything of this young lady's illness?"

"Yes," said the old man.

"We have no time to lose; I will question, and do you answer me." Noirtier made a sign that he was ready to answer. "Did you anticipate the accident which has happened to your granddaughter?"

"Yes." D'Avrigny reflected a moment; then approaching Noirtier:

"Pardon what I am going to say," added he, "but no indication should be neglected in this terrible situation. Did you see poor Barrois die?" Noirtier raised his eyes to heaven.

"Do you know of what he died!" asked d'Avrigny, placing his hand on Noirtier's shoulder.

"Yes," replied the old man.

"Do you think he died a natural death?" A sort of smile was discernible on the motionless lips of Noirtier.

"Then you have thought that Barrois was poisoned?"

"Yes."

"Do you think the poison he fell a victim to was intended for him?"

"No."

"Do you think the same hand which unintentionally struck Barrois has now attacked Valentine?"

"Yes."

"Then will she die too?" asked d'Avrigny, fixing his penetrating gaze on Noirtier. He watched the effect of this question on the old man.

"No," replied he with an air of triumph which would have puzzled the most clever diviner.

"Then you hope?" said d'Avrigny, with surprise.

"Yes."

"What do you hope?" The old man made him understand with his eyes that he could not answer.

"Ah, yes, it is true," murmured d'Avrigny. Then, turning to Noirtier,—"Do you hope the assassin will be tried?"

"No."

"Then you hope the poison will take no effect on Valentine?"

"Yes."

"It is no news to you," added d'Avrigny, "to tell you that an attempt has been made to poison her?" The old man made a sign that he entertained no doubt upon the subject. "Then how do you hope Valentine will escape?"

Noirtier kept his eyes steadfastly fixed on the same spot. D'Avrigny followed the direction and saw that they were fixed on a bottle containing the mixture which he took every morning. "Ah, indeed?" said d'Avrigny, struck with a sudden thought, "has it occurred to you"—Noirtier did not let him finish.

"Yes," said he.

"To prepare her system to resist poison?"

"Yes."

"By accustoming her by degrees—"

"Yes, yes, yes," said Noirtier, delighted to be understood.

"Of course. I had told you that there was brucine in the mixture I give you."

"Yes."

"And by accustoming her to that poison, you have endeavored to neutralize the effect of a similar poison?" Noirtier's joy continued. "And you have succeeded," exclaimed d'Avrigny. "Without that precaution Valentine would have died before assistance could have been procured. The dose has been excessive, but she has only been shaken by it; and this time, at any rate, Valentine will not die."

A superhuman joy expanded the old man's eyes, which were raised towards heaven with an expression of infinite gratitude. At this moment Villefort returned.

"Here, doctor," said he, "is what you sent me for."

"Was this prepared in your presence?"

"Yes," replied the procureur.

"Have you not let it go out of your hands?"

"No."

D'Avrigny took the bottle, poured some drops of the mixture it contained in the hollow of his hand, and swallowed them.

"Well," said he, "let us go to Valentine; I will give instructions to everyone, and you, M. de Villefort, will yourself see that no one deviates from them."

At the moment when d'Avrigny was returning to Valentine's room, accompanied by Villefort, an Italian priest, of serious demeanor and calm and firm tone, hired for his use the house adjoining the hotel of M. de Villefort. No one knew how the three former tenants of that house left it. About two hours afterwards its foundation was reported to be unsafe; but the report did not prevent the new occupant establishing himself there with his modest furniture the same day at five o'clock. The lease was drawn up for three, six, or nine years by the new tenant, who, according to the rule of the proprietor, paid six months in advance.

This new tenant, who, as we have said, was an Italian, was called Il Signor Giacomo Busoni. Workmen were immediately called in, and that same night the passengers at the end of the faubourg saw with surprise that carpenters and masons were occupied in repairing the lower part of the tottering house.

Study Guide Questions

For Students:

1. Why does M. de Villefort go to M. D'Avrigny?
2. Why does Morrel hurry to the Count's house?
3. What does the Count tell Maximillian Morrel about M. de Morcerf?

For Reading Club:

1. What secret does Maximillian share with the Count? Do you think the Count already knows it?
2. Discuss the information that M. Noirtier shares with M. D'Avrigny.
3. Discuss Maximillian's avowal. Why do you think he trusts the Count so much to share everything with him?

CHAPTER 95

Father and Daughter

We saw in a preceding chapter how Madame Danglars went formally to announce to Madame de Villefort the approaching marriage of Eugénie Danglars and M. Andrea Cavalcanti. This formal announcement, which implied or appeared to imply, the approval of all the persons concerned in this momentous affair, had been preceded by a scene to which our readers must be admitted. We beg them to take one step backward, and to transport themselves, the morning of that day of great catastrophes, into the showy, gilded salon we have before shown them, and which was the pride of its owner, Baron Danglars.

In this room, at about ten o'clock in the morning, the banker himself had been walking to and fro for some minutes thoughtfully and in evident uneasiness, watching both doors, and listening to every sound. When his patience was exhausted, he called his valet.

"Étienne," said he, "see why Mademoiselle Eugénie has asked me to meet her in the drawing-room, and why she makes me wait so long."

Having given this vent to his ill-humor, the baron became more calm; Mademoiselle Danglars had that morning requested an interview with her father, and had fixed on the gilded drawing-room as the spot. The singularity of this step, and above all its formality, had not a little surprised the banker, who had immediately obeyed his daughter by repairing first to the drawing-room. Étienne soon returned from his errand.

"Mademoiselle's lady's maid says, sir, that mademoiselle is finishing her toilette, and will be here shortly."

Danglars nodded, to signify that he was satisfied. To the world and to his servants Danglars assumed the character of the good-natured man and the indulgent father.

This was one of his parts in the popular comedy he was performing,—a make-up he had adopted and which suited him about as well as the masks worn on the classic stage by paternal actors, who seen from one side, were the image of geniality, and from the other showed lips drawn down in chronic ill-temper. Let us hasten to say that in private the genial side descended to the level of the other, so that generally the indulgent man disappeared to give place to the brutal husband and domineering father.

"Why the devil does that foolish girl, who pretends to wish to speak to me, not come into my study? and why on earth does she want to speak to me at all?"

He was turning this thought over in his brain for the twentieth time, when the door opened and Eugénie appeared, attired in a figured black satin dress, her hair dressed and gloves on, as if she were going to the Italian Opera.

"Well, Eugénie, what is it you want with me? and why in this solemn drawing-room when the study is so comfortable?"

"I quite understand why you ask, sir," said Eugénie, making a sign that her father might be seated, "and in fact your two questions suggest fully the theme of our conversation. I will answer them both, and contrary to the usual method, the last first, because it is the least difficult. I have chosen the drawing-room, sir, as our place of meeting, in order to avoid the disagreeable impressions and influences of a banker's study. Those gilded cashbooks, drawers locked like gates of fortresses, heaps of bank-bills, come from I know not where, and the quantities of letters from England, Holland, Spain, India, China, and Peru, have generally a strange influence on a father's mind, and make him forget that there is in the world an interest greater and more sacred than the good opinion of his correspondents. I have, therefore, chosen this drawing-room, where you see, smiling and happy in their magnificent frames, your portrait, mine, my mother's, and all sorts of rural landscapes and touching pastorals. I rely much on external impressions; perhaps, with regard to you, they are immaterial, but I should be no artist if I had not some fancies."

"Very well," replied M. Danglars, who had listened to all this preamble with imperturbable coolness, but without understanding a word, since like every man burdened with thoughts of the past, he was occupied with seeking the thread of his own ideas in those of the speaker.

"There is, then, the second point cleared up, or nearly so," said Eugénie, without the least confusion, and with that masculine pointedness which distinguished her gesture and her language; "and you appear satisfied with the explanation. Now, let us return to the first. You ask me why I have requested this interview; I will tell you in two words, sir; I will not marry count Andrea Cavalcanti."

Danglars leaped from his chair and raised his eyes and arms towards heaven.

"Yes, indeed, sir," continued Eugénie, still quite calm; "you are astonished, I see; for since this little affair began, I have not manifested the slightest opposition, and yet I am always sure, when the opportunity arrives, to oppose a determined and absolute will to people who have not consulted me, and things which displease me. However, this time, my tranquillity, or passiveness as philosophers say, proceeded from another source; it proceeded from a wish, like a submissive and devoted daughter" (a slight smile was observable on the purple lips of the young girl), "to practice obedience."

"Well?" asked Danglars.

"Well, sir," replied Eugénie, "I have tried to the very last and now that the moment has come, I feel in spite of all my efforts that it is impossible."

"But," said Danglars, whose weak mind was at first quite overwhelmed with the weight of this pitiless logic, marking evident premeditation and force of will, "what is your reason for this refusal, Eugénie? what reason do you assign?"

"My reason?" replied the young girl. "Well, it is not that the man is more ugly, more foolish, or more disagreeable than any other; no, M. Andrea Cavalcanti may appear to those who look at men's faces and figures as a very good specimen of his kind. It is not, either, that my heart is less touched by him than any other; that would be a schoolgirl's reason, which I consider quite beneath me. I actually love no one, sir; you know it, do you not? I do not then see why, without real necessity, I should encumber my life with a perpetual companion. Has not some sage said, 'Nothing too much'? and another, 'I carry all my effects with me'? I have been taught these two aphorisms in Latin and in Greek; one is, I believe, from Phædrus, and the other from Bias. Well, my dear father, in the shipwreck of life—for life is an eternal shipwreck of our hopes—I cast into the sea my useless encumbrance, that is all, and I remain with my own will, disposed to live perfectly alone, and consequently perfectly free."

"Unhappy girl, unhappy girl!" murmured Danglars, turning pale, for he knew from long experience the solidity of the obstacle he had so suddenly encountered.

"Unhappy girl," replied Eugénie, "unhappy girl, do you say, sir? No, indeed; the exclamation appears quite theatrical and affected. Happy, on the contrary, for what am I in want of? The world calls me beautiful. It is something to be well received. I like a favorable reception; it expands the countenance, and those around me do not then appear so ugly. I possess a share of wit, and a certain relative sensibility, which enables me to draw from life in general, for the support of mine, all I meet with that is good, like the monkey who cracks the nut to get at its contents. I am rich, for you have one of the first fortunes in France. I am your only daughter, and you are not so exacting as the fathers of the Porte Saint-Martin and Gaîté, who disinherit their daughters for not giving them grandchildren. Besides, the provident law has deprived you of the power to disinherit me, at least entirely, as it has also of the power to compel me to marry Monsieur This or Monsieur That. And so—being, beautiful, witty, somewhat talented, as the comic operas say, and rich—and that is happiness, sir—why do you call me unhappy?"

Danglars, seeing his daughter smiling, and proud even to insolence, could not entirely repress his brutal feelings, but they betrayed themselves only by an exclamation. Under the fixed and inquiring gaze levelled at him from under those beautiful black eyebrows, he prudently turned away, and calmed himself immediately, daunted by the power of a resolute mind.

"Truly, my daughter," replied he with a smile, "you are all you boast of being, excepting one thing; I will not too hastily tell you which, but would rather leave you to guess it."

Eugénie looked at Danglars, much surprised that one flower of her crown of pride, with which she had so superbly decked herself, should be disputed.

"My daughter," continued the banker, "you have perfectly explained to me the sentiments which influence a girl like you, who is determined she will not marry; now it remains for me to tell you the motives of a father like me, who has decided that his daughter shall marry."

Eugénie bowed, not as a submissive daughter, but as an adversary prepared for a discussion.

"My daughter," continued Danglars, "when a father asks his daughter to choose a husband, he has always some reason for wishing her to marry. Some are affected with the mania of which you spoke just now, that of living again in their grandchildren. This is not my weakness, I tell you at once; family joys have no charm for me. I may acknowledge this to a daughter whom I know to be philosophical enough to understand my indifference, and not to impute it to me as a crime."

"This is not to the purpose," said Eugénie; "let us speak candidly, sir; I admire candor."

"Oh," said Danglars, "I can, when circumstances render it desirable, adopt your system, although it may not be my general practice. I will therefore proceed. I have proposed to you to marry, not for your sake, for indeed I did not think of you in the least at the moment (you admire candor, and will now be satisfied, I hope); but because it suited me to marry you as soon as possible, on account of certain commercial speculations I am desirous of entering into." Eugénie became uneasy.

"It is just as I tell you, I assure you, and you must not be angry with me, for you have sought this disclosure. I do not willingly enter into arithmetical explanations with an artist like you, who fears to enter my study lest she should imbibe disagreeable or anti-poetic impressions and sensations. But in that same banker's study, where you very willingly presented yourself yesterday to ask for the thousand francs I give you monthly for pocket-money, you must know, my dear young lady, that many things may be learned, useful even to a girl who will not marry. There one may learn, for instance, what, out of regard to your nervous susceptibility, I will inform you of in the drawing-room, namely, that the credit of a banker is his physical and moral life; that credit sustains him as breath animates the body; and M. de Monte Cristo once gave me a lecture on that subject, which I have never forgotten. There we may learn that as credit sinks, the body becomes a corpse, and this is what must happen very soon to the banker who is proud to own so good a logician as you for his daughter."

But Eugénie, instead of stooping, drew herself up under the blow. "Ruined?" said she.

"Exactly, my daughter; that is precisely what I mean," said Danglars, almost digging his nails into his breast, while he preserved on his harsh features the smile of the heartless though clever man; "ruined—yes, that is it."

"Ah!" said Eugénie.

"Yes, ruined! Now it is revealed, this secret so full of horror, as the tragic poet says. Now, my daughter, learn from my lips how you may alleviate this misfortune, so far as it will affect you."

"Oh," cried Eugénie, "you are a bad physiognomist, if you imagine I deplore on my own account the catastrophe of which you warn me. I ruined? and what will that signify to me? Have I not my talent left? Can I not, like Pasta, Malibran, Grisi, acquire for myself what you would never have given me, whatever might have been your fortune, a hundred or a hundred and fifty thousand livres per annum, for which I shall be indebted to no one but myself; and which, instead of being given as you gave me those poor twelve thousand francs, with sour looks and reproaches for my prodigality, will be accompanied with acclamations, with bravos, and with flowers? And if I do not possess that talent, which your smiles prove to me you doubt, should I not still have that ardent love of independence, which will be a substitute for wealth, and which in my mind supersedes even the instinct of self-preservation? No, I grieve not on my own account, I shall always find a resource; my books, my pencils, my piano, all the things which cost but little, and which I shall be able to procure, will remain my own.

"Do you think that I sorrow for Madame Danglars? Undeceive yourself again; either I am greatly mistaken, or she has provided against the catastrophe which threatens you, and, which will pass over without affecting her. She has taken care for herself,—at least I hope so,—for her attention has not been diverted from her projects by watching over me. She has fostered my independence by professedly indulging my love for liberty. Oh, no, sir; from my childhood I have seen too much, and understood too much, of what has passed around me, for misfortune to have an undue power over me. From my earliest recollections, I have been beloved by no one—so much the worse; that has naturally led me to love no one—so much the better—now you have my profession of faith."

"Then," said Danglars, pale with anger, which was not at all due to offended paternal love,—"then, mademoiselle, you persist in your determination to accelerate my ruin?"

"Your ruin? I accelerate your ruin? What do you mean? I do not understand you."

"So much the better, I have a ray of hope left; listen."

"I am all attention," said Eugénie, looking so earnestly at her father that it was an effort for the latter to endure her unrelenting gaze.

"M. Cavalcanti," continued Danglars, "is about to marry you, and will place in my hands his fortune, amounting to three million livres."

"That is admirable!" said Eugénie with sovereign contempt, smoothing her gloves out one upon the other.

"You think I shall deprive you of those three millions," said Danglars; "but do not fear it. They are destined to produce at least ten. I and a brother banker have obtained a grant of a railway, the only industrial enterprise which in these days promises to make good the fabulous prospects that Law once held out to the eternally deluded Parisians, in the fantastic Mississippi scheme. As I look at it, a millionth part of a railway is worth fully as much as an acre of waste land on the banks of the Ohio. We make in our case a deposit, on a mortgage, which is an advance, as you see, since we gain at least ten, fifteen, twenty, or a hundred livres' worth of iron in exchange for our money. Well, within a week I am to deposit four millions for my share; the four millions, I promise you, will produce ten or twelve."

"But during my visit to you the day before yesterday, sir, which you appear to recollect so well," replied Eugénie, "I saw you arranging a deposit—is not that the term?—of five millions and a half; you even pointed it out to me in two drafts on the treasury, and you were astonished that so valuable a paper did not dazzle my eyes like lightning."

"Yes, but those five millions and a half are not mine, and are only a proof of the great confidence placed in me; my title of popular banker has gained me the confidence of charitable institutions, and the five millions and a half belong to them; at any other time I should not have hesitated to make use of them, but the great losses I have recently sustained are well known, and, as I told you, my credit is rather shaken. That deposit may be at any moment withdrawn, and if I had employed it for another purpose, I should bring on me a disgraceful bankruptcy. I do not despise bankruptcies, believe me, but they must be those which enrich, not those which ruin. Now, if you marry M. Cavalcanti, and I get the three millions, or even if it is thought I am going to get them, my credit will be restored, and my fortune, which for the last month or two has been swallowed up in gulfs which have been opened in my path by an inconceivable fatality, will revive. Do you understand me?"

"Perfectly; you pledge me for three millions, do you not?"

"The greater the amount, the more flattering it is to you; it gives you an idea of your value."

"Thank you. One word more, sir; do you promise me to make what use you can of the report of the fortune M. Cavalcanti will bring without touching the money? This is no act of selfishness, but of delicacy. I am willing to help rebuild your fortune, but I will not be an accomplice in the ruin of others."

"But since I tell you," cried Danglars, "that with these three million—"

"Do you expect to recover your position, sir, without touching those three million?"

"I hope so, if the marriage should take place and confirm my credit."

"Shall you be able to pay M. Cavalcanti the five hundred thousand francs you promise for my dowry?"

"He shall receive them on returning from the mayor's[13]."

"Very well!"

"What next? what more do you want?"

"I wish to know if, in demanding my signature, you leave me entirely free in my person?"

"Absolutely."

"Then, as I said before, sir,—very well; I am ready to marry M. Cavalcanti."

"But what are you up to?"

"Ah, that is my affair. What advantage should I have over you, if knowing your secret I were to tell you mine?"

Danglars bit his lips. "Then," said he, "you are ready to pay the official visits, which are absolutely indispensable?"

"Yes," replied Eugénie.

"And to sign the contract in three days?"

"Yes."

"Then, in my turn, I also say, very well!"

---

[13] The performance of the civil marriage.

Danglars pressed his daughter's hand in his. But, extraordinary to relate, the father did not say, "Thank you, my child," nor did the daughter smile at her father.

"Is the conference ended?" asked Eugénie, rising.

Danglars motioned that he had nothing more to say. Five minutes afterwards the piano resounded to the touch of Mademoiselle d'Armilly's fingers, and Mademoiselle Danglars was singing Brabantio's malediction on Desdemona. At the end of the piece Étienne entered, and announced to Eugénie that the horses were to the carriage, and that the baroness was waiting for her to pay her visits. We have seen them at Villefort's; they proceeded then on their course.

Study Guide Questions

For Students:

1. What does Eugénie tell her father about her upcoming marriage?
2. What are Danglars' motives behind Eugénie's wedding?
3. On what condition does Eugénie agree to marry Cavalcanti?

For Reading Club:

1. Discuss Eugénie's reason for not getting married. Do you think such reasons exist in contemporary society?
2. Discuss Eugénie's concept of happiness. Do you agree with it?
3. Discuss the relationship between father and daughter. Do you think such relationships exist in contemporary society?

VOLUME FIVE

CHAPTER 96

The Contract

Three days after the scene we have just described, namely towards five o'clock in the afternoon of the day fixed for the signature of the contract between Mademoiselle Eugénie Danglars and Andrea Cavalcanti, whom the banker persisted in calling prince, a fresh breeze was stirring the leaves in the little garden in front of the Count of Monte Cristo's house, and the count was preparing to go out. While his horses were impatiently pawing the ground, held in by the coachman, who had been seated a quarter of an hour on his box, the elegant phaeton with which we are familiar rapidly turned the angle of the entrance-gate, and cast out on the doorsteps M. Andrea Cavalcanti, as decked up and gay as if he were going to marry a princess.

He inquired after the count with his usual familiarity, and ascending lightly to the first story met him at the top of the stairs.

The count stopped on seeing the young man. As for Andrea, he was launched, and when he was once launched nothing stopped him.

"Ah, good morning, my dear count," said he.

"Ah, M. Andrea," said the latter, with his half-jesting tone; "how do you do?"

"Charmingly, as you see. I am come to talk to you about a thousand things; but, first tell me, were you going out or just returned?"

"I was going out, sir."

"Then, in order not to hinder you, I will get up with you if you please in your carriage, and Tom shall follow with my phaeton in tow."

"No," said the count, with an imperceptible smile of contempt, for he had no wish to be seen in the young man's society,—"no; I prefer listening to you here, my dear M. Andrea; we can chat better in-doors, and there is no coachman to overhear our conversation."

The count returned to a small drawing-room on the first floor, sat down, and crossing his legs motioned to the young man to take a seat also. Andrea assumed his gayest manner.

"You know, my dear count," said he, "the ceremony is to take place this evening. At nine o'clock the contract is to be signed at my father-in-law's."

"Ah, indeed?" said Monte Cristo.

"What; is it news to you? Has not M. Danglars informed you of the ceremony?"

"Oh, yes," said the count; "I received a letter from him yesterday, but I do not think the hour was mentioned."

"Possibly my father-in-law trusted to its general notoriety."

"Well," said Monte Cristo, "you are fortunate, M. Cavalcanti; it is a most suitable alliance you are contracting, and Mademoiselle Danglars is a handsome girl."

"Yes, indeed she is," replied Cavalcanti, in a very modest tone.

"Above all, she is very rich,—at least, I believe so," said Monte Cristo.

"Very rich, do you think?" replied the young man.

"Doubtless; it is said M. Danglars conceals at least half of his fortune."

"And he acknowledges fifteen or twenty millions," said Andrea with a look sparkling with joy.

"Without reckoning," added Monte Cristo, "that he is on the eve of entering into a sort of speculation already in vogue in the United States and in England, but quite novel in France."

"Yes, yes, I know what you mean,—the railway, of which he has obtained the grant, is it not?"

"Precisely; it is generally believed he will gain ten millions by that affair."

"Ten millions! Do you think so? It is magnificent!" said Cavalcanti, who was quite confounded at the metallic sound of these golden words.

"Without reckoning," replied Monte Cristo, "that all his fortune will come to you, and justly too, since Mademoiselle Danglars is an only daughter. Besides, your own fortune, as your father assured me, is almost equal to that of your betrothed. But enough of money matters. Do you know, M. Andrea, I think you have managed this affair rather skilfully?"

"Not badly, by any means," said the young man; "I was born for a diplomatist."

"Well, you must become a diplomatist; diplomacy, you know, is something that is not to be acquired; it is instinctive. Have you lost your heart?"

"Indeed, I fear it," replied Andrea, in the tone in which he had heard Dorante or Valère reply to Alceste[14] at the Théâtre Français.

"Is your love returned?"

"I suppose so," said Andrea with a triumphant smile, "since I am accepted. But I must not forget one grand point."

"Which?"

"That I have been singularly assisted."

"Nonsense."

"I have, indeed."

"By circumstances?"

"No; by you."

"By me? Not at all, prince," said Monte Cristo laying a marked stress on the title, "what have I done for you? Are not your name, your social position, and your merit sufficient?"

"No," said Andrea,—"no; it is useless for you to say so, count. I maintain that the position of a man like you has done more than my name, my social position, and my merit."

"You are completely mistaken, sir," said Monte Cristo coldly, who felt the perfidious manœuvre of the young man, and understood the bearing of his words; "you only acquired my protection after the influence and fortune of your father had been ascertained; for, after all, who procured for me, who had never seen either you or your illustrious father, the pleasure of your acquaintance?—two of my good friends, Lord Wilmore and the Abbé Busoni. What encouraged me not to become your surety, but to patronize you?—your father's name, so well known in Italy and so highly honored. Personally, I do not know you."

This calm tone and perfect ease made Andrea feel that he was, for the moment, restrained by a more muscular hand than his own, and that the restraint could not be easily broken through.

"Oh, then my father has really a very large fortune, count?"

"It appears so, sir," replied Monte Cristo.

"Do you know if the marriage settlement he promised me has come?"

"I have been advised of it."

"But the three millions?"

"The three millions are probably on the road."

"Then I shall really have them?"

---

[14] In Molière's comedy, *Le Misanthrope*.

"Oh, well," said the count, "I do not think you have yet known the want of money."

Andrea was so surprised that he pondered the matter for a moment. Then, arousing from his reverie:

"Now, sir, I have one request to make to you, which you will understand, even if it should be disagreeable to you."

"Proceed," said Monte Cristo.

"I have formed an acquaintance, thanks to my good fortune, with many noted persons, and have, at least for the moment, a crowd of friends. But marrying, as I am about to do, before all Paris, I ought to be supported by an illustrious name, and in the absence of the paternal hand some powerful one ought to lead me to the altar; now, my father is not coming to Paris, is he?"

"He is old, covered with wounds, and suffers dreadfully, he says, in travelling."

"I understand; well, I am come to ask a favor of you."

"Of me?"

"Yes, of you."

"And pray what may it be?"

"Well, to take his part."

"Ah, my dear sir! What?—after the varied relations I have had the happiness to sustain towards you, can it be that you know me so little as to ask such a thing? Ask me to lend you half a million and, although such a loan is somewhat rare, on my honor, you would annoy me less! Know, then, what I thought I had already told you, that in participation in this world's affairs, more especially in their moral aspects, the Count of Monte Cristo has never ceased to entertain the scruples and even the superstitions of the East. I, who have a seraglio at Cairo, one at Smyrna, and one at Constantinople, preside at a wedding?—never!"

"Then you refuse me?"

"Decidedly; and were you my son or my brother I would refuse you in the same way."

"But what must be done?" said Andrea, disappointed.

"You said just now that you had a hundred friends."

"Very true, but you introduced me at M. Danglars'."

"Not at all! Let us recall the exact facts. You met him at a dinner party at my house, and you introduced yourself at his house; that is a totally different affair."

"Yes, but, by my marriage, you have forwarded that."

"I?—not in the least, I beg you to believe. Recollect what I told you when you asked me to propose you. 'Oh, I never make matches, my dear prince, it is my settled principle.'" Andrea bit his lips.

"But, at least, you will be there?"

"Will all Paris be there?"

"Oh, certainly."

"Well, like all Paris, I shall be there too," said the count.

"And will you sign the contract?"

"I see no objection to that; my scruples do not go thus far."

"Well, since you will grant me no more, I must be content with what you give me. But one word more, count."

"What is it?"

"Advice."

"Be careful; advice is worse than a service."

"Oh, you can give me this without compromising yourself."

"Tell me what it is."

"Is my wife's fortune five hundred thousand livres?"

"That is the sum M. Danglars himself announced."

"Must I receive it, or leave it in the hands of the notary?"

"This is the way such affairs are generally arranged when it is wished to do them stylishly: Your two solicitors appoint a meeting, when the contract is signed, for the next or the following day; then they exchange the two portions, for which they each give a receipt; then, when the marriage is celebrated, they place the amount at your disposal as the chief member of the alliance."

"Because," said Andrea, with a certain ill-concealed uneasiness, "I thought I heard my father-in-law say that he intended embarking our property in that famous railway affair of which you spoke just now."

"Well," replied Monte Cristo, "it will be the way, everybody says, of trebling your fortune in twelve months. Baron Danglars is a good father, and knows how to calculate."

"In that case," said Andrea, "everything is all right, excepting your refusal, which quite grieves me."

"You must attribute it only to natural scruples under similar circumstances."

"Well," said Andrea, "let it be as you wish. This evening, then, at nine o'clock."

"Adieu till then."

Notwithstanding a slight resistance on the part of Monte Cristo, whose lips turned pale, but who preserved his ceremonious smile, Andrea seized the count's hand, pressed it, jumped into his phaeton, and disappeared.

The four or five remaining hours before nine o'clock arrived, Andrea employed in riding, paying visits,—designed to induce those of whom he had spoken to appear at the banker's in their gayest equipages,—dazzling them by promises of shares in schemes which have since turned every brain, and in which Danglars was just taking the initiative.

In fact, at half-past eight in the evening the grand salon, the gallery adjoining, and the three other drawing-rooms on the same floor, were filled with a perfumed crowd, who sympathized but little in the event, but who all participated in that love of being present wherever there is anything fresh to be seen. An Academician would say that the entertainments of the fashionable world are collections of flowers which attract inconstant butterflies, famished bees, and buzzing drones.

No one could deny that the rooms were splendidly illuminated; the light streamed forth on the gilt mouldings and the silk hangings; and all the bad taste of decorations, which had only their richness to boast of, shone in its splendor. Mademoiselle Eugénie was dressed with elegant simplicity in a figured white silk dress, and a white rose half concealed in her jet black hair was her only ornament, unaccompanied by a single jewel. Her eyes, however, betrayed that perfect confidence which contradicted the girlish simplicity of this modest attire.

Madame Danglars was chatting at a short distance with Debray, Beauchamp, and Château-Renaud. Debray was admitted to the house for this grand ceremony, but on the same plane with everyone else, and without any particular privilege. M. Danglars, surrounded by deputies and men connected with the revenue, was explaining a new theory of taxation which he intended to adopt when the course of events had compelled the government to call him into the ministry. Andrea, on whose arm hung one of the most consummate dandies of the Opera, was explaining to him rather cleverly, since he was obliged to be bold to appear at ease, his future projects, and the new luxuries he meant to introduce to Parisian fashions with his hundred and seventy-five thousand livres per annum.

The crowd moved to and fro in the rooms like an ebb and flow of turquoises, rubies, emeralds, opals, and diamonds. As usual, the oldest women were the most decorated, and the ugliest the most conspicuous. If there was a beautiful lily, or a sweet rose, you had to search for it, concealed in some corner behind a mother with a turban, or an aunt with a bird-of-paradise.

At each moment, in the midst of the crowd, the buzzing, and the laughter, the door-keeper's voice was heard announcing some name well known in the financial department, respected in the army, or illustrious in the literary world, and which was acknowledged by a slight movement in the different groups. But for one whose privilege it was to agitate that ocean of human waves, how many were received with a look of indifference or a sneer of disdain!

At the moment when the hand of the massive time-piece, representing Endymion asleep, pointed to nine on its golden face, and the hammer, the faithful type of mechanical thought, struck nine times, the name of the Count of Monte Cristo resounded in its turn, and as if by an electric shock all the assembly turned towards the door. The count was dressed in black and with his habitual simplicity; his white waistcoat displayed his expansive noble chest and his black stock was singularly noticeable because of its contrast with the deadly paleness of his face. His only jewellery was a chain, so fine that the slender gold thread was scarcely perceptible on his white waistcoat.

A circle was immediately formed around the door. The count perceived at one glance Madame Danglars at one end of the drawing-room, M. Danglars at the other, and Eugénie in front of him. He first advanced towards the baroness, who was chatting with Madame de Villefort, who had come alone, Valentine being still an invalid; and without turning aside, so clear was the road left for him, he passed from the baroness to Eugénie, whom he complimented in such rapid and measured terms, that the proud artist was quite struck. Near her was Mademoiselle Louise d'Armilly, who thanked the count for the letters of introduction he had so kindly given her for Italy, which she intended immediately to make use of. On leaving these ladies he found himself with Danglars, who had advanced to meet him.

Having accomplished these three social duties, Monte Cristo stopped, looking around him with that expression peculiar to a certain class, which seems to say, "I have done my duty, now let others do theirs."

Andrea, who was in an adjoining room, had shared in the sensation caused by the arrival of Monte Cristo, and now came forward to pay his respects to the count. He found him completely surrounded; all were eager to speak to him, as is always the case with those whose words are few and weighty. The solicitors arrived at this moment and arranged their scrawled papers on the velvet cloth embroidered with gold which covered the table prepared for the signature; it was a gilt table supported on lions' claws. One of the notaries sat down, the other remained standing. They were about to proceed to the reading of the contract, which half Paris assembled was to sign. All took their places, or rather the ladies formed a circle, while the gentlemen (more indifferent to the restraints of what Boileau calls the *style énergique*) commented on the feverish agitation of Andrea, on M. Danglars' riveted attention, Eugénie's composure, and the light and sprightly manner in which the baroness treated this important affair.

The contract was read during a profound silence. But as soon as it was finished, the buzz was redoubled through all the drawing-rooms; the brilliant sums, the rolling millions which were to be at the command of the two young people, and which crowned the display of the wedding presents and the young lady's diamonds, which had been made in a room entirely appropriated for that purpose, had exercised to the full their delusions over the envious assembly.

Mademoiselle Danglars' charms were heightened in the opinion of the young men, and for the moment seemed to outvie the sun in splendor. As for the ladies, it is needless to say that while they coveted the millions, they thought they did not need them for themselves, as they were beautiful enough without them. Andrea, surrounded by his friends, complimented, flattered, beginning to believe in the reality of his dream, was almost bewildered. The notary solemnly took the pen, flourished it above his head, and said:

"Gentlemen, we are about to sign the contract."

The baron was to sign first, then the representative of M. Cavalcanti, senior, then the baroness, afterwards the "future couple," as they are styled in the abominable phraseology of legal documents.

The baron took the pen and signed, then the representative. The baroness approached, leaning on Madame de Villefort's arm.

"My dear," said she, as she took the pen, "is it not vexatious? An unexpected incident, in the affair of murder and theft at the Count of Monte Cristo's, in which he nearly fell a victim, deprives us of the pleasure of seeing M. de Villefort."

"Indeed?" said M. Danglars, in the same tone in which he would have said, "Oh, well, what do I care?"

"As a matter of fact," said Monte Cristo, approaching, "I am much afraid that I am the involuntary cause of his absence."

"What, you, count?" said Madame Danglars, signing; "if you are, take care, for I shall never forgive you."

Andrea pricked up his ears.

"But it is not my fault, as I shall endeavor to prove."

Everyone listened eagerly; Monte Cristo who so rarely opened his lips, was about to speak.

"You remember," said the count, during the most profound silence, "that the unhappy wretch who came to rob me died at my house; the supposition is that he was stabbed by his accomplice, on attempting to leave it."

"Yes," said Danglars.

"In order that his wounds might be examined he was undressed, and his clothes were thrown into a corner, where the police picked them up, with the exception of the waistcoat, which they overlooked."

Andrea turned pale, and drew towards the door; he saw a cloud rising in the horizon, which appeared to forebode a coming storm.

"Well, this waistcoat was discovered today, covered with blood, and with a hole over the heart." The ladies screamed, and two or three prepared to faint. "It was brought to me. No one could guess what the dirty rag could be; I alone suspected that it was the waistcoat of the murdered man. My valet, in examining this mournful relic, felt a paper in the pocket and drew it out; it was a letter addressed to you, baron."

"To me?" cried Danglars.

"Yes, indeed, to you; I succeeded in deciphering your name under the blood with which the letter was stained," replied Monte Cristo, amid the general outburst of amazement.

"But," asked Madame Danglars, looking at her husband with uneasiness, "how could that prevent M. de Villefort—"

"In this simple way, madame," replied Monte Cristo; "the waistcoat and the letter were both what is termed circumstantial evidence; I therefore sent them to the king's attorney. You understand, my dear baron, that legal methods are the safest in criminal cases; it was, perhaps, some plot against you." Andrea looked steadily at Monte Cristo and disappeared in the second drawing-room.

"Possibly," said Danglars; "was not this murdered man an old galley-slave?"

"Yes," replied the count; "a felon named Caderousse." Danglars turned slightly pale; Andrea reached the anteroom beyond the little drawing-room.

"But go on signing," said Monte Cristo; "I perceive that my story has caused a general emotion, and I beg to apologize to you, baroness, and to Mademoiselle Danglars."

The baroness, who had signed, returned the pen to the notary.

"Prince Cavalcanti," said the latter; "Prince Cavalcanti, where are you?"

"Andrea, Andrea," repeated several young people, who were already on sufficiently intimate terms with him to call him by his Christian name.

"Call the prince; inform him that it is his turn to sign," cried Danglars to one of the floorkeepers.

But at the same instant the crowd of guests rushed in alarm into the principal salon as if some frightful monster had entered the apartments, *quærens quem devoret.* There was, indeed, reason to retreat, to be alarmed, and to scream. An officer was placing two soldiers at the door of each drawing-room, and was advancing towards Danglars, preceded by a commissary of police, girded with his scarf. Madame Danglars uttered a scream and fainted. Danglars, who thought himself threatened (certain consciences are never calm),—Danglars even before his guests showed a countenance of abject terror.

"What is the matter, sir?" asked Monte Cristo, advancing to meet the commissioner.

"Which of you gentlemen," asked the magistrate, without replying to the count, "answers to the name of Andrea Cavalcanti?"

A cry of astonishment was heard from all parts of the room. They searched; they questioned.

"But who then is Andrea Cavalcanti?" asked Danglars in amazement.

"A galley-slave, escaped from confinement at Toulon."

"And what crime has he committed?"

"He is accused," said the commissary with his inflexible voice, "of having assassinated the man named Caderousse, his former companion in prison, at the moment he was making his escape from the house of the Count of Monte Cristo."

Monte Cristo cast a rapid glance around him. Andrea was gone.

Study Guide Questions

For Students:

1. What favor does Cavalcanti ask of Monte Cristo?
2. What does the Count send to M. de Villefort?
3. What happens at the end of this chapter that prevents the wedding?

For Reading Club:

1. Discuss how the Count tempts Cavalcanti. Do you think such temptations still work?
2. Discuss the nature of the contract.
3. Discuss the story shared by the Count and how it impacts Danglars and Andrea.

CHAPTER 97

The Departure for Belgium

A few minutes after the scene of confusion produced in the salons of M. Danglars by the unexpected appearance of the brigade of soldiers, and by the disclosure which had followed, the mansion was deserted with as much rapidity as if a case of plague or of cholera morbus had broken out among the guests.

In a few minutes, through all the doors, down all the staircases, by every exit, everyone hastened to retire, or rather to fly; for it was a situation where the ordinary condolences,—which even the best friends are so eager to offer in great catastrophes,—were seen to be utterly futile. There remained in the banker's house only Danglars, closeted in his study, and making his statement to the officer of gendarmes; Madame Danglars, terrified, in the boudoir with which we are acquainted; and Eugénie, who with haughty air and disdainful lip had retired to her room with her inseparable companion, Mademoiselle Louise d'Armilly.

As for the numerous servants (more numerous that evening than usual, for their number was augmented by cooks and butlers from the Café de Paris), venting on their employers their anger at what they termed the insult to which they had been subjected, they collected in groups in the hall, in the kitchens, or in their rooms, thinking very little of their duty, which was thus naturally interrupted. Of all this household, only two persons deserve our notice; these are Mademoiselle Eugénie Danglars and Mademoiselle Louise d'Armilly.

The betrothed had retired, as we said, with haughty air, disdainful lip, and the demeanor of an outraged queen, followed by her companion, who was paler and more disturbed than herself. On reaching her room Eugénie locked her door, while Louise fell on a chair.

"Ah, what a dreadful thing," said the young musician; "who would have suspected it? M. Andrea Cavalcanti a murderer—a galley-slave escaped—a convict!"

An ironical smile curled the lip of Eugénie. "In truth, I was fated," said she. "I escaped the Morcerf only to fall into the Cavalcanti."

"Oh, do not confound the two, Eugénie."

"Hold your tongue! The men are all infamous, and I am happy to be able now to do more than detest them—I despise them."

"What shall we do?" asked Louise.

"What shall we do?"

"Yes."

"Why, the same we had intended doing three days since—set off."

"What?—although you are not now going to be married, you intend still—"

"Listen, Louise. I hate this life of the fashionable world, always ordered, measured, ruled, like our music-paper. What I have always wished for, desired, and coveted, is the life of an artist, free and independent, relying only on my own resources, and accountable only to myself. Remain here? What for?—that they may try, a month hence, to marry me again; and to whom?—M. Debray, perhaps, as it was once proposed. No, Louise, no! This evening's adventure will serve for my excuse. I did not seek one, I did not ask for one. God sends me this, and I hail it joyfully!"

"How strong and courageous you are!" said the fair, frail girl to her brunette companion.

"Did you not yet know me? Come, Louise, let us talk of our affairs. The post-chaise—"

"Was happily bought three days since."

"Have you had it sent where we are to go for it?"

"Yes."

"Our passport?"

"Here it is."

And Eugénie, with her usual precision, opened a printed paper, and read:

"M. Léon d'Armilly, twenty years of age; profession, artist; hair black, eyes black; travelling with his sister."

"Capital! How did you get this passport?"

"When I went to ask M. de Monte Cristo for letters to the directors of the theatres at Rome and Naples, I expressed my fears of travelling as a woman; he perfectly understood them, and undertook to procure for me a man's passport, and two days after I received this, to which I have added with my own hand, 'travelling with his sister.'"

"Well," said Eugénie cheerfully, "we have then only to pack up our trunks; we shall start the evening of the signing of the contract, instead of the evening of the wedding—that is all."

"But consider the matter seriously, Eugénie!"

"Oh, I am done with considering! I am tired of hearing only of market reports, of the end of the month, of the rise and fall of Spanish funds, of Haitian bonds. Instead of that, Louise—do you understand?—air, liberty, melody of birds, plains of Lombardy, Venetian canals, Roman palaces, the Bay of Naples. How much have we, Louise?"

The young girl to whom this question was addressed drew from an inlaid secretaire a small portfolio with a lock, in which she counted twenty-three bank-notes.

"Twenty-three thousand francs," said she.

"And as much, at least, in pearls, diamonds, and jewels," said Eugénie. "We are rich. With forty-five thousand francs we can live like princesses for two years, and comfortably for four; but before six months—you with your music, and I with my voice—we shall double our capital. Come, you shall take charge of the money, I of the jewel-box; so that if one of us had the misfortune to lose her treasure, the other would still have hers left. Now, the portmanteau—let us make haste—the portmanteau!"

"Stop!" said Louise, going to listen at Madame Danglars' door.

"What do you fear?"

"That we may be discovered."

"The door is locked."

"They may tell us to open it."

"They may if they like, but we will not."

"You are a perfect Amazon, Eugénie!" And the two young girls began to heap into a trunk all the things they thought they should require.

"There now," said Eugénie, "while I change my costume do you lock the portmanteau." Louise pressed with all the strength of her little hands on the top of the portmanteau.

"But I cannot," said she; "I am not strong enough; do you shut it."

"Ah, you do well to ask," said Eugénie, laughing; "I forgot that I was Hercules, and you only the pale Omphale!"

And the young girl, kneeling on the top, pressed the two parts of the portmanteau together, and Mademoiselle d'Armilly passed the bolt of the padlock through. When this was done, Eugénie opened a drawer, of which she kept the key, and took from it a wadded violet silk travelling cloak.

"Here," said she, "you see I have thought of everything; with this cloak you will not be cold."

"But you?"

"Oh, I am never cold, you know! Besides, with these men's clothes—"

"Will you dress here?"

"Certainly."

"Shall you have time?"

"Do not be uneasy, you little coward! All our servants are busy, discussing the grand affair. Besides, what is there astonishing, when you think of the grief I ought to be in, that I shut myself up?—tell me!"

"No, truly—you comfort me."

"Come and help me."

From the same drawer she took a man's complete costume, from the boots to the coat, and a provision of linen, where there was nothing superfluous, but every requisite. Then, with a promptitude which indicated that this was not the first time she had amused herself by adopting the garb of the opposite sex, Eugénie drew on the boots and pantaloons, tied her cravat, buttoned her waistcoat up to the throat, and put on a coat which admirably fitted her beautiful figure.

"Oh, that is very good—indeed, it is very good!" said Louise, looking at her with admiration; "but that beautiful black hair, those magnificent braids, which made all the ladies sigh with envy,—will they go under a man's hat like the one I see down there?"

"You shall see," said Eugénie. And with her left hand seizing the thick mass, which her long fingers could scarcely grasp, she took in her right hand a pair of long scissors, and soon the steel met through the rich and splendid hair, which fell in a cluster at her feet as she leaned back to keep it from her coat. Then she grasped the front hair, which she also cut off, without expressing the least regret; on the contrary, her eyes sparkled with greater pleasure than usual under her ebony eyebrows.

"Oh, the magnificent hair!" said Louise, with regret.

"And am I not a hundred times better thus?" cried Eugénie, smoothing the scattered curls of her hair, which had now quite a masculine appearance; "and do you not think me handsomer so?"

"Oh, you are beautiful—always beautiful!" cried Louise. "Now, where are you going?"

"To Brussels, if you like; it is the nearest frontier. We can go to Brussels, Liège, Aix-la-Chapelle; then up the Rhine to Strasbourg. We will cross Switzerland, and go down into Italy by the Saint-Gothard. Will that do?"

"Yes."

"What are you looking at?"

"I am looking at you; indeed you are adorable like that! One would say you were carrying me off."

"And they would be right, *pardieu!*"

"Oh, I think you swore, Eugénie."

And the two young girls, whom everyone might have thought plunged in grief, the one on her own account, the other from interest in her friend, burst out laughing, as they cleared away every visible trace of the disorder which had naturally accompanied the preparations for their escape. Then, having blown out the lights, the two fugitives, looking and listening eagerly, with outstretched necks, opened the door of a dressing-room which led by a side staircase down to the yard,—Eugénie going first, and holding with one arm the portmanteau, which by the opposite handle Mademoiselle d'Armilly scarcely raised with both hands. The yard was empty; the clock was striking twelve. The porter was not yet gone to bed. Eugénie approached softly, and saw the old man sleeping soundly in an armchair in his lodge. She returned to Louise, took up the portmanteau, which she had placed for a moment on the ground, and they reached the archway under the shadow of the wall.

Eugénie concealed Louise in an angle of the gateway, so that if the porter chanced to awake he might see but one person. Then placing herself in the full light of the lamp which lit the yard:

"Gate!" cried she, with her finest contralto voice, and rapping at the window.

The porter got up as Eugénie expected, and even advanced some steps to recognize the person who was going out, but seeing a young man striking his boot impatiently with his riding-whip, he opened it immediately. Louise slid through the half-open gate like a snake, and bounded lightly forward. Eugénie, apparently calm, although in all probability her heart beat somewhat faster than usual, went out in her turn.

A porter was passing and they gave him the portmanteau; then the two young girls, having told him to take it to No. 36, Rue de la Victoire, walked behind this man, whose presence comforted Louise. As for Eugénie, she was as strong as a Judith or a Delilah. They arrived at the appointed spot. Eugénie ordered the porter to put down the portmanteau, gave him some pieces of money, and having rapped at the shutter sent him away. The shutter where Eugénie had rapped was that of a little laundress, who had been previously warned, and was not yet gone to bed. She opened the door.

"Mademoiselle," said Eugénie, "let the porter get the post-chaise from the coach-house, and fetch some post-horses from the hotel. Here are five francs for his trouble."

"Indeed," said Louise, "I admire you, and I could almost say respect you." The laundress looked on in astonishment, but as she had been promised twenty louis, she made no remark.

In a quarter of an hour the porter returned with a post-boy and horses, which were harnessed, and put in the post-chaise in a minute, while the porter fastened the portmanteau on with the assistance of a cord and strap.

"Here is the passport," said the postilion, "which way are we going, young gentleman?"

"To Fontainebleau," replied Eugénie with an almost masculine voice.

"What do you say?" said Louise.

"I am giving them the slip," said Eugénie; "this woman to whom we have given twenty louis may betray us for forty; we will soon alter our direction."

And the young girl jumped into the britzka, which was admirably arranged for sleeping in, without scarcely touching the step.

"You are always right," said the music teacher, seating herself by the side of her friend.

A quarter of an hour afterwards the postilion, having been put in the right road, passed with a crack of his whip through the gateway of the Barrière Saint-Martin.

"Ah," said Louise, breathing freely, "here we are out of Paris."

"Yes, my dear, the abduction is an accomplished fact," replied Eugénie.

"Yes, and without violence," said Louise.

"I shall bring that forward as an extenuating circumstance," replied Eugénie.

These words were lost in the noise which the carriage made in rolling over the pavement of La Villette. M. Danglars no longer had a daughter.

Study Guide Questions

For Students:

1. What does Eugénie want to do after her marriage is broken off?
2. What is written on the passport that d'Armilly gives to Eugénie? Who helps her procure it?
3. Who takes the disguise of a man and why?

For Reading Club:

1. Discuss the relationship between Louise d'Armilly and Eugénie Danglars.
2. Discuss the theme of feminism with reference to the chapter.
3. Discuss the metaphor of Hercules for Eugénie and Amphale for Louise, what does it tell you about their relationship?

CHAPTER 98

The Bell and Bottle Tavern

And now let us leave Mademoiselle Danglars and her friend pursuing their way to Brussels, and return to poor Andrea Cavalcanti, so inopportunely interrupted in his rise to fortune. Notwithstanding his youth, Master Andrea was a very skilful and intelligent boy. We have seen that on the first rumor which reached the salon he had gradually approached the door, and crossing two or three rooms at last disappeared. But we have forgotten to mention one circumstance, which nevertheless ought not to be omitted; in one of the rooms he crossed, the *trousseau* of the bride-elect was on exhibition. There were caskets of diamonds, cashmere shawls, Valenciennes lace, English veils, and in fact all the tempting things, the bare mention of which makes the hearts of young girls bound with joy, and which is called the *corbeille*.[15] Now, in passing through this room, Andrea proved himself not only to be clever and intelligent, but also provident, for he helped himself to the most valuable of the ornaments before him.

Furnished with this plunder, Andrea leaped with a lighter heart from the window, intending to slip through the hands of the gendarmes. Tall and well proportioned as an ancient gladiator, and muscular as a Spartan, he walked for a quarter of an hour without knowing where to direct his steps, actuated by the sole idea of getting away from the spot where if he lingered he knew that he would surely be taken. Having passed through the Rue du Mont-Blanc, guided by the instinct which leads thieves always to take the safest path, he found himself at the end of the Rue La Fayette. There he stopped, breathless and panting. He was quite alone; on one side was the vast wilderness of the Saint-Lazare, on the other, Paris enshrouded in darkness.

[15] Literally, "the basket," because wedding gifts were originally brought in such a receptacle.

"Am I to be captured?" he cried; "no, not if I can use more activity than my enemies. My safety is now a mere question of speed."

At this moment he saw a cab at the top of the Faubourg Poissonnière. The dull driver, smoking his pipe, was plodding along toward the limits of the Faubourg Saint-Denis, where no doubt he ordinarily had his station.

"Ho, friend!" said Benedetto.

"What do you want, sir?" asked the driver.

"Is your horse tired?"

"Tired? oh, yes, tired enough—he has done nothing the whole of this blessed day! Four wretched fares, and twenty sous over, making in all seven francs, are all that I have earned, and I ought to take ten to the owner."

"Will you add these twenty francs to the seven you have?"

"With pleasure, sir; twenty francs are not to be despised. Tell me what I am to do for this."

"A very easy thing, if your horse isn't tired."

"I tell you he'll go like the wind,—only tell me which way to drive."

"Towards the Louvres."

"Ah, I know the way—you get good sweetened rum over there."

"Exactly so; I merely wish to overtake one of my friends, with whom I am going to hunt tomorrow at Chapelle-en-Serval. He should have waited for me here with a cabriolet till half-past eleven; it is twelve, and, tired of waiting, he must have gone on."

"It is likely."

"Well, will you try and overtake him?"

"Nothing I should like better."

"If you do not overtake him before we reach Bourget you shall have twenty francs; if not before Louvres, thirty."

"And if we do overtake him?"

"Forty," said Andrea, after a moment's hesitation, at the end of which he remembered that he might safely promise.

"That's all right," said the man; "hop in, and we're off! Who-o-o-pla!"

Andrea got into the cab, which passed rapidly through the Faubourg Saint-Denis, along the Faubourg Saint-Martin, crossed the barrier, and threaded its way through the interminable Villette. They never overtook the chimerical friend, yet Andrea frequently inquired of people on foot whom he passed and at the inns which were not yet closed, for a green cabriolet and bay horse; and as there are a great many cabriolets to be seen on the road to the Low Countries, and as nine-tenths of them are green, the inquiries increased at every step. Everyone had just seen it pass; it was only five hundred, two hundred, one hundred steps in advance; at length they reached it, but it was not the friend. Once the cab was also passed by a calash rapidly whirled along by two post-horses.

"Ah," said Cavalcanti to himself, "if I only had that britzka, those two good post-horses, and above all the passport that carries them on!" And he sighed deeply.

The calash contained Mademoiselle Danglars and Mademoiselle d'Armilly.

"Hurry, hurry!" said Andrea, "we must overtake him soon."

And the poor horse resumed the desperate gallop it had kept up since leaving the barrier, and arrived steaming at Louvres.

"Certainly," said Andrea, "I shall not overtake my friend, but I shall kill your horse, therefore I had better stop. Here are thirty francs; I will sleep at the *Cheval Rouge*, and will secure a place in the first coach. Good-night, friend."

And Andrea, after placing six pieces of five francs each in the man's hand, leaped lightly on to the pathway. The cabman joyfully pocketed the sum, and turned back on his road to Paris. Andrea pretended to go towards the hotel of the *Cheval Rouge*, but after leaning an instant against the door, and hearing the last sound of the cab, which was disappearing from view, he went on his road, and with a lusty stride soon traversed the space of two leagues. Then he rested; he must be near Chapelle-en-Serval, where he pretended to be going.

It was not fatigue that stayed Andrea here; it was that he might form some resolution, adopt some plan. It would be impossible to make use of a diligence, equally so to engage post-horses; to travel either way a passport was necessary. It was still more impossible to remain in the department of the Oise, one of the most open and strictly guarded in France; this was quite out of the question, especially to a man like Andrea, perfectly conversant with criminal matters.

He sat down by the side of the moat, buried his face in his hands and reflected. Ten minutes after he raised his head; his resolution was made. He threw some dust over the topcoat, which he had found time to unhook from the antechamber and button over his ball costume, and going to Chapelle-en-Serval he knocked loudly at the door of the only inn in the place.

The host opened.

"My friend," said Andrea, "I was coming from Mortefontaine to Senlis, when my horse, which is a troublesome creature, stumbled and threw me. I must reach Compiègne tonight, or I shall cause deep anxiety to my family. Could you let me hire a horse of you?"

An innkeeper has always a horse to let, whether it be good or bad. The host called the stable-boy, and ordered him to saddle *Le Blanc* then he awoke his son, a child of seven years, whom he ordered to ride before the gentleman and bring back the horse. Andrea gave the innkeeper twenty francs, and in taking them from his pocket dropped a visiting card. This belonged to one of his friends at the Café de Paris, so that the innkeeper, picking it up after Andrea had left, was convinced that he had let his horse to the Count of Mauléon, 25 Rue Saint-Dominique, that being the name and address on the card.

Le Blanc was not a fast animal, but he kept up an easy, steady pace; in three hours and a half Andrea had traversed the nine leagues which separated him from Compiègne, and four o'clock struck as he reached the place where the coaches stop. There is an excellent tavern at Compiègne, well remembered by those who have ever been there. Andrea, who had often stayed there in his rides about Paris, recollected the Bell and Bottle inn; he turned around, saw the sign by the light of a reflected lamp, and having dismissed the child, giving him all the small coin he had about him, he began knocking at the door, very reasonably concluding that having now three or four hours before him he had best fortify himself against the fatigues of the morrow by a sound sleep and a good supper. A waiter opened the door.

"My friend," said Andrea, "I have been dining at Saint-Jean-aux-Bois, and expected to catch the coach which passes by at midnight, but like a fool I have lost my way, and have been walking for the last four hours in the forest. Show me into one of those pretty little rooms which overlook the court, and bring me a cold fowl and a bottle of Bordeaux."

The waiter had no suspicions; Andrea spoke with perfect composure, he had a cigar in his mouth, and his hands in the pocket of his top coat; his clothes were fashionably made, his chin smooth, his boots irreproachable; he looked merely as if he had stayed out very late, that was all. While the waiter was preparing his room, the hostess arose; Andrea assumed his most charming smile, and asked if he could have No. 3, which he had occupied on his last stay at Compiègne. Unfortunately, No. 3 was engaged by a young man who was travelling with his sister. Andrea appeared in despair, but consoled himself when the hostess assured him that No. 7, prepared for him, was situated precisely the same as No. 3, and while warming his feet and chatting about the last races at Chantilly, he waited until they announced his room to be ready.

Andrea had not spoken without cause of the pretty rooms looking out upon the court of the Bell Hotel, which with its triple galleries like those of a theatre, with the jessamine and clematis twining round the light columns, forms one of the prettiest entrances to an inn that you can imagine. The fowl was tender, the wine old, the fire clear and sparkling, and Andrea was surprised to find himself eating with as good an appetite as though nothing had happened. Then he went to bed and almost immediately fell into that deep sleep which is sure to visit men of twenty years of age, even when they are torn with remorse. Now, here we are obliged to own that Andrea ought to have felt remorse, but that he did not.

This was the plan which had appealed to him to afford the best chance of his security. Before daybreak he would awake, leave the inn after rigorously paying his bill, and reaching the forest, he would, under pretence of making studies in painting, test the hospitality of some peasants, procure himself the dress of a woodcutter and a hatchet, casting off the lion's skin to assume that of the woodman; then, with his hands covered with dirt, his hair darkened by means of a leaden comb, his complexion embrowned with a preparation for which one of his old comrades had given him the recipe, he intended, by following the wooded districts, to reach the nearest frontier, walking by night and sleeping in the day in the forests and quarries, and only entering inhabited regions to buy a loaf from time to time.

Once past the frontier, Andrea proposed making money of his diamonds; and by uniting the proceeds to ten bank-notes he always carried about with him in case of accident, he would then find himself possessor of about 50,000 livres, which he philosophically considered as no very deplorable condition after all. Moreover, he reckoned much on the interest of the Danglars to hush up the rumor of their own misadventures. These were the reasons which, added to the fatigue, caused Andrea to sleep so soundly. In order that he might wake early he did not close the shutters, but contented himself with bolting the door and placing on the table an unclasped and long-pointed knife, whose temper he well knew, and which was never absent from him.

About seven in the morning Andrea was awakened by a ray of sunlight, which played, warm and brilliant, upon his face. In all well-organized brains, the predominating idea—and there always is one—is sure to be the last thought before sleeping, and the first upon waking in the morning. Andrea had scarcely opened his eyes when his predominating idea presented itself, and whispered in his ear that he had slept too long. He jumped out of bed and ran to the window. A gendarme was crossing the court. A gendarme is one of the most striking objects in the world, even to a man void of uneasiness; but for one who has a timid conscience, and with good cause too, the yellow, blue, and white uniform is really very alarming.

"Why is that gendarme there?" asked Andrea of himself.

Then, all at once, he replied, with that logic which the reader has, doubtless, remarked in him, "There is nothing astonishing in seeing a gendarme at an inn; instead of being astonished, let me dress myself." And the youth dressed himself with a facility his valet de chambre had failed to rob him of during the two months of fashionable life he had led in Paris.

"Now then," said Andrea, while dressing himself, "I'll wait till he leaves, and then I'll slip away."

And, saying this, Andrea, who had now put on his boots and cravat, stole gently to the window, and a second time lifted up the muslin curtain. Not only was the first gendarme still there, but the young man now perceived a second yellow, blue, and white uniform at the foot of the staircase, the only one by which he could descend, while a third, on horseback, holding a musket in his fist, was posted as a sentinel at the great street-door which alone afforded the means of egress. The appearance of the third gendarme settled the matter, for a crowd of curious loungers was extended before him, effectually blocking the entrance to the hotel.

"They're after me!" was Andrea's first thought. "*Diable!*"

A pallor overspread the young man's forehead, and he looked around him with anxiety. His room, like all those on the same floor, had but one outlet to the gallery in the sight of everybody. "I am lost!" was his second thought; and, indeed, for a man in Andrea's situation, an arrest meant the assizes, trial, and death,—death without mercy or delay.

For a moment he convulsively pressed his head within his hands, and during that brief period he became nearly mad with terror; but soon a ray of hope glimmered in the multitude of thoughts which bewildered his mind, and a faint smile played upon his white lips and pallid cheeks. He looked around and saw the objects of his search upon the chimney-piece; they were a pen, ink, and paper. With forced composure he dipped the pen in the ink, and wrote the following lines upon a sheet of paper:

"I have no money to pay my bill, but I am not a dishonest man; I leave behind me as a pledge this pin, worth ten times the amount. I shall be excused for leaving at daybreak, for I was ashamed."

He then drew the pin from his cravat and placed it on the paper. This done, instead of leaving the door fastened, he drew back the bolts and even placed the door ajar, as though he had left the room, forgetting to close it, and slipping into the chimney like a man accustomed to that kind of gymnastic exercise, after replacing the chimney-board, which represented Achilles with Deidamia, and effacing the very marks of his feet upon the ashes, he commenced climbing the hollow tunnel, which afforded him the only means of escape left.

At this precise time, the first gendarme Andrea had noticed walked upstairs, preceded by the commissary of police, and supported by the second gendarme who guarded the staircase and was himself reinforced by the one stationed at the door.

Andrea was indebted for this visit to the following circumstances. At daybreak, the telegraphs were set at work in all directions, and almost immediately the authorities in every district had exerted their utmost endeavors to arrest the murderer of Caderousse. Compiègne, that royal residence and fortified town, is well furnished with authorities, gendarmes, and commissaries of police; they therefore began operations as soon as the telegraphic despatch arrived, and the Bell and Bottle being the best-known hotel in the town, they had naturally directed their first inquiries there.

Now, besides the reports of the sentinels guarding the Hôtel de Ville, which is next door to the Bell and Bottle, it had been stated by others that a number of travellers had arrived during the night. The sentinel who was relieved at six o'clock in the morning, remembered perfectly that, just as he was taking his post a few minutes past four, a young man arrived on horseback, with a little boy before him. The young man, having dismissed the boy and horse, knocked at the door of the hotel, which was opened, and again closed after his entrance. This late arrival had attracted much suspicion, and the young man being no other than Andrea, the commissary and gendarme, who was a brigadier, directed their steps towards his room. They found the door ajar.

"Oh, oh," said the brigadier, who thoroughly understood the trick; "a bad sign to find the door open! I would rather find it triply bolted."

And, indeed, the little note and pin upon the table confirmed, or rather corroborated, the sad truth. Andrea had fled. We say corroborated, because the brigadier was too experienced to be convinced by a single proof. He glanced around, looked in the bed, shook the curtains, opened the closets, and finally stopped at the chimney. Andrea had taken the precaution to leave no traces of his feet in the ashes, but still it was an outlet, and in this light was not to be passed over without serious investigation.

The brigadier sent for some sticks and straw, and having filled the chimney with them, set a light to it. The fire crackled, and the smoke ascended like the dull vapor from a volcano; but still no prisoner fell down, as they expected. The fact was, that Andrea, at war with society ever since his youth, was quite as deep as a gendarme, even though he were advanced to the rank of brigadier, and quite prepared for the fire, he had climbed out on the roof and was crouching down against the chimney-pots.

At one time he thought he was saved, for he heard the brigadier exclaim in a loud voice, to the two gendarmes, "He is not here!" But venturing to peep, he perceived that the latter, instead of retiring, as might have been reasonably expected upon this announcement, were watching with increased attention.

It was now his turn to look about him; the Hôtel de Ville, a massive sixteenth century building, was on his right; anyone could descend from the openings in the tower, and examine every corner of the roof below, and Andrea expected momentarily to see the head of a gendarme appear at one of these openings. If once discovered, he knew he would be lost, for the roof afforded no chance of escape; he therefore resolved to descend, not through the same chimney by which he had come up, but by a similar one conducting to another room.

He looked around for a chimney from which no smoke issued, and having reached it, he disappeared through the orifice without being seen by anyone. At the same minute, one of the little windows of the Hôtel de Ville was thrown open, and the head of a gendarme appeared. For an instant it remained motionless as one of the stone decorations of the building, then after a long sigh of disappointment the head disappeared. The brigadier, calm and dignified as the law he represented, passed through the crowd, without answering the thousand questions addressed to him, and re-entered the hotel.

"Well?" asked the two gendarmes.

"Well, my boys," said the brigadier, "the brigand must really have escaped early this morning; but we will send to the Villers-Coterets and Noyon roads, and search the forest, when we shall catch him, no doubt."

The honorable functionary had scarcely expressed himself thus, in that intonation which is peculiar to brigadiers of the gendarmerie, when a loud scream, accompanied by the violent ringing of a bell, resounded through the court of the hotel.

"Ah, what is that?" cried the brigadier.

"Some traveller seems impatient," said the host. "What number was it that rang?"

"Number 3."

"Run, waiter!"

At this moment the screams and ringing were redoubled.

"Aha!" said the brigadier, stopping the servant, "the person who is ringing appears to want something more than a waiter; we will attend upon him with a gendarme. Who occupies Number 3?"

"The little fellow who arrived last night in a post-chaise with his sister, and who asked for an apartment with two beds."

The bell here rang for the third time, with another shriek of anguish.

"Follow me, Mr. Commissary!" said the brigadier; "tread in my steps."

"Wait an instant," said the host; "Number 3 has two staircases,—inside and outside."

"Good," said the brigadier. "I will take charge of the inside one. Are the carbines loaded?"

"Yes, brigadier."

"Well, you guard the exterior, and if he attempts to fly, fire upon him; he must be a great criminal, from what the telegraph says."

The brigadier, followed by the commissary, disappeared by the inside staircase, accompanied by the noise which his assertions respecting Andrea had excited in the crowd.

This is what had happened: Andrea had very cleverly managed to descend two-thirds of the chimney, but then his foot slipped, and notwithstanding his endeavors, he came into the room with more speed and noise than he intended. It would have signified little had the room been empty, but unfortunately it was occupied. Two ladies, sleeping in one bed, were awakened by the noise, and fixing their eyes upon the spot whence the sound proceeded, they saw a man. One of these ladies, the fair one, uttered those terrible shrieks which resounded through the house, while the other, rushing to the bell-rope, rang with all her strength. Andrea, as we can see, was surrounded by misfortune.

"For pity's sake," he cried, pale and bewildered, without seeing whom he was addressing,—"for pity's sake do not call assistance! Save me!—I will not harm you."

"Andrea, the murderer!" cried one of the ladies.

"Eugénie! Mademoiselle Danglars!" exclaimed Andrea, stupefied.

"Help, help!" cried Mademoiselle d'Armilly, taking the bell from her companion's hand, and ringing it yet more violently.

"Save me, I am pursued!" said Andrea, clasping his hands. "For pity, for mercy's sake do not deliver me up!"

"It is too late, they are coming," said Eugénie.

"Well, conceal me somewhere; you can say you were needlessly alarmed; you can turn their suspicions and save my life!"

The two ladies, pressing closely to one another, and drawing the bedclothes tightly around them, remained silent to this supplicating voice, repugnance and fear taking possession of their minds.

"Well, be it so," at length said Eugénie; "return by the same road you came, and we will say nothing about you, unhappy wretch."

"Here he is, here he is!" cried a voice from the landing; "here he is! I see him!"

The brigadier had put his eye to the keyhole, and had discovered Andrea in a posture of entreaty. A violent blow from the butt end of the musket burst open the lock, two more forced out the bolts, and the broken door fell in. Andrea ran to the other door, leading to the gallery, ready to rush out; but he was stopped short, and he stood with his body a little thrown back, pale, and with the useless knife in his clenched hand.

"Fly, then!" cried Mademoiselle d'Armilly, whose pity returned as her fears diminished; "fly!"

"Or kill yourself!" said Eugénie (in a tone which a Vestal in the amphitheatre would have used, when urging the victorious gladiator to finish his vanquished adversary). Andrea shuddered, and looked on the young girl with an expression which proved how little he understood such ferocious honor.

"Kill myself?" he cried, throwing down his knife; "why should I do so?"

"Why, you said," answered Mademoiselle Danglars, "that you would be condemned to die like the worst criminals."

"Bah," said Cavalcanti, crossing his arms, "one has friends."

The brigadier advanced to him, sword in hand.

"Come, come," said Andrea, "sheathe your sword, my fine fellow; there is no occasion to make such a fuss, since I give myself up;" and he held out his hands to be manacled.

The two girls looked with horror upon this shameful metamorphosis, the man of the world shaking off his covering and appearing as a galley-slave. Andrea turned towards them, and with an impertinent smile asked, "Have you any message for your father, Mademoiselle Danglars, for in all probability I shall return to Paris?"

Eugénie covered her face with her hands.

"Oh, oh!" said Andrea, "you need not be ashamed, even though you did post after me. Was I not nearly your husband?"

And with this raillery Andrea went out, leaving the two girls a prey to their own feelings of shame, and to the comments of the crowd. An hour after they stepped into their calash, both dressed in feminine attire. The gate of the hotel had been closed to screen them from sight, but they were forced, when the door was open, to pass through a throng of curious glances and whispering voices.

Eugénie closed her eyes; but though she could not see, she could hear, and the sneers of the crowd reached her in the carriage.

"Oh, why is not the world a wilderness?" she exclaimed, throwing herself into the arms of Mademoiselle d'Armilly, her eyes sparkling with the same kind of rage which made Nero wish that the Roman world had but one neck, that he might sever it at a single blow.

The next day they stopped at the Hôtel de Flandre, at Brussels. The same evening Andrea was incarcerated in the Conciergerie.

Study Guide Questions

For Students:

1. Where does Benedetto go?
2. From where does Benedetto get a horse?
3. Which other couple is staying in The Bell and Bottle Tavern?

For Reading Club:

1. Do you think money plays a vital role in Benedetto's escape?
2. Why do you think Benedetto feels no remorse at all? Do you think such selfishness is part of contemporary society?
3. Discuss how Benedetto tries to escape and does he succeed in it.

CHAPTER 99

The Law

We have seen how quietly Mademoiselle Danglars and Mademoiselle d'Armilly accomplished their transformation and flight; the fact being that everyone was too much occupied in his or her own affairs to think of theirs.

We will leave the banker contemplating the enormous magnitude of his debt before the phantom of bankruptcy, and follow the baroness, who after being momentarily crushed under the weight of the blow which had struck her, had gone to seek her usual adviser, Lucien Debray. The baroness had looked forward to this marriage as a means of ridding her of a guardianship which, over a girl of Eugénie's character, could not fail to be rather a troublesome undertaking; for in the tacit relations which maintain the bond of family union, the mother, to maintain her ascendancy over her daughter, must never fail to be a model of wisdom and a type of perfection.

Now, Madame Danglars feared Eugénie's sagacity and the influence of Mademoiselle d'Armilly; she had frequently observed the contemptuous expression with which her daughter looked upon Debray,—an expression which seemed to imply that she understood all her mother's amorous and pecuniary relationships with the intimate secretary; moreover, she saw that Eugénie detested Debray, not only because he was a source of dissension and scandal under the paternal roof, but because she had at once classed him in that catalogue of bipeds whom Plato endeavors to withdraw from the appellation of men, and whom Diogenes designated as animals upon two legs without feathers.

Unfortunately, in this world of ours, each person views things through a certain medium, and so is prevented from seeing in the same light as others, and Madame Danglars, therefore, very much regretted that the marriage of Eugénie had not taken place, not only because the match was good, and likely to insure the happiness of her child, but because it would also set her at liberty. She ran therefore to Debray, who, after having, like the rest of Paris, witnessed the contract scene and the scandal attending it, had retired in haste to his club, where he was chatting with some friends upon the events which served as a subject of conversation for three-fourths of that city known as the capital of the world.

At the precise time when Madame Danglars, dressed in black and concealed in a long veil, was ascending the stairs leading to Debray's apartments, notwithstanding the assurances of the concierge that the young man was not at home, Debray was occupied in repelling the insinuations of a friend, who tried to persuade him that after the terrible scene which had just taken place he ought, as a friend of the family, to marry Mademoiselle Danglars and her two millions. Debray did not defend himself very warmly, for the idea had sometimes crossed his mind; still, when he recollected the independent, proud spirit of Eugénie, he positively rejected it as utterly impossible, though the same thought again continually recurred and found a resting-place in his heart. Tea, play, and the conversation, which had become interesting during the discussion of such serious affairs, lasted till one o'clock in the morning.

Meanwhile Madame Danglars, veiled and uneasy, awaited the return of Debray in the little green room, seated between two baskets of flowers, which she had that morning sent, and which, it must be confessed, Debray had himself arranged and watered with so much care that his absence was half excused in the eyes of the poor woman.

At twenty minutes to twelve, Madame Danglars, tired of waiting, returned home. Women of a certain grade are like prosperous grisettes in one respect, they seldom return home after twelve o'clock. The baroness returned to the hotel with as much caution as Eugénie used in leaving it; she ran lightly upstairs, and with an aching heart entered her apartment, contiguous, as we know, to that of Eugénie. She was fearful of exciting any remark, and believed firmly in her daughter's innocence and fidelity to the paternal roof. She listened at Eugénie's door, and hearing no sound tried to enter, but the bolts were in place. Madame Danglars then concluded that the young girl had been overcome with the terrible excitement of the evening, and had gone to bed and to sleep. She called the maid and questioned her.

"Mademoiselle Eugénie," said the maid, "retired to her apartment with Mademoiselle d'Armilly; they then took tea together, after which they desired me to leave, saying that they needed me no longer."

Since then the maid had been below, and like everyone else she thought the young ladies were in their own room; Madame Danglars, therefore, went to bed without a shadow of suspicion, and began to muse over the recent events. In proportion as her memory became clearer, the occurrences of the evening were revealed in their true light; what she had taken for confusion was a tumult; what she had regarded as something distressing, was in reality a disgrace. And then the baroness remembered that she had felt no pity for poor Mercédès, who had been afflicted with as severe a blow through her husband and son.

"Eugénie," she said to herself, "is lost, and so are we. The affair, as it will be reported, will cover us with shame; for in a society such as ours satire inflicts a painful and incurable wound. How fortunate that Eugénie is possessed of that strange character which has so often made me tremble!"

And her glance was turned towards heaven, where a mysterious Providence disposes all things, and out of a fault, nay, even a vice, sometimes produces a blessing. And then her thoughts, cleaving through space like a bird in the air, rested on Cavalcanti. This Andrea was a wretch, a robber, an assassin, and yet his manners showed the effects of a sort of education, if not a complete one; he had been presented to the world with the appearance of an immense fortune, supported by an honorable name. How could she extricate herself from this labyrinth? To whom would she apply to help her out of this painful situation? Debray, to whom she had run, with the first instinct of a woman towards the man she loves, and who yet betrays her,—Debray could but give her advice, she must apply to someone more powerful than he.

The baroness then thought of M. de Villefort. It was M. de Villefort who had remorselessly brought misfortune into her family, as though they had been strangers. But, no; on reflection, the procureur was not a merciless man; and it was not the magistrate, slave to his duties, but the friend, the loyal friend, who roughly but firmly cut into the very core of the corruption; it was not the executioner, but the surgeon, who wished to withdraw the honor of Danglars from ignominious association with the disgraced young man they had presented to the world as their son-in-law. And since Villefort, the friend of Danglars, had acted in this way, no one could suppose that he had been previously acquainted with, or had lent himself to, any of Andrea's intrigues. Villefort's conduct, therefore, upon reflection, appeared to the baroness as if shaped for their mutual advantage. But the inflexibility of the procureur should stop there; she would see him the next day, and if she could not make him fail in his duties as a magistrate, she would, at least, obtain all the indulgence he could allow. She would invoke the past, recall old recollections; she would supplicate him by the remembrance of guilty, yet happy days. M. de Villefort would stifle the affair; he had only to turn his eyes on one side, and allow Andrea to fly, and follow up the crime under that shadow of guilt called contempt of court. And after this reasoning she slept easily.

At nine o'clock next morning she arose, and without ringing for her maid or giving the least sign of her activity, she dressed herself in the same simple style as on the previous night; then running downstairs, she left the hotel, walked to the Rue de Provence, called a cab, and drove to M. de Villefort's house.

For the last month this wretched house had presented the gloomy appearance of a lazaretto infected with the plague. Some of the apartments were closed within and without; the shutters were only opened to admit a minute's air, showing the scared face of a footman, and immediately afterwards the window would be closed, like a gravestone falling on a sepulchre, and the neighbors would say to each other in a low voice, "Will there be another funeral today at the procureur's house?"

Madame Danglars involuntarily shuddered at the desolate aspect of the mansion; descending from the cab, she approached the door with trembling knees, and rang the bell. Three times did the bell ring with a dull, heavy sound, seeming to participate, in the general sadness, before the concierge appeared and peeped through the door, which he opened just wide enough to allow his words to be heard. He saw a lady, a fashionable, elegantly dressed lady, and yet the door remained almost closed.

"Do you intend opening the door?" said the baroness.

"First, madame, who are you?"

"Who am I? You know me well enough."

"We no longer know anyone, madame."

"You must be mad, my friend," said the baroness.

"Where do you come from?"

"Oh, this is too much!"

"Madame, these are my orders; excuse me. Your name?"

"The baroness Danglars; you have seen me twenty times."

"Possibly, madame. And now, what do you want?"

"Oh, how extraordinary! I shall complain to M. de Villefort of the impertinence of his servants."

"Madame, this is precaution, not impertinence; no one enters here without an order from M. d'Avrigny, or without speaking to the procureur."

"Well, I have business with the procureur."

"Is it pressing business?"

"You can imagine so, since I have not even brought my carriage out yet. But enough of this—here is my card, take it to your master."

"Madame will await my return?"

"Yes; go."

The concierge closed the door, leaving Madame Danglars in the street. She had not long to wait; directly afterwards the door was opened wide enough to admit her, and when she had passed through, it was again shut. Without losing sight of her for an instant, the concierge took a whistle from his pocket as soon as they entered the court, and blew it. The valet de chambre appeared on the door-steps.

"You will excuse this poor fellow, madame," he said, as he preceded the baroness, "but his orders are precise, and M. de Villefort begged me to tell you that he could not act otherwise."

In the court showing his merchandise, was a tradesman who had been admitted with the same precautions. The baroness ascended the steps; she felt herself strongly infected with the sadness which seemed to magnify her own, and still guided by the valet de chambre, who never lost sight of her for an instant, she was introduced to the magistrate's study.

Preoccupied as Madame Danglars had been with the object of her visit, the treatment she had received from these underlings appeared to her so insulting, that she began by complaining of it. But Villefort, raising his head, bowed down by grief, looked up at her with so sad a smile that her complaints died upon her lips.

"Forgive my servants," he said, "for a terror I cannot blame them for; from being suspected they have become suspicious."

Madame Danglars had often heard of the terror to which the magistrate alluded, but without the evidence of her own eyesight she could never have believed that the sentiment had been carried so far.

"You too, then, are unhappy?" she said.

"Yes, madame," replied the magistrate.

"Then you pity me!"

"Sincerely, madame."

"And you understand what brings me here?"

"You wish to speak to me about the circumstance which has just happened?"

"Yes, sir,—a fearful misfortune."

"You mean a mischance."

"A mischance?" repeated the baroness.

"Alas, madame," said the procureur with his imperturbable calmness of manner, "I consider those alone misfortunes which are irreparable."

"And do you suppose this will be forgotten?"

"Everything will be forgotten, madame," said Villefort. "Your daughter will be married tomorrow, if not today—in a week, if not tomorrow; and I do not think you can regret the intended husband of your daughter."

Madame Danglars gazed on Villefort, stupefied to find him so almost insultingly calm. "Am I come to a friend?" she asked in a tone full of mournful dignity.

"You know that you are, madame," said Villefort, whose pale cheeks became slightly flushed as he gave her the assurance. And truly this assurance carried him back to different events from those now occupying the baroness and him.

"Well, then, be more affectionate, my dear Villefort," said the baroness. "Speak to me not as a magistrate, but as a friend; and when I am in bitter anguish of spirit, do not tell me that I ought to be gay." Villefort bowed.

"When I hear misfortunes named, madame," he said, "I have within the last few months contracted the bad habit of thinking of my own, and then I cannot help drawing up an egotistical parallel in my mind. That is the reason that by the side of my misfortunes yours appear to me mere mischances; that is why my dreadful position makes yours appear enviable. But this annoys you; let us change the subject. You were saying, madame—"

"I came to ask you, my friend," said the baroness, "what will be done with this impostor?"

"Impostor," repeated Villefort; "certainly, madame, you appear to extenuate some cases, and exaggerate others. Impostor, indeed!—M. Andrea Cavalcanti, or rather M. Benedetto, is nothing more nor less than an assassin!"

"Sir, I do not deny the justice of your correction, but the more severely you arm yourself against that unfortunate man, the more deeply will you strike our family. Come, forget him for a moment, and instead of pursuing him, let him go."

"You are too late, madame; the orders are issued."

"Well, should he be arrested—do they think they will arrest him?"

"I hope so."

"If they should arrest him (I know that sometimes prisons afford means of escape), will you leave him in prison?"

The procureur shook his head.

"At least keep him there till my daughter be married."

"Impossible, madame; justice has its formalities."

"What, even for me?" said the baroness, half jesting, half in earnest.

"For all, even for myself among the rest," replied Villefort.

"Ah!" exclaimed the baroness, without expressing the ideas which the exclamation betrayed. Villefort looked at her with that piercing glance which reads the secrets of the heart.

"Yes, I know what you mean," he said; "you refer to the terrible rumors spread abroad in the world, that the deaths which have kept me in mourning for the last three months, and from which Valentine has only escaped by a miracle, have not happened by natural means."

"I was not thinking of that," replied Madame Danglars quickly.

"Yes, you were thinking of it, and with justice. You could not help thinking of it, and saying to yourself, 'you, who pursue crime so vindictively, answer now, why are there unpunished crimes in your dwelling?'" The baroness became pale. "You were saying this, were you not?"

"Well, I own it."

"I will answer you."

Villefort drew his armchair nearer to Madame Danglars; then resting both hands upon his desk he said in a voice more hollow than usual:

"There are crimes which remain unpunished because the criminals are unknown, and we might strike the innocent instead of the guilty; but when the culprits are discovered" (Villefort here extended his hand toward a large crucifix placed opposite to his desk)—"when they are discovered, I swear to you, by all I hold most sacred, that whoever they may be they shall die. Now, after the oath I have just taken, and which I will keep, madame, dare you ask for mercy for that wretch!"

"But, sir, are you sure he is as guilty as they say?"

"Listen; this is his description: 'Benedetto, condemned, at the age of sixteen, for five years to the galleys for forgery.' He promised well, as you see—first a runaway, then an assassin."

"And who is this wretch?"

"Who can tell?—a vagabond, a Corsican."

"Has no one owned him?"

"No one; his parents are unknown."

"But who was the man who brought him from Lucca?"

"Another rascal like himself, perhaps his accomplice." The baroness clasped her hands.

"Villefort," she exclaimed in her softest and most captivating manner.

"For Heaven's sake, madame," said Villefort, with a firmness of expression not altogether free from harshness—"for Heaven's sake, do not ask pardon of me for a guilty wretch! What am I?—the law. Has the law any eyes to witness your grief? Has the law ears to be melted by your sweet voice? Has the law a memory for all those soft recollections you endeavor to recall? No, madame; the law has commanded, and when it commands it strikes. You will tell me that I am a living being, and not a code—a man, and not a volume. Look at me, madame—look around me. Has mankind treated me as a brother? Have men loved me? Have they spared me? Has anyone shown the mercy towards me that you now ask at my hands? No, madame, they struck me, always struck me!

“Woman, siren that you are, do you persist in fixing on me that fascinating eye, which reminds me that I ought to blush? Well, be it so; let me blush for the faults you know, and perhaps—perhaps for even more than those! But having sinned myself,—it may be more deeply than others,—I never rest till I have torn the disguises from my fellow-creatures, and found out their weaknesses. I have always found them; and more,—I repeat it with joy, with triumph,—I have always found some proof of human perversity or error. Every criminal I condemn seems to me living evidence that I am not a hideous exception to the rest. Alas, alas, alas; all the world is wicked; let us therefore strike at wickedness!”

Villefort pronounced these last words with a feverish rage, which gave a ferocious eloquence to his words.

“But”‘ said Madame Danglars, resolving to make a last effort, “this young man, though a murderer, is an orphan, abandoned by everybody.”

“So much the worse, or rather, so much the better; it has been so ordained that he may have none to weep his fate.”

“But this is trampling on the weak, sir.”

“The weakness of a murderer!”

“His dishonor reflects upon us.”

“Is not death in my house?”

“Oh, sir,” exclaimed the baroness, “you are without pity for others, well, then, I tell you they will have no mercy on you!”

“Be it so!” said Villefort, raising his arms to heaven with a threatening gesture.

“At least, delay the trial till the next assizes; we shall then have six months before us.”

“No, madame,” said Villefort; “instructions have been given. There are yet five days left; five days are more than I require. Do you not think that I also long for forgetfulness? While working night and day, I sometimes lose all recollection of the past, and then I experience the same sort of happiness I can imagine the dead feel; still, it is better than suffering.”

“But, sir, he has fled; let him escape—inaction is a pardonable offence.”

“I tell you it is too late; early this morning the telegraph was employed, and at this very minute—”

“Sir,” said the valet de chambre, entering the room, “a dragoon has brought this despatch from the Minister of the Interior.”

Villefort seized the letter, and hastily broke the seal. Madame Danglars trembled with fear; Villefort started with joy.

"Arrested!" he exclaimed; "he was taken at Compiègne, and all is over."

Madame Danglars rose from her seat, pale and cold.

"Adieu, sir," she said.

"Adieu, madame," replied the king's attorney, as in an almost joyful manner he conducted her to the door. Then, turning to his desk, he said, striking the letter with the back of his right hand:

"Come, I had a forgery, three robberies, and two cases of arson, I only wanted a murder, and here it is. It will be a splendid session!"

Study Guide Questions

For Students:

1. What is the disgrace that befalls Danglars' family?
2. Why does Madame Danglars decide to go to M. de Villefort?
3. What does M. de Villefort say about the law?

For Reading Club:

1. How does the chapter comment on motherhood?
2. Compare and contrast the character of Madame Danglars with Mademoiselle Eugénie.
3. Discuss the statement, "in a society such as ours, satire inflicts a painful and incurable wound."

CHAPTER 100

The Apparition

As the procureur had told Madame Danglars, Valentine was not yet recovered. Bowed down with fatigue, she was indeed confined to her bed; and it was in her own room, and from the lips of Madame de Villefort, that she heard all the strange events we have related; we mean the flight of Eugénie and the arrest of Andrea Cavalcanti, or rather Benedetto, together with the accusation of murder pronounced against him. But Valentine was so weak that this recital scarcely produced the same effect it would have done had she been in her usual state of health. Indeed, her brain was only the seat of vague ideas, and confused forms, mingled with strange fancies, alone presented themselves before her eyes.

During the daytime Valentine's perceptions remained tolerably clear, owing to the constant presence of M. Noirtier, who caused himself to be carried to his granddaughter's room, and watched her with his paternal tenderness; Villefort also, on his return from the law courts, frequently passed an hour or two with his father and child.

At six o'clock Villefort retired to his study, at eight M. d'Avrigny himself arrived, bringing the night draught prepared for the young girl, and then M. Noirtier was carried away. A nurse of the doctor's choice succeeded them, and never left till about ten or eleven o'clock, when Valentine was asleep. As she went downstairs she gave the keys of Valentine's room to M. de Villefort, so that no one could reach the sick-room excepting through that of Madame de Villefort and little Edward.

Every morning Morrel called on Noirtier to receive news of Valentine, and, extraordinary as it seemed, each day found him less uneasy. Certainly, though Valentine still labored under dreadful nervous excitement, she was better; and moreover, Monte Cristo had told him when, half distracted, he had rushed to the count's house, that if she were not dead in two hours she would be saved. Now four days had elapsed, and Valentine still lived.

The nervous excitement of which we speak pursued Valentine even in her sleep, or rather in that state of somnolence which succeeded her waking hours; it was then, in the silence of night, in the dim light shed from the alabaster lamp on the chimney-piece, that she saw the shadows pass and repass which hover over the bed of sickness, and fan the fever with their trembling wings. First she fancied she saw her stepmother threatening her, then Morrel stretched his arms towards her; sometimes mere strangers, like the Count of Monte Cristo came to visit her; even the very furniture, in these moments of delirium, seemed to move, and this state lasted till about three o'clock in the morning, when a deep, heavy slumber overcame the young girl, from which she did not awake till daylight.

On the evening of the day on which Valentine had learned of the flight of Eugénie and the arrest of Benedetto,—Villefort having retired as well as Noirtier and d'Avrigny,—her thoughts wandered in a confused maze, alternately reviewing her own situation and the events she had just heard.

Eleven o'clock had struck. The nurse, having placed the beverage prepared by the doctor within reach of the patient, and locked the door, was listening with terror to the comments of the servants in the kitchen, and storing her memory with all the horrible stories which had for some months past amused the occupants of the antechambers in the house of the king's attorney. Meanwhile an unexpected scene was passing in the room which had been so carefully locked.

Ten minutes had elapsed since the nurse had left; Valentine, who for the last hour had been suffering from the fever which returned nightly, incapable of controlling her ideas, was forced to yield to the excitement which exhausted itself in producing and reproducing a succession and recurrence of the same fancies and images. The night-lamp threw out countless rays, each resolving itself into some strange form to her disordered imagination, when suddenly by its flickering light Valentine thought she saw the door of her library, which was in the recess by the chimney-piece, open slowly, though she in vain listened for the sound of the hinges on which it turned.

At any other time Valentine would have seized the silken bell-pull and summoned assistance, but nothing astonished her in her present situation. Her reason told her that all the visions she beheld were but the children of her imagination, and the conviction was strengthened by the fact that in the morning no traces remained of the nocturnal phantoms, who disappeared with the coming of daylight.

From behind the door a human figure appeared, but the girl was too familiar with such apparitions to be alarmed, and therefore only stared, hoping to recognize Morrel.

The figure advanced towards the bed and appeared to listen with profound attention. At this moment a ray of light glanced across the face of the midnight visitor.

"It is not he," she murmured, and waited, in the assurance that this was but a dream, for the man to disappear or assume some other form. Still, she felt her pulse, and finding it throb violently she remembered that the best method of dispelling such illusions was to drink, for a draught of the beverage prepared by the doctor to allay her fever seemed to cause a reaction of the brain, and for a short time she suffered less. Valentine therefore reached her hand towards the glass, but as soon as her trembling arm left the bed the apparition advanced more quickly towards her, and approached the young girl so closely that she fancied she heard his breath, and felt the pressure of his hand.

This time the illusion, or rather the reality, surpassed anything Valentine had before experienced; she began to believe herself really alive and awake, and the belief that her reason was this time not deceived made her shudder. The pressure she felt was evidently intended to arrest her arm, and she slowly withdrew it. Then the figure, from whom she could not detach her eyes, and who appeared more protecting than menacing, took the glass, and walking towards the night-light held it up, as if to test its transparency. This did not seem sufficient; the man, or rather the ghost—for he trod so softly that no sound was heard—then poured out about a spoonful into the glass, and drank it.

Valentine witnessed this scene with a sentiment of stupefaction. Every minute she had expected that it would vanish and give place to another vision; but the man, instead of dissolving like a shadow, again approached her, and said in an agitated voice, "Now you may drink."

Valentine shuddered. It was the first time one of these visions had ever addressed her in a living voice, and she was about to utter an exclamation. The man placed his finger on her lips.

"The Count of Monte Cristo!" she murmured.

It was easy to see that no doubt now remained in the young girl's mind as to the reality of the scene; her eyes started with terror, her hands trembled, and she rapidly drew the bedclothes closer to her. Still, the presence of Monte Cristo at such an hour, his mysterious, fanciful, and extraordinary entrance into her room through the wall, might well seem impossibilities to her shattered reason.

"Do not call anyone—do not be alarmed," said the count; "do not let a shade of suspicion or uneasiness remain in your breast; the man standing before you, Valentine (for this time it is no ghost), is nothing more than the tenderest father and the most respectful friend you could dream of."

Valentine could not reply; the voice which indicated the real presence of a being in the room, alarmed her so much that she feared to utter a syllable; still the expression of her eyes seemed to inquire, "If your intentions are pure, why are you here?" The count's marvellous sagacity understood all that was passing in the young girl's mind.

"Listen to me," he said, "or, rather, look upon me; look at my face, paler even than usual, and my eyes, red with weariness—for four days I have not closed them, for I have been constantly watching you, to protect and preserve you for Maximilian."

The blood mounted rapidly to the cheeks of Valentine, for the name just announced by the count dispelled all the fear with which his presence had inspired her.

"Maximilian!" she exclaimed, and so sweet did the sound appear to her, that she repeated it—"Maximilian!—has he then owned all to you?"

"Everything. He told me your life was his, and I have promised him that you shall live."

"You have promised him that I shall live?"

"Yes."

"But, sir, you spoke of vigilance and protection. Are you a doctor?"

"Yes; the best you could have at the present time, believe me."

"But you say you have watched?" said Valentine uneasily; "where have you been?—I have not seen you."

The count extended his hand towards the library.

"I was hidden behind that door," he said, "which leads into the next house, which I have rented."

Valentine turned her eyes away, and, with an indignant expression of pride and modest fear, exclaimed:

"Sir, I think you have been guilty of an unparalleled intrusion, and that what you call protection is more like an insult."

"Valentine," he answered, "during my long watch over you, all I have observed has been what people visited you, what nourishment was prepared, and what beverage was served; then, when the latter appeared dangerous to me, I entered, as I have now done, and substituted, in the place of the poison, a healthful draught; which, instead of producing the death intended, caused life to circulate in your veins."

"Poison—death!" exclaimed Valentine, half believing herself under the influence of some feverish hallucination; "what are you saying, sir?"

"Hush, my child," said Monte Cristo, again placing his finger upon her lips, "I did say poison and death. But drink some of this;" and the count took a bottle from his pocket, containing a red liquid, of which he poured a few drops into the glass. "Drink this, and then take nothing more tonight."

Valentine stretched out her hand, but scarcely had she touched the glass when she drew back in fear. Monte Cristo took the glass, drank half its contents, and then presented it to Valentine, who smiled and swallowed the rest.

"Oh, yes," she exclaimed, "I recognize the flavor of my nocturnal beverage which refreshed me so much, and seemed to ease my aching brain. Thank you, sir, thank you!"

"This is how you have lived during the last four nights, Valentine," said the count. "But, oh, how I passed that time! Oh, the wretched hours I have endured—the torture to which I have submitted when I saw the deadly poison poured into your glass, and how I trembled lest you should drink it before I could find time to throw it away!"

"Sir," said Valentine, at the height of her terror, "you say you endured tortures when you saw the deadly poison poured into my glass; but if you saw this, you must also have seen the person who poured it?"

"Yes."

Valentine raised herself in bed, and drew over her chest, which appeared whiter than snow, the embroidered cambric, still moist with the cold dews of delirium, to which were now added those of terror. "You saw the person?" repeated the young girl.

"Yes," repeated the count.

"What you tell me is horrible, sir. You wish to make me believe something too dreadful. What?—attempt to murder me in my father's house, in my room, on my bed of sickness? Oh, leave me, sir; you are tempting me—you make me doubt the goodness of Providence—it is impossible, it cannot be!"

"Are you the first that this hand has stricken? Have you not seen M. de Saint-Méran, Madame de Saint-Méran, Barrois, all fall? Would not M. Noirtier also have fallen a victim, had not the treatment he has been pursuing for the last three years neutralized the effects of the poison?"

"Oh, Heaven," said Valentine; "is this the reason why grandpapa has made me share all his beverages during the last month?"

"And have they all tasted of a slightly bitter flavor, like that of dried orange-peel?"

"Oh, yes, yes!"

"Then that explains all," said Monte Cristo. "Your grandfather knows, then, that a poisoner lives here; perhaps he even suspects the person. He has been fortifying you, his beloved child, against the fatal effects of the poison, which has failed because your system was already impregnated with it. But even this would have availed little against a more deadly medium of death employed four days ago, which is generally but too fatal."

"But who, then, is this assassin, this murderer?"

"Let me also ask you a question. Have you never seen anyone enter your room at night?"

"Oh, yes; I have frequently seen shadows pass close to me, approach, and disappear; but I took them for visions raised by my feverish imagination, and indeed when you entered I thought I was under the influence of delirium."

"Then you do not know who it is that attempts your life?"

"No," said Valentine; "who could desire my death?"

"You shall know it now, then," said Monte Cristo, listening.

"How do you mean?" said Valentine, looking anxiously around.

"Because you are not feverish or delirious tonight, but thoroughly awake; midnight is striking, which is the hour murderers choose."

"Oh, heavens," exclaimed Valentine, wiping off the drops which ran down her forehead. Midnight struck slowly and sadly; every hour seemed to strike with leaden weight upon the heart of the poor girl.

"Valentine," said the count, "summon up all your courage; still the beatings of your heart; do not let a sound escape you, and feign to be asleep; then you will see."

Valentine seized the count's hand. "I think I hear a noise," she said; "leave me."

"Good-bye, for the present," replied the count, walking upon tiptoe towards the library door, and smiling with an expression so sad and paternal that the young girl's heart was filled with gratitude.

Before closing the door he turned around once more, and said, "Not a movement—not a word; let them think you asleep, or perhaps you may be killed before I have the power of helping you."

And with this fearful injunction the count disappeared through the door, which noiselessly closed after him.

Study Guide Questions

For Students:

1. What is Valentine's current condition?
2. Who comes to Valentine's room and what does he do?
3. How does the Count keep an eye on Valentine?

For Reading Club:

1. Do you think revenge can often engulf the innocent?
2. Who do you think is poisoning everybody in Villefort's house and why?
3. How does the Count help Valentine?

CHAPTER 101

Locusta

Valentine was alone; two other clocks, slower than that of Saint-Philippe-du-Roule, struck the hour of midnight from different directions, and excepting the rumbling of a few carriages all was silent. Then Valentine's attention was engrossed by the clock in her room, which marked the seconds. She began counting them, remarking that they were much slower than the beatings of her heart; and still she doubted,—the inoffensive Valentine could not imagine that anyone should desire her death. Why should they? To what end? What had she done to excite the malice of an enemy?

There was no fear of her falling asleep. One terrible idea pressed upon her mind,—that someone existed in the world who had attempted to assassinate her, and who was about to endeavor to do so again. Supposing this person, wearied at the inefficacy of the poison, should, as Monte Cristo intimated, have recourse to steel!—What if the count should have no time to run to her rescue!—What if her last moments were approaching, and she should never again see Morrel!

When this terrible chain of ideas presented itself, Valentine was nearly persuaded to ring the bell, and call for help. But through the door she fancied she saw the luminous eye of the count—that eye which lived in her memory, and the recollection overwhelmed her with so much shame that she asked herself whether any amount of gratitude could ever repay his adventurous and devoted friendship.

Twenty minutes, twenty tedious minutes, passed thus, then ten more, and at last the clock struck the half-hour.

Just then the sound of finger-nails slightly grating against the door of the library informed Valentine that the count was still watching, and recommended her to do the same; at the same time, on the opposite side, that is towards Edward's room, Valentine fancied that she heard the creaking of the floor; she listened attentively, holding her breath till she was nearly suffocated; the lock turned, and the door slowly opened. Valentine had raised herself upon her elbow, and had scarcely time to throw herself down on the bed and shade her eyes with her arm; then, trembling, agitated, and her heart beating with indescribable terror, she awaited the event.

Someone approached the bed and drew back the curtains. Valentine summoned every effort, and breathed with that regular respiration which announces tranquil sleep.

"Valentine!" said a low voice.

The girl shuddered to the heart but did not reply.

"Valentine," repeated the same voice.

Still silent: Valentine had promised not to wake. Then everything was still, excepting that Valentine heard the almost noiseless sound of some liquid being poured into the glass she had just emptied. Then she ventured to open her eyelids, and glance over her extended arm. She saw a woman in a white dressing-gown pouring a liquor from a phial into her glass. During this short time Valentine must have held her breath, or moved in some slight degree, for the woman, disturbed, stopped and leaned over the bed, in order the better to ascertain whether Valentine slept: it was Madame de Villefort.

On recognizing her step-mother, Valentine could not repress a shudder, which caused a vibration in the bed. Madame de Villefort instantly stepped back close to the wall, and there, shaded by the bed-curtains, she silently and attentively watched the slightest movement of Valentine. The latter recollected the terrible caution of Monte Cristo; she fancied that the hand not holding the phial clasped a long sharp knife. Then collecting all her remaining strength, she forced herself to close her eyes; but this simple operation upon the most delicate organs of our frame, generally so easy to accomplish, became almost impossible at this moment, so much did curiosity struggle to retain the eyelid open and learn the truth. Madame de Villefort, however, reassured by the silence, which was alone disturbed by the regular breathing of Valentine, again extended her hand, and half hidden by the curtains succeeded in emptying the contents of the phial into the glass. Then she retired so gently that Valentine did not know she had left the room. She only witnessed the withdrawal of the arm—the fair round arm of a woman but twenty-five years old, and who yet spread death around her.

It is impossible to describe the sensations experienced by Valentine during the minute and a half Madame de Villefort remained in the room.

The grating against the library-door aroused the young girl from the stupor in which she was plunged, and which almost amounted to insensibility. She raised her head with an effort. The noiseless door again turned on its hinges, and the Count of Monte Cristo reappeared.

"Well," said he, "do you still doubt?"

"Oh," murmured the young girl.

"Have you seen?"

"Alas!"

"Did you recognize?" Valentine groaned.

"Oh, yes;" she said, "I saw, but I cannot believe!"

"Would you rather die, then, and cause Maximilian's death?"

"Oh," repeated the young girl, almost bewildered, "can I not leave the house?—can I not escape?"

"Valentine, the hand which now threatens you will pursue you everywhere; your servants will be seduced with gold, and death will be offered to you disguised in every shape. You will find it in the water you drink from the spring, in the fruit you pluck from the tree."

"But did you not say that my kind grandfather's precaution had neutralized the poison?"

"Yes, but not against a strong dose; the poison will be changed, and the quantity increased." He took the glass and raised it to his lips. "It is already done," he said; "brucine is no longer employed, but a simple narcotic! I can recognize the flavor of the alcohol in which it has been dissolved. If you had taken what Madame de Villefort has poured into your glass, Valentine—Valentine—you would have been doomed!"

"But," exclaimed the young girl, "why am I thus pursued?"

"Why?—are you so kind—so good—so unsuspicious of ill, that you cannot understand, Valentine?"

"No, I have never injured her."

"But you are rich, Valentine; you have 200,000 livres a year, and you prevent her son from enjoying these 200,000 livres."

"How so? The fortune is not her gift, but is inherited from my relations."

"Certainly; and that is why M. and Madame de Saint-Méran have died; that is why M. Noirtier was sentenced the day he made you his heir; that is why you, in your turn, are to die—it is because your father would inherit your property, and your brother, his only son, succeed to his."

"Edward? Poor child! Are all these crimes committed on his account?"

"Ah, then you at length understand?"

"Heaven grant that this may not be visited upon him!"

"Valentine, you are an angel!"

"But why is my grandfather allowed to live?"

"It was considered, that you dead, the fortune would naturally revert to your brother, unless he were disinherited; and besides, the crime appearing useless, it would be folly to commit it."

"And is it possible that this frightful combination of crimes has been invented by a woman?"

"Do you recollect in the arbor of the Hôtel des Postes, at Perugia, seeing a man in a brown cloak, whom your stepmother was questioning upon *aqua tofana*? Well, ever since then, the infernal project has been ripening in her brain."

"Ah, then, indeed, sir," said the sweet girl, bathed in tears, "I see that I am condemned to die!"

"No, Valentine, for I have foreseen all their plots; no, your enemy is conquered since we know her, and you will live, Valentine—live to be happy yourself, and to confer happiness upon a noble heart; but to insure this you must rely on me."

"Command me, sir—what am I to do?"

"You must blindly take what I give you."

"Alas, were it only for my own sake, I should prefer to die!"

"You must not confide in anyone—not even in your father."

"My father is not engaged in this fearful plot, is he, sir?" asked Valentine, clasping her hands.

"No; and yet your father, a man accustomed to judicial accusations, ought to have known that all these deaths have not happened naturally; it is he who should have watched over you—he should have occupied my place—he should have emptied that glass—he should have risen against the assassin. Spectre against spectre!" he murmured in a low voice, as he concluded his sentence.

"Sir," said Valentine, "I will do all I can to live, for there are two beings who love me and will die if I die—my grandfather and Maximilian."

"I will watch over them as I have over you."

"Well, sir, do as you will with me;" and then she added, in a low voice, "oh, heavens, what will befall me?"

"Whatever may happen, Valentine, do not be alarmed; though you suffer; though you lose sight, hearing, consciousness, fear nothing; though you should awake and be ignorant where you are, still do not fear; even though you should find yourself in a sepulchral vault or coffin. Reassure yourself, then, and say to yourself: 'At this moment, a friend, a father, who lives for my happiness and that of Maximilian, watches over me!'"

"Alas, alas, what a fearful extremity!"

"Valentine, would you rather denounce your stepmother?"

"I would rather die a hundred times—oh, yes, die!"

"No, you will not die; but will you promise me, whatever happens, that you will not complain, but hope?"

"I will think of Maximilian!"

"You are my own darling child, Valentine! I alone can save you, and I will."

Valentine in the extremity of her terror joined her hands,—for she felt that the moment had arrived to ask for courage,—and began to pray, and while uttering little more than incoherent words, she forgot that her white shoulders had no other covering than her long hair, and that the pulsations of her heart could be seen through the lace of her nightdress. Monte Cristo gently laid his hand on the young girl's arm, drew the velvet coverlet close to her throat, and said with a paternal smile:

"My child, believe in my devotion to you as you believe in the goodness of Providence and the love of Maximilian." Valentine gave him a look full of gratitude, and remained as docile as a child.

Then he drew from his waistcoat-pocket the little emerald box, raised the golden lid, and took from it a pastille about the size of a pea, which he placed in her hand. She took it, and looked attentively on the count; there was an expression on the face of her intrepid protector which commanded her veneration. She evidently interrogated him by her look.

"Yes," said he.

Valentine carried the pastille to her mouth, and swallowed it.

"And now, my dear child, adieu for the present. I will try and gain a little sleep, for you are saved."

"Go," said Valentine, "whatever happens, I promise you not to fear."

Monte Cristo for some time kept his eyes fixed on the young girl, who gradually fell asleep, yielding to the effects of the narcotic the count had given her. Then he took the glass, emptied three parts of the contents in the fireplace, that it might be supposed Valentine had taken it, and replaced it on the table; then he disappeared, after throwing a farewell glance on Valentine, who slept with the confidence and innocence of an angel at the feet of the Lord.

Study Guide Questions

For Students:

1. Who is trying to poison Valentine?
2. What is the poisoner's motive?
3. Why and how does the Count empty Valentine's glass?

For Reading Club:

1. Discuss Madame de. Villefort's character and what is ironic about her actions?
2. Do you think maternal love can justify Madame de. Villefort's crimes?
3. How do you think the chapter reveals the dysfunctionality of a family?

CHAPTER 102

Valentine

The night-light continued to burn on the chimney-piece, exhausting the last drops of oil which floated on the surface of the water. The globe of the lamp appeared of a reddish hue, and the flame, brightening before it expired, threw out the last flickerings which in an inanimate object have been so often compared with the convulsions of a human creature in its final agonies. A dull and dismal light was shed over the bedclothes and curtains surrounding the young girl. All noise in the streets had ceased, and the silence was frightful.

It was then that the door of Edward's room opened, and a head we have before noticed appeared in the glass opposite; it was Madame de Villefort, who came to witness the effects of the drink she had prepared. She stopped in the doorway, listened for a moment to the flickering of the lamp, the only sound in that deserted room, and then advanced to the table to see if Valentine's glass were empty. It was still about a quarter full, as we before stated. Madame de Villefort emptied the contents into the ashes, which she disturbed that they might the more readily absorb the liquid; then she carefully rinsed the glass, and wiping it with her handkerchief replaced it on the table.

If anyone could have looked into the room just then he would have noticed the hesitation with which Madame de Villefort approached the bed and looked fixedly on Valentine. The dim light, the profound silence, and the gloomy thoughts inspired by the hour, and still more by her own conscience, all combined to produce a sensation of fear; the poisoner was terrified at the contemplation of her own work.

At length she rallied, drew aside the curtain, and leaning over the pillow gazed intently on Valentine. The young girl no longer breathed, no breath issued through the half-closed teeth; the white lips no longer quivered—the eyes were suffused with a bluish vapor, and the long black lashes rested on a cheek white as wax. Madame de

Villefort gazed upon the face so expressive even in its stillness; then she ventured to raise the coverlet and press her hand upon the young girl's heart. It was cold and motionless. She only felt the pulsation in her own fingers, and withdrew her hand with a shudder. One arm was hanging out of the bed; from shoulder to elbow it was moulded after the arms of Germain Pillon's "Graces,"[16] but the fore-arm seemed to be slightly distorted by convulsion, and the hand, so delicately formed, was resting with stiff outstretched fingers on the framework of the bed. The nails, too, were turning blue.

Madame de Villefort had no longer any doubt; all was over—she had consummated the last terrible work she had to accomplish. There was no more to do in the room, so the poisoner retired stealthily, as though fearing to hear the sound of her own footsteps; but as she withdrew she still held aside the curtain, absorbed in the irresistible attraction always exerted by the picture of death, so long as it is merely mysterious and does not excite disgust.

The minutes passed; Madame de Villefort could not drop the curtain which she held like a funeral pall over the head of Valentine. She was lost in reverie, and the reverie of crime is remorse.

Just then the lamp again flickered; the noise startled Madame de Villefort, who shuddered and dropped the curtain. Immediately afterwards the light expired, and the room was plunged in frightful obscurity, while the clock at that minute struck half-past four.

Overpowered with agitation, the poisoner succeeded in groping her way to the door, and reached her room in an agony of fear. The darkness lasted two hours longer; then by degrees a cold light crept through the Venetian blinds, until at length it revealed the objects in the room.

About this time the nurse's cough was heard on the stairs and the woman entered the room with a cup in her hand. To the tender eye of a father or a lover, the first glance would have sufficed to reveal Valentine's condition; but to this hireling, Valentine only appeared to sleep.

"Good," she exclaimed, approaching the table, "she has taken part of her draught; the glass is three-quarters empty."

Then she went to the fireplace and lit the fire, and although she had just left her bed, she could not resist the temptation offered by Valentine's sleep, so she threw herself into an armchair to snatch a little more rest. The clock striking eight awoke her.

---

[16] Germain Pillon was a famous French sculptor (1535-1598). His best known work is "The Three Graces," now in the Louvre.

Astonished at the prolonged slumber of the patient, and frightened to see that the arm was still hanging out of the bed, she advanced towards Valentine, and for the first time noticed the white lips. She tried to replace the arm, but it moved with a frightful rigidity which could not deceive a sick-nurse. She screamed aloud; then running to the door exclaimed:

"Help, help!"

"What is the matter?" asked M. d'Avrigny, at the foot of the stairs, it being the hour he usually visited her.

"What is it?" asked Villefort, rushing from his room. "Doctor, do you hear them call for help?"

"Yes, yes; let us hasten up; it was in Valentine's room."

But before the doctor and the father could reach the room, the servants who were on the same floor had entered, and seeing Valentine pale and motionless on her bed, they lifted up their hands towards heaven and stood transfixed, as though struck by lightening.

"Call Madame de Villefort!—Wake Madame de Villefort!" cried the procureur from the door of his chamber, which apparently he scarcely dared to leave. But instead of obeying him, the servants stood watching M. d'Avrigny, who ran to Valentine, and raised her in his arms.

"What?—this one, too?" he exclaimed. "Oh, where will be the end?"

Villefort rushed into the room.

"What are you saying, doctor?" he exclaimed, raising his hands to heaven.

"I say that Valentine is dead!" replied d'Avrigny, in a voice terrible in its solemn calmness.

M. de Villefort staggered and buried his head in the bed. On the exclamation of the doctor and the cry of the father, the servants all fled with muttered imprecations; they were heard running down the stairs and through the long passages, then there was a rush in the court, afterwards all was still; they had, one and all, deserted the accursed house.

Just then, Madame de Villefort, in the act of slipping on her dressing-gown, threw aside the drapery and for a moment stood motionless, as though interrogating the occupants of the room, while she endeavored to call up some rebellious tears. On a sudden she stepped, or rather bounded, with outstretched arms, towards the table. She saw d'Avrigny curiously examining the glass, which she felt certain of having emptied during the night. It was now a third full, just as it was when she threw the contents into the ashes. The spectre of Valentine rising before the poisoner would have alarmed her less. It was, indeed, the same color as the draught she had poured into the glass, and which Valentine had drunk; it was indeed the poison, which could not deceive M. d'Avrigny, which he now examined so closely; it was doubtless a miracle from heaven, that, notwithstanding her precautions, there should be some trace, some proof remaining to reveal the crime.

While Madame de Villefort remained rooted to the spot like a statue of terror, and Villefort, with his head hidden in the bedclothes, saw nothing around him, d'Avrigny approached the window, that he might the better examine the contents of the glass, and dipping the tip of his finger in, tasted it.

"Ah," he exclaimed, "it is no longer brucine that is used; let me see what it is!"

Then he ran to one of the cupboards in Valentine's room, which had been transformed into a medicine closet, and taking from its silver case a small bottle of nitric acid, dropped a little of it into the liquor, which immediately changed to a blood-red color.

"Ah," exclaimed d'Avrigny, in a voice in which the horror of a judge unveiling the truth was mingled with the delight of a student making a discovery.

Madame de Villefort was overpowered; her eyes first flashed and then swam, she staggered towards the door and disappeared. Directly afterwards the distant sound of a heavy weight falling on the ground was heard, but no one paid any attention to it; the nurse was engaged in watching the chemical analysis, and Villefort was still absorbed in grief. M. d'Avrigny alone had followed Madame de Villefort with his eyes, and watched her hurried retreat. He lifted up the drapery over the entrance to Edward's room, and his eye reaching as far as Madame de Villefort's apartment, he beheld her extended lifeless on the floor.

"Go to the assistance of Madame de Villefort," he said to the nurse. "Madame de Villefort is ill."

"But Mademoiselle de Villefort—" stammered the nurse.

"Mademoiselle de Villefort no longer requires help," said d'Avrigny, "since she is dead."

"Dead,—dead!" groaned forth Villefort, in a paroxysm of grief, which was the more terrible from the novelty of the sensation in the iron heart of that man.

"Dead!" repeated a third voice. "Who said Valentine was dead?"

The two men turned round, and saw Morrel standing at the door, pale and terror-stricken. This is what had happened. At the usual time, Morrel had presented himself at the little door leading to Noirtier's room. Contrary to custom, the door was open, and having no occasion to ring he entered. He waited for a moment in the hall and called for a servant to conduct him to M. Noirtier; but no one answered, the servants having, as we know, deserted the house. Morrel had no particular reason for uneasiness;

Monte Cristo had promised him that Valentine should live, and so far he had always fulfilled his word. Every night the count had given him news, which was the next morning confirmed by Noirtier. Still this extraordinary silence appeared strange to him, and he called a second and third time; still no answer. Then he determined to go up. Noirtier's room was opened, like all the rest. The first thing he saw was the old man sitting in his armchair in his usual place, but his eyes expressed alarm, which was confirmed by the pallor which overspread his features.

"How are you, sir?" asked Morrel, with a sickness of heart.

"Well," answered the old man, by closing his eyes; but his appearance manifested increasing uneasiness.

"You are thoughtful, sir," continued Morrel; "you want something; shall I call one of the servants?"

"Yes," replied Noirtier.

Morrel pulled the bell, but though he nearly broke the cord no one answered. He turned towards Noirtier; the pallor and anguish expressed on his countenance momentarily increased.

"Oh," exclaimed Morrel, "why do they not come? Is anyone ill in the house?" The eyes of Noirtier seemed as though they would start from their sockets. "What is the matter? You alarm me. Valentine? Valentine?"

"Yes, yes," signed Noirtier.

Maximilian tried to speak, but he could articulate nothing; he staggered, and supported himself against the wainscot. Then he pointed to the door.

"Yes, yes, yes!" continued the old man.

Maximilian rushed up the little staircase, while Noirtier's eyes seemed to say,—"Quicker, quicker!"

In a minute the young man darted through several rooms, till at length he reached Valentine's.

There was no occasion to push the door, it was wide open. A sob was the only sound he heard. He saw as though in a mist, a black figure kneeling and buried in a confused mass of white drapery. A terrible fear transfixed him. It was then he heard a voice exclaim "Valentine is dead!" and another voice which, like an echo repeated:

"Dead,—dead!"

Study Guide Questions

For Students:

1. Who is declared dead by D'Avrigny?
2. How does Madame de. Villefort react to Valentine's death?
3. How does Maxmillian come to know of Valentine's tragic fate?

For Reading Club:

1. Do you think Madame de. Villefort is remorseful or merely panicked?
2. Discuss the chaos in Villefort's house.
3. Do you think Valentine's suffering is underserved? Why or why not?

CHAPTER 103

Maximilian

Villefort rose, half-ashamed of being surprised in such a paroxysm of grief. The terrible office he had held for twenty-five years had succeeded in making him more or less than man. His glance, at first wandering, fixed itself upon Morrel. "Who are you, sir," he asked, "that forget that this is not the manner to enter a house stricken with death? Go, sir, go!"

But Morrel remained motionless; he could not detach his eyes from that disordered bed, and the pale corpse of the young girl who was lying on it.

"Go!—do you hear?" said Villefort, while d'Avrigny advanced to lead Morrel out. Maximilian stared for a moment at the corpse, gazed all around the room, then upon the two men; he opened his mouth to speak, but finding it impossible to give utterance to the innumerable ideas that occupied his brain, he went out, thrusting his hands through his hair in such a manner that Villefort and d'Avrigny, for a moment diverted from the engrossing topic, exchanged glances, which seemed to say,—"He is mad!"

But in less than five minutes the staircase groaned beneath an extraordinary weight. Morrel was seen carrying, with superhuman strength, the armchair containing Noirtier upstairs. When he reached the landing he placed the armchair on the floor and rapidly rolled it into Valentine's room. This could only have been accomplished by means of unnatural strength supplied by powerful excitement. But the most fearful spectacle was Noirtier being pushed towards the bed, his face expressing all his meaning, and his eyes supplying the want of every other faculty. That pale face and flaming glance appeared to Villefort like a frightful apparition. Each time he had been brought into contact with his father, something terrible had happened.

"See what they have done!" cried Morrel, with one hand leaning on the back of the chair, and the other extended towards Valentine. "See, my father, see!"

Villefort drew back and looked with astonishment on the young man, who, almost a stranger to him, called Noirtier his father. At this moment the whole soul of the old man seemed centred in his eyes which became bloodshot; the veins of the throat swelled; his cheeks and temples became purple, as though he was struck with epilepsy; nothing was wanting to complete this but the utterance of a cry. And the cry issued from his pores, if we may thus speak—a cry frightful in its silence. D'Avrigny rushed towards the old man and made him inhale a powerful restorative.

"Sir," cried Morrel, seizing the moist hand of the paralytic, "they ask me who I am, and what right I have to be here. Oh, you know it, tell them, tell them!" And the young man's voice was choked by sobs.

As for the old man, his chest heaved with his panting respiration. One could have thought that he was undergoing the agonies preceding death. At length, happier than the young man, who sobbed without weeping, tears glistened in the eyes of Noirtier.

"Tell them," said Morrel in a hoarse voice, "tell them that I am her betrothed. Tell them she was my beloved, my noble girl, my only blessing in the world. Tell them—oh, tell them, that corpse belongs to me!"

The young man overwhelmed by the weight of his anguish, fell heavily on his knees before the bed, which his fingers grasped with convulsive energy. D'Avrigny, unable to bear the sight of this touching emotion, turned away; and Villefort, without seeking any further explanation, and attracted towards him by the irresistible magnetism which draws us towards those who have loved the people for whom we mourn, extended his hand towards the young man.

But Morrel saw nothing; he had grasped the hand of Valentine, and unable to weep vented his agony in groans as he bit the sheets. For some time nothing was heard in that chamber but sobs, exclamations, and prayers. At length Villefort, the most composed of all, spoke:

"Sir," said he to Maximilian, "you say you loved Valentine, that you were betrothed to her. I knew nothing of this engagement, of this love, yet I, her father, forgive you, for I see that your grief is real and deep; and besides my own sorrow is too great for anger to find a place in my heart. But you see that the angel whom you hoped for has left this earth—she has nothing more to do with the adoration of men. Take a last farewell, sir, of her sad remains; take the hand you expected to possess once more within your own, and then separate yourself from her forever. Valentine now requires only the ministrations of the priest."

"You are mistaken, sir," exclaimed Morrel, raising himself on one knee, his heart pierced by a more acute pang than any he had yet felt—"you are mistaken; Valentine, dying as she has, not only requires a priest, but an avenger. *You*, M. de Villefort, send for the priest; *I* will be the avenger."

"What do you mean, sir?" asked Villefort, trembling at the new idea inspired by the delirium of Morrel.

"I tell you, sir, that two persons exist in you; the father has mourned sufficiently, now let the procureur fulfil his office."

The eyes of Noirtier glistened, and d'Avrigny approached.

"Gentlemen," said Morrel, reading all that passed through the minds of the witnesses to the scene, "I know what I am saying, and you know as well as I do what I am about to say—Valentine has been assassinated!"

Villefort hung his head, d'Avrigny approached nearer, and Noirtier said "Yes" with his eyes.

"Now, sir," continued Morrel, "in these days no one can disappear by violent means without some inquiries being made as to the cause of her disappearance, even were she not a young, beautiful, and adorable creature like Valentine. Now, M. le Procureur du Roi," said Morrel with increasing vehemence, "no mercy is allowed; I denounce the crime; it is your place to seek the assassin."

The young man's implacable eyes interrogated Villefort, who, on his side, glanced from Noirtier to d'Avrigny. But instead of finding sympathy in the eyes of the doctor and his father, he only saw an expression as inflexible as that of Maximilian.

"Yes," indicated the old man.

"Assuredly," said d'Avrigny.

"Sir," said Villefort, striving to struggle against this triple force and his own emotion,—"sir, you are deceived; no one commits crimes here. I am stricken by fate. It is horrible, indeed, but no one assassinates."

The eyes of Noirtier lighted up with rage, and d'Avrigny prepared to speak. Morrel, however, extended his arm, and commanded silence.

"And I say that murders *are* committed here," said Morrel, whose voice, though lower in tone, lost none of its terrible distinctness: "I tell you that this is the fourth victim within the last four months. I tell you, Valentine's life was attempted by poison four days ago, though she escaped, owing to the precautions of M. Noirtier. I tell you that the dose has been double, the poison changed, and that this time it has succeeded. I tell you that you know these things as well as I do, since this gentleman has forewarned you, both as a doctor and as a friend."

"Oh, you rave, sir," exclaimed Villefort, in vain endeavoring to escape the net in which he was taken.

"I rave?" said Morrel; "well, then, I appeal to M. d'Avrigny himself. Ask him, sir, if he recollects the words he uttered in the garden of this house on the night of Madame de Saint-Méran's death. You thought yourselves alone, and talked about that tragical death, and the fatality you mentioned then is the same which has caused the murder of Valentine." Villefort and d'Avrigny exchanged looks.

"Yes, yes," continued Morrel; "recall the scene, for the words you thought were only given to silence and solitude fell into my ears. Certainly, after witnessing the culpable indolence manifested by M. de Villefort towards his own relations, I ought to have denounced him to the authorities; then I should not have been an accomplice to thy death, as I now am, sweet, beloved Valentine; but the accomplice shall become the avenger. This fourth murder is apparent to all, and if thy father abandon thee, Valentine, it is I, and I swear it, that shall pursue the assassin."

And this time, as though nature had at least taken compassion on the vigorous frame, nearly bursting with its own strength, the words of Morrel were stifled in his throat; his breast heaved; the tears, so long rebellious, gushed from his eyes; and he threw himself weeping on his knees by the side of the bed.

Then d'Avrigny spoke. "And I, too," he exclaimed in a low voice, "I unite with M. Morrel in demanding justice for crime; my blood boils at the idea of having encouraged a murderer by my cowardly concession."

"Oh, merciful Heavens!" murmured Villefort. Morrel raised his head, and reading the eyes of the old man, which gleamed with unnatural lustre,—

"Stay," he said, "M. Noirtier wishes to speak."

"Yes," indicated Noirtier, with an expression the more terrible, from all his faculties being centred in his glance.

"Do you know the assassin?" asked Morrel.

"Yes," replied Noirtier.

"And will you direct us?" exclaimed the young man. "Listen, M. d'Avrigny, listen!"

Noirtier looked upon Morrel with one of those melancholy smiles which had so often made Valentine happy, and thus fixed his attention. Then, having riveted the eyes of his interlocutor on his own, he glanced towards the door.

"Do you wish me to leave?" said Morrel, sadly.

"Yes," replied Noirtier.

"Alas, alas, sir, have pity on me!"

The old man's eyes remained fixed on the door.

"May I, at least, return?" asked Morrel.

"Yes."

"Must I leave alone?"

"No."

"Whom am I to take with me? The procureur?"

"No."

"The doctor?"

"Yes."

"You wish to remain alone with M. de Villefort?"

"Yes."

"But can he understand you?"

"Yes."

"Oh," said Villefort, inexpressibly delighted to think that the inquiries were to be made by him alone,—"oh, be satisfied, I can understand my father." While uttering these words with this expression of joy, his teeth clashed together violently.

D'Avrigny took the young man's arm, and led him out of the room. A more than deathlike silence then reigned in the house. At the end of a quarter of an hour a faltering footstep was heard, and Villefort appeared at the door of the apartment where d'Avrigny and Morrel had been staying, one absorbed in meditation, the other in grief.

"You can come," he said, and led them back to Noirtier.

Morrel looked attentively on Villefort. His face was livid, large drops rolled down his face, and in his fingers he held the fragments of a quill pen which he had torn to atoms.

"Gentlemen," he said in a hoarse voice, "give me your word of honor that this horrible secret shall forever remain buried amongst ourselves!" The two men drew back.

"I entreat you—" continued Villefort.

"But," said Morrel, "the culprit—the murderer—the assassin."

"Do not alarm yourself, sir; justice will be done," said Villefort. "My father has revealed the culprit's name; my father thirsts for revenge as much as you do, yet even he conjures you as I do to keep this secret. Do you not, father?"

"Yes," resolutely replied Noirtier. Morrel suffered an exclamation of horror and surprise to escape him.

"Oh, sir," said Villefort, arresting Maximilian by the arm, "if my father, the inflexible man, makes this request, it is because he knows, be assured, that Valentine will be terribly revenged. Is it not so, father?"

The old man made a sign in the affirmative. Villefort continued:

"He knows me, and I have pledged my word to him. Rest assured, gentlemen, that within three days, in a less time than justice would demand, the revenge I shall have taken for the murder of my child will be such as to make the boldest heart tremble;"

and as he spoke these words he ground his teeth, and grasped the old man's senseless hand.

"Will this promise be fulfilled, M. Noirtier?" asked Morrel, while d'Avrigny looked inquiringly.

"Yes," replied Noirtier with an expression of sinister joy.

"Swear, then," said Villefort, joining the hands of Morrel and d'Avrigny, "swear that you will spare the honor of my house, and leave me to avenge my child."

D'Avrigny turned round and uttered a very feeble "Yes," but Morrel, disengaging his hand, rushed to the bed, and after having pressed the cold lips of Valentine with his own, hurriedly left, uttering a long, deep groan of despair and anguish.

We have before stated that all the servants had fled. M. de Villefort was therefore obliged to request M. d'Avrigny to superintend all the arrangements consequent upon a death in a large city, more especially a death under such suspicious circumstances.

It was something terrible to witness the silent agony, the mute despair of Noirtier, whose tears silently rolled down his cheeks. Villefort retired to his study, and d'Avrigny left to summon the doctor of the mayoralty, whose office it is to examine bodies after decease, and who is expressly named "the doctor of the dead." M. Noirtier could not be persuaded to quit his grandchild. At the end of a quarter of an hour M. d'Avrigny returned with his associate; they found the outer gate closed, and not a servant remaining in the house; Villefort himself was obliged to open to them. But he stopped on the landing; he had not the courage to again visit the death chamber. The two doctors, therefore, entered the room alone. Noirtier was near the bed, pale, motionless, and silent as the corpse. The district doctor approached with the indifference of a man accustomed to spend half his time amongst the dead; he then lifted the sheet which was placed over the face, and just unclosed the lips.

"Alas," said d'Avrigny, "she is indeed dead, poor child!"

"Yes," answered the doctor laconically, dropping the sheet he had raised. Noirtier uttered a kind of hoarse, rattling sound; the old man's eyes sparkled, and the good doctor understood that he wished to behold his child. He therefore approached the bed, and while his companion was dipping the fingers with which he had touched the lips of the corpse in chloride of lime, he uncovered the calm and pale face, which looked like that of a sleeping angel.

A tear, which appeared in the old man's eye, expressed his thanks to the doctor. The doctor of the dead then laid his permit on the corner of the table, and having fulfilled his duty, was conducted out by d'Avrigny. Villefort met them at the door of his study; having in a few words thanked the district doctor, he turned to d'Avrigny, and said:

"And now the priest."

"Is there any particular priest you wish to pray with Valentine?" asked d'Avrigny.

"No." said Villefort; "fetch the nearest."

"The nearest," said the district doctor, "is a good Italian abbé, who lives next door to you. Shall I call on him as I pass?"

"D'Avrigny," said Villefort, "be so kind, I beseech you, as to accompany this gentleman. Here is the key of the door, so that you can go in and out as you please; you will bring the priest with you, and will oblige me by introducing him into my child's room."

"Do you wish to see him?"

"I only wish to be alone. You will excuse me, will you not? A priest can understand a father's grief."

And M. de Villefort, giving the key to d'Avrigny, again bade farewell to the strange doctor, and retired to his study, where he began to work. For some temperaments work is a remedy for all afflictions.

As the doctors entered the street, they saw a man in a cassock standing on the threshold of the next door.

"This is the abbé of whom I spoke," said the doctor to d'Avrigny. D'Avrigny accosted the priest.

"Sir," he said, "are you disposed to confer a great obligation on an unhappy father who has just lost his daughter? I mean M. de Villefort, the king's attorney."

"Ah," said the priest, in a marked Italian accent; "yes, I have heard that death is in that house."

"Then I need not tell you what kind of service he requires of you."

"I was about to offer myself, sir," said the priest; "it is our mission to forestall our duties."

"It is a young girl."

"I know it, sir; the servants who fled from the house informed me. I also know that her name is Valentine, and I have already prayed for her."

"Thank you, sir," said d'Avrigny; "since you have commenced your sacred office, deign to continue it. Come and watch by the dead, and all the wretched family will be grateful to you."

"I am going, sir; and I do not hesitate to say that no prayers will be more fervent than mine."

D'Avrigny took the priest's hand, and without meeting Villefort, who was engaged in his study, they reached Valentine's room, which on the following night was to be occupied by the undertakers. On entering the room, Noirtier's eyes met those of the abbé, and no doubt he read some particular expression in them, for he remained in the room. D'Avrigny recommended the attention of the priest to the living as well as to the dead, and the abbé promised to devote his prayers to Valentine and his attentions to Noirtier.

In order, doubtless, that he might not be disturbed while fulfilling his sacred mission, the priest rose as soon as d'Avrigny departed, and not only bolted the door through which the doctor had just left, but also that leading to Madame de Villefort's room.

Study Guide Questions

For Students:

1. To whom does Maximillian go after knowing that Valentine is dead?
2. Does Valentine die of illness or has she been murdered?
3. Who is the priest called for Valentine?

For Reading Club:

1. Discuss Maximillian's grief. Do you think such love exists in the modern world?
2. Do you believe Villefort has been stricken by fate or his past crimes?
3. How do you think the chapter comments on the theme of undeserved suffering?

CHAPTER 104

Danglars' Signature

The next morning dawned dull and cloudy. During the night the undertakers had executed their melancholy office, and wrapped the corpse in the winding-sheet, which, whatever may be said about the equality of death, is at least a last proof of the luxury so pleasing in life. This winding-sheet was nothing more than a beautiful piece of cambric, which the young girl had bought a fortnight before.

During the evening two men, engaged for the purpose, had carried Noirtier from Valentine's room into his own, and contrary to all expectation there was no difficulty in withdrawing him from his child. The Abbé Busoni had watched till daylight, and then left without calling anyone. D'Avrigny returned about eight o'clock in the morning; he met Villefort on his way to Noirtier's room, and accompanied him to see how the old man had slept. They found him in the large armchair, which served him for a bed, enjoying a calm, nay, almost a smiling sleep. They both stood in amazement at the door.

"See," said d'Avrigny to Villefort, "nature knows how to alleviate the deepest sorrow. No one can say that M. Noirtier did not love his child, and yet he sleeps."

"Yes, you are right," replied Villefort, surprised; "he sleeps, indeed! And this is the more strange, since the least contradiction keeps him awake all night."

"Grief has stunned him," replied d'Avrigny; and they both returned thoughtfully to the procureur's study.

"See, I have not slept," said Villefort, showing his undisturbed bed; "grief does not stun me. I have not been in bed for two nights; but then look at my desk; see what I have written during these two days and nights. I have filled those papers, and have made out the accusation against the assassin Benedetto. Oh, work, work,—my passion, my joy, my delight,—it is for thee to alleviate my sorrows!" and he convulsively grasped the hand of d'Avrigny.

"Do you require my services now?" asked d'Avrigny.

"No," said Villefort; "only return again at eleven o'clock; at twelve the—the—oh, Heavens, my poor, poor child!" and the procureur again becoming a man, lifted up his eyes and groaned.

"Shall you be present in the reception-room?"

"No; I have a cousin who has undertaken this sad office. I shall work, doctor—when I work I forget everything."

And, indeed, no sooner had the doctor left the room, than he was again absorbed in work. On the doorsteps d'Avrigny met the cousin whom Villefort had mentioned, a personage as insignificant in our story as in the world he occupied—one of those beings designed from their birth to make themselves useful to others. He was punctual, dressed in black, with crape around his hat, and presented himself at his cousin's with a face made up for the occasion, and which he could alter as might be required.

At eleven o'clock the mourning-coaches rolled into the paved court, and the Rue du Faubourg Saint-Honoré was filled with a crowd of idlers, equally pleased to witness the festivities or the mourning of the rich, and who rush with the same avidity to a funeral procession as to the marriage of a duchess.

Gradually the reception-room filled, and some of our old friends made their appearance—we mean Debray, Château-Renaud, and Beauchamp, accompanied by all the leading men of the day at the bar, in literature, or the army, for M. de Villefort moved in the first Parisian circles, less owing to his social position than to his personal merit.

The cousin standing at the door ushered in the guests, and it was rather a relief to the indifferent to see a person as unmoved as themselves, and who did not exact a mournful face or force tears, as would have been the case with a father, a brother, or a lover. Those who were acquainted soon formed into little groups. One of them was made of Debray, Château-Renaud, and Beauchamp.

"Poor girl," said Debray, like the rest, paying an involuntary tribute to the sad event,—"poor girl, so young, so rich, so beautiful! Could you have imagined this scene, Château-Renaud, when we saw her, at the most three weeks ago, about to sign that contract?"

"Indeed, no," said Château-Renaud."

"Did you know her?"

"I spoke to her once or twice at Madame de Morcerf's, among the rest; she appeared to me charming, though rather melancholy. Where is her stepmother? Do you know?"

"She is spending the day with the wife of the worthy gentleman who is receiving us."

"Who is he?"

"Whom do you mean?"

"The gentleman who receives us? Is he a deputy?"

"Oh, no. I am condemned to witness those gentlemen every day," said Beauchamp; "but he is perfectly unknown to me."

"Have you mentioned this death in your paper?"

"It has been mentioned, but the article is not mine; indeed, I doubt if it will please M. Villefort, for it says that if four successive deaths had happened anywhere else than in the house of the king's attorney, he would have interested himself somewhat more about it."

"Still," said Château-Renaud, "Dr. d'Avrigny, who attends my mother, declares he is in despair about it. But whom are you seeking, Debray?"

"I am seeking the Count of Monte Cristo" said the young man.

"I met him on the boulevard, on my way here," said Beauchamp. "I think he is about to leave Paris; he was going to his banker."

"His banker? Danglars is his banker, is he not?" asked Château-Renaud of Debray.

"I believe so," replied the secretary with slight uneasiness. "But Monte Cristo is not the only one I miss here; I do not see Morrel."

"Morrel? Do they know him?" asked Château-Renaud. "I think he has only been introduced to Madame de Villefort."

"Still, he ought to have been here," said Debray; "I wonder what will be talked about tonight; this funeral is the news of the day. But hush, here comes our minister of justice; he will feel obliged to make some little speech to the cousin," and the three young men drew near to listen.

Beauchamp told the truth when he said that on his way to the funeral he had met Monte Cristo, who was directing his steps towards the Rue de la Chaussée d'Antin, to M. Danglars'. The banker saw the carriage of the count enter the courtyard, and advanced to meet him with a sad, though affable smile.

"Well," said he, extending his hand to Monte Cristo, "I suppose you have come to sympathize with me, for indeed misfortune has taken possession of my house. When I perceived you, I was just asking myself whether I had not wished harm towards those poor Morcerfs, which would have justified the proverb of 'He who wishes misfortunes to happen to others experiences them himself.' Well, on my word of honor, I answered, 'No!' I wished no ill to Morcerf; he was a little proud, perhaps, for a man who like myself has risen from nothing; but we all have our faults. Do you know, count, that persons of our time of life—not that you belong to the class, you are still a young man,—but as I was saying, persons of our time of life have been very unfortunate this year. For example, look at the puritanical procureur, who has just lost his daughter, and in fact nearly all his family, in so singular a manner; Morcerf dishonored and dead; and then myself covered with ridicule through the villany of Benedetto; besides—"

"Besides what?" asked the Count.

"Alas, do you not know?"

"What new calamity?"

"My daughter—"

"Mademoiselle Danglars?"

"Eugénie has left us!"

"Good heavens, what are you telling me?"

"The truth, my dear count. Oh, how happy you must be in not having either wife or children!"

"Do you think so?"

"Indeed I do."

"And so Mademoiselle Danglars—"

"She could not endure the insult offered to us by that wretch, so she asked permission to travel."

"And is she gone?"

"The other night she left."

"With Madame Danglars?"

"No, with a relation. But still, we have quite lost our dear Eugénie; for I doubt whether her pride will ever allow her to return to France."

"Still, baron," said Monte Cristo, "family griefs, or indeed any other affliction which would crush a man whose child was his only treasure, are endurable to a millionaire. Philosophers may well say, and practical men will always support the opinion, that money mitigates many trials; and if you admit the efficacy of this sovereign balm, you ought to be very easily consoled—you, the king of finance, the focus of immeasurable power."

Danglars looked at him askance, as though to ascertain whether he spoke seriously.

"Yes," he answered, "if a fortune brings consolation, I ought to be consoled; I am rich."

"So rich, dear sir, that your fortune resembles the pyramids; if you wished to demolish them you could not, and if it were possible, you would not dare!"

Danglars smiled at the good-natured pleasantry of the count. "That reminds me," he said, "that when you entered I was on the point of signing five little bonds; I have already signed two: will you allow me to do the same to the others?"

"Pray do so."

There was a moment's silence, during which the noise of the banker's pen was alone heard, while Monte Cristo examined the gilt mouldings on the ceiling.

"Are they Spanish, Haitian, or Neapolitan bonds?" said Monte Cristo.

"No," said Danglars, smiling, "they are bonds on the bank of France, payable to bearer. Stay, count," he added, "you, who may be called the emperor, if I claim the title of king of finance, have you many pieces of paper of this size, each worth a million?"

The count took into his hands the papers, which Danglars had so proudly presented to him, and read:—

"'To the Governor of the Bank. Please pay to my order, from the fund deposited by me, the sum of a million, and charge the same to my account.

"Baron Danglars.'"

"One, two, three, four, five," said Monte Cristo; "five millions—why what a Crœsus you are!"

"This is how I transact business," said Danglars.

"It is really wonderful," said the count; "above all, if, as I suppose, it is payable at sight."

"It is, indeed," said Danglars.

"It is a fine thing to have such credit; really, it is only in France these things are done. Five millions on five little scraps of paper!—it must be seen to be believed."

"You do not doubt it?"

"No!"

"You say so with an accent—stay, you shall be convinced; take my clerk to the bank, and you will see him leave it with an order on the Treasury for the same sum."

"No," said Monte Cristo folding the five notes, "most decidedly not; the thing is so curious, I will make the experiment myself. I am credited on you for six millions. I have drawn nine hundred thousand francs, you therefore still owe me five millions and a hundred thousand francs. I will take the five scraps of paper that I now hold as bonds, with your signature alone, and here is a receipt in full for the six millions between us. I had prepared it beforehand, for I am much in want of money today."

And Monte Cristo placed the bonds in his pocket with one hand, while with the other he held out the receipt to Danglars. If a thunderbolt had fallen at the banker's feet, he could not have experienced greater terror.

"What," he stammered, "do you mean to keep that money? Excuse me, excuse me, but I owe this money to the charity fund,—a deposit which I promised to pay this morning."

"Oh, well, then," said Monte Cristo, "I am not particular about these five notes, pay me in a different form; I wished, from curiosity, to take these, that I might be able to say that without any advice or preparation the house of Danglars had paid me five millions without a minute's delay; it would have been remarkable. But here are your bonds; pay me differently;" and he held the bonds towards Danglars, who seized them like a vulture extending its claws to withhold the food that is being wrested from its grasp.

Suddenly he rallied, made a violent effort to restrain himself, and then a smile gradually widened the features of his disturbed countenance.

"Certainly," he said, "your receipt is money."

"Oh dear, yes; and if you were at Rome, the house of Thomson & French would make no more difficulty about paying the money on my receipt than you have just done."

"Pardon me, count, pardon me."

"Then I may keep this money?"

"Yes," said Danglars, while the perspiration started from the roots of his hair. "Yes, keep it—keep it."

Monte Cristo replaced the notes in his pocket with that indescribable expression which seemed to say, "Come, reflect; if you repent there is still time."

"No," said Danglars, "no, decidedly no; keep my signatures. But you know none are so formal as bankers in transacting business; I intended this money for the charity fund, and I seemed to be robbing them if I did not pay them with these precise bonds. How absurd—as if one crown were not as good as another. Excuse me;" and he began to laugh loudly, but nervously.

"Certainly, I excuse you," said Monte Cristo graciously, "and pocket them." And he placed the bonds in his pocket-book.

"But," said Danglars, "there is still a sum of one hundred thousand francs?"

"Oh, a mere nothing," said Monte Cristo. "The balance would come to about that sum; but keep it, and we shall be quits."

"Count," said Danglars, "are you speaking seriously?"

"I never joke with bankers," said Monte Cristo in a freezing manner, which repelled impertinence; and he turned to the door, just as the valet de chambre announced:

"M. de Boville, Receiver-General of the charities."

"*Ma foi*," said Monte Cristo; "I think I arrived just in time to obtain your signatures, or they would have been disputed with me."

Danglars again became pale, and hastened to conduct the count out. Monte Cristo exchanged a ceremonious bow with M. de Boville, who was standing in the waiting-room, and who was introduced into Danglars' room as soon as the count had left.

The count's serious face was illumined by a faint smile, as he noticed the portfolio which the receiver-general held in his hand. At the door he found his carriage, and was immediately driven to the bank. Meanwhile Danglars, repressing all emotion, advanced to meet the receiver-general. We need not say that a smile of condescension was stamped upon his lips.

"Good-morning, creditor," said he; "for I wager anything it is the creditor who visits me."

"You are right, baron," answered M. de Boville; "the charities present themselves to you through me; the widows and orphans depute me to receive alms to the amount of five millions from you."

"And yet they say orphans are to be pitied," said Danglars, wishing to prolong the jest. "Poor things!"

"Here I am in their name," said M. de Boville; "but did you receive my letter yesterday?"

"Yes."

"I have brought my receipt."

"My dear M. de Boville, your widows and orphans must oblige me by waiting twenty-four hours, since M. de Monte Cristo whom you just saw leaving here—you did see him, I think?"

"Yes; well?"

"Well, M. de Monte Cristo has just carried off their five millions."

"How so?"

"The count has an unlimited credit upon me; a credit opened by Thomson & French, of Rome; he came to demand five millions at once, which I paid him with checks on the bank. My funds are deposited there, and you can understand that if I draw out ten millions on the same day it will appear rather strange to the governor. Two days will be a different thing," said Danglars, smiling.

"Come," said Boville, with a tone of entire incredulity, "five millions to that gentleman who just left, and who bowed to me as though he knew me?"

"Perhaps he knows you, though you do not know him; M. de Monte Cristo knows everybody."

"Five millions!"

"Here is his receipt. Believe your own eyes." M. de Boville took the paper Danglars presented him, and read:

"Received of Baron Danglars the sum of five million one hundred thousand francs, to be repaid on demand by the house of Thomson & French of Rome."

"It is really true," said M. de Boville.

"Do you know the house of Thomson & French?"

"Yes, I once had business to transact with it to the amount of 200,000 francs; but since then I have not heard it mentioned."

"It is one of the best houses in Europe," said Danglars, carelessly throwing down the receipt on his desk.

"And he had five millions in your hands alone! Why, this Count of Monte Cristo must be a nabob?"

"Indeed I do not know what he is; he has three unlimited credits—one on me, one on Rothschild, one on Lafitte; and, you see," he added carelessly, "he has given me the preference, by leaving a balance of 100,000 francs."

M. de Boville manifested signs of extraordinary admiration.

"I must visit him," he said, "and obtain some pious grant from him."

"Oh, you may make sure of him; his charities alone amount to 20,000 francs a month."

"It is magnificent! I will set before him the example of Madame de Morcerf and her son."

"What example?"

"They gave all their fortune to the hospitals."

"What fortune?"

"Their own—M. de Morcerf's, who is deceased."

"For what reason?"

"Because they would not spend money so guiltily acquired."

"And what are they to live upon?"

"The mother retires into the country, and the son enters the army."

"Well, I must confess, these are scruples."

"I registered their deed of gift yesterday."

"And how much did they possess?"

"Oh, not much—from twelve to thirteen hundred thousand francs. But to return to our millions."

"Certainly," said Danglars, in the most natural tone in the world. "Are you then pressed for this money?"

"Yes; for the examination of our cash takes place tomorrow."

"Tomorrow? Why did you not tell me so before? Why, it is as good as a century! At what hour does the examination take place?"

"At two o'clock."

"Send at twelve," said Danglars, smiling.

M. de Boville said nothing, but nodded his head, and took up the portfolio.

"Now I think of it, you can do better," said Danglars.

"How do you mean?"

"The receipt of M. de Monte Cristo is as good as money; take it to Rothschild's or Lafitte's, and they will take it off your hands at once."

"What, though payable at Rome?"

"Certainly; it will only cost you a discount of 5,000 or 6,000 francs."

The receiver started back.

"*Ma foi!*" he said, "I prefer waiting till tomorrow. What a proposition!"

"I thought, perhaps," said Danglars with supreme impertinence, "that you had a deficiency to make up?"

"Indeed," said the receiver.

"And if that were the case it would be worth while to make some sacrifice."

"Thank you, no, sir."

"Then it will be tomorrow."

"Yes; but without fail."

"Ah, you are laughing at me; send tomorrow at twelve, and the bank shall be notified."

"I will come myself."

"Better still, since it will afford me the pleasure of seeing you." They shook hands.

"By the way," said M. de Boville, "are you not going to the funeral of poor Mademoiselle de Villefort, which I met on my road here?"

"No," said the banker; "I have appeared rather ridiculous since that affair of Benedetto, so I remain in the background."

"Bah, you are wrong. How were you to blame in that affair?"

"Listen—when one bears an irreproachable name, as I do, one is rather sensitive."

"Everybody pities you, sir; and, above all, Mademoiselle Danglars!"

"Poor Eugénie!" said Danglars; "do you know she is going to embrace a religious life?"

"No."

"Alas, it is unhappily but too true. The day after the event, she decided on leaving Paris with a nun of her acquaintance; they are gone to seek a very strict convent in Italy or Spain."

"Oh, it is terrible!" and M. de Boville retired with this exclamation, after expressing acute sympathy with the father. But he had scarcely left before Danglars, with an energy of action those can alone understand who have seen Robert Macaire represented by Frédérick,[17] exclaimed:

"Fool!"

Then enclosing Monte Cristo's receipt in a little pocket-book, he added:—"Yes, come at twelve o'clock; I shall then be far away."

Then he double-locked his door, emptied all his drawers, collected about fifty thousand francs in bank-notes, burned several papers, left others exposed to view, and then commenced writing a letter which he addressed:

"To Madame la Baronne Danglars."

"I will place it on her table myself tonight," he murmured. Then taking a passport from his drawer he said,—"Good, it is available for two months longer."

[17] Frédérick Lemaître—French actor (1800-1876). Robert Macaire is the hero of two favorite melodramas—"Chien de Montargis" and "Chien d'Aubry"—and the name is applied to bold criminals as a term of derision.

Study Guide Questions

For Students:

1. What does Danglars tell the Count?
2. What does Danglars give to the Count?
3. Who is M. de Boville and why does he come to meet Danglars?

For Reading Club:

1. Discuss the statement, "nature knows how to alleviate the deepest sorrows."
2. Do you think Danglars' signature will ruin him?
3. Where do you think Eugénie has gone?

CHAPTER 105

The Cemetery of Père-Lachaise

M. de Boville had indeed met the funeral procession which was taking Valentine to her last home on earth. The weather was dull and stormy, a cold wind shook the few remaining yellow leaves from the boughs of the trees, and scattered them among the crowd which filled the boulevards. M. de Villefort, a true Parisian, considered the cemetery of Père-Lachaise alone worthy of receiving the mortal remains of a Parisian family; there alone the corpses belonging to him would be surrounded by worthy associates. He had therefore purchased a vault, which was quickly occupied by members of his family. On the front of the monument was inscribed: "The families of Saint-Méran and Villefort," for such had been the last wish expressed by poor Renée, Valentine's mother. The pompous procession therefore wended its way towards Père-Lachaise from the Faubourg Saint-Honoré. Having crossed Paris, it passed through the Faubourg du Temple, then leaving the exterior boulevards, it reached the cemetery. More than fifty private carriages followed the twenty mourning-coaches, and behind them more than five hundred persons joined in the procession on foot.

These last consisted of all the young people whom Valentine's death had struck like a thunderbolt, and who, notwithstanding the raw chilliness of the season, could not refrain from paying a last tribute to the memory of the beautiful, chaste, and adorable girl, thus cut off in the flower of her youth.

As they left Paris, an equipage with four horses, at full speed, was seen to draw up suddenly; it contained Monte Cristo. The count left the carriage and mingled in the crowd who followed on foot. Château-Renaud perceived him and immediately alighting from his *coupé*, joined him; Beauchamp did the same.

The count looked attentively through every opening in the crowd; he was evidently watching for someone, but his search ended in disappointment.

"Where is Morrel?" he asked; "do either of these gentlemen know where he is?"

"We have already asked that question," said Château-Renaud, "for none of us has seen him."

The count was silent, but continued to gaze around him. At length they arrived at the cemetery. The piercing eye of Monte Cristo glanced through clusters of bushes and trees, and was soon relieved from all anxiety, for seeing a shadow glide between the yew-trees, Monte Cristo recognized him whom he sought.

One funeral is generally very much like another in this magnificent metropolis. Black figures are seen scattered over the long white avenues; the silence of earth and heaven is alone broken by the noise made by the crackling branches of hedges planted around the monuments; then follows the melancholy chant of the priests, mingled now and then with a sob of anguish, escaping from some woman concealed behind a mass of flowers.

The shadow Monte Cristo had noticed passed rapidly behind the tomb of Abélard and Héloïse, placed itself close to the heads of the horses belonging to the hearse, and following the undertaker's men, arrived with them at the spot appointed for the burial. Each person's attention was occupied. Monte Cristo saw nothing but the shadow, which no one else observed. Twice the count left the ranks to see whether the object of his interest had any concealed weapon beneath his clothes. When the procession stopped, this shadow was recognized as Morrel, who, with his coat buttoned up to his throat, his face livid, and convulsively crushing his hat between his fingers, leaned against a tree, situated on an elevation commanding the mausoleum, so that none of the funeral details could escape his observation.

Everything was conducted in the usual manner. A few men, the least impressed of all by the scene, pronounced a discourse, some deploring this premature death, others expatiating on the grief of the father, and one very ingenious person quoting the fact that Valentine had solicited pardon of her father for criminals on whom the arm of justice was ready to fall—until at length they exhausted their stores of metaphor and mournful speeches, elaborate variations on the stanzas of Malherbe to Du Périer.

Monte Cristo heard and saw nothing, or rather he only saw Morrel, whose calmness had a frightful effect on those who knew what was passing in his heart.

"See," said Beauchamp, pointing out Morrel to Debray. "What is he doing up there?" And they called Château-Renaud's attention to him.

"How pale he is!" said Château-Renaud, shuddering.

"He is cold," said Debray.

"Not at all," said Château-Renaud, slowly; "I think he is violently agitated. He is very susceptible."

"Bah," said Debray; "he scarcely knew Mademoiselle de Villefort; you said so yourself."

"True. Still I remember he danced three times with her at Madame de Morcerf's. Do you recollect that ball, count, where you produced such an effect?"

"No, I do not," replied Monte Cristo, without even knowing of what or to whom he was speaking, so much was he occupied in watching Morrel, who was holding his breath with emotion.

"The discourse is over; farewell, gentlemen," said the count, unceremoniously.

And he disappeared without anyone seeing whither he went.

The funeral being over, the guests returned to Paris. Château-Renaud looked for a moment for Morrel; but while they were watching the departure of the count, Morrel had quitted his post, and Château-Renaud, failing in his search, joined Debray and Beauchamp.

Monte Cristo concealed himself behind a large tomb and awaited the arrival of Morrel, who by degrees approached the tomb now abandoned by spectators and workmen. Morrel threw a glance around, but before it reached the spot occupied by Monte Cristo the latter had advanced yet nearer, still unperceived. The young man knelt down. The count, with outstretched neck and glaring eyes, stood in an attitude ready to pounce upon Morrel upon the first occasion. Morrel bent his head till it touched the stone, then clutching the grating with both hands, he murmured:

"Oh, Valentine!"

The count's heart was pierced by the utterance of these two words; he stepped forward, and touching the young man's shoulder, said:

"I was looking for you, my friend." Monte Cristo expected a burst of passion, but he was deceived, for Morrel turning round, said calmly,—

"You see I was praying." The scrutinizing glance of the count searched the young man from head to foot. He then seemed more easy.

"Shall I drive you back to Paris?" he asked.

"No, thank you."

"Do you wish anything?"

"Leave me to pray."

The count withdrew without opposition, but it was only to place himself in a situation where he could watch every movement of Morrel, who at length arose, brushed the dust from his knees, and turned towards Paris, without once looking back. He walked slowly down the Rue de la Roquette. The count, dismissing his carriage, followed him about a hundred paces behind. Maximilian crossed the canal and entered the Rue Meslay by the boulevards.

Five minutes after the door had been closed on Morrel's entrance, it was again opened for the count. Julie was at the entrance of the garden, where she was attentively watching Penelon, who, entering with zeal into his profession of gardener, was very busy grafting some Bengal roses. "Ah, count," she exclaimed, with the delight manifested by every member of the family whenever he visited the Rue Meslay.

"Maximilian has just returned, has he not, madame?" asked the count.

"Yes, I think I saw him pass; but pray, call Emmanuel."

"Excuse me, madame, but I must go up to Maximilian's room this instant," replied Monte Cristo, "I have something of the greatest importance to tell him."

"Go, then," she said with a charming smile, which accompanied him until he had disappeared.

Monte Cristo soon ran up the staircase conducting from the ground floor to Maximilian's room; when he reached the landing he listened attentively, but all was still. Like many old houses occupied by a single family, the room door was panelled with glass; but it was locked, Maximilian was shut in, and it was impossible to see what was passing in the room, because a red curtain was drawn before the glass. The count's anxiety was manifested by a bright color which seldom appeared on the face of that imperturbable man.

"What shall I do!" he uttered, and reflected for a moment; "shall I ring? No, the sound of a bell, announcing a visitor, will but accelerate the resolution of one in Maximilian's situation, and then the bell would be followed by a louder noise."

Monte Cristo trembled from head to foot and as if his determination had been taken with the rapidity of lightning, he struck one of the panes of glass with his elbow; the glass was shivered to atoms, then withdrawing the curtain he saw Morrel, who had been writing at his desk, bound from his seat at the noise of the broken window.

"I beg a thousand pardons," said the count, "there is nothing the matter, but I slipped down and broke one of your panes of glass with my elbow. Since it is opened, I will take advantage of it to enter your room; do not disturb yourself—do not disturb yourself!"

And passing his hand through the broken glass, the count opened the door. Morrel, evidently discomposed, came to meet Monte Cristo less with the intention of receiving him than to exclude his entry.

"*Ma foi,*" said Monte Cristo, rubbing his elbow, "it's all your servant's fault; your stairs are so polished, it is like walking on glass."

"Are you hurt, sir?" coldly asked Morrel.

"I believe not. But what are you about there? You were writing."

"I?"

"Your fingers are stained with ink."

"Ah, true, I was writing. I do sometimes, soldier though I am."

Monte Cristo advanced into the room; Maximilian was obliged to let him pass, but he followed him.

"You were writing?" said Monte Cristo with a searching look.

"I have already had the honor of telling you I was," said Morrel.

The count looked around him.

"Your pistols are beside your desk," said Monte Cristo, pointing with his finger to the pistols on the table.

"I am on the point of starting on a journey," replied Morrel disdainfully.

"My friend," exclaimed Monte Cristo in a tone of exquisite sweetness.

"Sir?"

"My friend, my dear Maximilian, do not make a hasty resolution, I entreat you."

"I make a hasty resolution?" said Morrel, shrugging his shoulders; "is there anything extraordinary in a journey?"

"Maximilian," said the count, "let us both lay aside the mask we have assumed. You no more deceive me with that false calmness than I impose upon you with my frivolous solicitude. You can understand, can you not, that to have acted as I have done, to have broken that glass, to have intruded on the solitude of a friend—you can understand that, to have done all this, I must have been actuated by real uneasiness, or rather by a terrible conviction. Morrel, you are going to destroy yourself!"

"Indeed, count," said Morrel, shuddering; "what has put this into your head?"

"I tell you that you are about to destroy yourself," continued the count, "and here is proof of what I say;" and, approaching the desk, he removed the sheet of paper which Morrel had placed over the letter he had begun, and took the latter in his hands.

Morrel rushed forward to tear it from him, but Monte Cristo perceiving his intention, seized his wrist with his iron grasp.

"You wish to destroy yourself," said the count; "you have written it."

"Well," said Morrel, changing his expression of calmness for one of violence—"well, and if I do intend to turn this pistol against myself, who shall prevent me—who will dare prevent me? All my hopes are blighted, my heart is broken, my life a burden, everything around me is sad and mournful; earth has become distasteful to me, and human voices distract me. It is a mercy to let me die, for if I live I shall lose my reason and become mad. When, sir, I tell you all this with tears of heartfelt anguish, can you reply that I am wrong, can you prevent my putting an end to my miserable existence? Tell me, sir, could you have the courage to do so?"

"Yes, Morrel," said Monte Cristo, with a calmness which contrasted strangely with the young man's excitement; "yes, I would do so."

"You?" exclaimed Morrel, with increasing anger and reproach—"you, who have deceived me with false hopes, who have cheered and soothed me with vain promises, when I might, if not have saved her, at least have seen her die in my arms! You, who pretend to understand everything, even the hidden sources of knowledge,—and who enact the part of a guardian angel upon earth, and could not even find an antidote to a poison administered to a young girl! Ah, sir, indeed you would inspire me with pity, were you not hateful in my eyes."

"Morrel—"

"Yes; you tell me to lay aside the mask, and I will do so, be satisfied! When you spoke to me at the cemetery, I answered you—my heart was softened; when you arrived here, I allowed you to enter. But since you abuse my confidence, since you have devised a new torture after I thought I had exhausted them all, then, Count of Monte Cristo my pretended benefactor—then, Count of Monte Cristo, the universal guardian, be satisfied, you shall witness the death of your friend;" and Morrel, with a maniacal laugh, again rushed towards the pistols.

"And I again repeat, you shall not commit suicide."

"Prevent me, then!" replied Morrel, with another struggle, which, like the first, failed in releasing him from the count's iron grasp.

"I will prevent you."

"And who are you, then, that arrogate to yourself this tyrannical right over free and rational beings?"

"Who am I?" repeated Monte Cristo. "Listen; I am the only man in the world having the right to say to you, 'Morrel, your father's son shall not die today;'" and Monte Cristo, with an expression of majesty and sublimity, advanced with arms folded toward the young man, who, involuntarily overcome by the commanding manner of this man, recoiled a step.

"Why do you mention my father?" stammered he; "why do you mingle a recollection of him with the affairs of today?"

"Because I am he who saved your father's life when he wished to destroy himself, as you do today—because I am the man who sent the purse to your young sister, and the *Pharaon* to old Morrel—because I am the Edmond Dantès who nursed you, a child, on my knees."

Morrel made another step back, staggering, breathless, crushed; then all his strength give way, and he fell prostrate at the feet of Monte Cristo. Then his admirable nature underwent a complete and sudden revulsion; he arose, rushed out of the room and to the stairs, exclaiming energetically, "Julie, Julie—Emmanuel, Emmanuel!"

Monte Cristo endeavored also to leave, but Maximilian would have died rather than relax his hold of the handle of the door, which he closed upon the count. Julie, Emmanuel, and some of the servants, ran up in alarm on hearing the cries of Maximilian. Morrel seized their hands, and opening the door exclaimed in a voice choked with sobs:

"On your knees—on your knees—he is our benefactor—the saviour of our father! He is—"

He would have added "Edmond Dantès," but the count seized his arm and prevented him.

Julie threw herself into the arms of the count; Emmanuel embraced him as a guardian angel; Morrel again fell on his knees, and struck the ground with his forehead. Then the iron-hearted man felt his heart swell in his breast; a flame seemed to rush from his throat to his eyes, he bent his head and wept. For a while nothing was heard in the room but a succession of sobs, while the incense from their grateful hearts mounted to heaven. Julie had scarcely recovered from her deep emotion when she rushed out of the room, descended to the next floor, ran into the drawing-room with childlike joy and raised the crystal globe which covered the purse given by the unknown of the Allées de Meilhan. Meanwhile, Emmanuel in a broken voice said to the count:

"Oh, count, how could you, hearing us so often speak of our unknown benefactor, seeing us pay such homage of gratitude and adoration to his memory,—how could you continue so long without discovering yourself to us? Oh, it was cruel to us, and—dare I say it?—to you also."

"Listen, my friends," said the count—"I may call you so since we have really been friends for the last eleven years—the discovery of this secret has been occasioned by a great event which you must never know. I wished to bury it during my whole life in my own bosom, but your brother Maximilian wrested it from me by a violence he repents of now, I am sure."

Then turning around, and seeing that Morrel, still on his knees, had thrown himself into an armchair, he added in a low voice, pressing Emmanuel's hand significantly, "Watch over him."

"Why so?" asked the young man, surprised.

"I cannot explain myself; but watch over him." Emmanuel looked around the room and caught sight of the pistols; his eyes rested on the weapons, and he pointed to them. Monte Cristo bent his head. Emmanuel went towards the pistols.

"Leave them," said Monte Cristo. Then walking towards Morrel, he took his hand; the tumultuous agitation of the young man was succeeded by a profound stupor. Julie returned, holding the silken purse in her hands, while tears of joy rolled down her cheeks, like dewdrops on the rose.

"Here is the relic," she said; "do not think it will be less dear to us now we are acquainted with our benefactor!"

"My child," said Monte Cristo, coloring, "allow me to take back that purse? Since you now know my face, I wish to be remembered alone through the affection I hope you will grant me.

"Oh," said Julie, pressing the purse to her heart, "no, no, I beseech you do not take it, for some unhappy day you will leave us, will you not?"

"You have guessed rightly, madame," replied Monte Cristo, smiling; "in a week I shall have left this country, where so many persons who merit the vengeance of Heaven lived happily, while my father perished of hunger and grief."

While announcing his departure, the count fixed his eyes on Morrel, and remarked that the words, "I shall have left this country," had failed to rouse him from his lethargy. He then saw that he must make another struggle against the grief of his friend, and taking the hands of Emmanuel and Julie, which he pressed within his own, he said with the mild authority of a father:

"My kind friends, leave me alone with Maximilian."

Julie saw the means offered of carrying off her precious relic, which Monte Cristo had forgotten. She drew her husband to the door. "Let us leave them," she said.

The count was alone with Morrel, who remained motionless as a statue.

"Come," said Monte-Cristo, touching his shoulder with his finger, "are you a man again, Maximilian?"

"Yes; for I begin to suffer again."

The count frowned, apparently in gloomy hesitation.

"Maximilian, Maximilian," he said, "the ideas you yield to are unworthy of a Christian."

"Oh, do not fear, my friend," said Morrel, raising his head, and smiling with a sweet expression on the count; "I shall no longer attempt my life."

"Then we are to have no more pistols—no more despair?"

"No; I have found a better remedy for my grief than either a bullet or a knife."

"Poor fellow, what is it?"

"My grief will kill me of itself."

"My friend," said Monte Cristo, with an expression of melancholy equal to his own, "listen to me. One day, in a moment of despair like yours, since it led to a similar resolution, I also wished to kill myself; one day your father, equally desperate, wished to kill himself too. If anyone had said to your father, at the moment he raised the pistol to his head—if anyone had told me, when in my prison I pushed back the food I had not tasted for three days—if anyone had said to either of us then, 'Live—the day will come when you will be happy, and will bless life!'—no matter whose voice had spoken, we should have heard him with the smile of doubt, or the anguish of incredulity,—and yet how many times has your father blessed life while embracing you—how often have I myself—"

"Ah," exclaimed Morrel, interrupting the count, "you had only lost your liberty, my father had only lost his fortune, but I have lost Valentine."

"Look at me," said Monte Cristo, with that expression which sometimes made him so eloquent and persuasive—"look at me. There are no tears in my eyes, nor is there fever in my veins, yet I see you suffer—you, Maximilian, whom I love as my own son. Well, does not this tell you that in grief, as in life, there is always something to look forward to beyond? Now, if I entreat, if I order you to live, Morrel, it is in the conviction that one day you will thank me for having preserved your life."

"Oh, heavens," said the young man, "oh, heavens—what are you saying, count? Take care. But perhaps you have never loved!"

"Child!" replied the count.

"I mean, as I love. You see, I have been a soldier ever since I attained manhood. I reached the age of twenty-nine without loving, for none of the feelings I before then experienced merit the appellation of love. Well, at twenty-nine I saw Valentine; for two years I have loved her, for two years I have seen written in her heart, as in a book, all the virtues of a daughter and wife. Count, to possess Valentine would have been a happiness too infinite, too ecstatic, too complete, too divine for this world, since it has been denied me; but without Valentine the earth is desolate."

"I have told you to hope," said the count.

"Then have a care, I repeat, for you seek to persuade me, and if you succeed I should lose my reason, for I should hope that I could again behold Valentine."

The count smiled.

"My friend, my father," said Morrel with excitement, "have a care, I again repeat, for the power you wield over me alarms me. Weigh your words before you speak, for my eyes have already become brighter, and my heart beats strongly; be cautious, or you will make me believe in supernatural agencies. I must obey you, though you bade me call forth the dead or walk upon the water."

"Hope, my friend," repeated the count.

"Ah," said Morrel, falling from the height of excitement to the abyss of despair—"ah, you are playing with me, like those good, or rather selfish mothers who soothe their children with honeyed words, because their screams annoy them. No, my friend, I was wrong to caution you; do not fear, I will bury my grief so deep in my heart, I will disguise it so, that you shall not even care to sympathize with me. Adieu, my friend, adieu!"

"On the contrary," said the count, "after this time you must live with me—you must not leave me, and in a week we shall have left France behind us."

"And you still bid me hope?"

"I tell you to hope, because I have a method of curing you."

"Count, you render me sadder than before, if it be possible. You think the result of this blow has been to produce an ordinary grief, and you would cure it by an ordinary remedy—change of scene." And Morrel dropped his head with disdainful incredulity.

"What can I say more?" asked Monte Cristo. "I have confidence in the remedy I propose, and only ask you to permit me to assure you of its efficacy."

"Count, you prolong my agony."

"Then," said the count, "your feeble spirit will not even grant me the trial I request? Come—do you know of what the Count of Monte Cristo is capable? do you know that he holds terrestrial beings under his control? nay, that he can almost work a miracle? Well, wait for the miracle I hope to accomplish, or—"

"Or?" repeated Morrel.

"Or, take care, Morrel, lest I call you ungrateful."

"Have pity on me, count!"

"I feel so much pity towards you, Maximilian, that—listen to me attentively—if I do not cure you in a month, to the day, to the very hour, mark my words, Morrel, I will place loaded pistols before you, and a cup of the deadliest Italian poison—a poison more sure and prompt than that which has killed Valentine."

"Will you promise me?"

"Yes; for I am a man, and have suffered like yourself, and also contemplated suicide; indeed, often since misfortune has left me I have longed for the delights of an eternal sleep."

"But you are sure you will promise me this?" said Morrel, intoxicated.

"I not only promise, but swear it!" said Monte Cristo extending his hand.

"In a month, then, on your honor, if I am not consoled, you will let me take my life into my own hands, and whatever may happen you will not call me ungrateful?"

"In a month, to the day, the very hour and the date is a sacred one, Maximilian. I do not know whether you remember that this is the 5th of September; it is ten years today since I saved your father's life, who wished to die."

Morrel seized the count's hand and kissed it; the count allowed him to pay the homage he felt due to him.

"In a month you will find on the table, at which we shall be then sitting, good pistols and a delicious draught; but, on the other hand, you must promise me not to attempt your life before that time."

"Oh, I also swear it!"

Monte Cristo drew the young man towards him, and pressed him for some time to his heart. "And now," he said, "after today, you will come and live with me; you can occupy Haydée's apartment, and my daughter will at least be replaced by my son."

"Haydée?" said Morrel, "what has become of her?"

"She departed last night."

"To leave you?"

"To wait for me. Hold yourself ready then to join me at the Champs-Élysées, and lead me out of this house without anyone seeing my departure."

Maximilian hung his head, and obeyed with childlike reverence.

Study Guide Questions

For Students:

1. What is Morrel doing when the Count visits him?
2. Who intends to commit suicide in this chapter and why?
3. How does Dantès reveal the truth about his identity before Morrel?

For Reading Club:

1. Discuss the scenes in The Cemetery of Père-Lachaise.
2. Discuss your views on suicide. Do you think it is justified?
3. How does the Count motivate Morrel?

CHAPTER 106

Dividing the Proceeds

The apartment on the first floor of the house in the Rue Saint-Germain-des-Prés, where Albert de Morcerf had selected a home for his mother, was let to a very mysterious person. This was a man whose face the concierge himself had never seen, for in the winter his chin was buried in one of the large red handkerchiefs worn by gentlemen's coachmen on a cold night, and in the summer he made a point of always blowing his nose just as he approached the door. Contrary to custom, this gentleman had not been watched, for as the report ran that he was a person of high rank, and one who would allow no impertinent interference, his *incognito* was strictly respected.

His visits were tolerably regular, though occasionally he appeared a little before or after his time, but generally, both in summer and winter, he took possession of his apartment about four o'clock, though he never spent the night there. At half-past three in the winter the fire was lighted by the discreet servant, who had the superintendence of the little apartment, and in the summer ices were placed on the table at the same hour. At four o'clock, as we have already stated, the mysterious personage arrived.

Twenty minutes afterwards a carriage stopped at the house, a lady alighted in a black or dark blue dress, and always thickly veiled; she passed like a shadow through the lodge, and ran upstairs without a sound escaping under the touch of her light foot. No one ever asked her where she was going. Her face, therefore, like that of the gentleman, was perfectly unknown to the two concierges, who were perhaps unequalled throughout the capital for discretion. We need not say she stopped at the first floor. Then she tapped in a peculiar manner at a door, which after being opened to admit her was again fastened, and curiosity penetrated no farther. They used the same precautions in leaving as in entering the house. The lady always left first, and as soon as she had stepped into her carriage, it drove away, sometimes towards the right hand, sometimes to the left; then about twenty minutes afterwards the gentleman would also leave, buried in his cravat or concealed by his handkerchief.

The day after Monte Cristo had called upon Danglars, the mysterious lodger entered at ten o'clock in the morning instead of four in the afternoon. Almost directly afterwards, without the usual interval of time, a cab arrived, and the veiled lady ran hastily upstairs. The door opened, but before it could be closed, the lady exclaimed:

"Oh, Lucien—oh, my friend!"

The concierge therefore heard for the first time that the lodger's name was Lucien; still, as he was the very perfection of a door-keeper, he made up his mind not to tell his wife.

"Well, what is the matter, my dear?" asked the gentleman whose name the lady's agitation revealed; "tell me what is the matter."

"Oh, Lucien, can I confide in you?"

"Of course, you know you can do so. But what can be the matter? Your note of this morning has completely bewildered me. This precipitation—this unusual appointment. Come, ease me of my anxiety, or else frighten me at once."

"Lucien, a great event has happened!" said the lady, glancing inquiringly at Lucien,—"M. Danglars left last night!"

"Left?—M. Danglars left? Where has he gone?"

"I do not know."

"What do you mean? Has he gone intending not to return?"

"Undoubtedly;—at ten o'clock at night his horses took him to the barrier of Charenton; there a post-chaise was waiting for him—he entered it with his valet de chambre, saying that he was going to Fontainebleau."

"Then what did you mean—"

"Stay—he left a letter for me."

"A letter?"

"Yes; read it."

And the baroness took from her pocket a letter which she gave to Debray. Debray paused a moment before reading, as if trying to guess its contents, or perhaps while making up his mind how to act, whatever it might contain. No doubt his ideas were arranged in a few minutes, for he began reading the letter which caused so much uneasiness in the heart of the baroness, and which ran as follows:

"'Madame and most faithful wife.'"

Debray mechanically stopped and looked at the baroness, whose face became covered with blushes.

"Read," she said.

Debray continued:

"'When you receive this, you will no longer have a husband. Oh, you need not be alarmed, you will only have lost him as you have lost your daughter; I mean that I shall be travelling on one of the thirty or forty roads leading out of France. I owe you some explanations for my conduct, and as you are a woman that can perfectly understand me, I will give them. Listen, then. I received this morning five millions which I paid away; almost directly afterwards another demand for the same sum was presented to me; I put this creditor off till tomorrow and I intend leaving today, to escape that tomorrow, which would be rather too unpleasant for me to endure. You understand this, do you not, my most precious wife? I say you understand this, because you are as conversant with my affairs as I am; indeed, I think you understand them better, since I am ignorant of what has become of a considerable portion of my fortune, once very tolerable, while I am sure, madame, that you know perfectly well. For women have infallible instincts; they can even explain the marvellous by an algebraic calculation they have invented; but I, who only understand my own figures, know nothing more than that one day these figures deceived me. Have you admired the rapidity of my fall? Have you been slightly dazzled at the sudden fusion of my ingots? I confess I have seen nothing but the fire; let us hope you have found some gold among the ashes. With this consoling idea, I leave you, madame, and most prudent wife, without any conscientious reproach for abandoning you; you have friends left, and the ashes I have already mentioned, and above all the liberty I hasten to restore to you. And here, madame, I must add another word of explanation. So long as I hoped you were working for the good of our house and for the fortune of our daughter, I philosophically closed my eyes; but as you have transformed that house into a vast ruin I will not be the foundation of another man's fortune. You were rich when I married you, but little respected. Excuse me for speaking so very candidly, but as this is intended only for ourselves, I do not see why I should weigh my words. I have augmented our fortune, and it has continued to increase during the last fifteen years, till extraordinary and unexpected catastrophes have suddenly overturned it,—without any fault of mine, I can honestly declare. You, madame, have only sought to increase your own, and I am convinced that you have succeeded. I leave you, therefore, as I took you,—rich, but little respected. Adieu! I also intend from this time to work on my own account. Accept my acknowledgments for the example you have set me, and which I intend following.

"'Your very devoted husband,

"'Baron Danglars.'"

The baroness had watched Debray while he read this long and painful letter, and saw him, notwithstanding his self-control, change color once or twice. When he had ended the perusal, he folded the letter and resumed his pensive attitude.

"Well?" asked Madame Danglars, with an anxiety easy to be understood.

"Well, madame?" unhesitatingly repeated Debray.

"With what ideas does that letter inspire you?"

"Oh, it is simple enough, madame; it inspires me with the idea that M. Danglars has left suspiciously."

"Certainly; but is this all you have to say to me?"

"I do not understand you," said Debray with freezing coldness.

"He is gone! Gone, never to return!"

"Oh, madame, do not think that!"

"I tell you he will never return. I know his character; he is inflexible in any resolutions formed for his own interests. If he could have made any use of me, he would have taken me with him; he leaves me in Paris, as our separation will conduce to his benefit;—therefore he has gone, and I am free forever," added Madame Danglars, in the same supplicating tone.

Debray, instead of answering, allowed her to remain in an attitude of nervous inquiry.

"Well?" she said at length, "do you not answer me?"

"I have but one question to ask you,—what do you intend to do?"

"I was going to ask you," replied the baroness with a beating heart.

"Ah, then, you wish to ask advice of me?"

"Yes; I do wish to ask your advice," said Madame Danglars with anxious expectation.

"Then if you wish to take my advice," said the young man coldly, "I would recommend you to travel."

"To travel!" she murmured.

"Certainly; as M. Danglars says, you are rich, and perfectly free. In my opinion, a withdrawal from Paris is absolutely necessary after the double catastrophe of Mademoiselle Danglars' broken contract and M. Danglars' disappearance. The world will think you abandoned and poor, for the wife of a bankrupt would never be forgiven, were she to keep up an appearance of opulence. You have only to remain in Paris for about a fortnight, telling the world you are abandoned, and relating the details of this desertion to your best friends, who will soon spread the report. Then you can quit your house, leaving your jewels and giving up your jointure, and everyone's mouth will be filled with praises of your disinterestedness. They will know you are deserted, and think you also poor, for I alone know your real financial position, and am quite ready to give up my accounts as an honest partner."

The dread with which the pale and motionless baroness listened to this, was equalled by the calm indifference with which Debray had spoken.

"Deserted?" she repeated; "ah, yes, I am, indeed, deserted! You are right, sir, and no one can doubt my position."

These were the only words that this proud and violently enamoured woman could utter in response to Debray.

"But then you are rich,—very rich, indeed," continued Debray, taking out some papers from his pocket-book, which he spread upon the table. Madame Danglars did not see them; she was engaged in stilling the beatings of her heart, and restraining the tears which were ready to gush forth. At length a sense of dignity prevailed, and if she did not entirely master her agitation, she at least succeeded in preventing the fall of a single tear.

"Madame," said Debray, "it is nearly six months since we have been associated. You furnished a principal of 100,000 francs. Our partnership began in the month of April. In May we commenced operations, and in the course of the month gained 450,000 francs. In June the profit amounted to 900,000. In July we added 1,700,000 francs,—it was, you know, the month of the Spanish bonds. In August we lost 300,000 francs at the beginning of the month, but on the 13th we made up for it, and we now find that our accounts, reckoning from the first day of partnership up to yesterday, when I closed them, showed a capital of 2,400,000 francs, that is, 1,200,000 for each of us. Now, madame," said Debray, delivering up his accounts in the methodical manner of a stockbroker, "there are still 80,000 francs, the interest of this money, in my hands."

"But," said the baroness, "I thought you never put the money out to interest."

"Excuse me, madame," said Debray coldly, "I had your permission to do so, and I have made use of it. There are, then, 40,000 francs for your share, besides the 100,000 you furnished me to begin with, making in all 1,340,000 francs for your portion. Now, madame, I took the precaution of drawing out your money the day before yesterday; it is not long ago, you see, and I was in continual expectation of being called on to deliver up my accounts. There is your money,—half in bank-notes, the other half in checks payable to bearer. I say *there*, for as I did not consider my house safe enough, or lawyers sufficiently discreet, and as landed property carries evidence with it, and moreover since you have no right to possess anything independent of your husband, I have kept this sum, now your whole fortune, in a chest concealed under that closet, and for greater security I myself concealed it there.

"Now, madame," continued Debray, first opening the closet, then the chest;—"now, madame, here are 800 notes of 1,000 francs each, resembling, as you see, a large book bound in iron; to this I add a certificate in the funds of 25,000 francs; then, for the odd cash, making I think about 110,000 francs, here is a check upon my banker, who, not being M. Danglars, will pay you the amount, you may rest assured."

Madame Danglars mechanically took the check, the bond, and the heap of bank-notes. This enormous fortune made no great appearance on the table. Madame Danglars, with tearless eyes, but with her breast heaving with concealed emotion, placed the bank-notes in her bag, put the certificate and check into her pocket-book, and then, standing pale and mute, awaited one kind word of consolation.

But she waited in vain.

"Now, madame," said Debray, "you have a splendid fortune, an income of about 60,000 livres a year, which is enormous for a woman who cannot keep an establishment here for a year, at least. You will be able to indulge all your fancies; besides, should you find your income insufficient, you can, for the sake of the past, madame, make use of mine; and I am ready to offer you all I possess, on loan."

"Thank you, sir—thank you," replied the baroness; "you forget that what you have just paid me is much more than a poor woman requires, who intends for some time, at least, to retire from the world."

Debray was, for a moment, surprised, but immediately recovering himself, he bowed with an air which seemed to say, "As you please, madame."

Madame Danglars had until then, perhaps, hoped for something; but when she saw the careless bow of Debray, and the glance by which it was accompanied, together with his significant silence, she raised her head, and without passion or violence or even hesitation, ran downstairs, disdaining to address a last farewell to one who could thus part from her.

"Bah," said Debray, when she had left, "these are fine projects! She will remain at home, read novels, and speculate at cards, since she can no longer do so on the Bourse."

Then taking up his account book, he cancelled with the greatest care all the entries of the amounts he had just paid away.

"I have 1,060,000 francs remaining," he said. "What a pity Mademoiselle de Villefort is dead! She suited me in every respect, and I would have married her."

And he calmly waited until the twenty minutes had elapsed after Madame Danglars' departure before he left the house. During this time he occupied himself in making figures, with his watch by his side.

Asmodeus—that diabolical personage, who would have been created by every fertile imagination if Le Sage had not acquired the priority in his great masterpiece—

would have enjoyed a singular spectacle, if he had lifted up the roof of the little house in the Rue Saint-Germain-des-Prés, while Debray was casting up his figures.

Above the room in which Debray had been dividing two millions and a half with Madame Danglars was another, inhabited by persons who have played too prominent a part in the incidents we have related for their appearance not to create some interest.

Mercédès and Albert were in that room.

Mercédès was much changed within the last few days; not that even in her days of fortune she had ever dressed with the magnificent display which makes us no longer able to recognize a woman when she appears in a plain and simple attire; nor indeed, had she fallen into that state of depression where it is impossible to conceal the garb of misery; no, the change in Mercédès was that her eye no longer sparkled, her lips no longer smiled, and there was now a hesitation in uttering the words which formerly sprang so fluently from her ready wit.

It was not poverty which had broken her spirit; it was not a want of courage which rendered her poverty burdensome. Mercédès, although deposed from the exalted position she had occupied, lost in the sphere she had now chosen, like a person passing from a room splendidly lighted into utter darkness, appeared like a queen, fallen from her palace to a hovel, and who, reduced to strict necessity, could neither become reconciled to the earthen vessels she was herself forced to place upon the table, nor to the humble pallet which had become her bed.

The beautiful Catalane and noble countess had lost both her proud glance and charming smile, because she saw nothing but misery around her; the walls were hung with one of the gray papers which economical landlords choose as not likely to show the dirt; the floor was uncarpeted; the furniture attracted the attention to the poor attempt at luxury; indeed, everything offended eyes accustomed to refinement and elegance.

Madame de Morcerf had lived there since leaving her house; the continual silence of the spot oppressed her; still, seeing that Albert continually watched her countenance to judge the state of her feelings, she constrained herself to assume a monotonous smile of the lips alone, which, contrasted with the sweet and beaming expression that usually shone from her eyes, seemed like "moonlight on a statue,"—yielding light without warmth.

Albert, too, was ill at ease; the remains of luxury prevented him from sinking into his actual position. If he wished to go out without gloves, his hands appeared too white; if he wished to walk through the town, his boots seemed too highly polished. Yet these two noble and intelligent creatures, united by the indissoluble ties of maternal and filial love, had succeeded in tacitly understanding one another, and economizing their stores, and Albert had been able to tell his mother without extorting a change of countenance:

"Mother, we have no more money."

Mercédès had never known misery; she had often, in her youth, spoken of poverty, but between want and necessity, those synonymous words, there is a wide difference.

Amongst the Catalans, Mercédès wished for a thousand things, but still she never really wanted any. So long as the nets were good, they caught fish; and so long as they sold their fish, they were able to buy twine for new nets. And then, shut out from friendship, having but one affection, which could not be mixed up with her ordinary pursuits, she thought of herself—of no one but herself. Upon the little she earned she lived as well as she could; now there were two to be supported, and nothing to live upon.

Winter approached. Mercédès had no fire in that cold and naked room—she, who was accustomed to stoves which heated the house from the hall to the boudoir; she had not even one little flower—she whose apartment had been a conservatory of costly exotics. But she had her son. Hitherto the excitement of fulfilling a duty had sustained them. Excitement, like enthusiasm, sometimes renders us unconscious to the things of earth. But the excitement had calmed down, and they felt themselves obliged to descend from dreams to reality; after having exhausted the ideal, they found they must talk of the actual.

"Mother," exclaimed Albert, just as Madame Danglars was descending the stairs, "let us reckon our riches, if you please; I want capital to build my plans upon."

"Capital—nothing!" replied Mercédès with a mournful smile.

"No, mother,—capital 3,000 francs. And I have an idea of our leading a delightful life upon this 3,000 francs."

"Child!" sighed Mercédès.

"Alas, dear mother," said the young man, "I have unhappily spent too much of your money not to know the value of it. These 3,000 francs are enormous, and I intend building upon this foundation a miraculous certainty for the future."

"You say this, my dear boy; but do you think we ought to accept these 3,000 francs?" said Mercédès, coloring.

"I think so," answered Albert in a firm tone. "We will accept them the more readily, since we have them not here; you know they are buried in the garden of the little house in the Allées de Meilhan, at Marseilles. With 200 francs we can reach Marseilles."

"With 200 francs?—are you sure, Albert?"

"Oh, as for that, I have made inquiries respecting the diligences and steamboats, and my calculations are made. You will take your place in the *coupé* to Châlons. You see, mother, I treat you handsomely for thirty-five francs."

Albert then took a pen, and wrote:

Frs.	
Coupé, thirty-five francs	35.
From Châlons to Lyons you will go on by the steamboat	6.
From Lyons to Avignon (still by steamboat)	16.
From Avignon to Marseilles, seven francs	7.
Expenses on the road, about fifty francs	50.
Total	114 frs.

"Let us put down 120," added Albert, smiling. "You see I am generous, am I not, mother?"

"But you, my poor child?"

"I? do you not see that I reserve eighty francs for myself? A young man does not require luxuries; besides, I know what travelling is."

"With a post-chaise and valet de chambre?"

"Any way, mother."

"Well, be it so. But these 200 francs?"

"Here they are, and 200 more besides. See, I have sold my watch for 100 francs, and the guard and seals for 300. How fortunate that the ornaments were worth more than the watch. Still the same story of superfluities! Now I think we are rich, since instead of the 114 francs we require for the journey we find ourselves in possession of 250."

"But we owe something in this house?"

"Thirty francs; but I pay that out of my 150 francs,—that is understood,—and as I require only eighty francs for my journey, you see I am overwhelmed with luxury. But that is not all. What do you say to this, mother?"

And Albert took out of a little pocket-book with golden clasps, a remnant of his old fancies, or perhaps a tender souvenir from one of the mysterious and veiled ladies who used to knock at his little door,—Albert took out of this pocket-book a note of 1,000 francs.

"What is this?" asked Mercédès.

"A thousand francs."

"But whence have you obtained them?"

"Listen to me, mother, and do not yield too much to agitation." And Albert, rising, kissed his mother on both cheeks, then stood looking at her. "You cannot imagine, mother, how beautiful I think you!" said the young man, impressed with a profound feeling of filial love. "You are, indeed, the most beautiful and most noble woman I ever saw!"

"Dear child!" said Mercédès, endeavoring in vain to restrain a tear which glistened in the corner of her eye. "Indeed, you only wanted misfortune to change my love for you to admiration. I am not unhappy while I possess my son!"

"Ah, just so," said Albert; "here begins the trial. Do you know the decision we have come to, mother?"

"Have we come to any?"

"Yes; it is decided that you are to live at Marseilles, and that I am to leave for Africa, where I will earn for myself the right to use the name I now bear, instead of the one I have thrown aside." Mercédès sighed. "Well, mother, I yesterday engaged myself as substitute in the Spahis,"[18] added the young man, lowering his eyes with a certain feeling of shame, for even he was unconscious of the sublimity of his self-abasement. "I thought my body was my own, and that I might sell it. I yesterday took the place of another. I sold myself for more than I thought I was worth," he added, attempting to smile; "I fetched 2,000 francs."

"Then these 1,000 francs—" said Mercédès, shuddering.

"Are the half of the sum, mother; the other will be paid in a year."

Mercédès raised her eyes to heaven with an expression it would be impossible to describe, and tears, which had hitherto been restrained, now yielded to her emotion, and ran down her cheeks.

"The price of his blood!" she murmured.

"Yes, if I am killed," said Albert, laughing. "But I assure you, mother, I have a strong intention of defending my person, and I never felt half so strong an inclination to live as I do now."

"Merciful Heavens!"

"Besides, mother, why should you make up your mind that I am to be killed? Has Lamoricière, that Ney of the South, been killed? Has Changarnier been killed? Has Bedeau been killed? Has Morrel, whom we know, been killed? Think of your joy, mother, when you see me return with an embroidered uniform! I declare, I expect to look magnificent in it, and chose that regiment only from vanity."

---

[18] The Spahis are French cavalry reserved for service in Africa.

Mercédès sighed while endeavoring to smile; the devoted mother felt that she ought not to allow the whole weight of the sacrifice to fall upon her son.

"Well, now you understand, mother!" continued Albert; "here are more than 4,000 francs settled on you; upon these you can live at least two years."

"Do you think so?" said Mercédès.

These words were uttered in so mournful a tone that their real meaning did not escape Albert; he felt his heart beat, and taking his mother's hand within his own he said, tenderly:

"Yes, you will live!"

"I shall live!—then you will not leave me, Albert?"

"Mother, I must go," said Albert in a firm, calm voice; "you love me too well to wish me to remain useless and idle with you; besides, I have signed."

"You will obey your own wish and the will of Heaven!"

"Not my own wish, mother, but reason—necessity. Are we not two despairing creatures? What is life to you?—Nothing. What is life to me?—Very little without you, mother; for believe me, but for you I should have ceased to live on the day I doubted my father and renounced his name. Well, I will live, if you promise me still to hope; and if you grant me the care of your future prospects, you will redouble my strength. Then I will go to the governor of Algeria; he has a royal heart, and is essentially a soldier; I will tell him my gloomy story. I will beg him to turn his eyes now and then towards me, and if he keep his word and interest himself for me, in six months I shall be an officer, or dead. If I am an officer, your fortune is certain, for I shall have money enough for both, and, moreover, a name we shall both be proud of, since it will be our own. If I am killed—well then mother, you can also die, and there will be an end of our misfortunes."

"It is well," replied Mercédès, with her eloquent glance; "you are right, my love; let us prove to those who are watching our actions that we are worthy of compassion."

"But let us not yield to gloomy apprehensions," said the young man; "I assure you we are, or rather we shall be, very happy. You are a woman at once full of spirit and resignation; I have become simple in my tastes, and am without passion, I hope. Once in service, I shall be rich—once in M. Dantès' house, you will be at rest. Let us strive, I beseech you,—let us strive to be cheerful."

"Yes, let us strive, for you ought to live, and to be happy, Albert."

"And so our division is made, mother," said the young man, affecting ease of mind. "We can now part; come, I shall engage your passage."

"And you, my dear boy?"

"I shall stay here for a few days longer; we must accustom ourselves to parting. I want recommendations and some information relative to Africa. I will join you again at Marseilles."

"Well, be it so—let us part," said Mercédès, folding around her shoulders the only shawl she had taken away, and which accidentally happened to be a valuable black cashmere. Albert gathered up his papers hastily, rang the bell to pay the thirty francs he owed to the landlord, and offering his arm to his mother, they descended the stairs.

Someone was walking down before them, and this person, hearing the rustling of a silk dress, turned around. "Debray!" muttered Albert.

"You, Morcerf?" replied the secretary, resting on the stairs. Curiosity had vanquished the desire of preserving his *incognito*, and he was recognized. It was, indeed, strange in this unknown spot to find the young man whose misfortunes had made so much noise in Paris.

"Morcerf!" repeated Debray. Then noticing in the dim light the still youthful and veiled figure of Madame de Morcerf:

"Pardon me," he added with a smile, "I leave you, Albert." Albert understood his thoughts.

"Mother," he said, turning towards Mercédès, "this is M. Debray, secretary of the Minister for the Interior, once a friend of mine."

"How once?" stammered Debray; "what do you mean?"

"I say so, M. Debray, because I have no friends now, and I ought not to have any. I thank you for having recognized me, sir." Debray stepped forward, and cordially pressed the hand of his interlocutor.

"Believe me, dear Albert," he said, with all the emotion he was capable of feeling,—"believe me, I feel deeply for your misfortunes, and if in any way I can serve you, I am yours."

"Thank you, sir," said Albert, smiling. "In the midst of our misfortunes, we are still rich enough not to require assistance from anyone. We are leaving Paris, and when our journey is paid, we shall have 5,000 francs left."

The blood mounted to the temples of Debray, who held a million in his pocket-book, and unimaginative as he was he could not help reflecting that the same house had contained two women, one of whom, justly dishonored, had left it poor with 1,500,000 francs under her cloak, while the other, unjustly stricken, but sublime in her misfortune, was yet rich with a few deniers. This parallel disturbed his usual politeness, the philosophy he witnessed appalled him, he muttered a few words of general civility and ran downstairs.

That day the minister's clerks and the subordinates had a great deal to put up with from his ill-humor. But that same night, he found himself the possessor of a fine house, situated on the Boulevard de la Madeleine, and an income of 50,000 livres.

The next day, just as Debray was signing the deed, that is about five o'clock in the afternoon, Madame de Morcerf, after having affectionately embraced her son, entered the *coupé* of the diligence, which closed upon her.

A man was hidden in Lafitte's banking-house, behind one of the little arched windows which are placed above each desk; he saw Mercédès enter the diligence, and he also saw Albert withdraw. Then he passed his hand across his forehead, which was clouded with doubt.

"Alas," he exclaimed, "how can I restore the happiness I have taken away from these poor innocent creatures? God help me!"

Study Guide Questions

For Students:

1. Where does Danglars go?
2. What does Debray advise Madame Danglars?
3. What is the current state of Mercédès and Albert?

For Reading Club:

1. Discuss the letter that Danglars leaves for his wife.
2. Do you think Madame Danglars has been ruined or liberated?
3. Discuss the division that takes place in the chapter.

CHAPTER 107

The Lions' Den

One division of La Force, in which the most dangerous and desperate prisoners are confined, is called the court of Saint-Bernard. The prisoners, in their expressive language, have named it the "Lions' Den," probably because the captives possess teeth which frequently gnaw the bars, and sometimes the keepers also. It is a prison within a prison; the walls are double the thickness of the rest. The gratings are every day carefully examined by jailers, whose herculean proportions and cold pitiless expression prove them to have been chosen to reign over their subjects for their superior activity and intelligence.

The courtyard of this quarter is enclosed by enormous walls, over which the sun glances obliquely, when it deigns to penetrate into this gulf of moral and physical deformity. On this paved yard are to be seen,—pacing to and fro from morning till night, pale, careworn, and haggard, like so many shadows,—the men whom justice holds beneath the steel she is sharpening. There, crouched against the side of the wall which attracts and retains the most heat, they may be seen sometimes talking to one another, but more frequently alone, watching the door, which sometimes opens to call forth one from the gloomy assemblage, or to throw in another outcast from society.

The court of Saint-Bernard has its own particular apartment for the reception of guests; it is a long rectangle, divided by two upright gratings placed at a distance of three feet from one another to prevent a visitor from shaking hands with or passing anything to the prisoners. It is a wretched, damp, nay, even horrible spot, more especially when we consider the agonizing conferences which have taken place between those iron bars. And yet, frightful though this spot may be, it is looked upon as a kind of paradise by the men whose days are numbered; it is so rare for them to leave the Lions' Den for any other place than the barrier Saint-Jacques, the galleys! or solitary confinement.

In the court which we have attempted to describe, and from which a damp vapor was rising, a young man with his hands in his pockets, who had excited much curiosity among the inhabitants of the "Den," might be seen walking. The cut of his clothes would have made him pass for an elegant man, if those clothes had not been torn to shreds; still they did not show signs of wear, and the fine cloth, beneath the careful hands of the prisoner, soon recovered its gloss in the parts which were still perfect, for the wearer tried his best to make it assume the appearance of a new coat. He bestowed the same attention upon the cambric front of a shirt, which had considerably changed in color since his entrance into the prison, and he polished his varnished boots with the corner of a handkerchief embroidered with initials surmounted by a coronet.

Some of the inmates of the "Lions' Den" were watching the operations of the prisoner's toilet with considerable interest.

"See, the prince is pluming himself," said one of the thieves.

"He's a fine looking fellow," said another; "if he had only a comb and hair-grease, he'd take the shine off the gentlemen in white kids."

"His coat looks nearly new, and his boots are brilliant. It is pleasant to have such well-dressed brethren; and those gendarmes behaved shamefully. What jealousy; to tear such clothes!"

"He looks like a big-bug," said another; "dresses in fine style. And, then, to be here so young! Oh, what larks!"

Meanwhile the object of this hideous admiration approached the wicket, against which one of the keepers was leaning.

"Come, sir," he said, "lend me twenty francs; you will soon be paid; you run no risks with me. Remember, I have relations who possess more millions than you have deniers. Come, I beseech you, lend me twenty francs, so that I may buy a dressing-gown; it is intolerable always to be in a coat and boots! And what a coat, sir, for a prince of the Cavalcanti!"

The keeper turned his back, and shrugged his shoulders; he did not even laugh at what would have caused anyone else to do so; he had heard so many utter the same things,—indeed, he heard nothing else.

"Come," said Andrea, "you are a man void of compassion; I'll have you turned out."

This made the keeper turn around, and he burst into a loud laugh. The prisoners then approached and formed a circle.

"I tell you that with that wretched sum," continued Andrea, "I could obtain a coat, and a room in which to receive the illustrious visitor I am daily expecting."

"Of course—of course," said the prisoners;—"anyone can see he's a gentleman!"

"Well, then, lend him the twenty francs," said the keeper, leaning on the other shoulder; "surely you will not refuse a comrade!"

"I am no comrade of these people," said the young man, proudly, "you have no right to insult me thus."

The thieves looked at one another with low murmurs, and a storm gathered over the head of the aristocratic prisoner, raised less by his own words than by the manner of the keeper. The latter, sure of quelling the tempest when the waves became too violent, allowed them to rise to a certain pitch that he might be revenged on the importunate Andrea, and besides it would afford him some recreation during the long day.

The thieves had already approached Andrea, some screaming, *"La savate—La savate!"*[19] a cruel operation, which consists in cuffing a comrade who may have fallen into disgrace, not with an old shoe, but with an iron-heeled one. Others proposed the *anguille*, another kind of recreation, in which a handkerchief is filled with sand, pebbles, and two-sous pieces, when they have them, which the wretches beat like a flail over the head and shoulders of the unhappy sufferer.

"Let us horsewhip the fine gentleman!" said others.

But Andrea, turning towards them, winked his eyes, rolled his tongue around his cheeks, and smacked his lips in a manner equivalent to a hundred words among the bandits when forced to be silent. It was a Masonic sign Caderousse had taught him. He was immediately recognized as one of them; the handkerchief was thrown down, and the iron-heeled shoe replaced on the foot of the wretch to whom it belonged.

Some voices were heard to say that the gentleman was right; that he intended to be civil, in his way, and that they would set the example of liberty of conscience,—and the mob retired. The keeper was so stupefied at this scene that he took Andrea by the hands and began examining his person, attributing the sudden submission of the inmates of the Lions' Den to something more substantial than mere fascination.

Andrea made no resistance, although he protested against it. Suddenly a voice was heard at the wicket.

"Benedetto!" exclaimed an inspector. The keeper relaxed his hold.

"I am called," said Andrea.

"To the visitors' room!" said the same voice.

"You see someone pays me a visit. Ah, my dear sir, you will see whether a Cavalcanti is to be treated like a common person!"

[19] *Savate*: an old shoe.

And Andrea, gliding through the court like a black shadow, rushed out through the wicket, leaving his comrades, and even the keeper, lost in wonder. Certainly a call to the visitors' room had scarcely astonished Andrea less than themselves, for the wily youth, instead of making use of his privilege of waiting to be claimed on his entry into La Force, had maintained a rigid silence.

"Everything," he said, "proves me to be under the protection of some powerful person,—this sudden fortune, the facility with which I have overcome all obstacles, an unexpected family and an illustrious name awarded to me, gold showered down upon me, and the most splendid alliances about to be entered into. An unhappy lapse of fortune and the absence of my protector have cast me down, certainly, but not forever. The hand which has retreated for a while will be again stretched forth to save me at the very moment when I shall think myself sinking into the abyss. Why should I risk an imprudent step? It might alienate my protector. He has two means of extricating me from this dilemma,—the one by a mysterious escape, managed through bribery; the other by buying off my judges with gold. I will say and do nothing until I am convinced that he has quite abandoned me, and then—"

Andrea had formed a plan which was tolerably clever. The unfortunate youth was intrepid in the attack, and rude in the defence. He had borne with the public prison, and with privations of all sorts; still, by degrees nature, or rather custom, had prevailed, and he suffered from being naked, dirty, and hungry. It was at this moment of discomfort that the inspector's voice called him to the visiting-room. Andrea felt his heart leap with joy. It was too soon for a visit from the examining magistrate, and too late for one from the director of the prison, or the doctor; it must, then, be the visitor he hoped for. Behind the grating of the room into which Andrea had been led, he saw, while his eyes dilated with surprise, the dark and intelligent face of M. Bertuccio, who was also gazing with sad astonishment upon the iron bars, the bolted doors, and the shadow which moved behind the other grating.

"Ah," said Andrea, deeply affected.

"Good morning, Benedetto," said Bertuccio, with his deep, hollow voice.

"You—you?" said the young man, looking fearfully around him.

"Do you not recognize me, unhappy child?"

"Silence,—be silent!" said Andrea, who knew the delicate sense of hearing possessed by the walls; "for Heaven's sake, do not speak so loud!"

"You wish to speak with me alone, do you not?" said Bertuccio.

"Oh, yes."

"That is well."

And Bertuccio, feeling in his pocket, signed to a keeper whom he saw through the window of the wicket.

"Read?" he said.

"What is that?" asked Andrea.

"An order to conduct you to a room, and to leave you there to talk to me."

"Oh," cried Andrea, leaping with joy. Then he mentally added,—"Still my unknown protector! I am not forgotten. They wish for secrecy, since we are to converse in a private room. I understand, Bertuccio has been sent by my protector."

The keeper spoke for a moment with an official, then opened the iron gates and conducted Andrea to a room on the first floor. The room was whitewashed, as is the custom in prisons, but it looked quite brilliant to a prisoner, though a stove, a bed, a chair, and a table formed the whole of its sumptuous furniture. Bertuccio sat down upon the chair, Andrea threw himself upon the bed; the keeper retired.

"Now," said the steward, "what have you to tell me?"

"And you?" said Andrea.

"You speak first."

"Oh, no. You must have much to tell me, since you have come to seek me."

"Well, be it so. You have continued your course of villany; you have robbed—you have assassinated."

"Well, I should say! If you had me taken to a private room only to tell me this, you might have saved yourself the trouble. I know all these things. But there are some with which, on the contrary, I am not acquainted. Let us talk of those, if you please. Who sent you?"

"Come, come, you are going on quickly, M. Benedetto!"

"Yes, and to the point. Let us dispense with useless words. Who sends you?"

"No one."

"How did you know I was in prison?"

"I recognized you, some time since, as the insolent dandy who so gracefully mounted his horse in the Champs-Élysées."

"Oh, the Champs-Élysées? Ah, yes; we burn, as they say at the game of pincette. The Champs-Élysées? Come, let us talk a little about my father."

"Who, then, am I?"

"You, sir?—you are my adopted father. But it was not you, I presume, who placed at my disposal 100,000 francs, which I spent in four or five months; it was not you who manufactured an Italian gentleman for my father; it was not you who introduced me into the world, and had me invited to a certain dinner at Auteuil, which I fancy I am eating at this moment, in company with the most distinguished people in Paris—

amongst the rest with a certain procureur, whose acquaintance I did very wrong not to cultivate, for he would have been very useful to me just now;—it was not you, in fact, who bailed me for one or two millions, when the fatal discovery of my little secret took place. Come, speak, my worthy Corsican, speak!"

"What do you wish me to say?"

"I will help you. You were speaking of the Champs-Élysées just now, worthy foster-father."

"Well?"

"Well, in the Champs-Élysées there resides a very rich gentleman."

"At whose house you robbed and murdered, did you not?"

"I believe I did."

"The Count of Monte Cristo?"

"'Tis you who have named him, as M. Racine says. Well, am I to rush into his arms, and strain him to my heart, crying, 'My father, my father!' like Monsieur Pixérécourt."[20]

"Do not let us jest," gravely replied Bertuccio, "and dare not to utter that name again as you have pronounced it."

"Bah," said Andrea, a little overcome, by the solemnity of Bertuccio's manner, "why not?"

"Because the person who bears it is too highly favored by Heaven to be the father of such a wretch as you."

"Oh, these are fine words."

"And there will be fine doings, if you do not take care."

"Menaces—I do not fear them. I will say—"

"Do you think you are engaged with a pygmy like yourself?" said Bertuccio, in so calm a tone, and with so steadfast a look, that Andrea was moved to the very soul. "Do you think you have to do with galley-slaves, or novices in the world? Benedetto, you are fallen into terrible hands; they are ready to open for you—make use of them. Do not play with the thunderbolt they have laid aside for a moment, but which they can take up again instantly, if you attempt to intercept their movements."

"My father—I will know who my father is," said the obstinate youth; "I will perish if I must, but I *will* know it. What does scandal signify to me? What possessions, what reputation, what 'pull,' as Beauchamp says,—have I? You great people always lose something by scandal, notwithstanding your millions. Come, who is my father?"

"I came to tell you."

---

[20] Guilbert de Pixérécourt, French dramatist (1773-1844).

"Ah," cried Benedetto, his eyes sparkling with joy. Just then the door opened, and the jailer, addressing himself to Bertuccio, said:

"Excuse me, sir, but the examining magistrate is waiting for the prisoner."

"And so closes our interview," said Andrea to the worthy steward; "I wish the troublesome fellow were at the devil!"

"I will return tomorrow," said Bertuccio.

"Good! Gendarmes, I am at your service. Ah, sir, do leave a few crowns for me at the gate that I may have some things I am in need of!"

"It shall be done," replied Bertuccio.

Andrea extended his hand; Bertuccio kept his own in his pocket, and merely jingled a few pieces of money.

"That's what I mean," said Andrea, endeavoring to smile, quite overcome by the strange tranquillity of Bertuccio.

"Can I be deceived?" he murmured, as he stepped into the oblong and grated vehicle which they call "the salad basket."

"Never mind, we shall see! Tomorrow, then!" he added, turning towards Bertuccio.

"Tomorrow!" replied the steward.

Study Guide Questions

For Students:

1. What is the Lions' Den?
2. Who is in the Court of Saint-Bernard?
3. Who comes to visit Benedetto in prison?

For Reading Club:

1. Considering the character of Benedetto, do you think some people never change?
2. Discuss the conversation between Benedetto and Bertuccio.
3. Do you think Benedetto could have been a different man if he had lived with his parents?

CHAPTER 108

The Judge

We remember that the Abbé Busoni remained alone with Noirtier in the chamber of death, and that the old man and the priest were the sole guardians of the young girl's body. Perhaps it was the Christian exhortations of the abbé, perhaps his kind charity, perhaps his persuasive words, which had restored the courage of Noirtier, for ever since he had conversed with the priest his violent despair had yielded to a calm resignation which surprised all who knew his excessive affection for Valentine.

M. de Villefort had not seen his father since the morning of the death. The whole establishment had been changed; another valet was engaged for himself, a new servant for Noirtier, two women had entered Madame de Villefort's service,—in fact, everywhere, to the concierge and coachmen, new faces were presented to the different masters of the house, thus widening the division which had always existed between the members of the same family. The assizes, also, were about to begin, and Villefort, shut up in his room, exerted himself with feverish anxiety in drawing up the case against the murderer of Caderousse. This affair, like all those in which the Count of Monte Cristo had interfered, caused a great sensation in Paris. The proofs were certainly not convincing, since they rested upon a few words written by an escaped galley-slave on his death-bed, and who might have been actuated by hatred or revenge in accusing his companion. But the mind of the procureur was made up; he felt assured that Benedetto was guilty, and he hoped by his skill in conducting this aggravated case to flatter his self-love, which was about the only vulnerable point left in his frozen heart.

The case was therefore prepared owing to the incessant labor of Villefort, who wished it to be the first on the list in the coming assizes. He had been obliged to seclude himself more than ever, to evade the enormous number of applications presented to him for the purpose of obtaining tickets of admission to the court on the day of trial.

And then so short a time had elapsed since the death of poor Valentine, and the gloom which overshadowed the house was so recent, that no one wondered to see the father so absorbed in his professional duties, which were the only means he had of dissipating his grief.

Once only had Villefort seen his father; it was the day after that upon which Bertuccio had paid his second visit to Benedetto, when the latter was to learn his father's name. The magistrate, harassed and fatigued, had descended to the garden of his house, and in a gloomy mood, similar to that in which Tarquin lopped off the tallest poppies, he began knocking off with his cane the long and dying branches of the rose-trees, which, placed along the avenue, seemed like the spectres of the brilliant flowers which had bloomed in the past season.

More than once he had reached that part of the garden where the famous boarded gate stood overlooking the deserted enclosure, always returning by the same path, to begin his walk again, at the same pace and with the same gesture, when he accidentally turned his eyes towards the house, whence he heard the noisy play of his son, who had returned from school to spend the Sunday and Monday with his mother.

While doing so, he observed M. Noirtier at one of the open windows, where the old man had been placed that he might enjoy the last rays of the sun which yet yielded some heat, and was now shining upon the dying flowers and red leaves of the creeper which twined around the balcony.

The eye of the old man was riveted upon a spot which Villefort could scarcely distinguish. His glance was so full of hate, of ferocity, and savage impatience, that Villefort turned out of the path he had been pursuing, to see upon what person this dark look was directed.

Then he saw beneath a thick clump of linden-trees, which were nearly divested of foliage, Madame de Villefort sitting with a book in her hand, the perusal of which she frequently interrupted to smile upon her son, or to throw back his elastic ball, which he obstinately threw from the drawing-room into the garden.

Villefort became pale; he understood the old man's meaning.

Noirtier continued to look at the same object, but suddenly his glance was transferred from the wife to the husband, and Villefort himself had to submit to the searching investigation of eyes, which, while changing their direction and even their language, had lost none of their menacing expression. Madame de Villefort, unconscious of the passions that exhausted their fire over her head, at that moment held her son's ball, and was making signs to him to reclaim it with a kiss. Edward begged for a long while, the maternal kiss probably not offering sufficient recompense for the trouble he must take to obtain it; however at length he decided, leaped out of the window into a cluster of heliotropes and daisies, and ran to his mother, his forehead streaming with perspiration. Madame de Villefort wiped his forehead, pressed her lips upon it, and sent him back with the ball in one hand and some bonbons in the other.

Villefort, drawn by an irresistible attraction, like that of the bird to the serpent, walked towards the house. As he approached it, Noirtier's gaze followed him, and his eyes appeared of such a fiery brightness that Villefort felt them pierce to the depths of his heart. In that earnest look might be read a deep reproach, as well as a terrible menace. Then Noirtier raised his eyes to heaven, as though to remind his son of a forgotten oath.

"It is well, sir," replied Villefort from below,—"it is well; have patience but one day longer; what I have said I will do."

Noirtier seemed to be calmed by these words, and turned his eyes with indifference to the other side. Villefort violently unbuttoned his greatcoat, which seemed to strangle him, and passing his livid hand across his forehead, entered his study.

The night was cold and still; the family had all retired to rest but Villefort, who alone remained up, and worked till five o'clock in the morning, reviewing the last interrogatories made the night before by the examining magistrates, compiling the depositions of the witnesses, and putting the finishing stroke to the deed of accusation, which was one of the most energetic and best conceived of any he had yet delivered.

The next day, Monday, was the first sitting of the assizes. The morning dawned dull and gloomy, and Villefort saw the dim gray light shine upon the lines he had traced in red ink. The magistrate had slept for a short time while the lamp sent forth its final struggles; its flickerings awoke him, and he found his fingers as damp and purple as though they had been dipped in blood.

He opened the window; a bright yellow streak crossed the sky, and seemed to divide in half the poplars, which stood out in black relief on the horizon. In the clover-fields beyond the chestnut-trees, a lark was mounting up to heaven, while pouring out her clear morning song. The damps of the dew bathed the head of Villefort, and refreshed his memory.

"Today," he said with an effort,—"today the man who holds the blade of justice must strike wherever there is guilt."

Involuntarily his eyes wandered towards the window of Noirtier's room, where he had seen him the preceding night. The curtain was drawn, and yet the image of his father was so vivid to his mind that he addressed the closed window as though it had been open, and as if through the opening he had beheld the menacing old man.

"Yes," he murmured,—"yes, be satisfied."

His head dropped upon his chest, and in this position he paced his study; then he threw himself, dressed as he was, upon a sofa, less to sleep than to rest his limbs, cramped with cold and study. By degrees everyone awoke. Villefort, from his study, heard the successive noises which accompany the life of a house,—the opening and shutting of doors, the ringing of Madame de Villefort's bell, to summon the waiting-maid, mingled with the first shouts of the child, who rose full of the enjoyment of his age. Villefort also rang; his new valet brought him the papers, and with them a cup of chocolate.

"What are you bringing me?" said he.

"A cup of chocolate."

"I did not ask for it. Who has paid me this attention?"

"My mistress, sir. She said you would have to speak a great deal in the murder case, and that you should take something to keep up your strength;" and the valet placed the cup on the table nearest to the sofa, which was, like all the rest, covered with papers.

The valet then left the room. Villefort looked for an instant with a gloomy expression, then, suddenly, taking it up with a nervous motion, he swallowed its contents at one draught. It might have been thought that he hoped the beverage would be mortal, and that he sought for death to deliver him from a duty which he would rather die than fulfil. He then rose, and paced his room with a smile it would have been terrible to witness. The chocolate was inoffensive, for M. de Villefort felt no effects.

The breakfast-hour arrived, but M. de Villefort was not at table. The valet re-entered.

"Madame de Villefort wishes to remind you, sir," he said, "that eleven o'clock has just struck, and that the trial commences at twelve."

"Well," said Villefort, "what then?"

"Madame de Villefort is dressed; she is quite ready, and wishes to know if she is to accompany you, sir?"

"Where to?"

"To the Palais."

"What to do?"

"My mistress wishes much to be present at the trial."

"Ah," said Villefort, with a startling accent; "does she wish that?"

The servant drew back and said, "If you wish to go alone, sir, I will go and tell my mistress."

Villefort remained silent for a moment, and dented his pale cheeks with his nails.

"Tell your mistress," he at length answered, "that I wish to speak to her, and I beg she will wait for me in her own room."

"Yes, sir."

"Then come to dress and shave me."

"Directly, sir."

The valet re-appeared almost instantly, and, having shaved his master, assisted him to dress entirely in black. When he had finished, he said:

"My mistress said she should expect you, sir, as soon as you had finished dressing."

"I am going to her."

And Villefort, with his papers under his arm and hat in hand, directed his steps toward the apartment of his wife.

At the door he paused for a moment to wipe his damp, pale brow. He then entered the room. Madame de Villefort was sitting on an ottoman and impatiently turning over the leaves of some newspapers and pamphlets which young Edward, by way of amusing himself, was tearing to pieces before his mother could finish reading them. She was dressed to go out, her bonnet was placed beside her on a chair, and her gloves were on her hands.

"Ah, here you are, monsieur," she said in her naturally calm voice; "but how pale you are! Have you been working all night? Why did you not come down to breakfast? Well, will you take me, or shall I take Edward?"

Madame de Villefort had multiplied her questions in order to gain one answer, but to all her inquiries M. de Villefort remained mute and cold as a statue.

"Edward," said Villefort, fixing an imperious glance on the child, "go and play in the drawing-room, my dear; I wish to speak to your mamma."

Madame de Villefort shuddered at the sight of that cold countenance, that resolute tone, and the awfully strange preliminaries. Edward raised his head, looked at his mother, and then, finding that she did not confirm the order, began cutting off the heads of his leaden soldiers.

"Edward," cried M. de Villefort, so harshly that the child started up from the floor, "do you hear me?—Go!"

The child, unaccustomed to such treatment, arose, pale and trembling; it would be difficult to say whether his emotion were caused by fear or passion. His father went up to him, took him in his arms, and kissed his forehead.

"Go," he said: "go, my child." Edward ran out.

M. de Villefort went to the door, which he closed behind the child, and bolted.

"Dear me!" said the young woman, endeavoring to read her husband's inmost thoughts, while a smile passed over her countenance which froze the impassibility of Villefort; "what is the matter?"

"Madame, where do you keep the poison you generally use?" said the magistrate, without any introduction, placing himself between his wife and the door.

Madame de Villefort must have experienced something of the sensation of a bird which, looking up, sees the murderous trap closing over its head.

A hoarse, broken tone, which was neither a cry nor a sigh, escaped from her, while she became deadly pale.

"Monsieur," she said, "I—I do not understand you."

And, in her first paroxysm of terror, she had raised herself from the sofa, in the next, stronger very likely than the other, she fell down again on the cushions.

"I asked you," continued Villefort, in a perfectly calm tone, "where you conceal the poison by the aid of which you have killed my father-in-law, M. de Saint-Méran, my mother-in-law, Madame de Saint-Méran, Barrois, and my daughter Valentine."

"Ah, sir," exclaimed Madame de Villefort, clasping her hands, "what do you say?"

"It is not for you to interrogate, but to answer."

"Is it to the judge or to the husband?" stammered Madame de Villefort.

"To the judge—to the judge, madame!" It was terrible to behold the frightful pallor of that woman, the anguish of her look, the trembling of her whole frame.

"Ah, sir," she muttered, "ah, sir," and this was all.

"You do not answer, madame!" exclaimed the terrible interrogator. Then he added, with a smile yet more terrible than his anger, "It is true, then; you do not deny it!" She moved forward. "And you cannot deny it!" added Villefort, extending his hand toward her, as though to seize her in the name of justice. "You have accomplished these different crimes with impudent address, but which could only deceive those whose affections for you blinded them. Since the death of Madame de Saint-Méran, I have known that a poisoner lived in my house. M. d'Avrigny warned me of it. After the death of Barrois my suspicions were directed towards an angel,—those suspicions which, even when there is no crime, are always alive in my heart; but after the death of Valentine, there has been no doubt in my mind, madame, and not only in mine, but in those of others; thus your crime, known by two persons, suspected by many, will soon become public, and, as I told you just now, you no longer speak to the husband, but to the judge."

The young woman hid her face in her hands.

"Oh, sir," she stammered, "I beseech you, do not believe appearances."

"Are you, then, a coward?" cried Villefort, in a contemptuous voice. "But I have always observed that poisoners were cowards. Can you be a coward, you, who have had the courage to witness the death of two old men and a young girl murdered by you?"

"Sir! sir!"

"Can you be a coward?" continued Villefort, with increasing excitement, "you, who could count, one by one, the minutes of four death agonies? *You*, who have arranged your infernal plans, and removed the beverages with a talent and precision almost miraculous? Have you, then, who have calculated everything with such nicety, have you forgotten to calculate one thing—I mean where the revelation of your crimes will lead you to? Oh, it is impossible—you must have saved some surer, more subtle and deadly poison than any other, that you might escape the punishment that you deserve. You have done this—I hope so, at least."

Madame de Villefort stretched out her hands, and fell on her knees.

"I understand," he said, "you confess; but a confession made to the judges, a confession made at the last moment, extorted when the crime cannot be denied, diminishes not the punishment inflicted on the guilty!"

"The punishment?" exclaimed Madame de Villefort, "the punishment, monsieur? Twice you have pronounced that word!"

"Certainly. Did you hope to escape it because you were four times guilty? Did you think the punishment would be withheld because you are the wife of him who pronounces it?—No, madame, no; the scaffold awaits the poisoner, whoever she may be, unless, as I just said, the poisoner has taken the precaution of keeping for herself a few drops of her deadliest poison."

Madame de Villefort uttered a wild cry, and a hideous and uncontrollable terror spread over her distorted features.

"Oh, do not fear the scaffold, madame," said the magistrate; "I will not dishonor you, since that would be dishonor to myself; no, if you have heard me distinctly, you will understand that you are not to die on the scaffold."

"No, I do not understand; what do you mean?" stammered the unhappy woman, completely overwhelmed.

"I mean that the wife of the first magistrate in the capital shall not, by her infamy, soil an unblemished name; that she shall not, with one blow, dishonor her husband and her child."

"No, no—oh, no!"

"Well, madame, it will be a laudable action on your part, and I will thank you for it!"

"You will thank me—for what?"

"For what you have just said."

"What did I say? Oh, my brain whirls; I no longer understand anything. Oh, my God, my God!"

And she rose, with her hair dishevelled, and her lips foaming.

"Have you answered the question I put to you on entering the room?—where do you keep the poison you generally use, madame?"

Madame de Villefort raised her arms to heaven, and convulsively struck one hand against the other.

"No, no," she vociferated, "no, you cannot wish that!"

"What I do not wish, madame, is that you should perish on the scaffold. Do you understand?" asked Villefort.

"Oh, mercy, mercy, monsieur!"

"What I require is, that justice be done. I am on the earth to punish, madame," he added, with a flaming glance; "any other woman, were it the queen herself, I would send to the executioner; but to you I shall be merciful. To you I will say, 'Have you not, madame, put aside some of the surest, deadliest, most speedy poison?'"

"Oh, pardon me, sir; let me live!"

"She is cowardly," said Villefort.

"Reflect that I am your wife!"

"You are a poisoner."

"In the name of Heaven!"

"No!"

"In the name of the love you once bore me!"

"No, no!"

"In the name of our child! Ah, for the sake of our child, let me live!"

"No, no, no, I tell you; one day, if I allow you to live, you will perhaps kill him, as you have the others!"

"I?—I kill my boy?" cried the distracted mother, rushing toward Villefort; "I kill my son? Ha, ha, ha!" and a frightful, demoniac laugh finished the sentence, which was lost in a hoarse rattle.

Madame de Villefort fell at her husband's feet. He approached her.

"Think of it, madame," he said; "if, on my return, justice has not been satisfied, I will denounce you with my own mouth, and arrest you with my own hands!"

She listened, panting, overwhelmed, crushed; her eye alone lived, and glared horribly.

"Do you understand me?" he said. "I am going down there to pronounce the sentence of death against a murderer. If I find you alive on my return, you shall sleep tonight in the conciergerie."

Madame de Villefort sighed; her nerves gave way, and she sunk on the carpet. The king's attorney seemed to experience a sensation of pity; he looked upon her less severely, and, bowing to her, said slowly:

"Farewell, madame, farewell!"

That farewell struck Madame de Villefort like the executioner's knife. She fainted. The procureur went out, after having double-locked the door.

Study Guide Questions

For Students:

1. Who wishes to accompany M. de Villefort to Palais de Justice?
2. What does M. de Villefort ask Madame Villefort when he goes to meet her?
3. What is the option given by Me. de Villefort to Madame Villefort?

For Reading Club:

1. How do you think Villefort's fate suggests the presence of a stronger judge?
2. Do you feel pity for Villefort or is his plight justified?
3. Discuss Villefort's character as a judge. Do you think he always stands with the truth?

CHAPTER 109

The Assizes

The Benedetto affair, as it was called at the Palais, and by people in general, had produced a tremendous sensation. Frequenting the Café de Paris, the Boulevard de Gand, and the Bois de Boulogne, during his brief career of splendor, the false Cavalcanti had formed a host of acquaintances. The papers had related his various adventures, both as the man of fashion and the galley-slave; and as everyone who had been personally acquainted with Prince Andrea Cavalcanti experienced a lively curiosity in his fate, they all determined to spare no trouble in endeavoring to witness the trial of M. Benedetto for the murder of his comrade in chains.

In the eyes of many, Benedetto appeared, if not a victim to, at least an instance of, the fallibility of the law. M. Cavalcanti, his father, had been seen in Paris, and it was expected that he would re-appear to claim the illustrious outcast. Many, also, who were not aware of the circumstances attending his withdrawal from Paris, were struck with the worthy appearance, the gentlemanly bearing, and the knowledge of the world displayed by the old patrician, who certainly played the nobleman very well, so long as he said nothing, and made no arithmetical calculations.

As for the accused himself, many remembered him as being so amiable, so handsome, and so liberal, that they chose to think him the victim of some conspiracy, since in this world large fortunes frequently excite the malevolence and jealousy of some unknown enemy.

Everyone, therefore, ran to the court; some to witness the sight, others to comment upon it. From seven o'clock in the morning a crowd was stationed at the iron gates, and an hour before the trial commenced the hall was full of the privileged. Before the entrance of the magistrates, and indeed frequently afterwards, a court of justice, on days when some especial trial is to take place, resembles a drawing-room where many persons recognize each other and converse if they can do so without losing their seats; or, if they are separated by too great a number of lawyers, communicate by signs.

It was one of the magnificent autumn days which make amends for a short summer; the clouds which M. de Villefort had perceived at sunrise had all disappeared as if by magic, and one of the softest and most brilliant days of September shone forth in all its splendor.

Beauchamp, one of the kings of the press, and therefore claiming the right of a throne everywhere, was eying everybody through his monocle. He perceived Château-Renaud and Debray, who had just gained the good graces of a sergeant-at-arms, and who had persuaded the latter to let them stand before, instead of behind him, as they ought to have done. The worthy sergeant had recognized the minister's secretary and the millionnaire, and, by way of paying extra attention to his noble neighbors, promised to keep their places while they paid a visit to Beauchamp.

"Well," said Beauchamp, "we shall see our friend!"

"Yes, indeed!" replied Debray. "That worthy prince. Deuce take those Italian princes!"

"A man, too, who could boast of Dante for a genealogist, and could reckon back to the *Divina Comedia.*"

"A nobility of the rope!" said Château-Renaud phlegmatically.

"He will be condemned, will he not?" asked Debray of Beauchamp.

"My dear fellow, I think we should ask you that question; you know such news much better than we do. Did you see the president at the minister's last night?"

"Yes."

"What did he say?"

"Something which will surprise you."

"Oh, make haste and tell me, then; it is a long time since that has happened."

"Well, he told me that Benedetto, who is considered a serpent of subtlety and a giant of cunning, is really but a very commonplace, silly rascal, and altogether unworthy of the experiments that will be made on his phrenological organs after his death."

"Bah," said Beauchamp, "he played the prince very well."

"Yes, for you who detest those unhappy princes, Beauchamp, and are always delighted to find fault with them; but not for me, who discover a gentleman by instinct, and who scent out an aristocratic family like a very bloodhound of heraldry."

"Then you never believed in the principality?"

"Yes.—in the principality, but not in the prince."

"Not so bad," said Beauchamp; "still, I assure you, he passed very well with many people; I saw him at the ministers' houses."

"Ah, yes," said Château-Renaud. "The idea of thinking ministers understand anything about princes!"

"There is something in what you have just said," said Beauchamp, laughing.

"But," said Debray to Beauchamp, "if I spoke to the president, *you* must have been with the procureur."

"It was an impossibility; for the last week M. de Villefort has secluded himself. It is natural enough; this strange chain of domestic afflictions, followed by the no less strange death of his daughter—"

"Strange? What do you mean, Beauchamp?"

"Oh, yes; do you pretend that all this has been unobserved at the minister's?" said Beauchamp, placing his eye-glass in his eye, where he tried to make it remain.

"My dear sir," said Château-Renaud, "allow me to tell you that you do not understand that manœuvre with the eye-glass half so well as Debray. Give him a lesson, Debray."

"Stay," said Beauchamp, "surely I am not deceived."

"What is it?"

"It is she!"

"Whom do you mean?"

"They said she had left."

"Mademoiselle Eugénie?" said Château-Renaud; "has she returned?"

"No, but her mother."

"Madame Danglars? Nonsense! Impossible!" said Château-Renaud; "only ten days after the flight of her daughter, and three days from the bankruptcy of her husband?"

Debray colored slightly, and followed with his eyes the direction of Beauchamp's glance.

"Come," he said, "it is only a veiled lady, some foreign princess, perhaps the mother of Cavalcanti. But you were just speaking on a very interesting topic, Beauchamp."

"I?"

"Yes; you were telling us about the extraordinary death of Valentine."

"Ah, yes, so I was. But how is it that Madame de Villefort is not here?"

"Poor, dear woman," said Debray, "she is no doubt occupied in distilling balm for the hospitals, or in making cosmetics for herself or friends. Do you know she spends two or three thousand crowns a year in this amusement? But I wonder she is not here. I should have been pleased to see her, for I like her very much."

"And I hate her," said Château-Renaud.

"Why?"

"I do not know. Why do we love? Why do we hate? I detest her, from antipathy."

"Or, rather, by instinct."

"Perhaps so. But to return to what you were saying, Beauchamp."

"Well, do you know why they die so multitudinously at M. de Villefort's?"

"'Multitudinously' is good," said Château-Renaud.

"My good fellow, you'll find the word in Saint-Simon."

"But the thing itself is at M. de Villefort's; but let's get back to the subject."

"Talking of that," said Debray, "Madame was making inquiries about that house, which for the last three months has been hung with black."

"Who is Madame?" asked Château-Renaud.

"The minister's wife, *pardieu!*"

"Oh, your pardon! I never visit ministers; I leave that to the princes."

"Really, you were only before sparkling, but now you are brilliant; take compassion on us, or, like Jupiter, you will wither us up."

"I will not speak again," said Château-Renaud; "pray have compassion upon me, and do not take up every word I say."

"Come, let us endeavor to get to the end of our story, Beauchamp; I told you that yesterday Madame made inquiries of me upon the subject; enlighten me, and I will then communicate my information to her."

"Well, gentlemen, the reason people die so multitudinously (I like the word) at M. de Villefort's is that there is an assassin in the house!"

The two young men shuddered, for the same idea had more than once occurred to them.

"And who is the assassin;" they asked together.

"Young Edward!" A burst of laughter from the auditors did not in the least disconcert the speaker, who continued,—"Yes, gentlemen; Edward, the infant phenomenon, who is quite an adept in the art of killing."

"You are jesting."

"Not at all. I yesterday engaged a servant, who had just left M. de Villefort—I intend sending him away tomorrow, for he eats so enormously, to make up for the fast imposed upon him by his terror in that house. Well, now listen."

"We are listening."

"It appears the dear child has obtained possession of a bottle containing some drug, which he every now and then uses against those who have displeased him. First, M. and Madame de Saint-Méran incurred his displeasure, so he poured out three drops of his elixir—three drops were sufficient; then followed Barrois, the old servant of M. Noirtier, who sometimes rebuffed this little wretch—he therefore received the same quantity of the elixir; the same happened to Valentine, of whom he was jealous; he gave her the same dose as the others, and all was over for her as well as the rest."

"Why, what nonsense are you telling us?" said Château-Renaud.

"Yes, it is an extraordinary story," said Beauchamp; "is it not?"

"It is absurd," said Debray.

"Ah," said Beauchamp, "you doubt me? Well, you can ask my servant, or rather him who will no longer be my servant tomorrow, it was the talk of the house."

"And this elixir, where is it? what is it?"

"The child conceals it."

"But where did he find it?"

"In his mother's laboratory."

"Does his mother then, keep poisons in her laboratory?"

"How can I tell? You are questioning me like a king's attorney. I only repeat what I have been told, and like my informant I can do no more. The poor devil would eat nothing, from fear."

"It is incredible!"

"No, my dear fellow, it is not at all incredible. You saw the child pass through the Rue Richelieu last year, who amused himself with killing his brothers and sisters by sticking pins in their ears while they slept. The generation who follow us are very precocious."

"Come, Beauchamp," said Château-Renaud, "I will bet anything you do not believe a word of all you have been telling us. But I do not see the Count of Monte Cristo here."

"He is worn out," said Debray; "besides, he could not well appear in public, since he has been the dupe of the Cavalcanti, who, it appears, presented themselves to him with false letters of credit, and cheated him out of 100,000 francs upon the hypothesis of this principality."

"By the way, M. de Château-Renaud," asked Beauchamp, "how is Morrel?"

"*Ma foi*, I have called three times without once seeing him. Still, his sister did not seem uneasy, and told me that though she had not seen him for two or three days, she was sure he was well."

"Ah, now I think of it, the Count of Monte Cristo cannot appear in the hall," said Beauchamp.

"Why not?"

"Because he is an actor in the drama."

"Has he assassinated anyone, then?"

"No, on the contrary, they wished to assassinate him. You know that it was in leaving his house that M. de Caderousse was murdered by his friend Benedetto. You know that the famous waistcoat was found in his house, containing the letter which stopped the signature of the marriage-contract. Do you see the waistcoat? There it is, all blood-stained, on the desk, as a testimony of the crime."

"Ah, very good."

"Hush, gentlemen, here is the court; let us go back to our places."

A noise was heard in the hall; the sergeant called his two patrons with an energetic "hem!" and the door-keeper appearing, called out with that shrill voice peculiar to his order, ever since the days of Beaumarchais:

"The court, gentlemen!"

Study Guide Questions

For Students:

1. Why is the Benedetto affair so talked about?
2. What do the papers print about the false Cavalcanti?
3. Who according to Beauchamp has poisoned Valentine and why?

For Reading Club:

1. Why do you think most of the people think of Benedetto as a victim?
2. Discuss why the narrator compares the court of justice to a drawing room.
3. Many chapters start with different characters gossiping about the affairs of the town. Why do you think Dumas has opted for this style of introductions?

CHAPTER 110

The Indictment

The judges took their places in the midst of the most profound silence; the jury took their seats; M. de Villefort, the object of unusual attention, and we had almost said of general admiration, sat in the armchair and cast a tranquil glance around him. Everyone looked with astonishment on that grave and severe face, whose calm expression personal griefs had been unable to disturb, and the aspect of a man who was a stranger to all human emotions excited something very like terror.

"Gendarmes," said the president, "lead in the accused."

At these words the public attention became more intense, and all eyes were turned towards the door through which Benedetto was to enter. The door soon opened and the accused appeared.

The same impression was experienced by all present, and no one was deceived by the expression of his countenance. His features bore no sign of that deep emotion which stops the beating of the heart and blanches the cheek. His hands, gracefully placed, one upon his hat, the other in the opening of his white waistcoat, were not at all tremulous; his eye was calm and even brilliant. Scarcely had he entered the hall when he glanced at the whole body of magistrates and assistants; his eye rested longer on the president, and still more so on the king's attorney.

By the side of Andrea was stationed the lawyer who was to conduct his defence, and who had been appointed by the court, for Andrea disdained to pay any attention to those details, to which he appeared to attach no importance. The lawyer was a young man with light hair whose face expressed a hundred times more emotion than that which characterized the prisoner.

The president called for the indictment, revised as we know, by the clever and implacable pen of Villefort. During the reading of this, which was long, the public attention was continually drawn towards Andrea, who bore the inspection with Spartan unconcern. Villefort had never been so concise and eloquent. The crime was depicted in the most vivid colors; the former life of the prisoner, his transformation, a review of his life from the earliest period, were set forth with all the talent that a knowledge of human life could furnish to a mind like that of the procureur. Benedetto was thus forever condemned in public opinion before the sentence of the law could be pronounced.

Andrea paid no attention to the successive charges which were brought against him. M. de Villefort, who examined him attentively, and who no doubt practiced upon him all the psychological studies he was accustomed to use, in vain endeavored to make him lower his eyes, notwithstanding the depth and profundity of his gaze. At length the reading of the indictment was ended.

"Accused," said the president, "your name and surname?"

Andrea arose.

"Excuse me, Mr. President," he said, in a clear voice, "but I see you are going to adopt a course of questions through which I cannot follow you. I have an idea, which I will explain by and by, of making an exception to the usual form of accusation. Allow me, then, if you please, to answer in different order, or I will not do so at all."

The astonished president looked at the jury, who in turn looked at Villefort. The whole assembly manifested great surprise, but Andrea appeared quite unmoved.

"Your age?" said the president; "will you answer that question?"

"I will answer that question, as well as the rest, Mr. President, but in its turn."

"Your age?" repeated the president.

"I am twenty-one years old, or rather I shall be in a few days, as I was born the night of the 27th of September, 1817."

M. de Villefort, who was busy taking down some notes, raised his head at the mention of this date.

"Where were you born?" continued the president.

"At Auteuil, near Paris."

M. de Villefort a second time raised his head, looked at Benedetto as if he had been gazing at the head of Medusa, and became livid. As for Benedetto, he gracefully wiped his lips with a fine cambric pocket-handkerchief.

"Your profession?"

"First I was a forger," answered Andrea, as calmly as possible; "then I became a thief, and lately have become an assassin."

A murmur, or rather storm, of indignation burst from all parts of the assembly. The judges themselves appeared to be stupefied, and the jury manifested tokens of disgust for a cynicism so unexpected in a man of fashion. M. de Villefort pressed his hand upon his brow, which, at first pale, had become red and burning; then he suddenly arose and looked around as though he had lost his senses—he wanted air.

"Are you looking for anything, Mr. Procureur?" asked Benedetto, with his most ingratiating smile.

M. de Villefort answered nothing, but sat, or rather threw himself down again upon his chair.

"And now, prisoner, will you consent to tell your name?" said the president. "The brutal affectation with which you have enumerated and classified your crimes calls for a severe reprimand on the part of the court, both in the name of morality, and for the respect due to humanity. You appear to consider this a point of honor, and it may be for this reason, that you have delayed acknowledging your name. You wished it to be preceded by all these titles."

"It is quite wonderful, Mr. President, how entirely you have read my thoughts," said Benedetto, in his softest voice and most polite manner. "This is, indeed, the reason why I begged you to alter the order of the questions."

The public astonishment had reached its height. There was no longer any deceit or bravado in the manner of the accused. The audience felt that a startling revelation was to follow this ominous prelude.

"Well," said the president; "your name?"

"I cannot tell you my name, since I do not know it; but I know my father's, and can tell it to you."

A painful giddiness overwhelmed Villefort; great drops of acrid sweat fell from his face upon the papers which he held in his convulsed hand.

"Repeat your father's name," said the president.

Not a whisper, not a breath, was heard in that vast assembly; everyone waited anxiously.

"My father is king's attorney," replied Andrea calmly.

"King's attorney?" said the president, stupefied, and without noticing the agitation which spread over the face of M. de Villefort; "king's attorney?"

"Yes; and if you wish to know his name, I will tell it,—he is named Villefort."

The explosion, which had been so long restrained from a feeling of respect to the court of justice, now burst forth like thunder from the breasts of all present; the court itself did not seek to restrain the feelings of the audience. The exclamations, the insults addressed to Benedetto, who remained perfectly unconcerned, the energetic gestures, the movement of the gendarmes, the sneers of the scum of the crowd always sure to rise to the surface in case of any disturbance—all this lasted five minutes, before the door-keepers and magistrates were able to restore silence. In the midst of this tumult the voice of the president was heard to exclaim:

"Are you playing with justice, accused, and do you dare set your fellow-citizens an example of disorder which even in these times has never been equalled?"

Several persons hurried up to M. de Villefort, who sat half bowed over in his chair, offering him consolation, encouragement, and protestations of zeal and sympathy. Order was re-established in the hall, except that a few people still moved about and whispered to one another. A lady, it was said, had just fainted; they had supplied her with a smelling-bottle, and she had recovered. During the scene of tumult, Andrea had turned his smiling face towards the assembly; then, leaning with one hand on the oaken rail of the dock, in the most graceful attitude possible, he said:

"Gentlemen, I assure you I had no idea of insulting the court, or of making a useless disturbance in the presence of this honorable assembly. They ask my age; I tell it. They ask where I was born; I answer. They ask my name, I cannot give it, since my parents abandoned me. But though I cannot give my own name, not possessing one, I can tell them my father's. Now I repeat, my father is named M. de Villefort, and I am ready to prove it."

There was an energy, a conviction, and a sincerity in the manner of the young man, which silenced the tumult. All eyes were turned for a moment towards the procureur, who sat as motionless as though a thunderbolt had changed him into a corpse.

"Gentlemen," said Andrea, commanding silence by his voice and manner; "I owe you the proofs and explanations of what I have said."

"But," said the irritated president, "you called yourself Benedetto, declared yourself an orphan, and claimed Corsica as your country."

"I said anything I pleased, in order that the solemn declaration I have just made should not be withheld, which otherwise would certainly have been the case. I now repeat that I was born at Auteuil on the night of the 27th of September, 1817, and that I am the son of the procureur, M. de Villefort. Do you wish for any further details? I will give them. I was born in No. 28, Rue de la Fontaine, in a room hung with red damask; my father took me in his arms, telling my mother I was dead, wrapped me in a napkin marked with an H and an N, and carried me into a garden, where he buried me alive."

A shudder ran through the assembly when they saw that the confidence of the prisoner increased in proportion to the terror of M. de Villefort.

"But how have you become acquainted with all these details?" asked the president.

"I will tell you, Mr. President. A man who had sworn vengeance against my father, and had long watched his opportunity to kill him, had introduced himself that night into the garden in which my father buried me. He was concealed in a thicket; he saw my father bury something in the ground, and stabbed him; then thinking the deposit might contain some treasure he turned up the ground, and found me still living. The man carried me to the foundling asylum, where I was registered under the number 37. Three months afterwards, a woman travelled from Rogliano to Paris to fetch me, and having claimed me as her son, carried me away. Thus, you see, though born in Paris, I was brought up in Corsica."

There was a moment's silence, during which one could have fancied the hall empty, so profound was the stillness.

"Proceed," said the president.

"Certainly, I might have lived happily amongst those good people, who adored me, but my perverse disposition prevailed over the virtues which my adopted mother endeavored to instil into my heart. I increased in wickedness till I committed crime. One day when I cursed Providence for making me so wicked, and ordaining me to such a fate, my adopted father said to me, 'Do not blaspheme, unhappy child, the crime is that of your father, not yours,—of your father, who consigned you to hell if you died, and to misery if a miracle preserved you alive.' After that I ceased to blaspheme, but I cursed my father. That is why I have uttered the words for which you blame me; that is why I have filled this whole assembly with horror. If I have committed an additional crime, punish me, but if you will allow that ever since the day of my birth my fate has been sad, bitter, and lamentable, then pity me."

"But your mother?" asked the president.

"My mother thought me dead; she is not guilty. I did not even wish to know her name, nor do I know it."

Just then a piercing cry, ending in a sob, burst from the centre of the crowd, who encircled the lady who had before fainted, and who now fell into a violent fit of hysterics. She was carried out of the hall, the thick veil which concealed her face dropped off, and Madame Danglars was recognized. Notwithstanding his shattered nerves, the ringing sensation in his ears, and the madness which turned his brain, Villefort rose as he perceived her.

"The proofs, the proofs!" said the president; "remember this tissue of horrors must be supported by the clearest proofs."

"The proofs?" said Benedetto, laughing; "do you want proofs?"

"Yes."

"Well, then, look at M. de Villefort, and then ask me for proofs."

Everyone turned towards the procureur, who, unable to bear the universal gaze now riveted on him alone, advanced staggering into the midst of the tribunal, with his hair dishevelled and his face indented with the mark of his nails. The whole assembly uttered a long murmur of astonishment.

"Father," said Benedetto, "I am asked for proofs, do you wish me to give them?"

"No, no, it is useless," stammered M. de Villefort in a hoarse voice; "no, it is useless!"

"How useless?" cried the president, "what do you mean?"

"I mean that I feel it impossible to struggle against this deadly weight which crushes me. Gentlemen, I know I am in the hands of an avenging God! We need no proofs; everything relating to this young man is true."

A dull, gloomy silence, like that which precedes some awful phenomenon of nature, pervaded the assembly, who shuddered in dismay.

"What, M. de Villefort," cried the president, "do you yield to an hallucination? What, are you no longer in possession of your senses? This strange, unexpected, terrible accusation has disordered your reason. Come, recover."

The procureur dropped his head; his teeth chattered like those of a man under a violent attack of fever, and yet he was deadly pale.

"I am in possession of all my senses, sir," he said; "my body alone suffers, as you may suppose. I acknowledge myself guilty of all the young man has brought against me, and from this hour hold myself under the authority of the procureur who will succeed me."

And as he spoke these words with a hoarse, choking voice, he staggered towards the door, which was mechanically opened by a door-keeper. The whole assembly were dumb with astonishment at the revelation and confession which had produced a catastrophe so different from that which had been expected during the last fortnight by the Parisian world.

"Well," said Beauchamp, "let them now say that drama is unnatural!"

"*Ma foi!*" said Château-Renaud, "I would rather end my career like M. de Morcerf; a pistol-shot seems quite delightful compared with this catastrophe."

"And moreover, it kills," said Beauchamp.

"And to think that I had an idea of marrying his daughter," said Debray. "She did well to die, poor girl!"

"The sitting is adjourned, gentlemen," said the president; "fresh inquiries will be made, and the case will be tried next session by another magistrate."

As for Andrea, who was calm and more interesting than ever, he left the hall, escorted by gendarmes, who involuntarily paid him some attention.

"Well, what do you think of this, my fine fellow?" asked Debray of the sergeant-at-arms, slipping a louis into his hand.

"There will be extenuating circumstances," he replied.

Study Guide Questions

For Students:

1. Why does M. de Villefort feel uncomfortable during Benedetto's trial?
2. What does Benedetto say about his parents?
3. What is Villefort's final reaction by the end of the chapter?

For Reading Club:

1. Briefly discuss what happens at the trial.
2. Compare Villefort's crime with his wife's crime.
3. Do you think Villefort could have refuted Benedetto's claims?

CHAPTER 111

Expiation

Notwithstanding the density of the crowd, M. de Villefort saw it open before him. There is something so awe-inspiring in great afflictions that even in the worst times the first emotion of a crowd has generally been to sympathize with the sufferer in a great catastrophe. Many people have been assassinated in a tumult, but even criminals have rarely been insulted during trial. Thus Villefort passed through the mass of spectators and officers of the Palais, and withdrew. Though he had acknowledged his guilt, he was protected by his grief. There are some situations which men understand by instinct, but which reason is powerless to explain; in such cases the greatest poet is he who gives utterance to the most natural and vehement outburst of sorrow. Those who hear the bitter cry are as much impressed as if they listened to an entire poem, and when the sufferer is sincere they are right in regarding his outburst as sublime.

It would be difficult to describe the state of stupor in which Villefort left the Palais. Every pulse beat with feverish excitement, every nerve was strained, every vein swollen, and every part of his body seemed to suffer distinctly from the rest, thus multiplying his agony a thousand-fold. He made his way along the corridors through force of habit; he threw aside his magisterial robe, not out of deference to etiquette, but because it was an unbearable burden, a veritable garb of Nessus, insatiate in torture. Having staggered as far as the Rue Dauphine, he perceived his carriage, awoke his sleeping coachman by opening the door himself, threw himself on the cushions, and pointed towards the Faubourg Saint-Honoré; the carriage drove on.

All the weight of his fallen fortune seemed suddenly to crush him; he could not foresee the consequences; he could not contemplate the future with the indifference of the hardened criminal who merely faces a contingency already familiar.

God was still in his heart. "God," he murmured, not knowing what he said,—"God—God!" Behind the event that had overwhelmed him he saw the hand of God. The carriage rolled rapidly onward. Villefort, while turning restlessly on the cushions, felt something press against him. He put out his hand to remove the object; it was a fan which Madame de Villefort had left in the carriage; this fan awakened a recollection which darted through his mind like lightning. He thought of his wife.

"Oh!" he exclaimed, as though a red-hot iron were piercing his heart.

During the last hour his own crime had alone been presented to his mind; now another object, not less terrible, suddenly presented itself. His wife! He had just acted the inexorable judge with her, he had condemned her to death, and she, crushed by remorse, struck with terror, covered with the shame inspired by the eloquence of *his* irreproachable virtue,—she, a poor, weak woman, without help or the power of defending herself against his absolute and supreme will,—she might at that very moment, perhaps, be preparing to die!

An hour had elapsed since her condemnation; at that moment, doubtless, she was recalling all her crimes to her memory; she was asking pardon for her sins; perhaps she was even writing a letter imploring forgiveness from her virtuous husband—a forgiveness she was purchasing with her death! Villefort again groaned with anguish and despair.

"Ah," he exclaimed, "that woman became criminal only from associating with me! I carried the infection of crime with me, and she has caught it as she would the typhus fever, the cholera, the plague! And yet I have punished her—I have dared to tell her—*I* have—'Repent and die!' But no, she must not die; she shall live, and with me. We will flee from Paris and go as far as the earth reaches. I told her of the scaffold; oh, Heavens, I forgot that it awaits me also! How could I pronounce that word? Yes, we will fly; I will confess all to her,—I will tell her daily that I also have committed a crime!—Oh, what an alliance—the tiger and the serpent; worthy wife of such as I am! She *must* live that my infamy may diminish hers."

And Villefort dashed open the window in front of the carriage.

"Faster, faster!" he cried, in a tone which electrified the coachman. The horses, impelled by fear, flew towards the house.

"Yes, yes," repeated Villefort, as he approached his home—"yes, that woman must live; she must repent, and educate my son, the sole survivor, with the exception of the indestructible old man, of the wreck of my house. She loves him; it was for his sake she has committed these crimes. We ought never to despair of softening the heart of a mother who loves her child. She will repent, and no one will know that she has been guilty. The events which have taken place in my house, though they now occupy the public mind, will be forgotten in time, or if, indeed, a few enemies should persist in remembering them, why then I will add them to my list of crimes. What will it signify if one, two, or three more are added? My wife and child shall escape from this gulf, carrying treasures with them; she will live and may yet be happy, since her child, in whom all her love is centred, will be with her. I shall have performed a good action, and my heart will be lighter."

And the procureur breathed more freely than he had done for some time.

The carriage stopped at the door of the house. Villefort leaped out of the carriage, and saw that his servants were surprised at his early return; he could read no other expression on their features. Neither of them spoke to him; they merely stood aside to let him pass by, as usual, nothing more. As he passed by M. Noirtier's room, he perceived two figures through the half-open door; but he experienced no curiosity to know who was visiting his father; anxiety carried him on further.

"Come," he said, as he ascended the stairs leading to his wife's room, "nothing is changed here."

He then closed the door of the landing.

"No one must disturb us," he said; "I must speak freely to her, accuse myself, and say"—he approached the door, touched the crystal handle, which yielded to his hand. "Not locked," he cried; "that is well."

And he entered the little room in which Edward slept; for though the child went to school during the day, his mother could not allow him to be separated from her at night. With a single glance Villefort's eye ran through the room.

"Not here," he said; "doubtless she is in her bedroom." He rushed towards the door, found it bolted, and stopped, shuddering.

"Héloïse!" he cried. He fancied he heard the sound of a piece of furniture being removed.

"Héloïse!" he repeated.

"Who is there?" answered the voice of her he sought. He thought that voice more feeble than usual.

"Open the door!" cried Villefort. "Open; it is I."

But notwithstanding this request, notwithstanding the tone of anguish in which it was uttered, the door remained closed. Villefort burst it open with a violent blow. At the entrance of the room which led to her boudoir, Madame de Villefort was standing erect, pale, her features contracted, and her eyes glaring horribly.

"Héloïse, Héloïse!" he said, "what is the matter? Speak!" The young woman extended her stiff white hands towards him.

"It is done, monsieur," she said with a rattling noise which seemed to tear her throat. "What more do you want?" and she fell full length on the floor.

Villefort ran to her and seized her hand, which convulsively clasped a crystal bottle with a golden stopper. Madame de Villefort was dead. Villefort, maddened with horror, stepped back to the threshhold of the door, fixing his eyes on the corpse.

"My son!" he exclaimed suddenly, "where is my son?—Edward, Edward!" and he rushed out of the room, still crying, "Edward, Edward!" The name was pronounced in such a tone of anguish that the servants ran up.

"Where is my son?" asked Villefort; "let him be removed from the house, that he may not see—"

"Master Edward is not downstairs, sir," replied the valet.

"Then he must be playing in the garden; go and see."

"No, sir; Madame de Villefort sent for him half an hour ago; he went into her room, and has not been downstairs since."

A cold perspiration burst out on Villefort's brow; his legs trembled, and his thoughts flew about madly in his brain like the wheels of a disordered watch.

"In Madame de Villefort's room?" he murmured and slowly returned, with one hand wiping his forehead, and with the other supporting himself against the wall. To enter the room he must again see the body of his unfortunate wife. To call Edward he must reawaken the echo of that room which now appeared like a sepulchre; to speak seemed like violating the silence of the tomb. His tongue was paralyzed in his mouth.

"Edward!" he stammered—"Edward!"

The child did not answer. Where, then, could he be, if he had entered his mother's room and not since returned? He stepped forward. The corpse of Madame de Villefort was stretched across the doorway leading to the room in which Edward must be; those glaring eyes seemed to watch over the threshold, and the lips bore the stamp of a terrible and mysterious irony. Through the open door was visible a portion of the boudoir, containing an upright piano and a blue satin couch. Villefort stepped forward two or three paces, and beheld his child lying—no doubt asleep—on the sofa. The unhappy man uttered an exclamation of joy; a ray of light seemed to penetrate the abyss of despair and darkness. He had only to step over the corpse, enter the boudoir, take the child in his arms, and flee far, far away.

Villefort was no longer the civilized man; he was a tiger hurt unto death, gnashing his teeth in his wound. He no longer feared realities, but phantoms. He leaped over the corpse as if it had been a burning brazier. He took the child in his arms, embraced him, shook him, called him, but the child made no response. He pressed his burning lips to the cheeks, but they were icy cold and pale; he felt the stiffened limbs; he pressed his hand upon the heart, but it no longer beat,—the child was dead.

A folded paper fell from Edward's breast. Villefort, thunderstruck, fell upon his knees; the child dropped from his arms, and rolled on the floor by the side of its mother. He picked up the paper, and, recognizing his wife's writing, ran his eyes rapidly over its contents; it ran as follows:

"You know that I was a good mother, since it was for my son's sake I became criminal. A good mother cannot depart without her son."

Villefort could not believe his eyes,—he could not believe his reason; he dragged himself towards the child's body, and examined it as a lioness contemplates its dead cub. Then a piercing cry escaped from his breast, and he cried,

"Still the hand of God."

The presence of the two victims alarmed him; he could not bear solitude shared only by two corpses. Until then he had been sustained by rage, by his strength of mind, by despair, by the supreme agony which led the Titans to scale the heavens, and Ajax to defy the gods. He now arose, his head bowed beneath the weight of grief, and, shaking his damp, dishevelled hair, he who had never felt compassion for anyone determined to seek his father, that he might have someone to whom he could relate his misfortunes,—someone by whose side he might weep.

He descended the little staircase with which we are acquainted, and entered Noirtier's room. The old man appeared to be listening attentively and as affectionately as his infirmities would allow to the Abbé Busoni, who looked cold and calm, as usual. Villefort, perceiving the abbé, passed his hand across his brow. The past came to him like one of those waves whose wrath foams fiercer than the others.

He recollected the call he had made upon him after the dinner at Auteuil, and then the visit the abbé had himself paid to his house on the day of Valentine's death.

"You here, sir!" he exclaimed; "do you, then, never appear but to act as an escort to death?"

Busoni turned around, and, perceiving the excitement depicted on the magistrate's face, the savage lustre of his eyes, he understood that the revelation had been made at the assizes; but beyond this he was ignorant.

"I came to pray over the body of your daughter."

"And now why are you here?"

"I come to tell you that you have sufficiently repaid your debt, and that from this moment I will pray to God to forgive you, as I do."

"Good heavens!" exclaimed Villefort, stepping back fearfully, "surely that is not the voice of the Abbé Busoni!"

"No!" The abbé threw off his wig, shook his head, and his hair, no longer confined, fell in black masses around his manly face.

"It is the face of the Count of Monte Cristo!" exclaimed the procureur, with a haggard expression.

"You are not exactly right, M. Procureur; you must go farther back."

"That voice, that voice!—where did I first hear it?"

"You heard it for the first time at Marseilles, twenty-three years ago, the day of your marriage with Mademoiselle de Saint-Méran. Refer to your papers."

"You are not Busoni?—you are not Monte Cristo? Oh, heavens! you are, then, some secret, implacable, and mortal enemy! I must have wronged you in some way at Marseilles. Oh, woe to me!"

"Yes; you are now on the right path," said the count, crossing his arms over his broad chest; "search—search!"

"But what have I done to you?" exclaimed Villefort, whose mind was balancing between reason and insanity, in that cloud which is neither a dream nor reality; "what have I done to you? Tell me, then! Speak!"

"You condemned me to a horrible, tedious death; you killed my father; you deprived me of liberty, of love, and happiness."

"Who are you, then? Who are you?"

"I am the spectre of a wretch you buried in the dungeons of the Château d'If. God gave that spectre the form of the Count of Monte Cristo when he at length issued from his tomb, enriched him with gold and diamonds, and led him to you!"

"Ah, I recognize you—I recognize you!" exclaimed the king's attorney; "you are—"

"I am Edmond Dantès!"

"You are Edmond Dantès," cried Villefort, seizing the count by the wrist; "then come here!"

And up the stairs he dragged Monte Cristo; who, ignorant of what had happened, followed him in astonishment, foreseeing some new catastrophe.

"There, Edmond Dantès!" he said, pointing to the bodies of his wife and child, "see, are you well avenged?"

Monte Cristo became pale at this horrible sight; he felt that he had passed beyond the bounds of vengeance, and that he could no longer say, "God is for and with me." With an expression of indescribable anguish he threw himself upon the body of the child, reopened its eyes, felt its pulse, and then rushed with him into Valentine's room, of which he double-locked the door.

"My child," cried Villefort, "he carries away the body of my child! Oh, curses, woe, death to you!"

He tried to follow Monte Cristo; but as though in a dream he was transfixed to the spot,—his eyes glared as though they were starting through the sockets; he griped the flesh on his chest until his nails were stained with blood; the veins of his temples swelled and boiled as though they would burst their narrow boundary, and deluge his brain with living fire. This lasted several minutes, until the frightful overturn of reason was accomplished; then uttering a loud cry followed by a burst of laughter, he rushed down the stairs.

A quarter of an hour afterwards the door of Valentine's room opened, and Monte Cristo reappeared. Pale, with a dull eye and heavy heart, all the noble features of that face, usually so calm and serene, were overcast by grief. In his arms he held the child, whom no skill had been able to recall to life. Bending on one knee, he placed it reverently by the side of its mother, with its head upon her breast. Then, rising, he went out, and meeting a servant on the stairs, he asked:

"Where is M. de Villefort?"

The servant, instead of answering, pointed to the garden. Monte Cristo ran down the steps, and advancing towards the spot designated beheld Villefort, encircled by his servants, with a spade in his hand, and digging the earth with fury.

"It is not here!" he cried. "It is not here!"

And then he moved farther on, and began again to dig.

Monte Cristo approached him, and said in a low voice, with an expression almost humble:

"Sir, you have indeed lost a son; but—"

Villefort interrupted him; he had neither listened nor heard.

"Oh, I *will* find it," he cried; "you may pretend he is not here, but I *will* find him, though I dig forever!"

Monte Cristo drew back in horror.

"Oh," he said, "he is mad!" And as though he feared that the walls of the accursed house would crumble around him, he rushed into the street, for the first time doubting whether he had the right to do as he had done. "Oh, enough of this,—enough of this," he cried; "let me save the last." On entering his house, he met Morrel, who wandered about like a ghost awaiting the heavenly mandate for return to the tomb.

"Prepare yourself, Maximilian," he said with a smile; "we leave Paris tomorrow."

"Have you nothing more to do there?" asked Morrel.

"No," replied Monte Cristo; "God grant I may not have done too much already."

The next day they indeed left, accompanied only by Baptistin. Haydée had taken away Ali, and Bertuccio remained with Noirtier.

Study Guide Questions

For Students:

1. Who dies in the Villefort house?
2. Where does Villefort find a note from his wife and what is written on it?
3. Who is sitting with M. Noiriter?

For Reading Club:

1. Villefort calls his wife “Héloïse” for the first time in the book. What does it tell you about the husband/wife relationship in the 19th Century?
2. How does Edmond Dantès reveal himself before Villefort?
3. Discuss Dantès’ reaction to Edward’s death. To what extent do you think he is responsible for the tragedy that befalls the child?

CHAPTER 112

The Departure

The recent events formed the theme of conversation throughout all Paris. Emmanuel and his wife conversed with natural astonishment in their little apartment in the Rue Meslay upon the three successive, sudden, and most unexpected catastrophes of Morcerf, Danglars, and Villefort. Maximilian, who was paying them a visit, listened to their conversation, or rather was present at it, plunged in his accustomed state of apathy.

"Indeed," said Julie, "might we not almost fancy, Emmanuel, that those people, so rich, so happy but yesterday, had forgotten in their prosperity that an evil genius—like the wicked fairies in Perrault's stories who present themselves unbidden at a wedding or baptism—hovered over them, and appeared all at once to revenge himself for their fatal neglect?"

"What a dire misfortune!" said Emmanuel, thinking of Morcerf and Danglars.

"What dreadful sufferings!" said Julie, remembering Valentine, but whom, with a delicacy natural to women, she did not name before her brother.

"If the Supreme Being has directed the fatal blow," said Emmanuel, "it must be that he in his great goodness has perceived nothing in the past lives of these people to merit mitigation of their awful punishment."

"Do you not form a very rash judgment, Emmanuel?" said Julie. "When my father, with a pistol in his hand, was once on the point of committing suicide, had anyone then said, 'This man deserves his misery,' would not that person have been deceived?"

"Yes; but your father was not allowed to fall. A being was commissioned to arrest the fatal hand of death about to descend on him."

Emmanuel had scarcely uttered these words when the sound of the bell was heard, the well-known signal given by the porter that a visitor had arrived. Nearly at the same instant the door was opened and the Count of Monte Cristo appeared on the threshold. The young people uttered a cry of joy, while Maximilian raised his head, but let it fall again immediately.

"Maximilian," said the count, without appearing to notice the different impressions which his presence produced on the little circle, "I come to seek you."

"To seek me?" repeated Morrel, as if awakening from a dream.

"Yes," said Monte Cristo; "has it not been agreed that I should take you with me, and did I not tell you yesterday to prepare for departure?"

"I am ready," said Maximilian; "I came expressly to wish them farewell."

"Whither are you going, count?" asked Julie.

"In the first instance to Marseilles, madame."

"To Marseilles!" exclaimed the young couple.

"Yes, and I take your brother with me."

"Oh, count." said Julie, "will you restore him to us cured of his melancholy?" Morrel turned away to conceal the confusion of his countenance.

"You perceive, then, that he is not happy?" said the count.

"Yes," replied the young woman; "and fear much that he finds our home but a dull one."

"I will undertake to divert him," replied the count.

"I am ready to accompany you, sir," said Maximilian. "Adieu, my kind friends! Emmanuel—Julie—farewell!"

"How farewell?" exclaimed Julie; "do you leave us thus, so suddenly, without any preparations for your journey, without even a passport?"

"Needless delays but increase the grief of parting," said Monte Cristo, "and Maximilian has doubtless provided himself with everything requisite; at least, I advised him to do so."

"I have a passport, and my clothes are ready packed," said Morrel in his tranquil but mournful manner.

"Good," said Monte Cristo, smiling; "in these prompt arrangements we recognize the order of a well-disciplined soldier."

"And you leave us," said Julie, "at a moment's warning? you do not give us a day—no, not even an hour before your departure?"

"My carriage is at the door, madame, and I must be in Rome in five days."

"But does Maximilian go to Rome?" exclaimed Emmanuel.

"I am going wherever it may please the count to take me," said Morrel, with a smile full of grief; "I am under his orders for the next month."

"Oh, heavens, how strangely he expresses himself, count!" said Julie.

"Maximilian goes with *me*," said the count, in his kindest and most persuasive manner; "therefore do not make yourself uneasy on your brother's account."

"Once more farewell, my dear sister; Emmanuel, adieu!" Morrel repeated.

"His carelessness and indifference touch me to the heart," said Julie. "Oh, Maximilian, Maximilian, you are certainly concealing something from us."

"Pshaw!" said Monte Cristo, "you will see him return to you gay, smiling, and joyful."

Maximilian cast a look of disdain, almost of anger, on the count.

"We must leave you," said Monte Cristo.

"Before you quit us, count," said Julie, "will you permit us to express to you all that the other day—"

"Madame," interrupted the count, taking her two hands in his, "all that you could say in words would never express what I read in your eyes; the thoughts of your heart are fully understood by mine. Like benefactors in romances, I should have left you without seeing you again, but that would have been a virtue beyond my strength, because I am a weak and vain man, fond of the tender, kind, and thankful glances of my fellow-creatures. On the eve of departure I carry my egotism so far as to say, 'Do not forget me, my kind friends, for probably you will never see me again.'"

"Never see you again?" exclaimed Emmanuel, while two large tears rolled down Julie's cheeks, "never behold you again? It is not a man, then, but some angel that leaves us, and this angel is on the point of returning to heaven after having appeared on earth to do good."

"Say not so," quickly returned Monte Cristo—"say not so, my friends; angels never err, celestial beings remain where they wish to be. Fate is not more powerful than they; it is they who, on the contrary, overcome fate. No, Emmanuel, I am but a man, and your admiration is as unmerited as your words are sacrilegious."

And pressing his lips on the hand of Julie, who rushed into his arms, he extended his other hand to Emmanuel; then tearing himself from this abode of peace and happiness, he made a sign to Maximilian, who followed him passively, with the indifference which had been perceptible in him ever since the death of Valentine had so stunned him.

"Restore my brother to peace and happiness," whispered Julie to Monte Cristo. And the count pressed her hand in reply, as he had done eleven years before on the staircase leading to Morrel's study.

"You still confide, then, in Sinbad the Sailor?" asked he, smiling.

"Oh, yes," was the ready answer.

"Well, then, sleep in peace, and put your trust in the Lord."

As we have before said, the post-chaise was waiting; four powerful horses were already pawing the ground with impatience, while Ali, apparently just arrived from a long walk, was standing at the foot of the steps, his face bathed in perspiration.

"Well," asked the count in Arabic, "have you been to see the old man?" Ali made a sign in the affirmative.

"And have you placed the letter before him, as I ordered you to do?"

The slave respectfully signalized that he had.

"And what did he say, or rather do?" Ali placed himself in the light, so that his master might see him distinctly, and then imitating in his intelligent manner the countenance of the old man, he closed his eyes, as Noirtier was in the custom of doing when saying "Yes."

"Good; he accepts," said Monte Cristo. "Now let us go."

These words had scarcely escaped him, when the carriage was on its way, and the feet of the horses struck a shower of sparks from the pavement. Maximilian settled himself in his corner without uttering a word. Half an hour had passed when the carriage stopped suddenly; the count had just pulled the silken check-string, which was fastened to Ali's finger. The Nubian immediately descended and opened the carriage door. It was a lovely starlight night—they had just reached the top of the hill Villejuif, from whence Paris appears like a sombre sea tossing its millions of phosphoric waves into light—waves indeed more noisy, more passionate, more changeable, more furious, more greedy, than those of the tempestuous ocean,—waves which never rest as those of the sea sometimes do,—waves ever dashing, ever foaming, ever ingulfing what falls within their grasp.

The count stood alone, and at a sign from his hand, the carriage went on for a short distance. With folded arms, he gazed for some time upon the great city. When he had fixed his piercing look on this modern Babylon, which equally engages the contemplation of the religious enthusiast, the materialist, and the scoffer,—

"Great city," murmured he, inclining his head, and joining his hands as if in prayer, "less than six months have elapsed since first I entered thy gates. I believe that the Spirit of God led my steps to thee and that he also enables me to quit thee in triumph; the secret cause of my presence within thy walls I have confided alone to him who only has had the power to read my heart. God only knows that I retire from thee without pride or hatred, but not without many regrets; he only knows that the power confided to me has never been made subservient to my personal good or to any useless cause. Oh, great city, it is in thy palpitating bosom that I have found that which I sought; like a patient miner, I have dug deep into thy very entrails to root out evil thence. Now my work is accomplished, my mission is terminated, now thou canst neither afford me pain nor pleasure. Adieu, Paris, adieu!"

His look wandered over the vast plain like that of some genius of the night; he passed his hand over his brow, got into the carriage, the door was closed on him, and the vehicle quickly disappeared down the other side of the hill in a whirlwind of dust and noise.

Ten leagues were passed and not a single word was uttered. Morrel was dreaming, and Monte Cristo was looking at the dreamer.

"Morrel," said the count to him at length, "do you repent having followed me?"

"No, count; but to leave Paris—"

"If I thought happiness might await you in Paris, Morrel, I would have left you there."

"Valentine reposes within the walls of Paris, and to leave Paris is like losing her a second time."

"Maximilian," said the count, "the friends that we have lost do not repose in the bosom of the earth, but are buried deep in our hearts, and it has been thus ordained that we may always be accompanied by them. I have two friends, who in this way never depart from me; the one who gave me being, and the other who conferred knowledge and intelligence on me. Their spirits live in me. I consult them when doubtful, and if I ever do any good, it is due to their beneficent counsels. Listen to the voice of your heart, Morrel, and ask it whether you ought to preserve this melancholy exterior towards me."

"My friend," said Maximilian, "the voice of my heart is very sorrowful, and promises me nothing but misfortune."

"It is the way of weakened minds to see everything through a black cloud. The soul forms its own horizons; your soul is darkened, and consequently the sky of the future appears stormy and unpromising."

"That may possibly be true," said Maximilian, and he again subsided into his thoughtful mood.

The journey was performed with that marvellous rapidity which the unlimited power of the count ever commanded. Towns fled from them like shadows on their path, and trees shaken by the first winds of autumn seemed like giants madly rushing on to meet them, and retreating as rapidly when once reached. The following morning they arrived at Châlons, where the count's steamboat waited for them. Without the loss of an instant, the carriage was placed on board and the two travellers embarked without delay. The boat was built for speed; her two paddle-wheels were like two wings with which she skimmed the water like a bird.

Morrel was not insensible to that sensation of delight which is generally experienced in passing rapidly through the air, and the wind which occasionally raised the hair from his forehead seemed on the point of dispelling momentarily the clouds collected there.

As the distance increased between the travellers and Paris, almost superhuman serenity appeared to surround the count; he might have been taken for an exile about to revisit his native land.

Ere long Marseilles presented herself to view,—Marseilles, white, fervid, full of life and energy,—Marseilles, the younger sister of Tyre and Carthage, the successor to them in the empire of the Mediterranean,—Marseilles, old, yet always young. Powerful memories were stirred within them by the sight of the round tower, Fort Saint-Nicolas, the City Hall designed by Puget,[21] the port with its brick quays, where they had both played in childhood, and it was with one accord that they stopped on the Canebière.

A vessel was setting sail for Algiers, on board of which the bustle usually attending departure prevailed. The passengers and their relations crowded on the deck, friends taking a tender but sorrowful leave of each other, some weeping, others noisy in their grief, the whole forming a spectacle that might be exciting even to those who witnessed similar sights daily, but which had no power to disturb the current of thought that had taken possession of the mind of Maximilian from the moment he had set foot on the broad pavement of the quay.

"Here," said he, leaning heavily on the arm of Monte Cristo,—"here is the spot where my father stopped, when the *Pharaon* entered the port; it was here that the good old man, whom you saved from death and dishonor, threw himself into my arms. I yet feel his warm tears on my face, and his were not the only tears shed, for many who witnessed our meeting wept also."

Monte Cristo gently smiled and said,—"I was there;" at the same time pointing to the corner of a street. As he spoke, and in the very direction he indicated, a groan, expressive of bitter grief, was heard, and a woman was seen waving her hand to a passenger on board the vessel about to sail. Monte Cristo looked at her with an emotion that must have been remarked by Morrel had not his eyes been fixed on the vessel.

"Oh, heavens!" exclaimed Morrel, "I do not deceive myself—that young man who is waving his hat, that youth in the uniform of a lieutenant, is Albert de Morcerf!"

"Yes," said Monte Cristo, "I recognized him."

"How so?—you were looking the other way."

---

[21] Gaspard Puget, the sculptor-architect, was born at Marseilles in 1615.

The count smiled, as he was in the habit of doing when he did not want to make any reply, and he again turned towards the veiled woman, who soon disappeared at the corner of the street. Turning to his friend:

"Dear Maximilian," said the count, "have you nothing to do in this land?"

"I have to weep over the grave of my father," replied Morrel in a broken voice.

"Well, then, go,—wait for me there, and I will soon join you."

"You leave me, then?"

"Yes; I also have a pious visit to pay."

Morrel allowed his hand to fall into that which the count extended to him; then with an inexpressibly sorrowful inclination of the head he quitted the count and bent his steps to the east of the city. Monte Cristo remained on the same spot until Maximilian was out of sight; he then walked slowly towards the Allées de Meilhan to seek out a small house with which our readers were made familiar at the beginning of this story.

It yet stood, under the shade of the fine avenue of lime-trees, which forms one of the most frequent walks of the idlers of Marseilles, covered by an immense vine, which spreads its aged and blackened branches over the stone front, burnt yellow by the ardent sun of the south. Two stone steps worn away by the friction of many feet led to the door, which was made of three planks; the door had never been painted or varnished, so great cracks yawned in it during the dry season to close again when the rains came on. The house, with all its crumbling antiquity and apparent misery, was yet cheerful and picturesque, and was the same that old Dantès formerly inhabited—the only difference being that the old man occupied merely the garret, while the whole house was now placed at the command of Mercédès by the count.

The woman whom the count had seen leave the ship with so much regret entered this house; she had scarcely closed the door after her when Monte Cristo appeared at the corner of a street, so that he found and lost her again almost at the same instant. The worn out steps were old acquaintances of his; he knew better than anyone else how to open that weather-beaten door with the large headed nail which served to raise the latch within. He entered without knocking, or giving any other intimation of his presence, as if he had been a friend or the master of the place. At the end of a passage paved with bricks, was a little garden, bathed in sunshine, and rich in warmth and light. In this garden Mercédès had found, at the place indicated by the count, the sum of money which he, through a sense of delicacy, had described as having been placed there twenty-four years previously. The trees of the garden were easily seen from the steps of the street-door.

Monte Cristo, on stepping into the house, heard a sigh that was almost a deep sob; he looked in the direction whence it came, and there under an arbor of Virginia jessamine,[22] with its thick foliage and beautiful long purple flowers, he saw Mercédès seated, with her head bowed, and weeping bitterly. She had raised her veil, and with her face hidden by her hands was giving free scope to the sighs and tears which had been so long restrained by the presence of her son.

Monte Cristo advanced a few steps, which were heard on the gravel. Mercédès raised her head, and uttered a cry of terror on beholding a man before her.

"Madame," said the count, "it is no longer in my power to restore you to happiness, but I offer you consolation; will you deign to accept it as coming from a friend?"

"I am, indeed, most wretched," replied Mercédès. "Alone in the world, I had but my son, and he has left me!"

"He possesses a noble heart, madame," replied the count, "and he has acted rightly. He feels that every man owes a tribute to his country; some contribute their talents, others their industry; these devote their blood, those their nightly labors, to the same cause. Had he remained with you, his life must have become a hateful burden, nor would he have participated in your griefs. He will increase in strength and honor by struggling with adversity, which he will convert into prosperity. Leave him to build up the future for you, and I venture to say you will confide it to safe hands."

"Oh," replied the wretched woman, mournfully shaking her head, "the prosperity of which you speak, and which, from the bottom of my heart, I pray God in his mercy to grant him, I can never enjoy. The bitter cup of adversity has been drained by me to the very dregs, and I feel that the grave is not far distant. You have acted kindly, count, in bringing me back to the place where I have enjoyed so much bliss. I ought to meet death on the same spot where happiness was once all my own."

"Alas," said Monte Cristo, "your words sear and embitter my heart, the more so as you have every reason to hate me. I have been the cause of all your misfortunes; but why do you pity, instead of blaming me? You render me still more unhappy—"

"Hate you, blame you—*you*, Edmond! Hate, reproach, the man that has spared my son's life! For was it not your fatal and sanguinary intention to destroy that son of whom M. de Morcerf was so proud? Oh, look at me closely, and discover, if you can, even the semblance of a reproach in me."

---

[22] The Carolina—not Virginia—jessamine, *gelsemium sempervirens* (properly speaking not a jessamine at all) has yellow blossoms. The reference is no doubt to the *Wistaria frutescens.*—Ed.

The count looked up and fixed his eyes on Mercédès, who arose partly from her seat and extended both her hands towards him.

"Oh, look at me," continued she, with a feeling of profound melancholy, "my eyes no longer dazzle by their brilliancy, for the time has long fled since I used to smile on Edmond Dantès, who anxiously looked out for me from the window of yonder garret, then inhabited by his old father. Years of grief have created an abyss between those days and the present. I neither reproach you nor hate you, my friend. Oh, no, Edmond, it is myself that I blame, myself that I hate! Oh, miserable creature that I am!" cried she, clasping her hands, and raising her eyes to heaven. "I once possessed piety, innocence, and love, the three ingredients of the happiness of angels, and now what am I?"

Monte Cristo approached her, and silently took her hand.

"No," said she, withdrawing it gently—"no, my friend, touch me not. You have spared me, yet of all those who have fallen under your vengeance I was the most guilty. They were influenced by hatred, by avarice, and by self-love; but I was base, and for want of courage acted against my judgment. Nay, do not press my hand, Edmond; you are thinking, I am sure, of some kind speech to console me, but do not utter it to me, reserve it for others more worthy of your kindness. See" (and she exposed her face completely to view)—"see, misfortune has silvered my hair, my eyes have shed so many tears that they are encircled by a rim of purple, and my brow is wrinkled. You, Edmond, on the contrary,—you are still young, handsome, dignified; it is because you have had faith; because you have had strength, because you have had trust in God, and God has sustained you. But as for me, I have been a coward; I have denied God and he has abandoned me."

Mercédès burst into tears; her woman's heart was breaking under its load of memories. Monte Cristo took her hand and imprinted a kiss on it; but she herself felt that it was a kiss of no greater warmth than he would have bestowed on the hand of some marble statue of a saint.

"It often happens," continued she, "that a first fault destroys the prospects of a whole life. I believed you dead; why did I survive you? What good has it done me to mourn for you eternally in the secret recesses of my heart?—only to make a woman of thirty-nine look like a woman of fifty. Why, having recognized you, and I the only one to do so—why was I able to save my son alone? Ought I not also to have rescued the man that I had accepted for a husband, guilty though he were? Yet I let him die! What do I say? Oh, merciful heavens, was I not accessory to his death by my supine insensibility, by my contempt for him, not remembering, or not willing to remember, that it was for my sake he had become a traitor and a perjurer? In what am I benefited by accompanying my son so far, since I now abandon him, and allow him to depart alone to the baneful climate of Africa? Oh, I have been base, cowardly, I tell you; I have abjured my affections, and like all renegades I am of evil omen to those who surround me!"

"No, Mercédès," said Monte Cristo, "no; you judge yourself with too much severity. You are a noble-minded woman, and it was your grief that disarmed me. Still I was but an agent, led on by an invisible and offended Deity, who chose not to withhold the fatal blow that I was destined to hurl. I take that God to witness, at whose feet I have prostrated myself daily for the last ten years, that I would have sacrificed my life to you, and with my life the projects that were indissolubly linked with it. But—and I say it with some pride, Mercédès—God needed me, and I lived. Examine the past and the present, and endeavor to dive into futurity, and then say whether I am not a divine instrument. The most dreadful misfortunes, the most frightful sufferings, the abandonment of all those who loved me, the persecution of those who did not know me, formed the trials of my youth; when suddenly, from captivity, solitude, misery, I was restored to light and liberty, and became the possessor of a fortune so brilliant, so unbounded, so unheard-of, that I must have been blind not to be conscious that God had endowed me with it to work out his own great designs. From that time I looked upon this fortune as something confided to me for a particular purpose. Not a thought was given to a life which you once, Mercédès, had the power to render blissful; not one hour of peaceful calm was mine; but I felt myself driven on like an exterminating angel. Like adventurous captains about to embark on some enterprise full of danger, I laid in my provisions, I loaded my weapons, I collected every means of attack and defence; I inured my body to the most violent exercises, my soul to the bitterest trials; I taught my arm to slay, my eyes to behold excruciating sufferings, and my mouth to smile at the most horrid spectacles. Good-natured, confiding, and forgiving as I had been, I became revengeful, cunning, and wicked, or rather, immovable as fate. Then I launched out into the path that was opened to me. I overcame every obstacle, and reached the goal; but woe to those who stood in my pathway!"

"Enough," said Mercédès; "enough, Edmond! Believe me, that she who alone recognized you has been the only one to comprehend you; and had she crossed your path, and you had crushed her like glass, still, Edmond, still she must have admired you! Like the gulf between me and the past, there is an abyss between you, Edmond, and the rest of mankind; and I tell you freely that the comparison I draw between you and other men will ever be one of my greatest tortures. No, there is nothing in the world to resemble you in worth and goodness! But we must say farewell, Edmond, and let us part."

"Before I leave you, Mercédès, have you no request to make?" said the count.

"I desire but one thing in this world, Edmond,—the happiness of my son."

"Pray to the Almighty to spare his life, and I will take upon myself to promote his happiness."

"Thank you, Edmond."

"But have you no request to make for yourself, Mercédès?"

"For myself I want nothing. I live, as it were, between two graves. One is that of Edmond Dantès, lost to me long, long since. He had my love! That word ill becomes my faded lip now, but it is a memory dear to my heart, and one that I would not lose for all that the world contains. The other grave is that of the man who met his death from the hand of Edmond Dantès. I approve of the deed, but I must pray for the dead."

"Your son shall be happy, Mercédès," repeated the count.

"Then I shall enjoy as much happiness as this world can possibly confer."

"But what are your intentions?"

Mercédès smiled sadly.

"To say that I shall live here, like the Mercédès of other times, gaining my bread by labor, would not be true, nor would you believe me. I have no longer the strength to do anything but to spend my days in prayer. However, I shall have no occasion to work, for the little sum of money buried by you, and which I found in the place you mentioned, will be sufficient to maintain me. Rumor will probably be busy respecting me, my occupations, my manner of living—that will signify but little, that concerns God, you, and myself."

"Mercédès," said the count, "I do not say it to blame you, but you made an unnecessary sacrifice in relinquishing the whole of the fortune amassed by M. de Morcerf; half of it at least by right belonged to you, in virtue of your vigilance and economy."

"I perceive what you are intending to propose to me; but I cannot accept it, Edmond—my son would not permit it."

"Nothing shall be done without the full approbation of Albert de Morcerf. I will make myself acquainted with his intentions and will submit to them. But if he be willing to accept my offers, will you oppose them?"

"You well know, Edmond, that I am no longer a reasoning creature; I have no will, unless it be the will never to decide. I have been so overwhelmed by the many storms that have broken over my head, that I am become passive in the hands of the Almighty, like a sparrow in the talons of an eagle. I live, because it is not ordained for me to die. If succor be sent to me, I will accept it."

"Ah, madame," said Monte Cristo, "you should not talk thus! It is not so we should evince our resignation to the will of heaven; on the contrary, we are all free agents."

"Alas!" exclaimed Mercédès, "if it were so, if I possessed free-will, but without the power to render that will efficacious, it would drive me to despair."

Monte Cristo dropped his head and shrank from the vehemence of her grief.

"Will you not even say you will see me again?" he asked.

"On the contrary, we shall meet again," said Mercédès, pointing to heaven with solemnity. "I tell you so to prove to you that I still hope."

And after pressing her own trembling hand upon that of the count, Mercédès rushed up the stairs and disappeared. Monte Cristo slowly left the house and turned towards the quay. But Mercédès did not witness his departure, although she was seated at the little window of the room which had been occupied by old Dantès. Her eyes were straining to see the ship which was carrying her son over the vast sea; but still her voice involuntarily murmured softly:

"Edmond, Edmond, Edmond!"

Study Guide Questions

For Students:

1. Whose departure is mentioned at the beginning of the chapter?
2. Where is the Count going?
3. What duty does the Count assign to Ali?

For Reading Club:

1. Discuss why the Count is leaving Paris.
2. Do you think the Count has any regrets?
3. Discuss the Count's prayer at the end of the chapter.

CHAPTER 113

The Past

The count departed with a sad heart from the house in which he had left Mercédès, probably never to behold her again. Since the death of little Edward a great change had taken place in Monte Cristo. Having reached the summit of his vengeance by a long and tortuous path, he saw an abyss of doubt yawning before him. More than this, the conversation which had just taken place between Mercédès and himself had awakened so many recollections in his heart that he felt it necessary to combat with them. A man of the count's temperament could not long indulge in that melancholy which can exist in common minds, but which destroys superior ones. He thought he must have made an error in his calculations if he now found cause to blame himself.

"I cannot have deceived myself," he said; "I must look upon the past in a false light. What!" he continued, "can I have been following a false path?—can the end which I proposed be a mistaken end?—can one hour have sufficed to prove to an architect that the work upon which he founded all his hopes was an impossible, if not a sacrilegious, undertaking? I cannot reconcile myself to this idea—it would madden me. The reason why I am now dissatisfied is that I have not a clear appreciation of the past. The past, like the country through which we walk, becomes indistinct as we advance. My position is like that of a person wounded in a dream; he feels the wound, though he cannot recollect when he received it.

"Come, then, thou regenerate man, thou extravagant prodigal, thou awakened sleeper, thou all-powerful visionary, thou invincible millionaire,—once again review thy past life of starvation and wretchedness, revisit the scenes where fate and misfortune conducted, and where despair received thee. Too many diamonds, too much gold and splendor, are now reflected by the mirror in which Monte Cristo seeks to behold Dantès. Hide thy diamonds, bury thy gold, shroud thy splendor, exchange riches for poverty, liberty for a prison, a living body for a corpse!"

As he thus reasoned, Monte Cristo walked down the Rue de la Caisserie. It was the same through which, twenty-four years ago, he had been conducted by a silent and nocturnal guard; the houses, today so smiling and animated, were on that night dark, mute, and closed.

"And yet they were the same," murmured Monte Cristo, "only now it is broad daylight instead of night; it is the sun which brightens the place, and makes it appear so cheerful."

He proceeded towards the quay by the Rue Saint-Laurent, and advanced to the Consigne; it was the point where he had embarked. A pleasure-boat with striped awning was going by. Monte Cristo called the owner, who immediately rowed up to him with the eagerness of a boatman hoping for a good fare.

The weather was magnificent, and the excursion a treat. The sun, red and flaming, was sinking into the embrace of the welcoming ocean. The sea, smooth as crystal, was now and then disturbed by the leaping of fish, which were pursued by some unseen enemy and sought for safety in another element; while on the extreme verge of the horizon might be seen the fishermen's boats, white and graceful as the sea-gull, or the merchant vessels bound for Corsica or Spain.

But notwithstanding the serene sky, the gracefully formed boats, and the golden light in which the whole scene was bathed, the Count of Monte Cristo, wrapped in his cloak, could think only of this terrible voyage, the details of which were one by one recalled to his memory. The solitary light burning at the Catalans; that first sight of the Château d'If, which told him whither they were leading him; the struggle with the gendarmes when he wished to throw himself overboard; his despair when he found himself vanquished, and the sensation when the muzzle of the carbine touched his forehead—all these were brought before him in vivid and frightful reality.

Like the streams which the heat of the summer has dried up, and which after the autumnal storms gradually begin oozing drop by drop, so did the count feel his heart gradually fill with the bitterness which formerly nearly overwhelmed Edmond Dantès. Clear sky, swift-flitting boats, and brilliant sunshine disappeared; the heavens were hung with black, and the gigantic structure of the Château d'If seemed like the phantom of a mortal enemy. As they reached the shore, the count instinctively shrunk to the extreme end of the boat, and the owner was obliged to call out, in his sweetest tone of voice:

"Sir, we are at the landing."

Monte Cristo remembered that on that very spot, on the same rock, he had been violently dragged by the guards, who forced him to ascend the slope at the points of their bayonets. The journey had seemed very long to Dantès, but Monte Cristo found it equally short. Each stroke of the oar seemed to awaken a new throng of ideas, which sprang up with the flying spray of the sea.

There had been no prisoners confined in the Château d'If since the revolution of July; it was only inhabited by a guard, kept there for the prevention of smuggling. A concierge waited at the door to exhibit to visitors this monument of curiosity, once a scene of terror.

The count inquired whether any of the ancient jailers were still there; but they had all been pensioned, or had passed on to some other employment. The concierge who attended him had only been there since 1830. He visited his own dungeon. He again beheld the dull light vainly endeavoring to penetrate the narrow opening. His eyes rested upon the spot where had stood his bed, since then removed, and behind the bed the new stones indicated where the breach made by the Abbé Faria had been. Monte Cristo felt his limbs tremble; he seated himself upon a log of wood.

"Are there any stories connected with this prison besides the one relating to the poisoning of Mirabeau?" asked the count; "are there any traditions respecting these dismal abodes,—in which it is difficult to believe men can ever have imprisoned their fellow-creatures?"

"Yes, sir; indeed, the jailer Antoine told me one connected with this very dungeon."

Monte Cristo shuddered; Antoine had been his jailer. He had almost forgotten his name and face, but at the mention of the name he recalled his person as he used to see it, the face encircled by a beard, wearing the brown jacket, the bunch of keys, the jingling of which he still seemed to hear. The count turned around, and fancied he saw him in the corridor, rendered still darker by the torch carried by the concierge.

"Would you like to hear the story, sir?"

"Yes; relate it," said Monte Cristo, pressing his hand to his heart to still its violent beatings; he felt afraid of hearing his own history.

"This dungeon," said the concierge, "was, it appears, some time ago occupied by a very dangerous prisoner, the more so since he was full of industry. Another person was confined in the Château at the same time, but he was not wicked, he was only a poor mad priest."

"Ah, indeed?—mad!" repeated Monte Cristo; "and what was his mania?"

"He offered millions to anyone who would set him at liberty."

Monte Cristo raised his eyes, but he could not see the heavens; there was a stone veil between him and the firmament. He thought that there had been no less thick a veil before the eyes of those to whom Faria offered the treasures.

"Could the prisoners see each other?" he asked.

"Oh, no, sir, it was expressly forbidden; but they eluded the vigilance of the guards, and made a passage from one dungeon to the other."

"And which of them made this passage?"

"Oh, it must have been the young man, certainly, for he was strong and industrious, while the abbé was aged and weak; besides, his mind was too vacillating to allow him to carry out an idea."

"Blind fools!" murmured the count.

"However, be that as it may, the young man made a tunnel, how or by what means no one knows; but he made it, and there is the evidence yet remaining of his work. Do you see it?" and the man held the torch to the wall.

"Ah, yes; I see," said the count, in a voice hoarse from emotion.

"The result was that the two men communicated with one another; how long they did so, nobody knows. One day the old man fell ill and died. Now guess what the young one did?"

"Tell me."

"He carried off the corpse, which he placed in his own bed with its face to the wall; then he entered the empty dungeon, closed the entrance, and slipped into the sack which had contained the dead body. Did you ever hear of such an idea?"

Monte Cristo closed his eyes, and seemed again to experience all the sensations he had felt when the coarse canvas, yet moist with the cold dews of death, had touched his face.

The jailer continued:

"Now this was his project. He fancied that they buried the dead at the Château d'If, and imagining they would not expend much labor on the grave of a prisoner, he calculated on raising the earth with his shoulders, but unfortunately their arrangements at the Château frustrated his projects. They never buried the dead; they merely attached a heavy cannon-ball to the feet, and then threw them into the sea. This is what was done. The young man was thrown from the top of the rock; the corpse was found on the bed next day, and the whole truth was guessed, for the men who performed the office then mentioned what they had not dared to speak of before, that at the moment the corpse was thrown into the deep, they heard a shriek, which was almost immediately stifled by the water in which it disappeared."

The count breathed with difficulty; the cold drops ran down his forehead, and his heart was full of anguish.

"No," he muttered, "the doubt I felt was but the commencement of forgetfulness; but here the wound reopens, and the heart again thirsts for vengeance. And the prisoner," he continued aloud, "was he ever heard of afterwards?"

"Oh, no; of course not. You can understand that one of two things must have happened; he must either have fallen flat, in which case the blow, from a height of ninety feet, must have killed him instantly, or he must have fallen upright, and then the weight would have dragged him to the bottom, where he remained—poor fellow!"

"Then you pity him?" said the count.

"*Ma foi*, yes; though he was in his own element."

"What do you mean?"

"The report was that he had been a naval officer, who had been confined for plotting with the Bonapartists."

"Great is truth," muttered the count, "fire cannot burn, nor water drown it! Thus the poor sailor lives in the recollection of those who narrate his history; his terrible story is recited in the chimney-corner, and a shudder is felt at the description of his transit through the air to be swallowed by the deep." Then, the count added aloud, "Was his name ever known?"

"Oh, yes; but only as No. 34."

"Oh, Villefort, Villefort," murmured the count, "this scene must often have haunted thy sleepless hours!"

"Do you wish to see anything more, sir?" said the concierge.

"Yes, especially if you will show me the poor abbé's room."

"Ah! No. 27."

"Yes; No. 27." repeated the count, who seemed to hear the voice of the abbé answering him in those very words through the wall when asked his name.

"Come, sir."

"Wait," said Monte Cristo, "I wish to take one final glance around this room."

"This is fortunate," said the guide; "I have forgotten the other key."

"Go and fetch it."

"I will leave you the torch, sir."

"No, take it away; I can see in the dark."

"Why, you are like No. 34. They said he was so accustomed to darkness that he could see a pin in the darkest corner of his dungeon."

"He spent fourteen years to arrive at that," muttered the count.

The guide carried away the torch. The count had spoken correctly. Scarcely had a few seconds elapsed, ere he saw everything as distinctly as by daylight. Then he looked around him, and really recognized his dungeon.

"Yes," he said, "there is the stone upon which I used to sit; there is the impression made by my shoulders on the wall; there is the mark of my blood made when one day I dashed my head against the wall. Oh, those figures, how well I remember them! I made them one day to calculate the age of my father, that I might know whether I should find him still living, and that of Mercédès, to know if I should find her still free. After finishing that calculation, I had a minute's hope. I did not reckon upon hunger and infidelity!" and a bitter laugh escaped the count.

He saw in fancy the burial of his father, and the marriage of Mercédès. On the other side of the dungeon he perceived an inscription, the white letters of which were still visible on the green wall:

"'*Oh, God!*'" he read, "'*preserve my memory!*'"

"Oh, yes," he cried, "that was my only prayer at last; I no longer begged for liberty, but memory; I dreaded to become mad and forgetful. Oh, God, thou hast preserved my memory; I thank thee, I thank thee!"

At this moment the light of the torch was reflected on the wall; the guide was coming; Monte Cristo went to meet him.

"Follow me, sir;" and without ascending the stairs the guide conducted him by a subterraneous passage to another entrance. There, again, Monte Cristo was assailed by a multitude of thoughts. The first thing that met his eye was the meridian, drawn by the abbé on the wall, by which he calculated the time; then he saw the remains of the bed on which the poor prisoner had died. The sight of this, instead of exciting the anguish experienced by the count in the dungeon, filled his heart with a soft and grateful sentiment, and tears fell from his eyes.

"This is where the mad abbé was kept, sir, and that is where the young man entered;" and the guide pointed to the opening, which had remained unclosed. "From the appearance of the stone," he continued, "a learned gentleman discovered that the prisoners might have communicated together for ten years. Poor things! Those must have been ten weary years."

Dantès took some louis from his pocket, and gave them to the man who had twice unconsciously pitied him. The guide took them, thinking them merely a few pieces of little value; but the light of the torch revealed their true worth.

"Sir," he said, "you have made a mistake; you have given me gold."

"I know it."

The concierge looked upon the count with surprise.

"Sir," he cried, scarcely able to believe his good fortune—"sir, I cannot understand your generosity!"

"Oh, it is very simple, my good fellow; I have been a sailor, and your story touched me more than it would others."

"Then, sir, since you are so liberal, I ought to offer you something."

"What have you to offer to me, my friend? Shells? Straw-work? Thank you!"

"No, sir, neither of those; something connected with this story."

"Really? What is it?"

"Listen," said the guide; "I said to myself, 'Something is always left in a cell inhabited by one prisoner for fifteen years,' so I began to sound the wall."

"Ah," cried Monte Cristo, remembering the abbé's two hiding-places.

"After some search, I found that the floor gave a hollow sound near the head of the bed, and at the hearth."

"Yes," said the count, "yes."

"I raised the stones, and found—"

"A rope-ladder and some tools?"

"How do you know that?" asked the guide in astonishment.

"I do not know—I only guess it, because that sort of thing is generally found in prisoners' cells."

"Yes, sir, a rope-ladder and tools."

"And have you them yet?"

"No, sir; I sold them to visitors, who considered them great curiosities; but I have still something left."

"What is it?" asked the count, impatiently.

"A sort of book, written upon strips of cloth."

"Go and fetch it, my good fellow; and if it be what I hope, you will do well."

"I will run for it, sir;" and the guide went out.

Then the count knelt down by the side of the bed, which death had converted into an altar.

"Oh, second father," he exclaimed, "thou who hast given me liberty, knowledge, riches; thou who, like beings of a superior order to ourselves, couldst understand the science of good and evil; if in the depths of the tomb there still remain something within us which can respond to the voice of those who are left on earth; if after death the soul ever revisit the places where we have lived and suffered,—then, noble heart, sublime soul, then I conjure thee by the paternal love thou didst bear me, by the filial obedience I vowed to thee, grant me some sign, some revelation! Remove from me the remains of doubt, which, if it change not to conviction, must become remorse!" The count bowed his head, and clasped his hands together.

"Here, sir," said a voice behind him.

Monte Cristo shuddered, and arose. The concierge held out the strips of cloth upon which the Abbé Faria had spread the riches of his mind. The manuscript was the great work by the Abbé Faria upon the kingdoms of Italy. The count seized it hastily, his eyes immediately fell upon the epigraph, and he read:

"Thou shalt tear out the dragons' teeth, and shall trample the lions under foot, saith the Lord."

"Ah," he exclaimed, "here is my answer. Thanks, father, thanks." And feeling in his pocket, he took thence a small pocket-book, which contained ten bank-notes, each of 1,000 francs.

"Here," he said, "take this pocket-book."

"Do you give it to me?"

"Yes; but only on condition that you will not open it till I am gone;" and placing in his breast the treasure he had just found, which was more valuable to him than the richest jewel, he rushed out of the corridor, and reaching his boat, cried, "To Marseilles!"

Then, as he departed, he fixed his eyes upon the gloomy prison.

"Woe," he cried, "to those who confined me in that wretched prison; and woe to those who forgot that I was there!"

As he repassed the Catalans, the count turned around and burying his head in his cloak murmured the name of a woman. The victory was complete; twice he had overcome his doubts. The name he pronounced, in a voice of tenderness, amounting almost to love, was that of Haydée.

On landing, the count turned towards the cemetery, where he felt sure of finding Morrel. He, too, ten years ago, had piously sought out a tomb, and sought it vainly. He, who returned to France with millions, had been unable to find the grave of his father, who had perished from hunger. Morrel had indeed placed a cross over the spot, but it had fallen down and the grave-digger had burnt it, as he did all the old wood in the churchyard.

The worthy merchant had been more fortunate. Dying in the arms of his children, he had been by them laid by the side of his wife, who had preceded him in eternity by two years. Two large slabs of marble, on which were inscribed their names, were placed on either side of a little enclosure, railed in, and shaded by four cypress-trees. Morrel was leaning against one of these, mechanically fixing his eyes on the graves. His grief was so profound that he was nearly unconscious.

"Maximilian," said the count, "you should not look on the graves, but there;" and he pointed upwards.

"The dead are everywhere," said Morrel; "did you not yourself tell me so as we left Paris?"

"Maximilian," said the count, "you asked me during the journey to allow you to remain some days at Marseilles. Do you still wish to do so?"

"I have no wishes, count; only I fancy I could pass the time less painfully here than anywhere else."

"So much the better, for I must leave you; but I carry your word with me, do I not?"

"Ah, count, I shall forget it."

"No, you will not forget it, because you are a man of honor, Morrel, because you have taken an oath, and are about to do so again."

"Oh, count, have pity upon me. I am so unhappy."

"I have known a man much more unfortunate than you, Morrel."

"Impossible!"

"Alas," said Monte Cristo, "it is the infirmity of our nature always to believe ourselves much more unhappy than those who groan by our sides!"

"What can be more wretched than the man who has lost all he loved and desired in the world?"

"Listen, Morrel, and pay attention to what I am about to tell you. I knew a man who like you had fixed all his hopes of happiness upon a woman. He was young, he had an old father whom he loved, a betrothed bride whom he adored. He was about to marry her, when one of the caprices of fate,—which would almost make us doubt the goodness of Providence, if that Providence did not afterwards reveal itself by proving that all is but a means of conducting to an end,—one of those caprices deprived him of his mistress, of the future of which he had dreamed (for in his blindness he forgot he could only read the present), and cast him into a dungeon."

"Ah," said Morrel, "one quits a dungeon in a week, a month, or a year."

"He remained there fourteen years, Morrel," said the count, placing his hand on the young man's shoulder. Maximilian shuddered.

"Fourteen years!" he muttered.

"Fourteen years!" repeated the count. "During that time he had many moments of despair. He also, Morrel, like you, considered himself the unhappiest of men."

"Well?" asked Morrel.

"Well, at the height of his despair God assisted him through human means. At first, perhaps, he did not recognize the infinite mercy of the Lord, but at last he took patience and waited. One day he miraculously left the prison, transformed, rich, powerful. His first cry was for his father; but that father was dead."

"My father, too, is dead," said Morrel.

"Yes; but your father died in your arms, happy, respected, rich, and full of years; his father died poor, despairing, almost doubtful of Providence; and when his son sought his grave ten years afterwards, his tomb had disappeared, and no one could say, 'There sleeps the father you so well loved.'"

"Oh!" exclaimed Morrel.

"He was, then, a more unhappy son than you, Morrel, for he could not even find his father's grave."

"But then he had the woman he loved still remaining?"

"You are deceived, Morrel, that woman—"

"She was dead?"

"Worse than that, she was faithless, and had married one of the persecutors of her betrothed. You see, then, Morrel, that he was a more unhappy lover than you."

"And has he found consolation?"

"He has at least found peace."

"And does he ever expect to be happy?"

"He hopes so, Maximilian."

The young man's head fell on his breast.

"You have my promise," he said, after a minute's pause, extending his hand to Monte Cristo. "Only remember—"

"On the 5th of October, Morrel, I shall expect you at the Island of Monte Cristo. On the 4th a yacht will wait for you in the port of Bastia, it will be called the *Eurus*. You will give your name to the captain, who will bring you to me. It is understood—is it not?"

"But, count, do you remember that the 5th of October—"

"Child," replied the count, "not to know the value of a man's word! I have told you twenty times that if you wish to die on that day, I will assist you. Morrel, farewell!"

"Do you leave me?"

"Yes; I have business in Italy. I leave you alone in your struggle with misfortune—alone with that strong-winged eagle which God sends to bear aloft the elect to his feet. The story of Ganymede, Maximilian, is not a fable, but an allegory."

"When do you leave?"

"Immediately; the steamer waits, and in an hour I shall be far from you. Will you accompany me to the harbor, Maximilian?"

"I am entirely yours, count."

Morrel accompanied the count to the harbor. The white steam was ascending like a plume of feathers from the black chimney. The steamer soon disappeared, and in an hour afterwards, as the count had said, was scarcely distinguishable in the horizon amidst the fogs of the night.

Study Guide Questions

For Students:

1. Where does Dantès meet Mercédès and what is the request she makes?
2. Where does Edmond go after meeting Mercédès and why?
3. What does the janitor give to the Count?

For Reading Club:

1. How do you think Mercédès' decision about herself affirms gender stereotypes? Do you think she could have made a different decision?
2. What is the story that the janitor tells the Count of old times, compare it with the original story.
3. Discuss the inscription Dantès reads in his cell.

CHAPTER 114

Peppino

At the same time that the steamer disappeared behind Cape Morgiou, a man travelling post on the road from Florence to Rome had just passed the little town of Aquapendente. He was travelling fast enough to cover a great deal of ground without exciting suspicion. This man was dressed in a greatcoat, or rather a surtout, a little worse for the journey, but which exhibited the ribbon of the Legion of Honor still fresh and brilliant, a decoration which also ornamented the under coat. He might be recognized, not only by these signs, but also from the accent with which he spoke to the postilion, as a Frenchman.

Another proof that he was a native of the universal country was apparent in the fact of his knowing no other Italian words than the terms used in music, and which like the "goddam" of Figaro, served all possible linguistic requirements. "*Allegro!*" he called out to the postilions at every ascent. "*Moderato!*" he cried as they descended. And heaven knows there are hills enough between Rome and Florence by the way of Aquapendente! These two words greatly amused the men to whom they were addressed. On reaching La Storta, the point from whence Rome is first visible, the traveller evinced none of the enthusiastic curiosity which usually leads strangers to stand up and endeavor to catch sight of the dome of Saint Peter's, which may be seen long before any other object is distinguishable. No, he merely drew a pocketbook from his pocket, and took from it a paper folded in four, and after having examined it in a manner almost reverential, he said:

"Good! I have it still!"

The carriage entered by the Porta del Popolo, turned to the left, and stopped at the Hôtel d'Espagne. Old Pastrini, our former acquaintance, received the traveller at the door, hat in hand. The traveller alighted, ordered a good dinner, and inquired the address of the house of Thomson & French, which was immediately given to him, as it was one of the most celebrated in Rome. It was situated in the Via dei Banchi, near St. Peter's.

In Rome, as everywhere else, the arrival of a post-chaise is an event. Ten young descendants of Marius and the Gracchi, barefooted and out at elbows, with one hand resting on the hip and the other gracefully curved above the head, stared at the traveller, the post-chaise, and the horses; to these were added about fifty little vagabonds from the Papal States, who earned a pittance by diving into the Tiber at high water from the bridge of St. Angelo. Now, as these street Arabs of Rome, more fortunate than those of Paris, understand every language, more especially the French, they heard the traveller order an apartment, a dinner, and finally inquire the way to the house of Thomson & French.

The result was that when the new-comer left the hotel with the *cicerone*, a man detached himself from the rest of the idlers, and without having been seen by the traveller, and appearing to excite no attention from the guide, followed the stranger with as much skill as a Parisian police agent would have used.

The Frenchman had been so impatient to reach the house of Thomson & French that he would not wait for the horses to be harnessed, but left word for the carriage to overtake him on the road, or to wait for him at the bankers' door. He reached it before the carriage arrived. The Frenchman entered, leaving in the anteroom his guide, who immediately entered into conversation with two or three of the industrious idlers who are always to be found in Rome at the doors of banking-houses, churches, museums, or theatres. With the Frenchman, the man who had followed him entered too; the Frenchman knocked at the inner door, and entered the first room; his shadow did the same.

"Messrs. Thomson & French?" inquired the stranger.

An attendant arose at a sign from a confidential clerk at the first desk.

"Whom shall I announce?" said the attendant.

"Baron Danglars."

"Follow me," said the man.

A door opened, through which the attendant and the baron disappeared. The man who had followed Danglars sat down on a bench. The clerk continued to write for the next five minutes; the man preserved profound silence, and remained perfectly motionless. Then the pen of the clerk ceased to move over the paper; he raised his head, and appearing to be perfectly sure of privacy:

"Ah, ha," he said, "here you are, Peppino!"

"Yes," was the laconic reply. "You have found out that there is something worth having about this large gentleman?"

"There is no great merit due to me, for we were informed of it."

"You know his business here, then."

"*Pardieu*, he has come to draw, but I don't know how much!"

"You will know presently, my friend."

"Very well, only do not give me false information as you did the other day."

"What do you mean?—of whom do you speak? Was it the Englishman who carried off 3,000 crowns from here the other day?"

"No; he really had 3,000 crowns, and we found them. I mean the Russian prince, who you said had 30,000 livres, and we only found 22,000."

"You must have searched badly."

"Luigi Vampa himself searched."

"In that case he must either have paid his debts—"

"A Russian do that?"

"Or spent the money?"

"Possibly, after all."

"Certainly. But you must let me make my observations, or the Frenchman will transact his business without my knowing the sum."

Peppino nodded, and taking a rosary from his pocket began to mutter a few prayers while the clerk disappeared through the same door by which Danglars and the attendant had gone out. At the expiration of ten minutes the clerk returned with a beaming countenance.

"Well?" asked Peppino of his friend.

"Joy, joy—the sum is large!"

"Five or six millions, is it not?"

"Yes, you know the amount."

"On the receipt of the Count of Monte Cristo?"

"Why, how came you to be so well acquainted with all this?"

"I told you we were informed beforehand."

"Then why do you apply to me?"

"That I may be sure I have the right man."

"Yes, it is indeed he. Five millions—a pretty sum, eh, Peppino?"

"Hush—here is our man!" The clerk seized his pen, and Peppino his beads; one was writing and the other praying when the door opened. Danglars looked radiant with joy; the banker accompanied him to the door. Peppino followed Danglars.

According to the arrangements, the carriage was waiting at the door. The guide held the door open. Guides are useful people, who will turn their hands to anything. Danglars leaped into the carriage like a young man of twenty. The *cicerone* reclosed the door, and sprang up by the side of the coachman. Peppino mounted the seat behind.

"Will your excellency visit Saint Peter's?" asked the *cicerone*.

"I did not come to Rome to see," said Danglars aloud; then he added softly, with an avaricious smile, "I came to touch!" and he rapped his pocket-book, in which he had just placed a letter.

"Then your excellency is going—"

"To the hotel."

"Casa Pastrini!" said the *cicerone* to the coachman, and the carriage drove rapidly on.

Ten minutes afterwards the baron entered his apartment, and Peppino stationed himself on the bench outside the door of the hotel, after having whispered something in the ear of one of the descendants of Marius and the Gracchi whom we noticed at the beginning of the chapter, who immediately ran down the road leading to the Capitol at his fullest speed. Danglars was tired and sleepy; he therefore went to bed, placing his pocketbook under his pillow. Peppino had a little spare time, so he had a game of *morra* with the facchini, lost three crowns, and then to console himself drank a bottle of Orvieto.

The next morning Danglars awoke late, though he went to bed so early; he had not slept well for five or six nights, even if he had slept at all. He breakfasted heartily, and caring little, as he said, for the beauties of the Eternal City, ordered post-horses at noon. But Danglars had not reckoned upon the formalities of the police and the idleness of the posting-master. The horses only arrived at two o'clock, and the *cicerone* did not bring the passport till three.

All these preparations had collected a number of idlers round the door of Signor Pastrini's; the descendants of Marius and the Gracchi were also not wanting. The baron walked triumphantly through the crowd, who for the sake of gain styled him "your excellency." As Danglars had hitherto contented himself with being called a baron, he felt rather flattered at the title of excellency, and distributed a dozen silver coins among the beggars, who were ready, for twelve more, to call him "your highness."

"Which road?" asked the postilion in Italian.

"The Ancona road," replied the baron. Signor Pastrini interpreted the question and answer, and the horses galloped off.

Danglars intended travelling to Venice, where he would receive one part of his fortune, and then proceeding to Vienna, where he would find the rest, he meant to take up his residence in the latter town, which he had been told was a city of pleasure.

He had scarcely advanced three leagues out of Rome when daylight began to disappear. Danglars had not intended starting so late, or he would have remained; he put his head out and asked the postilion how long it would be before they reached the next town. "*Non capisco*" (do not understand), was the reply. Danglars bent his head, which he meant to imply, "Very well." The carriage again moved on.

"I will stop at the first posting-house," said Danglars to himself.

He still felt the same self-satisfaction which he had experienced the previous evening, and which had procured him so good a night's rest. He was luxuriously stretched in a good English calash, with double springs; he was drawn by four good horses, at full gallop; he knew the relay to be at a distance of seven leagues. What subject of meditation could present itself to the banker, so fortunately become bankrupt?

Danglars thought for ten minutes about his wife in Paris; another ten minutes about his daughter travelling with Mademoiselle d'Armilly; the same period was given to his creditors, and the manner in which he intended spending their money; and then, having no subject left for contemplation, he shut his eyes, and fell asleep. Now and then a jolt more violent than the rest caused him to open his eyes; then he felt that he was still being carried with great rapidity over the same country, thickly strewn with broken aqueducts, which looked like granite giants petrified while running a race. But the night was cold, dull, and rainy, and it was much more pleasant for a traveller to remain in the warm carriage than to put his head out of the window to make inquiries of a postilion whose only answer was "*Non capisco.*"

Danglars therefore continued to sleep, saying to himself that he would be sure to awake at the posting-house. The carriage stopped. Danglars fancied that they had reached the long-desired point; he opened his eyes and looked through the window, expecting to find himself in the midst of some town, or at least village; but he saw nothing except what seemed like a ruin, where three or four men went and came like shadows.

Danglars waited a moment, expecting the postilion to come and demand payment with the termination of his stage. He intended taking advantage of the opportunity to make fresh inquiries of the new conductor; but the horses were unharnessed, and others put in their places, without anyone claiming money from the traveller. Danglars, astonished, opened the door; but a strong hand pushed him back, and the carriage rolled on. The baron was completely roused.

"Eh?" he said to the postilion, "eh, *mio caro?*"

This was another little piece of Italian the baron had learned from hearing his daughter sing Italian duets with Cavalcanti. But *mio caro* did not reply. Danglars then opened the window.

"Come, my friend," he said, thrusting his hand through the opening, "where are we going?"

"*Dentro la testa!*" answered a solemn and imperious voice, accompanied by a menacing gesture.

Danglars thought *dentro la testa* meant, "Put in your head!" He was making rapid progress in Italian. He obeyed, not without some uneasiness, which, momentarily increasing, caused his mind, instead of being as unoccupied as it was when he began his journey, to fill with ideas which were very likely to keep a traveller awake, more especially one in such a situation as Danglars. His eyes acquired that quality which in the first moment of strong emotion enables them to see distinctly, and which afterwards fails from being too much taxed. Before we are alarmed, we see correctly; when we are alarmed, we see double; and when we have been alarmed, we see nothing but trouble. Danglars observed a man in a cloak galloping at the right hand of the carriage.

"Some gendarme!" he exclaimed. "Can I have been intercepted by French telegrams to the pontifical authorities?"

He resolved to end his anxiety. "Where are you taking me?" he asked.

"*Dentro la testa*," replied the same voice, with the same menacing accent.

Danglars turned to the left; another man on horseback was galloping on that side.

"Decidedly," said Danglars, with the perspiration on his forehead, "I must be under arrest." And he threw himself back in the calash, not this time to sleep, but to think.

Directly afterwards the moon rose. He then saw the great aqueducts, those stone phantoms which he had before remarked, only then they were on the right hand, now they were on the left. He understood that they had described a circle, and were bringing him back to Rome.

"Oh, unfortunate!" he cried, "they must have obtained my arrest."

The carriage continued to roll on with frightful speed. An hour of terror elapsed, for every spot they passed showed that they were on the road back. At length he saw a dark mass, against which it seemed as if the carriage was about to dash; but the vehicle turned to one side, leaving the barrier behind and Danglars saw that it was one of the ramparts encircling Rome.

"*Mon dieu!*" cried Danglars, "we are not returning to Rome; then it is not justice which is pursuing me! Gracious heavens; another idea presents itself—what if they should be—"

His hair stood on end. He remembered those interesting stories, so little believed in Paris, respecting Roman bandits; he remembered the adventures that Albert de Morcerf had related when it was intended that he should marry Mademoiselle Eugénie. "They are robbers, perhaps," he muttered.

Just then the carriage rolled on something harder than gravel road. Danglars hazarded a look on both sides of the road, and perceived monuments of a singular form, and his mind now recalled all the details Morcerf had related, and comparing them with his own situation, he felt sure that he must be on the Appian Way. On the left, in a sort of valley, he perceived a circular excavation. It was Caracalla's circus. On a word from the man who rode at the side of the carriage, it stopped. At the same time the door was opened. "*Scendi!*" exclaimed a commanding voice.

Danglars instantly descended; although he did not yet speak Italian, he understood it very well. More dead than alive, he looked around him. Four men surrounded him, besides the postilion.

"*Di quà*," said one of the men, descending a little path leading out of the Appian Way. Danglars followed his guide without opposition, and had no occasion to turn around to see whether the three others were following him. Still it appeared as though they were stationed at equal distances from one another, like sentinels. After walking for about ten minutes, during which Danglars did not exchange a single word with his guide, he found himself between a hillock and a clump of high weeds; three men, standing silent, formed a triangle, of which he was the centre. He wished to speak, but his tongue refused to move.

"*Avanti!*" said the same sharp and imperative voice.

This time Danglars had double reason to understand, for if the word and gesture had not explained the speaker's meaning, it was clearly expressed by the man walking behind him, who pushed him so rudely that he struck against the guide. This guide was our friend Peppino, who dashed into the thicket of high weeds, through a path which none but lizards or polecats could have imagined to be an open road.

Peppino stopped before a rock overhung by thick hedges; the rock, half open, afforded a passage to the young man, who disappeared like the evil spirits in the fairy tales. The voice and gesture of the man who followed Danglars ordered him to do the same. There was no longer any doubt, the bankrupt was in the hands of Roman banditti. Danglars acquitted himself like a man placed between two dangerous positions, and who is rendered brave by fear. Notwithstanding his large stomach, certainly not intended to penetrate the fissures of the Campagna, he slid down like Peppino, and closing his eyes fell upon his feet. As he touched the ground, he opened his eyes.

The path was wide, but dark. Peppino, who cared little for being recognized now that he was in his own territories, struck a light and lit a torch. Two other men descended after Danglars forming the rearguard, and pushing Danglars whenever he happened to stop, they came by a gentle declivity to the intersection of two corridors. The walls were hollowed out in sepulchres, one above the other, and which seemed in contrast with the white stones to open their large dark eyes, like those which we see on the faces of the dead. A sentinel struck the rings of his carbine against his left hand.

"Who comes there?" he cried.

"A friend, a friend!" said Peppino; "but where is the captain?"

"There," said the sentinel, pointing over his shoulder to a spacious crypt, hollowed out of the rock, the lights from which shone into the passage through the large arched openings.

"Fine spoil, captain, fine spoil!" said Peppino in Italian, and taking Danglars by the collar of his coat he dragged him to an opening resembling a door, through which they entered the apartment which the captain appeared to have made his dwelling-place.

"Is this the man?" asked the captain, who was attentively reading Plutarch's *Life of Alexander*.

"Himself, captain—himself."

"Very well, show him to me."

At this rather impertinent order, Peppino raised his torch to the face of Danglars, who hastily withdrew that he might not have his eyelashes burnt. His agitated features presented the appearance of pale and hideous terror.

"The man is tired," said the captain, "conduct him to his bed."

"Oh," murmured Danglars, "that bed is probably one of the coffins hollowed in the wall, and the sleep I shall enjoy will be death from one of the poniards I see glistening in the darkness."

From their beds of dried leaves or wolf-skins at the back of the chamber now arose the companions of the man who had been found by Albert de Morcerf reading *Cæsar's Commentaries*, and by Danglars studying the *Life of Alexander*. The banker uttered a groan and followed his guide; he neither supplicated nor exclaimed. He no longer possessed strength, will, power, or feeling; he followed where they led him. At length he found himself at the foot of a staircase, and he mechanically lifted his foot five or six times. Then a low door was opened before him, and bending his head to avoid striking his forehead he entered a small room cut out of the rock. The cell was clean, though empty, and dry, though situated at an immeasurable distance under the earth. A bed of dried grass covered with goat-skins was placed in one corner. Danglars brightened up on beholding it, fancying that it gave some promise of safety.

"Oh, God be praised," he said; "it is a real bed!"

This was the second time within the hour that he had invoked the name of God. He had not done so for ten years before.

"*Ecco!*" said the guide, and pushing Danglars into the cell, he closed the door upon him.

A bolt grated and Danglars was a prisoner. If there had been no bolt, it would have been impossible for him to pass through the midst of the garrison who held the catacombs of St. Sebastian, encamped round a master whom our readers must have recognized as the famous Luigi Vampa.

Danglars, too, had recognized the bandit, whose existence he would not believe when Albert de Morcerf mentioned him in Paris; and not only did he recognize him, but the cell in which Albert had been confined, and which was probably kept for the accommodation of strangers. These recollections were dwelt upon with some pleasure by Danglars, and restored him to some degree of tranquillity. Since the bandits had not despatched him at once, he felt that they would not kill him at all. They had arrested him for the purpose of robbery, and as he had only a few louis about him, he doubted not he would be ransomed.

He remembered that Morcerf had been taxed at 4,000 crowns, and as he considered himself of much greater importance than Morcerf he fixed his own price at 8,000 crowns. Eight thousand crowns amounted to 48,000 livres; he would then have about 5,050,000 francs left. With this sum he could manage to keep out of difficulties. Therefore, tolerably secure in being able to extricate himself from his position, provided he were not rated at the unreasonable sum of 5,050,000 francs, he stretched himself on his bed, and after turning over two or three times, fell asleep with the tranquillity of the hero whose life Luigi Vampa was studying.

Study Guide Questions

For Students:

1. Who is looking for the House of Thomson and French?
2. What is Danglars doing in Rome?
3. Who captures Danglars?

For Reading Club:

1. Discuss the role of Peppino in this chapter.
2. Discuss what happens to Danglars in Rome.
3. Discuss Danglars' thoughts at the end of the chapter.

CHAPTER 115

Luigi Vampa's Bill of Fare

We awake from every sleep except the one dreaded by Danglars. He awoke. To a Parisian accustomed to silken curtains, walls hung with velvet drapery, and the soft perfume of burning wood, the white smoke of which diffuses itself in graceful curves around the room, the appearance of the whitewashed cell which greeted his eyes on awakening seemed like the continuation of some disagreeable dream. But in such a situation a single moment suffices to change the strongest doubt into certainty.

"Yes, yes," he murmured, "I am in the hands of the brigands of whom Albert de Morcerf spoke." His first idea was to breathe, that he might know whether he was wounded. He borrowed this from *Don Quixote*, the only book he had ever read, but which he still slightly remembered.

"No," he cried, "they have not wounded, but perhaps they have robbed me!" and he thrust his hands into his pockets. They were untouched; the hundred louis he had reserved for his journey from Rome to Venice were in his trousers pocket, and in that of his greatcoat he found the little note-case containing his letter of credit for 5,050,000 francs.

"Singular bandits!" he exclaimed; "they have left me my purse and pocket-book. As I was saying last night, they intend me to be ransomed. Hello, here is my watch! Let me see what time it is."

Danglars' watch, one of Breguet's repeaters, which he had carefully wound up on the previous night, struck half past five. Without this, Danglars would have been quite ignorant of the time, for daylight did not reach his cell. Should he demand an explanation from the bandits, or should he wait patiently for them to propose it? The last alternative seemed the most prudent, so he waited until twelve o'clock. During all this time a sentinel, who had been relieved at eight o'clock, had been watching his door.

Danglars suddenly felt a strong inclination to see the person who kept watch over him. He had noticed that a few rays, not of daylight, but from a lamp, penetrated through the ill-joined planks of the door; he approached just as the brigand was refreshing himself with a mouthful of brandy, which, owing to the leathern bottle containing it, sent forth an odor which was extremely unpleasant to Danglars. "Faugh!" he exclaimed, retreating to the farther corner of his cell.

At twelve this man was replaced by another functionary, and Danglars, wishing to catch sight of his new guardian, approached the door again.

He was an athletic, gigantic bandit, with large eyes, thick lips, and a flat nose; his red hair fell in dishevelled masses like snakes around his shoulders.

"Ah, ha," cried Danglars, "this fellow is more like an ogre than anything else; however, I am rather too old and tough to be very good eating!"

We see that Danglars was collected enough to jest; at the same time, as though to disprove the ogreish propensities, the man took some black bread, cheese, and onions from his wallet, which he began devouring voraciously.

"May I be hanged," said Danglars, glancing at the bandit's dinner through the crevices of the door,—"may I be hanged if I can understand how people can eat such filth!" and he withdrew to seat himself upon his goat-skin, which reminded him of the smell of the brandy.

But the mysteries of nature are incomprehensible, and there are certain invitations contained in even the coarsest food which appeal very irresistibly to a fasting stomach. Danglars felt his own not to be very well supplied just then, and gradually the man appeared less ugly, the bread less black, and the cheese more fresh, while those dreadful vulgar onions recalled to his mind certain sauces and side-dishes, which his cook prepared in a very superior manner whenever he said, "Monsieur Deniseau, let me have a nice little fricassee today." He got up and knocked on the door; the bandit raised his head. Danglars knew that he was heard, so he redoubled his blows.

"*Che cosa?*" asked the bandit.

"Come, come," said Danglars, tapping his fingers against the door, "I think it is quite time to think of giving me something to eat!"

But whether he did not understand him, or whether he had received no orders respecting the nourishment of Danglars, the giant, without answering, went on with his dinner. Danglars' feelings were hurt, and not wishing to put himself under obligations to the brute, the banker threw himself down again on his goat-skin and did not breathe another word.

Four hours passed by and the giant was replaced by another bandit. Danglars, who really began to experience sundry gnawings at the stomach, arose softly, again applied his eye to the crack of the door, and recognized the intelligent countenance of his guide. It was, indeed, Peppino who was preparing to mount guard as comfortably as possible by seating himself opposite to the door, and placing between his legs an earthen pan, containing chick-peas stewed with bacon. Near the pan he also placed a pretty little basket of Villetri grapes and a flask of Orvieto. Peppino was decidedly an epicure. Danglars watched these preparations and his mouth watered.

"Come," he said to himself, "let me try if he will be more tractable than the other;" and he tapped gently at the door.

"*On y va*," (coming) exclaimed Peppino, who from frequenting the house of Signor Pastrini understood French perfectly in all its idioms.

Danglars immediately recognized him as the man who had called out in such a furious manner, "Put in your head!" But this was not the time for recrimination, so he assumed his most agreeable manner and said with a gracious smile:

"Excuse me, sir, but are they not going to give me any dinner?"

"Does your excellency happen to be hungry?"

"Happen to be hungry,—that's pretty good, when I haven't eaten for twenty-four hours!" muttered Danglars. Then he added aloud, "Yes, sir, I am hungry—very hungry."

"And your excellency wants something to eat?"

"At once, if possible"

"Nothing easier," said Peppino. "Here you can get anything you want; by paying for it, of course, as among honest folk."

"Of course!" cried Danglars. "Although, in justice, the people who arrest and imprison you, ought, at least, to feed you."

"That is not the custom, excellency," said Peppino.

"A bad reason," replied Danglars, who reckoned on conciliating his keeper; "but I am content. Let me have some dinner!"

"At once! What would your excellency like?"

And Peppino placed his pan on the ground, so that the steam rose directly under the nostrils of Danglars. "Give your orders."

"Have you kitchens here?"

"Kitchens?—of course—complete ones."

"And cooks?"

"Excellent!"

"Well, a fowl, fish, game,—it signifies little, so that I eat."

"As your excellency pleases. You mentioned a fowl, I think?"

"Yes, a fowl."

Peppino, turning around, shouted, "A fowl for his excellency!" His voice yet echoed in the archway when a handsome, graceful, and half-naked young man appeared, bearing a fowl in a silver dish on his head, without the assistance of his hands.

"I could almost believe myself at the Café de Paris," murmured Danglars.

"Here, your excellency," said Peppino, taking the fowl from the young bandit and placing it on the worm-eaten table, which with the stool and the goat-skin bed formed the entire furniture of the cell. Danglars asked for a knife and fork.

"Here, excellency," said Peppino, offering him a little blunt knife and a boxwood fork. Danglars took the knife in one hand and the fork in the other, and was about to cut up the fowl.

"Pardon me, excellency," said Peppino, placing his hand on the banker's shoulder; "people pay here before they eat. They might not be satisfied, and—"

"Ah, ha," thought Danglars, "this is not so much like Paris, except that I shall probably be skinned! Never mind, I'll fix that all right. I have always heard how cheap poultry is in Italy; I should think a fowl is worth about twelve sous at Rome.—There," he said, throwing a louis down.

Peppino picked up the louis, and Danglars again prepared to carve the fowl.

"Stay a moment, your excellency," said Peppino, rising; "you still owe me something."

"I said they would skin me," thought Danglars; but resolving to resist the extortion, he said, "Come, how much do I owe you for this fowl?"

"Your excellency has given me a louis on account."

"A louis on account for a fowl?"

"Certainly; and your excellency now owes me 4,999 louis."

Danglars opened his enormous eyes on hearing this gigantic joke.

"Very droll," he muttered, "very droll indeed," and he again began to carve the fowl, when Peppino stopped the baron's right hand with his left, and held out his other hand.

"Come, now," he said.

"Is it not a joke?" said Danglars.

"We never joke," replied Peppino, solemn as a Quaker.

"What! A hundred thousand francs for a fowl!"

"Ah, excellency, you cannot imagine how hard it is to rear fowls in these horrible caves!"

"Come, come, this is very droll—very amusing—I allow; but, as I am very hungry, pray allow me to eat. Stay, here is another louis for you."

"Then that will make only 4,998 louis more," said Peppino with the same indifference. "I shall get them all in time."

"Oh, as for that," said Danglars, angry at this prolongation of the jest,—"as for that you won't get them at all. Go to the devil! You do not know with whom you have to deal!"

Peppino made a sign, and the youth hastily removed the fowl. Danglars threw himself upon his goat-skin, and Peppino, reclosing the door, again began eating his peas and bacon. Though Danglars could not see Peppino, the noise of his teeth allowed no doubt as to his occupation. He was certainly eating, and noisily too, like an ill-bred man. "Brute!" said Danglars. Peppino pretended not to hear him, and without even turning his head continued to eat slowly. Danglars' stomach felt so empty, that it seemed as if it would be impossible ever to fill it again; still he had patience for another half-hour, which appeared to him like a century. He again arose and went to the door.

"Come, sir, do not keep me starving here any longer, but tell me what they want."

"Nay, your excellency, it is you who should tell us what you want. Give your orders, and we will execute them."

"Then open the door directly." Peppino obeyed. "Now look here, I want something to eat! To eat—do you hear?"

"Are you hungry?"

"Come, you understand me."

"What would your excellency like to eat?"

"A piece of dry bread, since the fowls are beyond all price in this accursed place."

"Bread? Very well. Holloa, there, some bread!" he called. The youth brought a small loaf. "How much?" asked Danglars.

"Four thousand nine hundred and ninety-eight louis," said Peppino; "You have paid two louis in advance."

"What? One hundred thousand francs for a loaf?"

"One hundred thousand francs," repeated Peppino.

"But you only asked 100,000 francs for a fowl!"

"We have a fixed price for all our provisions. It signifies nothing whether you eat much or little—whether you have ten dishes or one—it is always the same price."

"What, still keeping up this silly jest? My dear fellow, it is perfectly ridiculous—stupid! You had better tell me at once that you intend starving me to death."

"Oh, dear, no, your excellency, unless you intend to commit suicide. Pay and eat."

"And what am I to pay with, brute?" said Danglars, enraged. "Do you suppose I carry 100,000 francs in my pocket?"

"Your excellency has 5,050,000 francs in your pocket; that will be fifty fowls at 100,000 francs apiece, and half a fowl for the 50,000."

Danglars shuddered. The bandage fell from his eyes, and he understood the joke, which he did not think quite so stupid as he had done just before.

"Come," he said, "if I pay you the 100,000 francs, will you be satisfied, and allow me to eat at my ease?"

"Certainly," said Peppino.

"But how can I pay them?"

"Oh, nothing easier; you have an account open with Messrs. Thomson & French, Via dei Banchi, Rome; give me a draft for 4,998 louis on these gentlemen, and our banker shall take it." Danglars thought it as well to comply with a good grace, so he took the pen, ink, and paper Peppino offered him, wrote the draft, and signed it.

"Here," he said, "here is a draft at sight."

"And here is your fowl."

Danglars sighed while he carved the fowl; it appeared very thin for the price it had cost. As for Peppino, he examined the paper attentively, put it into his pocket, and continued eating his peas.

Study Guide Questions

For Students:

1. Where does Danglars find himself when he wakes up?
2. What does Peppino do when Danglars ask for food?
3. How much does Danglars pay for a fowl?

For Reading Club:

1. How does the chapter show that *pride hath a fall*?
2. Discuss what happens to Danglars after he wakes up.
3. How does Peppino exploit Danglars?

CHAPTER 116

The Pardon

The next day Danglars was again hungry; certainly the air of that dungeon was very provocative of appetite. The prisoner expected that he would be at no expense that day, for like an economical man he had concealed half of his fowl and a piece of the bread in the corner of his cell. But he had no sooner eaten than he felt thirsty; he had forgotten that. He struggled against his thirst till his tongue clave to the roof of his mouth; then, no longer able to resist, he called out. The sentinel opened the door; it was a new face. He thought it would be better to transact business with his old acquaintance, so he sent for Peppino.

"Here I am, your excellency," said Peppino, with an eagerness which Danglars thought favorable to him. "What do you want?"

"Something to drink."

"Your excellency knows that wine is beyond all price near Rome."

"Then give me water," cried Danglars, endeavoring to parry the blow.

"Oh, water is even more scarce than wine, your excellency,—there has been such a drought."

"Come," thought Danglars, "it is the same old story." And while he smiled as he attempted to regard the affair as a joke, he felt his temples get moist with perspiration.

"Come, my friend," said Danglars, seeing that he made no impression on Peppino, "you will not refuse me a glass of wine?"

"I have already told you that we do not sell at retail."

"Well, then, let me have a bottle of the least expensive."

"They are all the same price."

"And what is that?"

"Twenty-five thousand francs a bottle."

"Tell me," cried Danglars, in a tone whose bitterness Harpagon[23] alone has been capable of revealing—"tell me that you wish to despoil me of all; it will be sooner over than devouring me piecemeal."

"It is possible such may be the master's intention."

"The master?—who is he?"

"The person to whom you were conducted yesterday."

"Where is he?"

"Here."

"Let me see him."

"Certainly."

And the next moment Luigi Vampa appeared before Danglars.

"You sent for me?" he said to the prisoner.

"Are you, sir, the chief of the people who brought me here?"

"Yes, your excellency. What then?"

"How much do you require for my ransom?"

"Merely the 5,000,000 you have about you." Danglars felt a dreadful spasm dart through his heart.

"But this is all I have left in the world," he said, "out of an immense fortune. If you deprive me of that, take away my life also."

"We are forbidden to shed your blood."

"And by whom are you forbidden?"

"By him we obey."

"You do, then, obey someone?"

"Yes, a chief."

"I thought you said you were the chief?"

"So I am of these men; but there is another over me."

"And did your superior order you to treat me in this way?"

"Yes."

"But my purse will be exhausted."

"Probably."

"Come," said Danglars, "will you take a million?"

"No."

"Two millions?—three?—four? Come, four? I will give them to you on condition that you let me go."

---

[23] The miser in Molière's comedy of *L'Avare*.—Ed.

"Why do you offer me 4,000,000 for what is worth 5,000,000? This is a kind of usury, banker, that I do not understand."

"Take all, then—take all, I tell you, and kill me!"

"Come, come, calm yourself. You will excite your blood, and that would produce an appetite it would require a million a day to satisfy. Be more economical."

"But when I have no more money left to pay you?" asked the infuriated Danglars.

"Then you must suffer hunger."

"Suffer hunger?" said Danglars, becoming pale.

"Most likely," replied Vampa coolly.

"But you say you do not wish to kill me?"

"No."

"And yet you will let me perish with hunger?"

"Ah, that is a different thing."

"Well, then, wretches," cried Danglars, "I will defy your infamous calculations—I would rather die at once! You may torture, torment, kill me, but you shall not have my signature again!"

"As your excellency pleases," said Vampa, as he left the cell.

Danglars, raving, threw himself on the goat-skin. Who could these men be? Who was the invisible chief? What could be his intentions towards him? And why, when everyone else was allowed to be ransomed, might he not also be? Oh, yes; certainly a speedy, violent death would be a fine means of deceiving these remorseless enemies, who appeared to pursue him with such incomprehensible vengeance. But to die? For the first time in his life, Danglars contemplated death with a mixture of dread and desire; the time had come when the implacable spectre, which exists in the mind of every human creature, arrested his attention and called out with every pulsation of his heart, "Thou shalt die!"

Danglars resembled a timid animal excited in the chase; first it flies, then despairs, and at last, by the very force of desperation, sometimes succeeds in eluding its pursuers. Danglars meditated an escape; but the walls were solid rock, a man was sitting reading at the only outlet to the cell, and behind that man shapes armed with guns continually passed. His resolution not to sign lasted two days, after which he offered a million for some food. They sent him a magnificent supper, and took his million.

From this time the prisoner resolved to suffer no longer, but to have everything he wanted. At the end of twelve days, after having made a splendid dinner, he reckoned his accounts, and found that he had only 50,000 francs left. Then a strange reaction took place; he who had just abandoned 5,000,000 endeavored to save the 50,000 francs he had left, and sooner than give them up he resolved to enter again upon a life of privation—he was deluded by the hopefulness that is a premonition of madness.

He, who for so long a time had forgotten God, began to think that miracles were possible—that the accursed cavern might be discovered by the officers of the Papal States, who would release him; that then he would have 50,000 remaining, which would be sufficient to save him from starvation; and finally he prayed that this sum might be preserved to him, and as he prayed he wept. Three days passed thus, during which his prayers were frequent, if not heartfelt. Sometimes he was delirious, and fancied he saw an old man stretched on a pallet; he, also, was dying of hunger.

On the fourth, he was no longer a man, but a living corpse. He had picked up every crumb that had been left from his former meals, and was beginning to eat the matting which covered the floor of his cell. Then he entreated Peppino, as he would a guardian angel, to give him food; he offered him 1,000 francs for a mouthful of bread. But Peppino did not answer. On the fifth day he dragged himself to the door of the cell.

"Are you not a Christian?" he said, falling on his knees. "Do you wish to assassinate a man who, in the eyes of Heaven, is a brother? Oh, my former friends, my former friends!" he murmured, and fell with his face to the ground. Then rising in despair, he exclaimed, "The chief, the chief!"

"Here I am," said Vampa, instantly appearing; "what do you want?"

"Take my last gold," muttered Danglars, holding out his pocket-book, "and let me live here; I ask no more for liberty—I only ask to live!"

"Then you suffer a great deal?"

"Oh, yes, yes, cruelly!"

"Still, there have been men who suffered more than you."

"I do not think so."

"Yes; those who have died of hunger."

Danglars thought of the old man whom, in his hours of delirium, he had seen groaning on his bed. He struck his forehead on the ground and groaned. "Yes," he said, "there have been some who have suffered more than I have, but then they must have been martyrs at least."

"Do you repent?" asked a deep, solemn voice, which caused Danglars' hair to stand on end. His feeble eyes endeavored to distinguish objects, and behind the bandit he saw a man enveloped in a cloak, half lost in the shadow of a stone column.

"Of what must I repent?" stammered Danglars.

"Of the evil you have done," said the voice.

"Oh, yes; oh, yes, I do indeed repent." And he struck his breast with his emaciated fist.

"Then I forgive you," said the man, dropping his cloak, and advancing to the light.

"The Count of Monte Cristo!" said Danglars, more pale from terror than he had been just before from hunger and misery.

"You are mistaken—I am not the Count of Monte Cristo."

"Then who are you?"

"I am he whom you sold and dishonored—I am he whose betrothed you prostituted—I am he upon whom you trampled that you might raise yourself to fortune—I am he whose father you condemned to die of hunger—I am he whom you also condemned to starvation, and who yet forgives you, because he hopes to be forgiven—I am Edmond Dantès!"

Danglars uttered a cry, and fell prostrate.

"Rise," said the count, "your life is safe; the same good fortune has not happened to your accomplices—one is mad, the other dead. Keep the 50,000 francs you have left—I give them to you. The 5,000,000 you stole from the hospitals has been restored to them by an unknown hand. And now eat and drink; I will entertain you tonight. Vampa, when this man is satisfied, let him be free."

Danglars remained prostrate while the count withdrew; when he raised his head he saw disappearing down the passage nothing but a shadow, before which the bandits bowed.

According to the count's directions, Danglars was waited on by Vampa, who brought him the best wine and fruits of Italy; then, having conducted him to the road, and pointed to the post-chaise, left him leaning against a tree. He remained there all night, not knowing where he was. When daylight dawned he saw that he was near a stream; he was thirsty, and dragged himself towards it. As he stooped down to drink, he saw that his hair had become entirely white.

Study Guide Questions

For Students:

1. How much does a bottle of wine cost?
2. What does Danglars decide to do after his chat with Vampa?
3. How much does Danglars spend on food?

For Reading Club:

1. How does the chapter comment on the futility of money and social status?
2. Do you think men like Danglars only remember God in adversity?
3. Why does Edmond forgive his worst enemy? Do you think this pardon justifies his previous acts?

CHAPTER 117

The Fifth of October

It was about six o'clock in the evening; an opal-colored light, through which an autumnal sun shed its golden rays, descended on the blue ocean. The heat of the day had gradually decreased, and a light breeze arose, seeming like the respiration of nature on awakening from the burning siesta of the south. A delicious zephyr played along the coasts of the Mediterranean, and wafted from shore to shore the sweet perfume of plants, mingled with the fresh smell of the sea.

A light yacht, chaste and elegant in its form, was gliding amidst the first dews of night over the immense lake, extending from Gibraltar to the Dardanelles, and from Tunis to Venice. The vessel resembled a swan with its wings opened towards the wind, gliding on the water. It advanced swiftly and gracefully, leaving behind it a glittering stretch of foam. By degrees the sun disappeared behind the western horizon; but as though to prove the truth of the fanciful ideas in heathen mythology, its indiscreet rays reappeared on the summit of every wave, as if the god of fire had just sunk upon the bosom of Amphitrite, who in vain endeavored to hide her lover beneath her azure mantle.

The yacht moved rapidly on, though there did not appear to be sufficient wind to ruffle the curls on the head of a young girl. Standing on the prow was a tall man, of a dark complexion, who saw with dilating eyes that they were approaching a dark mass of land in the shape of a cone, which rose from the midst of the waves like the hat of a Catalan.

"Is that Monte Cristo?" asked the traveller, to whose orders the yacht was for the time submitted, in a melancholy voice.

"Yes, your excellency," said the captain, "we have reached it."

"We have reached it!" repeated the traveller in an accent of indescribable sadness.

Then he added, in a low tone, "Yes; that is the haven."

And then he again plunged into a train of thought, the character of which was better revealed by a sad smile, than it would have been by tears. A few minutes afterwards a flash of light, which was extinguished instantly, was seen on the land, and the sound of firearms reached the yacht.

"Your excellency," said the captain, "that was the land signal, will you answer yourself?"

"What signal?"

The captain pointed towards the island, up the side of which ascended a volume of smoke, increasing as it rose.

"Ah, yes," he said, as if awaking from a dream. "Give it to me."

The captain gave him a loaded carbine; the traveller slowly raised it, and fired in the air. Ten minutes afterwards, the sails were furled, and they cast anchor about a hundred fathoms from the little harbor. The gig was already lowered, and in it were four oarsmen and a coxswain. The traveller descended, and instead of sitting down at the stern of the boat, which had been decorated with a blue carpet for his accommodation, stood up with his arms crossed. The rowers waited, their oars half lifted out of the water, like birds drying their wings.

"Give way," said the traveller. The eight oars fell into the sea simultaneously without splashing a drop of water, and the boat, yielding to the impulsion, glided forward. In an instant they found themselves in a little harbor, formed in a natural creek; the boat grounded on the fine sand.

"Will your excellency be so good as to mount the shoulders of two of our men, they will carry you ashore?" The young man answered this invitation with a gesture of indifference, and stepped out of the boat; the sea immediately rose to his waist.

"Ah, your excellency," murmured the pilot, "you should not have done so; our master will scold us for it."

The young man continued to advance, following the sailors, who chose a firm footing. Thirty strides brought them to dry land; the young man stamped on the ground to shake off the wet, and looked around for someone to show him his road, for it was quite dark. Just as he turned, a hand rested on his shoulder, and a voice which made him shudder exclaimed:

"Good-evening, Maximilian; you are punctual, thank you!"

"Ah, is it you, count?" said the young man, in an almost joyful accent, pressing Monte Cristo's hand with both his own.

"Yes; you see I am as exact as you are. But you are dripping, my dear fellow; you must change your clothes, as Calypso said to Telemachus. Come, I have a habitation prepared for you in which you will soon forget fatigue and cold."

Monte Cristo perceived that the young man had turned around; indeed, Morrel saw with surprise that the men who had brought him had left without being paid, or uttering a word. Already the sound of their oars might be heard as they returned to the yacht.

"Oh, yes," said the count, "you are looking for the sailors."

"Yes, I paid them nothing, and yet they are gone."

"Never mind that, Maximilian," said Monte Cristo, smiling. "I have made an agreement with the navy, that the access to my island shall be free of all charge. I have made a bargain."

Morrel looked at the count with surprise. "Count," he said, "you are not the same here as in Paris."

"How so?"

"Here you laugh." The count's brow became clouded.

"You are right to recall me to myself, Maximilian," he said; "I was delighted to see you again, and forgot for the moment that all happiness is fleeting."

"Oh, no, no, count," cried Maximilian, seizing the count's hands, "pray laugh; be happy, and prove to me, by your indifference, that life is endurable to sufferers. Oh, how charitable, kind, and good you are; you affect this gayety to inspire me with courage."

"You are wrong, Morrel; I was really happy."

"Then you forget me, so much the better."

"How so?"

"Yes; for as the gladiator said to the emperor, when he entered the arena, 'He who is about to die salutes you.'"

"Then you are not consoled?" asked the count, surprised.

"Oh," exclaimed Morrel, with a glance full of bitter reproach, "do you think it possible that I could be?"

"Listen," said the count. "Do you understand the meaning of my words? You cannot take me for a commonplace man, a mere rattle, emitting a vague and senseless noise. When I ask you if you are consoled, I speak to you as a man for whom the human heart has no secrets. Well, Morrel, let us both examine the depths of your heart. Do you still feel the same feverish impatience of grief which made you start like a wounded lion? Have you still that devouring thirst which can only be appeased in the grave? Are you still actuated by the regret which drags the living to the pursuit of death; or are you only suffering from the prostration of fatigue and the weariness of hope deferred? Has the loss of memory rendered it impossible for you to weep? Oh, my dear friend, if this be the case,—if you can no longer weep, if your frozen heart be dead, if you put all your trust in God, then, Maximilian, you are consoled—do not complain."

"Count," said Morrel, in a firm and at the same time soft voice, "listen to me, as to a man whose thoughts are raised to heaven, though he remains on earth; I come to die in the arms of a friend. Certainly, there are people whom I love. I love my sister Julie,—I love her husband Emmanuel; but I require a strong mind to smile on my last moments. My sister would be bathed in tears and fainting; I could not bear to see her suffer. Emmanuel would tear the weapon from my hand, and alarm the house with his cries. You, count, who are more than mortal, will, I am sure, lead me to death by a pleasant path, will you not?"

"My friend," said the count, "I have still one doubt,—are you weak enough to pride yourself upon your sufferings?"

"No, indeed,—I am calm," said Morrel, giving his hand to the count; "my pulse does not beat slower or faster than usual. No, I feel that I have reached the goal, and I will go no farther. You told me to wait and hope; do you know what you did, unfortunate adviser? I waited a month, or rather I suffered for a month! I did hope (man is a poor wretched creature), I did hope. What I cannot tell,—something wonderful, an absurdity, a miracle,—of what nature he alone can tell who has mingled with our reason that folly we call hope. Yes, I did wait—yes, I did hope, count, and during this quarter of an hour we have been talking together, you have unconsciously wounded, tortured my heart, for every word you have uttered proved that there was no hope for me. Oh, count, I shall sleep calmly, deliciously in the arms of death."

Morrel uttered these words with an energy which made the count shudder.

"My friend," continued Morrel, "you named the fifth of October as the end of the period of waiting,—today is the fifth of October," he took out his watch, "it is now nine o'clock,—I have yet three hours to live."

"Be it so," said the count, "come." Morrel mechanically followed the count, and they had entered the grotto before he perceived it. He felt a carpet under his feet, a door opened, perfumes surrounded him, and a brilliant light dazzled his eyes. Morrel hesitated to advance; he dreaded the enervating effect of all that he saw. Monte Cristo drew him in gently.

"Why should we not spend the last three hours remaining to us of life, like those ancient Romans, who when condemned by Nero, their emperor and heir, sat down at a table covered with flowers, and gently glided into death, amid the perfume of heliotropes and roses?"

Morrel smiled. "As you please," he said; "death is always death,—that is forgetfulness, repose, exclusion from life, and therefore from grief."

He sat down, and Monte Cristo placed himself opposite to him. They were in the marvellous dining-room before described, where the statues had baskets on their heads always filled with fruits and flowers. Morrel had looked carelessly around, and had probably noticed nothing.

"Let us talk like men," he said, looking at the count.

"Go on!"

"Count," said Morrel, "you are the epitome of all human knowledge, and you seem like a being descended from a wiser and more advanced world than ours."

"There is something true in what you say," said the count, with that smile which made him so handsome; "I have descended from a planet called grief."

"I believe all you tell me without questioning its meaning; for instance, you told me to live, and I did live; you told me to hope, and I almost did so. I am almost inclined to ask you, as though you had experienced death, 'is it painful to die?'"

Monte Cristo looked upon Morrel with indescribable tenderness. "Yes," he said, "yes, doubtless it is painful, if you violently break the outer covering which obstinately begs for life. If you plunge a dagger into your flesh, if you insinuate a bullet into your brain, which the least shock disorders,—then certainly, you will suffer pain, and you will repent quitting a life for a repose you have bought at so dear a price."

"Yes; I know that there is a secret of luxury and pain in death, as well as in life; the only thing is to understand it."

"You have spoken truly, Maximilian; according to the care we bestow upon it, death is either a friend who rocks us gently as a nurse, or an enemy who violently drags the soul from the body. Some day, when the world is much older, and when mankind will be masters of all the destructive powers in nature, to serve for the general good of humanity; when mankind, as you were just saying, have discovered the secrets of death, then that death will become as sweet and voluptuous as a slumber in the arms of your beloved."

"And if you wished to die, you would choose this death, count?"

"Yes."

Morrel extended his hand. "Now I understand," he said, "why you had me brought here to this desolate spot, in the midst of the ocean, to this subterranean palace; it was because you loved me, was it not, count? It was because you loved me well enough to give me one of those sweet means of death of which we were speaking; a death without agony, a death which allows me to fade away while pronouncing Valentine's name and pressing your hand."

"Yes, you have guessed rightly, Morrel," said the count, "that is what I intended."

"Thanks; the idea that tomorrow I shall no longer suffer, is sweet to my heart."

"Do you then regret nothing?"

"No," replied Morrel.

"Not even me?" asked the count with deep emotion. Morrel's clear eye was for the moment clouded, then it shone with unusual lustre, and a large tear rolled down his cheek.

"What," said the count, "do you still regret anything in the world, and yet die?"

"Oh, I entreat you," exclaimed Morrel in a low voice, "do not speak another word, count; do not prolong my punishment."

The count fancied that he was yielding, and this belief revived the horrible doubt that had overwhelmed him at the Château d'If.

"I am endeavoring," he thought, "to make this man happy; I look upon this restitution as a weight thrown into the scale to balance the evil I have wrought. Now, supposing I am deceived, supposing this man has not been unhappy enough to merit happiness. Alas, what would become of me who can only atone for evil by doing good?"

Then he said aloud: "Listen, Morrel, I see your grief is great, but still you do not like to risk your soul." Morrel smiled sadly.

"Count," he said, "I swear to you my soul is no longer my own."

"Maximilian, you know I have no relation in the world. I have accustomed myself to regard you as my son: well, then, to save my son, I will sacrifice my life, nay, even my fortune."

"What do you mean?"

"I mean, that you wish to quit life because you do not understand all the enjoyments which are the fruits of a large fortune. Morrel, I possess nearly a hundred millions and I give them to you; with such a fortune you can attain every wish. Are you ambitious? Every career is open to you. Overturn the world, change its character, yield to mad ideas, be even criminal—but live."

"Count, I have your word," said Morrel coldly; then taking out his watch, he added, "It is half-past eleven."

"Morrel, can you intend it in my house, under my very eyes?"

"Then let me go," said Maximilian, "or I shall think you did not love me for my own sake, but for yours;" and he arose.

"It is well," said Monte Cristo whose countenance brightened at these words; "you wish it—you are inflexible. Yes, as you said, you are indeed wretched and a miracle alone can cure you. Sit down, Morrel, and wait."

Morrel obeyed; the count arose, and unlocking a closet with a key suspended from his gold chain, took from it a little silver casket, beautifully carved and chased, the corners of which represented four bending figures, similar to the Caryatides, the forms of women, symbols of the angels aspiring to heaven.

He placed the casket on the table; then opening it took out a little golden box, the top of which flew open when touched by a secret spring. This box contained an unctuous substance partly solid, of which it was impossible to discover the color, owing to the reflection of the polished gold, sapphires, rubies, emeralds, which ornamented the box. It was a mixed mass of blue, red, and gold.

The count took out a small quantity of this with a gilt spoon, and offered it to Morrel, fixing a long steadfast glance upon him. It was then observable that the substance was greenish.

"This is what you asked for," he said, "and what I promised to give you."

"I thank you from the depths of my heart," said the young man, taking the spoon from the hands of Monte Cristo. The count took another spoon, and again dipped it into the golden box. "What are you going to do, my friend?" asked Morrel, arresting his hand.

"Well, the fact is, Morrel, I was thinking that I too am weary of life, and since an opportunity presents itself—"

"Stay!" said the young man. "You who love, and are beloved; you, who have faith and hope,—oh, do not follow my example. In your case it would be a crime. Adieu, my noble and generous friend, adieu; I will go and tell Valentine what you have done for me."

And slowly, though without any hesitation, only waiting to press the count's hand fervently, he swallowed the mysterious substance offered by Monte Cristo. Then they were both silent. Ali, mute and attentive, brought the pipes and coffee, and disappeared. By degrees, the light of the lamps gradually faded in the hands of the marble statues which held them, and the perfumes appeared less powerful to Morrel. Seated opposite to him, Monte Cristo watched him in the shadow, and Morrel saw nothing but the bright eyes of the count. An overpowering sadness took possession of the young man, his hands relaxed their hold, the objects in the room gradually lost their form and color, and his disturbed vision seemed to perceive doors and curtains open in the wall.

"Friend," he cried, "I feel that I am dying; thanks!"

He made a last effort to extend his hand, but it fell powerless beside him. Then it appeared to him that Monte Cristo smiled, not with the strange and fearful expression which had sometimes revealed to him the secrets of his heart, but with the benevolent kindness of a father for a child. At the same time the count appeared to increase in stature, his form, nearly double its usual height, stood out in relief against the red tapestry, his black hair was thrown back, and he stood in the attitude of an avenging angel. Morrel, overpowered, turned around in the armchair; a delicious torpor permeated every vein. A change of ideas presented themselves to his brain, like a new design on the kaleidoscope. Enervated, prostrate, and breathless, he became unconscious of outward objects; he seemed to be entering that vague delirium preceding death. He wished once again to press the count's hand, but his own was immovable. He wished to articulate a last farewell, but his tongue lay motionless and heavy in his throat, like a stone at the mouth of a sepulchre. Involuntarily his languid eyes closed, and still through his eyelashes a well-known form seemed to move amid the obscurity with which he thought himself enveloped.

The count had just opened a door. Immediately a brilliant light from the next room, or rather from the palace adjoining, shone upon the room in which he was gently gliding into his last sleep. Then he saw a woman of marvellous beauty appear on the threshold of the door separating the two rooms. Pale, and sweetly smiling, she looked like an angel of mercy conjuring the angel of vengeance.

"Is it heaven that opens before me?" thought the dying man; "that angel resembles the one I have lost."

Monte Cristo pointed out Morrel to the young woman, who advanced towards him with clasped hands and a smile upon her lips.

"Valentine, Valentine!" he mentally ejaculated; but his lips uttered no sound, and as though all his strength were centred in that internal emotion, he sighed and closed his eyes. Valentine rushed towards him; his lips again moved.

"He is calling you," said the count; "he to whom you have confided your destiny—he from whom death would have separated you, calls you to him. Happily, I vanquished death. Henceforth, Valentine, you will never again be separated on earth, since he has rushed into death to find you. Without me, you would both have died. May God accept my atonement in the preservation of these two existences!"

Valentine seized the count's hand, and in her irresistible impulse of joy carried it to her lips.

"Oh, thank me again!" said the count; "tell me till you are weary, that I have restored you to happiness; you do not know how much I require this assurance."

"Oh, yes, yes, I thank you with all my heart," said Valentine; "and if you doubt the sincerity of my gratitude, oh, then, ask Haydée! ask my beloved sister Haydée, who ever since our departure from France, has caused me to wait patiently for this happy day, while talking to me of you."

"You then love Haydée?" asked Monte Cristo with an emotion he in vain endeavored to dissimulate.

"Oh, yes, with all my soul."

"Well, then, listen, Valentine," said the count; "I have a favor to ask of you."

"Of me? Oh, am I happy enough for that?"

"Yes; you have called Haydée your sister,—let her become so indeed, Valentine; render her all the gratitude you fancy that you owe to me; protect her, for" (the count's voice was thick with emotion) "henceforth she will be alone in the world."

"Alone in the world!" repeated a voice behind the count, "and why?"

Monte Cristo turned around; Haydée was standing pale, motionless, looking at the count with an expression of fearful amazement.

"Because tomorrow, Haydée, you will be free; you will then assume your proper position in society, for I will not allow my destiny to overshadow yours. Daughter of a prince, I restore to you the riches and name of your father."

Haydée became pale, and lifting her transparent hands to heaven, exclaimed in a voice stifled with tears, "Then you leave me, my lord?"

"Haydée, Haydée, you are young and beautiful; forget even my name, and be happy."

"It is well," said Haydée; "your order shall be executed, my lord; I will forget even your name, and be happy." And she stepped back to retire.

"Oh, heavens," exclaimed Valentine, who was supporting the head of Morrel on her shoulder, "do you not see how pale she is? Do you not see how she suffers?"

Haydée answered with a heartrending expression,

"Why should he understand this, my sister? He is my master, and I am his slave; he has the right to notice nothing."

The count shuddered at the tones of a voice which penetrated the inmost recesses of his heart; his eyes met those of the young girl and he could not bear their brilliancy.

"Oh, heavens," exclaimed Monte Cristo, "can my suspicions be correct? Haydée, would it please you not to leave me?"

"I am young," gently replied Haydée; "I love the life you have made so sweet to me, and I should be sorry to die."

"You mean, then, that if I leave you, Haydée—"

"I should die; yes, my lord."

"Do you then love me?"

"Oh, Valentine, he asks if I love him. Valentine, tell him if you love Maximilian."

The count felt his heart dilate and throb; he opened his arms, and Haydée, uttering a cry, sprang into them.

"Oh, yes," she cried, "I do love you! I love you as one loves a father, brother, husband! I love you as my life, for you are the best, the noblest of created beings!"

"Let it be, then, as you wish, sweet angel; God has sustained me in my struggle with my enemies, and has given me this reward; he will not let me end my triumph in suffering; I wished to punish myself, but he has pardoned me. Love me then, Haydée! Who knows? perhaps your love will make me forget all that I do not wish to remember."

"What do you mean, my lord?"

"I mean that one word from you has enlightened me more than twenty years of slow experience; I have but you in the world, Haydée; through you I again take hold on life, through you I shall suffer, through you rejoice."

"Do you hear him, Valentine?" exclaimed Haydée; "he says that through me he will suffer—through *me*, who would yield my life for his."

The count withdrew for a moment. "Have I discovered the truth?" he said; "but whether it be for recompense or punishment, I accept my fate. Come, Haydée, come!" and throwing his arm around the young girl's waist, he pressed the hand of Valentine, and disappeared.

An hour had nearly passed, during which Valentine, breathless and motionless, watched steadfastly over Morrel. At length she felt his heart beat, a faint breath played upon his lips, a slight shudder, announcing the return of life, passed through the young man's frame. At length his eyes opened, but they were at first fixed and expressionless; then sight returned, and with it feeling and grief.

"Oh," he cried, in an accent of despair, "the count has deceived me; I am yet living;" and extending his hand towards the table, he seized a knife.

"Dearest," exclaimed Valentine, with her adorable smile, "awake, and look at me!" Morrel uttered a loud exclamation, and frantic, doubtful, dazzled, as though by a celestial vision, he fell upon his knees.

The next morning at daybreak, Valentine and Morrel were walking arm-in-arm on the seashore, Valentine relating how Monte Cristo had appeared in her room, explained everything, revealed the crime, and, finally, how he had saved her life by enabling her to simulate death.

They had found the door of the grotto opened, and gone forth; on the azure dome of heaven still glittered a few remaining stars.

Morrel soon perceived a man standing among the rocks, apparently awaiting a sign from them to advance, and pointed him out to Valentine.

"Ah, it is Jacopo," she said, "the captain of the yacht;" and she beckoned him towards them.

"Do you wish to speak to us?" asked Morrel.

"I have a letter to give you from the count."

"From the count!" murmured the two young people.

"Yes; read it."

Morrel opened the letter, and read:

"My Dear Maximilian,

"There is a felucca for you at anchor. Jacopo will carry you to Leghorn, where Monsieur Noirtier awaits his granddaughter, whom he wishes to bless before you lead her to the altar. All that is in this grotto, my friend, my house in the Champs-Élysées, and my château at Tréport, are the marriage gifts bestowed by Edmond Dantès upon the son of his old master, Morrel. Mademoiselle de Villefort will share them with you; for I entreat her to give to the poor the immense fortune reverting to her from her father, now a madman, and her brother who died last September with his mother. Tell the angel who will watch over your future destiny, Morrel, to pray sometimes for a man, who, like Satan, thought himself for an instant equal to God, but who now acknowledges with Christian humility that God alone possesses supreme power and infinite wisdom. Perhaps those prayers may soften the remorse he feels in his heart. As for you, Morrel, this is the secret of my conduct towards you. There is neither happiness nor misery in the world; there is only the comparison of one state with another, nothing more. He who has felt the deepest grief is best able to experience supreme happiness. We must have felt what it is to die, Morrel, that we may appreciate the enjoyments of living.

"Live, then, and be happy, beloved children of my heart, and never forget that until the day when God shall deign to reveal the future to man, all human wisdom is summed up in these two words,—'*Wait and hope.*'—Your friend,

"Edmond Dantès, *Count of Monte Cristo.*"

During the perusal of this letter, which informed Valentine for the first time of the madness of her father and the death of her brother, she became pale, a heavy sigh escaped from her bosom, and tears, not the less painful because they were silent, ran down her cheeks; her happiness cost her very dear.

Morrel looked around uneasily.

"But," he said, "the count's generosity is too overwhelming; Valentine will be satisfied with my humble fortune. Where is the count, friend? Lead me to him."

Jacopo pointed towards the horizon.

"What do you mean?" asked Valentine. "Where is the count?—where is Haydée?"

"Look!" said Jacopo.

The eyes of both were fixed upon the spot indicated by the sailor, and on the blue line separating the sky from the Mediterranean Sea, they perceived a large white sail.

"Gone," said Morrel; "gone!—adieu, my friend—adieu, my father!"

"Gone," murmured Valentine; "adieu, my sweet Haydée—adieu, my sister!"

"Who can say whether we shall ever see them again?" said Morrel with tearful eyes.

"Darling," replied Valentine, "has not the count just told us that all human wisdom is summed up in two words:

"'*Wait and hope* (Fac et spera)!'"

Study Guide Questions

For Students:

1. Who arrives on the isle of Monte Cristo?
2. What happens to Haydée?
3. What happens to Morrel?

For Reading Club:

1. Discuss and compare the happy ending of Valentine and Haydée with Eugénie and Mercédès. Do you think the author favors females who are sweet and submissive?
2. What is written in the letter that Dantès leave for Morrel?
3. Discuss the ending of the novel.

Made in the USA
Columbia, SC
16 October 2024